# MATCH ME SIDNEY!

## THE NO EXIT PRESS CRIME ANTHOLOGY

**NO EXIT PRESS**

1989

No Exit Press
18 Coleswood Road
Harpenden, Herts AL5 1EQ

British Library Cataloguing in Publishing Data available

ISBN 0 948353 59 7

This edition limited to 2,000 copies only.

### Acknowledgements

Mysterious Press for the stories by George Chesboro, Max Allan Collins,
Michael Collins, Wayne Dundee, Loren Estelman, Sue Grafton, Rob Kantner,
John Lutz & Josh Pachter, Arthur Lyons, Bill Pronzini, Robert Randisi,
James Reasoner & L. J. Washburn in the collection 'An Eye for Justice'.

Maxim Jakubowski for the Top Ten Books and authors.

Robert Hale for permission to publish 'Phantom Lady'.

A. M. Heath for permission to reprint 'Students of Disaster'.

Curtis Brown for permission to reprint 'Speciality of the House'.

Graham Lovatt for compiling the crime diary.

Argosy Communications Inc. for permission to reprint 'The Morgue's Our Home'
from the December 1936, Dime Detective Magazine.

The following booksellers for help in finding material:
Heroes, Murder One and Post Mortem Books.

Printed by The Guernsey Press Co. Ltd.,
Guernsey, Channel Islands.

# CONTENTS

# GEORGE C. CHESBRO

# CANDALA

*Perhaps the most unusual P.I. to appear in this collection is George C. Chesbro's dwarf detective Robert "Mongo the Magnificent" Frederickson. Mongo is an ex-circus performer turned criminology professor, who works on the side as a P.I. Many of Mongo's recent cases have entered into the realm of the fantastic, but in "Candala" Mongo deals with an uncommon case involving a common problem: the unforeseen consequences of bigotry gone mad.*

## 1

Indiri Tamidian wafted into my downtown office like a gossamer breath of incense from some Hindu temple in her native India. Her young, lithe body rippled beneath the rustling silk folds of her sari; her coal black eyes, sheened by that enormous zest for life which was Indiri's very quintessence, smoldered in their sockets. Blue-black hair tumbled to her shoulders, perfectly complementing the translucent, light chocolate colored flesh of her face. Indiri was stunningly beautiful. And troubled; the light from her eyes could not disguise the fact that she had been crying.

Self-pity, unexpected and unbidden, welled up within me like a poisonous cloud, a hated stench from a dark, secret place deep inside my soul. Some thoughts have teeth; just as it is dangerous for an artist to search too hard for the murky headwaters of his power, it is folly for a dwarf to entertain romantic thoughts of beautiful women. I fall into the second category.

I pushed the cloud back to its wet place and clamped the lid on. I stood and smiled as Indiri glanced around her.

"So this is where the famous criminologist spends his time when he's not teaching," Indiri said with a forced gaiety that fell just short of its mark.

7

I grunted. "You could have seen the criminology professor anytime on campus, even if you are majoring in agriculture," I said easily. "You didn't have to come all the way down here."

"I didn't come to see the professor," Indiri said, leaning forward on my desk. "I came to see the detective. I would like to hire you."

"Now what would a lovely, intelligent young woman like you want with a seedy private detective?" Immediately my smile faded. The girl's flesh had paled, isolating the painted ceremonial dot in the center of her forehead, lending it the appearance of an accusing third eye. It had been a stupid thing to say. Worse, it had sounded patronizing, and Indiri Tamidian was not a woman to be patronized. "How can I help you, Indiri?"

"I want you to find out what's bothering Pram."

"What makes you think anything is bothering him?"

"He hasn't called or come to see me for a week. Yesterday I went over to his room and he refused to see me."

I turned away before my first reaction could wander across my face. Pram Sakhuntala was one of my graduate students, and a friend of sorts. A good athlete, Pram often worked out with me in the gym as I struggled to retain and polish the skills that were a legacy of the nightmare years I had spent headlining with the circus as Mongo the Magnificent. Like Indiri, Pram was part of a U.N.-funded exchange program designed to train promising young Indians for eventual return to their own land, where their newly acquired skills could be put to optimum use. Pram was taking a degree in sociology, which explained his presence in one of my criminology sections. He was also Indiri's fiancé and lover. Or had been. Losing interest in a woman like Indiri might be an indication that Pram was losing his mind, but that was his business. It certainly did not seem the proper concern of a private detective, and that's what I told Indiri.

"No, Dr. Frederickson, you don't understand," Indiri said, shaking her head. "There would be no problem if it were simply a matter of Pram not loving me anymore. That I could understand and accept. But he *does* love me, as I love him. I know that because I see it in his eyes; I feel it. Perhaps that sounds silly, but it is true."

It did not sound silly; Indiri came from a people who had produced the *Kama Sutra*, a land where life is always a question of basics. "Still, you don't have any idea what could have caused him to stop seeing you?"

"I'm not sure," Indiri said hesitantly.

"But you do have a suspicion."

"Yes. Do you know Dr. Dev Reja?"

"Dev Reja. He's chairman of Far Eastern Studies." I knew him, and didn't like him. He strode about the campus with all the imperiousness of a reincarnated Gautama Buddha with none of the Buddha's compensating humility.

"Yes," Indiri said softly. "He is also the advisor to the Indo-American Student Union, and coordinator of our exchange program. Last week Pram told me that Dr. Dev Reja had asked to speak with him. I don't know if there's any connection, but it was after that meeting that Pram changed toward me."

It suddenly occurred to me that I had not seen Pram for more than a week. He had missed my last class. This, in itself, was not significant. At least it hadn't seemed so at the time.

"What could Dev Reja have said to Pram that would cause him to change his attitude toward you?"

"That is what I would like you to find out for me, Dr. Frederickson."

I absently scratched my head. Indiri reached for her purse and I asked her what she was doing.

"I don't know how much you charge for your services," the girl said, looking straight into my eyes. "I don't have too much—"

"I only charge for cases," I said abruptly. "So far, this doesn't look like anything I could help you with." Tears welled in Indiri's eyes. "Not yet, it doesn't," I added quickly. "First I'll have to talk to Dr. Dev Reja before I can decide whether or not there's going to be any money in this for me. If I think there's anything I can do, we'll talk about fees later."

I was beginning to feel like the editor of an advice to the lovelorn column, but the look Indiri gave me shook me right down to my rather modest dwarf toes and made it all worthwhile.

## 2

Famous. That was the word Indiri had used—half in jest, half seriously—to describe me. It was true that I'd generated some heat and some headlines with my last two cases, both of which I'd literally stumbled across. But *famous*? Perhaps. I never gave it much thought. I'd had enough of fame; Mongo the Magnificent had been famous, and that kind of freak fame had almost destroyed me. What Indiri—or anyone else, for that matter, with the possible exceptions of my parents and Garth, my six-foot police detective brother—could not be expected to understand were the special needs and perspective of a four-foot-seven-inch dwarf with an I.Q. of 156 who had been forced to finance his way to a Ph.D. by working in a circus, *entertaining* people who saw nothing more than a freak who just happened to be a highly gifted tumbler and acrobat. Long ago I had developed the habit of not looking back, even to yesterday. There were just too many seemingly impossible obstacles I had already crossed, not to mention the ones coming up; the look of disbelief in the eyes of an unsuspecting client seeing me for the first time, choking back laughter at the idea of a *dwarf* trying to make it as a private detective.

I squeezed the genie of my past back into its psychic bottle as I neared the building housing the Center for Far Eastern Studies. Mahajar Dev Reja was in his office. I knocked and went in.

Dev Reja continued working at his desk a full minute before finally glancing up and acknowledging my presence. In the meantime I had glanced around his office; elephant tusks and other Indian trinkets cluttered the walls. I found the display rather gauche compared to the Indian presence Indiri carried *within* her. Finally Dev Reja stood up and nodded to me.

"I'm Frederickson," I said, extending my hand. "I don't think we've ever been formally introduced. I teach criminology."

Dev Reja considered my hand in such a way that he gave the impression he believed dwarfism might be catching. But I left it there and finally he took it.

"Frederickson," Dev Reja said. "You're the circus performer I've heard so much about."

"Ex-performer," I said quickly. "Actually, I'd like to speak to you about a mutual acquaintance. Pram Sakhuntala."

That raised Dev Reja's eyebrows a notch and I thought I detected a slight flush high on his cheekbones.

"My time is limited, Mr.—Dr.—Frederickson. How does your business with Pram Sakhuntala concern me?"

I decided there was just no way to sneak up on it. "Pram has been having some difficulty in my class," I lied. "There's an indication his troubles may stem from a talk he had with you." It wasn't diplomatic, but Dev Reja didn't exactly bring out the rosy side of my personality. "I thought I would see if there was any way I could help."

"He *told* you of our conversation?" This time his reaction was much more obvious and recognizable; it was called anger. I said nothing. *"Candala!"* Dev Reja hissed. It sounded like a curse.

"How's that?"

"Pram asked you to come and see me?"

*"Is* Pram in some kind of trouble?"

Dev Reja's sudden calm was costing him. "It must have occurred to you before you came here that any discussion Pram and I may have had would be none of your business. You were right."

I didn't have to be told that the interview was at an end. I turned and walked to the door past a blown-up photograph of a tiger in an Indian jungle. It was night and the eyes of the startled beast glittered like fractured diamonds in the light of the enterprising photographer's flash. In the background the under-brush was impenetrably dark and tangled. I wondered what had happened to the man who took the shot.

Pram showed up at the gym that evening for our scheduled workout. His usually expressive mouth was set in a grim line and he looked shaky. I made small talk as we rolled out the mats and began our warm-up exercises. Soon Pram's finely sculpted body began to glisten, and he seemed to relax as his tension melted and merged with the sweat flowing from his pores.

"Pram, what's a 'candala'?"

His reaction was immediate and shocking. Pram blanched bone white, then jumped up and away as though I had grazed his stomach with a white-hot poker.

"Where did you hear that?" His words came at me like bullets from the smoking barrel of a machine gun.

"Oh, Dr. Dev Reja dropped it in conversation the other day and I didn't have time to ask him what it meant."

"He was talking about me, wasn't he?!"

Pram's face and voice were a torrent of emotions, a river of tortured human feeling I was not yet prepared to cross. I'd stuck my foot in the water and found it icy cold and dark. I backed out.

"As far as I know, it had nothing to do with you," I said lamely. Pram wasn't fooled.

"You don't usually lie, Professor. Why are you lying now?"

"What's a 'candala,' Pram? Why don't you tell me what's bothering you?"

"What right do you have to ask me these questions?"

"None."

"Where did you get the idea of going to see Dr. Dev Reja?"

Like it or not, it seemed I'd just been pushed right into the middle of the water. This time I struck out for the other side. "Indiri's been hurt and confused by the way you've been acting," I said evenly. "Not hurt for herself, but for you. She thinks you may be in some kind of trouble, and she asked me to try to help if I can. She loves you very much, Pram. You must know that. If you are in trouble, I can't help you unless you tell me what it's all about."

Pram blinked rapidly. His skin had taken on a greenish pallor and for a moment I thought he would be sick. The fire in his eyes was now banked back to a dull glow as he seemed to stare through and beyond me. Suddenly he turned and, still in his gym clothes, walked out of the gym and into the night. I let him go. I had already said too much for a man who was working blind.

I showered and dressed, then made my way over to the women's residence where Indiri was staying. I called her room and she immediately came down to meet me in the lobby. I wasted no time.

"Indiri, what's a 'candala'?"

The question obviously caught her by surprise. "It's a term used to refer to a person of very low caste," she said quietly, after a long hesitation. "A candala is what you in the West could call an 'untouchable.' But it is even worse—I'm sorry to have to tell you these things, Dr. Frederickson. I love my country, but I am so ashamed of the evil that is our caste system. Mahatma Gandhi taught us that it was evil, and every one of our leaders have followed his example. Still, it persists. I am afraid it is just too deeply ingrained in the souls of our people."

"Don't apologize, Indiri. India has no monopoly on prejudice."

"It's not the same, Dr. Frederickson. You cannot fully understand the meaning and implications of *caste* unless you are Indian."

I wondered. I had a few black friends who might give her an argument, but I didn't say anything.

"Actually," Indiri continued, "the most common name for an untouchable is 'sutra.' A candala is—or was—even lower."

"Was?"

"You rarely hear the word anymore, except as a curse. Once, a candala was considered absolutely apart from other men. Such a man could be killed on the spot if he so much as allowed his shadow to touch that of a man in a higher caste. However, over the centuries it was realized that this practice ran counter to the basic Indian philosophy that every man, no matter how 'low,' had *some* place in the social system. In Indian minds—and in day-to-day life—the concept of candala fell under the weight of its own illogic."

"Go on."

"Candalas were forced to wear wooden clappers around their necks to warn other people of their presence. They were allowed to work only as executioners and burial attendants. They were used to cremate corpses, then forced to wear the dead man's clothing."

I shuddered involuntarily. "Who decides who's who in this system?"

"It is usually a question of birth. A person normally belongs to the caste his parents belonged to, except in the case of illegitimate children who are automatically considered sutras."

"What about Pram?" I said, watching Indiri carefully. "Could he be a sutra, or even a candala?"

I had expected some kind of reaction, but not laughter. It just didn't go with our conversation. "I'm sorry, Dr. Frederickson," Indiri said, reading my face. "That just struck me as being funny. Pram's family is Ksatriyana, the same as mine."

"Where does a Ksatriyana fit into the social scheme of things?"

"A Ksatriyana is very high," she said. I decided it was to her credit that she didn't blush. "Ksatriyana is almost interchangeable with Brahman, which is usually considered the highest caste. Buddha himself was a Ksatriyana. A member of such a family could never be considered a sutra, much less a candala."

"What about Dr. Dev Reja? What's his pedigree?"

"He is a Brahman."

I nodded. I had no time to answer Indiri's unspoken questions; I still had too many of my own. I thanked her and left. The subject of our conversation had left a dusty residue on the lining of my mind and I gulped thirstily at the cool night air.

I needed an excuse to speak to Pram so I picked up his clothes from the common locker we shared in the gym and cut across the campus to his residence.

It was a small building, a cottage really, converted into apartments for those who preferred a certain kind of rickety individuality to the steel-and-glass anonymity of the high-rise student dorms. There was a light on in Pram's second-floor room. I went inside and up the creaking stairs. The rap of my knuckles on the door coincided with another sound that could have been a chair tipping over onto the floor. I raised my hand to knock again, and froze. There was a new sound, barely perceptible but real nonetheless; it was the strangling rasp of a man choking to death.

I grabbed the knob and twisted. The door was locked. I had about three feet of space on the landing and I used every inch of it as I stepped back and leaped forward, kipping off the floor, kicking out with my heel at the door just above the lock. It gave. The door flew open and I hit the floor, slapping the wood with my hands to absorb the shock and immediately springing to my feet. The scene in the room branded its image on my mind even as I leaped to right the fallen chair.

Two factors were responsible for the fact that Pram was still alive: He had changed his mind at the last moment, and he was a lousy hangman to begin with. The knot in the plastic clothesline had not been tied properly and there had not been enough slack to break his neck; he had sagged rather than fallen through the air. His fingers clawed at the thin line, then slipped off. His legs thrashed in the air a good two feet above the floor; his eyes bulged and his tongue, thick and black, protruded from his dry lips like an obscene worm. His face was blue. He had already lost control of his sphincter and the air was filled with a sour, fetid smell.

I quickly righted the chair and placed it beneath the flailing feet, one of which caught me in the side of the head, stunning me. I fought off the dizziness and grabbed his ankles, forcing his feet onto the chair. That wasn't going to be enough. A half-dead, panic-stricken man with a rope around his neck choking the life out of him doesn't just calmly stand up on a chair. I jumped up beside him, bracing and lifting him by his belt while, with the other hand, I stretched up and went to work on the knot in the clothesline. Finally it came loose and Pram suddenly went limp. I ducked and let Pram's body fall over my shoulder. I got down off the chair and carried him to the bed. I put my ear to his chest; he was still breathing, but just barely. I grabbed the phone and called for an ambulance. After that I called my brother.

## 3

Pram's larynx wasn't damaged and, with a little difficulty, he could manage to talk; but he wasn't doing any of it to Garth. "What can I tell you, Mongo?" Garth said. He pointed to the closed door of Pram's hospital room where we had just spent a fruitless half hour trying to get Pram to open up about what had prompted him to try to take his own life. "He says nobody's done anything to him. Actually, by attempting suicide, he's the one who's broken the law."

I muttered a carefully selected obscenity.

"I didn't say I was going to press charges against him," Garth grunted. "I'm just trying to tell you that I'm not going to press charges against anyone else either. I can't. Whatever bad blood there is between your friend and this Dev Reja, it obviously isn't a police matter. Not until and unless some complaint is made."

I was convinced that Pram's act was linked to Dev Reja, and I'd hoped that a talk with Pram would provide the basis for charges of harassment—or worse—against the other man. Pram had refused to even discuss the matter, just as he had refused to let Indiri even see him. I thanked my brother for his time and walked him to the elevator. Then I went back to Pram's room.

I paused at the side of the bed, staring down at the young man in it who would not meet my gaze. The fiery rope burns on his neck were concealed beneath bandages, but the medication assailed my nostrils. I lifted my hands in a helpless gesture and sat down in a chair beside the bed, just beyond Pram's field of vision.

"It does have something to do with Dev Reja, doesn't it, Pram?" I said after a long pause.

"What I did was a terrible act of cowardice," Pram croaked into the silence. "I must learn to accept. I *will* learn to accept and live my life as it is meant to be lived."

"Accept what?" I said very carefully, leaning forward.

Tears welled up in Pram's eyes, brimmed at the lids, then rolled down his cheeks. He made no move to wipe them away. "My birth," he said in a tortured whisper. "I must learn to accept the fact of my birth."

"What are you talking about? You are a Ksatriyana. Indiri told me."

Pram shook his head. "I am a . . . sutra." I tried to think of a way to frame my next question, but it wasn't necessary. Now Pram's words flowed out of him like pus from a ruptured boil. "You see, I am adopted," Pram continued. "That I knew. What I did not know is that I am illegitimate, and that my real mother was a sutra. Therefore, on *two* counts, I am a sutra. Dr. Dev Reja discovered this because he has access to the birth records of all the Indian exchange students. He had no reason to tell me until he found out that Indiri and I intended to marry. It was only then that he felt the need to warn me."

"*Warn* you?" The words stuck in my throat.

"A sutra cannot marry a Ksatriyana. It would not be right." I started to speak but Pram cut me off, closing his eyes and shaking his head as though he was in great pain. "I cannot explain," he said, squeezing the words out through lips that had suddenly become dry and cracked. "You must simply accept what I tell you and know that it is true. I know why Dr. Dev Reja called me a candala; he thought I had gone to you to discuss something which has nothing to do with someone who is not Indian. It does not matter that it was said in anger, or that he was mistaken in thinking it was me who had come to you; he was right about me being a candala. I have proved it by my actions. I have behaved like a coward. It is in my blood."

"If you want to call yourself a fool, I might agree with you," I said evenly. "Do you think Indiri gives a damn what caste you come from?" There was a rage building inside me and I had to struggle to keep it from tainting my words.

Pram suddenly looked up at me. Now, for the first time, life had returned to his eyes, but it was a perverted life, burning with all the intensity of a fuse on a time bomb. "Having Indiri know of my low station would only increase my humiliation. I have told you what you wanted to know, Dr. Frederickson. Now you must promise to leave me alone and to interfere no further."

"You haven't told me anything that makes any sense," I said, standing up and leaning on the side of the bed. "A few days ago you were a fairly good-looking young man, a better than average student deeply loved by the most beautiful girl on campus. Now you've refused to even see that girl and, a few hours ago, you tried to take your own life. You're falling apart, and all because some silly bastard called you a *name!* Explain *that* to me!"

I paused and took a deep breath. I realized that my bedside manner might leave something to be desired, but at the moment I felt Pram needed something stronger than sympathy; something like a kick in the ass. "*I'm* not going to tell Indiri," I said heatedly. "*You* are. And you're going to apologize to her for acting like such a . . . jerk. Then maybe the three of us can go out for a drink and discuss the curious vagaries of the human mind." I smiled to soften the blow of my words, but Pram continued to stare blankly, shaking his head.

"I am a candala," he said, his words strung together like a chant. "What I did was an act of pride. Candalas are not allowed pride. I must learn to accept what my life has—"

I couldn't stand the monotonous tones, the corroding, poisonous mist that was creeping into his brain and shining out through his eyes; I struck at that sick light with my hand. Pram took the blow across his face without flinching, as if it was someone else I had hit. The nurse who had come into the room had no doubts as to whom I had hit and she didn't like it one bit. I shook off her hand and screamed into Pram's face.

"A name means nothing!" I shouted, my voice trembling with rage. "What the hell's the *matter* with you?! You can't allow yourself to be defined by someone else! You must define *yourself!* Only *you* can determine what you are. Now stop talking crazy and pull yourself together!"

But I was the one being pulled—out of the room by two very husky young interns. I continued to scream at the dull-faced youth in the bed even as they pulled me out through the door. I could not explain my own behavior, except in terms of blind rage and hatred in the presence of some great evil that I was unable to even see, much less fight.

Outside in the corridor I braced my heels against the tiles of the floor. "Get your goddam hands off me," I said quietly. The two men released me and I hurried out of the hospital, anxious to get home and into a hot bath. Still, I suspected even then that the smell I carried with me out of that room was in my mind, and would not be so easily expunged.

"He's changed, Dr. Frederickson," Indiri sobbed. I pushed back from my desk and the Indian girl rushed into my arms. I held her until the violent shuddering of her shoulders began to subside.

"He's told you what the problem is?" Pram had been released

from the hospital that morning, and it had been my suggestion that Indiri go to meet him.

Indiri nodded. "He's becoming what Dr. Dev Reja says he is."

I didn't need Indiri to tell me that. I knew the psychiatrist assigned to Pram and a little gentle prodding had elicited the opinion that Pram had, indeed, accepted Dev Reja's definition of himself and was adjusting his personality, character, and behavior accordingly. It had all been couched in psychiatric mumbo jumbo, but I had read Jean Paul Sartre's existential masterpiece, *Saint Genet*, and that was all the explanation I needed.

"How do you feel about what he told you?" I said gently. Indiri's eyes were suddenly dry and flashing angrily. "Sorry," I added quickly. "I just had to be sure where we stood."

"What can we do, Dr. Frederickson?"

If she was surprised when I didn't answer she didn't show it. Perhaps she hadn't really expected a reply, or perhaps she already knew the answer. And I knew that I was afraid, afraid as I had not been since, as a child, I had first learned I was different from other children and had lain awake at night listening to strange sounds inside my mind.

## 4

I burst into the room and slammed the door behind me. My timing was perfect; Dev Reja was about halfway through his lecture.

"Ladies and gentlemen," I intoned, "class is dismissed. Professor Dev Reja and I have business to discuss."

Dev Reja and the students stared at me, uncomprehending. Dev Reja recovered first, drawing himself up to his full height and stalking across the room. I stepped around him and positioned myself behind his lectern. "Dismiss them now," I said, drumming my fingers on the wood, "or I deliver my own impromptu lecture on bigotry, Indian style."

That stopped him. Dev Reja glared at me, then waved his hand in the direction of the students. The students rose and filed quickly out of the room, embarrassed, eager to escape the suppressed anger that crackled in the air like heat lightning before a summer storm.

"What do you think you're doing, Frederickson?" Dev Reja's voice shook with outrage. "This behavior is an utter breach of professional ethics, not to mention common courtesy. I will have this brought up—"

"Shut up," I said easily. It caught him by surprise and stopped the flow of words. He stared at me, his mouth open. My own voice was calm, completely belying the anger and frustration behind the words. "If there's anyone who should be brought before the Ethics Committee, it's you. You're absolutely unfit to teach."

Dev Reja walked past me to the window, but not before I caught a flash of what looked like pain in his eyes. I found that incongruous in Dev Reja, and it slowed me. But not for long.

"Let me tell you exactly what you're going to do," I said to the broad back. "I don't pretend to understand all that's involved in this caste business, but I certainly can recognize rank prejudice when I see it. For some reason that's completely beyond me, Pram has accepted what you told him about himself, and it's destroying him. Do you know that he tried to kill himself?"

"Of course I know, you fool," Dev Reja said, wheeling on me. I was startled to see that the other man's eyes were glistening with tears. I was prepared for anything but that. I continued with what I had come to say, but the rage was largely dissipated; now I was close to pleading.

"You're the one who put this 'untouchable' crap into his head, Dev Reja, and you're the one who's going to have to take it out. I don't care how you do it; just do it. Tell him you were mistaken; tell him he's really the reincarnation of Buddha, or Gandhi. Anything. Just make it so that Pram can get back to the business of living. If you don't, you can be certain that I'm going to make your stay at this university—and in this country—very uncomfortable. I'll start with our Ethics Committee, then work my way up to your embassy. I don't think they'd like it if they knew you were airing India's dirty laundry on an American campus."

"There's nothing that can be done now," Dev Reja said in a tortured voice that grated on my senses precisely because it did not fit the script I had written for this confrontation. Dev Reja was not reacting the way I had expected him to.

"What kind of man are you, Dev Reja?"

"I am an Indian."

"Uh-huh. Like Hitler was a German."

The remark had no seeming effect on the other man and I found that disappointing.

"Dr. Frederickson, may I speak to you for a few minutes without any interruption?"

"Be my guest."

"I detest the caste system, as any right-thinking man detests a system that traps and dehumanizes men. However, I can assure you that Pram's mentality and way of looking at things is much more representative of Indian thinking than is mine. The caste system is a stain upon our national character, just as your enslavement and discrimination against blacks is a stain upon yours. But it *does* exist, and must be dealt with. The ways of India are deeply ingrained in the human being that is Pram Sakhuntala. I can assure you this is true. I know Pram much better than you do, and his reaction to the information I gave him proves that I am correct."

"Then why did you give him that information? Why did you give him something you knew he probably couldn't handle?"

"Because it was inevitable," Dev Reja said quietly. "You see, Dr. Frederickson, you or I could have overcome this thing. Pram cannot, simply because he is not strong enough. Because he is weak, and because he would have found out anyway, for reasons which I think will become clear to you, he would have destroyed himself, and Indiri as well. This way, there is a great deal of pain for Pram, but the catastrophe that would otherwise be is prevented."

"I don't understand."

"Pram was going to marry a Ksatriyana. Don't you suppose Indiri's family would have checked the circumstances of Pram's birth before they allowed such a marriage to take place? I tell you they would, and then things would have been much worse for everyone involved."

"But he could have married her and lived here."

"Ah, Dr. Frederickson, he could *still* do that, couldn't he? But I think you will agree that that does not seem likely. You see, what you fail to understand is that Pram is an *Indian*, and his roots are in India. Pram's adoptive parents are extremely liberal and far-seeing people. Not at all like most people in India, in the United States or, for that matter, in the world. Pram himself failed to learn the great truth that was implicit in his adoption. I know that if Pram was to attempt to return to India and marry Indiri—as he would most certainly have done if I had not told him what I did— he would have been ridiculed and derided by Indiri's family; perhaps even stoned for even presuming to do such a thing. In

other words, Dr. Frederickson, Pram has the same options he had
before: to marry Indiri or not; to live here or in India. I'm sure
Indiri is as indifferent to Pram's origins as his own family is. He is
not able to do this because, as you say, the knowledge that *he*
could come from sutra origins is destroying him. You see, in
effect, Pram is prejudiced against himself. I had hoped that telling
him the truth as I did would give him time to adjust, to prepare
himself."

I suddenly felt sick at the image of a young man doing battle
with shadows; Pram had had a glittering treasure within his grasp
and had ended with an empty pot at the end of a fake rainbow.
And all because of a label he had swallowed and internalized but
which, for him, was no more digestible than a stone.

"I didn't know you'd said those things to him," I said lamely.
"But now he's obsessed with this candala thing."

"I'm afraid you'll have to take the responsibility for that, Dr.
Frederickson."

"You said it."

"In anger, without thinking. You felt the need to repeat it."

I could feel a cloak of guilt settling over my shoulders. I made
no attempt to shrug it off for the simple reason that Dev Reja was
right.

"It doesn't really matter, Dr. Frederickson. Even without you
the problem would still remain. However, now I am curious.
What would you have done in my place?"

I wished I had an answer. I didn't. I was in over my head and
knew it.

"All right," I said resignedly, "what do we do now?"

"What we have been doing," Dev Reja said. "Help Pram the
best we can, each in our own way."

"He has a psychiatrist looking after him now. The university
insisted."

"That's good as far as it goes," Dev Reja said, looking down at
his hands. "Still, you and I and Indiri must continue to talk to
him, to try to make him see what you wanted him to see: that a
man is not a label. If he is to marry Indiri and return to India, he
must strengthen himself; he must prepare an inner defense
against the people who will consider his love a crime."

"Yes," I said, "I think I see." It was all I said, and I could only
hope Dev Reja could sense all of the other things I might have
said. I turned and walked out of the classroom, closing the door
quietly behind me.

* * *

Pram's soul was rotting before my eyes. He came to class, but it was merely a habitual response and did not reflect a desire to actually learn anything. Once I asked him how he could expect to be a successful sociologist if he failed his courses; he had stared at me blankly, as though my words had no meaning.

He no longer bathed, and his body smelled. The wound on his throat had become infected and suppurating; Pram had wrapped it in a dirty rag which he did not bother to change. His very presence had become anathema to the rest of his class, and it was only with the greatest difficulty that I managed to get through each lecture that Pram attended. Soon I wished he would no longer come, and this realization only added to my own growing sense of horror. He came to see me each day, but only because I asked him to. Each day I talked, and Pram sat and gave the semblance of attention. But that was all he gave, and it was not difficult to see that my words had no effect; I could not even be sure he heard them. After a while he would ask permission to leave and I would walk him to the door, fighting back the urge to scream at him, to beat him with my fists.

The infected wound landed him back in the hospital. Three days later I was awakened in the middle of the night by the insistent ring of the telephone. I picked it up and Indiri's voice cut through me like a knife.

"Dr. Frederickson! It's Pram! I think something terrible is going to happen!"

Her words were shrill, strung together like knots in a wire about to snap. "Easy, Indiri. Slow down and tell me exactly what's happened."

"Something woke me up a few minutes ago," she said, her heavy breathing punctuating each word. "I got up and went to the window. Pram was standing on the lawn, staring up at my window."

"Did he say anything, make any signal that he wanted to talk to you?"

"No. He ran when he saw me." Her voice broke off in a shudder, then resumed in the frightened croak of an old woman. "He was wearing two wooden blocks on a string around his neck."

"Wooden blocks?"

"Clappers," Indiri sobbed. "Like a candala might wear. Do you remember what I told you?"

I remembered. "In what direction was he running?"

"I'm not sure, but I think Dr. Dev Reja's house is in that direction."

I slammed down the phone and yanked on enough clothes to keep from being arrested. Then, still without knowing exactly why, I found myself running through the night.

My own apartment was a block and a half off campus, about a half mile from Dev Reja's on-campus residence. I hurdled a low brick wall on the east side of the campus and pumped my arms as I raced across the rolling green lawns.

I ran in a panic, pursued by thoughts of clappers and corpses. My lungs burned and my legs felt like slabs of dough; then a new surge of adrenalin flowed and I ran. And ran.

The door to Dev Reja's house was ajar, the light on in the living room. I took the porch steps three at a time, tripped over the door jamb and sprawled headlong on the living room floor. I rolled to my feet; and froze.

Pram might have been waiting for me, or simply lost in thought, groping for some last thread of sanity down in the black, ether depths where his mind had gone. My mouth opened, but no sound came out. Pram's eyes were like two dull marbles, too large for his face and totally unseeing.

Dev Reja's naked corpse lay on the floor. The handle of a kitchen knife protruded from between the shoulder blades. The clothes Dev Reja should have been wearing were loosely draped over Pram. The room reeked with the smell of gasoline.

Candala. Pram had made the final identification, embracing it completely.

I saw Pram's hand move and heard something that sounded like the scratching of a match; my yell was lost in the sudden explosion of fire. Pram and the corpse beside him blossomed into an obscene flower of flame: its petals seared my flesh as I stepped forward.

I backed up slowly, shielding my face with my hands. Deep inside the deadly pocket of fire Pram's charred body rocked back and forth, then fell across Dev Reja's corpse. I gagged on the smell of cooking flesh.

Somewhere, thousands of miles and years from what was happening in the room, I heard the scream of fire engines, their wailing moans blending with my own.

# MAX ALLAN COLLINS

# MARBLE MILDRED

*"Marble Mildred" is another of Max Collins's miniature historical gems featuring P.I. Nathan Heller, an ex-cop in the corrupt Chicago of the 1930s. The first Heller novel,* True Detective, *won the Shamus Award for Best P.I. Novel of 1983. The subsequent Heller novels,* True Crime *and* The Million-Dollar Wound, *were nominated for the same award in 1984 and 1986. Max Collins has had a Nate Heller story in each of the three PWA anthologies; this is the lengthiest, and the best.*

In June 1936, Chicago was in the midst of the Great Depression and a sweltering summer, and I was in the midst of Chicago. Specifically, on this Tuesday afternoon, the ninth to be exact, I was sitting on a sofa in the minuscule lobby of the Van Buren Hotel. The sofa had seen better days, and so had the hotel. The Van Buren was no flophouse, merely a moderately rundown residential hotel just west of the El tracks, near the LaSalle Street Station.

Divorce work wasn't the bread and butter of the A-1 Detective Agency, but we didn't turn it away. I use the editorial "we," but actually there was only one of us, me, Nathan Heller, "president" of the firm. And despite my high-flown title, I was just a down-at-the-heels dick reading a racing form in a seedy hotel's seedy lobby, waiting to see if a certain husband showed up in the company of another woman.

Another woman, that is, than the one he was married to; the dumpy, dusky dame who'd come to my office yesterday.

"I'm not as good-looking as I was fourteen years ago," she'd said, coyly, her voice honeyed by a Southern drawl, "but I'm a darn sight younger looking than *some* women I know."

"You're a very handsome woman, Mrs. Bolton," I said, smiling, figuring she was fifty if she was a day, "and I'm sure there's nothing to your suspicions."

She had been a looker once, but she'd run to fat, and her badly hennaed hair and overdone makeup were no help; nor was the raccoon stole she wore over a faded floral print housedress. The stole looked a bit ratty and in any case was hardly called for in this weather.

"Mr. Heller, they are more than suspicions. My husband is a successful businessman, with an office in the financial district. He is easy prey to gold diggers."

The strained formality of her tone made the raccoon stole make sense, somehow.

"This isn't the first time you've suspected him of infidelity."

"Unfortunately, no."

"Are you hoping for reconciliation, or has a lawyer advised you to establish grounds for divorce?"

"At this point," she said, calmly, the Southern drawl making her words seem more casual than they were, "I wish only to know. Can you understand that, Mr. Heller?"

"Certainly. I'm afraid I'll need some details . . ."

She had them. Though they lived in Hyde Park, a quiet, quietly well-off residential area, Bolton was keeping a room at the Van Buren Hotel, a few blocks down the street from the very office in which we sat. Mrs. Bolton believed that he went to the hotel on assignations while pretending to leave town on business trips.

"How did you happen to find that out?" I asked her.

"His secretary told me," she said, with a crinkly little smile, proud of herself.

"Are you sure you need a detective? You seem to be doing pretty well on your own . . ."

The smile disappeared and she seemed quite serious now, digging into her big black purse and coming back with a folded wad of cash. She thrust it across the desk toward me, as if daring me to take it.

I don't take dares, but I do take money. And there was plenty of it: a hundred in tens and fives.

"My rate's ten dollars a day and expenses," I said, reluctantly, the notion of refusing money going against the grain. "A thirty-dollar retainer would be plenty . . ."

She nodded curtly. "I'd prefer you accept that. But it's all I can afford, remember; when it's gone, it's gone."

I wrote her out a receipt and told her I hoped to refund some of the money, though of course I hoped the opposite, and that I hoped to be able to dispel her fears about her husband's fidelity, though there was little hope of that, either. Hope was in short supply in Chicago, these days.

Right now, she said, Joe was supposedly on a business trip; but the secretary had called to confide in Mrs. Bolton that her husband had been in the office all day.

I had to ask the usual questions. She gave me a complete description (and a photo she'd had foresight to bring), his business address, working hours, a list of places he was known to frequent.

And, so, I had staked out the hotel yesterday, starting late afternoon. I didn't start in the lobby. The hotel was a walk-up, the lobby on the second floor; the first floor leased out to a saloon, in the window of which I sat nursing beers and watching people stroll by. One of them, finally, was Joseph Bolton, a tall, nattily attired businessman about ten years his wife's junior; he was pleasant looking, but with his wire-rimmed glasses and receding brown hair was no Robert Taylor.

Nor was he enjoying feminine company, unless said company was already up in the hotel room before I'd arrived on the scene. I followed him up the stairs to the glorified landing of a lobby, where I paused at the desk while he went on up the next flight of stairs (there were no elevators in the Van Buren) and, after buying a newspaper from the desk clerk, went up to his floor, the third of the four-story hotel, and watched from around a corner as he entered his room.

Back down in the lobby, I approached the desk clerk, an older guy with rheumy eyes and a blue bow tie. I offered him a buck for the name of the guest in Room 3C.

"Bolton," he said.

"You're kidding," I said. "Let me see the register." I hadn't bothered coming in earlier to bribe a look because I figured Bolton would be here under an assumed name.

"What it's worth to you?" he asked.

"I already paid," I said, and turned his register around and looked in it. Joseph Bolton it was. Using his own goddamn name. That was a first.

"Any women?" I asked.

"Not that I know of," he said.

"Regular customer?"

"He's been living here a couple months."

"Living here? He's here every night?"

"I dunno. He pays his six bits a day, is all I know. I don't tuck him in."

I gave the guy half a buck to let me rent his threadbare sofa. Sat for another couple of hours and followed two women upstairs. Both seemed to be hookers; neither stopped at Bolton's room.

At a little after eight, Bolton left the hotel and I followed him over to Adams Street, to the Berghoff, the best German restaurant for the money in the Loop. What the hell—I hadn't eaten yet either. We both dined alone.

That night I phoned Mrs. Bolton with my report, such as it was.

"He has a woman in his room," she insisted.

"It's possible," I allowed.

"Stay on the job," she said, and hung up.

I stayed on the job. That is, the next afternoon I returned to the Van Buren Hotel, or anyway to the saloon underneath it, and drank beers and watched the world go by. Now and then the world would go up the hotel stairs. Men I ignored; women that looked like hookers I ignored. One woman, who showed up around four-thirty, I did not ignore.

She was as slender and attractive a woman as Mildred Bolton was not, though she was only a few years younger. And her wardrobe was considerably more stylish than my client's—high-collared white dress with a bright colorful figured print, white gloves, white shoes, a felt hat with a wide turned-down brim.

She did not look like the sort of woman who would be stopping in at the Van Buren Hotel, but stop in she did.

So did I. I trailed her up to the third floor, where she was met at the door of Bolton's room by a male figure. I just got a glimpse of the guy, but he didn't seem to be Bolton. She went inside.

I used a pay phone in the saloon downstairs and called Mrs. Bolton in Hyde Park.

"I can be there in forty minutes," she said.

"What are you talking about?"

"I want to catch them together. I'm going to claw that hussy's eyes out."

"Mrs. Bolton, you don't want to do that . . ."

"I most certainly do. You can go home, Mr. Heller. You've done your job, and nicely."

And she had hung up.

I'd mentioned to her that the man in her husband's room did

not seem to be her husband, but that apparently didn't matter. Now I had a choice: I could walk back up to my office and write Mrs. Bolton out a check refunding seventy of her hundred dollars, goddamnit (ten bucks a day, ten bucks expenses—she'd pay for my bribes and beers).

Or I could do the Christian thing and wait around and try to defuse this thing before it got even uglier.

I decided to do the latter. Not because it was the Christian thing—I wasn't a Christian, after all—but because I might be able to convince Mrs. Bolton she needed a few more days' work out of me, to figure out what was really going on here. It seemed to me she could use a little more substantial information, if a divorce was to come out of this. It also seemed to me I could use the money.

I don't know how she arrived—whether by El or streetcar or bus or auto—but as fast as she was walking, it could've been on foot. She was red in the face, eyes hard and round as marbles, fists churning as she strode, her head floating above the incongruous raccoon stole.

I hopped off my bar stool and caught her at the sidewalk.

"Don't go in there, Mrs. Bolton," I said, taking her arm gently.

She swung it away from me, held her head back and, short as she was, looked down at me, nostrils flared. I felt like a matador who dropped his cape.

"You've been discharged for the day, Mr. Heller," she said.

"You still need my help. You're not going about this the right way."

With indignation she began, "My husband . . ."

"Your husband isn't in there. He doesn't even get off work till six."

She swallowed. The redness of her face seemed to fade some; I was quieting her down.

Then fucking fate stepped in, in the form of that swanky dame in the felt hat, who picked that very moment to come strolling out of the Van Buren Hotel like it was the goddamn Palmer House. On her arm was a young man, perhaps eighteen, perhaps twenty, in a cream-color seersucker suit and a gold tie, with a pale complexion and sky-blue eyes and corn-silk blond hair. He and the woman on his arm shared the same sensitive mouth.

"Whore!" somebody shouted.

Who else? My client.

I put my hand over my face and shook my head and wished I was dead, or at least in my office.

"Degenerate!" Mrs. Bolton sang out. She rushed toward the slender woman, who reared back, properly horrified. The young man gripped the woman's arm tightly; whether to protect her or himself, it wasn't quite clear.

Well, the sidewalks were filled with people who'd gotten off work, heading for the El or the LaSalle Street Station, so we had an audience. Yes we did.

And Mrs. Bolton was standing nose to nose with the startled woman, saying defiantly, "I am *Mrs.* Bolton—you've been up to see my husband!"

"Why, Mrs. Bolton," the woman said, backing away as best she could. "Your husband is not in his room."

"Liar!"

"If he were in the room, I wouldn't have been in there myself, I assure you."

"Lying whore . . ."

"Okay," I said, wading in, taking Mrs. Bolton by the arm, less gently this time, "that's enough."

"Don't talk to my mother that way," the young man said to Mrs. Bolton.

"I'll talk to her any way I like, you little degenerate."

And the young man slapped my client. It was a loud, ringing slap, and drew blood from one corner of her wide mouth.

I pointed a finger at the kid's nose. "That wasn't nice. Back away."

My client's eyes were glittering; she was smiling, a blood-flecked smile that wasn't the sanest thing I ever saw. Despite the gleeful expression, she began to scream things at the couple: "Whore! Degenerate!"

"Oh Christ," I said, wishing I'd listened to my old man and finished college.

We were encircled by a crowd who watched all this with bemused interest, some people smiling, others frowning, others frankly amazed. In the street the clop-clop of an approaching mounted police officer, interrupted in the pursuit of parking violators, cut through the din. A tall, lanky officer, he climbed off his mount and pushed through the crowd.

"What's going on here?" he asked.

"This little degenerate hit me," my client said, wearing her bloody mouth and her righteous indignation like medals, and she grabbed the kid by the tie and yanked the poor son of a bitch by it, jerking him silly.

It made me laugh. It was amusing only in a sick way, but I was sick enough to appreciate it.

"That'll be all of that," the officer said. "Now what happened here?"

I filled him in, in a general way, while my client interrupted with occasional non sequiturs; the mother and son just stood there looking chagrined about being the center of attention for perhaps a score of onlookers.

"I want that dirty little brute arrested," Mrs. Bolton said, through an off-white picket fence of clenched teeth. "I'm a victim of assault!"

The poor shaken kid was hardly a brute, and he was cleaner than most, but he admitted having struck her, when the officer asked him.

"I'm going to have to take you in, son," the officer said.

The boy looked like he might cry. Head bowed, he shrugged and his mother, eyes brimming with tears herself, hugged him.

The officer went to a call box and summoned a squad car and soon the boy was sent away, the mother waiting pitifully at the curb as the car pulled off, the boy's pale face looking back, a sad cameo in the window.

I was at my client's side.

"Let me help you get home, Mrs. Bolton," I said, taking her arm again.

She smiled tightly, patronizingly, withdrew her arm. "I'm fine, Mr. Heller. I can take care of myself. I thank you for your assistance."

And she rolled like a tank through what remained of the crowd, toward the El station.

I stood there a while, trying to gather my wits; it would have taken a better detective than yours truly to find them, however, so, finally, I approached the shattered woman who still stood at the curb. The crowd was gone. So was the mounted officer. All that remained were a few horse apples and me.

"I'm sorry about all that," I told her.

She looked at me, her face smooth, her eyes sad; they were a darker blue than her son's. "What's your role in this?"

"I'm an investigator. Mrs. Bolton suspects her husband of infidelity."

She laughed harshly—a very harsh laugh for such a refined woman. "My understanding is that Mrs. Bolton has suspected that for some fourteen years—and without foundation. But at this point, it would seem moot, one would think."

"Moot? What are you talking about?"

"The Boltons have been separated for months. Mr. Bolton is suing her for divorce."

"What? Since when?"

"Why, since January."

"Then Bolton *does* live at the Van Buren Hotel, here?"

"Yes. My brother and I have known Mr. Bolton for years. My son Charles came up to Chicago recently, to find work, and Joe— Mr. Bolton—is helping him find a job."

"You're, uh, not from Chicago?"

"I live in Woodstock. I'm a widow. Have you any other questions?"

"Excuse me, ma'am. I'm sorry about this. Really. My client misled me about a few things." I tipped my hat to her.

She warmed up a bit; gave me a smile. Tentative, but a smile. "Your apology is accepted, mister . . . ?"

"Heller," I said. "Nathan. And your name?"

"Marie Winston," she said, and extended her gloved hand. I grasped it, smiled.

"Well," I said, shrugged, smiled, tipped my hat again, and headed back for my office.

It wasn't the first time a client had lied to me, and it sure wouldn't be the last. But I'd never been lied to in quite this way. For one thing, I wasn't sure Mildred Bolton knew she *was* lying. This lady clearly did not have all her marbles.

I put the hundred bucks in the bank and the matter out of my mind, until I received a phone call, on the afternoon of June 14.

"This is Marie Winston, Mr. Heller. Do you remember me?"

At first, frankly, I didn't; but I said, "Certainly. What can I do for you, Mrs. Winston?"

"That . . . incident out in front of the Van Buren Hotel last Wednesday, which you witnessed . . ."

"Oh yes. What about it?"

"Mrs. Bolton has insisted on pressing charges. I wonder if you could appear in police court tomorrow morning, and explain what happened?"

"Well . . ."

"Mr. Heller, I would greatly appreciate it."

I don't like turning down attractive women, even on the telephone; but there was more to it than that: the emotion in her voice got to me.

"Well, sure," I said.

So the next morning I headed over to the south Loop police court and spoke my piece. I kept to the facts, which I felt would pretty much exonerate all concerned. The circumstances were, as they say, extenuating.

Mildred Bolton, who glared at me as if I'd betrayed her, approached the bench and spoke of the young man's "unprovoked assault." She claimed to be suffering physically and mentally from the blow she'd received. The latter, at least, was believable. Her eyes were round and wild as she answered the judge's questions.

When the judge fined young Winston one hundred dollars, Mrs. Bolton stood in her place in the gallery and began to clap. Loudly. The judge looked at her, too startled to rap his gavel and demand order; then she flounced out of the courtroom very girlishly, tossing her raccoon stole over her shoulder, exulting in her victory.

An embarrassed silence fell across the room. And it's hard to embarrass hookers, a brace of which were awaiting their turn at the docket.

Then the judge pounded his gavel and said, "The court vacates this young man's fine."

Winston, who'd been hangdog throughout the proceedings, brightened like his switch had been turned on. He pumped his lawyer's hand and turned to his mother, seated behind him just beyond the railing, and they hugged.

On the way out Marie Winston, smiling gently, touched my arm and said, "Thank you very much, Mr. Heller."

"I don't think I made much difference."

"I think you did. The judge vacated the fine, after all."

"Hell, I had nothing to do with that. Mildred was your star witness."

"In a way I guess she was."

"I notice her husband wasn't here."

Son Charles spoke up. "No, he's at work. He . . . well, he thought it was better he not be here. We figured *that woman* would be here, after all."

"'That woman' is sick."

"In the head," Charles said bitterly.

"That's right. You or I could be sick that way, too. Somebody ought to help her."

Marie Winston, straining to find some compassion for Mildred Bolton, said, "Who would you suggest?"

"Damnit," I said, "the husband. He's been with her fourteen years. She didn't get this way overnight. The way I see it, he's got a responsibility to get her some goddamn *help* before he dumps her by the side of the road."

Mrs. Winston smiled at that, some compassion coming through after all. "You have a very modern point of view, Mr. Heller."

"Not really. I'm not even used to talkies yet. Anyway, I'll see you, Mrs. Winston. Charles."

And I left the graystone building and climbed in my '32 Auburn and drove back to my office. I parked in the alley, in my space, and walked over to the Berghoff for lunch. I think I hoped to find Bolton there. But he wasn't.

I went back to the office and puttered a while; I had a pile of retail credit-risk checks to whittle away at.

Hell with it, I thought, and walked over to Bolton's office building, a narrow, fifteen-story, white granite structure just behind the Federal Reserve on West Jackson, next to the El. Bolton was doing all right—better than me, certainly—but as a broker he was in the financial district only by a hair. No doubt he was a relatively small-time insurance broker, making twenty or twenty-five grand a year. Big money by my standards, but a lot of guys over at the Board of Trade spilled more than that.

There was no lobby really, just a wide hall between facing rows of shops—newsstand, travel agency, cigar store. The uniformed elevator operator, a skinny, pockmarked guy about my age, was waiting for a passenger. I was it.

"Tenth floor," I told him, and he took me up.

He was pulling open the cage doors when we heard the air crack, three times.

"What the hell was that?" he said.

"It wasn't a car backfiring," I said. "You better stay here."

I moved cautiously out into the hall. The elevators came up a central shaft, with a squared-off "c" of offices all about. I glanced quickly at the names on the pebbled glass in the wood-partition walls, and finally lit upon BOLTON AND SCHMIDT, INSURANCE BROKERS. I swallowed and moved cautiously in that direction as the door flew open and a young woman flew out—a dark-haired dish of maybe twenty with wide eyes and a face drained of blood, her silk stockings flashing as she rushed my way.

She fell into my arms and I said, "Are you wounded?"

"No," she swallowed, "but somebody is."

The poor kid was gasping for air; I hauled her toward the bank of elevators. Even under the strain, I was enjoying the feel and smell of her.

"You wouldn't be Joseph Bolton's secretary, by any chance?" I asked, helping her onto the elevator.

She nodded, eyes still huge.

"Take her down," I told the operator.

And I headed back for that office. I was nearly there when I met Joseph Bolton, as he lurched down the hall. He had a gun in his hand. His light brown suitcoat was splotched with blood in several places; so was his right arm. He wasn't wearing his eyeglasses, which made his face seem naked somehow. His expression seemed at once frightened, pained, and sorrowful.

He staggered toward me like a child taking its first steps, and I held my arms out to him like daddy. But they were more likely his last steps: he fell to the marble floor and began to writhe, tracing abstract designs in his own blood on the smooth surface.

I moved toward him and he pointed the gun at me, a little .32 revolver. "Stay away! Stay away!"

"Okay, bud, okay," I said.

I heard someone laughing.

A woman.

I looked up and in the office doorway, feet planted like a giant surveying a puny world, was dumpy little Mildred, in her floral housedress and raccoon stole. Her mug was split in a big goofy smile.

"Don't pay any attention to him, Mr. Heller," she said, lightly. "He's just faking."

"He's shot to shit, lady!" I said.

Keeping their distance out of respect and fear were various tenth-floor tenants, standing near their various offices, as if witnessing some strange performance.

"Keep her away from me!" Bolton managed to shout. His mouth was bubbling with blood. His body moved slowly across the marble floor like a slug, leaving a slimy red trail.

I moved to Mrs. Bolton, stood between her and Bolton. "You just take it easy . . ."

Mrs. Bolton, giggling, peeked out from in back of me. "Look at him, fooling everybody."

"You behave," I told her. Then I called out to a businessman of about fifty near the elevators. I asked him if there were any doctors in the building, and he said yes, and I said then for Christsake go get one.

"Why don't you get up and stop faking?" she said teasingly to her fallen husband, the Southern drawl dripping off her words. She craned her neck around me to see him, like she couldn't bear to miss a moment of the show.

"Keep her away! Keep her away!"

Bolton continued to writhe like a wounded snake, but he kept clutching that gun, and wouldn't let anyone near him. He would cry out that he couldn't breathe, beating his legs against the floor, but he seemed always conscious of his wife's presence. He would move his head so as to keep my body between him and her round cold glittering eyes.

"Don't you mind Joe, Mr. Heller. He's just putting on an act."

If so, I had a hunch it was his final performance.

And now he began to scream in pain.

I approached him and he looked at me with tears in his eyes, eyes that bore the confusion of a child in pain, and he relented, allowed me to come close, handed me the gun, like he was offering a gift. I accepted it, by the nose of the thing, and dropped it in my pocket.

"Did you shoot yourself, Mr. Bolton?" I asked him.

"Keep that woman away from me," he managed, lips bloody.

"He's not really hurt," his wife said, mincingly, from the office doorway.

"Did your wife shoot you?"

"Just keep her away . . ."

Two people in white came rushing toward us—a doctor and a nurse—and I stepped aside, but the doctor, a middle-aged, rather heavyset man with glasses, asked if I'd give him a hand. I said sure and pitched in.

Bolton was a big man, nearly two hundred pounds I'd say, and pretty much dead weight; we staggered toward the elevator like drunks. Like Bolton himself had staggered toward me, actually. The nurse tagged along.

So did Mrs. Bolton.

The nurse, young, blond, slender, did her best to keep Mrs. Bolton out of the elevator, but Mrs. Bolton pushed her way through like a fullback. The doctor and I, bracing Bolton, couldn't help the young nurse.

Bolton, barely conscious, said, "Please . . . please, keep her away."

"Now, now," Mrs. Bolton said, the violence of her entry into the elevator forgotten (by her), standing almost primly, hands folded over the big black purse, "everything will be all right, dear. You'll see."

Bolton began to moan; the pain it suggested wasn't entirely physical.

On the thirteenth floor, a second doctor met us and took my place hauling Bolton, and I went ahead and opened the door onto a waiting room where patients, having witnessed the doctor and nurse race madly out of the office, were milling about expectantly. The nurse guided the doctors and their burden down a hall into an X-ray room. The nurse shut the door on them and faced Mrs. Bolton with a firm look.

"I'm sorry, Mrs. Bolton, you'll have to wait."

"Is that so?" she said.

"Mrs. Bolton," I said, touching her arm.

She glared at me. "Who invited you?"

I resisted the urge to say, *you did, you fucking cow,* and just stood back while she moved up and down the narrow corridor between the offices and examining rooms, searching for a door that would lead her to her beloved husband. She trundled up and down, grunting, talking to herself, and the nurse looked at me helplessly.

"She *is* the wife," I said, with a facial shrug.

The nurse sighed heavily and went to a door adjacent to the X-ray room and called out to Mrs. Bolton; Mrs. Bolton whirled and looked at her fiercely.

"You can view your husband's treatment from in here," the nurse said.

Mrs. Bolton smiled in tight triumph and drove her taxicab of a body into the room. I followed her. Don't ask me why.

A wide glass panel looked in on the X-ray room. Mrs. Bolton climbed onto an examination table, got up on her knees, and watched the flurry of activity beyond the glass, as her husband lay on a table being attended by the pair of frantic doctors.

"Did you shoot him, Mrs. Bolton?" I asked her.

She frowned but did not look at me. "Are *you* still here?"

"You lied to me, Mrs. Bolton."

"No, I didn't. And I didn't shoot him, either."

"What happened in there?"

"I never touched that gun." She was moving her head side to side, like somebody in the bleachers trying to see past the person sitting in front.

"Did your husband shoot himself?"

She made a childishly smug face. "Joe's just faking to get everybody's sympathy. He's not really hurt."

The door opened behind me and I turned to see a police officer step in.

The officer frowned at us, and shook his head as if to say "Oh, no." It was an understandable response: it was the same cop, the mounted officer, who'd come upon the disturbance outside the Van Buren Hotel. Not surprising, really—this part of the Loop was his beat, or anyway his horse's.

He crooked his finger for me to step out in the hall and I did.

"I heard a murder was being committed up on the tenth floor of 166," he explained, meaning 166 West Jackson. "Do you know what happened? Did you see it?"

I told him what I knew, which for somebody on the scene was damned little.

"Did she do it?" the officer asked.

"The gun was in the husband's hand," I shrugged. "Speaking of which . . ."

And I took the little revolver out of my pocket, holding the gun by its nose again.

"What make is this?" the officer said, taking it.

"I don't recognize it."

He read off the side: "Narizmande Eibar Spair. Thirty-two caliber."

"It got the job done."

He held the gun so that his hand avoided the grip; tried to break it open, but couldn't.

"What's wrong with this thing?" he said.

"The trigger's been snapped on empty shells, I'd say. After six slugs were gone, the shooter kept shooting. Just once around wouldn't drive the shells into the barrel like that."

"Judas," the officer said.

The X-ray room's door opened and the doctor I'd shared the elevator and Bolton's dead weight with stepped into the hall, bloody and bowed.

"He's dead," the doctor said, wearily. "Choked to death on his own blood, poor bastard."

I said nothing; just glanced at the cop, who shrugged.

"The wife's in there," I said, pointing.

But I was pointing to Mrs. Bolton, who had stepped out into the hall. She was smiling pleasantly.

She said, "You're not going to frighten me about Joe. He's a great big man and as strong as a horse. Of course, I begin to think he ought to go to the hospital this time—for a while."

"Mrs. Bolton," the doctor said, flatly, with no sympathy whatsoever, "your husband is dead."

Like a spiteful brat, she stuck out her tongue. "Liar," she said.

The doctor sighed, turned to the cop. "Shall I call the morgue, or would you like the honor?"

"You should make the call, Doctor," the officer said.

Mrs. Bolton moved slowly toward the door to the X-ray room, from which the other doctor, his smock blood-spattered, emerged. She seemed to lose her footing, then, and I took her arm yet again. This time she accepted the help. I walked her into the room and she approached the body, stroked its brow with stubby fingers.

"I can't believe he'd go," she said.

From behind me, the doctor said, "He's dead, Mrs. Bolton. Please leave the room."

Still stroking her late husband's brow, she said, "He feels cold. So cold."

She kissed his cheek.

Then she smiled down at the body and patted its head, as one might a sleeping child, and said, "He's got a beautiful head, hasn't he?"

The officer stepped into the room and said, "You'd better come along with me, Mrs. Bolton. Captain Stege wants to talk to you."

"You're making a terrible mistake. I didn't shoot him."

He took her arm; she assumed a regal posture. He asked her if she would like him to notify any relatives or friends.

"I have no relatives or friends," she said, proudly. "I never had anybody or wanted anybody except Joe."

A crowd was waiting on the street. Damn near a mob, and at the forefront were the newshounds, legmen and cameramen alike. Cameras were clicking away as Davis of the *News* and a couple of others blocked the car waiting at the curb to take Mrs. Bolton to the Homicide Bureau. The mounted cop, with her in tow, brushed them and their questions aside and soon the car, with her in it, was inching into the late afternoon traffic. The reporters and photogs began flagging cabs to take quick pursuit, but snide, boyish Davis lingered to ask me a question.

"What were you doing here, Heller?"

"Getting a hangnail looked at up at the doctor's office."

"Fuck, Heller, you got blood all over you!"

I shrugged, lifted my middle finger. "Hell of a hangnail."

He smirked and I smirked and pushed through the crowd and hoofed it back to my office.

I was sitting at my desk, about an hour later, when the phone rang.

"Get your ass over here!"

"Captain Stege?"

"No, Walter Winchell. You were an eyewitness to a homicide, Heller! Get your ass over here!"

The phone clicked in my ear and I shrugged to nobody and got my hat and went over to the First District Station, entering off Eleventh. It was a new, modern, nondescript high rise; if this was the future, who needed it.

In Stege's clean little office, from behind his desk, the clean little cop looked out his black-rimmed, round-lensed glasses at me and said, "Did you see her do it?"

"I told the officer at the scene all about it, Captain."

"You didn't make a statement."

"Get a stenographer in here and I will."

He did and I did.

That seemed to cool the stocky little cop down. He and I had been adversaries once, though were getting along better these days. But there was still a strain.

Thought gripped his doughy, owlish countenance. "How do you read it, Heller?"

"I don't know. He had the gun. Maybe it was suicide."

"Everybody in that building agrees with you. Bolton's been having a lot of trouble with his better half. They think she drove him to suicide, finally. But there's a hitch."

"Yeah?"

"Suicides don't usually shoot themselves five times, two of 'em in the back."

I had to give him that.

"You think she's nuts?" Stege asked.

"Nuttier than a fruitcake."

"Maybe. But that was murder—premeditated."

"Oh, I doubt that, Captain. Don't you know a crime of passion when you see it? Doesn't the unwritten law apply to women as well as men?"

"The answer to your question is yes to the first, and no to the second. You want to see something?"

"Sure."

From his desk he handed me a small slip of paper.

It was a receipt for a gun sold on June 11 by the Hammond Loan Company of Hammond, Indiana, to a Mrs. Sarah Weston.

"That was in her purse," Stege said, smugly. "Along with a powder puff, a hanky, and some prayer leaflets."

"And you think Sarah Weston is just a name Mrs. Bolton used to buy the .32 from the pawn shop?"

"Certainly. And that slip—found in a narrow side pocket in the lining of her purse—proves premeditation."

"Does it, Captain?" I said, smiling, standing, hat in hand. "It seems to me premeditation would have warned her to get *rid* of that receipt. But then, what do I know? I'm not cop." From the doorway I said, "Just a detective."

And I left him there to mull that over.

In the corridor, on my way out, Sam Backus buttonholed me.

"Got a minute for a pal, Nate?"

"Sam, if we were pals, I'd see you someplace besides court."

Sam was with the Public Defender's office, and I'd bumped into him from time to time, dating back to my cop days. He was a conscientious and skillful attorney who, in better times, might have had a lucrative private practice; in times like these, he was glad to have a job. Sam's sharp features and receding hairline gave the smallish man a ferretlike appearance; he was similarly intense, too.

"My client says she employed you to do some work for her," he said, in a rush. "She'd like you to continue—"

"Wait a minute, wait a minute—your client? Not Mrs. Mildred Bolton?"

"Yes."

"She's poison. You're on your own."

"She tells me you were given a hundred-dollar retainer."

"Well, that's true, but I figured I earned it."

"She figures you owe her some work, or some dough."

"Sam, she lied to me. She misrepresented herself and her intentions." I was walking out the building and he was staying right with me.

"She's a disturbed individual. And she's maintaining she didn't kill her husband."

"They got her cold." I told him about Stege's evidence.

"It could've been planted," he said, meaning the receipt. "Look, Bolton's secretary was up there, and Mrs. Bolton says he and the girl—an Angela something, sounds like 'who-you'—were having an affair."

"I thought the affair was supposed to be with Marie Winston."

"Her, too. Bolton must've been a real ladies' man. And the Winston woman was up there at that office this afternoon, too, before the shooting."

"Was she there during the shooting, though?"

"I don't know. I need to find out. The Public Defender's office doesn't have an investigative staff, you know that, Nate. And I can't afford to hire anybody, and I don't have the time to do the legwork myself. You owe her some days. Deliver."

He had a point.

I gathered some names from Sam, and the next morning I began to interview the participants.

"An affair with Joe?" Angela Houyoux said. "Why, that's nonsense."

We were in the outer office of BOLTON AND SCHMIDT. She'd given me the nickel tour of the place: one outer office, and two inner ones, the one to the south having been Bolton's. The crime scene told me nothing. Angela, the sweet-smelling dark-haired beauty who'd tumbled into my arms and the elevator yesterday, did.

"I was rather shaken by Mrs. Bolton's behavior at first—and his. But then it became rather routine to come to the office and find the glass in the door broken, or Mr. Bolton with his hands cut from taking a knife away from Mrs. Bolton. After a few weeks, I grew quite accustomed to having dictation interrupted while Mr. and Mrs. Bolton scuffled and fought and yelled. Lately they argued about Mrs. Winston a lot."

"How was your relationship with Mrs. Bolton?"

"Spotty, I guess you'd call it. Sometimes she'd seem to think I was interested in her husband. Other times she'd confide in me like a sister. I never said much to her. I'd just shrug my shoulders or just look at her kind of sympathetic. I had the feeling she didn't have anybody else to talk to about this. She'd cry and say her husband was unfaithful—I didn't dare point out they'd been separated for a year and that Mr. Bolton had filed for divorce and all. One time . . . well, maybe I shouldn't say it."

"Say it."

"One time she said she 'just might kill' her husband. She said they never convict a woman for murder in Cook County."

Others in the building at West Jackson told similar tales. Bolton's business partner, Schmidt, wondered why Bolton bothered to get an injunction to keep his wife out of the office, but then refused to mail her her temporary alimony, giving her a reason to come to the office all the time.

"He would dole out the money, two or three dollars at a time," Schmidt said. "He could have paid her what she had coming for a month, or at least a week—Joe made decent money. It would've got rid of her. Why parcel it out?"

The elevator operator I'd met yesterday had a particularly wild yarn.

"Yesterday, early afternoon, Mr. Bolton got on at the ninth floor. He seemed in an awful hurry and said, 'Shoot me up to eleven.' I had a signal to stop at ten, so I made the stop and Mrs. Bolton came charging aboard. Mr. Bolton was right next to me. He kind of hid behind me and said, 'For God's sake, she'll kill us both!' I sort of forced the door closed on her, and she stood there in the corridor and raised her fist and said, 'Goddamnit, I'll fix you!' I guess she meant Bolton, not me."

"Apparently."

"Anyway, I took him up to eleven and he kind of sighed and as he got off he said, 'It's just hell, isn't it?' I said it was a damn shame he couldn't do anything about it."

"This was yesterday."

"Yes, sir. Not long before he was killed."

"Did it occur to you, at the time, it might lead to that?"

"No, sir. It was pretty typical, actually. I helped him escape from her before. And I kept her from getting on the elevator downstairs, sometimes. After all, he had an injunction to keep her from 'molesting him at his place of business,' he said."

Even the heavyset doctor up on thirteen found time for me.

"I think they were *both* sick," he said, rather bitterly I thought.

"What do you mean, Doctor?"

"I mean that I've administered more first aid to that man than a battlefield physician. That woman has beaten her husband, cut him with a knife, with a razor, created commotions and scenes with such regularity that the patrol wagon coming for Mildred is a commonplace occurrence on West Jackson."

"How well did you know Bolton?"

"We were friendly. God knows I spent enough time with him, patching him up. He should've been a much more successful man than he was, you know. She drove him out of one job and another. I never understood him."

"Oh?"

"Well, they live, or lived, in Hyde Park. That's a university neighborhood. Fairly refined, very intellectual, really."

"Was Bolton a scholar?"

"He had bookish interests. He liked having the University of Chicago handy. Now why would a man of his sensibilities endure a violent harridan like Mildred Bolton?"

"In my trade, Doc," I said, "we call that a mystery."

I talked to more people. I talked to a pretty blond legal secretary named Peggy O'Reilly who, in 1933, had been employed by Ocean Accident and Guarantee Company. Joseph Bolton, Jr., had been a business associate there.

"His desk was four feet from mine," she said. "But I never went out with him. There was no social contact whatsoever, but Mrs. Bolton didn't believe that. She came into the office and accused me of—well, called me a 'dirty hussy,' if you must know. I asked her to step out into the hall where we wouldn't attract so much attention, and she did—and proceeded to tear my clothes off me. She tore the clothes off my body, scratched my neck, my face, kicked me, it was horrible. The attention it attracted . . . oh, dear. Several hundred people witnessed the sight—two nice men pulled her off of me. I was badly bruised and out of the office a week. When I came back, Mr. Bolton had been discharged."

A pattern was forming here, one I'd seen before; but usually it was the wife who was battered and yet somehow endured and even encouraged the twisted union. Only Bolton was a battered husband, a strapping man who never turned physically on his abusing wife; his only punishment had been to withhold that money from her, dole it out a few bucks at a time. That was the only satisfaction, the only revenge, he'd been able to extract.

At the Van Buren Hotel I knocked on the door of what had been Bolton's room. 3C.

Young Charles Winston answered. He looked terrible. Pale as milk, only not near as healthy. Eyes bloodshot. He was in a T-shirt and boxer shorts. The other times I'd seen him he'd been fully and even nattily attired.

"Put some clothes on," I said. "We have to talk."

In the saloon below the hotel we did that very thing.

"Joe was a great guy," he said, eyes brimming with tears. He would have cried into his beer, only he was having a mixed drink. I was picking up the tab, so Mildred Bolton was buying it.

"Is your mother still in town?"

He looked up with sharp curiosity. "No. She's back in Woodstock. Why?"

"She was up at the office shortly before Bolton was killed."

"I know. I was there, too."

"Oh?" Now, that was news.

"We went right over, after the hearing."

"To tell him how it came out?"

"Yes, and to thank him. You see, after that incident out in front, last Wednesday, when they took me off to jail, Mother went to see Joe. They met at the Twelfth Street Bus Depot. She asked him if he would take care of my bail—she could have had her brother do it, in the morning, but I'd have had to spend the night in jail first." He smiled fondly. "Joe went right over to the police station with the money and got me out."

"That was white of him."

"Sure was. Then we met Mother over at the taproom of the Auditorium Hotel."

Very posh digs; interesting place for folks who lived at the Van Buren to be hanging out.

"Unfortunately, I'd taken time to stop back at the hotel to pick up some packages my mother had left behind. Mrs. Bolton must've been waiting here for me. She followed me to the Auditorium taproom, where she attacked me with her fists, and told the crowd in no uncertain terms, and in a voice to wake the dead, that my mother was"—he shook his head—"'nothing but a whore' and such. Finally the management ejected her."

"Was your mother in love with Joe?"

He looked at me sharply. "Of course not. They were friendly. That's the extent of it."

"When did you and your mother leave Bolton's office?"

"Yesterday? About one-thirty. Mrs. Bolton was announced as being in the outer office, and we just got the hell out."

"Neither of you lingered."

"No. Are you going to talk to my mother?"

"Probably."

"I wish you wouldn't," he said glumly.

I drank my beer, studying the kid.

"Maybe I won't have to," I said, smiled at him, patted his shoulder, and left.

I met with public defender Backus in a small interrogation room at the First District Station.

"Your client is guilty," I said.

I was sitting. He was standing. Pacing.

"The secretary was in the outer office at all times," I said. "In view of other witnesses. The Winstons left around one-thirty. They were seen leaving by the elevator operator on duty."

"One of them could have sneaked back up the stairs . . ."

"I don't think so. Anyway, this meeting ends my participation, other than a report I'll type up for you. I've used up the hundred."

From my notes I read off summaries of the various interviews I'd conducted. He finally sat, sweat beading his brow, eyes slitted behind the glasses.

"She says she didn't do it," he said.

"She says a lot of things. I think you can get her off, anyway."

He smirked. "Are you a lawyer now?"

"No. Just a guy who's been in the thick of this bizarre fucking case since day one."

"I bow to your experience if not expertise."

"You can plead her insane, Sam."

"A very tough defense to pull off, and besides, she won't hear of it. She wants no psychiatrists, no alienists involved."

"You can still get her off."

"How in hell?"

I let some air out. "I'm going to have to talk to her before I say any more. It's going to have to be up to her."

"You can't tell me?"

"You're not my client."

Mildred Bolton was.

And she was ushered into the interrogation room by a matron who then waited outside the door. She wore the same floral print dress, but the raccoon stole was gone. She smiled faintly upon seeing me, sat across from me.

"You been having fun with the press, Mildred, haven't you?"

"I sure have. They call me 'Marble Mildred.' They think I'm cold."

"They think it's unusual for a widow to joke about her dead husband."

"They're silly people. They asked me the name of my attorney and I said, 'Horsefeathers.'" She laughed. That struck her very funny; she was proud of herself over that witty remark.

"I'm glad you can find something to smile about."

"I'm getting hundreds of letters, you know. Fan mail! They say, 'You should have killed him whether you did or not.' I'm not the only woman wronged in Chicago, you know."

"They've got you dead bang, Mildred. I've seen some of the evidence. I've talked to the witnesses."

"Did you talk to Mrs. Winston? It was her fault, you know. Her and that . . . that boy."

"You went to see Joe after the boy was fined in court."

"Yes! I called him and told him that the little degenerate had been convicted and fined. Then I asked Joe, did he have any money, because I didn't have anything to eat, and he said yes. So I went to the office and when I got there he tried to give me a check for ten dollars. I said, 'I guess you're going to pay that boy's fine and that's why you haven't any money for me.' He said, 'That's all you're going to get.' And I said, 'Do you mean for a whole *week*? To pay rent out of and eat on?' He said, 'Yes, that's all you get.'"

"He was punishing you."

"I suppose. We argued for about an hour and then he said he had business on another floor—that boy's lawyer is on the ninth floor, you know—and I followed him, chased him to the elevator, but he got away. I went back and said to Miss Houyoux, 'He ran away from me.' I waited in his office and in about an hour he came back. I said, 'Joe, I have been your wife for fourteen years and I think I deserve more respect and better treatment than that.' He just leaned back in his chair so cocky and said, 'You know what you are?' And then he said it."

"Said it?"

She swallowed; for the first time, those marble eyes filled with tears. "He said, 'You're just a dirty old bitch.' Then he said it again. Then I said, 'Just a dirty old bitch for fourteen years?' And I pointed the gun at him."

"Where was it?"

"It was on his desk where I put it. It was in a blue box I carried in with me."

"What did you do with it, Mildred?"

"The box?"

"The gun."

"Oh. That. I fired it at him."

I gave her a handkerchief and she dabbed her eyes with it. "How many times did you fire the gun, Mildred?"

"I don't know. He fell over in his chair and then he got up and came toward me and he said, 'Give me that gun, give me that gun.' I said, 'No, I'm going to finish myself now. Let go of me because my hand is on the trigger!'" Her teeth were clenched. "He struggled with me, and his glasses got knocked off, but he got the gun from my hand and he went out in the hall with it. I followed him, but then I turned and went back in his office. I was going to jump out of the window, but I heard him scream in the hall and I ran to him. The gun was lying beside him and I reached for it, but he reached and got it first. I went back in the office."

"Why?"

"To jump out the window, I told you. But I just couldn't leave him. I started to go back out and when I opened the door some people were around. You were one of them, Mr. Heller."

"Where did you get that gun, Mildred?"

"At a pawn shop in Hammond, Indiana."

"To kill Joe?"

"To kill myself."

"But you didn't."

"I'm sorry I didn't. I had plenty of time to do it at home, but I wanted to do it in his office. I wanted to embarrass him."

"He was shot in the back, Mildred. Twice."

"I don't know about that. Maybe his body turned when I was firing. I don't know. I don't remember."

"You know that the prosecution will not buy your suicide claims."

"They are *not* claims!"

"I know they aren't. But they won't buy them. They'll tell the judge and the jury that all your talk of suicide is just a clever excuse to get around planning Joe's murder. In other words, that you premeditated the killing and supplied yourself with a gun— and a reason for having a gun."

"I don't know about those things."

"Would you like to walk away from this?"

"Well, of course. I'm not crazy."

Right.

"You can, I think. But it's going to be hard on you. They're going to paint you as a shrew. As a brutal woman who battered her husband. They'll suggest that Bolton was too much of a gentleman for his own good, that he should have struck back at you, physically."

She giggled. "He wasn't such a gentleman."

"Really?"

"He wasn't what you think at all. Not at all."

"What do you mean, Mildred?"

"We were married for fourteen years before he tried to get rid of me. That's a long time."

"It sure is. What is it about your husband that we're getting wrong?"

"I haven't said."

"I know that. Tell me."

"I won't tell you. I've never told a living soul. I never will."

"I think you should. I think you need to."

"I won't. I won't now. I won't ever."

"There were no other women, were there, Mildred?"

"There were countless women, countless!"

"Like Marie Winston."

"She was the worst!"

"What about her son?"

"That little . . ." She stopped herself.

"That little degenerate? That's what you seem to always call him."

She nodded, pursing her thin wide lips.

"Joe was living in a fleabag hotel," I said. "A guy with *his* money. Why?"

"It was close to his work."

"Relatively. I think it had to do with who he was living with. A young man."

"A lot of men room together."

"There were no other women, were there, Mildred? Your husband used you to hide behind, didn't he, for many years."

She was crying now. The marble woman was crying now. "I loved him. I loved him."

"I know you did. And I don't know when you discovered it. Maybe you never did, really. Maybe you just suspected, and couldn't bring yourself to admit it. Then, after he left you, after he moved out of the house, you finally decided to find out, really find out. You hired me, springing for a hundred precious bucks you'd scrimped and saved, knowing I might find things out you'd want kept quiet. Knowing I might confirm the suspicions that drove you bughouse for years."

"Stop it . . . please stop it . . ."

"Your refined husband who liked to be near a college campus. You knew there were affairs. And there were. But not with women."

She stood, squeezing my hanky in one fist. "I don't have to listen to this!"

"You do if you want to be a free woman. The unwritten law doesn't seem to apply to women as equally as it does to men. But if you tell the truth about your husband—about just who it was he was seeing behind your back—I guarantee you no jury will convict you."

Her mouth was trembling.

I stood. "It's up to you, Mildred."

"Are you going to tell Mr. Backus?"

"No. You're my client. I'll respect your wishes."

"I wish you would just go. Just go, Mr. Heller."

I went.

I told Backus nothing except that I would suggest he introduce expert testimony from an alienist. He didn't. His client wouldn't hear of it.

The papers continued to have a great time with Marble Mildred. She got to know the boys of the press, became bosom buddies with the sob sisters, warned cameramen not to take a profile pic or she'd break their lens, shouted greetings and wisecracks to one and all. She laughed and talked; being on trial for murder was a lark to her.

Of course, as the trial wore on, she grew less boisterous, even became sullen at times. On the stand she told her story more or less straight, but minus any hint her husband was bent. The prosecution, as I had told her they would, ridiculed her statement that she'd bought the .32 to do herself in. The prosecutor extolled "motherhood and wifehood," but expressed "the utmost comtempt for Mildred Bolton." She was described as "dirt," "filth," "vicious," and more. She was sentenced to die in the electric chair.

She didn't want an appeal, a new trial.

"As far as I am concerned," she told the stunned judge, "I am perfectly satisfied with things as they now stand."

But Cook County was squeamish about electrocuting a woman; just half an hour before the execution was to take place, hair shaved above one ear, wearing special females-only electrocution shorts, Mildred was spared by Governor Horner.

Mildred, who'd been strangely blissful in contemplation of her electrocution, was less pleased with her new sentence of 199 years. Nonetheless she was a model prisoner, until August 29, 1943, when she was found slumped in her cell, wrists slashed. She had managed to smuggle some scissors in. It took her hours to die. Sitting in the darkness, waiting for the blood to empty out of her.

She left a note, stuck to one wall:

To whom it may concern. In the event of my death do not notify anybody or try to get in touch with family or friends. I wish to die as I have lived, completely alone.

What she said was true, but I wondered if I was the only person alive who knew that it hadn't been by choice.

AUTHOR'S NOTE: I wish to acknowledge the true-crime article "Joseph Bolton, the Almost Indestructible Husband" by Nellise Child. Also helpful was the Mildred Bolton entry in *Find the Woman* by Jay Robert Nash. And my thanks to my research associate George Hagenauer. Most names in the preceding fact-based story have been changed or at least altered (exceptions include the Boltons and Captain Stege); fact, speculation, and fiction are freely mixed therein.

# MICHAEL COLLINS

# BLACK IN THE SNOW

*Michael Collins's first Dan Fortune novel,* Act of Fear, *won the Mystery Writers of America Edgar Award for Best First Novel of 1967. In February of 1988 the new Fortune novel,* Red Rosa, *was published by Donald I. Fine. That makes Fortune presently one of the longest continuously running P.I. series.*

*Michael Collins is a past president of PWA, and has also written mystery series as John Crowe, Mark Sadler, and William Arden. Under his real name, Dennis Lynds, he has written novels and works of short fiction.*

*"Black in the Snow" marks Fortune's second appearance in a PWA anthology.*

No more than a black spot in the unbroken snow.

The February afternoon sun reflected from the windows of the silent suburban house, and I looked at the small black dog dead in the white expanse of the Ralstons' front yard. On the distant parkway the traffic throbbed in its endless stream, but on the snow, and in the white frame house with the green shutters, nothing moved.

"It ought to be an easy one, Fortune," the lawyer had said. "George Ralston never hurt a fly. A solid man, an executive. Married twenty years. No children, they lived well. Middle-class people with their own home, bank accounts, the works."

"What does Ralston say happened?"

"He hasn't any idea. Too broken up and under sedation to think about it," the lawyer said. "But it has to be robbery, some nut on the loose. They have a lot of burglaries out in Manhasset; Anna Ralston and the dog must have surprised the bastard and he killed them."

"How?"

"Knife." The lawyer shuddered and shook his head. "The dog

had its throat cut, Anna Ralston was stabbed twice. In the
stomach and under the ribs. Blood all over the pantry. George
Ralston doesn't kill that way, has a wall of guns to use."

"They find the weapon?"

The lawyer nodded. "It was next to the woman. A butcher
knife from the kitchen."

"Their kitchen? It was their knife?"

"That's what I mean. Anna Ralston walked in, some junkie
burglar panicked. Blood all over and none on George Ralston."

"Any prints?"

"Smudges. You know prints on a wood-handled knife."

"Why are they holding him?"

"Nothing was stolen," the lawyer said. "The house wasn't
broken into, no tracks in the snow. Some neighbor heard the
Ralstons in a screaming fight the night before, and George's alibi
isn't airtight. He was in Great Neck that afternoon, but could
have gotten home an hour or two before he did."

"What's Ralston's story?"

"He stopped in a couple of bars, no one saw him. When he got
home he found her dead in the pantry. He doesn't remember
much after that except he called the police."

Lawyers see what they want to see, believe what they have to
believe, tell an investigator just enough so he can find what they
want him to find.

"Why the dog, Counsellor? Why kill the dog?"

"Maybe it attacked the killer."

"What kind of dog?"

Even he had the grace to look away. "Pomeranian."

"Some thief."

Lawyers don't give up easily. Without hard evidence, one
theory is as good as another.

"Look," the lawyer said, "the wife always had a dog. Four in
the twenty years they were married. Small dogs, maybe because
she was small herself, Ralston says. He's a big guy, burly, used to
work in the factory where he's vice president now. He says she
was always with the dog. She carried them around with her
everywhere. So when she surprised the thief she had the dog. It
got in the way or he had to stop its barking."

And then threw the dead dog out into the snow? Why? The
lawyer would have had an answer, but I didn't. I stood in the
evening winter light and looked at the silent suburban house and

saw a small black dog dead in the snow without footprints or any other tracks leading to it.

There were drops of blood in the center of the pale carpeting in the hallway to the front door, and then no more until the narrow pantry behind the kitchen. The large, formal living room was immaculate, with green brocade period furniture, the dining room furnished in light, delicate woods from what could have been the same antique period. The silver on the sideboard was rubbed to a soft glow and probably used every day.

I stood in the doorway between the dining room and kitchen and imagined the Ralstons eating dinner every night in the spotless formal room with its perpetually polished silver. Two middle-aged people alone at the long table. He, from what the lawyer said, a big, burly man who liked shirtsleeves; she a small, slender woman still pretty and birdlike, the small black dog at her feet if not in her lap. It was a picture violence had no place in. Boredom, maybe, but not violence.

The windowless pantry across the kitchen held a different picture. Blood black on the walls, the floor, even the ceiling. The random slashing of a psychotic, or terrified amateur, or drug-crazed thief? I let my eyes take it in, squatted down to study the floor. The blanket and basket of the dog's bed were soaked with blood, and the floor around it was literally coated. The killings must have happened there, and without much struggle, the spattered blood thin on the walls and ceiling. Savage, yes, but not the pattern of a random, senseless slashing.

The kitchen with its flowered curtains was polished but not immaculate: a dirty cup and saucer in the sink; a plate with a soggy crust; the coffee maker still with stale coffee; one chair moved from the kitchen table to the wall telephone. I looked again at the well-used dining room with everything in its proper place, at the living room barely dusty even after a week of being untouched, and then went upstairs.

There were two bedrooms, a small sewing-and-plant room with a half-greenhouse wall, and a den-office.

The faint sound came from below.

A key turning softly in the front door.

Footsteps of someone trying to be soundless. Inside the den-office I stood back behind the door. Who had a key beside me, George Ralston, and the police?

Then she was in the room. A woman with dark hair, slim and more than attractive, but with the hands of over forty.

"George?"

I stepped out. "You often meet George here?"

"Jesus!" She jumped a foot and turned scared. "Who . . . who are you?"

"Did Mrs. Ralston know about you and George?"

Her eyes were brown and confused. "You're the police? Have you found anything? I mean, the man—"

"Private detective," I said. "I've found something now. You want to tell me about you and George?"

The brown eyes blinked. "George and me?" She shook her head. "No, I'm his sister. You thought George—?"

Guns hung all over the den walls: modern military rifles and pistols, even a light machine gun, as the lawyer had said. But he had forgotten to mention, or hadn't known, that they were all inoperative. No matter how violent George Ralston got, they were no more than clubs.

"Private detective?" the sister said.

"His lawyer hired me."

"Then they think George could have—!"

"What do you think, Miss Ralston?"

"Mrs. Deming," she said. "Sarah. I think they're insane."

"Someone killed her and the dog."

The desk was piled with books, pamphlets, letters. There was a TV set, a small refrigerator to save trips downstairs for beer, and a convertible couch that had been used and left open. Someone had slept in the den sometime before the killings, and no one had made the bed.

"George drinks," Sarah Deming said. "Anna wouldn't let him sleep with her when he was drunk."

"Which came first?" I said.

"What?"

"Which came first, not sleeping together or his drinking?"

She flushed. "I wouldn't know. Perhaps a little of both."

Between the guns on the wall above the desk were photographs of men in heavy shoes and work clothes inside a factory. Only one face was in all the photos: a big, heavyset young man with a wide grin and his arms around his buddies.

"George is proud of having worked with his hands," Sarah Deming said. "Down on the factory floor with the real workers.

He's never really gotten used to being an executive, goes out with
his old work friends when he drinks."

"He drinks a lot?"

She shrugged. "Enough, mister . . . ?"

"Dan Fortune. Were they having any trouble, Mrs. Deming?"

"Make it Sarah, okay? Deming and I busted a long time ago."
She smiled for the first time. It was a nice smile that faded almost
at once. "No trouble I know except his drinking. That bothered
her a lot. She even had a plan to get him to stop."

"She talked to you about it?"

"To all of us. The Wednesday afternoon coffee club just the day
before she . . . died. She started talking about George."

*They sit in the green brocade living room. Five ladies around the coffee
table eating small cakes, talking.*

*"I'm not sure when he changed," Anna Ralston says. "He always
drank, mostly beer with his friends. I never liked it, but he didn't drink
when we were together, so it wasn't that important. But now he's
drinking all the time."*

*Anna holds the small dog in her lap, a black puff of fur. A nervous ball
of fur, its eyes fixed on Miss Guilfoyle as she speaks. Anna strokes the
tiny dog, soothes, reassures. The dog turns its fox-like face up to her, its
small blue tongue out.*

*"I don't know why men have to drink," Miss Guilfoyle says. She sells a
little real estate, inherited a house from her brother, almost married a
man named Donald once, and has never forgotten. "Not that Donald
drank. That wasn't our problem."*

*Grace Hill says, "My Fred says George can be very insulting when he's
had too much, especially in the executive lounge."*

*"I'm sorry, Grace. You see, it's even affecting his work now. Something
has to be done."*

*"He's forty-six," Sarah says. "Maybe it's change of life."*

*Barbara Oliveri giggles. "Men do get moody around fifty."*

*Anna says, "It's a wife's job to help her husband; my mother always
told me, be a jump ahead of him."*

*"You've got some plan for old George," Sarah says.*

*Anna nods. "It came to me this morning when I was combing Mitzi."*

*She smiles down at the dog curled into her lap. The small dog lays back
its ears and closes its eyes, oblivious now that its mistress is talking,
going to sleep while its body continues to twitch in the nervousness of all
small animals.*

*Anna smiles at her friends. "I've decided to buy George a dog of his
own. I suddenly realized how unfair I've been. He's wanted a big dog ever*

*since he had to give that collie away before we were married. Don't you
think it's a fine idea?"*

"It would certainly give him something to do beside drink," Miss
Guilfoyle says.

Grace Hill isn't sure. "Two dogs are a lot of trouble."

"Especially a big dog," Barbara Oliveri says.

"Have you told him?" Sarah asks.

"I'm going to tell him tonight," Anna says, satisfied. "I think it's a
wonderful idea. Mitzi means so much to me."

I said, "Did she get him the dog?"

"No," Sarah Deming said.

We had moved on to the front bedroom. It was a large, light
bedroom that faced the front lawn with its evening sun glare
reflecting off the snow. Outside, the small smudge of black still lay
motionless in the expanse of white. Inside, a queen-sized bed had
only one side slept in. It was unmade, too.

"Did she make the beds first or last?" I asked.

"In the morning," Sarah Deming said. "Always. She cleaned
like a temple every day, beds first."

The bedroom had a feminine, girlish aura: pastel pinks and
yellows; ruffles and skirts on the chairs and vanity; dried
corsages, old programs, high school pennants; yellowed photos
on the walls. In the photos a girl in longish fifties dresses, and an
older couple in dark, reserved clothes, mingled with small
Oriental people in Japanese kimonos and polyglot Western garb.

"Anna and her parents," Sarah Deming said. "Missionaries in
Japan all through the war and after. Anna was born over there."

"Where are they now?"

"Dead. Her father died soon after they came back in the late
fifties, her mother only five years ago. I met her a few times when
she came to visit, didn't like her much. A real sour type full of
pronouncements and wise sayings. A chip on her shoulder about
something, probably the wicked world."

"Where did they go after Japan?"

"Nowhere. There was some trouble. They retired as missionaries when they got back. Anna didn't like to talk about it."

Nothing on the second floor showed evidence of an intruder as
far as I could tell, and we went downstairs. Nothing in the whole
house indicated an intruder. We stood in the kitchen.

"Was your brother messing around, Sarah? Another woman?"

"So they do think George killed her!"

"They don't know who killed her. Or why."

She shook her head, angry. "He just drank. Most people don't go to the effort of breaking out when they're comfortable, do they? Anna's mother said it: 'Give a man a home, take care of him, that's all he really needs.' Anna was good at that."

"Then he had a reason to break out?"

"He had a reason to drink." She shook her head. "He wasn't happy, hadn't been for years, but he wasn't the type to go to another woman."

"What about her? His drinking bothered her a lot."

"Anna? God no! She had her house, her duties, and her dogs. She always had her dogs. Mitzi was the fourth since they were married. She got the first one while George was still on the factory floor and they had a small apartment in Queens."

"Any enemies? Maybe from the past? In Japan? Something to do with her parents? With their work?"

She shook her head. "I wouldn't know about that." She looked at me. "I just know George didn't kill her."

I wished I knew as much. Lawyers don't hire a detective to prove their client guilty. I wanted to talk to the neighbors, but it was dinnertime in the suburbs, the men coming home. No one would want to talk now, and I needed a beer.

"Buy you a drink?"

Sarah Deming smiled. "Why not. As long as you're on our side. You are on our side?"

"I'll do my best."

The tavern was on the water overlooking Manhasset Bay. We both had Amstel Lights. She hadn't even asked about my missing arm.

"Why didn't she buy the dog for George?"

"He didn't want it." She poured the last of her beer. "You always knew George was home because her dog started barking. That evening Mitzi barked even before we heard the garage door open. He always came in and sat in his big armchair, his suitcoat off, his feet up on another chair. Anna hated that, but she never said anything because her mother told her you had to put up with things men did, make allowances. That was one of the mother's favorite sayings. Anna didn't always follow it with George, but that night she was eager to tell him her big idea."

*"Two dogs are too much trouble, Anna."*

*"You always wanted your own dog, George. A nice big one. You can fence in the backyard, even build a doghouse."*

*"The yard for my dog, eh?"*

*"A house is no place for a big dog. Certainly not a male."*

*George begins to laugh. "We could mate him to Mitzi. God, can you see the pups? Mitzi and a Great Dane?"*

*Sarah laughs, too. Anna doesn't laugh. The small dog raises its head on Anna's lap, its eyes watchful, alert. Anna holds the dog with both hands.*

*George shrugs. "I don't need a dog, Anna."*

*"You've always said you'd like a big dog."*

*"I don't need another damned dog!" George is up, walks to the liquor cabinet, pours a whiskey. "Anyone else?"*

*"I'll have a beer," Sarah says.*

*Anna says nothing; the dog only watches, its lips skinned back from small, pointed teeth as it senses George Ralston's anger. George brings beer in a glass from the kitchen for Sarah, sits down again in his chair, and stares moodily at his whiskey.*

*"A real dog'd be nice. One you can tell what it is. With those little ones of yours I forget which was which. Never could tell one of the damned things from another."*

*"That's ridiculous!" Anna snaps. "Mitzi's a Pom. Mrs. Ching was a Peke and so was Dodo. Suzy Q was a King Charles."*

*"Remember the collie I had when we met? Admiral? We mated him once, got half the litter. I think Ed Riley had one, dead now, of course. I saw Ed the other day down on the plant floor."*

*"I don't see how you could possibly confuse a Pom with a Peke or a King Charles."*

*"Sometimes I wish I'd stayed in the plant. Work hard all week, booze and whore on the weekend."*

*"I don't allow words like that, George!"*

*He drinks. "It's just a word, Anna."*

*"Sometimes I wish I'd never married you!"*

*He stands, drains his glass. "So do I."*

*"Go and drink!" Her voice is shrill. "Go and get drunk!"*

*The small dog barks, teeth bared in Anna's lap, its high, yapping bark as shrill as her voice.*

*"Why not? Falling-down drunk."*

*The dog goes on barking until the back door slams shut. Then it stops, looks alertly up at its mistress for approval. Anna strokes it.*

Sarah Deming swirled her second Amstel. "The dog stopped the moment George was gone, and Anna got up and started to wash the glasses, straighten up, and get ready for the Girls' Club meeting she was having later. As if nothing had happened."

"Or as if it had happened a lot of times before."

She drank. "I suppose."

"What did you do?"

"Helped Anna, then went home."

"Where's home?"

"A few blocks from here. Deming at least left me a house."

"I'll escort you home after some dinner."

She smiled. "Not tonight, Dan. I'm . . . I'm still upset. You can't think George . . . ? Not George."

"No," I said, "not George."

It was never George. I paid for the drinks, watched her drive off, then headed for the parkway into the city.

Next morning I lay in bed in my loft and thought. Then I got dressed, put a long scarf under my duffel against the wind that blew the old snow river to river, went out and had some breakfast at the diner on Eighth Avenue, and called on my client.

"No evidence of a burglar around the house." I took the chair facing his desk. "I don't think there was an intruder."

"You talk to the neighbors? Any other burglaries around?"

A lawyer's job is get his client off. Innocent or guilty.

"The cops'll have done that."

"The cops aren't talking to me," the lawyer said, "but they must have something. They released George Ralston this morning."

"They make an arrest?"

"Not that I heard. I'm paying you to find out what the cops have and maybe more, not make guesses."

I went up to the main library and checked old newspapers from the late fifties, the publications of missionary societies. Then I drove my rental car out to the Nassau County Medical Center in East Meadow. The pathologist on duty read my credentials and the papers from the lawyer.

"What do you want to know about Anna Ralston?"

"Time of death first."

He opened a file. "Between four or five P.M. the afternoon she was found."

"Did she have scratches on her hands? Maybe her face? Rips in her clothes besides the knife wounds?"

He looked up at me. "You know something the police don't?"

"Then there are scratches?"

"Deep ones on both hands, even her face. Rips on the top of her dress that probably weren't the knife."

"Thanks."

If they'd released George Ralston the case probably hadn't gone to Mineola Homicide yet, so I drove to the Sixth Precinct in Manhasset. Frank Domenici was on the case. We'd worked together maybe three years ago.

"You don't buy the burglar theory?" I asked.

"Nothing to back it up yet."

"But you let George Ralston go."

"Only as far as home. He's got a so-so alibi, psychiatrist says he's really broken up, and we can't figure a motive."

"Not enough to hold him, but he's still your best bet?"

"Until somebody hands us the crazy burglar, or a stoned vagrant with red hands."

"Tell me about the screaming fight made you hold Ralston in the first place."

Domenici shrugged. "The next-door neighbor couldn't sleep the night before the killing, went out for a walk in the snow with his dog. He was right out front when he saw the light go on in the bedroom. He noticed because it was after two A.M., and he'd never known Anna Ralston to be up past eleven tops."

"Which bedroom?"

"The front," Domenici said. "The neighbor hears Ralston laugh, drunk and slurring which wasn't unusual, and say Anna gave him an idea. The neighbor hears her say, 'Go to bed, George.'"

"She made him sleep in his office when he was drunk."

"What else is new?" Domenici said. "Only he won't go to bed, says something about old Mitzi earning her keep. She tells him to look at the time. The neighbor can see his shadow weaving around while he talks about money, and she's starting to yell."

"What about the dog?"

"It's up there, the neighbor hears it growling and yapping. Ralston's voice turns nasty, says something about 'upside down,' and the wife flips out. She's yelling 'animal,' and 'pig,' and the dog's barking like crazy, and Ralston's staggering around and laughing loud and nasty, and the wife screams not to touch her and get out, and finally Ralston leaves after yelling about tomorrow, and damned bitch, and like that."

"The neighbor didn't hear what about tomorrow?"

Domenici shook his head. "It's all silent after that, the neighbor goes on walking his dog. When he comes back the light's still on in the bedroom; he can hear her sort of singing real soft but can't hear the words. He goes home to bed, but he wakes up again around dawn and the light's still on. He doesn't hear anything more until Ralston starts bumping things in the kitchen and finally goes to work. He swears the light looked still on in the bedroom, but he didn't hear the wife moving around the way she usually did before he had to leave himself. He got back late, we were already there, and Anna Ralston was dead."

"Can I make a phone call?"

"Is it about the case?"

"Yes. You have Ralston's office number?"

He gave it to me. I dialed, told Ralston's secretary, Miss Kerry, who I was and what I wanted. I heard the protectiveness in her voice. She wanted to help Ralston's lawyer, but she didn't want to say anything that might make Ralston look bad.

"He left about three that afternoon, was going to a kennel in Great Neck. That's all I know, Mr. Fortune."

"When did Anna Ralston call?"

There was a silence. "About four. How did you know she called?"

"What did she want, Miss Kerry?"

"To talk to Mr. Ralston. It wasn't unusual."

"I'm sure it wasn't. What did you tell her?"

"That he'd already left."

"What did she say?"

"She asked where he'd gone."

"Did you tell her?"

"Yes."

"What did she say then?"

"She thanked me and hung up."

I thanked her, hung up, and stood up. Domenici watched me.

"Let's go talk to George Ralston," I said.

"Am I going to like what we talk about?"

"I don't know," I said.

George Ralston sat in the immaculate, green antique living room that wasn't so immaculate now, dust already on the brocade.

"There wasn't any burglar, Mr. Ralston," I said. "No dope addict, no psycho or punk vagrant."

"Yes," Ralston said. "He came in and killed Anna."

I said, "You want me to tell what happened the night before and when you got home, or do you want to tell us?"

I had his attention, but he said nothing.

"A neighbor heard the fight," I said. "Not all the words, but I think I can fill in most of them. When I get it wrong, you correct me. You'd argued about her getting you a big dog, a yard dog, a male dog, and you went out and got pretty plastered and staggered home late. She was asleep, but you turned on the light, woke her up. You had this idea of your own."

*Anna Ralston looks up at George's red face grinning down at her. He's drunk. Mitzi growls on the bed beside her. She only slowly becomes aware of what he is saying.*

"... got a great idea. Yessir. Know what gave me the idea? You did, with your big male dog."

"Go to bed, George."

"I'm in this bar, told this guy about you having all these damned little bitches and wanting to get me a big one and he said there was more money in little dogs than big ones. He says everyone wants small dog pups for apartments and that's when it hit me. Real pedigree pups're worth plenty. About time that Mitzi earned her damned keep."

"You're drunk! Look at the time."

*George sits heavily on the bed. Anna shrinks, holds the covers to her chin.*

*George grins.* "Mate her with a real good stud and the pups'll be worth a hell of a lot of money."

*Anna is pale.* "Mitzi's much too small. Go to bed now."

"Supposed to be small. Smaller they are, more the pups're worth. Use a small stud. Feisty little stud shove it to her good." *George laughs.* "Guy says the bitches get so scared they try 'n hide with the damn little hard stud after 'em."

*Anna's voice in a rage of anger.* "Go to bed, George!"

*Mitzi, curled against her mistress on the bed, growls. Anna holds the covers tight, her voice angry, almost violent, with a trembling violence that alarms the dog, its neck fur bristling. Its lips skin back over sharp teeth. George still laughs.*

"After they get it you got to hold them upside down so the stuff doesn't run out. Can you see it? Old Mitzi fucked good and upside down?"

*Then Anna is shouting, screaming in the pink and lace late-night bedroom. The small dog barks, snarling and barking and shrinking against its mistress. Anna drops the covers, holds the dog against her.* "You leave my baby alone! You animal! No one is going to hurt my little Mitzi. Get away. Animal! Pig! Don't you touch my baby! Never! Animal!"

*George gets to his feet, sways.* "Tomorrow. Some damn good out of her."

*Anna is trembling and shaking. She holds the dog, croons, "My poor Mitzi. Poor helpless little girl. He won't touch you, no. My little girl."*

*George glares at the small woman in the thin nightgown, and the small black dog held against her. "Damned little bitch."*

*He blinks at them, turns and staggers out and down the hall to fall onto the already opened sofa bed in his office-den. The house becomes silent except for the low snarls of the frightened dog and the thin, soothing voice of Anna as she croons to the little dog. The light does not go out.*

*Anna Ralston sits in the neat bed barely disturbed by her small body and holds the dog until it stops shivering and goes to sleep against her. She still doesn't turn out the light, sits the rest of the night holding the dog and watching the half-open door of her bedroom and the unseen office-den along the hall where the faint snores of George Ralston go on and on. Until the sky outside lightens into a morning gray. Until the alarm she had set in George's den last night to wake him for work goes off. Until George staggers up, swearing and groaning, bumps down stairs, crashes around the kitchen, goes out and drives off. Until the sun is up and long after.*

*She sits in the bed holding the dog until the morning is half gone. Then she turns off the light, dresses, goes down and feeds the small dog. After that she sits by the kitchen telephone and waits. She does not make the beds, dust, run the vacuum, clean George's breakfast dishes from the kitchen, put her polished house in order. She waits by the telephone. Because George will call to apologize. She knows he will call. But he doesn't, and at four P.M. she calls his office. She talks to his secretary. She hangs up. She calls Mitzi to her.*

*"Come here, little girl. Come to mother, little girl."*

*Then she takes the butcher knife from the drawer.*

"You didn't call," I said to George Ralston where he sat in the antique brocade chair. "You always called after a fight to apologize, say you were sorry. This time you didn't. You went to a kennel in Great Neck."

Ralston looked at his thick, heavy hands. "I was still mad. I went to the kennel, but only to ask about a dog for me. Then I changed my mind, didn't want a damned dog, stopped in some bars."

"She'd grown up in Japan," I said. "Her father was accused of chasing girls. It was hushed up, but they were forced to leave Japan. Her mother probably never let him forget it. Or Anna. She took the knife and the dog into the pantry. She cut the dog's throat. It struggled and clawed and bit. There were scratches all over her hands, her face. Then she used the knife on herself."

George Ralston's voice was flat and empty. "They were in the pantry. On the floor as if they were asleep. She was still holding the knife in her. I took her dress and pulled the knife out. I picked up the dog. It was stiff, not much blood. I suppose I carried it all the way to the front door. I don't remember that part. I threw it out into the snow. I remember that. I threw that goddamned little bitch of a dog that had killed my wife out into the goddamned snow!"

Domenici and I waited, but Ralston said nothing more. Just sat there and stared at his hands and at nothing.

"You didn't want anyone to know she'd killed herself," I said. "Maybe you didn't want to believe it yourself."

Ralston still looked only at his hands. "She never wanted me, sex, not from the start. I don't know why she married me."

"Because she was supposed to marry," I said. "She had to get married to someone. Her mother would have told her that."

He looked up at us. "The last few years there was nothing. I stank, I was coarse, I drank too much, I was an animal." An expression almost of surprise. "Married twenty years, I never saw her naked."

Domenici asked him to go to the precinct to make a statement. I rode with them to my rented car, called Sarah Deming, and asked her to dinner. Over coffee I told her. She cried. We went home to her place. Neither of us wanted to be alone.

# WAYNE D. DUNDEE

# THE JUDAS TARGET

*Wayne Dundee's Joe Hannibal appeared in the second PWA anthology,* Mean Streets, *in a story called "Body Count." It collected nominations for an Edgar, a Shamus, and an Anthony (the award presented by crime-fiction fans). In 1988 the first Hannibal novel,* Burning Season, *will be published by St. Martin's Press. Wayne is also the publisher and editor of* Hardboiled, *a small-press fiction magazine specializing in tough, hard fiction written by established pros and newcomers alike. In fact,* Hardboiled *is one of the few training grounds there are for new writers, which was Wayne's intention from the beginning. At the present time, he is serving as a member of the Board of Directors of PWA.*

*In a relatively short time Wayne has established himself as a writer to watch. We feel that "The Judas Target" will only add to his growing reputation.*

"**E**ver see one of those el cheapo kung fu movies?" The Bomber asked rhetorically. "You know, the kind where every time somebody gets hit, it sounds like a five-pound T-bone landing on the sidewalk after being dropped out of an upstairs window? Well, that's how it sounded when the bullet smacked into the brick wall beside my head. Like a loud slap. The report of the gun came a fraction of a second later and then brick fragments were stinging the side of my face and that's when it finally dawned on me that somebody had taken a shot at me."

"Just one shot?" I said.

He shrugged his massive shoulders. "Far as I could tell. I didn't exactly stand around counting, you know? I got the hell off those

67

steps, did a swan dive down behind a row of garbage cans. All the clanging and banging I did when I landed, I probably wouldn't have heard if they'd fired a dozen more times. But the police only found evidence of one slug, the one that hit the wall where I'd been standing."

"Those lab boys don't miss too damn much," I allowed. "If there'd been more than one shot, they would have found some indication. Funny, though, that whoever opened up on you only fired the once."

"So what are you—disappointed he didn't make Swiss cheese out of me?"

"Of course not. It just seems strange that somebody would go to all the trouble of setting up an ambush and then spend only one bullet. Let's face it, those garbage cans didn't offer much protection. Almost anything bigger than a BB gun can penetrate that cheap galvanized steel. Why not at least throw a few random rounds into them in hopes of scoring a lucky hit?"

The Bomber screwed up his face and thought about it. "Maybe when they saw me dive off those steps," he suggested, "they thought they'd hit me and I fell."

"Or maybe," Liz offered from her side of the bar, "they mistook Bomber for somebody else and didn't realize their mistake until after they'd taken that first shot."

"Come on," I said. "How the hell could you mistake The Bomber for somebody else? You see that many guys walking around who stand six-six and weigh over three hundred pounds? Besides, what about the car that tried to run him down the other day? Were they after somebody else, too?"

Liz's pretty face reddened—first with embarrassment, then with defensive anger. "You can just climb down off your high horse, Joe Hannibal," she snapped. "If I'm not making any sense, it's because this whole business has me scared half to death. You're supposed to be the hotshot private eye, *you* tell *me* what's going on then."

It was quarter of ten in the morning and the three of us were huddled in the preopening hour stillness of The Bomb Shelter, the State Street bar owned and operated by my mountainous pal. If the name Bomber Brannigan is familiar to you, you're showing your age as a sports fan. Before retiring from the ring wars to turn The Bomb Shelter into one of Rockford's most popular watering holes, The Bomber spent several years as a top-ranked heavyweight boxer and then nearly two decades as one of the biggest draws on the pro wrestling circuit.

Liz is Liz Grimaldi, Bomber's gal Friday and a special kind of friend to me. It had been a phone call from her that had awakened me earlier that morning and informed me that another attempt had been made on The Bomber's life, this time a shooting in the side alley adjacent to the bar after he'd closed up last night and was leaving to go home. Less than forty-eight hours before that, a late-model sedan (reported stolen and later found abandoned) had tried to run him down in a shopping center parking lot. I'd already known about the parking lot incident, but like everyone else (including The Bomber) had managed to convince myself that it was just one of those freaky things that sometimes happen and not really a deliberate attack. But this time they'd left no room for doubt. They were playing with guns, and that's about as deliberate as you can get.

"What's going on," I replied to Liz, "is that somebody's apparently trying to kill Bomber here. The question is, why? And—ultimately—who?"

The Bomber grunted. "You sound just like the cops. 'Any idea *why* someone wants you dead, Mr. Brannigan? Any idea *who* dislikes you enough to try and kill you, Mr. Brannigan?' Christ, their questions can get on your nerves almost as bad as the thought of some whacko running around out there with your name at the top of his hit list."

"They're only trying to do their jobs and—just incidentally— save your ass," I pointed out. "I hope you had sense enough to cooperate and not get sore and clam up on them?"

"Yeah, yeah, of course I cooperated. You think I like any of this? It's just that I didn't have any answers for them because I don't know of anybody who'd want to kill me. Christ knows you don't get to be my age without making a few enemies. But not the kind who'd run you down with a car or blow your brains out in an alley, for crying out loud. Besides, most of the enemies I made— and *enemies* is really too strong a word—were back when I was making my living in the ring."

"You may have to go back that far," I told him. "Sometimes hatred can build up inside a person for years before it builds up enough pressure to drive them to murder."

Bomber and I were perched on stools, sipping coffee from thick, old-fashioned mugs, while Liz was behind the bar, rattling around in glassware between contributions to the conversation. She stopped rattling now and said, "Anyway, what you said isn't entirely the truth, Bomber. I can think of at least two run-ins you've had in the past six months with guys I certainly wouldn't consider incapable of murder."

The Bomber made a face. "Aw, Liz, you know you overreact. Jeez, I can't sic the cops on everybody I've had a barroom argument with."

"Why not? Haven't you ever heard the expression 'Better safe than sorry'? We're talking about your life here, you stubborn mule. And the way I remember it, those were a little more than simple barroom arguments."

I said, "Somebody mind telling me just what it is you're talking about?"

Bomber and Liz glared at each other. After several seconds, he made a condescending gesture with his hand. "Go ahead, you're the one who started it."

It turned out that a few months back The Bomber had butted heads with a local pimp who called himself Sweet Thomas. Sweet had decided to expand his territory that spring and had started dropping off girls to work the bars along this previously unclaimed stretch of State Street. After Bomber had run the girls out of his place three nights in a row, the pimp stopped by one afternoon to try and grease the way. First he offered money, then he made thinly veiled threats. Bomber's response had been classic Bomber: Without saying a word he'd reached out and gently but firmly removed Sweet's trademark hundred-dollar hat, taken a huge bite out of the brim, than spat the chewed remains in the gaping pimp's face. The Bomb Shelter hadn't been visited by Sweet Thomas or any of his girls since. But they continued to work the surrounding blocks and rumor had it that Sweet on more than one occasion had vowed to make Bomber "spit his own damn honky blood the way he spit my hat, man."

More recently, there'd been some trouble with a guy named Mallory, the estranged boyfriend of a young woman The Bomber had employed briefly as a dancer. When the dancer ditched him and moved on, Mallory had continued to hang around, bitter, heartbroken, unshakably convinced that Bomber knew something of his errant girlfriend's whereabouts. There had been a number of drunken accusations and arguments before he was finally barred from The Bomb Shelter. But Mallory had a reputation for being a hothead and a bully and he, too, had been heard threatening to "get" The Bomber.

As I listened to Liz recount the two incidents, I remembered hearing about them back when they occurred. There'd been no reason to stick my nose in, either time. Bomber is a big boy and he seemed to have things under control. In the wake of the recent murder attempts, however—and particularly with no other murder suspects at hand—I found myself agreeing with Liz that Sweet Thomas and Mallory rated a closer look.

"Hell, Joe," Bomber protested. "They're just a couple punks who like to hear themselves blow. The two of them put together wouldn't have enough balls to actually come after me."

"Not head-on maybe," I said. "But they sound exactly like the kind who wouldn't be above staging an ambush in an alley. Besides, you got any better leads?"

He shook his head sullenly. "I already told you I don't."

"All right then. If it'll make you feel any better, we can leave the cops out of it for the time being. I got nothing much going right now; I'll do some poking around myself." I drained my coffee mug, stood, jabbed an admonishing finger. "In the meantime, you keep a low profile and rack your brain for any more possibilities. I don't care how far back you have to go or how trivial it might seem, I want the names of everybody you've had any kind of serious conflict with and/or who's threatened you in any way. It wouldn't be a bad idea to write them down. Don't make faces, just do it. I'll check back later."

By six o'clock that evening, I was back to square one. Sweet Thomas and Mallory had both checked out clean—well, clean as far as having anything to do with the attempts on Bomber's life.

Mallory had been in the county lockup for the past week and would remain there for quite a while longer, serving time on a DUI charge he couldn't post bail for. And Sweet Thomas had just been released from a three-day stint in Swedish American with seventy-odd stitches adorning his chest and one forearm, the result of one of his girls turning on him when he tried batting her around for not bringing in enough money.

I'd considered the possibility of one of them having hired somebody to hit The Bomber. In Mallory's case it seemed laughable. And when I suggested the idea to Sweet Thomas, he denied it vehemently. Inasmuch as I'd threatened to reopen his stitches one at a time if I thought he even *might* be lying, his denial had sounded sincere.

So, despite my earlier stated intentions, the end of the day found me seated in a little coffee shop around the corner from police headquarters, hashing over the whole thing with Lieutenant of Detectives Ed Terry. Terry is my best contact with the RPD and, though I wouldn't go so far as to call him a friend, over the years we've developed a working relationship we can both live with. He knew The Bomber and knew of our friendship, so while he couldn't officially condone my involvement, he at least understood my interest in the matter.

"What you ought to do," he said as he stirred a second heaping teaspoon of sugar into his coffee, "is get Bomber out of the city for a while. Whoever's behind this thing is keyed up, anxious, pissed off because he's failed twice already. If you suddenly take away his target it'll increase the pressure on him, maybe make him do something to show his hand. At the same time, it would give us some breathing room, more opportunity to work the streets, lean on our snitches, until we turn up some kind of lead. With no suspects—hell, we didn't even have Sweet Thomas and this Mallory—that's the only way we've got to play it."

"What's to prevent the guy from just laying low until The Bomber returns?" I asked.

The lieutenant shrugged. "It could happen that way, I suppose. But I don't see this character as being that cool. First he tries to be a little tricky by using an automobile; when that doesn't work, he resorts pretty quickly to a gun. I read that as a kind of growing desperation. Plus he's got to know his quarry is alerted now; that should make him even more desperate."

"The Bomber's been after me to go up into Wisconsin with him and do some fishing before cold weather sets in," I mused. "Might not be a bad time to take him up on it. I'm damn sure not tied down by a heavy caseload right now. We could rent a cabin on some out-of-the-way little lake for a week or so and give this whole mess down here a chance to come to a head."

Terry nodded. "Sounds like just the ticket to me. You'd even be along to act as bodyguard in case the trouble somehow followed him up there."

* * *

To say that Bomber wasn't very receptive to the idea when I tried it on him a couple hours later would be something of an understatement.

"I never ran away from a fight in my life," he exploded, "and I'm damn sure not going to start now!"

"You wouldn't be running away," I tried to explain. "You'd be turning the tables on whoever's out to get you by taking control of the situation away from them. The way it is now, they can keep trying for you whenever and wherever they want—until they get the job done."

"I'm not running and that's that," he said stubbornly, then turned and stalked away to busy himself elsewhere.

The Bomb Shelter was doing exceptionally good business for a weeknight. Cindy, one of the most popular dancers, was gyrating energetically up on the go-go stage and the predominately male crowd seemed duly appreciative. I noticed Liz was still on hand, sharing bartending duties with Bomber and Old Charley. She normally opened up in the morning, took care of the lunch-hour crowd, and was gone by six. It was obvious she was hanging around tonight to keep an eye on The Bomber. Despite his hulking size, he brings out the mother hen in her. Of course, I do, too, but that's another story.

I brooded through the rest of my beer, didn't order another. I decided there was no sense badgering Bomber anymore tonight. I knew him too well for that. In the morning, I'd put a bug in Liz's ear. She had a knack for being able to get him to do things when no one else could.

I left around nine. I drove to Dan's Dog House on Broadway and ordered two kraut dogs with the works. Dan Modesto and his wife, Sunshine, are the last of the original hippies. Dan is a bearded, wiry little runt who looks for all the world like Charles Manson, while Sunshine is a shapely, stunning blond Amazon who hasn't aged a minute since the middle 1960s. Ironically, despite the success of their unpretentious little hot dog stand, both are staunch vegetarians who wouldn't eat their own fare on a bet. But somehow that doesn't prevent them from preparing and serving the best red-hots on the planet. As a lifelong aficionado of the vastly underrated, much maligned, generally ill-treated great American hot dog, it took me about three seconds to sniff out the Dog House after it opened, and I've been going back several times a week ever since.

Business was slow this night so Dan and Sunshine had a Scrabble board set up in one of the corner booths. After I'd finished my kraut dogs, I surprised myself by accepting their invitation to join in. I quickly discovered that my usually mellow, laid-back hosts took their board games very seriously. The play was intense. We won a game each and it was sometime after midnight when we were going to the wire on the tie breaker. I managed to pull it out by adding *I-O-N* to DIVERS and ending up on a double-word-value square with DIVERSION for twenty-six points.

It was only later that I would look back and recognize the omenlike significance of the word.

Half past one found me parked across the street and down slightly from The Bomb Shelter. I could see any comings and goings through the establishment's front door and I also had a good view down the length of the alley where the shooting had taken place last night. Tonight—well, it was morning now if you want to be technical—The Bomber's big Buick was parked at the curb near the mouth of the alley instead of in the back where he usually kept it. So at least he was showing enough good sense not to invite trouble.

The September night was cool, with a gusting wind that rocked my old Mustang on its worn springs. I sat and smoked, watching, taking occasional hits from the glove compartment flask, ruminating.

Bomber Brannigan. Big, gregarious bear. Sucker for dewy-eyed blondes and hard-luck stories. Always willing to loan you a few bucks even when he really couldn't spare it, or to extend your bar tab for another day or another week. Wouldn't hesitate to bust your head if you caused trouble in his place, then turn around and offer to help pay the emergency room fees or go your bail if the cops threw you in the clink over it. Who the hell would want to murder a guy like that? It just didn't figure.

Any way I looked at it, it had to go back to Bomber's past. Someone from some incident he either wasn't admitting to or didn't recognize as a danger. I had to believe it was the latter—I couldn't picture him keeping something from both me and Liz, especially not under the circumstances. The problem, then, was getting him to realize who it might be.

By two o'clock my rear end was falling asleep and I had gas from the additional kraut dog I'd eaten before leaving Dan's. If I hadn't had the bourbon to comfort me, I might have decided this stakeout wasn't necessary after all.

I'd figured Bomber was safe enough in the midst of The Bomb Shelter's crowd, but I wanted to be around when he closed up tonight to make sure there were no repeats of last night's incident. I hadn't bothered mentioning this to him because he was already in a funk and undoubtedly would have objected. So if he caught me at it, he'd be sore as hell. But I could live with that. And, more to the point, so could he.

Twice I spotted police squad cars circling the block and one of them even made a pass down through the alley. I had a feeling Ed Terry had something to do with that. He maybe couldn't assign a man full time to The Bomber, but at least he could see to it that there was some extra attention given.

At two-thirty, with the last of the drinking crowd herded out ahead of them, the lights inside The Bomb Shelter winked off and Liz, Old Charley, and Bomber emerged together from the front door. They stood talking for a minute or so, then Liz and Old Charley headed east down the sidewalk. I could see Liz's VW Bug parked in the block and knew that Old Charley's hotel was just a couple blocks farther.

Bomber stood watching until Liz reached her car before turning and heading for his own. He paused at the mouth of the alley for a moment and glared into it as if daring it to cause him some trouble this night. Then he continued on to the Buick, unlocked the driver's door, pulled it open. Instead of getting in, however, he froze suddenly and craned his neck to peer back at the alley as if he'd heard something there. He stood like that for maybe five seconds, listening intently, then eased the door shut and started toward the alley.

I felt the short hairs on the back of my neck stand up. My left hand reached for the door handle, my right snaked inside my jacket and closed around the butt of the .45 nestled there in its shoulder holster. I don't always carry the big gun. My everyday walkaround piece is a two-shot .22 magnum derringer clipped inside my right boot. But when I know in advance I could be walking into a hard scene, I'll drag out the manstopper.

Because I had the car windows rolled up against the cool night air, whatever The Bomber had heard hadn't reached my ears. But whatever it was, I didn't like it.

I shouldered open the door and piled out of the Mustang. I'd just opened my mouth to call out when the night split wide open. A ball of brilliant light seemed to fill the inside of Bomber's Buick and then grow to envelop the entire vehicle. A dull, jarring boom hammered my ears and shook the macadam underneath my feet. And out of the brilliant light shot a gigantic, orange-gold, fiery hot fist that knocked me down and sent me rolling into unconsciousness.

"The explosives were fastened underneath the car, directly below the driver's seat, and rigged to the doorlatch mechanism," Ed Terry explained. "When the door was opened, a timer was activated and twenty seconds later—ka-blooey!"

"Twenty seconds," I said. "About the average amount of time it would take someone to get in their car, get settled, maybe even fasten their seat belt so they'd feel nice and secure."

"Exactly. If The Bomber hadn't heard that noise in the alley after he opened his door and started over to investigate . . . well, we'd probably be talking about so much burnt meat in the morgue right now."

"What did he hear anyway? Did he ever say?"

"The sound of breaking glass. When my men checked, they found a freshly broken beer bottle beside one of the garbage cans. The can was pretty full, it could have rolled out on its own or maybe been knocked out by a cat or rat or something."

I nodded. "It would've had to have been something like that. There was no person in that alley, I'm sure of that. I had it under surveillance for over an hour." I sat on the edge of the hospital bed and began pulling on my socks. "The Bomber's being released this morning, too, right?"

"Uh-huh. They kept him overnight for observation, same as you. You two were both damn lucky to get away with only your pinfeathers singed and your eardrums rattled."

"Pinfeathers singed. That's real cute." I reached up and gently touched my left cheek. It smarted like hell and I knew from looking in the mirror that it was as red as a scalded lobster. "I won't be able to shave for a week."

"Shouldn't be a problem. You take Bomber up to that fishing

lake like we talked about and the both of you can let your beards grow, pretend you're regular mountain men or something."

I grunted. "He hasn't agreed to go yet. But I've got Liz working on him right now. She was here a little while ago and I told her your idea, how getting Bomber out of town might help."

Twenty minutes later, after I'd fought off a hatchet-faced old nurse armed with a wheelchair she was bound and determined I was going to let her push me away in, the elevator doors opened and Terry and I emerged into the hospital's main lobby. Liz and The Bomber were waiting for us. Terry went over and stood with them while I went to the front desk and made arrangements on my bill.

When I joined the others, Bomber regarded me with a skeptically arched brow. The back of his head and neck were lumpy with bandages.

"You look like a boiled tomato," he observed.

"Thanks," I replied. "You, you sort of resemble a giant Q-Tip."

"That's what you get for poking your nose in where you weren't invited, you know."

I shrugged. "Just looking out for my interests. You're the only bartender in town lets me run a tab. Anything happened to you, I might have to start drinking water part of the time."

"Why don't you two save the Frick and Frack routine," Liz suggested, "until you're up in the middle of some Wisconsin lake where no one else has to suffer through it?"

I glanced at her, then back at Bomber. "The Lone Ranger here finally agree to go?" I asked.

"That's exactly *why* he agreed to go," Liz said. "I pointed out to him that he's *not* the Lone Ranger. He's surrounded by a lot of friends. As crazy as this thing is getting, the next explosion might go off *inside* The Bomb Shelter and hurt—maybe kill—dozens of innocent people."

The Bomber looked at a spot on the floor, said nothing. I saw his jaw muscles clench and unclench.

"It really is a smart move," Ed Terry said. "It's just a matter of time before we get a line on this asshole. The bombing was a big mistake. It's pretty hard to cover your tracks once you start messing with explosives."

The fishing lodge we selected was on Dogleg Lake, about two hundred and fifty miles up into Wisconsin. Since it was the off-season, we had no trouble getting reservations on short notice. Less than three hours after being released from the hospital—the backseat of my Mustang piled with beer and gear—we'd put Rockford behind us and were across the state line. "Let's do it," The Bomber had said, "before I change my mind."

The last sliver of sunlight was sinking behind the jack pines when we arrived at the lodge. The manager, a guy named Hogan, showed us to our cabin, explaining the camp's simple setup and its rules and regs as we climbed a grassy incline that sloped up from the gravel parking lot.

"That pier down there," he said, pointing, "goes with your cabin. I'll have a boat brought around and tied there, motor all gassed up and ready, so you can get as early a start as you want in the morning. The walleyes have been hitting real good on live minnows all week. I've got plenty of those at the bait shop, any time you want to stop and get some."

The cabin was a low-ceilinged, single-room affair with kitchen facilities at one end and a broad fireplace flanked by sturdy bunk beds at the other. When Hogan was ready to leave us to our own devices, he paused in the doorway and said, "Oh, yeah, one more thing. About the lake. I was out just a little while ago and saw that some of the warning buoys are gone again. Damn kids keep cutting them loose, think it's real cute I guess. I'd like to catch 'em at it one of these times, show 'em how cute a boot in the ass is. But anyway, stay clear of the north end of the lake. Too many shallow spots there, especially after a dry summer like we've just had. The whole section is ribbed with sand and gravel bars just under the surface of the water. Hard to see, but pure hell on boat bottoms and propellers, take my word for it. I'll get the buoys back in place sometime tomorrow."

After Hogan had gone, while The Bomber set to work making a batch of his "world-famous, gonad-grabbing, high-tech, industri-al-strength" chili for supper, I lugged the rest of our gear up from the car. On my last trip, I stopped at the old-fashioned, booth-type pay phone outside the bait shop and called Liz at The Bomb Shelter. I told her we'd arrived okay, that the lodge appeared rustic but comfortable, and suggested boastfully that she bone up on her fish-cleaning skills because we'd probably have to rent a U-Haul to carry home our catch. Before ringing off, she made me promise to call frequently and said she'd let us know if Lieutenant Terry came up with anything on their end.

Bomber's chili lived up to its high standards. I demonstrated my appreciation by eating three bowlfuls. I washed it down with twice that many cans of cold Michelob mined from the depths of one of the ice-filled coolers.

Later, before nodding off, I lay for a time in the dark and tried to fit some of the pieces of this potentially deadly puzzle together in my mind. A part of me, too, felt as if we were running away from the problem, and yet everything Ed Terry said had made sense. But who would want to kill Bomber in the first place? That's what it all kept coming back to, and that's where it all fell apart. Sleep finally nudged aside the scattered pieces and unanswered questions and, for a while at least, made them go away.

Armed with Thermoses of coffee, fishing poles, and a bucket of minnows, we were out on the lake before dawn the next morning. A storm had blown through during the night, leaving in its wake an overcast sky and a stiff breeze that churned the gunmetal-gray water into shifting sheets of corrugated steel.

Wherever those hard-hitting walleyes Hogan had told us about were, we never found them. After nearly four hours, out of patience and out of coffee, bellies growling for breakfast, we were ready to head in.

Bomber fired up the outboard with one pull of the starter cord. But then, before it had taken us more than twenty yards, the motor abruptly coughed a couple times and died. A dozen more yanks failed to revive it.

"Damn!" The Bomber muttered after unscrewing the cap and peering into the gas tank. "Dry as a bone. Looks like our friend Hogan forgot about the 'gassed up and ready' part when he brought this baby around last night."

"Swell," I said.

I looked around us. The lake, as its name implied, was a rectangularish body of water bent more or less in the middle like a dog's leg. It was three, three-and-a-half-miles long and about two miles at its widest. We were above the point of the inner bend, well out of sight of our lodge and nearly three-quarters of a mile from the nearest shore. I could see a couple cabins on the shoreline, but there were no signs of activity around them. We hadn't seen another boat on the water all morning.

"Only one thing to do," Bomber said matter-of-factly. "That's break out the oars and make for shore the hard way."

"Swell," I said again.

We dragged the oars out from under the seats, fastened them into their locks, flipped a coin to see who took first turn. I lost.

Given my inexperience and the roughness of the water, I hardly sent us streaking on our way. After fifteen minutes of tugging and puffing, I'd maybe equaled the distance the motor had propelled us in a matter of seconds.

Just as he was getting ready to spell me, The Bomber suddenly leaned out to gaze past my shoulder. "Don't look now," he said, "but I think I'm about to get beat out of my turn."

I twisted around in my seat. Another boat, a twelve-footer almost identical to ours, was cutting across the water toward us.

"Swell," I panted.

The craft's single occupant was a guy in his middle thirties, tall, slightly built, with a rust-colored beard and a baseball cap pulled low over his eyes. He guided his boat alongside ours, cut the motor to idle, regarded us from under the long bill of his cap.

"Trouble, fellas?"

"Out of gas," The Bomber answered. "Guy at the lodge where we're staying was supposed to've filled it for us. We never thought to check."

The guy in the cap nodded. "Happens. Hate to admit how many times I've been in the same pickle. Let me maneuver up in front of you, then you can tie on with your anchor line there and I'll tow you in. You'll row your guts out trying to get anywhere in this chop."

"Tell me about it," I muttered.

He had us secured in a matter of minutes. All the while his boat's motor gurgled reassuringly.

"There now," our rescuer said. "Looks like we can be on our way."

"Sounds good to me," The Bomber replied, grinning.

As Bomber and I settled back in our boat, the guy in the cap leaned forward in his and busied himself for a moment with the tarp roll at his feet. When he straightened up and turned back toward us, he held a sawed-off shotgun leveled calmly, menacingly in our direction. He said, "But there is one more little thing."

The grin froze on Bomber's face. I felt my guts jump into a knot and Ed Terry's words echoed hauntingly through my mind: "You'd even be along to act as bodyguard in case the trouble somehow followed Bomber up there."

When I found my voice, it was a sandpapery rasp. I said, "What the hell is this? Somebody's sick idea of a joke?"

The guy in the cap shook his head. "No joke, Hannibal. No joke at all."

"How do you know my name?" I demanded.

"Oh, I know a lot of things about you, Hannibal. I know, for instance, about the derringer you always carry in your boot, and I know how you sometimes back it up with a heavier piece. Judging from the bulge under your jacket, I'd say this is one of those times. I guess I should be flattered, since the extra firepower is probably in honor of me. I think you can understand, though, how I'd feel better if you were unarmed. So, one at a time, very slowly, using only the thumb and forefinger of your left hand, I want you to take the pieces out and drop them over the side."

There's no arguing with a shotgun. I did as he said.

After my weapons had disappeared into the gray water, he said, "You still don't see it, do you? You still don't recognize me. But you recognized me okay seven years ago, you bastard. Think back. It was your testimony that put me away, and I swore then that I'd get even. Maybe you forgot over the years, but I never did. Never for a fucking minute!"

He swept his cap off with a dramatic gesture and suddenly I knew who the hell he was. He'd lost some weight in seven years, turned harder around the eyes and mouth. The beard was new and so was the rusty brown color it and his hair had been dyed. It had been his hair as a matter of fact—so pale and so fine that the pinkish color of his scalp showed through—that had earned him his nickname, the only name I ever knew him by.

I said it out loud now. "Pinky Bascomb."

"Jackpot, shamus," he confirmed with a cold smile.

My brain was reeling. This was crazy. Had we come all this way, gone to all this trouble to avoid Bomber's would-be murderer—only to be cornered by a vengeance-crazed killer from *my* past?

Bascomb produced a pair of silvery handcuffs and tossed them to me. I made the catch out of reflex.

"Link up with your oversized buddy there. Now!" He made a jabbing motion with the sawed-off to emphasize the command.

As I cuffed his right wrist to my left, Bomber said, "Who is this guy, Joe? What the hell's going on?"

"What's going on," Bascomb answered him, "is revenge. Your

friend there is about to pay for sticking his nose in my business
seven long years ago."

"Yeah," I said. "Pinky and one of his punk cohorts had a real
sweet 'business,' Bomber. Think back, you ought to remember.
Whenever they needed a little extra spending money they'd
knock over an all-night convenience store and, just for kicks,
pistol-whip the clerk. Two of those clerks died. One of the stores
that hadn't been hit yet hired me to provide some extra security,
and when Pinky and his pal finally got around to us, I was there
waiting. I blew his partner away with my first shot because he
had guts enough to stand his ground. But I only managed to
wound Pinky in his yellow streak as he was running away. The
police dragnet got him a couple hours later, though, and, like he
said, my testimony put him away. It's just too damn bad my aim
was a little off that night."

"Too bad, all right," Bascomb agreed icily. "Too bad for *you*. The
only thing that kept me going all that time in the joint—kept me
on my best behavior so I could make early release—was the
thought of you and how I was going to make my payback. In case
you're interested, I'm loving every fucking second of it so far.
Revenge truly is sweet. And the fact that I'm going to take your
friend down with you—just the way you took my friend down—
makes it even sweeter."

"Why? The score you have to settle is with me. Bomber's no
part of it."

"But of course he's part of it. He's a very important part. After
all, he was my Judas goat. Or, more accurately, I guess I should
call him my Judas target. At any rate, he's the one who led you
here . . . to your slaughter."

I saw it then. All of it. The pieces of the puzzle came together
with a mind-jarring snap and the insane brilliance of the completed picture they made was a frightening thing to comprehend.

"So it was you," I said. "All along it's been you. Those attempts
on The Bomber's life were never meant to succeed—they were
only staged to draw me into the picture. Because of our
friendship, you knew that sooner or later I'd get involved. It was
your intention all along to kill us both, knowing everyone had
been misled and would assume Bomber was the primary target
and I was just unlucky enough to get caught in the crunch."

Bascomb actually beamed. "Exactly. If I'd gone directly after
you, how long do you think it would have taken before some

enterprising cop or newspaper reporter would have remembered me and my courtroom threats? A man in your business has plenty of enemies, and I would have been on the list. When they checked and found I'd recently made parole, I would have shot right to the top. No matter what kind of alibi I rigged up, the fucking pigs would have stayed on my ass. There's nothing those bastards like better than hassling ex-cons."

"The attempted rundown with the car and the shooting would've been easy enough to stage," I said. "But how did you know how to rig the bomb? How could you be sure Bomber would walk away from his car before it went off?"

"Because you big macho types are all alike. Predictable. I knew if he heard a noise in that alley he'd feel obligated to go check it out. As far as the bomb, well, if you just keep your mouth shut and your ears open, it's amazing what you can learn in the joint."

"But you weren't in that alley," I insisted. "I was watching."

"I was watching, too, from the roof of The Bomb Shelter. When I saw Brannigan open his car door, I dropped the beer bottle down beside the garbage cans. Simple as that. The only hard part was restraining myself from putting a bullet in you right then and there. You made such a perfect target, sitting across the street so conveniently framed in your car window."

"This your doing, too?" The Bomber asked, indicating our outboard's empty gas tank with a jerk of his head.

Bascomb nodded. "That it is. So you see, your man Hogan was dependable after all. You can die with your faith in mankind restored."

"How did you find us up here?" I said, remembering the various checks I'd made and the driving tricks I'd pulled to make certain we weren't followed.

"Ah, yes. Have to admit you did catch me by surprise when you left the city the way you did. Very unmacho, that. As I saw it, the only move I had left then was to pry your whereabouts out of your lady friend at The Bomb Shelter. I was working my way up to that when you obligingly made your phone call last night, Hannibal. I happened to be sitting at the bar nearby and overheard her end of the conversation. Afterwards, I heard her telling one of the dancers about it and she mentioned Dogleg Lake. She had no way of knowing, of course, but she saved herself a good deal of unpleasantness with that. On the other hand, she denied me a bit of pleasure. Maybe when we're finished here, I'll go back and look her up again . . . just for the hell of it."

Bomber tensed like a steel cable beside me. "You sick son of a bitch."

Bascomb's face tightened above the lethal black mouths of the shotgun. "Enough talk. We'll get to shore and finish this. Chained together like you are, you gotta know you have no chance of rushing me or jumping over the side and escaping. One wrong move from either of you and I let go with both barrels. You'd be two piles of hamburger. If you're smart, you'll sit still and live as long as you can."

Like I said, there's no arguing with a shotgun.

Bascomb nudged open the throttle and we began moving across the lake . . . toward whatever end he had in mind for Bomber and me. He swung north, taking us further away from the lodge and away from the cabins I'd spotted earlier. In the distance I could see a heavily wooded shoreline at the end of the lake, with no cabins or piers anywhere in sight.

My mind raced, trying to figure some way around that damned sawed-off. The wind blew cold and bitter against my face, yet under my jacket I was dripping sweat. In the final analysis, I knew, there was no way I was going to let Bascomb pump a slug in me without putting up a fight, no matter how hopeless the odds. And I knew Bomber well enough to know he'd feel the same way. Big macho types, Bascomb had called us. Predictable. Yeah, well, fuck that. If you're going to go down it's a hell of a lot better to go down swinging, that's all. So when the time came—

And then it hit me. What Hogan had said about the north end of the lake. Warning buoys down. Sand and gravel bars just under the surface of the water. Stay away from there.

That was exactly where Bascomb was taking us. Wherever he had gotten his boat, he had not received the same warning.

I glanced at The Bomber. If he shared my realization, he showed no sign. I tensed myself and tried to think of a way to warn him. Bascomb sat sideways in his seat, taking his eyes off us very seldom, steering mainly by peripheral vision. The shoreline loomed ever closer.

Even though I was scanning the water intently, I missed the gravel bar that nailed us. Bascomb's boat bottomed out with a sharp scratching sound followed instantly by the metallic *whang!*

of the propeller impacting. Our craft, weighted down by two bigger men and thus riding lower in the water, hit harder still.

We pitched forward, somersaulting, spinning wildly through the air. Fishing gear and minnow bait swirled around us like shrapnel. Hitting the water was like hitting a wall. My wrist and shoulder shrieked with agony as Bomber's weight—on the other end of the handcuff chain—twisted savagely away from me.

Everything was upside down and crazy for several seconds. Cold black water. Bubbles. Pain. Panic.

My head and shoulders broke to the surface. I sucked in great mouthfuls of air and found that if I just put my feet down I was in water barely chest high. Bomber surfaced beside me, coughing and cursing. When he lifted his face, it was chalky white and his eyes were pain-dulled. Red tendrils of blood began rising up, clouding the water around him.

I clutched him to me. Through clenched teeth he said, "Damn propeller caught me just before we hit the water. Pretty bad I think; I can hardly move my left leg."

The propeller. I could still hear its irritating buzz. I looked around.

Bascomb's boat, tilted onto one side, was lodged on the gravel bar. The motor had flipped up on its hinges from the impact, but was still running at three-quarter throttle, the propeller blades chewing the air. The towline had snapped and our boat had ended up several yards beyond, upside down, split open, sinking fast.

And then I saw Bascomb. He came around the end of his boat. He had a gash above one eye that left a watery smear of blood across his forehead. There was no sign of the shotgun. Instead, he carried one of the oars like a baseball bat.

"You're still mine, Hannibal," he crowed maniacally. "Damn you to hell, you're still mine!"

He moved toward me, the oar raised to swing.

With my left arm badly wrenched and chained to Bomber's injured bulk, I was one-handed and practically immobile. I looked around wildly for some sort of weapon to defend myself with, but there was none to be had.

"I'm going to club you, Hannibal," Bascomb jeered. "I'm going to club you to death like a gaffed mackerel."

He swung, a vicious downward chop with the edge of the oar's paddle end. Somehow, I got out of the way. He swung again almost immediately, this time a swooping blow that skimmed the surface of the water. He caught a piece of my good shoulder with that one, but nothing serious.

I backpedaled frantically, dragging Bomber along with me.

Bascomb circled. He moved into slightly shallower water and poised to strike again.

The Bomber sagged against me, seemingly on the verge of passing out. I shook him and swore at him, shouting for him to hang on. If he blacked out, became totally dead weight on the other end of that chain, neither of us had a prayer.

Bascomb swung again, and again I somehow managed to dodge it. But my breath was starting to come in ragged gasps and the water running down my face was as much from sweat as it was from being dunked in the lake. This deadly game of cat and mouse was incredibly exhausting, and I wouldn't be able to keep it up for very long.

And then, on the other side of Bascomb, something caught my eye. His boat moved! The vibrations from the still-running motor were causing it to shift on the gravel bar.

As Bascomb's shoulder muscles bunched for a fourth swing, the craft abruptly slid down off the crown of the bar and righted itself in the water with a wet slap. This last movement caused the motor to drop back down. The propeller bit deep into the wind-whipped waves and the boat shot forward.

Even if I'd wanted to, I never had a chance to warn him.

The prow caught Bascomb square between the shoulder blades. I heard his spine snap above the growl of the motor and saw him go down like a wrecking-balled wall. The boat veered away at impact and began moving parallel with the shoreline. It traveled only a couple dozen yards before striking another gravel bar. This time the motor stalled.

The silence was a sudden, overwhelming thing.

They didn't find Pinky Bascomb's body until the following spring. I had a few bad nights that winter, waking from cold-sweat dreams with chilling visions of Pinky rising up through the ice, clutching a frost-covered shotgun, eyes still burning red with vengeance. I was through the worst of it by the time his remains finally washed up.

After I'd gotten The Bomber to shore, I'd been able to stanch the bleeding of his wound pretty effectively with strips torn from my shirt. The propeller blades had caught him low on the hip and back slightly, toward the buttock, an area of the body where there are no big blood vessels.

I'd broken our handcuff chain between two rocks, then fashioned Bomber a crutch from the oar Bascomb had tried to split my skull with. With me supporting him on one side and the oar crutch on the other, we'd made our way along the shoreline until we reached a cabin where we were able to phone for medical assistance and the police.

I guess the bottom line on the whole thing is the pact Bomber and I made shortly after his release from the hospital. You should probably know about it in case you ever stop by The Bomb Shelter for a couple cold ones. It goes simply like this: The next time we hear somebody blowing about what a great Wisconsin fishing trip they've had, we vowed that one of us is going to march over and belt that person right in the mouth.

# LOREN D. ESTLEMAN

# STATE OF GRACE

*Loren D. Estleman is one of today's finest practitioners of the P.I. form. This is a belief widely held, and reinforced by novels like* Every Brilliant Eye *(1986),* Lady Yesterday *(1987), and his Shamus Award–winning* Sugartown *(1985). All of these novels featured his Detroit-based P.I. Amos Walker. "State of Grace," however, introduces a new—and quite "different"—character. We think you'll find Ralph Poteet gives Walker a run for his money in his first appearance, anywhere.*

"Ralph? This is Lyla."

"Who the hell is Lyla?"

"Lyla Dane. I live in the apartment above you, for chrissake. We see each other every day."

"The hooker."

"You live over a dirty bookstore. What do you want for a neighbor, a freaking rocket scientist?"

Ralph Poteet sat up in bed and rumpled his mouse-colored hair. He fumbled the alarm clock off the night table and held it very close to his good eye. He laid it facedown and scowled at the receiver in his hand. "It's two-thirty ayem."

"Thanks. My watch stopped and I knew if I called you you'd tell me what time it is. Listen, you're like a cop, right?"

"Not at two-thirty ayem."

"I'll give you a hundred dollars to come up here now."

He blew his nose on the sheet. "Ain't that supposed to be the other way around?"

"You coming up or not? You're not the only dick in town. I just called you because you're handy."

"What's the squeal?"

"I got a dead priest in my bed."

He said he was on his way and hung up. A square gin bottle slid off the blanket. He caught it before it hit the floor, but it was

89

empty and he dropped it. He put on his Tyrolean hat with a feather in the band, found his suitpants on the floor half under the bed, and pulled them on over his pajamas. He stuck bare feet into his loafers and because it was October he pulled on his suitcoat, grunting with the effort. He was forty-three years old and forty pounds overweight. He looked for his gun just because it was 2:30 A.M., couldn't find it, and went out.

Lyla Dane was just five feet and ninety pounds in a pink kimono and slippers with carnations on the toes. She wore her black hair in a pageboy like Anna May Wong, but the Oriental effect fell short of her round Occidental face. "You look like crap," she told Ralph at the door.

"That's what two hours' sleep will do for you. Where's the hundred?"

"Don't you want to see the stiff first?"

"What do I look like, a pervert?"

"Yes." She opened a drawer in the telephone stand and counted a hundred in twenties and tens into his palm.

He stuck the money in a pocket and followed her through a small living room decorated by K-Mart into a smaller bedroom containing a Queen Anne bed that had cost twice as much as all the other furniture combined and took up most of the space in the room. The rest of the space was taken up by Monsignor John Breame, pastor of St. Boniface, a cathedral Ralph sometimes used to exchange pictures for money, although not so much lately because the divorce business was on the slide. He recognized the monsignor's pontifical belly under the flesh-colored satin sheet that barely covered it. The monsignor's face was purple.

"He a regular?" Ralph found a Diamond matchstick in his suitcoat pocket and stuck the end between his teeth.

"Couple of times a month. Tonight I thought he was breathing a little hard after. Then he wasn't."

"What do you want me to do?"

"Get rid of him, what else? Cops find him here the Christers'll run me out on a cross. I got a business to run."

"Cost you another hundred."

"I just gave you a hundred."

"You're lucky I don't charge by the pound. Look at that gut."

"*You* look at it. He liked the missionary position."

"What else would he?"

She got the hundred and gave it to him. He told her to leave. "Where'll I go?"

"There's beds all over town. You probably been in half of them. Or go find an all-night movie if you don't feel like working. Don't come back before dawn."

She dressed and went out after emptying the money drawer into a shoulder bag she took with her. When she was gone Ralph helped himself to a Budweiser from her refrigerator and looked up a number in the city directory and called it from the telephone in the living room. A voice like ground glass answered.

"Bishop Stoneman?" Ralph asked.

"It's three ayem," said the voice.

"Thank you. My name is Ralph Poteet. I'm a private detective. I'm sorry to have to inform you Monsignor Breame is dead."

"Mary Mother of God! What happened?"

"I'm no expert. It looks like a heart attack."

"Mary Mother of God. In bed?"

"Yeah."

"Was he—do you know if he was in a state of grace?"

"That's what I wanted to talk to you about," Ralph said.

The man Bishop Stoneman sent was tall and gaunt, with a complexion like wet pulp and colorless hair cropped down to stubble. He had on a black coat buttoned to the neck and looked like an early martyr. He said his name was Morgan. Together they wrapped the monsignor in the soiled bedding and carried him down three flights of stairs, stopping a dozen times to rest, and laid him on the backseat of a big Buick Electra parked between streetlamps. Ralph stood guard at the car while Morgan went back up for the monsignor's clothes. It was nearly 4:00 A.M. and their only witness was a skinny cat who lost interest after a few minutes and stuck one leg up in the air to lick itself.

After a long time Morgan came down and threw the bundle onto the front seat and gave Ralph an envelope containing a hundred dollars. He said he'd handle it from there. Ralph watched him drive off and went back up to bed. He was very tired and didn't wake up until the fire sirens were grinding down in front of the building. He hadn't even heard the explosion when Lyla Dane returned to her apartment at dawn.

"Go away."

"That's no way to talk to your partner," Ralph said.

"Ex-partner. You got the boot and I did, too. Now I'm giving it to you. Go away."

Dale English was a special investigator with the sheriff's department who kept his office in the City-County Building. He had a monolithic face and fierce black eyebrows like Lincoln's, creating an effect he tried to soften with pink shirts and knobby knitted ties. He and Ralph had shared a city prowl car for two years, until some evidence turned up missing from the property room. Both had been dismissed, English without prejudice because unlike the case with Ralph, none of the incriminating items had been found in English's possession.

"The boot didn't hurt you none," Ralph said.

"No, it just cost me my wife and my kid and seven years' seniority. I'd be a lieutenant now."

Ralph lowered his bulk onto the vinyl-and-aluminum chair in front of English's desk. "I wouldn't hang this on you if I could go to the city cops. Somebody's out to kill me."

"Tell whoever it is I said good luck."

"I ain't kidding."

"Me neither."

"You know that hooker got blown up this morning?"

"The gas explosion? I read about it."

"Yeah, well, it wasn't no accident. I'm betting the arson boys find a circuit breaker in the wall switch. You know what that means."

"Sure. Somebody lets himself in and turns on the gas and puts a breaker in the switch so when the guy comes home the spark blows him to hell. What was the hooker into and what was your angle?"

"It's more like who was into the hooker." Ralph told him the rest.

"This the same Monsignor Breame was found by an altar boy counting angels in his bed at the St. Boniface rectory this morning?" English asked.

"Thanks to me and this bug Morgan."

"So what do you want?"

"Hell, protection. The blowup was meant for me. Morgan thought I'd be going back to that same apartment and set it up while I was waiting for him to come down with Breame's clothes."

"Bishops don't kill people over priests that can't keep their vows in their pants."

Ralph screwed up his good eye. Its mate looked like a sour ball someone had spat out. "What world you living in? Shape the Church is in, he'd do just that to keep it quiet."

"Go away, Ralph."

"Well, pick up Morgan at least. He can't be hard to find. He looks like one of those devout creeps you see skulking around in paintings of the Crucifixion."

"I don't have jurisdiction in the city."

"That ain't why you won't do it. Hey, I told IAD you didn't have nothing to do with what went down in Property."

"It would've carried more weight if you'd submitted to a lie detector test. Mine was inconclusive." He paged through a report on his desk without looking at it. "I'll run the name Morgan and the description you gave me through the computer and see what it coughs up. There won't be anything."

"Thanks, buddy."

"You sure you didn't take pictures? It'd be your style to try and put the squeeze on a bishop."

"I thought about it, but my camera's in hock." Ralph got up. "You can get me at my place. They got the fire out before it reached my floor."

"That was lucky. Gin flames are the hardest to put out."

He was driving a brand-new red Riviera he had promised to sell for a lawyer friend who was serving two years for suborning to commit perjury, only he hadn't gotten around to it yet. He parked in a handicapped zone near his building and climbed stairs smelling of smoke and firemen's rubber boots. Inside his apartment, which was also his office, he rewound the tape on his answering machine and played back a threatening call from a loan shark named Zwingman, a reminder from a dentist's receptionist with a Nutra-Sweet voice that last month's root canal was still unpaid for, and a message from a heavy breather that he had to play back three times before deciding it was a man. He was staring toward the door, his attention on the tape, when a square of white paper slithered over the threshold.

That day he was wearing his legal gun, a short-nosed .38 Colt, in a clip on his belt, and an orphan High Standard .22 magnum derringer in an ankle holster. Drawing the Colt, he lunged and tore open the door just in time to hear the street door closing below. He swung around and crossed to the street window. Through it he saw a narrow figure in a long black coat and the back of a close-cropped head crossing against traffic to the other side. The man rounded the corner and vanished.

Ralph holstered the revolver and picked up the note. It was addressed to him in a round, shaped hand.

> Mr. Poteet:
>     If it is not inconvenient, your presence at my home could prove to your advantage and mine.
>                                          Cordially,
>                                          Philip Stoneman,
>                                          Bishop-in-Ordinary

Clipped to it was a hundred-dollar bill.

Bishop Stoneman lived in a refurbished brownstone in a neighborhood that the city had reclaimed from slum by evicting its residents and sandblasting graffiti off the buildings. The bell was answered by a youngish bald man in a dark suit and clerical collar who introduced himself as Brother Edwards and directed Ralph to a curving staircase, then retired to be seen no more. Ralph didn't hear Morgan climbing behind him until something hard probed his right kidney. A hand patted him down and removed the Colt from its clip. "End of the hall."

The bishop was a tall old man, nearly as thin as Morgan, with iron-gray hair and a face that fell away to the white shackle of his collar. He rose from behind a redwood desk to greet his visitor in an old-fashioned black frock that made him look like a crow. The room was large and square and smelled of leather from the books on the built-in shelves and pipe tobacco. Morgan entered behind Ralph and closed the door.

"Thank you for coming, Mr. Poteet. Please sit down."

"Thank Ben Franklin." But he settled into a deep leather chair that gripped his buttocks like a big hand in a soft glove.

"I'm grateful for this chance to thank you in person," Stoneman said, sitting in his big swivel. "I'm very disappointed in Monsignor Breame. I'd hoped that he would take my place at the head of the diocese."

"You bucking for cardinal?"

He smiled. "I suppose you've shown yourself worthy of confidence. Yes, His Holiness has offered me the red hat. The appointment will be announced next month."

"That why you tried to croak me? I guess your right bower cashing in in a hooker's bed would look bad in Rome."

One corner of the desk supported a silver tray containing two long-stemmed glasses and a cut-crystal decanter half full of ruby liquid. Stoneman removed the stopper and filled both glasses. "This is an excellent Madeira. I confess that the austere life allows me two mild vices. The other is tobacco."

"What are we celebrating?" Ralph didn't pick up his glass.

"Your new appointment as chief of diocesan security. The position pays well and the hours are regular."

"In return for which I forget about Monsignor Breame?"

"And entrust all related material to me. You took pictures, of course." Stoneman sipped from his glass.

Ralph lifted his. "I'd be pretty stupid not to, considering what happened to Lyla Dane."

"I heard about the tragedy. That child's soul could have been saved."

"You should've thought about that before your boy Morgan croaked her." Ralph gulped off half his wine. It tasted bitter.

The bishop laid a bony hand atop an ancient ornate Bible on the desk. His guest thought he was about to swear his innocence. "This belonged to St. Thomas. More, not Aquinas. I have a weakness for religious antiques."

"Thought you only had two vices." The air in the room stirred slightly. Ralph turned to see who had entered, but his vision was thickening. Morgan was a shimmering shadow. The glass dropped from Ralph's hand. He bent to retrieve it and came up with the derringer. Stoneman's shout echoed. Ralph fired twice at the shadow and pitched headfirst into its depths.

He awoke feeling pretty much the way he did most mornings, with his head throbbing and his stomach turning over. He wanted to turn over with it, but he was stretched out on a hard, flat surface with his ankles strapped down and his arms tied above his head. He was looking up at water-stained tile. His joints ached.

"The sedative was in the stem of your glass," Stoneman was saying. He was out of Ralph's sight and Ralph had the impression he'd been talking for a while. "You've been out for two hours. The unpleasant effect is temporary, rather like a hangover."

"Did I get him?" Ralph's tongue moved sluggishly.

"No, you missed rather badly. It required persuasion to get

Morgan to carry you down here to the basement instead of killing
you on the spot. He was quite upset."

Ralph squirmed. There was something familiar about the
position he was tied in. For some reason he thought of Mrs.
Thornton, his ninth-grade American Lit. teacher. *What is the
significance of Poe's "Pit and the Pendulum" to the transcendentalist
movement?* His organs shriveled.

"Another antique," said the bishop. "The Inquisition did not
end when General Lasalle entered Madrid, but went on for
several years in the provinces. This particular rack was still in use
after Torquemada's death. The gears are original. The wheel is
new, and of course I had to replace the ropes. Morgan?"

A shoe scraped the floor and a spoked shadow fluttered across
Ralph's vision. His arms tightened. He gasped.

"That's enough. We don't want to put Mr. Poteet back under."
To Ralph: "Morgan just returned from your apartment. He found
neither pictures nor film nor even a camera. Where are they?"

"I was lying. I didn't take no pictures."

"Morgan."

Ralph shrieked.

"Enough! His Holiness is sensitive about scandal, Mr. Poteet. I
won't have Monsignor Breame's indiscretions bar me from the
Vatican. Who is keeping the pictures for you?"

"There ain't no pictures, honest."

"Morgan!"

A socket started to slip. Ralph screamed and blubbered.

"Enough!" Stoneman's fallen-away face moved into Ralph's
vision. His eyes were fanatic. "A few more turns will sever your
spine. You could be spoon-fed for the rest of your life. Do you
think that after failing to kill you in that apartment I would
hesitate to cripple you? Where are the pictures?"

"I didn't take none!"

"Morgan!"

"*No!*" It ended in a howl. His armpits were on fire. The ropes
creaked.

"Police! Don't move!"

The bishop's face jerked away. The spoked shadow fluttered.
The tension went out of Ralph's arms suddenly, and relief poured
into his joints. A shot flattened the air. Two more answered it.
Something struck the bench Ralph was lying on and drove a
splinter into his back. He thought at first he was shot, but the pain
was nothing; he'd just been through worse. He squirmed onto his

hip and saw Morgan, one black-clad arm stained and glistening, leveling a heavy automatic at a target behind Ralph's back. Scrambling out of the line of fire, Ralph jerked his bound hands and the rack's wheel, six feet in diameter with handles bristling from it like a ship's helm, spun around. One of the handles slapped the gun from Morgan's hand. Something cracked past Ralph's left ear and Morgan fell back against the tile wall and slid down it. The shooting stopped.

Ralph wriggled onto his other hip. A man he didn't know in a houndstooth coat with a revolver in his hand had Bishop Stoneman spread-eagled against a wall and was groping in his robes for weapons. Dale English came off the stairs with the Ruger he had been carrying since Ralph was his partner. He bent over Morgan on the floor, then straightened and holstered the gun. He looked at Ralph. "I guess you're okay."

"I am if you got a pocketknife."

"Arson boys found the circuit breaker in the wall switch just like you said." He cut Ralph's arms free and sawed through the straps on his ankles. "When you didn't answer your telephone I went to your place and found Stoneman's note."

"He confessed to the hooker's murder."

"I know. I heard him."

"How the hell long were you listening?"

"We had to have enough to pin him to it, didn't we?"

"You son of a bitch. You just wanted to hear me holler."

"Couldn't help it. You sure got lungs."

"I got to go to the toilet."

"Stick around after," English said. "I need a statement to hand to the city boys. They won't like County sticking its face in this."

Ralph hobbled upstairs. When he was through in the bathroom he found his hat and coat and headed out. At the front door he turned around and went back into the bishop's study, where he hoisted Thomas More's Bible under one arm. He knew a bookseller who would probably give him at least a hundred for it.

# SUE GRAFTON

# NON SUNG SMOKE

*With four novels in her alphabetized Kinsey Millhone series (and several short stories), Sue Grafton has racked up a Shamus Award ("B" Is for Burglar, Best Novel of 1985), and three Anthony Awards ("B" Is for Burglar, Best Novel of 1985; "C" Is for Corpse, Best Novel of 1986; and "The Parker Shotgun," Best Short Story of 1986). "The Parker Shotgun" appeared in* Mean Streets.

*"Non Sung Smoke" makes her a strong contender for awards next year, as well.*

The day was an odd one, brooding and chill, sunlight alternating with an erratic wind that was being pushed toward California in advance of a tropical storm called Bo. It was late September in Santa Teresa. Instead of the usual Indian summer, we were caught up in vague presentiments of the long, gray winter to come. I found myself pulling sweaters out of my bottom drawer and I went to the office smelling of moth balls and last year's cologne.

I spent the morning caught up in routine paperwork which usually leaves me feeling productive, but this was the end of a dull week and I was so bored I would have taken on just about anything. The young woman showed up just before lunch, announcing herself with a tentative tap on my office door. She couldn't have been more than twenty, with a sultry, pornographic face and a tumble of long dark hair. She was wearing an outfit that suggested she hadn't gone home the night before unless, of course, she simply favored low-cut sequined cocktail dresses at noon. Her spike heels were a dyed-to-match green and her legs were bare. She moved over to my desk with an air of uncertainty, like someone just learning to roller skate.

"Hi, how are you? Have a seat," I said.

She sank into a chair. "Thanks. I'm Mona Starling. I guess you're Kinsey Millhone, huh."

"Yes, that's right."

"Are you really a private detective?"

"Licensed and bonded," I said.

"Are you single?"

I did a combination nod and shrug which I hoped would cover two divorces and my current happily *un*married state.

"Great," she said, "then you'll understand. God, I can't believe I'm really doing this. I've never hired a detective, but I don't know what else to do."

"What's going on?"

She blushed, maybe from nervousness, maybe from embarrassment, but the heightened coloring only made her green eyes more vivid. She shifted in her seat, the sequins on her dress winking merrily. Something about her posture made me downgrade her age. She looked barely old enough to drive.

"I hope you don't think this is dumb. I . . . uh, ran into this guy last night and we really hit it off. He told me his name was Gage. I don't know if that's true or not. Sometimes guys make up names, you know, like if they're married or maybe not sure they want to see you again. Anyway, we had a terrific time, only he left without telling me how to get in touch. I was just wondering how much it might cost to find out who he is."

"How do you know he won't get in touch with you?"

"Well, he might. I mean, I'll give him a couple of days of course. All I'm asking for is his name and address. Just in case."

"I take it you'll want his phone number, too."

She laughed uneasily. "Well, yeah."

"What if he doesn't want to renew the acquaintance?"

"Oh, I wouldn't bother him if he felt that way. I know it looks like a pickup, but it really wasn't. For me, at any rate. I don't want him to think it was casual on my part."

"I take it you were . . . ah, *intimate*," I said.

"Un-uh, we just balled, but it was incredible and I'd really like to see him again."

Reluctantly, I pulled out a legal pad and made a note. "Where'd you meet this man?"

"I ran into him at Mooter's. He talked like he hung out there a lot. The music was so loud we were having to shout, so after a while we went to the bar next door where it was quiet. We talked for hours. I know what you're going to say. Like why don't I let well enough alone or something, but I just can't."

"Why not go back to Mooter's and ask around?"

"Well, I would, but I, uh, have this boyfriend who's really jealous and he'd figure it out. If I even look at another guy, he has this incredible ESP reaction. He's spooky sometimes."

"How'd you get away with it last night?"

"He was working, so I was on my own," she said. "Say you'll help me, okay? Please? I've been cruising around all night looking for his car. He lives somewhere in Montebello, I'm almost sure."

"I can probably find him, Mona, but my services aren't cheap."

"I don't care," she said. "That's fine. I have money. Just tell me how much."

I debated briefly and finally asked her for fifty bucks. I didn't have the heart to charge my usual rates. I didn't really want her business, but it was better than typing up file notes for the case I'd just done. She put a fifty-dollar bill on my desk and I wrote out a receipt, bypassing my standard contract. As young as she was, I wasn't sure it'd be binding anyway.

I jotted down a description of the man named Gage. He sounded like every stud on the prowl I've ever seen. Early thirties, five foot ten, good build, dark hair, dark moustache, great smile, and a dimple in his chin. I was prepared to keep writing, but that was the extent of it. For all of their alleged hours of conversation, she knew precious little about him. I quizzed her at length about hobbies, interests, what sort of work he did. The only real information she could give me was that he drove an old silver Jaguar which is where they "got it on" (her parlance, not mine) the first time. The second time was at her place. After that, he apparently disappeared like a puff of smoke. Real soul mates, these two. I didn't want to tell her what an old story it was. In Santa Teresa, the eligible men are so much in demand they can do anything they want. I took her address and telephone number and said I'd get back to her. As soon as she left, I picked up my handbag and car keys. I had a few personal errands to run and figured I'd tuck her business in when I was finished with my own.

Mooter's is one of a number of bars on the Santa Teresa singles' circuit. By night, it's crowded and impossibly noisy. Happy Hour features well drinks for fifty cents and the bartender rings a gong for every five-dollar tip. The tables are small, jammed together around a dance floor the size of a boxing ring. The walls are covered with caricatures of celebrities, possibly purchased from some other bar, as they seem to be signed and dedicated to someone named Stan whom nobody's ever heard of. An ex-husband of mine played jazz piano there once upon a time, but I hadn't been in for years.

I arrived that afternoon at two, just in time to watch the place being opened up. Two men, day drinkers by the look of them, edged in ahead of me and took up what I surmised were habitual perches at one end of the bar. They were exchanging the kind of pleasantries that suggest daily contact of no particular depth. The man who let us in apparently doubled as bartender and bouncer. He was in his thirties, with curly blond hair, and a T-shirt reading BOUNCER stretched across an impressively muscular chest. His arms were so big I thought he might rip his sleeves out when he flexed.

I found an empty stool at the far end of the bar and waited while he made a couple of martinis for the two men who'd come in with me. A waitress appeared for work, taking off her coat as she moved through the bar to the kitchen area.

The bartender then ambled in my direction with an inquiring look.

"I'll have a wine spritzer," I said.

A skinny guy with a guitar case came into the bar behind me. When the bartender saw him, he grinned. "Hey, how's it goin'? How's Fresno?"

They shook hands and the guy took a stool two down from mine. "Hot. And dull, but Mary Jane's was fine. We really packed 'em in."

"Smirnoff on the rocks?"

"Nah, not today. Gimme a beer instead. Bud'll do."

The bartender pulled one for him and set his drink on the bar at the same time I got mine. I wondered what it must be like to hang out all day in saloons, nursing beers, shooting the shit with idlers and ne'er-do-wells. The waitress came out of the kitchen, tying an apron around her waist. She took a sandwich order from the guys at the far end of the bar. The other fellow and I both declined when she asked if we were interested in lunch. She began to busy herself with napkins and flatware.

The bartender caught my eye. "You want to run a tab?"

I shook my head. "This is fine," I said. "I'm trying to get in touch with a guy who was in here last night."

"Good luck. The place was a zoo."

"Apparently, he's a regular. I thought you might identify him from a description."

"What's he done?"

"Not a thing. From what I was told, he picked up a young lady and ran out on her afterward. She wants to get in touch with him, that's all."

He stood and looked at me. "You're a private detective."

"That's right."

He and the other fellow exchanged a look.

The fellow said, "Help the woman. This is great."

The bartender shrugged. "Sure, why not? What's he look like?"

The waitress paused, listening in on the conversation with interest.

I mentioned the first name and description Mona'd given me. "The only other thing I know about him is he drives an old silver Jaguar."

"Gage Vesca," the other fellow said promptly.

The bartender said, "Yeah, that's him."

"You know how I might get in touch?"

The other fellow shook his head and the bartender shrugged. "All I know is he's a jerk. The guy's got a vanity license plate reads STALYUN if that tells you anything. Besides that, he just got married a couple months back. He's bad news. Better warn your client. He'll screw anything that moves."

"I'll pass the word. Thanks." I put a five-dollar bill on the bar and hopped down off the stool, leaving the spritzer untouched.

"Hey, who's the babe?" the bartender asked.

"Can't tell you that," I said, as I picked up my bag.

The waitress spoke up. "Well, I know which one she's talking about. That girl in the green-sequined dress."

I went back to my office and checked the telephone book. No listing for Vescas of any kind. Information didn't have him either, so I put in a call to a friend of mine at the DMV who plugged the license plate into the computer. The name Gage Vesca came up, with an address in Montebello. I used my crisscross directory for a match and came up with the phone number, which I dialed just to see if it was good. As soon as the maid said "Vesca residence," I hung up.

I put in a call to Mona Starling and gave her what I had, including the warning about his marital status and his character references which were poor. She didn't seem to care. After that, I figured if she pursued him, it was her lookout . . . and his. She thanked me profusely before she rang off, relief audible in her voice.

That was Saturday.

Monday morning, I opened my front door, picked up the paper, and caught the headlines about Gage Vesca's death.

"Shit!"

He'd been shot in the head at close range sometime between two and six A.M. on Sunday, then crammed into the trunk of his Jaguar and left in the long-term parking lot at the airport. Maybe somebody hoped the body wouldn't be discovered for days. Time enough to set up an alibi or pull a disappearing act. As it was, the hood had popped open and a passerby had spotted him. My hands were starting to shake. What kind of chump had I been?

I tried Mona Starling's number and got a busy signal. I threw some clothes on, grabbed my car keys, and headed over to the Frontage Road address she'd given me. As I chirped to a stop out front, a Yellow cab pulled away from the curb with a lone passenger. I checked the house number. A duplex. I figured the odds were even that I'd just watched Mona split. She must have seen the headlines about the same time I did.

I took off again, craning for sight of the taxi somewhere ahead. Beyond the next intersection, there was a freeway on-ramp. I caught a flash of yellow and pursued it. By keeping my foot to the floor and judiciously changing lanes, I managed to slide in right behind the taxi as it took the airport exit. By the time the cab deposited Mona at the curb out in front, I was squealing into the short-term lot with the parking ticket held between my teeth. I shoved it in my handbag and ran.

The airport at Santa Teresa only has five gates, and it didn't take much detecting to figure out which one was correct. United was announcing a final boarding call for a flight to San Francisco. I used the fifty bucks Mona'd paid me to snag a seat and a boarding pass from a startled reservations clerk and then I headed for the gate. I had no luggage and nothing on me to set off the security alarm as I whipped through. I flashed my ticket, opened the double doors, and raced across the tarmac for the plane, taking the portable boarding stairs two at a time. The flight attendant pulled the door shut behind me. I was in.

I spotted Mona eight rows back in a window seat on the left-hand side, her face turned away from me. This time she was wearing jeans and an oversized shirt. The aisle seat was occupied, but the middle was empty. The plane was still sitting on the runway, engines revving, as I bumped across some guy's knees, saying, "'scuse me, pardon me," and popped in beside Ms. Starling. She turned a blanched face toward me and a little cry escaped. "What are you doing here?"

"See if you can guess."

"I didn't do it," she whispered hoarsely.

"Yeah, right. I bet. That's probably why you got on a plane the minute the story broke," I said.

"That's *not* what happened."

"The hell it's not!"

The man on my left leaned forward and looked at us quizzically.

"The fellow she picked up Friday night got killed," I said, conversationally. I pointed my index finger at my head like a gun and fired. He decided to mind his own business, which suited me. Mona got to her feet and tried to squeeze past. All I had to do was extend my knees and she was trapped. Other people were taking an interest by now. She did a quick survey of the situation, rolled her eyes, and sat down again. "Let's get off the plane. I'll explain in a minute. Just don't make a scene," she said, the color high in her cheeks.

"Hey, let's not cause you any embarrassment," I said. "A man was murdered. That's all we're talking about."

"I know he's dead," she hissed, "but I'm innocent. I swear to God."

We got up together and bumped and thumped across the man's knees, heading down the aisle toward the door. The flight attendant was peeved, but she let us deplane.

We went upstairs to the airport bar and found a little table at the rear. When the waitress came, I shook my head, but Mona ordered a Pink Squirrel. The waitress had questions about her age, but I had to question her taste. A Pink Squirrel? Mona had pulled her wallet out and the waitress scrutinized her California driver's license, checking Mona's face against the stamp-sized color photograph, apparently satisfied at the match. As she passed the wallet back to Mona, I snagged it and peeked at the license myself. She was twenty-one by a month. The address was

the same one she'd given me. The waitress disappeared and
Mona snatched her wallet, shoving it down in her purse again.

"What was that for?" she said sulkily.

"Just checking. You want to tell me what's going on?"

She picked up a packet of airport matches and began to bend
the cover back and forth. "I lied to you."

"This comes as no surprise," I said. "What's the truth?"

"Well, I did pick him up, but we didn't screw. I just told you
that because I couldn't think of any other reason I'd want his
home address."

"Why *did* you want it?"

She broke off eye contact. "He stole something and I had to get
it back."

I stared at her. "Let me take a flyer," I said. "It had to be
something illegal or you'd have told me about it right up front. Or
reported it to the cops. So it must be dope. Was it coke or grass?"

She was wide-eyed. "Grass, but how did you know?"

"Just tell me the rest," I replied with a shake of my head. I love
the young. They're always amazed that we know anything.

Mona glanced up to my right.

The waitress was approaching with her tray. She set an airport
cocktail napkin on the table and placed the Pink Squirrel on it.
"That'll be three-fifty."

Mona took five ones from her billfold and waved her off. She
sipped at the drink and shivered. The concoction was the same
pink as bubble gum, which made me shiver a bit as well. She
licked her lips. "My boyfriend got a lid of this really incredible
grass. 'Non Sung Smoke' it's called, from the town of Non Sung
in Thailand."

"Never heard of it," I said. "Not that I'm any connoisseur."

"Well, me neither, but he paid like two thousand dollars for it
and he'd only smoked one joint. The guy he got it from said half a
hit would put you away so we weren't going to smoke it every
day. Just special occasions."

"Pretty high-class stuff at those rates."

"The best."

"And you told Gage."

"Well, yeah," she said reluctantly. "We met and we started
talking. He said he needed to score some pot so I mentioned it. I
wasn't going to sell him ours. I just thought he might try it and
then if he was interested, maybe we could get some for him.
When we got to my place, I went in the john while he rolled a

joint, and when I came out, he was gone and so was the dope. I had to take a cab back to Mooter's to pick up my car. I was in such a panic. I knew if Jerry found out he'd have a fit!"

"He's your boyfriend?"

"Right," she said, looking down at her lap. She began to blink rapidly and she put a trembling hand to her lips.

I gave her a verbal nudge, just to head off the tears. "Then what? After I gave you the phone number, you got in touch with Gage?"

She nodded mutely, then took a deep breath. "I had to wait till Jerry went off to work and then I called. Gage said—"

"Wait a minute. He answered the phone?"

"Uh-uh. She did. His wife, but I made sure she'd hung up the extension and then I talked so he only had to answer yes and no. I told him I knew he fucking stole the dope and I wanted it back like right then. I just screamed. I told him if he didn't get that shit back to me, he'd be sorry. He said he'd meet me in the parking lot at Mooter's after closing time."

"That was Saturday night?"

She nodded.

"All right. Then what?"

"That's all there was," she said. "I met him there at two-fifteen and he handed over the dope. I didn't even tell him what a shitheel he was. I just snatched the baggie, got back in my car, and came home. When I saw the headlines this morning, I thought I'd die!"

"Who else was aware of all this?"

"No one as far as I know."

"Didn't your boyfriend think it was odd you went out at two-fifteen?"

She shook her head. "I was back before he got home."

"Didn't he realize the dope had disappeared?"

"No, because I put it back before he even looked for it. He couldn't have known."

"What about Mooter's? Was there anyone else in the parking lot?"

"Not that I saw."

"No one coming or going from the bar?"

"Just the guy who runs the place."

"What about Mrs. Vesca? Could she have followed him?"

"Well, I asked him if she overheard my call and he said no. But

108 

she could have followed, I guess. I don't know what kind of car she drives, but she could have been parked on a side street."

"Aside from that, how could anyone connect you to Vesca's death? I don't understand why you decided to run."

Her voice dropped to a whisper. "My fingerprints have to be on that car. I was just in it two nights ago."

I studied the look in her eyes and I could feel my heart sink. "You have a record," I said.

"I was picked up for shoplifting once. But that's the only trouble I was ever in. Honestly."

"I think you ought to go to the cops with this. It's far better to be up front with them than to come up with lame excuses after they track you down, which I suspect they will."

"Oh, God, I'll die."

"No, you won't. You'll feel better. Now do what I say and I'll check the rest of it from my end."

"You will?"

"Of course!" I snapped. "If I hadn't found the guy for you, he might be okay. How do you think I feel?"

I followed the maid through the Vescas' house to the pool area at the rear, where one of the cabanas had been fitted out as a personal gym. There were seven weight machines bolted to the floor, which was padded with rubber matting. Mirrors lined three walls and sunlight streamed in the fourth. Katherine Vesca, in a hot-pink leotard and silver tights, was working on her abs, an unnecessary expenditure of energy from what I could see. She was thin as a snake. Her ash-blond hair was kept off her face by a band of pink chiffon and her gray eyes were cold. She blotted sweat from her neck as she glanced at my business card. "You're connected with the police?"

"Actually, I'm not, but I'm hoping you'll answer some questions anyway."

"Why should I?"

"I'm trying to get a line on your husband's killer just like they are."

"Why not leave it up to them?"

"I have some information they don't have yet. I thought I'd see what else I could add before I pass on the facts."

"The facts?"

"About his activities the last two days of his life."

She gave me a chilly smile and crossed to the leg-press

machine. She moved the pin down to the hundred-and-eighty-pound mark, then seated herself and started to do reps. "Fire away," she said.

"I understand a phone call came in sometime on Saturday," I said.

"That's right. A woman called. He went out to meet her quite late that night and he didn't come back. I never saw him again."

"Do you know what the call was about?"

"Sorry. He never said."

"Weren't you curious?"

"When I married Gage, I agreed that I wouldn't be 'curious' about anything he did."

"And he wasn't curious about you?"

"We had an open relationship. At his insistence, I might add. He was free to do anything he liked."

"And you didn't object?"

"Sometimes, but those were his terms and I agreed."

"What sort of work did he do?"

"He didn't. Neither of us worked. I have a business here in town and I derive income from that, among other things."

"Do you know if he was caught up in anything? A quarrel? Some kind of personal feud?"

"If so, he never mentioned it," she said. "He was not well liked, but I couldn't say he had enemies."

"Do you have a theory about who killed him?"

She finished ten reps and rested. "I wish I did."

"When's the funeral?" I asked.

"Tomorrow morning at ten. You're welcome to come. Then maybe there'll be two of us."

She gave me the name of the funeral home and I made a note.

"One more thing," I said. "What sort of business are you in? Could that be relevant?"

"I don't see how. I have a bar. Called Mooter's. It's managed by my brother, Jim."

When I walked in, he was washing beer mugs behind the bar, running each in turn across a rotating brush, then through a hot water rinse. To his right was a mounting pyramid of drying mugs, still radiating heat. Today he wore a bulging T-shirt imprinted with a slogan that read: ONE NIGHT OF BAD SEX IS STILL BETTER THAN A GOOD DAY AT WORK. He fixed a look on my face, smiling pleasantly. "How's it going?"

I perched on a bar stool. "Not bad," I said. "You're Jim?"

"That's me. And you're the lady P.I. I don't think you told me your name."

"Kinsey Millhone. I'm assuming you heard about Vesca's death?"

"Yeah, Jesus. Poor guy. Looks like somebody really cleaned his clock. Hope it wasn't the little gal he dumped the other night."

"That's always a possibility."

"You want a spritzer?"

"Sure," I said. "You have a good memory."

"For drinks," he said. "That's my job." He got out the jug wine and poured some in a glass, adding soda from the hose. He added a twist of lime and put the drink in front of me. "On the house."

"Thanks," I said. I took a sip. "How come you never said he was your brother-in-law?"

"How'd you find out about that?" he asked mildly.

"I talked to your sister. She mentioned it."

He shrugged. "Didn't seem pertinent."

I was puzzled by his attitude. He wasn't acting like a man with anything to hide. "Did you see him Saturday?"

"Saw his car at closing time. That was Sunday morning, actually. What's that got to do with it?"

"He must have been killed about then. The paper said sometime between two and six."

"I locked up here shortly after two. My buddy stopped by and picked me up right out front. I was in a poker game by two thirty-five, at a private club."

"You have witnesses?"

"Just the fifty other people in the place. I guess I could have shot the guy before my buddy showed up, but why would I do that? I had no axe to grind with him. I wasn't crazy about him, but I wouldn't plug the guy. My sister adored him. Why break her heart?"

Good question, I thought.

I returned to my office and sat down, tilting back in my swivel chair with my feet on the desk. I kept thinking Gage's death must be connected to the Non Sung Smoke, but I couldn't figure out quite how. I made a call to the Vesca house and was put on hold while the maid went to fetch Miss Katherine. She clicked on. "Yes?"

"Hello, Mrs. Vesca. This is Kinsey Millhone."

"Oh, hello. Sorry if I sounded abrupt. What can I do for you?"

"Just a question I forgot to ask you earlier. Did Gage ever mention something called Non Sung Smoke?"

"I don't think so. What is it?"

"A high-grade marijuana from Thailand. Two thousand bucks a lid. Apparently, he helped himself to somebody's stash on Friday night."

"Well, he did have some grass, but it couldn't be the same. He said it was junk. He was incensed that somebody hyped it to him."

"Really," I said, but it was more to myself than to her.

I headed down to the parking lot and retrieved my car. A dim understanding was beginning to form.

I knocked at the door of the duplex on Frontage Road. Mona answered, looking puzzled when she caught sight of me.

"Did you talk to the cops?" I asked.

"Not yet. I was just on my way. Why? What's up?"

"It occurred to me I might have misunderstood something you said to me. Friday night when you went out, you told me your boyfriend Jerry was at work. How come you had the nerve to stay out all night?"

"He was out of town," she said. "He got back Saturday afternoon about five."

"Couldn't he have arrived in Santa Teresa earlier that day?"

She shrugged. "I suppose so."

"What about Saturday when you met Gage in Mooter's parking lot? Was he working again?"

"Well, yes. He had a gig here in town. He got home about three," she said in the same bewildered tone.

"He's a musician, isn't he," I said.

"Wait a minute. What *is* this? What's it got to do with him?"

"A lot," he said from behind me. A choking arm slid around my neck and I was jerked half off my feet. I hung on, trying to ease the pressure on my windpipe. I could manage to breathe if I stood on tiptoe, but I couldn't do much else. Something hard was jammed into my ribs and I didn't think it was Jerry's fountain pen. Mona was astonished.

"Jerry! What the hell are you doing?" she yelped.

"Back up, bitch. Step back and let us in," he said between clenched teeth. I hung on, struggling, as he half-lifted, half-shoved me toward the threshold. He dragged me into the apartment and kicked the door shut. He pushed me down on the couch and stood there with his gun pointed right between my eyes. Hey, I was comfy. I wasn't going anyplace.

When I saw his face, of course, my suspicions were confirmed. Jerry was the fellow with the guitar case who'd sat next to me at Mooter's bar when I first went in. He wasn't a big guy—maybe five-eight, weighing in at a hundred and fifty-five—but he'd caught me by surprise. He was edgy and he had a crazy look in his eyes. I've noticed that in a pinch like this, my mind either goes completely blank or begins to compute at lightning speeds. I found myself staring at his gun, which was staring disconcertingly at me. It looked like a little Colt .32, a semiautomatic, almost a double for mine . . . locked at that moment in a briefcase in the backseat of my car. I bypassed the regrets and got straight to the point. Before being fired the first time, a semiautomatic has to be manually cocked, a maneuver that can be accomplished only with two hands. I couldn't remember hearing the sound of the slide being yanked before the nose of the gun was shoved into the small of my back. I wondered briefly if, in his haste to act, he hadn't had time to cock the gun.

"Hello, Jerry," I said. "Nice seeing you again. Why don't you tell Mona about your run-in with Gage?"

"*You* killed Gage?" she said, staring at him with disbelief.

"That's right, Mona, and I'm going to kill you, too. Just as soon as I figure out what to do with her." He kept his eyes on me, making sure I didn't move.

"But why? What did I do?" she gasped.

"Don't give me that," he said. "You balled the guy! Cattin' around in that green-sequined dress with your tits hangin' out and you pick up a scumbag like him! I told you I'd kill you if you ever did that to me."

"But I didn't. I swear it. All I did was bring him back here to try a hit of pot. Next thing I knew he'd stolen the whole lid."

"Bullshit!"

"No, it's not!"

I said, "She's telling the truth, Jerry. That's why she hired me."

Confused, he shot a look at her. "You never went to bed with him?"

"Jesus Christ, of course not. The guy was a creep! I'm not *that* low class!"

Jerry's hand began to tremble and his gaze darted back and

forth between her face and mine. "Then why'd you meet him again the next night?"

"To get the grass back. What else could I do? I didn't want you to know I'd been stiffed for two thousand dollars' worth of pot."

He stared at her, transfixed, and that's when I charged. I flew at him, head down, butting straight into his midriff, my momentum taking us both down in a heap. The gun skittered off across the floor. Mona leaped on him and punched him in the gut, using her body to hold him down while I scrambled over to the Colt. I snatched it up. Silly me. The sucker had been cocked the whole time. I was lucky I hadn't had my head blown off.

I could hear him yelling, "Jesus Christ, all right! Get off. I'm done." And then he lay there, winded. I kept the gun pointed steadily at body parts he treasured while Mona called the cops.

He rolled over on his side and sat up. I moved back a step. The wild look had left his eyes and he was starting to weep, still gasping and out of breath. "Oh, Jesus. I can't believe it."

Mona turned to him with a withering look. "It's too late for an attack of conscience, Jerry."

He shook his head. "You don't know the half of it, babe. You're not the one who got stiffed for the dope. I was."

She looked at him blankly. "Meaning what?"

"I paid two grand for garbage. That dope was crap. I didn't want to tell you I got taken in so I invented some bullshit about Non Sung Smoke. There's no such thing. I made it up."

It took an instant for the irony to penetrate. She sank down beside him. "Why didn't you trust me? Why didn't you just tell me the truth?"

His expression was bleak. "Why didn't you?"

The question hung between them like a cobweb, wavering in the autumn light.

By the time the cops came, they were huddled on the floor together, clinging to each other in despair.

The sight of them was almost enough to cure me of the lies I tell.

But not quite.

# ROB KANTNER

---

# LEFT FOR DEAD

*Rob Kantner won the 1986 Shamus Award for Best Paperback Novel with* The Back Door Man *(Bantam, 1986), his first novel, and the 1986 Shamus Award for Best Short Story with "Fly Away Home," which appeared in* Mean Streets. *His second "Ben Perkins" novel,* The Harder They Hit, *was published by Bantam in 1987, and the third,* Dirty Work, *will appear in December 1988.*

*It's rare to find a writer who is so at home with both the novel and short story forms, but then Rob has already proven himself a rare writer.*

*For further proof, read "Left for Dead."*

It wasn't a landing, it was a barely controlled crash. My ultralight hit on all three wheels of the tricycle gear simultaneously and, hurtling entirely too fast along the rock-hard, burned-out field, bounced from one wheel to another in rapid sequence as I fought the stick for control. A quiet voice in my mind speculated quite impersonally that any second a viciously errant gust of wind would catch one of the wings, flip the aircraft over, and smear me into a long red stain on the ground.

But the voice, for once, was wrong. I rolled to a stop, throttled down the 350cc Zenoah engine, and cut the ignition, leaving only the sound of the driving wind.

I clambered out of the open cockpit, shucked off my wool hood and heavy goggles, unzipped my black snowmobile suit halfway, and paced a small circle under the influence of maximum adrenaline, trying to figure out where I was and what the hell I'd do now.

The first part was relatively easy. I was somewhere in the middle of the twenty-five-hundred-acre Southern Michigan Wilderness Preserve, located roughly halfway between Detroit and Sturgis, in Whitlock County near the Ohio line. What the hell I'd

115

do now was, without doubt, wait. Wait for better weather. Even if I had to spend the night in this godforsaken place. I was lucky I'd gotten the aircraft down in one piece as it was.

I stopped pacing, zipped my suit back up against the October chill, and scanned the area. I was near the center of a large flat valley. Behind me was the westernmost fringe of the Irish Hills. Ahead was a mass of forest, as far as the eye could see. Nowhere were there people or signs of habitation. In a month or so the area would be covered with the first dusting of snow and peopled by red-coated hunters taking potshots at anything that moved, especially each other. A month after that there'd be snow on the ground, and crowds of snowmobilers and skiers. Now was the dead time, nobody around but little old me, an unscheduled visitor but pretty damn glad to be there, just the same.

The afternoon was wearing on, getting colder and windier by the moment. I grabbed the ultralight by the downtube and wheeled her along the hard ground till I reached the fringe of thick trees. I folded down the wings and, for extra measure, propped some rocks against the wheels. Then I ventured twenty feet or so into the woods and found a nice comfortable spot against a rock outcropping, the ground covered with a thick layer of leaves and humus, and tamped myself a place to rest. I lay down, propped my head against an old, rotting stump, and relaxed. Nothing to do but kill time till morning, maybe sleep if I could, later.

I had nothing to eat or drink, but I did have a handful of cigars tucked away, so the essentials were certainly taken care of. I extracted one, stuck it in my mouth, then dug beneath the snowsuit into my jeans pocket in search of a light. Found a wad of bills. A dead Michigan Lotto ticket. Some coins. And a loose .45 caliber bullet. Pretty typical pocket inventory—but no matches. I was starting to panic when I found my kitchen matches in the other pocket, sighed in relief, and flared one. I was just getting the cigar going when I heard the far-off scream.

I jerked upright, listening hard. Nothing. Could have been my imagination, I thought. Or maybe an animal. But I'm not known to imagine things. And, though I knew there were no settlements within twenty miles, I felt certain the scream was human. Female, flat, atonal, not expecting to be heard.

I sighed, hoisted myself to my feet, tucked my cigar away, and hoofed into the vast clearing. Still deserted. I stood still for a moment, hearing the scream again in my mind, then turned left and began to hike. I wasn't even sure the sound had come from that direction. I could very well have been wasting my time. But time was something I had plenty of just then, so I set out hiking.

The woods bent away to my left as the valley turned toward the west. I followed the curve down a gentle incline, and as the trees fell back I saw a cabin at the bottom of the slope, hard against a sudden, wooded rise.

I stopped for a minute and surveyed. The cabin looked small, maybe twenty by twenty, weathered planks topped by a rusted tin roof and a stone chimney, no porch. A gaunt wood-slat snow fence, bowed in spots, surrounded it. The dying grass had grown up tall here and was being whipped to and fro by the wind. Overall, the place looked like it had been built as an afterthought and not occupied much since then. Certainly it looked abandoned now.

I set out for it anyway. Even if there was no screamer to be found, a man-made shelter sure beat the hell out of a makeshift camp deep in the woods. As I drew nearer, I saw a narrow gap in the fence about twenty feet from the cabin, and a path beaten in the tall grass up to the door. To the right of the fence gap was a platform of rotting planks, probably the covering of an old disused well. Beyond that, in the corner of the makeshift yard, was a neatly stacked couple of cords of split, well-seasoned firewood. Back of the cabin I caught just a glimpse of a small, leaning, tin-roofed outhouse. Somebody had obviously put in some time here. How long ago, I had no idea.

I slowed my pace as I passed through the fence gap and ventured up to the door. Not a sound from anywhere, nothing but the wind. The rough-hewn plank door stood open a couple of inches. I looked at it for a minute, then pushed it open slowly on groaning iron hinges.

The inside smelled of old wood and mold. A two-man folding cot stood open on the plank floor, covered with a nondescript pile of gray army blankets. To the right, a wood table hung against the wall with a broad ceramic sink built into it, into which an iron hand pump dripped. On the left-hand wall, between the pair of dirty, cobwebby windows, stood a makeshift cabinet, its twin doors hanging open like a dead man's jaw, its contents indistinct in the darkness.

Dead ahead, to the right of the back door, was a large cobblestoned fireplace. Hanging above it was a dusty, rough-hewn mantel propped up by wrought-iron supports bolted into the plank wall.

And handcuffed to one of the iron supports was a woman. Tall. Short blond hair. Thin, frightened, obviously exhausted. And completely naked.

Her face changed when she saw me, went into shock. "Who the hell are *you?*"

Who the hell I am is Ben Perkins, and all I'd been trying to do that afternoon was get myself home after completing a quickie job for a client.

The night before, I'd been peaceably enjoying game two of the World Series when Tony Omaha had called, all in a lather. While the rest of the nation was engrossed in the I-70 Series, Tony was, as usual, competing in a top-secret, high-stakes poker tournament held annually at a lodge at Burns Point, down near the Ohio line. Normally, Tony does pretty well in those things. This time, he told me tersely, the cards weren't being too friendly. I knew very well what he meant—though I'm not in Tony's professional league—having held in my time plenty of hands composed of unmatched garbage cards.

But in today's session he'd felt the cards turning, he told me in all seriousness; all he needed was a fresh infusion of capital, and he'd be able to turn the thing around in the next day's session.

He wasn't putting the arm on me. All he wanted me to do was deliver some cash to him, cash which his wife had, waiting and ready. I told him I'd get it to him the next morning, and went back to the TV to watch the Royals take it on the chin. I didn't give the errand a second thought. Private detective work isn't all sleuthing; I've sort of broadened the definition to include anything that turns a more or less honest buck.

I picked up the cash first thing the next morning from Omaha's suspicious, yet resigned wife, and headed back to my apartment, having decided to fly down to Burns Point rather than drive. It was pushing mid-October, stretching the ultralight season a little; but the weather outlook was good, and this could very well be my last chance to fly this year. Besides, Burns Point was an eighty-mile drive, but only a sixty-mile flight. Furthermore, I'd just the weekend before completed the 350cc engine's five-hundred-hour rebuild, and a hop like this one would break in the work, securely reseating the components, just the thing to do prior to putting the aircraft away for the winter.

And it worked out great, the flight down, anyway. I coasted down at two thousand feet on a due southwest heading, dipped south when I reached the village of Burns Point, then approached the resort from due east and landed on the golf course. My arrival caused something of a sensation—in my snowmobile suit, black wool hood, and heavy goggles I looked a little like a Michigan Ninja—and Tony Omaha, obviously regarding my mode of arrival as a good omen, gave me half a G and urged me to stay for lunch and sit in on a few hands. I accepted the lunch but passed on the poker, refueled the aircraft, and taxied to the number six fairway, a four-hundred-yard par three bearing due west, for takeoff.

Even as the aircraft left the ground, I knew I was in for trouble. The formerly clear western horizon had scudded up with dirty clouds, obscuring the sun. From the powerful lift I felt upon leaving the ground, I knew the wind had picked up. And, as I made the big banking turn to head northeast, I felt an ominous tugging at the aircraft's thirty-eight-foot, nylon-coated wings. Wind gusts, and strong ones. A storm front was pulling in from the west. Fast.

My first thought was to put about five thousand feet beneath me and try to outrun the sucker. But the wind was from the tail, reducing my lift, and I could tell from the way the engine was laboring that I was sucking up a lot of gas. And as I flew, the wind gusts got progressively worse, making it hard to maintain a heading. I was being knocked around in the sky, and try as I might to stay calm, I began to sweat in my snowmobile suit, my heart pounding, every muscle in my body strung tight and trembling. I knew very well that an ultralight is purely for pleasure flying in absolutely benign skies. Any kind of rough weather up there can crumple you up like a paper cup and send you fluttering down in a lethal embrace of aluminum frame and nylon.

Nothing to do, then, but take her in as best I could. I made a long, sweeping, banking turn till I was headed south, and began to descend in a series of abrupt jerks. The land below flowed away on all sides of me in densely wooded hills and valleys as far as I could see. A couple of miles ahead I could see a reasonably wide valley running east-west, ending at a lake to the east and a large hill to the west. Have to take her down there. As to which direction, there was no contest. Left was downwind; in this wind it was practically impossible to land that way. So I began to swing to the right. Right for safe, I thought. Left for dead.

* * *

I didn't answer, being slightly taken aback at finding a naked
woman handcuffed in this shack out in the middle of nowhere.
She shrieked, eyes wild. "Who *are* you?"

"Perkins," I managed. I jerked a thumb over my shoulder. "I
was forced down—I heard—uh—"

She rattled the handcuff. "Get me loose! Please!"

"Oh sure, right." It wasn't quite that easy. There were no tools
to be found inside the cabin. I remembered the woodpile, trotted
out there, and found an old, heavy, rusted hatchet. She cringed as
I approached her with it. "Take it easy," I said. "Stretch the chain
tight against that mantel there." She did so and covered her eyes
with her free hand. I severed the chain with one hard chop. The
woman took two steps, fell to her knees, bent her head nearly to
her thighs, and began to cry. I lay the hatchet on the mantel and
examined the iron mantel support. It was scratched bright and
deep where the cuff hung. There were corresponding scratches,
livid ones, on her thin wrist. She'd been tugging at it for a while.

I looked at her. No point in questioning her till she'd calmed
down. "How about I step out, and you get yourself dressed."

She tossed her head back, ran her hand through her blond hair,
and got clumsily to her feet. "No"—she sniffed—"you just stay
put, it's all right." She walked uncertainly to the cot, rifled the
blankets, and found jeans and a heavy white ski sweater. She was
utterly unselfconscious as she dressed, and gave me an occasional
glance out of the corner of her eye, but said nothing. I leaned
against the mantel and watched her. She was a long-limbed one,
five-eight, one-ten, her hair a straight blond cap around high
cheekbones, deep eyes, a generous mouth, and snub nose.
Relatively young, in years anyway. Twenty-five, max. Pretty
tough, too, to compose herself so quickly after an experience like
this. Whatever *that* was.

"What's your name?" I asked.

"Jill. Jill Evans." She slid her bare feet into a pair of worn hiking
shoes and began to lace them up. "You're . . . Perkins, you
said?"

"Ben." Finished with her work, she clambered to her feet, went
to the pump, worked the handle till the rusty flow had passed,
then bent under and drank deeply. Wiping her mouth once, she
went back to the cot, wadded up a couple of blankets into a
makeshift pillow, and lay back with her head propped on them.

Though her face was slack with weariness, her light eyes were sharp and bright on me. "Oh God, that feels good," she sighed.

"How long you been penned up like that?" I asked.

"Two days, two whole days. I couldn't sit down, I couldn't sleep . . . it gets *cold* at night this time of year, and—"

"How'd you get here in the first place?" I interrupted.

"I was kidnaped," she replied. "They held me here till they got the ransom. Then they cuffed me there and split. Left me here, left for dead." She straightened vertical, forearms propped on her knees. "Hey, you got a car out there or something? I want to get the hell out of here."

For something to do, I ambled to the cupboard and peered inside. Not a hell of a lot there by way of food. Canned tomatoes, a couple of cans of SpaghettiOs, a spilled jar of Folger's instant. Some plastic utensils. And four cans of low-alcohol beer. As a matter of policy, I avoid any beer that sends me to the can cold sober; but, any port in a storm. I popped the top, took a slug, and turned to face her. "No car. I was flying an ultralight, the weather forced me down." I gestured at the darkening window. "Day's about gone, no getting out of here before morning."

She barely contained the shrillness in her voice. "I want to go home. My family's got to be scared sick worrying about me." She tossed her head. "Maybe I'll walk out. There's light left."

"Listen up, Jill, it's twenty-plus miles to the nearest phone, and after two days tied up like that you're in no shape to walk it, trust me."

Her face slackened with resignation. "You got that right. Oh well." Her eyes brightened above a narrow smile. "So it's just you and me here for the night, huh?"

"Sure do look that way." Every man's fantasy, I thought with sour amusement. The big heroic rescuer of a helpless kidnap victim, a natural blonde and thoroughly female (both verified beyond dispute), young, yet exuding experience from every pore. To the victor belong the spoils. Ha. I said, "You must be starving. Menu's kinda thin here, but I can hack open a can of SpaghettiOs for you if you want."

"Oh, not right now. I could use one of those beers, though."

I carried one to her. She popped the top and drank. I said, "Easy, now. Don't wanna lose your head or anything." She winked at me and drank some more. I glanced out the back window—sure enough, another woodpile back there, near the outhouse. I looked back at Jill. "Light's going quick. Think I'll fetch in some firewood and get something going. It'll be a cold one tonight."

Before she could answer, I was out the back door. The dead grass was knee high, and I waded through it toward the woodpile. The wind was strong and the temperature was dropping steadily; I began to feel a chill even inside my snowmobile suit. Got to get the fire going quick, I thought. Hope the wood's okay.

I didn't find out right away. Because, halfway to the woodpile, I stopped and froze, staring down. A man lay prone there, face down, inert. His suit jacket was jagged with an array of small, bloody holes, and he was quite dead.

I used the hatchet to whack some thin strips of well-seasoned maple, built a pyramid of them in the fireplace, fired them up with a kitchen match, then patiently began to feed heavier pieces to the gaining blaze as Jill Evans watched me from the cot.

Finally she said, "Aren't you going to ask me about it?"

I carefully laid a four-by-four hunk of wood on the blaze, then used a twig to relight my cigar, and faced her. "Ask you about what?"

"The body out there."

"Which body."

"The dead body."

"Oh, *that* body." I exhaled smoke and cleared my throat. "I figured you'd get around to it sooner or later."

The skin stretched taut over the good bones of her face, making her eyes look larger in the half-darkness. "He was one of the kidnapers," she whispered.

"How'd he get dead?" I asked.

"Some kind of argument with the other two men. I'm not sure what it was about . . . I was only half-listening. . . . Suddenly they hustled him out there and I heard shooting. . . . He never came back in. The others tied me up and left right after that. I assumed he was dead. I didn't ask. I was—I was scared they'd kill me, too."

"Might have been more merciful if they had, rather than leaving you tied up to freeze to death."

She got to her feet and walked over and sat cross-legged next to me in front of the growing fire. "You're probably right," she murmured. "But you know? All I wanted to do was live. For the

next minute, the next hour, the next day." She leaned her head
onto my shoulder and took my left hand in both of hers. "I had no
way of knowing someone like you would happen along. But you
did."

I squeezed her hand, broke from her gently, and stood.
"Getting warm in here. Think I'll shuck the suit."

"All right." I didn't have to look to see her smile.

I unzipped my black snowmobile suit down to the crotch and,
dancing awkwardly on each foot in sequence, tugged it off. Jill
rose, too, and stood very close to me, watching me with her
unreadable eyes, lips parted. As I tossed the suit away, Jill
reached up and began to unbutton my chambray shirt, the
handcuff clinking like a cheap bracelet on her wrist. I made no
move to interfere, just reached behind to the waistband of my
jeans and pulled out my .45 automatic. She stepped back from me
suddenly as I hefted it. "I'd better secure this somewhere."

She laughed nervously. "Packing, huh? How come?"

"Private detective. Standard equipment." I went to the cup-
board, laid the weapon down on the shelf, grabbed a large can of
SpaghettiOs, and began to wipe the dust off it with my shirttail.
"Hungry yet?"

She exhaled impatiently, then grabbed the hem of her sweater,
shimmied it off over her head, tossed it toward the cot, and shook
her head to loosen her fine blond hair. The firelight ran whitish-
gold fingers over her smooth shoulders, her up-aimed, arrogant
breasts. She threw her shoulders back and hooked her hands in
the empty belt loops of her jeans. "This answer your question?"

It was indeed a transfixing vision: the young half-dressed
woman, framed in the blaze of the fire which filled the cabin out
in the middle of darkening nowhere with sweet-smelling heat. I
grinned. "Look, it's been two days, you gotta eat. Get some of
this in you, then we'll sort out the other."

Long pause, then she sighed impatiently. "Oh, all right then."
She went to the cot, sat, flung one leg over the other; then, for
good measure, she pulled the ski sweater back on even though,
by then, it was getting quite warm in there.

I cleaved the top of the SpaghettiOs can with the hatchet,
wedged a respectable opening, then took it to her along with a
reasonably clean plastic fork and a freshly opened can of designer
beer. "Eat hearty," I advised. "Every bite now." She nodded
glumly at me and began to eat, taking about four swallows of beer
for every bite of cold spaghetti.

I took my time about stoking up the fire with fresh logs. It was roaring now, popping and sizzling, so hot that each fresh log fairly exploded into flames as I tossed it in. I sat down, leaning against the far wall, and smoked my cigar as Jill finished the spaghetti and tossed the empty can into the fire. She took a long draft of beer and licked her lips. Her eyes looked glassy as she said through numb lips, "Okay."

"Okay." I stood. "You get yourself ready, I got an urgent errand." She was unzipping her jeans as I went out the back door and pulled it shut behind me. The cold wind was steady and piercing as I loped through the tall grass to the privy. On my way back, I stopped at the body, fired up a kitchen match and, cupping it with my palm, lowered myself for a long look. Then I flipped the match away and walked slowly and deliberately back to the cabin.

Aside from the crackling roar of the fire, all was still and silent inside the cabin. Jill Evans lay sprawled on the cot, white legs spread, jeans hanging forgotten from one bare ankle. I walked softly to the cot and looked down at her for ten long breaths, then gently lifted her legs onto the cot and covered her with two of the blankets. She muttered vaguely and curled into a fetal position and buried her face in the coarse mattress.

I watched her for ten long heartbeats, then went silently out the front door. I was out there for a vigorous quarter hour, and when I got back I had to wash my hands in the icy pump water. Jill slept silently, almost invisible under the blankets. I tossed a couple more logs on the fire, shunted myself back into the snowsuit, stretched out on the hard plank floor by the fire and, using my hands as a wholly inadequate pillow, free-fell into inky black, totally dreamless sleep.

The explosion didn't just rouse me, it sent me nearly to the ceiling. I came fully awake on knees and fingertips, back arched like a bird dog, heart pounding supercharged adrenaline to every nerve. As the sound replayed in my mind, I relaxed. It had been nothing more than a superheated knot exploding in the dying coals of the fireplace.

I sat back on my rump, breathing hard. Dawn shot hard bright fingers of light through the dirty cabin windows. Birds chirped outside. The drone of the wind, a natural part of the environment the night before, was gone. It was early yet, somewhere between six and seven, but with the full break of day I knew that flying weather would be back.

Jill Evans had not moved, but suddenly I realized her eyes were open, and on me.

She pursed her lips, then licked them quite deliberately and rippled the blanket back off her. The ski sweater had bunched up under her breasts, leaving her bare from there down.

She said, "Come on now, Ben."

I got to my feet. "Better throw on a couple of logs. Getting chilly in here." Ignoring her skeptical look, I tossed on the last chunks of split maple, blew the coals, watched as the flames started their reddish-blue licks, then faced her.

She said in a hard voice, "Don't come near me with that damn snowsuit on."

"Oh. Certainly." I unzipped it, peeled it off, kicked it away, then sauntered to her and sat on the edge of the wobbly cot. With a faraway look in her eyes, she wandered her hands up my shirt and began to unbutton it. I said, "Look, I got a confession to make."

"Mm-hm."

"I believe in honesty in relationships."

"That's your confession?"

"Uh-huh. I don't want to get involved with you under false pretenses."

"Ooh." She finished the unbuttoning and ran her hands over my chest. "I'm not as complicated as you. All I want to do is screw."

I bent and gave her a quick, brushing, teasing kiss, and said very softly, "I just can't stop thinking about my daddy."

Her hands had deliberately wandered to my pants and were busily unsnapping and unzipping. "What about your daddy?"

"What he used to say."

"And what was that?"

"My daddy used to say . . . he told me . . . 'Never lay down with a woman who has more troubles than you.' . . . That's what my daddy always said."

She laughed, and prodded me gently, and I lifted myself just enough to enable her to pull my jeans down over my pelvis. "Sounds like good advice. But hey, Ben," she cooed, "I don't have any troubles. You fixed up the worst of 'em yesterday. And what troubles I have left," she breathed as I kicked my jeans back off one leg, then the other, "I think you're about to take care of for me. Mm. Yes, indeedy."

I lowered myself onto her, slid my left arm under her neck, and we enjoyed a long kiss of tongue tips. I looked into her bright eyes. "But see, that's the point. I don't think your troubles are over, I think they're just beginning."

She traced my eyebrows, cheekbones, mouth and chin with just the lightest touch of fingertips, intertwined her ankles with mine, and laughed softly.

I kissed her again, then raised myself on my palms and said in that same light, casual tone: "'Cause you ain't the victim, babe. You weren't the kidnapee. The kidna*per*, more like. Or one of 'em, anyhow."

She tried that laugh again, and though she was good, very *very* goddamned good, it sent back a hollow echo in that little cabin.

I disentangled my legs, negotiated myself a sitting position on the edge of the cot, and began pulling on my jeans. Out of the corner of my eye I saw her frowning as she propped her head on the heel of her palm. "That's a nasty, ugly thing to suggest, Ben Perkins."

"Oh yeah, I couldn't agree more. 'Specially since it happens to be true, now ain't it, little darlin'.'"

"This is starting to perturb me," she said, giving the blanket a deliberate jerk over her, "*totally*. You read me?"

I zipped and snapped my pants shut, stood, took a step toward the fire, then turned and faced her. "'Member what you said when I first busted in here? You said, 'Who the hell are you?' Like maybe you were expecting somebody else. *Not* like you weren't expecting to see anybody at all. Dig it?"

Her face was a smoldering mask, God knows what churning behind her eyes.

"And then that stiff out back," I added, jerking a thumb. "For a helpless, innocent kidnap victim, you were awful casual about that. And how come he's all dolled up in a business suit? A kidnaper, knowing he was going to spend some time out here, wouldn't dress up in some fancy business suit. Nope, he'd've fixed himself up with jeans. And a sweater. And boots. Sort of like *you*, kid . . . Then there was the way you reacted to my pistol. 'Packing, huh?' Not exactly civilian talk. And this seductress routine, that don't hang right with me either."

Her jaw was square and ugly. "I *liked* you, Ben."

"Oh yeah, sure. I don't think I'm completely disgusting to look at, but for a helpless, traumatized kidnap victim you sure seemed awful anxious to get me between the knees. That old soften-up stunt insults my intelligence, kiddo; it's older than running water."

"I won't repeat the mistake," she said pointedly.

"Suits me just fine," I answered, picking up my shirt.

"Me, too," said the male voice from the window. I whirled as glass crashed in, and saw twin shotgun barrels that were so large I almost didn't take notice of the muscle-bound grinner behind them.

Jill Evans jerked upright on the cot. "'Bout time you got here, Darrell!"

He was young, burr-cut, and a weight freak, judging from the way the veins and muscles stood out on his neck and arms. He wore a sleeveless bright orange hunting jacket and a big grin. "Took me some time, Jill. This ape been molesting you?"

"No way," she said disgustedly, then skooched off the cot and began pulling on her jeans. "What kept you?"

I slid my right hand into my jeans pocket.

"Took me a while to get the drop on Edgar," he said, keeping the twin barrels fixed on my chest. "Got it done late last night and drove like hell to get back here. He the one with the plane?"

She snapped her jeans closed. "Yeah, so what."

"Saw it out there, so I circled around with the Jeep and drove cross-country and snuck in here. Figured you had company."

She ignored him. "You got the money then?"

I sorted through my pocket silently and palmed the loose .45 bullet.

"All hundred G worth, out there in the Jeep." He glanced at me. "What do we do with him, tie him up?"

Her look at me was venomous. "I've got bigger plans than that. Get in here, Darrell."

"He got a gun or something?"

"Yeah. Wait a minute, cover him. I'll get it." She trotted to the cupboard and rescued my .45 automatic from the counter and swung around to hold it on me. "Okay. Come on in."

He gave us one appraising look, then disappeared from the window. We heard a clank, a thump, a "son of a bitch!" and as Jill glanced out I tossed the bullet at the fireplace. It landed soundlessly, hopefully—for me, anyway—in the flames somewhere.

Darrell came in the door, shotgun at port arms, grumbling. "Tripped over a damn bucket out there. Can't wait to get out of this pigpen." He stood at the opposite end of the cot from me, shotgun hung under his arm and aimed half downward. Judging from the way he posed, he was proud of his body; every muscle seemed to stand out whether there were clothes over it or not. His grin was bright and giddy and humorless. "So this fella happened by and turned you loose, huh, Jill?"

"No thanks to you, Darrell. I'd given up on you. I thought I was going to die here."

"Well, hey! You shouldn't have wasted old man Simmons."

I said, "Oh, Simmons the stiff lying out back there? The victim?"

"Shut up, Perkins," Jill said.

Darrell beamed. "Yeah, that's him all right; bigshot insurance man, richer'n God. You shoulda seen what Jill did to him. We'd gotten the ransom, we're all set to split; before Edgar and me know it Jill opens the back door and shoves Simmons out. He starts to run. She's carrying this twenty-two target revolver, single-action job, and she draws down on him, and cocks, and bang! Cocks it again, just as cool as could be, and bang! All six shots, the last four after he's on the ground."

I glanced at Jill, who held the heavy .45 in both hands aimed at me, and wondered how long it would take the bullet to explode, and where it would go when it did.

Darrell continued, "Well, Edgar got madder'n hell. Wasting Simmons wasn't part of the plan. He grabbed Jill and slapped her around and said to me, 'We're leaving this gun-happy bitch here, teach her a nice lesson.'"

"And you went along with him," Jill said hoarsely. "You helped him strip me and tie me up and you drove away with him."

"Hey sweetie, I had to! He had the gun and he'd of hurt me bad if I hadn't fallen into line." His smile became earnest. "You knew I'd come back for you, just as soon as I could."

"Yeah. I knew I could trust you, Darrell," she said sourly. She hefted the .45 and drew a bead on me, eyes narrow. "We'll argue about that later. First, a little target practice with our private detective friend here."

I took a deep breath, wondering *where the hell is that damn bullet*, and said, "Darrell, you better think about what she might do to you once you have your back turned."

He chuckled. "Sounds like one of them cute little private detective–type tricks. Divide and conquer and all that. No thanks." He looked at Jill. "Careful with that thing, babe. Aim low and leave some give in the wrists. That ain't no twenty-two that gives a snap and drills nice neat holes. That thing kicks like a mule. Built to stop, drop, and splatter."

"Good." I braced myself to jump, and then—finally—the bullet in the fireplace exploded.

I don't know where it went and I didn't take time out to check. I jumped as high as I could and came down with both feet on my end of the cot. The other end flew up like a runaway teeter-totter and caught Darrell under the elbows. The shotgun flew sideways and discharged both barrels, blowing out the front window. I had a quick sight of Jill leveling the .45 toward me, but I was nowhere around; I took a running, full-body leap at Darrell and plowed him back against the cabin wall with a crash.

There could be no Marquis of Queensbury niceties with this clown, and, moreover, I had to keep him from grabbing me or I'd be finished. Fortunately, big muscle-bound guys like him aren't all that fast. I came up with a knee to his groin, jinked back and, as he drove at me I took him by an elbow, pivoted, and threw him across the cot onto the floor. Jill danced back toward the fireplace, aiming, trying to get a clear field of fire, but I was on the move again as she aimed for me, diving across at Darrell as he sprang to his feet.

"Hold him still! Hold him *still!*" she muttered as I piled Darrell against the pump. He gave me a shot upside my head with a bricklike fist, and stars spotted my vision as I fell back. I was aware of Jill frozen in place just behind me, aiming for true now, and as Darrell moved in for me I took a wrist in both hands and jumped on one foot with both of mine and flung him toward me as hard as I could, dropping to the floor as I did so.

Completely off-balance, he fell straight at Jill, who apparently had maximum pressure on the trigger of the .45. The gun went off and Darrell flew back over me, clearing me easily, and landed suddenly inert at the wall. Judging from the looks of his head, he'd only been six inches from the .45 when Jill fired. Like the man said: stop, drop, and splatter.

I heard the .45 hit the floor as Jill screamed. I turned to see her holding her right wrist with her left hand, bending and gasping, face twisted with pain. I started for my feet, but she saw me and charged the door and disappeared outside. I stood, in no particular hurry to chase her. From outside I heard a shriek. Then silence.

I took several deep breaths, then put my snowsuit back on, trying not to look at Darrell as I did so. Then I retrieved and secured my .45 and trotted out the back door. It was a splendid Michigan October morning: pale blue sky, bright sun, just a hint of breeze. I had no trouble finding the Jeep back in the woods, and sauntered back to the cabin, carrying a vinyl airline carry-on bag under my arm. I circled the cabin to the front and walked up to the gap in the fence. The ground disappeared at that point, leaving a circle of black. I stepped toward the lip of the old disused well and looked down.

It was maybe fifteen feet deep, its walls old, rough discolored brick. At the bottom lay remnants of the old rotted boards that had covered the top, and atop these lay Jill Evans, on her side, one leg twisted oddly under her.

Her eyes looked very large in her pale pinched face. "You moved the fence," she said.

"Uh-huh. Last night, after you were asleep."

"You knew even then?"

"Let's just say I had my doubts."

"Oh, God." She squirmed and winced. "That was slick. Real slick, how you tricked me, Ben."

"Wasn't that much to it. All I did was move a section of fence, cover the well top with weeds, and tramp a new path up to it from the cabin door."

"I think my leg is broken," she said in a small voice.

"Doesn't surprise me a bit."

"How are you going to get me out?"

"Hadn't planned to, actually."

She swallowed and blinked and licked her lips. "You can't be serious."

"Am, too. You honest to God scare me, kid. I don't want you anywhere near me. Don't trust you, for some damn reason."

Her efforts to remain calm made her voice sound labored. "Is that—is that bag the money?"

"Uh-huh."

"A hundred thousand, cash."

"If you say so."

"We can—we can take it and go away—together, and—"

"Listen, even if I was the larcenous sort, no way am I going to spend the rest of my life with you in my backfield. Get real, here."

I started away. "Wait!" she shouted. I stepped back. Now, for

the first time, her voice was crushed, despairing, completely lost.
"How can you just leave me here like this?"

I considered. "Well, all I have to do is picture you standing at
the door of the cabin, drawing a bead on that poor old man and
putting six shots into him as he ran, four after he hit the ground.
That's how."

"I'll *die* here!" she sobbed.

"You, die? No way. The cops'll be here by afternoon. You're a
pretty tough chick, you'll keep till then."

"Heartless bastard!"

"Takes one to know one."

As I began the long hike toward the ultralight, I heard her
screaming obscenities. Gradually the voice faded and then
stopped entirely.

As I powered the ultralight into the air and swung northwest, it
idly occurred to me that I could, in fact, just keep the money and
sort of forget to call the cops. No one would ever know that I'd
ever been at the cabin.

Of course I did notify the police once I got home, but not
because I felt sorry for Jill Evans.

Quite the opposite.

# JOHN LUTZ AND JOSH PACHTER

# DDS 10752 LIBRA

*John Lutz is presently serving his second term as president of
PWA. He is also continuing to produce first-rate novels in two
P.I. series—those featuring "Nudger" (Ride the Lightning,
St. Martin's Press, 1987), and "Carver" (Scorcher, Henry
Holt, 1987). He is a past winner of the Shamus and Edgar
awards for short fiction, another example of that uncommon
writer adept at both the short and long forms. Here he joins
forces with Josh Pachter to give us a truly memorable Nudger
story.*

*Josh Pachter has been writing and publishing short stories
since he was eighteen years of age. He is the editor of one of the
best anthologies of recent years,* Top Crime, *and the editor
and publisher of* The Short Sheet, *a publication dedicated to
the short story.*

**D**wight Stone sat hunched over the telephone in the yellow
glow from the antique lamp atop his desk. His voice was pitched
low but excited. The huge oak rolltop was the dominant feature
of Stone's cluttered living room, which also served as his office.
Most of the furniture scattered around was ancient, because he
couldn't afford anything newer; the desk and lamp, legacies from
a long-dead aunt, were the only valuable pieces in the apartment.

A mischievous smile flickered briefly across his lips as he
cradled the receiver, but his clear brown eyes were still troubled.
He crossed to the tiny cubicle his landlord called a kitchenette,
made coffee on a hot plate, and carried a steaming mug back to
his desk. He pulled a blank expense account form from one of the
drawers and laboriously began to fill it in, now and then darting
out a hand for coffee or to work the cantankerous old adding
machine at his side. He was a large man, with too much
upholstery straining the material of his clothes; he and his
overstuffed furniture were perfectly compatible.

134 AN EYE FOR JUSTICE

In a silence between ratchety growls of the adding machine, Stone suddenly sat up straight. A slight noise from behind had alerted him. He turned, and saw the tarnished brass knob of the front door slowly rotating, heard a floorboard creak outside in the hall. Fear lanced through his bowels like a shaft of ice as he realized that he *had* been followed home, after all.

Fright momentarily numbed him. Like most small-town private investigators, he never carried a gun, didn't even own one. He regretted that now, because he had no illusions about who it was that stood outside his door. Or about what it was the man had come for.

True, the door was locked, but the lock was a joke and would offer little resistance. It would slow down the man outside for a moment, but it wouldn't stop him.

There wasn't much time. Within the next few minutes, Stone knew, he would be out of time forever.

Swallowing his terror, he scribbled hastily at the bottom of the paper he was working on. There was an ominous click from the doorway, and he dropped his pen and reached for one of the desk's many cubbyholes.

Seconds later, the apartment door swung open behind him.

Nudger watched the two detectives nosing around the ransacked apartment. The place was a mess. Stone hadn't been much of a housekeeper to begin with, and whoever had killed him had taken the time to toss the four small rooms with frantic thoroughness.

The policemen were both in their fifties; they moved with the studied nonchalance of the typical small-town cop. They were a team: one was named Byrnes (the plodder, Nudger soon decided), the other was Allen (the brains of the operation). Nudger resisted making the obvious crack about George and Gracie. He didn't figure this pair for a comedy act.

"Go through it again," said Byrnes, standing in the light from the front window. The lamp on the big old rolltop where Stone had died was still on. Nudger had found it on when he'd arrived, an hour earlier, and had left it that way. He hadn't touched the body, either; it lay slumped across the surface of the desk, as he had discovered it. The expression on the half of Stone's face he could see was twisted, terrorized. There was no blood on the desk or the floor, because the small-caliber bullet that had left a neat little hole in the back of Stone's head on entry hadn't come out the other side. Nudger was glad about that; he hated the sight of blood. Murder scared him plenty all by itself, without the accompanying gore.

"Stone had been hired to recover a set of drawings which had been stolen from the office of a fashion designer here in town," he said tiredly, starting in on the story for the third time. "He phoned me in the city last night and told me about the case. He'd only been brought in a couple of days ago, but he'd already managed to get his hands on the drawings. He was worried that the thief would try to get them back again, though, so he'd hidden them someplace where he was sure they'd be safe. He wouldn't tell me where they were, but he seemed pretty clear that the thief would never be able to find them. He was going to work up an expense account, he said, then catch some sleep. He wanted me to meet him here this morning and go with him to pick up the drawings and deliver them to his client. Just in case the thief tried to get him back, he said."

Byrnes and Allen listened impassively.

"When I showed up here," Nudger went on, "he didn't answer my knock. I slipped the lock with a credit card and came in to wait for him."

Byrnes stirred. "That's breaking and entering," he remarked.

Actually it was trespassing, but Nudger decided not to quibble. Somehow the time seemed wrong for a discussion of legal niceties. "Bull," he said. "Dwight Stone and I have been friends for years. I let myself in whenever I came calling and found him out. He didn't mind; he did the same thing at my place." He motioned toward the body at the desk. "Anyway, I found him like that and phoned the police immediately."

Allen's pale blue eyes were unreadable. If he held any particular opinion about Nudger's story, he wasn't letting it show. Byrnes, on the other hand, had a more provincial personality; he was making no effort to conceal his disdain for the hotshot city-slicker P.I.

"You didn't touch anything?" Allen asked.

"Of course not."

"Just like on TV," said Byrnes. Nudger couldn't tell if he was kidding.

"Tell us more about this case Stone was working on," Allen suggested.

"There's not much to tell. Geoffrey Devane's got a small but very successful fashion house here in your town. He does all the

designing himself, and employs about two-dozen people to
manufacture and market the clothing. When he opened up his
safe on Monday morning, the drawings for his spring line were
missing. Four of the people who work for him knew the
combination of the safe, and Devane figured one of the four must
have swiped the designs, planning on selling them to one of the
firm's competitors."

"Industrial espionage," Allen murmured.

"Exactly. Devane reported the theft, but the police didn't seem
very encouraging, so he decided to bring in a private investigator.
He got Stone's number out of the Yellow Pages, and it took
Dwight three days to pin down the thief's identity and recover the
drawings."

"Only the thief wanted them back"—Allen picked up the
narrative—"so he followed Stone home and killed him and
turned the place upside down looking for them."

"That's the way I figure it," Nudger agreed.

Allen trudged to the window, gazed outside, then turned to
face Nudger. He was framed by sunlight, and Nudger had to
squint to look at him. That was the sort of technique cops used on
suspects, not fellow professionals. Nudger's stomach twitched
out a warning. He thumbed back the foil on a roll of antacid
tablets and popped two of the chalky disks into his mouth.

"Nervous?" Allen asked.

"My stomach is. Almost always."

"Ulcer?"

"Don't know. Afraid to find out."

"Dumb."

"I guess."

"You say you used a credit card to slip the lock this morning?"

Nudger nodded. "The killer must have locked the door behind
him when he left last night."

"Why last night? Why not this morning, sometime before you
arrived?"

"The lamp on the desk," said Nudger. "It must have been dark
outside when Stone was shot, that's why he had it switched on."

"You look good for this, you know." Byrnes scowled. "In spite
of your pretty story." He seemed to relish the opportunity to
speak in Hollywood clichés.

"You mean I'm a suspect?" Nudger asked, as if the thought had
just now occurred to him. It was uncomfortable, standing there in
a room with two homicide detectives as they plied their trade. It

was uncomfortable standing there in a room with a dead body in it. The combination of cops and corpse was lousy. "Don't forget," he said to Allen, who seemed much the more open-minded of the two, "I'm the one who called this in in the first place."

"Subterfuge," Allen suggested. "You and Stone were pals. You figured we'd get around to you sooner or later, so you called in the murder to convince us you had nothing to do with it."

Now they were ganging up on him. It didn't seem fair. "I'm not that devious," Nudger said. "And what about the murder weapon? I'm not carrying a gun, and you haven't found one in the apartment. And the door was locked when I got here."

"That's *your* story," said Byrnes doggedly. He shot a glance at the corpse. "What's *his* story?"

"What about my motive?" Nudger tried.

"We might just find one."

Or invent one, Nudger thought. He popped another antacid tablet into his mouth. Small-town murder, small-town cops, small-town judge and jury. Put it all together and it might spell big-time trouble.

"Mind if I look at the desk for a minute?" he asked.

"Be our guest," Allen told him.

Nudger crossed the room, riffled through the papers on the rolltop's surface, explored its cubbyholes carefully.

"The expense account," he said at last, straightening and looking over at Allen. "Stone told me he was going to work it up for Devane after he got through talking with me, but there's no sign of the form on his desk."

"*You* say he told you," Byrnes reminded Nudger. "What *I* say is that you and Stone were together last night. You had an argument, or you've got some other motive we haven't tumbled to yet. You shot him, then realized we'd tie you to him eventually. So you went away and ditched the gun, then came back this morning so you could 'find' the body and call us in and feed us your carefully rehearsed version of the facts."

Nudger thought back over the last fifteen hours and realized he'd been completely alone between the time he'd hung up the phone after talking with Stone and his discovery of the body this morning. Alone on the phone with Stone; the words ran through his mind and kept him from thinking clearly. The law couldn't prove he was here when Stone was murdered, that was certain— but Nudger couldn't prove he wasn't here, either. His stomach dived and did a few tight loops.

"The fingerprint man and photographer ought to be here soon," Byrnes announced. "When they show up, we'll be leaving."

"I know," Nudger said. "You're going to take me downtown for another little chat."

"This *is* downtown," Allen told him. "You can call your lawyer from headquarters."

"I'll wait until I'm charged before I do that," Nudger muttered. He wasn't at all sure Byrnes and Allen had enough evidence to hold him on a murder rap.

Allen shrugged. Byrnes smiled. Nudger figured they probably thought they had enough.

Staring at the big rolltop desk and the position of the body, he had an idea. Or maybe it was just a final straw to clutch at before drowning in a sea of lawyers, judges, and jurors. And then jailers.

"Maybe he hid it," he said.

"Hid what?" That was Allen, of course. Byrnes had better things to do than pay attention to anything Nudger might offer.

"The expense account form. Stone was sitting at his desk when he was shot. What if he heard someone at the door behind him? He might have had just enough time to scrawl a message on that form and hide it from his killer."

"That's right," said Byrnes, deadpan, "he was working on his expenses when he bought it."

"Which would explain how come there's no expense account form in plain view on the desk now," Nudger continued. "He wrote a message on it and hid it before the killer entered the apartment."

That line of reasoning seemed to sway Allen slightly. He gave Nudger an encouraging smile. Byrnes looked like he was wishing they could wind this whole thing up, so he could file his report and head for home. Police work, this minor matter of the rest of Nudger's life, was apparently annoying him.

Nudger walked back to the desk, and neither officer moved to stop him.

"We looked and you looked," Byrnes said.

"Can I look again?"

"Why not?" Allen shrugged. "With a minimum of touching, please."

Nudger stood back from the desk and scanned it carefully.

Nothing he could see even remotely resembled an expense account form.

"We already checked under the body," said Byrnes, hoping to hurry things along. "We did everything but take the damn desk apart."

"You didn't look where you couldn't see, though, did you?"

"What do you mean?" Allen's forehead wrinkled with puzzlement.

Ignoring him, Nudger stepped to the desk and eased the rolltop down as far as possible, almost to the point where it would have touched Stone's body.

A printed form was attached to the accordion S-roll of the retractable top with a bit of cellophane tape. Stone must have had just enough time to use the tape, then push the rolltop up and out of sight before his murderer came into the room.

Nudger tore the form away from the wooden rolltop triumphantly. Byrnes and Allen had already moved to flank him, and the three of them read the combination of letters and numbers scribbled across the bottom of the sheet:

## DDS 10752 LIBRA

"Libra," said Byrnes, with a disgusted look at his partner. "Don't tell me this turns out to be another one of your damn zodiac cases."

"'Zodiac cases'?" Nudger repeated, turning the words into a question.

Allen frowned. "A couple years back," he explained, "I solved a case where a dying man's last word was *Gemini*, and Byrnes here thinks that makes me some kind of astrology expert."

"Libra," Byrnes grumbled. "And DDS. And 10752. What the hell's it all supposed to mean?"

Nudger fumbled with his roll of antacid tablets, then changed his mind and slipped the roll back into his pocket. "The DDS part I understand," he said. "Stone once told me he was born during Eisenhower's first presidential campaign. His parents were staunch Republicans, so they named him Dwight David. Which made his initials DDS."

"And," Allen mused, "he was born during Ike's campaign." He bent over the body and slid a thin billfold from the dead man's hip pocket. Unfolding it, he leafed through its half-dozen plastic windows until he located Stone's driver's license. "Uh-huh. He was born on October seventh, 1952: that's 10/7/52."

"Which makes him a Libra, all right," Byrnes contributed. "Same as my wife." Suddenly he faced Nudger and snapped, "What's *your* sign?"

"No smoking," Nudger told him.

"Get serious, tough guy."

"I'm not tough and I am serious. I don't have any idea what my sign is. My birthday's September thirteenth, does that help any?"

"Virgo," said Byrnes, as if a lot of things had just been explained.

"So the letters are his initials, the numbers are his birthdate, and Libra is his astrological sign," Allen nodded. "But—I mean, so *what?*"

"Maybe the killer was a Libra, too," Byrnes suggested feebly.

"Or a dentist," said Nudger, glad to see that the focus of the investigation had shifted away from him for a change. "DDS might stand for Doctor of Dental Surgery, you know, instead of Dwight David Stone."

Before Byrnes could formulate an appropriately snide comeback, the fingerprint man and photographer arrived. They turned out to be the same man, a wiry scarecrow with bristling gray hair and a genuine Speed Graphic camera, like the press used to rely on in the thirties and forties. Then a second man turned up, the county's medical examiner and town's mortician. There was a lot of versatility in this backwater. Stone hadn't had any family, and the M.E. was sizing up the furniture to see how big a funeral the estate could be expected to cover.

While the experts went about their tasks, Nudger, Byrnes, and Allen turned back to Dwight Stone's last desperate message.

"We oughta check his horoscope for today," Byrnes proposed.

Nudger thought that was as logical an idea as he'd heard so far.

"Never mind that," Allen said, snapping his fingers. There was a hunter's gleam in his eye. "Let's go."

"Go?" Byrnes asked gruffly. "Go where?"

"You'll see," said Allen. "And you're not going to like it when I tell you Nudger here gave me the idea."

"Me?" Nudger looked around blankly, making sure there was nobody else with that name in the apartment. "What'd I say?"

"You said maybe the killer was a dentist." Allen smiled mysteriously, and they couldn't get another word out of him.

They left Stone's apartment and crossed the street to a dusty unmarked car parked illegally next to a fire hydrant. Halfway to their destination, Nudger finally realized where they were headed, and why. He was impressed. Maybe there was something to be said for small-town detective work, after all.

If Allen turned out to be right, that is.

The building was suitably quiet. There were people there—old ladies in padded armchairs devouring Barbara Cartland romances, college types copying term papers from assorted encyclopedias, a prim woman with her hair in a bun pulling outdated periodicals out of plastic covers and replacing them with more recent issues—but all of them went about their business in silence.

It took only a few moments for Allen to find the shelf he was looking for, and he ran his index finger along the spines of the books lined up there until he reached one whose white gummed label read 107.52 and, beneath that, Mol. He eased the book from the shelf and pronounced its title aloud: *"Teaching Philosophy,* by Vincent Molloy. Should make fascinating reading, if that's the sort of reading that fascinates you. Me, I like the 87th Precinct."

There were several sheets of paper sandwiched between the book's removable dust jacket and permanent hard cover. Allen slid them free and unfolded them. Each page displayed a sketch of a woman dressed in delicate pastel clothing, and each drawing had been signed by Geoffrey Devane at the lower-right corner.

On the top sheet, in Dwight Stone's handwriting, the name of Devane's comptroller had been penciled in.

"I'm still not sure I understand it all," Byrnes said, as Nudger and the two detectives sat over coffee in a closet-sized office at headquarters. Luther Higham, Devane's comptroller, had confessed to the theft of the drawings and the murder of Dwight Stone, and was in a holding cell awaiting arraignment on charges of industrial espionage and murder.

Nudger was glad to explain. "Higham opened up the safe and stole his boss's drawings, planning to sell them to a competitor. But unfortunately—for the thief, that is—Stone was able to recover the sketches. He was afraid to keep them in his apartment, though, figuring—correctly, as it turned out—that the thief might know who he was and come after them. So he stashed them at the local library, figuring he and I would pick them up the next morning and deliver them to Devane."

Byrnes finished his coffee and set down his Styrofoam cup, still looking perplexed. "That much I get," he said. "And to make sure he wouldn't forget which book he'd hidden the drawings in, he used the volume whose call number matched his birthdate. But why did he put his initials on that note he left you? And why the hell did he bother writing down his sign?"

"They weren't his initials," said Allen. "And it wasn't his sign, either. It was Nudger who tipped me off to that, when he pointed out that DDS didn't *have* to stand for Dwight David Stone. Well, it didn't stand for a dentist, either: it stood for Dewey decimal system, the cataloging system used for classifying nonfiction books by subject. Stone was telling Nudger that he'd hidden the drawings in the book shelved under Number 107.52 according to the Dewey decimal system."

"But why Libra?" Byrnes demanded.

Nudger grinned. "Stone didn't have time to finish his message *and* hide it away before Devane's comptroller broke into his apartment. It was more important to hide it than to finish it, so he stopped writing, two letters before what he'd intended to be the end of the message, and counted on Nudger to realize what he meant."

"Library," Byrnes sighed. "Dewey decimal system number 107.52, in the public library."

"Only I managed to miss it," said Nudger. "I guess I'm not as bright as Stone thought. Good thing for me your partner worked it out."

Byrnes washed a hand across his face. "Yeah, sure is. Listen, Nudger, looks like I owe you an apology. I jump to conclusions, sometimes. It's a lousy habit, I know, but I do it anyway. Like with that astrology business—"

Nudger stood up from his straight-backed chair, feeling his stomach beginning to react to the acidic coffee he'd only half finished. He smiled and waved a hand negligently and said, "Forget the apology. Let's just say you owe me a decent cup of coffee. That stuff you guys drink is awful."

"Actually, we usually drink tea." Byrnes grinned. "So the Zodiac Detective here can read the leaves."

# ARTHUR LYONS

# DEAD COPY

*Arthur Lyons is a busy man, producing novels featuring his P.I., Jacob Asch (most recently* Fast Fade, The Mysterious Press, 1987), *compiling works of nonfiction (*Satan Wants You: The Cult of Devil Worship in America, The Mysterious Press, 1988), *and writing screenplays for his own books.*

*He has not written many short stories, however (a notable exception being "Missing in Miami," which appeared in* Mean Streets). *We are proud to feature one of those rare and delicious efforts in this volume.*

All in all, it was a perfect day for a funeral. A weepy drizzle fell steadily from the somber sky and there were rumblings of thunder from the north, carrying with them the threat of more gloom.

I didn't need thunder and rain to feel gloomy. As I watched the casket disappear into the ground I felt sad, and at the same time angry. Angry at myself and the capriciousness of the universe. You add up a man's life and what do you get? A hole in a hillside. Ten plus ten plus ten equals zero. The addition was screwy.

Steve Guttenberg and I had been close at one time, but our lives had gone off in different directions over the past six years—his in search of the Big Story, mine in search of whatever anyone paid me to search for, preferably in advance. We had talked on the phone several times during the past few months, always making the proverbial promises to get together for lunch. We never had; something I regretted now but could do nothing about because Steve had stepped off the wrong curb, canceling all future lunches.

The shovelful of dirt rattled off the top of the casket, the rabbi went into his ashes-to-ashes bit, and it was over. I waited for the crowd of well-wishers around Becky to dissipate, then went over.

She had always reminded me of a little doll, tiny and fragile and

143

cute, and she looked even more that way now, even dressed in black. She had cut her dark hair pixie-short and she was very pale, so that her skin and dark red lipstick looked almost like paint. She saw me and her big dark eyes filled with tears. "Oh, Jake. He was only thirty-three."

She fell into my arms and began to cry and I held her, feeling as if she would break if I squeezed too hard. I knew she wouldn't, though. She was a trench fighter. I remembered her eight years ago when Steve had been starting out as a cub reporter for the *Chronicle* and she had been holding down two jobs to keep them in Hamburger Helper.

She backed up and dabbed her eyes with a tissue. "I have to talk to you," she said, sniffling. "It's really important. Will you come over to the house?"

I was depressed enough and didn't feel like dragging out the mood, but there was an urgency in her request I couldn't turn down, and I told her I'd be there.

The house was a small, ranch-style place in the hills above Studio City. I parked the car at the first available curb space I could find and made a fifty-yard dash through the rain, which was heavy now. Becky greeted me at the front door and took my dripping overcoat, then whisked me into the den, past the two dozen or so people in the living room filling paper plates from the buffet table set up in the corner.

The den was a small, bookshelf-lined room with a desk, a small love seat, and a reclining leather chair. A portable electric typewriter sat on the desk—Steve's typewriter—and I felt slightly uneasy listening to its silence. She told me to sit down, which I did, and she shut the door. When she turned around her face looked feverish. "It wasn't an accident," she said quietly, locking stares with me. "They killed him, Jake. That car ran him down on purpose."

"Wait a minute," I said, trying to catch up. "Who is 'they'?"

"That's what I want you to find out." Her face was deadly serious. She sat down next to me on the love seat. "Steve was working on something, Jake. Something big. He said it was going to shake a lot of people up, and one of them was going to be Irving Sappherstein."

The name jarred me. Irving Sappherstein's legal clients included some of the West Coast kingpins of organized crime, and it was even rumored that the lawyer-businessman was in charge of all Syndicate financial investments from L.A. to Denver. But in spite of the fact that his name cropped up regularly in every major federal and local investigation of organized crime activity in southern California, no law enforcement agency had ever come close to making any allegations against Sappherstein stick. "What did Steve have on Sappherstein?"

"I don't know. All I know is that he was working day and night on it. He didn't come home until nearly two all last week. Whatever it was, something was supposed to be happening with it the day he died."

"Do you know what?"

She shook her head and looked down at the handkerchief she was twisting in her lap. "No, but it was something major, I think. Two days before he was killed he started acting real strange, as if something were really bothering him. I asked him what it was, but all he would say was that he couldn't tell me then, that I'd hear about it one way or another on Friday."

"The day he died," I said, mulling that one over. "What about his notes? Didn't he keep any about what he was doing?"

"Yes, but trying to decipher them is another thing. Joe Fitzpatrick is trying to do that now."

Another name that surprised me. "Joe Fitzpatrick the Pulitzer prize winner?"

She nodded. "Harry, Steve's editor, turned the notes over to him. He says Fitz was closer to what Steve was working on than anyone. Steve consulted him several times about it, I guess."

"Do the cops know about this?"

"I told Lefferts, the detective in charge of the case," she said in a slightly resentful tone, "but he didn't seem very impressed."

"Have they determined what Steve was doing at Plummer Park at ten-thirty at night?"

"Nobody has any idea. And the only people who saw him there were a young couple too distracted with each other to pay attention. They said they thought the car that hit him pulled out from the curb, but they weren't sure. They were pretty far away and it happened so fast."

I really didn't see what I could do about it that the entire staff of the *Chronicle* couldn't. "Fitzpatrick is one of the best around, Becky. If there's something wrong, he'll find it."

"*You're* the best," she said firmly. "Steve always said so. He said you were his mentor."

"Steve liked to exaggerate. I showed him a few tricks of the trade when he was starting out, that was all. Within a few months, he was making up his own."

"I'll pay you." Her eyes had that helpless, wounded look in them I hated to see.

"That isn't the point—"

"The point is he was your friend," she said, her voice suddenly brittle.

She was right, of course. I owed him that much. At the end of my career at the *Chronicle*, when I had been a rather unfashionable cause, Steve had never balked at backing me up even when it put him into direct conflict with management. Perhaps there was nothing to it. Perhaps he had just been the victim of some strung-out drunk driver who was on a bender because his wife had left him for a lineman for the phone company. But he had been a friend and I owed him a look-see. He would have done it for me.

I pointed at the closed door. "Is Fitzpatrick in there?"

"No. He was at the funeral, but he had to get back to the paper."

"Tell you what," I said. "I'll drop by and talk to him and see what he's gotten from Steve's notes."

"You don't have to," she said, getting up and walking around the desk. From the middle drawer, she pulled out a manila envelope and put it on top of the typewriter. "Steve always made an extra copy of his notes, in case something happened to the original."

She had me now. I told her to tend to her guests and shoved her out the door.

She was right about the notes—they were a mess—but after two hours, I'd managed to come up with a couple of intriguing items. Steve seemed to have been taking a close look at three companies—Thompson Paint and Varnish, Wil-Stick Glue Company, and Apex Steel Drum—in which Sappherstein was a major stockholder. Although Sappherstein was not an officer in any of the corporations, he did appear as an original incorporator of one, Apex. Indeed, Apex seemed to have been the focus of Steve's investigation; a log among the notes indicated that he had staked out the company on five different nights during the week prior to his death, which would be why he hadn't been getting home until two. Apparently nothing much had happened on those nights and the reason for the stakeouts was not among the notes. One thing that *was* among the notes that seemed totally unconnected to the rest of the file was one of the articles from Fitzpatrick's

Pulitzer prize–winning series on cocaine smuggling. It had appeared last year in the *Chronicle*. Passages in the text had been underlined, and in the margin Steve had scribbled, "S.B. 109." After unsuccessfully dwelling on the significance of S.B. 109 and the underlined passages for ten minutes or so, I put everything away in the desk drawer and went out to the living room.

The crowd had boiled down to half-a-dozen diehard friends and Becky managed to detach herself from their sympathetic cooing long enough to come over. "Well?"

"I'll do some nosing around and see what I can come up with."

She put a hand on my arm and smiled gratefully. "Thank you."

Her eyes were starting to get watery again. I told her I'd keep her informed and got out of there before the floodgates opened.

They had already opened outside, and all the way downtown my wipers fought a losing battle with the rain. From a pay phone in the lobby of the *Chronicle* I called Detective Lefferts at the LAPD, and found his interest in Becky's murder theory at least as tepid as she'd described. He seemed to get irritated when I brought it up, saying that he intended to look into it as soon as he checked out every body-and-fender shop in town for a late-model, green GM car, which was what they'd determined had hit Steve. He became even more irritated when I suggested they'd find the car about the time his seven-year-old needed a new pair of Nikes, and hung up on me.

The city room upstairs had the usual aura of frenzy when I popped in. There were a lot of new faces manning the desks, but some I knew, and others I could have happily gone another eight years without seeing. I recognized Fitzpatrick from the funeral. He had a long, narrow face with too much chin, and a long bony nose on which sat a pair of rimless glasses. His brown hair was parted on the side and slicked down, its neatness contrasting with the rumpled white shirt rolled up to the elbows and spotted with various stains.

He stood up and offered a thin, pale hand. "Sit down, Mr. Asch. It's a pleasure to finally meet you."

"Finally?" I asked, pulling up a chair.

He smiled and waved a hand at the reigning chaos. "You've achieved a permanent measure of fame around here. The man who went to jail before revealing his news sources, and all that. What can I do for you?"

"I understand Steve Guttenberg's notes have been turned over to you."

Behind the glasses, his small eyes were shiny and hard, like the backs of two brown beetles. "That's right."

"Have you determined yet what connection Steve was trying to make between Irving Sappherstein and Apex Steel Drum?"

The beetles jumped. "How did you know about that?"

"Becky has asked me to look into Steve's death. She has a copy of his notes."

He didn't seem too pleased about that, but I hadn't expected him to be. Investigative reporters as a rule don't like other people digging around in their stories. He shrugged and began toying with a pencil on the desk. "On paper, at least, Apex seems to be legit. It's a company that buys, repairs, and resells chemical storage drums. Aside from being a major stockholder, Sappherstein doesn't seem to have any interest in it."

"You say it's legit on paper. What about off paper?"

"I don't know."

"Why was Steve surveilling the place?"

"I don't know that, either."

"What did Steve talk about when he consulted you about the piece?"

He put down the pencil and began rubbing the back of his neck. "I've done a few organized crime pieces. Steve threw out some names and wanted to know what I knew about them."

"What names?"

"Sappherstein and a few of his business associates. Manny Rothstein, Jimmy Carnera."

"Did he ask any questions about drug connections?"

His tone grew wary. "Drug connections? No, why?"

"Your cocaine piece was in with his notes."

The beetles sought refuge in the cracks as the eyelids narrowed. "I don't know why. Steve never mentioned anything about drugs, if that's what he thought was going on."

"He'd written on the clipping," I said. " 'S.B. 109.' Does that mean anything to you?"

"No."

I had a feeling he knew more than he was telling, but there was no way he was going to give it to me, so I thanked him and stood up. To ease his reporter's paranoia, I said, "I reread your Pulitzer piece this afternoon. You're a hell of a writer. I just want you to know that if I find out anything, you'll get the exclusive."

His expression seemed to relax a bit. "I appreciate that," he said, offering his hand.

* * *

The rain had stopped late in the afternoon but the cloud cover was still thick at ten that night, which was good for me. The street I was parked on was wide and unlighted, lined with grimy industrial warehouses and storage yards, and Apex fit right in. A high wooden fence ran around the perimeter of the property, but I could see the hangarlike building through the chain-link gates pulled across the driveway. Two hours ago, two men had driven a four-ton, open-bed truck through the gates and had disappeared into the building. That had been the only activity of the night.

I unwrapped the ham sandwich I'd brought from home and had started to take a bite when headlights in my rearview mirror sent me sliding down in my seat. When the car drove by, I sat up and watched it pull over to the curb a hundred feet ahead, and its lights and engine go off. The car was easily in range of the 300mm lens attached to my Starlight Scope, and after getting the license number, I focused through the back window and waited for the driver to turn around. After a minute or two he did, and I unscrewed the bulb from the overhead light and slipped quietly out of the car.

Fitzpatrick jumped about a foot off the seat when I opened the passenger door of the Granada and got in. He let out the breath he was holding and said in an annoyed tone, "You scared the hell out of me. Where did you come from?"

"You know how sneaky we detectives are," I said, grinning. "I just thought since we both had the same idea, we might pool our efforts. Stakeouts can get pretty boring alone."

The wary look was back. He said hesitantly, "Okay, but I expect you to keep your word about me getting the exclusive."

"You got it."

He glanced down at the equipment in my hand. "What kind of camera is that?"

"Canon 35mm with a 300mm lens attached to a Starlight Scope with a focal plane iris for reading license plates."

"You like to come equipped."

"Boy Scout training."

We shared several Thermos cups of coffee laced with 100-proof bourbon and a lot of conversation over the next hour and a half, while we waited for something to happen. I found out he was thirty-nine and from Nebraska, a Columbia graduate, and had come West to work for the *Chronicle* three years ago after making a rep for himself as A Big Story man at the *Washington Post*. He had tried marriage for a short time but had given it up when he found it interfered with his work, which was his life. His goal had always been the Pulitzer and he had his break last year when he fell in with a group of coke smugglers and they had allowed him to accompany a shipment from South America.

At twelve-forty, conversation was put to an end by the sound of a motor starting up. I trained my scope on the building. A heavyset, dark-haired man opened the gates and the big open-bed truck rumbled through and stopped, heading away from us. I read off the license number to Fitzpatrick as the heavyset man repadlocked the gate and trotted to the truck. After they had gone down the street, we flipped a U and followed without lights until they turned right onto Santa Fe. The area was still heavily commercial and we hung back and tried to blend in with the few other headlights on the street. We crossed under the freeway and after half a mile, the truck's running lights disappeared. Fitzpatrick speeded up, then took his foot off the gas as we passed a big brick building sitting back from the street. The sign on the building said THOMPSON PAINT AND VARNISH. The truck was nowhere to be seen.

"I have one of those feelings," Fitzpatrick said.

"Yeah," I agreed.

We parked on a dark side street across from the building and waited. Twenty minutes later, the truck pulled out of the driveway of Thompson Paint and Varnish and headed back in the direction from which it had come. At the freeway, it got onto the westbound ramp.

The truck's running lights made it easy to follow and we were able to drop way back. Five miles later it swung onto the junction for the San Diego Freeway heading north, and we had to close some distance to make sure we didn't lose it. At the top of the Sepulveda pass the truck's blinker flashed, and it got off at the Mulholland exit.

A few turns later, and the city was only a memory. The fresh smells of the rain-soaked chaparral filled the car as we followed the narrow, two-lane road twisting into the hills. On our left the canyon dropped away sheerly, and occasionally, far down, I could see the rectangular light from a window. The truck was lost in the curves and we were traveling blind. Then suddenly, as we came around a hairpin, there it was right in front of us.

The truck was parked on a dirt turnout, its back end hanging over the edge of the canyon. The heavyset man and the driver were outside the cab and they watched us suspiciously as we passed. Around the next curve Fitzpatrick let me out and took off. I slid down the wet embankment and made my way as quietly as I could through the weeds, back toward the truck. The camera made it clumsy going, but that couldn't be helped; I had a feeling I was going to need it.

The two men were standing stiffly by the truck, listening to Fitzpatrick's engine die in the distance. When they were satisfied he wasn't coming back, they hopped up onto the truck bed and began shoving the half-dozen twenty-gallon steel drums they were carrying over the side of the canyon. They spent five minutes dumping the load and I spent an entire roll of film.

Ten minutes after they had gone Fitzpatrick pulled up, and I got in the car and asked for a flashlight. He said there was one in the glove compartment. I found it under a car rental receipt, snatched up the Thermos and, while Fitzpatrick rummaged around in his trunk for tools, started the long slide down the side of the canyon. Luckily, I didn't have to go to the bottom; one of the drums had lodged against a boulder halfway down the slope. Fitzpatrick joined me and together we pried off the lid.

"What do you think it is?" he asked as we were knocked back by the strong chemical smell. The liquid had an oily, green look to it.

"I don't know," I said, as I carefully ladled some of the stuff into the Thermos with the plastic cup. "I just hope it doesn't eat through the Thermos."

He shook his head. "I must admit I had my doubts, but I guess this clinches it. They must have spotted Steve tailing them one night and decided to have him hit."

"Maybe."

"What do you mean, 'maybe'?" he asked, almost angrily. "Do you know how much money is at stake here? The bastards have to be saving thousands a load dumping it this way instead of at a licensed toxic waste dump."

"If he tailed them, why wasn't it in his notes?"

"Maybe he didn't have time to write it down. Maybe they got to him before he could."

"If these guys hit Steve, they're either incredibly stupid or incredibly cocky. They know somebody is onto them and they conduct business as usual without taking the most minor security precautions? They let us follow them all over town without even checking to see if somebody is behind them? I don't buy it."

"Why should they check? They think they've eliminated the problem."

"Come on, Joe. Sappherstein is not dumb. He has to know that the *Chronicle* is not going to let one of its people get wiped out without looking into what he was working on."

He shook his head. "It's Sappherstein. I can feel it."

"Maybe you want to feel it."

His tone turned belligerent. "What do you mean by that?"

"Think what a story it would make. ORGANIZED CRIME'S POISON-OUS ROOTS EXTEND ALL THE WAY DOWN TO THE WATER TABLE. Quite a byline."

"Sappherstein had Steve killed," he said positively. "And I'm going to prove it. With or without your help."

The Thermos was still intact when we got back to the car, but my lungs felt as if they were going through a major meltdown. Fitzpatrick must have said a total of six words all the way back to Apex, which was all right with me. I had some thinking to do.

The next morning, I stopped at the camera store and put a rush on the film, then took the Thermos over to a lab and waited for the analysis. When it came in, I called Fitzpatrick. "Toluene, carbon tet, and cadmium," I read from the report. "Nice poisons all."

"I *knew* it," he said gleefully.

"You find out anything?"

"Some good, some bad. Alex Tartunian, the president of Apex, and Sappherstein were both officers in a plastics manufacturing business that went bankrupt a few years ago. That gives him a connection to management. But proving either of them are behind the illegal dumping is going to be tough. Apex leases its building and equipment and another company pays its payroll. If we're going to tie Sappherstein into it, we're going to have to establish a stronger connection than we have." His tone was friendly and he was talking in "we's." He must have forgotten our little difference of opinion last night. "You up for another stakeout tonight?"

"Eight o'clock?"

"Fine," he said. "Oh, and Asch, you know the paper will pay you a nice chunk of change for those pictures."

I couldn't keep the grin off my face. "I already thought of that."

The grin didn't last long. I was still bothered by the carelessness of those men last night. I called Becky and drove out to the valley.

I wanted to go through Steve's notes again, just to make sure I hadn't missed something.

When I related what we had found out, she wanted to immediately get on the phone to the cops. I told her that after discussing it, Fitzpatrick and I had decided to wait until we found out what other companies Apex was illegally dumping for and hand it to them in a nice, neat package they couldn't screw up. She reluctantly went along with the program and left me alone in the den.

Two hours later, I'd gone through Steve's notes three times without finding any indication Steve had witnessed a midnight dumping or had been spotted while surveilling Apex. He could have been spotted without knowing, of course, but if that had been the case, why didn't they take care of business there and then? Why wait until a day or two later, when he could have blown the whistle on the operation? Had it taken that long for the decision to be made and the order passed down? And if that had been the way it had happened, why hadn't Sappherstein or whoever tried to plug the leaks before ordering Steve hit? Sappherstein was a careful man; he would have wanted to find out what kind of incriminating evidence Steve had left behind before ordering something as drastic as an execution.

I picked up Fitzpatrick's cocaine article and stared at it. I could not shake the feeling that it was a missing piece of the puzzle. Why had Steve put it with his notes? The incongruity of it irritated me. I shifted my gaze to the bookcase next to the desk and let my eyes wander aimlessly, with my thoughts. They stopped wandering when they landed on a paperback book lying horizontally on top of the upright volumes. *Snow Bound* by Hugh Harris. I pulled it off the shelf.

It had been published four years ago, by a publishing house I had never heard of. There was a bookmark sticking out of the text. I knew what page it would be on and I knew what would be on the page, but I turned to it anyway.

Fitzpatrick was parked across from Apex when I pulled up and parked. It was eight-ten and the half moon put a silvery backing on the dissipating clouds. It was a fine night. Fitzpatrick greeted me cheerfully as I opened the door of the Granada. He offered me a cup of coffee from a new Thermos.

"No, thanks," I said, glancing across the street. "Any action?"

"Not yet." He looked at my empty hands. "You didn't bring your equipment?"

"I'm not going to be staying that long." I opened the glove compartment and pulled out the rental receipt I'd run across last night. "You rented this car on Saturday. What happened to your car? The 1963 green Firebird?"

His eyes became small and hard again. "It's being repaired. I blew a piston."

I put the receipt back and slammed the box shut. "Really? Where is it being worked on? Mexico? It couldn't be being done around here, unless, of course, you're chummy with some hot-car boys who don't advertise their skills."

He stiffened and looked at me as if I was wearing a bunch of bananas on my head. "What are you talking about?"

"The front end of your car is being repaired, not a piston. You hit Steve with it."

He kept the look on his face. I didn't mind. I went on: "I couldn't figure why Steve had your cocaine article among his notes. My mistake was thinking it had something to do with Apex. He consulted with you on the Wednesday he died, all right, but not to talk about Sappherstein. He wanted to talk about the fact that your Pulitzer story had been lifted from a little-known book called *Snow Bound*. It was all a lie. You never traveled with any coke dealers. Steve must have had his notes with him when you two met, and stuck the article among them."

His expression went blank and he turned away, rigidly. I said to his back: "Steve told his wife she would know all about what was bothering him on Friday. What did he do, give you a deadline to expose yourself?"

He turned back. The surface of his face rippled, then broke in a wave of anguish. "He gave me forty-eight hours to break the story any way I wanted, then he was going to break it himself. It would have made me a laughingstock. My career—my life—would have been over."

"So you killed him . . . then talked your editor into turning Steve's notes over to you. You had to find out if there was anything incriminating in them."

He grabbed the sleeve of my jacket and held on desperately. He looked dazed, like a punch-drunk fighter. "I didn't mean to. It just happened. We arranged to meet at Plummer Park that night to discuss things. I was already there when he got there. He got out of his car and started toward mine. I don't remember anything after that until I was miles away. I swear to God, I don't remember running him over."

He choked down a sob. I didn't know if he was telling the truth or getting his plea ready, although it didn't matter much. He went on: "That was the only time in my career I ever did anything like that, Asch. I was just all written out and I had a deadline. I'm sorry now the damned article attracted so much attention. The Pulitzer was something I'd wanted my whole life, and once I got it, it turned out to be a curse."

He was sorrier about the article than he was about the fact that he had killed a man. It made me feel good that I was out of the business. "Steve gave you forty-eight hours," I said, getting out of the car. "I'm giving you zip."

He called out to me as I walked back to my car, but I didn't turn around. I kept a keen ear for the sound of his engine starting, just in case he decided to go for two out of two, but nothing happened. He was still parked there when I drove away.

I called Becky from home and told her the story, then made myself a stiff drink and went to bed.

The next morning, I opened the paper to a black-and-white photograph of a smashed-down sardine can that had once been a car. The story beneath it said that Pulitzer prize–winning reporter Joe Fitzpatrick had been killed shortly before ten last night when his automobile had gone out of control and struck a freeway abutment. He should have been proud, wherever he was; he had made Page One.

# BILL PRONZINI

# INCIDENT IN A NEIGHBORHOOD TAVERN

*Bill Pronzini's "Nameless" detective is one of the more enduring P.I.s of the genre; he has been appearing in short stories and novels since the late 1960s.*

*Bill received a Shamus Award for Best Novel with* Hoodwink *(St. Martin's Press, 1981); for Best Short Story with "Cat's Paw" (1983); and in 1984 became the youngest recipient of PWA's Life Achievement Award, the "Eye." He also served as PWA's very first president.*

*Many of us presently toiling in the genre learned a lot about writing the P.I. story from reading Bill Pronzini. Now it's your turn to read—and enjoy.*

When the holdup went down I was sitting at the near end of the Foghorn Tavern's scarred mahogany bar talking to the owner, Matt Candiotti.

It was a little before seven of a midweek evening, lull-time in working-class neighborhood saloons like this one. Blue-collar locals would jam the place from four until about six-thirty, when the last of them headed home for dinner; the hard-core drinkers wouldn't begin filtering back in until about seven-thirty or eight. Right now there were only two customers, and the jukebox and computer hockey games were quiet. The TV over the back bar was on but with the sound turned down to a tolerable level. One of the customers, a porky guy in his fifties, drinking Anchor Steam out of the bottle, was watching the last of the NBC national news. The other customer, an equally porky and middle-aged

157

female barfly, half in the bag on red wine, was trying to convince
him to pay attention to her instead of Tom Brokaw.

I had a draft beer in front of me, but that wasn't the reason I
was there. I'd come to ask Candiotti, as I had asked two dozen
other merchants here in the Outer Mission, if he could offer any
leads on the rash of burglaries that were plaguing small busi-
nesses in the neighborhood. The police hadn't come up with
anything positive after six weeks, so a couple of the victims had
gotten up a fund and hired me to see what I could find out.
They'd picked me because I had been born and raised in the
Outer Mission, I still had friends and shirttail relatives living here,
and I understood the neighborhood a good deal better than any
other private detective in San Francisco.

But so far I wasn't having any more luck than the SFPD. None
of the merchants I'd spoken with today had given me any new
ideas, and Candiotti was proving to be no exception. He stood
slicing limes into wedges as we talked. They might have been
onions the way his long, mournful face was screwed up, like a
man trying to hold back tears. His gray-stubbled jowls wobbled
every time he shook his head. He reminded me of a tired old
hound, friendly and sad, as if life had dealt him a few kicks but
not quite enough to rob him of his good nature.

"Wish I could help," he said. "But hell, I don't hear nothing.
Must be pros from Hunters Point or the Fillmore, hah?"

Hunters Point and the Fillmore were black sections of the city,
which was a pretty good indicator of where his head was at. I
said, "Some of the others figure it for local talent."

"Out of this neighborhood, you mean?"

I nodded, drank some of my draft.

"Nah, I doubt it," he said. "Guys that organized, they don't
shit where they eat. Too smart, you know?"

"Maybe. Any break-ins or attempted break-ins here?"

"Not so far. I got bars on all the windows, double dead-bolt
locks on the storeroom door off the alley. Besides, what's for them
to steal besides a few cases of whiskey?"

"You don't keep cash on the premises overnight?"

"Fifty bucks in the till," Candiotti said, "that's all; that's my
limit. Everything else goes out of here when I close up, down to
the night deposit at the B of A on Mission. My mama didn't raise
no airheads." He scraped the lime wedges off his board, into a
plastic container, and racked the serrated knife he'd been using.

"One thing I did hear," he said. "I heard some of the loot turned up down in San Jose. You know about that?"

"Not much of a lead there. Secondhand dealer named Pitman had a few pieces of stereo equipment stolen from the factory outlet store on Geneva. Said he bought it from a guy at the San Jose flea market, somebody he didn't know, never saw before."

"Yeah, sure," Candiotti said wryly. "What do the cops think?"

"That Pitman bought it off a fence."

"Makes sense. So maybe the boosters are from San Jose, hah?"

"Could be," I said, and that was when the kid walked in.

He brought bad air in with him; I sensed it right away and so did Candiotti. We both glanced at the door when it opened, the way you do, but we didn't look away again once we saw him. He was in his early twenties, dark-skinned, dressed in chinos, a cotton windbreaker, sharp-toed shoes polished to a high gloss. But it was his eyes that put the chill on my neck, the sudden clutch of tension down low in my belly. They were bright, jumpy, on the wild side, and in the dim light of the Foghorn's interior, the pupils were so small they seemed nonexistent. He had one hand in his jacket pocket and I knew it was clamped around a gun even before he took it out and showed it to us.

He came up to the bar a few feet on my left, the gun jabbing the air in front of him. He couldn't hold it steady; it kept jerking up and down, from side to side, as if it had a kind of spasmodic life of its own. Behind me, at the other end of the bar, I heard Anchor Steam suck in his breath, the barfly make a sound like a stifled moan. I eased back a little on the stool, watching the gun and the kid's eyes flick from Candiotti to me to the two customers and back around again. Candiotti didn't move at all, just stood there staring with his hound's face screwed up in that holding-back-tears way.

"All right all right," the kid said. His voice was high pitched, excited, and there was drool at one corner of his mouth. You couldn't get much more stoned than he was and still function. Coke, crack, speed—maybe a combination. The gun that kept flicking this way and that was a goddamn Saturday Night Special. "Listen good, man, everybody listen good I don't want to kill none of you, man, but I will if I got to, you believe it?"

None of us said anything. None of us moved.

The kid had a folded-up paper sack in one pocket; he dragged it out with his free hand, dropped it, broke quickly at the middle to pick it up without lowering his gaze. When he straightened again there was sweat on his forehead, more drool coming out of his mouth. He threw the sack on the bar.

"Put the money in there Mr. Cyclone Man," he said to Candiotti. "All the money in the register but not the coins; I don't want the fuckin' coins, you hear me?"

Candiotti nodded; reached out slowly, caught up the sack, turned toward the back bar with his shoulders hunched up against his neck. When he punched No Sale on the register, the ringing thump of the cash drawer sliding open seemed overloud in the electric hush. For a few seconds the kid watched him scoop bills into the paper sack; then his eyes and the gun skittered my way again. I had looked into the muzzle of a handgun before and it was the same feeling each time: dull fear, helplessness, a kind of naked vulnerability.

"Your wallet on the bar, man, all your cash." The gun barrel and the wild eyes flicked away again, down the length of the plank, before I could move to comply. "You down there, dude, you and fat mama put your money on the bar. All of it, hurry up."

Each of us did as we were told. While I was getting my wallet out I managed to slide my right foot off the stool, onto the brass rail, and to get my right hand pressed tight against the beveled edge of the bar. If I had to make any sudden moves, I would need the leverage.

Candiotti finished loading the sack, turned from the register. There was a grayish cast to his face now—the wet gray color of fear. The kid said to him, "Pick up their money, put it in the sack with the rest. Come on come on come on!"

Candiotti went to the far end of the plank, scooped up the wallets belonging to Anchor Steam and the woman; then he came back my way, added my wallet to the contents of the paper sack, put the sack down carefully in front of the kid.

"Okay," the kid said, "okay all right." He glanced over his shoulder at the street door, as if he'd heard something there; but it stayed closed. He jerked his head around again. In his sweaty agitation the Saturday Night Special almost slipped free of his fingers; he fumbled a tighter grip on it, and when it didn't go off I let the breath I had been holding come out thin and slow between my teeth. The muscles in my shoulders and back were drawn so tight I was afraid they might cramp.

The kid reached out for the sack, dragged it in against his body. But he made no move to leave with it. Instead he said, "Now we go get the big pile, man."

Candiotti opened his mouth, closed it again. His eyes were almost as big and starey as the kid's.

"Come on Mr. Cyclone Man, the safe, the safe in your office. We goin' back there *now*."

"No money in that safe," Candiotti said in a thin, scratchy voice. "Nothing valuable."

"Oh man I'll kill you man I'll blow your fuckin' head off! I ain't playin' no games I want that money!"

He took two steps forward, jabbing with the gun up close to Candiotti's gray face. Candiotti backed off a step, brought his hands up, took a tremulous breath.

"All right," he said, "but I got to get the key to the office. It's in the register."

"Hurry up hurry up!"

Candiotti turned back to the register, rang it open, rummaged inside with his left hand. But with his right hand, shielded from the kid by his body, he eased up the top on a large wooden cigar box adjacent. The hand disappeared inside; came out again with metal in it, glinting in the back bar lights. I saw it and I wanted to yell at him, but it wouldn't have done any good, would only have warned the kid . . . and he was already turning with it, bringing it up with both hands now—the damn gun of his own he'd had hidden inside the cigar box. There was no time for me to do anything but shove away from the bar and sideways off the stool just as Candiotti opened fire.

The state he was in, the kid didn't realize what was happening until it was too late for him to react; he never even got a shot off. Candiotti's first slug knocked him halfway around, and one of the three others that followed it opened up his face like a piece of ripe fruit smacked by a hammer. He was dead before his body, driven backward, slammed into the cigarette machine near the door, slid down it to the floor.

The half-drunk woman was yelling in broken shrieks, as if she couldn't get enough air for a sustained scream. When I came up out of my crouch I saw that Anchor Steam had hold of her, clinging to her as much for support as in an effort to calm her down. Candiotti stood flat-footed, his arms down at his sides, the gun out of sight below the bar, staring at the bloody remains of the kid as if he couldn't believe what he was seeing, couldn't believe what he'd done.

Some of the tension in me eased as I went to the door, found the lock on its security gate, fastened it before anybody could come in off the street. The Saturday Night Special was still clutched in the kid's hand; I bent, pulled it free with my thumb and forefinger, broke the cylinder. It was loaded, all right—five cartridges. I dropped it into my jacket pocket, thought about checking the kid's clothing for identification, didn't do it. It wasn't any of my business, now, who he'd been. And I did not want to touch him or any part of him. There was a queasiness in my stomach, a fluttery weakness behind my knees—the same delayed reaction I always had to violence and death—and touching him would only make it worse.

To keep from looking at the red ruin of the kid's face, I pivoted back to the bar. Candiotti hadn't moved. Anchor Steam had gotten the woman to stop screeching and had coaxed her over to one of the handful of tables near the jukebox; now she was sobbing, "I've got to go home, I'm gonna be sick if I don't go home." But she didn't make any move to get up and neither did Anchor Steam.

I walked over near Candiotti, pushed hard words at him in an undertone. "That was a damn fool thing to do. You could have got us all killed."

"I know," he said. "I know."

"Why'd you do it?"

"I thought . . . hell, you saw the way he was waving that piece of his . . ."

"Yeah," I said. "Call the police. Nine-eleven."

"Nine-eleven. Okay."

"Put that gun of yours down first. On the bar."

He did that. There was a phone on the back bar; he went away to it in shaky strides. While he was talking to the Emergency operator I picked up his weapon, saw that it was a .32 Charter Arms revolver. I held it in my hand until Candiotti finished with the call, set it down again as he came back to where I stood.

"They'll have somebody here in five minutes," he said.

I said, "You know that kid?"

"Christ, no."

"Ever see him before? Here or anywhere else?"

"No."

"So how did he know about your safe?"

Candiotti blinked at me. "What?"

"The safe in your office. Street kid like that . . . how'd he know about it?"

"How should I know? What difference does it make?"

"He seemed to think you keep big money in that safe."

"Well, I don't. There's nothing in it."

"That's right, you told me you don't keep more than fifty bucks on the premises overnight. In the till."

"Yeah."

"Then why have you got a safe, if it's empty?"

Candiotti's eyes narrowed. "I used to keep my receipts in it, all right? Before all these burglaries started. Then I figured I'd be smarter to take the money to the bank every night."

"Sure, that explains it," I said. "Still, a kid like that, looking for a big score to feed his habit, he wasn't just after what was in the till and our wallets. No, it was as if he'd gotten wind of a heavy stash—a grand or more."

Nothing from Candiotti.

I watched him for a time. Then I said, "Big risk you took, using that .32 of yours. How come you didn't make your play the first time you went to the register? How come you waited until the kid mentioned your office safe?"

"I didn't like the way he was acting, like he might start shooting any second. I figured it was our only chance. Listen, what're you getting at, hah?"

"Another funny thing," I said, "is the way he called you 'Mr. Cyclone Man.' Now why would a hopped-up kid use a term like that to a bar owner he didn't know?"

"How the hell should I know?"

"Cyclone," I said. "What's a cyclone but a big destructive wind? Only one other thing I can think of."

"Yeah? What's that?"

"A fence. A cyclone fence."

Candiotti made a fidgety movement. Some of the wet gray pallor was beginning to spread across his cheeks again, like a fungus.

I said, "And a fence is somebody who receives and distributes stolen goods. A Mr. Fence Man. But then you know that, don't you, Candiotti? We were talking about that kind of fence before the kid came in . . . how Pitman, down in San Jose, bought some hot stereo equipment off of one. That fence could just as easily be operating here in San Francisco, though. Right here in this neighborhood, in fact. Hell, suppose the stuff taken in all those burglaries never left the neighborhood. Suppose it was brought to a place nearby and stored until it could be trucked out to other cities—a tavern storeroom, for instance. Might even be some of it is *still* in that storeroom. And the money he got for the rest he'd keep locked up in his safe, right? Who'd figure it? Except maybe a poor junkie who picked up a whisper on the street somewhere—"

Candiotti made a sudden grab for the .32, caught it up, backed up a step with it leveled at my chest. "You smart son of a bitch," he said. "I ought to kill you too."

"In front of witnesses? With the police due any minute?"

He glanced over at the two customers. The woman was still sobbing, lost in a bleak outpouring of self-pity; but Anchor Steam was staring our way, and from the expression on his face he'd heard every word of my exchange with Candiotti.

"There's still enough time for me to get clear," Candiotti said grimly. He was talking to himself, not to me. Sweat had plastered his lank hair to his forehead; the revolver was not quite steady in his hand. "Lock you up in my office, you and those two back there . . ."

"I don't think so," I said.

"Goddamn you, you think I won't use this gun again?"

"I *know* you won't use it. I emptied out the last two cartridges while you were on the phone."

I took the two shells out of my left-hand jacket pocket and held them up where he could see them. At the same time I got the kid's Saturday Night Special out of the other pocket, held it loosely pointed in his direction. "You want to put your piece down now, Candiotti? You've not going anywhere, not for a long time."

He put it down—dropped it clattering onto the bartop. And as he did his sad hound's face screwed up again, only this time he didn't even try to keep the wetness from leaking out of his eyes. He was leaning against the bar, crying like the woman, submerged in his own outpouring of self-pity, when the cops showed up a little while later.

# ROBERT J. RANDISI

# THE VANISHING VIRGIN

*Nick Delvecchio's first appearance in a novel was* No Exit From Brooklyn, *published by St. Martin's Press in 1987. His very first appearance was in a short story called "The Snaphaunce," which appeared in Wayne Dundee's* Hardboiled, *and was nominated for a Shamus Award as Best P.I. Short Story of 1985.*

*Join Delvecchio in Brooklyn as he looks for "The Vanishing Virgin."*

### 1

"One of my virgins has vanished," the man sitting across the table said.

I frowned at him. I'd heard of men collecting women before—harems, and all that—but virgins? What would one do with them?

"Perhaps I'd better explain," George Vanguard said.

"It would be appreciated."

I didn't usually talk like that, but there was something about Vanguard that brought it out in me.

He had called me earlier and asked for an appointment; I lied and told him that he was in luck, I'd had a cancellation. His name was George Vanguard and he was a playwright with a problem.

"You see," he began, "in my new play—which is now in rehearsals, by the way—the three central characters are virgins."

In this day and age? "Is it a fantasy?"

"How did you know?" he replied, looking at me with surprise and something akin to respect. It never hurts to impress a potential client early.

165

"I guessed. Go on, please."

"Yes, well, the girl who plays one of the virgins hasn't shown up for rehearsal in two days. It's wreaking havoc with my schedule, as I'm sure you can imagine."

The guy came off like a daisy, but I wanted to give him the benefit of the doubt—which was kind of hard to do with a fellow who wears a pink shirt and lavender jacket with matching kerchief.

"Indeed," I said.

"Well, that's it," he said, shrugging. "We simply *cannot* find her," he added, for dramatic effect.

"Have you tried her home?"

"Well, we've *called*, of course."

"You haven't gone to her place to check?"

"I simply don't have the *time*," he explained. "We're running rehearsals around her, but we can't do that *forever*. I'd like to hire you to find her within the next two days."

"Why the time limit?"

"Well, I don't *want* to replace her, she's *perfect* for the part, but in a few days that will be a moot point. I will simply be *forced* to replace her and continue rehearsals. We open next month, you know."

"On Broadway?"

"Off Broadway," he said, as if he were implying *who wants to be on Broadway?*

"I see. Do you have her address with you?"

"Well, of *course*," he scolded. His nose wrinkled when he scolded. I decided he was definitely gay—that's why I'm a *detective*.

He rattled off her address and I wrote it down on the doodle pad I carry in my pocket. It was in Manhattan, and *I* wrinkled *my* nose at the prospect of going across the bridge.

"My fee," I told him, "is twenty dollars an hour, plus expenses."

"My backers will pay it."

"I'll need a retainer," I said, firmly.

He wrinkled his nose and took out a checkbook. He signed with a flourish of loops and circles. It was a lavender check for three hundred and twenty dollars. Sixteen hours' work. I wondered if he expected those hours to be spread over two days. I've been known to work on a case like this for four hours a day, or

even two, in which case it stretched out. It depended on whether
or not I had other cases.

Which, at the moment, I did not.

Accepting the check I asked, "What about her friends?"

"What about them?"

"Who are they?"

"How should I know that? I don't socialize with the girl, for
heaven's sake," he said, as if the very thought of socializing with
a *woman* was appalling. "As for the other girls in the show, you
can come to the theater and I'll introduce you."

"Where are you rehearsing?"

He wrinkled his nose again.

"We simply could not get a theater in Manhattan, so we're
using an old movie theater in Bay Ridge. Do you know where Bay
Ridge is?"

"I can find it," I said, with my tongue in my cheek.

He gave me the address, a small theater on Third Avenue.

"When will you come down?"

"Are you rehearsing today?"

"Well, of *course*. That's where I should be *now*."

I checked my watch. Twelve-forty.

"After I check out the girl's apartment I'll come right over.
What's her name, by the way?"

"Oh, of course," he said, almost simpering, "how silly of us.
Her name is Amy Butterworth."

"What does she look like?"

"Oh, I'm terrible at describing *women*. I can do men much more
easily."

I believed him.

I smiled and said, "Give it your best shot."

"Let me see," he said, looking at the ceiling. "She's about
twenty-two, built rather petitely except for her breasts, which are
rather large for a girl her size. She's just right for the part, you
know, virginal, but with a touch of wanton, do you know what I
mean?"

"I believe so."

"She has blond hair, long," he said, touching his shoulders,
"blue eyes, and she laughs a lot. Does that help?"

"It'll do. I'll probably drop by the theater somewhere around
three, after I've been to her place and talked to the police."

"The police?" he said, alarmed. "Oh dear, we shouldn't have
any bad publicity."

"I'm just going to check with them and see if she's . . . turned up, anywhere, like in a hospital."

"Oh, I see. That makes sense."

"Thank you."

He rose and extended his hand for me to shake. I had already done that when he arrived, and I dreaded doing it again. He was tall, about six-one, but very thin, like a blade of pink-and-lavender grass. His eyes were a pale gray and slightly watery and he seemed as if he'd be the nervous type even under normal circumstances. His handshake hadn't gotten any firmer since his arrival, when it had felt like a warm, moist dishrag.

"Thank you ever so much, Mr. Delvecchio," he gushed, pumping my hand. I hate men who gush. "I'm sure my cast is just going to love you, but remember—my business before your pleasure, eh?" he said, trying in his own way to be slightly bawdy—I think.

"I'll keep that in mind."


## 2


The girl who opened Amy Butterworth's door had long dark hair, elegantly thin red lips, and two of the biggest breasts I'd ever seen. I got a real good look at them, too, because she was wearing a thin T-shirt on which someone had stenciled the words "Fly Me." Below that she was wearing tight designer jeans, no shoes, and red nail polish on her toes.

The apartment was on West Fifty-sixth Street in Manhattan, and I'd had to walk up four flights of stairs to knock on the door. I was acutely aware of the fact that I was soaking wet from perspiration, not all of it from exertion. I was experiencing the usual heebie-jeebies from crossing the bridge from Brooklyn to "the City."

"Hello," she said, cheerfully. "Can I help you?"

"Soon as I get my breath back you can," I said.

"You'll have to do better than that before I invite a strange man into my apartment," she said, thinking it was a compliment.

"The climb," I said, panting.

"Oh."

"And this heat doesn't help, either. Why don't they air-condition these halls?"

"Are you kidding? I had to buy my own window air conditioner."

I could feel the cool air coming out of her apartment, feeling cooler yet on my wet face.

"My name is Delvecchio, Nick Delvecchio. I'm a private investigator looking for Amy Butterworth."

"Do you have some I.D.?" she asked, like a true New Yorker.

I showed it to her and she stepped back and said, "All right, come on in and cool off."

"Thank you."

I entered and she shut the door behind us. She was tall, about five-nine in her bare feet. With heels she would be taller than me.

"I'm Amy's roommate. What's this about?"

"Have you seen her lately? Over the past few days?"

"No, I haven't seen her for three or four days, but that's not unusual."

"Oh? Why not? Does she stay away for days at a time?"

"No, I'm a stew."

"Pardon?"

"A stewardess—or flight attendant, as they now call us. I haven't been in town for days. I just got back today from London. Has something happened to her?"

"I hope not. May I sit down?"

"Oh, sure, sorry, please," she said, nervously. "My name's Lucy, Lucy Mills."

"Nick Delvecchio," I said.

"Can I ask who hired you to look for Amy, and why?"

"Sure. Do you know George Vanguard?"

"The playwright?"

"Yes. He's the man who hired me. Seems Amy hasn't shown up for rehearsals for two days, and he's worried."

"About his play, I'll bet."

"That may be, but he did hire me."

"He's a fag," she said with distaste. "He probably hassled Amy and she took off for a couple of days."

"You're not worried, then?"

"No," she said, shrugging. "She's an actress, isn't she? And she's everything an actresss should be: temperamental, sensitive, and a little nutty. She'll be back."

"Well, if you don't mind," I said, handing her one of the business cards I'd just had printed up. All they had on them was

my name, my occupation, and home phone. "If she shows up
within the next couple of days, would you give me a call?"

"I'm flying out again tomorrow night, but if she shows by then
I'll call you."

"I appreciate it."

She walked me to the door and said, "When I get back why
don't I check in with you again and see if you've found her. If not,
you might want to talk to me again."

I wondered if it would be presumptuous of me to read
something else into her offer. I figured I'd just have to wait and
see.

"That'd be fine," I said, and left.

## 3

Before going to the theater I called a detective in Missing
Persons I used to work with when I first became a cop. I asked if
they had anything on an Amy Butterworth, or anyone who fit her
description. Their listing was citywide, and if she'd been in a
hospital or morgue in any of the boroughs, they would have
known about it.

They didn't, which meant she wasn't in one of those places—or
maybe just not yet.

I got to the theater a little after three and rehearsals were in full
swing. I took a seat about halfway down and watched for a while,
waiting for an opening. It was hot as hell in there, and obvious
the air-conditioning was out of order. Still, I felt a lot better just
being back in Brooklyn.

"I won't tell them why you're here," Vanguard said, sitting next
to me. "You can do that individually."

"Fine."

"Until you speak to them privately, they'll probably just assume
that you're another backer."

"Good enough."

"Lord, I wish they'd fix the air-conditioning in here," he
bitched.

"It could be worse," I said. "We could be in Florida in July
instead of New York."

"True."

A woman started up the aisle toward us and Vanguard started

to get up, saying in a low tone, "Maybe I'd better introduce you to my director."

"Nick Delvecchio," he said aloud, "this is my assistant director, Sherry Logan."

"Mr. Delvecchio," she said, extending her hand as a man would.

Her grip was surprisingly firm. She was auburn-haired, with green eyes and a wide, full-lipped mouth. She reminded me very much of an actress I had seen in a private-eye movie my friend Billy Palmer had showed me, once. The film was called *P.J.*, and the actress's name was Gayle Hunnicut.

Unlike the actress, however, she was not tall—maybe five-four—and she was slim and small-breasted. Her mouth was very sensuous; the upper and lower lip were of equal fullness. A tendril of hair was plastered to her forehead by perspiration.

I placed her age at about twenty-eight, but she could have gone a couple of years in either direction with no problem. What with her job I figured her for closer to thirty than not.

"I'm pleased to meet you, Mr. Delvecchio. Are you interested in the theater?"

"Not particularly. Theater people, yes, but not the theater itself. I have to meet a few of the people here, but perhaps we could talk later, say over dinner?"

She frowned at my abrupt offer and asked, "About what?" She was polite, because she still wasn't sure that I wasn't a backer.

"Oh, about theater people."

Her puzzled frown turned shrewd.

"Anyone in particular?"

I handed her one of my cards and said, "Amy Butterworth."

She read the card and turned to Vanguard. "Oh, George, you didn't."

"I certainly did," he replied haughtily. "Cooperate with him, Sherry. Let me introduce him around and then you can talk to him."

"If you don't mind," I added. I didn't want her to be hostile.

She looked at me, parting her full lips and tapping her front teeth with my card.

"No, I guess I don't mind. I'll wait for you, Mr. Delvecchio, but this dinner is going to cost you."

"That's okay," I said, "I'm on an expense account."

Vanguard frowned, and then led me toward the stage. He introduced me around without saying who and what I was, and I could tell by the polite reception that he'd been right about everyone assuming I was a backer.

The male lead in the play was a fairly young, tall, slim, somewhat effeminate-looking man named Harry Wilkens. His handshake was firmer than Vanguard's, but not as firm as Sherry Logan's.

The second lead was a huskier man who seemed a bit old to be second lead actor in an off-Broadway play. His name was Jack Dwyer and he studied me long enough to make me uncomfortable. I had the feeling he wasn't accepting me for what I appeared to be.

Next I met the other two virgins.

Linda Pollard was a petite blonde with light blue eyes and a small mouth, kind of like Lana Turner when she was real young. She was extremely slim and delicate looking and—if her breasts hadn't been so small—she could have fit Amy Butterworth's description.

The other virgin was quite different; probably, I figured, by design. Her name was Onaly O'Toole, and I had to have that repeated to me before I understood that it was her stage name.

"I was an on-aly child," she said, as if she'd been explaining it for years.

She had the blackest hair I've ever seen, worn long and parted in the center. She was tall, about five-eight, and had an arresting face. Her eyes were brown and set just a bit too far apart. Her nose was too big, but not so much so that it would hamper her career any. She was as full-breasted as Linda Pollard was petite. *Virgin* was the last word that would come to mind to describe Onaly O'Toole.

It was obvious that this was not a dress rehearsal, as virtually all of these people were wearing T-shirts and jeans.

"Those are our lead players," Vanguard said after the intros had been made. "Now that they've met you they won't question your presence in the theater. You can talk to them now or at your convenience, just please keep in mind that there is a time limit. This is Wednesday. If you can't find Amy in time for Saturday rehearsal, I'm going to have to replace her."

"I understand."

He stepped away into the center of the stage and clapped his hands, reminding me very much of a teacher I'd had in the third grade. Thinking back, I could swear that he'd been gay, too.

I became aware of a presence behind me at that point and turned to find Sherry Logan.

"I don't mind an early dinner," she said.

"Doesn't he . . ."

"George can handle this himself. Besides, I want to talk about Amy."

"Why?"

"I want this show to go on without a hitch," she said. "It's important to me. Helping you find Amy can accomplish that."

"All right," I said, "an early dinner, it is."

## 4

She took me to a restaurant in the area—an air-conditioned restaurant—and after we ordered a couple of iced teas she said, "So tell me how I can help you?"

"Do you know Amy well?"

"Not very well. We've worked together once or twice before, but we're not what you'd call friends."

"Had she ever done a disappearing act any of those other times you worked with her?"

"Let me think." The waitress brought our drinks. "I'm sure she missed a rehearsal or two on occasion, but I wouldn't say it was a habit with her."

"Do you know any of her hangouts?"

"Only the usual theater places," she said, mentioning a few. "Some of the others might know something more specific."

"Who are her friends in the show? Who is she close to?"

"Linda," she said, without hesitation. "Linda and Amy are *very* close."

"I think you're trying to tell me something without telling me something," I said.

She smiled and said, "You really are a detective."

"Are you telling me that Linda and Amy were an item?"

"Well, it's pretty common knowledge that Linda and Amy were—are—lovers."

"You're sure of that?"

"They don't flaunt it, but yes, I'm sure."

"Is Vanguard aware of this?"

"Georgie is only aware of his performers as performers, not as people."

"Well then, I guess my next step is to talk to Linda."

"Take it easy on her, Nick," she said, using my first name very easily. "She's very young, and she's as fragile as she appears to be."

"Isn't that a hazard in your business?"

"Yes," she said, as our dinner arrived.

We talked about other things: my former profession as a boxer, and hers as an actress, before she decided to "switch sides," as she put it. This was actually her first chance to direct on her own—although it hardly seemed that way to me. She said that Vanguard was taking a big chance with her.

"It'll keep his budget down," she explained, being realistic. She seemed to have both feet firmly planted on the ground, and I liked that about her.

"As producer and author, Georgie will always be around with his two cents anyway, but I really am grateful for the opportunity he's given me."

"I wish you luck."

"Thank you."

"Can you tell me anything about the other people in the show?"

"Personal things, you mean?"

"That's what I mean, all right. What about Harry Wilkens? Is he involved with anyone? Or Onaly O'Toole?"

"Isn't that a great name?" she asked. "Her real name's Ann, but Onaly is a wonderful stage name." She shook her head and got back to my question. "Onaly keeps to herself, so I can't help you there—but Harry?" she said, smiling. "Georgie and Harry are *very, very* close."

"I see."

"Jack is this guy from the Midwest who was recommended to Georgie. I don't know much about him."

"I'll just have to ask him, then."

"There's only one thing I do know about him for sure."

"What's that?"

"He's not gay. He's been after me since we first met."

"Has he caught you?"

"Can I tell you anything else?"

"Yes," I said, "tell me about this play."

## 5

I got Linda's address from Sherry and decided to go and see her after our early dinner. The fact that Sherry insisted she go straight home—where her work awaited—certainly had a bearing on my decision.

"I'll see you tomorrow at the theater," she said, and we went our separate ways.

It was after six, but the heat was persisting.

Linda Pollard lived in an apartment on the Upper East Side of Manhattan, one that she should have had trouble paying for if she did not have a roommate, a rich daddy, or a sugar daddy. From what Sherry had told me about Amy and Linda, though, the latter seemed remote.

When she answered the door I had to explain who I was before she recognized me.

"I'm sorry," she said, frowning, "but what are you doing here?"

"I'd like to come in and talk to you, if I may."

Her eyes widened and she said, "I'm sorry, mister . . . ?"

"Delvecchio."

"I'm sorry, but maybe one of the other girls would—I mean, I don't—"

"You don't understand. I want to talk to you about Amy."

"Do you know Amy?" she asked. "Do you know where she is?" Her tone was desperate.

"No, but I'm looking for her." I took out my I.D. and showed it to her. "Vanguard hired me to try and find her."

"A private detective," she said, frowning at the card.

"May I come in?" I asked again, and this time she nodded and backed away from the door.

"Miss Pollard—"

"Linda, please."

"Linda . . . when was the last time you saw Amy?"

"We went shopping together three days ago."

"Where?"

"Oh, Fifth Avenue, Thirty-fourth Street, like that. Amy doesn't have any money, but I get some from . . . from home, so we shopped and I bought her something."

"And after that?"

"We had dinner, and then we went home. We had an early call the next morning."

"When you say you went home, does that mean . . ."

"She went to her apartment, and I came here."

"I see."

"She didn't show up the next day, or yesterday. I'm real worried. She really wanted this part. She wouldn't walk away from it, Mr. Delvecchio, not willingly."

I started to say "I see" again, but stopped myself and just nodded.

"Was anyone bothering her lately?"

"Georgie was yelling at her, but he does that sometimes."

"No, I mean were there any men following her, or calling her?"

"No, not that she mentioned."

"Would she have mentioned it to you?"

"Oh, definitely, either to me or Lucy. That's her roommate."

"I've met her." I hadn't asked her that question, though. It was as good a reason to go back as any.

"Amy didn't talk about leaving town?"

"She'd never leave, Mr. Delvecchio—"

"Nick."

"She wants to be an actress so much. This part meant *everything* to her."

This time I did say "I see," and immediately grimaced.

"Is there somewhere she would go if something was bothering her?"

"If something was bothering her, she'd come to me . . . Nick."

I stood and said, "Well, thank you for your help, Miss—Linda."

"If you find her, you'll let me know?"

"Yes, and if you hear from her, call me at this number," I said, giving her one of my cards. "Oh, by the way. Does she have any family in town?"

"She has no family anywhere, Nick. Neither of us do. That's why we became such good friends."

I nodded and said, "Thanks, Linda."

"Please," she said, grabbing my arm, "find her."

"I'm going to do my best."

I went home from Linda Pollard's apartment and ran into Sam in front of the building. Sam is Samantha Karson, my neighbor

across the hall. She's a romance writer who uses the name "Kit"
Karson on her books. A pale blonde who reminds me of a prettier
Sissy Spacek, she invited me to have a drink with her, and I
accepted. We went to a place that had opened up nearby called
the Can-U-Drop-Inn and sat at the bar.

"What do you know about the theater?" I asked her.

"Nothing."

"Big help."

"I try," she said.

I told her about the case and she listened quietly. She was real
good at listening. She wanted to break into the mystery field, and
she saw me as the source of her plots.

I finished my beer and climbed down off my stool.

"Going?"

I nodded. "I'm wiped. This heat wrings me out."

"Working tonight?" she asked.

I shook my head. "I'll go back to the theater in the morning and
talk to everyone. There's no point in pussyfooting around this
thing. If any of them know where she is, they'll tell me. If they
don't, it'll hold up the show."

"Good luck. I'm going to have another drink and get to know
the bartender."

"Why?" I asked. "This place will be closed in a month."

She shrugged and said, "I need a couple of drinks before I get
to work tonight."

Sam did most of her writing at night. Sometimes, if I listen real
hard, I can hear her typewriter going at three in the morning.

"Okay," I said. "I'll see you sometime tomorrow."

"I'll be in after three."

I nodded, shook hands, and went out into the waning heat. By
eight or nine o'clock, maybe it would even be down to eighty.


# 6

The next morning I had breakfast and headed for the theater.
When I got there, all the doors were open and the people inside
were complaining.

"Not only is it the heat," someone up on the stage was yelling,
"but now we've got this smell."

Vanguard called back petulantly, "I've opened the windows and doors. What more do you want?"

"Get somebody in here to find out what that smell is." I saw now that it was Onaly O'Toole who was complaining.

"Onaly—"

"God," she said, "it smells like something curled up in a corner and died."

I was halfway down the aisle now and the smell hit me. I stopped short, took a wary breath, and my stomach sank.

"George," I said.

He turned and saw me, waved a hand for me to wait.

"Vanguard!" I said, moving to him and grabbing his arm.

"What is it?"

"Get everyone out of here."

"What?"

"Out!" I said. "Get everyone out . . . now!"

"Why?"

"Take a deep breath, George."

He did and said, "I smell it, for heaven's sake; what can I do—"

"Get everyone out and I'll find out what the smell is. If it's what I think it is . . ." Actually, I knew what it was because I'd smelled it plenty of times when I was a cop.

"Oh my Lord," he said, his eyes widening.

"Exactly. Now come on, get everyone outside."

"All right, people," he shouted, "take five. Everyone outside."

The complaints started, but he was doing a good job of herding them out. As he passed me on his own way out I stopped him again.

"George, who's not here?"

"Uh, Dwyer, Jack Dwyer. He's not here yet, but I assumed he was just late."

"Where's the smell coming from?"

"There's a stairway backstage—stage right—that goes downstairs. It seems to be coming from there."

"What's down there?"

"It's used for storage."

"Okay. Go outside and wait for me."

He nodded and turned away, and I heard him say, "Linda, come on, love; let's go outside. You don't want to stay in here . . ."

". . . looking for my purse . . ."

The rest of what they were saying got lost as I made my way to

the stage. I hopped up and went backstage. I made like
Snagglepuss—"Exit, staaage right!"—and found the stairway.

He was right. The smell was stronger here, and was rising. I
went downstairs, breathing as shallowly as possible. I knew that
a civilian would be choking by now. I found myself in a small
hallway with two doors on the right and one on the left, directly
under the stage.

I checked the two on the right and found small storage rooms.
The smell was no stronger in either of them. That left the door
under the stage.

When I opened it I was hit first by a wave of air that might have
been coming from a furnace, and then by the smell. I took out my
handkerchief, held it over my mouth, and went inside.

I found her fairly easily. Someone had piled debris on top of
her, but the smell and insect activity led me right to her.

Whoever had killed her and put her down there had probably
figured to come back eventually and move her. What they hadn't
counted on was the air-conditioning going on the fritz. Amy—if it
was Amy, and I felt sure it was—had swelled up like a balloon
and done what a balloon does when it's filled too much. She was
as ripe as they come.

When I was on the job and we were called to the scene of a
D.O.A. what we usually did was drop a handful of coffee into a
frying pan. In moments the strong smell of burning coffee would
help dilute the odor of the corpse. I knew some cops who could
eat their lunch in the same room while waiting for the M.E. and
never miss a swallow. I wasn't one of them.

I turned to leave and saw her in the doorway.

"Linda," I said.

"My God," she said, "it smells terrible."

"Didn't expect that, did you?" I asked.

She had one hand over her mouth. In her other was a .22
caliber revolver.

"Where did you get the gun, Linda?"

"My father gave it to me when I told him I was moving to New
York. I carry it with me everywhere."

"And how did you come to use it on Amy?"

"We had a fight."

"Over . . . someone else?"

"I see you've heard the stories," she said, bitterly. "Amy and I
weren't lovers. In fact, we were hardly even friends. We just had
a lot in common."

"What changed that?"

"When she got the role as the first virgin, and I got the role as the third."

"And the second?"

"Onaly."

"What happened between you and Amy?"

"She got uppity when she landed the role of first virgin. That night we stayed to go over some lines, and we got into a fight. She said I was third virgin because I had third-virgin talent."

"That wasn't fair."

"No, it wasn't. I told her I could very easily be second virgin. She sneered and said the only way I could do that was if Onaly died."

"And you showed her different, didn't you?"

"That's right, I did," Linda Pollard said. "I showed her that I could move up by her dying."

"And how would you have moved up to first virgin, Linda? By killing Onaly?"

"I wouldn't kill Onaly," she said, staring at me strangely. "She's a nice girl."

"And Amy wasn't."

"No," Linda Pollard said. "She was a snot."

"Did you drag her down here by yourself?"

"I dragged her to the stairs and pushed her down, then pulled her in here and covered her. I didn't know where else to put her!"

Her eyes were tearing now from the smell, as mine were. I was so wet from perspiration that I felt as if I were standing in a pool.

"Come on, Linda. Let's go upstairs."

"No," she said, choking a bit, "you'll tell them."

"I'll have to."

"No!"

"Are you going to kill me, too?" I asked. My stomach was one big knot, waiting for her to pull the damned trigger.

"I . . . don't know."

She coughed then and I said, "Let's get out of here so we can talk, Linda."

"No, no!"

"Linda—"

I'd never seen anyone with such vacant eyes before. I knew she was going to fire and that there was nothing I could do about it. I leaped for her anyway, just as an arm came through the doorway behind her and a hand took hold of her arm as she squeezed the trigger. Jack Dwyer pushed her arm up and her shot went into the ceiling. He reached around with his other hand and twisted the gun away from her.

"Jesus Christ," he said, "let's get out of here!"

## 7

Dwyer had indeed arrived late and, when he saw everyone outside and smelled the scent of a ripe one, he knew what was going on. He asked Vanguard about it, and George had told him that I'd gone downstairs to find the source of the smell. As it turned out, he was an ex-cop, too, as well as sometime actor and sometime P.I. It was just coincidence that he happened to land this role, so that he could be around to save my life. He'd told George to call the police, and come downstairs after me.

He told me all this at the Can-U-Drop-Inn over a beer, after the police had come and taken Linda Pollard away. Vanguard gave everyone the day off so that the theater could be cleared of the smell, and maybe even get the AC fixed.

"Why did she go down there?" Dwyer wondered aloud.

"I guess she was afraid I'd find the body."

"And it never occurred to her that that's what smelled?"

I shrugged and said, "I guess she'd never smelled a ripe one before, Jack. A lot of people haven't had that pleasure. Speaking of ripe ones, what'll happen to the show now?"

"I guess Vanguard will find himself two more virgins," Dwyer answered.

"And what about you?"

"I've about had it with this show. Vanguard's a prima donna, the leading man's gay, Onaly's number one virgin now, and she can't act worth a damn. I think I'll head back home."

"That means he'll have to replace you, too."

"That shouldn't be too hard. Mine wasn't much of a part, anyway." He swirled the beer at the bottom of his bottle and said, "They never are."

"Well," I said, "you've got my vote for performer of the year, the way you performed in that basement. I can't give you a Tony Award, but I can buy you another drink."

"Well," he said fatalistically, "I guess that's a start."

# JAMES M. REASONER

## THE SAFEST PLACE
## IN THE WORLD

*James Reasoner and his wife, L.J. Washburn, represent the
first husband-and-wife team to appear in a PWA anthology.
They also represent two very special writing talents.*

*James's 1980 first novel* **Texas** **Wind** *(which introduced his
Texas P.I. "Cody") has become something of a cult classic, and
is to be reprinted by Black Lizard Books. Cody appears here in
a PWA anthology for the first time.*

The eye squinting at me over the sights of the automatic weapon
was pale gray and insane. One burst would just about cut me in
half.

The things a private eye gets into for his clients . . .

It began simply enough. All I would have to do, Connie Lamb
had said, was make friends with her ex-husband Roy. Roy had
legal custody of their son Jeremy, and Connie wanted to get the
boy back before Roy turned him into a killer.

She was pretty upset when she came into my office on Camp
Bowie Boulevard, on the west side of Fort Worth on the edge of
the museum district. Sensing that just being in a private investigator's office was adding to her nervousness, I took her a couple
of doors down the street to an ice cream place and calmed her
down over a couple of bowls of Fudge Ripple. It was summer,
after all, and what could be more soothing than a bowl of good ice
cream?

"Roy didn't have any trouble getting custody," Connie said.
"He did find me in bed with another man, after all. And I don't
have the greatest background in the world." Her spoon rattled
against the bowl as she put it down. "Before I was married I did a

lot of drugs and got busted for it a few times. I just thank God I didn't mess up my chromosomes and stuff. Jeremy was always a healthy little kid."

His mother was pretty healthy, too, I thought. She was a tall brunette, her hair cut fairly short, and though she had to be in her early thirties she looked ten years younger than that. Her figure was striking, to say the least, especially in tight blue jeans and a sleeveless jersey top. I told myself sternly that I should not be thinking semilecherous thoughts about a potential client in distress.

"Roy's lawyer brought all of that up, of course," she was saying. "I never had a chance. And naturally he made Roy sound like Ward Cleaver or somebody. It was disgusting." She looked out the window toward the traffic passing by on Camp Bowie, but I don't think she was seeing the cars. "I never had a chance. He's a goddamned *accountant*, after all."

I waited a moment, then asked, "How old is Jeremy now?"

"He's twelve. Roy's had him since he was nine. I guess Roy thought he wasn't old enough to brainwash until now."

"Brainwash is a strong word," I pointed out. "I suppose all parents try to mold their children in one way or another."

"He's taking Jeremy with him to that camp on weekends! He's taking him out there and teaching him how to kill!"

The ice cream parlor was doing brisk business on a hot afternoon like that one, and several people turned to look at our table. Connie's voice wasn't loud, but it carried a lot of intensity. I said, "Take it easy. I can understand you wanting to get your son back. Maybe I can help you."

"You can. If you can just get proof that Roy's getting Jeremy involved with all that paramilitary crap, I'm sure any judge would give him back to me."

I had an image in my mind of a twelve-year-old in fatigues and helmet, carrying an M-16. Maybe she had a point. A lot of judges I knew wouldn't look kindly on that sort of parental influence. If she could prove that she had cleaned up her act and wasn't sleeping around or doing drugs, she could stand a good chance of regaining custody.

"Tell me more about Roy," I said.

It was a common enough picture: Roy Lamb was an accountant, as she had told me, and worked at the livestock exchange for one of the cattle companies headquartered there. During the week he fit the stereotypical mild-mannered image of his profes-

THE SAFEST PLACE IN THE WORLD

sion. It was only on the weekends that he became a raving gun-
nut, to hear her tell it. He and some friends of his gathered out in
the boonies in Wise County, northwest of Fort Worth, and shot off
their rifles and machine guns, practiced military maneuvers, and
generally prepared themselves to survive once the godless
Communists came in and took over the United States.

"He thinks he's going to be a damned guerrilla fighter," Connie
said bitterly. "Either that, or the Russians will drop the bomb and
he'll be a survivalist. He's got his basement stocked with all kinds
of survival gear and food, and he's talking about buying a place
out in the country and building an underground bunker. Then
he'll move all the stuff out there. I tell you, Mr. Cody, it's kind of
scary."

"Was your husband like that before you married him?"

Connie shook her head. "It started about five years ago. I put
up with it for a couple of years, thinking that maybe Roy would
grow out of it. It was almost like he was a little kid playing soldier.
But he never changed. I was going to divorce him, but well, he
kind of got the goods on me first, if you know what I mean."

I knew what she meant, all right. And I wasn't sure that Jeremy
Lamb wouldn't be just as well off with his father as with her. That
wasn't my decision to make, though. My job was just to gather
evidence and turn it over to her. After that it was all up to her and
her ex-husband and the judicial system.

"Will you take the case?" she asked, staring pitifully across the
empty ice cream bowl at me.

"I'll look into it for you," I told her. I quoted her my daily rate
and she nodded and reached for her purse.

"I'll give you a check," she said.

"Let's walk back down to the office. We'll fill out a contract, and
you can give me a retainer then."

Back in the office, the business taken care of, she stood up and
extended a hand to me. I shook it, still vaguely uncomfortable
after all these years about shaking hands with women, and told
her I'd call her when I had something to report. She had already
given me Roy Lamb's address and phone number and told me
where he worked. All that information was written down in my
notebook. We were through for now, and I should have been
ready to go to work.

Her hand was cool and soft, though, and as she smiled at me
across the desk and said, "I know this will all work out," I knew
distinctly that I didn't want her to go yet. I wanted to come up

with some reason for her to stay a little longer, so that I could talk
to her and look into her dark brown eyes.

I kept my mouth shut and let out a sigh of relief when the door
shut behind her. The appeal she had been oozing had probably
been totally unconscious on her part, but I knew one thing.

I was too damned old for that sort of stuff.

Cowtown, the city where the West begins. That's what they used
to call Fort Worth. Still do, in the chamber of commerce
brochures. And the name is authentic enough. The Old West is
still alive in the spirit of the town, even after the influx of Yankees
during the seventies and eighties. The livestock industry has been
a vital part of the economy for over a hundred years.

But in some parts of town, Fort Worth is the city where the
Hype begins.

I sat in a restaurant in the Stockyards area and watched the
tourists in newly bought Stetsons as they gawked at longhorns
mounted on the walls and sat on bar stools shaped like saddles. I
was in a booth next to the wall, drinking dark beer and waiting for
Roy Lamb.

The livestock exchange building was only a few blocks away,
and Connie had told me that Roy often had lunch here. The day
before I had followed the same routine, but he hadn't shown up.

Today he did. He came in about ten minutes after noon,
wearing a suit and carrying a small briefcase. He was alone, so
maybe he planned on getting a little work done while he ate. He
was a little over six feet, with the beginnings of a paunch. His
light brown hair was carefully styled and brushed, and the
horned-rim glasses he wore were just the right touch with the
conservative gray suit. Just like Connie had described him. He
looked honest. I might have even trusted him with my money.

Of course, his honesty wasn't what was in question.

He cooperated by sitting at one of the tables between the bar
and the wall, where he would have a good view of the booth
where I was waiting. He set his briefcase down on the red-and-
white-checked tablecloth and sprung it open, taking out a sheaf of
papers. A waitress came over, and he ordered quickly, without
consulting a menu.

I picked up one of the magazines I had brought with me and
opened it up, holding it so that the cover was visible. I sipped my
beer and began reading an article about combat shotguns and

how they were perfect weapons for defending your family when it came time to ensure their survival.

I didn't look at Roy Lamb as I read.

I made it through that article and a couple of others on how to build a radiation detector from items you could find in an ordinary kitchen or some such, while Roy Lamb ate a chef's salad and drank a glass of iced tea. It looked like he wasn't going to pay any attention to me, and I was starting to wonder how many days I might have to do this.

But then he put his papers back in the briefcase, closed it, stood up. His eyes lit on the cover of the magazine, and he smiled.

A couple of steps brought him over beside my booth, and he said, "Say, I hate to bother you, but isn't that the new issue?"

I looked over the top of the magazine, keeping my face neutral, and said, "What? Oh, the magazine. Yeah, I just picked it up."

"I subscribe. My copy must be late this month. Hell of a magazine, isn't it?"

I laid the magazine down on the table, keeping my place with a finger. "Sure is," I agreed. "Lots of good information. We'd be better off if more people knew what was going on in the world."

"That's the truth," he said emphatically. He stuck out his hand. "Roy Lamb."

I shook hands and told him my name, then gestured at the other magazines on the seat beside me. "You read these, too?"

He leaned over slightly so that he could see their titles. "You bet. They're good magazines."

I nodded to the seat on the other side of the table. "You're welcome to look at these if you want. They're all new issues, and I'm just killing time waiting for a guy."

"Well . . ." Roy looked at his watch, and for a second I thought he was going to say that he had to get back to work. But then he said, "I don't have to get back right away. I got some work done while I was eating, so I think I can justify taking a few minutes off."

The few minutes turned out to be almost half an hour. He sat across from me and let me buy him another glass of iced tea, though he turned down my offer of a beer. We hit it off right away, flipping through the magazines and making comments on the articles. I'm no weapons expert, but you can't be in my line of work and not know something about guns, so I was able to keep up with what he was saying and add some remarks of my own. Anyway, Roy did most of the talking.

He was everything that Connie had told me he was. On the surface, a normal, likable guy, but his interest in guns bordered on passion. And his politics followed right along with the philosophies of the magazines. It all came down to us versus the Russians and us versus the subversive elements in our own country who wanted to bring us down. Of course, it was always possible that a great natural disaster, like the shifting of the earth's magnetic poles, would come along first and plunge the world into chaos, beating World War III to the punch.

Whatever catastrophe happened, it was going to be up to the average man to be prepared to defend himself and his family. To *survive* . . .

And I couldn't say, even to myself, that he was necessarily wrong. Something about his attitude made me a little uncomfortable, though. It was like he was anxious for something to happen, so that he could demonstrate just how well prepared he was.

You can make friends in a hurry if you get a man to talking about his hobby. By the time Roy had to get back to the livestock exchange building we were buddies, at least in his eyes. I told him I had lunch there frequently, and he said that he did, too. Even as I said, "Maybe we'll run into each other again," I knew damn well that we would.

That was a Tuesday. By Thursday night, when Connie Lamb called me wanting to know how things were progressing, I had had lunch with Roy twice more. He had told me about his son and the breakup of his marriage, and I had heard all about how Connie cheated on him, neglecting him and Jeremy to run around with men she met in bars. As I talked to Connie on the phone, I could hear talking and laughter and hard-driving music in the background, and I thought it was safe to assume she wasn't home studying her Sunday-school lesson.

None of my business.

I assured her that the job was going well. I had dropped a few hints already about wishing I could find a group in the area who thought the way I did, and Roy had said noncommittally that he had heard of such a group. I was sure that he was just checking with the leaders to make sure it was all right before he told me about it.

"Be sure you let me know what happens. They'll be going out to their camp this weekend. I'm certain of that. They always do."

"I'll keep you advised," I told her.

She partially covered the phone and yelled at somebody to hold on, that she was almost through, then said, "Thanks again, Mr. Cody. You don't know how much this means to me."

I told her she was welcome and hung up. I was earning my money on this one.

At lunch the next day, Roy was excited. Maybe it was the prospect of the weekend, maybe it was the fact that he was going to recruit a new member for his group.

"I spoke to some friends of mine," he told me, "some guys I go out in the field to train with. They said I could bring you with me this weekend."

"You're talking about organized survival training?" I asked.

"That's right. We rent a place out in the country, an old farm with about two hundred acres of land. It makes a great staging area."

"Military maneuvers?" I kept my voice down.

Roy nodded. "We've got a target range and an obstacle course and plenty of room for war games. It's quite a setup."

"Who runs it?"

"The commander is a man named Brian Hayes. He was a Green Beret colonel in 'Nam. Great guy. He's an expert in everything from demolitions to unarmed combat."

"Sounds great," I said enthusiastically. "What do I have to do to join?"

"Well, one of the troop has to sponsor you, but that's no problem. I'll be your sponsor. You come out this weekend and take part, and we see if you fit into the group. If you do, that's all there is to it. If for some reason you don't like it, well, there's no hard feelings. There are just a couple of things."

"Like what?"

"It'll cost you a couple hundred dollars."

"For a weekend?" I tried to sound suitably put out.

"It's worth it, Cody. The group furnishes all the uniforms and equipment."

"Including weapons?"

He nodded. "If you don't have your own. A lot of the guys already have their own armaments."

"Well, that sounds a little more reasonable, if the fee covers all that. What's the other thing?"

"Just a little background info on you, mainly your place of employment."

I was ready for that question, even though it hadn't come up so

far in our conversations. A friend of mine who worked at one of
the downtown banks was prepared to tell anybody who asked
that I was part of their security force. I told Roy the same thing,
and he nodded happily. He would pass it along to someone
higher up in the group, probably this Brian Hayes who ran the
thing. If the checking up didn't go too deep—and I had a feeling it
wouldn't—my story would be accepted, and so would I.

"How do I get to the place?" I asked.

"I can come by and pick you up," Roy said. "That is, if you
don't mind riding up with me."

"Not at all. That sounds fine."

"That'll give you a chance to meet my son Jeremy. He'll be
going with us."

I smiled. "After all you've told me, I'm looking forward to
meeting him."

"Yeah, he's a great kid. Twelve years old. Just the right age to
start teaching him how to be a real man."

"Damn right," I said.

He left first, heading back to his office. I stayed where I was for
a long time, drinking beer and watching the tourists soak up the
phony Western culture.

Jeremy was fairly tall for his age, with a touch of the gangliness
that went with being twelve. His hair was blond and short, and
his face had a scattering of freckles. He shook hands with me and
said he was glad to meet me, and I did the same.

"Didn't I tell you he was a great kid?" Roy asked, parental pride
strong in his voice.

Jeremy rode in the backseat of Roy's Volvo. Roy drove northwest out of Fort Worth toward Decatur. It was a typical summer
Saturday, already hot enough to make you sweat if you were
outside more than a minute. The sky was high and clear, the air
almost bone-dry.

Just the kind of day to go out in the country and play war.

Roy talked quite a bit, obviously excited at the prospect of
training over the weekend. He already had his camouflage
fatigues on, as did Jeremy, and I could see that the mental image I
had had of the boy as I talked to his mother a few days before
hadn't been far wrong. There was something ridiculous about the
whole situation.

"How many members do you have?" I asked Roy as we drove
through a little town called Alvord. There was a nudist colony

nearby, I remembered, where one of my more embarrassing cases had taken me.

"We have forty in the group right now," Roy replied, "but it's growing all the time. Small but vital, that's us."

Forty members at two hundred dollars a head. That was eight thousand dollars every weekend. Not a bad business. It sounded like ex-colonel Brian Hayes might be cleaning up.

Jeremy hadn't said much. I half-turned in the seat and asked him, "You enjoy the training, Jeremy?"

"You bet," he said. "Dad's teaching me how to shoot, and Colonel Hayes has already taught us how to kill an enemy with our bare hands, three different ways!"

There was a disturbing amount of enthusiasm in his voice, and suddenly Connie Lamb's barhopping didn't sound so much like a bad influence.

Roy said, "It's important to be prepared for the dangerous times that are coming, of course, but you'll see that one of the best things about the camp is that you can put all the mundane little details of your everyday life in perspective. For instance, I've been working on a deal for my bosses all week that's been a real killer. They're buying a big herd up in Jack County, and I've been putting the figures together for them. You wouldn't believe how many details there are to consider in a hundred-thousand-dollar deal, especially when it's a cash sale. But I can put all that behind me while I'm training this weekend."

He rattled on some more, but I didn't pay much attention. As far as I could tell, Jeremy was healthy and well cared for, at least physically. Roy and I had never talked about how much money he made, but he had to be doing all right to afford four hundred dollars every weekend for the two of them to go out to the camp. I knew he loved the boy, and Jeremy seemed to like him. I could see why a judge had given custody to Roy in the divorce action.

If it wasn't for all the paramilitary survivalism, I would have said that Jeremy would be a lot better off staying right where he was.

But I just couldn't reconcile that thinking with teaching a twelve-year-old three different ways to kill with his bare hands.

Roy turned off the highway onto an asphalt-topped county road and followed that for several miles, then turned again onto a dirt road. After a mile or so, I noticed that the land to the left of the road was now fenced. A high chain-link fence, in fact, that looked like it should have been topped with barbed wire but wasn't.

"That must be the place," I said, nodding toward the fenced-off property.

Roy glanced at me. "How did you know?"

"Lucky guess." I shrugged. "Figured you'd want your privacy. That's why the fence is there, isn't it?"

"Survival training is serious business," he said solemnly. "We don't want any of the locals blundering in and getting hurt. We get enough bad publicity."

"Boy, that's the truth." I made my voice sound bitter. "Damned newspaper and TV reporters never get things right. They always make things sound worse than they are."

"You are absolutely right, Cody. I've got a feeling you and the colonel are going to get along just fine. You'll be a regular in the group before you know it."

There was an open gate in the fence a little farther on. Roy turned in there. I was a little surprised there was no guard on the gate, but I thought I saw movement in a clump of oaks nearby. A hidden guard? That was a possibility.

The narrow driveway led through more trees, across a little dry wash, and up a hill. The old farmhouse sat among trees at the top of the hill. There were a couple dozen cars parked around on the grass.

The farmhouse looked like it had been there a long time, but it had been restored. Either that, or it had been cared for with great diligence. The wooden siding on its walls appeared newly whitewashed. The trim was painted dark brown. There were two floors, and a big porch ran the entire width of the house. A small group of men sat there in rocking chairs, waiting for something.

The something must have been us, because the men stood up and came to the edge of the porch to greet us. In the lead was a man in his forties, tall and athletic, with sandy hair and a heavy moustache. He wore dark, aviator-style sunglasses. The other men were a little younger, but they were cut from the same mold. A couple had short, neat beards. All of them wore fatigues and looked like they had probably been born in them.

The leader snapped a casual salute, which Roy and Jeremy returned crisply. He said, "Mornin', Mr. Lamb, Jeremy. This the new man you told me about?"

"That's right, Colonel," Roy said. He quickly introduced us, and the leader turned out to be Brian Hayes, as I had suspected.

His handshake was hard, almost painful, and I let myself wince a little bit.

"Glad to meet you, Mr. Cody," Hayes said. "It's always a pleasure to meet another man who believes in good old-fashioned American values."

"Nothing wrong with being a good old-fashioned American," I said.

"Of course there's nothing wrong with that. You have the fee for the weekend, I believe?"

I pulled out my wallet, gave him nine twenties and two tens. He took the bills and passed them on to one of the other men. A slight smile tugged at his lips. "We'll get you all set up," he told me. "Roy, why don't you and Jeremy go on down to the staging area after you draw your weapons from the armory. The rest of us will be down shortly, and we can get underway."

Hayes and one of the other men took me into the house while the rest of them marched off somewhere. The place was well appointed, especially the huge dining room which had been made by knocking out some walls and combining rooms. It was paneled in dark wood, with animal heads mounted on the walls, along with a collection of antique weapons. The long table was massive, made of thick slabs of wood. There was something about it that reminded me of an ancient mead hall, where the Viking warriors could gather and carouse after a hard day of pillaging.

In the back part of the house was another large room lined with metal lockers that would have looked right at home in any junior high. I was told that I could leave my clothes and personal possessions there.

They outfitted me with a set of fatigues. I felt silly, but I tried not to let that show. Get into the spirit of things, that's what I had to do. Get in there and play soldier with the rest of them.

I got the feeling that Hayes and his cadre weren't playing, though.

The armory was behind the house and had been a barn at one time. One of the men who had been on the porch was waiting there for us. He issued me an M-16. I checked the magazine. Empty.

"You'll be issued ammo for target practice later," Hayes told me. He picked up a bulky weapon that looked more like a kid's toy. "For maneuvers, we use these. They fire paint balls. I'm sure you've heard of them."

I had. They were a standard part of all these civilian war games. I had to admit, though, I was a little surprised they didn't use regular weapons and blanks. The atmosphere around the place was serious, almost grim.

Almost like it was the real thing, and not just play.

I was starting to get a bad feeling about this setup. I told myself I'd seen too many hokey TV shows that used paramilitary groups as villains, read too many action novels in that same vein. But something sure as hell wasn't right.

We went down the hill to the staging area.

Nearly all the group must have been in attendance that weekend, because there were at least thirty-five men waiting for the training to get underway. I saw a few teenagers, but no one else as young as Jeremy. And there were no women there, either. That made sense, though. To their way of thinking, it was part of a man's duty to protect defenseless females.

The men were all shapes and sizes, but they had one thing in common. With the exception of Hayes and his lieutenants, all of them looked out of place in the camouflage fatigues. They were trying hard to look like hardened survivalists, but something about them just didn't cut it. They looked like accountants and merchants and computer salesmen wearing funny outfits. I watched them as one of Hayes's subordinates put us through several drills, and though the members of the troop tried hard and made the right moves, there was more than a touch of clumsiness about them.

Maybe in a year or so, these guys might shape up and become good civilian soldiers. Maybe. Until then, they were no threat to godless Communists or anybody but themselves.

And Hayes and his men never stopped praising them and telling them what good fighting men they were turning into.

It was a scam, all right, I decided as I went through the drills and workouts with the rest of them. I was willing to bet that Hayes owned this place and that most of the eight thousand bucks a week went right into his pocket. He and his buddies, probably all of them combat vets from the same unit, had set up this deal to bilk a bunch of average guys who wanted to play at being commandos and guerrilla fighters. Not a bad idea, and obviously successful.

The most interesting part was that I couldn't see one damn thing illegal about it.

Nobody had hired me to get the goods on ex-colonel Brian

Hayes, though. I could testify in court that Roy Lamb was taking his son to a survival training camp where he was being taught how to kill some hypothetical "enemy." That was the extent of my job.

In the meantime, though, I was stuck out here for the rest of the weekend.

Late Saturday morning, unarmed combat training came up on the schedule. So far, I had managed to blend in with the other guys, but now Hayes surprised me by calling my name. "You're a newcomer here, Mr. Cody," he said with a tight little smile, "so I'm sure you won't mind if we see just what you can do."

I shrugged my shoulders. "You're in charge, Colonel."

He nodded. "That's right, mister." He gestured at one of his men. "You and Lieutenant Starnes here can put on a demonstration for us."

Starnes was a whipcord-thin man of medium height, quite likely fast and mean. He grinned at me and stepped forward.

I wiped sweat off my forehead. Starnes was eight or ten years younger than me and quite a bit lighter. But I didn't want to back down. Stupid male pride, maybe.

I grinned right back at him and handed my empty M-16 to Roy Lamb, who was standing nearby. "Sure, be glad to," I said.

"Be careful, Cody," Roy whispered to me. "Starnes is good."

I just nodded and turned back to face the lieutenant.

"You can start it off, mister," he rasped at me.

I didn't wait any longer. I swung a roundhouse punch, telegraphing it badly.

He twisted and let my fist go by, then lashed out and chopped me in the side. Pain shot through me. I tried to turn around and block the next blow, but it slipped past my guard and drove into my belly. Air puffed out of my lungs, leaving me gasping.

I saw the arrogant grin on Starnes's face as he moved in for the kill. So far, I hadn't put up much of a fight.

That was the way I had intended for it to go. I wanted to look just as clumsy and ineffectual as the rest of the troop. But Starnes had hurt me, and he had enjoyed it. I forgot what I had planned and let my instincts take over.

The punch he aimed at my jaw found only air.

Instead of letting him polish me off, I drove inside, putting my shoulder into his belly and bulling him backward. His balance went and he fell, and I landed right on top of him. I brought my right elbow up under his chin, knocking his head back so that it bounced off the hard ground. His throat was wide open, and I could have crushed his larynx and left him there to suffocate slowly.

My brain started functioning again just in time, and I slipped awkwardly off his body, making it look like I lost my balance. He hit me savagely in the kidney, and the groan I let out was genuine. I rolled away as he tried to stomp me in the head.

Then two of the other lieutenants had hold of his arms, dragging him back, and Hayes was stepping forward with a grin on his face. "You see what happens when you lose your temper, men," he called out. "Cody had an advantage for a moment, but he lost it because he wasn't in control of his anger. You have to channel your emotion, make it work for you, rather than letting it take control of you."

I knew it was bullshit, and maybe he did, too. The only one who had lost control was Starnes.

I got up and brushed myself off, retrieving my rifle from Roy Lamb. Hayes went on with the training schedule, and the little incident between me and Starnes was quickly forgotten.

Almost forgotten. There was an ache in my side that kept reminding me when I moved wrong.

Lunch in the big dining room was simple fare, light because of the heat. We got a short rest period after we ate, and then it was back to work. In the middle of the afternoon, I got a chance to talk to Jeremy alone, as both of us took a five-minute break under the shade of an oak tree.

"You enjoy this kind of stuff, Jeremy?" I asked him.

"Sure." He shrugged. "It's fun, shooting and fighting and things like that. It's important, too. Besides, it gives me a chance to spend more time with my dad."

"What do you do during the week? Don't you go to ball games or anything like that?" My old-fashioned attitudes were cropping up again, but I couldn't help it.

Jeremy shook his head. "I have to spend a lot of my time studying, you know. And Dad's always busy with his work, or with things like checking our food supply and replenishing it."

I looked away from him and grimaced. He sure as hell didn't sound much like a kid. I glanced back at him and asked, "Studying? You going to summer school or something?"

"No, sir. My dad gives me books and articles to read on survival preparedness and then quizzes me on them."

"We've got to be ready for whatever comes," Roy Lamb said from behind us.

I glanced up, wondering how much of the conversation he had overheard and whether he thought I was meddling. "You're sure right," I agreed with him. "Can't be too prepared."

He gave me a funny look anyway.

I was starting to wonder if it would be possible to get out of here tonight. My job was done, and I didn't see any point in prolonging it.

Hayes called us back into formation, and that ended my speculation for the moment.

I was sore by the time the day was over. As the sun finally set, Hayes gathered the whole group together and made a little speech to get our minds off our aching muscles.

"You'll read articles and hear people talk about where the safest place to be is in case of war, nuclear or otherwise. Well, I don't care if they say Australia or Idaho or Timbuktu." His voice rose in stirring tones. "The safest place in the world is the place a man is willing to defend with his life! Remember that the next time you look around your home."

It was effective rhetoric, and as we went in to supper, I could see the smiles on the faces of the men. They believed in what they were doing and in what they were hearing. Maybe, in the long run, it didn't really matter that Hayes was taking them for a ride.

Maybe they were getting their money's worth in heroic dreams alone.

Our time was our own after supper, so I decided to take a walk around the farm. There was no particular reason for it, just something to do to kill time. I didn't feel like sitting in the makeshift barracks on the second floor of the farmhouse and joining in one of the ongoing poker games.

I had showered and put my own clothes back on, and I suppose in the back of my mind was the thought that I could hike back to the highway and catch a ride back to Fort Worth, leaving this phony training camp behind me.

That was before I spotted the helicopter, though.

It was parked about a hundred yards away from the house in a little clearing in the trees. I hadn't spotted it earlier because it was covered with camo netting. I wouldn't have seen it now if I hadn't nearly run into one of the landing skids.

"What the hell?" I muttered.

There was nothing unusual in a helicopter, of course. It was a good-sized chopper, a four-man job, and that was about all I could tell about it under its camouflage. I couldn't help but wonder why it was hidden. Nobody had said anything about using a helicopter in our training, but maybe we just hadn't gotten to that yet.

The man behind me was good. I barely heard him in time to dodge the knife he tried to put in my back.

I went down, scissoring with my feet and catching his left leg at the knee. He stumbled and fell, but he held on to the knife and came back up onto his feet at the same time I did.

"This time I'll kill you, you son of a bitch!" Starnes hissed at me.

I held up my hands, palm out. "Wait a minute, Starnes!" I said quickly. "I was just taking a walk. No need to get upset."

"Don't give me that crap! What are you, a cop? You're sure as hell not one of those lard-ass toy soldiers!"

I shook my head. "I don't know what you're talking about."

"You could have had me this morning. You could have killed me, and you know it! The colonel told me to keep an eye on you."

So my bad feelings had been from more than the mild swindle Hayes was working on his "recruits." Starnes wanted me dead, and there had to be a reason for that.

"You'd better drop that knife, mister," I said coldly. "I'm from Military Intelligence, and we know all about your operation here."

He laughed.

It had been worth a try. Not much of one, maybe, but a try.

Starnes came at me, fast and vicious.

There was enough moonlight so that we weren't fighting in darkness, but it was still a desperate struggle among shadows. I blocked his first thrust and tried to get a hand on his wrist, but he was too slippery. He squirmed away and lashed at me backhanded. The point of the knife ripped my shirt and laid a shallow scratch across my stomach.

He was out of position for a split second, though. I kicked, burying the toe of my boot in his groin. He gave a strangled scream and hacked at me with the knife as I drove in on him. I knocked the blade aside and caught him flush on the jaw with a punch, putting all of my weight behind the blow. He went down hard and stayed down. I clutched my throbbing hand and hoped I hadn't broken a knuckle.

I hadn't, I decided after a few moments. Starnes was unconscious but alive. He'd probably be out a good while. The longer the better, as far as I was concerned. My shirt was wet with the blood leaking from the wound he had given me, and I didn't feel one damn bit guilty about kicking him in the balls.

There was a possibility that Starnes was just crazy and had decided to kill me because he thought I had shown him up that morning. I didn't think so, though. My gut told me that Hayes had given him the orders to kill if I got too close to something I shouldn't.

I suddenly wanted to get back to that armory and get my hands on a gun.

The armory was locked, so I had to give up that idea. Given time, I might have been able to pick the heavy padlock on the door, but I didn't think I had that much time. I circled around the house instead, finding a lighted window on the first floor. I was glad that the simulated hardships of survival training meant that there were no air conditioners in the place. The glass was up, and I could hear everything that Hayes and a couple of his men were saying inside.

"They're all accounted for except that Cody," one of the lieutenants said. "Everybody else is upstairs."

"I sent Starnes to keep an eye on Cody," Hayes told him. "He should be back soon."

"You think Cody's a cop?"

"It's possible," Hayes admitted. "More than likely, though, he's just a nosy bastard. He never should have taken Ed down like that in the unarmed combat drill. Ed'll kill him if he's got the least excuse."

"We don't need that," another voice said.

"We can handle it," Hayes assured him. "There are plenty of places on this farm where an unmarked grave will never be found. I grew up here, remember."

That confirmed one of my guesses. This was Hayes's place.

I heard the rattle of papers. "All right," Hayes went on, his voice stern now like he was conducting an operations briefing. In a way, I guess he was. "Here are the details of the deal. The meeting is at the main ranch house at eleven o'clock next Wednesday. Lamb's bosses will arrive right at eleven, and they'll have the cash with them. We land right behind their car, blocking them in. We waste them, take the briefcase with the money, and we're gone. Less than a minute on the ground if everything goes according to plan, and we'll practice enough Monday and Tuesday so that it *will* go according to plan. Once we're airborne again, we put napalm into the house so that there won't be any witnesses left. Any questions?"

"Sounds good, Colonel," one of the other men said. "Lamb doesn't suspect anything?"

"Hell, no," Hayes snorted. "I'm his trusted commanding officer. He thought I was sympathizing with him when he was bitching about setting up this cattle sale."

"Just like all the others," a man said, chuckling.

"Right. Just like all the others."

And they had thought that I was a security officer at a bank, with access to all sorts of information about money transfers and things like that. I wondered suddenly what kinds of jobs the other "troops" had. I was willing to bet that a lot of them involved money.

Targets for armed robberies from the sky, carried out with military precision.

I remembered hearing about a couple of heists like that over the last year or so, and as far as I knew, the men who had been responsible for them had never been caught. It wasn't the kind of deal you could pull all the time, but two or three jobs a year, if they were big enough, would make all this phony survival training worthwhile. Plus they were taking in the fees from the suckers who were unwittingly helping them.

This had gotten a lot more grim than just a custody hassle.

"Don't move, you son of a bitch!" a voice grated behind me.

Slowly, I turned my head, not wanting to alarm him. Starnes had come to sooner than I had hoped, and he had gotten a gun from somewhere. This wasn't an army-surplus M-16, though, but a full-sized Ingram MAC-10. And as I said, the eye squinting at me over the sights was pale gray and insane.

I stood as still as possible, trying not to even breathe.

"I oughta blow you away," Starnes rasped. "Now get inside, and keep your damn mouth shut!"

I walked slowly away from the window, Starnes right behind me, prodding me every few steps with the hard barrel of the Ingram.

I was getting mad again. I forced it down. There was no way in hell I could spin around and disarm him before he could squeeze off a burst.

We went up onto the porch and inside the house; the screen door slammed behind us. Starnes marched me down the hall toward the room where Hayes and the others had been having their meeting. They all jerked their heads around and stared when Starnes shoved me through the door.

"He was listening outside the window," Starnes said, "and he found the helicopter."

Hayes's face was tightly drawn as he looked at me. He had finally taken off the sunglasses, and I could see that his eyes were blue.

"All right," he said after a moment. "Take care of him, Starnes." There was no mercy on his face or in his voice, and the other men looked the same.

Starnes caught my collar and hustled me back outside.

I wasn't going to just stand still and let him kill me. Even if it was futile, I had to do *something*. I waited, trying to control my fear and anger, waited for the best moment.

It never came.

"I'm going to enjoy this," Starnes growled, pushing me into the woods behind the house, toward the chopper. "You been askin' for it, you goddamn smart ass."

"Cody!" a voice yelled behind us. "Hit the dirt!"

I reacted instinctively, doing like the voice said, diving to the ground as Starnes spun around and looked for a target. We both spotted him at the same time, standing about twenty yards away, a rifle in his hands. Starnes fired as I launched myself toward him.

I hit his knees as the Ingram ripped off a burst. He went down and I was all over him, clubbing my hands together and driving them into the back of his head. His face smashed into the ground, and I grabbed his hair and lifted him back up and slammed him down again several times. It wasn't until I rolled his limp body over and saw the blood and the distorted features that I saw the rough chunk of rock on the ground. The stains on the rock were dark in the moonlight.

I picked up the Ingram and ran over to where Roy Lamb writhed on the ground, his legs blown out from under him by the heavy slugs. The empty M-16 lay on the grass beside him.

Roy was crying almost silently. I knelt beside him, and he opened his eyes, focusing on me after a few seconds.

"Cody . . . ," he gasped. "Saw you and . . . Starnes . . . from the window . . . thought something was wrong . . ."

"You were right," I told him. "He was going to kill me."

"Wh-why . . . ?"

"Too long a story," I told him. "Hayes and the others, they're the bad guys, Roy. They're the real enemy. I've got to stop them, so I'll have to leave you here for a little while." I didn't like the way he was bleeding, but there was nothing I could do about extensive wounds like he had suffered.

"Jeremy . . . he's back there . . ."

"I'll get him out," I promised. "And then I'll come back for you."

His hand caught my arm, dug in painfully. "I . . . I'm sorry . . ."

"You saved my life, Roy. It's not your fault—"

I broke off. He was unconscious, his hand slipping off my arm.

I went back toward the house at a run, the Ingram cradled in my arms. I had fired one once, with a cop friend of mine at the police firing range, but I wasn't real confident about handling it. Maybe I wouldn't have to do any more shooting.

As I neared the porch, a shape came out of the shadows, and Hayes called to me, "Is that you, Starnes?"

I brought the Ingram up. "Hold it, Hayes!"

He went for the pistol holstered on his hip, and I knew it wasn't loaded with blanks. I hesitated, and he had the .45 all the way out of the holster before I pressed the trigger of the machine gun.

The recoil threatened to push the muzzle up. I held it down, squeezing off short bursts that chewed up the porch of the old house. Hayes grunted and folded up, the pistol falling from his hands and bouncing down the steps to the ground.

His men came boiling out of the house, but so did the trainees. I covered all of them with the Ingram and yelled for nobody to move. I spotted Jeremy in the crowd on the porch and called out to him. "Your dad's in the woods, Jeremy," I told him. "He's been hurt."

He came off the porch and ran past me while I kept the rest of them under the gun. I backed off, then turned and hurried into the darkness after Jeremy.

There was plenty of confusion behind me, and I expected Hayes's men to be after me in a matter of minutes. Moving Roy Lamb might not be a good idea, but I didn't see that I had any choice.

I found Jeremy beside him. I pulled the kid to his feet and shoved the Ingram into his hand. "You've fired a gun before," I told him. "Just be careful." Then I bent to pick up Roy, who was still out cold. I had in mind that we'd head for the helicopter. I didn't think they'd risk shooting it up.

I heard car doors slamming, the roar of engines. Headlights lanced through the woods, then turned and went away, and all I could see was the red glow of taillights as the cars raced toward the highway.

They were pulling out.

All of them.

I figured it was a trap, but with Hayes dead, the others must have thought it made more sense to cut and run. With everything that had happened, there would be no chance of continuing with the survival camp scheme.

I would have liked to wait until morning before catfooting back up to the house, but with Roy badly injured, there wasn't that much time. I found that I was worried for nothing. The place was deserted, and the phone still worked. I got hold of the operator and started yelling for help as loud as I could.

Then I went back into the woods to wait with Jeremy and his father.

"What do you mean you won't testify?" Connie Lamb asked me, her voice rising stridently. "It's not bad enough that the damn reporters are making out that Roy's a hero, and now you say you won't tell the truth!"

"The truth is your husband saved my life," I told her flatly. "He's going to be in a wheelchair the rest of his life as it is. I'm not going to help take his son away from him."

She leaned over the desk in my office, glaring at me. "He wouldn't have gotten shot if he hadn't been out there at that camp with those other lunatics!"

"You may have a point there," I admitted. "But he went up against one of those lunatics armed only with an empty rifle he was using to practice field-stripping methods. And he saved my life."

"You keep coming back to that!"

"It is pretty important to me," I said.

"I'll have you subpoenaed."

I shrugged. "Go to it. But it won't look good, having to haul me into court. And once I'm on the stand, I'll have to offer my testimony that Roy saved my life and helped capture a band of ruthless criminals. That won't help your case, either."

She stared at me for a long moment, then turned and stalked out of the office. Even after all that had happened, I couldn't help but admire the rear view.

The rest of Hayes's men had been rounded up, and a few of the recruits had even come forward to tell the cops about the operation of the camp. It was going to be a nice mess before it was all cleaned up, but I had a feeling when the investigation was over, there would be several military-flavored robberies cleared up.

As for me, I was back in Fort Worth, definitely not a safe place. Less than ten miles from my office was Carswell Air Force Base, with its long-range bombers that made it a prime target for a Russian attack. Not to mention the damage that would be done to the agriculture and oil industries if the city was suddenly vaporized by the godless Communists. The safest place in the world? Not here.

Besides, my office rent was due in a few days and Connie Lamb had decided not to pay me the rest of the money she owed me. Unless another case came along in a hurry, I was going to be in trouble.

I locked the door and went across the street to commune with the spirits of Remington and Russell. Then, maybe, a bowl of ice cream . . . ?

# L.J. WASHBURN

# HOLLYWOOD GUNS

*We are proud to be able to claim that we introduced L.J. Washburn's P.I. Hallam, in* The Eyes Have It, *with her story entitled simply "Hallam."*

*Since then this cowboy who has outlived the days of the old West to become a gun-toting P.I. and stuntman in 1920s Hollywood has appeared in* Hardboiled, A Matter Of Crime, *and in his first novel,* Wild Night *(Tor, 1987). A second Hallam novel has also been scheduled to be published by Tor.*

*Now Hallam is back—still the freshest, most original P.I. to appear in some years.*

Hallam's Colt jammed just as he was about to shoot William S. Hart.

Hallam said, "Dammit!" and glared down at the revolver. Bill Hart, who was directing as well as starring in the picture, merely shrugged his shoulders and called, "Cut!" in that deep, resonant voice of his.

"Sorry, Bill," Hallam said as he drew back the hammer of the Colt and studied it. "Looks like the sear's busted."

"Don't worry about it, Lucas. The script called for you to miss me anyway," Hart pointed out. He held out his hand. "Mind if I take a look?"

Hallam handed over the Colt, knowing that Hart was a westerner like himself and not some play-acting dude from back East. Hart handed the weapon back after a moment's study of it and agreed with Hallam's conclusion.

"I imagine that old hog-leg's seen a lot of use," he said.

Hallam grinned, hefting the Colt. "Had it, man and boy, nigh onto forty years."

"I have a pair of six-shooters that belonged to Billy the Kid. Did you and young Bonney ever cross paths, by any chance?"

Hallam shook his head. "He was a few years before my time. Not much, mind you."

Nearby, an assistant director sweated and watched the two older men talking. He was wearing an open-throated sport shirt and jodhpurs, which was quite a contrast to the dusty range clothes worn by Hallam and Bill Hart. In the wilds of Bronson Canyon, where the company was shooting today, the A.D. looked more like he was in costume than Hallam and Hart did.

They looked right at home.

"Excuse me, Mr. Hart," the A.D. finally said. "Are we going to try to set up for another shot?"

Hart glanced around at the crowd of people, momentarily forgotten as he and Hallam had looked at the broken gun. He looked back at Hallam. "Feel like doing the scene with another gun, Lucas? We could start from the top so there wouldn't be any problem with continuity."

Hallam removed the battered, broad-brimmed hat from his head and ran his fingers around the inside of the band, wiping away the sweat. His craggy face with its drooping gray moustache was thoughtful. "Wouldn't really seem right," he said after a moment.

Hart nodded. "That's what I thought. Man gets used to his own gun." He turned to the A.D. "Might as well get the chase out of the way, Marty."

The young man nodded, hurrying off to confer with the cameraman and round up the riding extras that would be needed to film the scene. Hallam slid the Colt back in its holster and said, "Reckon it won't matter while I'm just ridin'. I can get it fixed tomorrow."

"Are you going to take it to Old Bob?" Hart asked.

"Where else? Old Bob's the best damn gunsmith in Hollywood."

The sign painted on the window of the little shop read HOLLYWOOD GUNS. The place was far out on Sunset, on the edge of town in an area where the rents were low. Inside, it was musty and a little gloomy, but as Hallam opened the door the next day, he thought that it was one of his favorite places in California.

There were guns everywhere you looked in the front part of the store, rifles and shotguns in racks along the walls, handguns of all kinds in glass-topped display cases. A wooden counter ran through the middle of the room. The back section was cluttered with metal racks and workbenches and guns in various states of disrepair. That was where Old Bob did his gunsmithing. There was also a small back room where ammunition was stored.

Hallam had never heard Old Bob called anything else. He didn't know the man's last name. But he was a familiar figure as he sat on a tall stool behind the counter, fiddling with a little nickel-plated .25. He was a small, wizened man in his sixties, with a few strands of hair plastered across a bald head and a wispy growth of whiskers on his chin. His dark eyes lit up as he saw Hallam come into the shop.

"Well, if it ain't the actor!" he said mockingly. "How's the picture business, Fairbanks?"

Hallam grinned, used to the old codger riding him. Of course, Bob wasn't that much older than Hallam himself. But hell, Hallam didn't mind being a codger.

He hauled out the broken Colt and laid it on the counter. "Got a busted sear," he said. "Reckon you can fix it?"

Old Bob snorted derisively. "Can I fix it? Of course I can fix it!" He picked up the Colt and sniffed it, wrinkling his nose. "Don't you ever clean this damn thing?"

Hallam ignored the question and said, "Time's money. How soon can you have it ready?"

"You picture people," Old Bob growled. "Hurry up, hurry up. That's all you do. Then you stand around."

Hallam put his hands on the counter. "How long?"

Old Bob shrugged and said, "Give me a couple of hours."

Hallam nodded. He turned to leave the shop, but he paused in front of a small stretch of wall where there were no gun racks. Instead, the wall was covered with yellowed newspaper clippings, some of them dating back to the 1870s. Hallam always got a kick out of reading them. Old Bob had one interest besides guns, and that was outlaws.

The stories had been cut out of papers all over the country. Evidently Old Bob had traveled a lot in his younger days. The clippings told of bank robberies and stagecoach holdups, train robbers and shootists and road agents. All the famous desperadoes were there—the James boys, the Daltons and the Youngers, Bill Doolin, Bitter Creek Newcomb, Jake Fentress and his backshooting brother Leroy, the Wild Bunch, Ben Thompson, King Fisher, John Wesley Harding . . . Nearly every outlaw Hallam had ever heard of was up on that wall, represented by the colorful writing of the journalists of those wild days.

Hallam had crossed paths with a few of those lawbreakers, had traded lead with some of them. In fact, one of the clippings contained a group photograph of the posse that had rounded up a gang of train robbers in Arizona, and Hallam was right there, a lot of years younger and serving as a deputy. Old Bob had been excited to meet one of the men pictured in his collection, and it had been an even bigger thrill when Hallam had brought Al Jennings around to meet him. Hallam didn't know the Oklahoma badman well, but he had made a few pictures with him.

"Relivin' past glories, Lucas?" Old Bob asked from his seat behind the counter, and the irascible tone was gone from his voice now.

Hallam shook his head. "Them days weren't so glorious, most of the time. Lots of hard work and gettin' shot at."

"You still a detective?"

"When somebody wants to hire me," Hallam said, nodding. He divided his time between movie work and being a private detective. Between the two jobs, he made a decent living.

Old Bob shook his head. "Must not be much of a challenge, chasin' crooks these days. The country's grown up a mighty sorry crop of desperadoes."

"Oh, there's still a few wild and woolly ones out there," Hallam said.

"Not like the old days," Old Bob insisted.

"Hell," Hallam said with a grin, "what is?"

With a wave of his hand, he went out the door and wandered down the street.

There was a diner a couple of blocks away, and he settled in there to drink several cups of coffee and read a paper that a previous customer had left behind. There was a lot of tension in the world, as usual. That seemed to be something that just went with modern times. Back East in New York and Chicago the gangsters were shooting each other up, also as usual. Hallam was glad he was in sunny Southern California.

There was crime out here too, though. As he scanned the paper, he saw stories about a man going insane and shooting his wife and in-laws, a payroll robbery in Glendale, a gun battle between two rival groups of rumrunners, and a swindle that had left several people penniless. Only the lunatic had been caught. The cops were still looking for the folks who had pulled all the other jobs.

Hallam turned the pages to the trade news. A new studio had

opened for business down on Poverty Row, and he was sure they'd be grinding out Westerns, just like all the other Gower Gulch outfits. Good news for him and all the others like him, the riding extras and the wranglers and the stuntmen who had found a home in the moving pictures.

It was hot in the diner, the one fan not stirring up much air. Hallam was used to heat, though, having lived in the Southwest most of his life. Hollywood was nothing compared to the deserts of Texas and New Mexico and Arizona. The time passed fairly quickly and when he checked his turnip, he saw that he ought to be heading back to Old Bob's to check and see if the Colt was ready.

Before, the old man had been alone in the shop. This time there was another customer, a tall man in a suit who was studying some of the pistols in the display cases. He glanced up at Hallam and then went back to looking at the guns.

Old Bob was sitting stiffly on his stool, and he didn't return Hallam's nod of greeting. He was probably feeling touchy again, Hallam thought. "Got the Colt ready yet?" he asked.

Old Bob squinted at him. "What's that name again?" He held up a hand as Hallam frowned. Before Hallam could say anything, Bob went on, "Oh, yeah, I remember now. Fentress, ain't it? Had a Colt with a busted sear."

Hallam nodded slowly. "That's right."

"Got 'er ready for you, Mr. Fentress." Old Bob reached under the counter and pulled out Hallam's Colt. "Be five dollars," he said as he handed it over.

Hallam took the gun and pulled out his wallet, gave a five-dollar bill to Old Bob. "Thanks," he said.

"Welcome," the gunsmith grunted. Hallam turned to go out, but Old Bob stopped him by saying, "You wouldn't be any relation to Leroy Fentress, would you?"

Hallam shook his head. "Never heard of him."

"Thought you might've been. I seen ol' Leroy not long ago."

Hallam smiled politely. "'Fraid I don't know the man, friend." He left the shop after nodding politely to the other customer.

Hallam walked to his flivver parked at the curb nearby, got in, drove away. He turned at the next corner and went around the block. There was a vacant lot behind the shop called Hollywood Guns. Hallam parked next to it, then reached into the glove box and took out a box of shells. He thumbed the cartridges into the cylinder of the Colt.

He wished there was more cover leading up to the back door of Old Bob's place. There was only one window on the rear wall, though, and it was fairly grimy. He'd just have to chance it.

Hallam got out of the car, went toward the building at a run.

He lifted a booted foot and drove it against the back door, his heel slamming into the panel beside the knob. The wood splintered and the door smashed back against the wall.

Hallam went through low, the boom of a gun filling his ears. He saw the muzzle flash off to his left and dove to the floor, rolling and tracking the Colt in that direction. He just had time to hope that Old Bob had done a good job repairing it before he triggered off two fast shots.

Both of them hit their target, smashing into the chest of the man crouched in the shadows of the back room and driving him back against the wall. The pistol he held slipped from his fingers and thudded to the floor. The man slid down the wall into a sitting position. His eyes were staring at Hallam, but they weren't seeing him. All the life was gone from them.

Hallam was back on his feet before the echoes of his shots had died away. A thick curtain covered the opening in the partition between the back room and the rest of the shop. Hallam bulled through it, his eyes scanning the room and finding the man who had pretended to be a customer. The man had a pistol out now and was trying to find something at which to fire it.

Old Bob was still on the stool. Hallam kicked out, upsetting the stool and sending the old man flying. He crashed behind the relative safety of the counter as Hallam leveled the Colt at the other man and yelled, "Hold it!"

The man jerked his gun toward Hallam and got off a shot. The slug whined past Hallam's head and punched through the partition behind him. Hallam fired once. The heavy bullet from the Colt caught the man in the shoulder, shattering bone and shredding muscle. The man flopped to the floor, his gun spinning away. He gobbled in pain for a few seconds before shock knocked him out.

From the floor behind the counter, Old Bob looked up at Hallam and asked, "T'other one?"

"Dead in the back," Hallam said shortly. His face was grim as he looked at the sprawled figure of the second gunman. "What the hell was that all about?"

Old Bob got to his feet, brushing himself off. He reached under the counter and brought out a bulky machine gun. "Feller got too attached to his gun," he said. "Thing kept jammin' up on him, so he brought it in to be fixed before him and the other one took off. They was on the run, somethin' about a payroll robbery they pulled in Glendale. Been layin' low for a few days, but the cops were closin' in on them. They were goin' to try to head back East, where they come from. Right talkative pair. 'Course, they figgered to kill me when they left, so's I couldn't send the cops after 'em."

Hallam shook his head. "Damned foolish."

"That they were," Old Bob agreed.

Hallam glared at him. "I'm talkin' about *you*. Startin' a shoot-out in here like that."

"Hell, boy, I knew you'd pick up on it when I called you by Jake Fentress's name. I just threw in that bit about Leroy so's you'd know there was one hidin' in the back. Knew you'd remember the Fentress boys and understand what I was gettin' at."

"I'd've looked a mite embarrassed if that gent had turned out to be a real customer." Hallam grimaced. "I'm gettin' too old to be goin' around bustin' in doors and wavin' guns around. Besides," he added, "what if them two had dropped me, instead of the other way around? Then there'd be two of us dead."

Old Bob shook his head slowly. "I knew you could take 'em. Ain't I been tellin' you? These owlhoots today ain't real desperadoes! Now if it had been Frank and Jesse James, or the Daltons . . ."

Hallam just shook his head and went to see if he could keep the wounded man from bleeding to death before the cops and ambulances got there.

## MURDER ONE'S TOP TEN PAPERBACKS
### 8/88 to 7/89

| | | |
|---|---|---|
| 1. | Thomas Harris | *Red Dragon* |
| 2. | Robert B Parker | *Pale Kings and Princes* |
| 3. | Andrew Vachss | *Flood and Strega* |
| 4. | Charles Willeford | *The Hoke Moseley Series* |
| 5. | Reginald Hill | *Underworld* |
| 6. | Rohase Piercy | *My Dearest Holmes* |
| 7. | Sara Paretsky | *Bitter Medicine* |
| 8. | Stephen Dobyns | *Cold Dog Soup* |
| 9. | Barbara Wilson | *The Dog Collar Murders* |
| 10. | Jen Green (ed.) | *Reader, I Murdered Him* |

## MURDER ONE'S TOP TEN HARDCOVERS
### 8/88 to 7/89

| | | |
|---|---|---|
| 1. | Ruth Rendell | *The Bridesmaid* |
| 2. | Dick Francis | *The Edge* |
| 3. | Ellis Peters | *The Heretic's Apprentice* |
| 4. | Ellis Peters | *A Rare Benedictine* |
| 5. | Elmore Leonard | *Freaky Deaky* |
| 6. | Thomas Harris | *The Silence of the Lambs* |
| 7. | Emma Lathen | *Something in the Air* |
| 8. | Sara Paretsky | *Toxic Shock* |
| 9. | Sara Caudwell | *The Sirens Sang of Murder* |
| 10. | Francis Nevins | *First You Dream, Then You Die. The Biography of Cornell Woolrich* |

# MURDER ONE'S TOP SELLING AUTHORS
### (in alphabetical order)

Margery     ALLINGHAM
Robert     BARNARD
Lawrence     BLOCK
Frederic     BROWN
Robert     CAMPBELL
John D     CARR (also as Carter DICKSON)
Sarah     CAUDWELL
Amanda     CROSS
James     CRUMLEY
Stephen     DOBYNS
James     ELLROY
Loren     ESTLEMAN
Michael     GILBERT
Sue     GRAFTON
George V     HIGGINS
Reginald     HILL
Tony     HILLERMAN
Elmore     LEONARD
Ed     McBAIN
John D     MACDONALD
Ross     MACDONALD
Charlotte     MACLEOD
Sara     PARETSKY
Robert B     PARKER
Elizabeth     PETERS (also as Barbara MICHAELS)
Ellis     PETERS
Ruth     RENDELL
Rex     STOUT
Jim     THOMPSON
Andrew     VACHSS
Donald     WESTLAKE (also as Richard STARK, Tucker COE and Samuel HOLT)
Charles     WILLEFORD
Cornell     WOOLRICH

*All these books and authors plus many more are available from Murder One, the specialist crime bookshop at 23 Denmark Street, London WC2H 8NN. Telephone 01-497 2200.*

# PHANTOM LADY

## ONE

## The Hundred and Fiftieth Day Before the Execution

SIX P.M.

The night was young, and so was he. But the night was sweet, and
he was sour. You could see it coming from yards away, that sullen
look on his face. It was one of those sustained angers, pent-up but
smouldering, that last for hours sometimes. It was a shame, too,
because it was all out of tune with everything around him. It was
the one jarring note in the whole scene.

It was an evening in May, at the get-together hour. The hour
when half the town, under thirty, has slicked back its hair and given
its billfold a refill and sauntered jauntily forth to keep *that date*.
And the other half of the town, still under thirty, has powdered its
nose and put on something special and tripped blithely forth to
keep that *same date*. Everywhere you looked the two halves of the
town were getting together. On every corner, in every restaurant
and bar, outside drugstores and inside hotel-lobbies and under
jewellery-store clocks, and darned near every place there was that
somebody else hadn't beat them to first. And the same old stuff
went around and around, old as the hills but always new. "Here I
am. Been waiting long?" "You look swell. Where'll we go?"

That was the kind of an evening it was. The sky was rouge-red
in the west, as though it was all dolled-up for a date itself, and it
was using a couple of stars for diamond clips to hold up in
evening-gown. Neons were beginning to wink out along the
street-vistas, flirting with the passers-by like everyone else was
tonight, and taxi-horns were chirping, and everyone was going
some place, all at one time. The air wasn't just air, it was aerated
champagne, with a whiff of City for good measure, and if you
didn't watch out it went to your head. Or maybe your heart.

And there he went, pushing that sore face in front of him,
spoiling the whole scene. People glancing at him as he strode by
wondered what he had to be that ill-tempered about. It wasn't his

215

216

health. Anyone that could swing along at the gait he was must be
in the pink of condition. It wasn't his circumstances. His clothes
had that carelessly expensive hang that can't be faked. It wasn't his
age. If he had thirty beat at all, it was by months, not years. He
wouldn't have been half bad-looking if he'd given his features a
chance to unpucker. You could tell that around the edges where
the scowl was thin.

He went striding along with that chip-on-the-shoulder look, his
mouth a down-turned ellipse, a horseshoe stuck under his nose.
The topcoat slung cross the crook of his arm bobbed up and down
with the momentum of his pace. His hat was too far back on his
head and it had a dent in the wrong place, as though he'd punched
it on without adjusting it afterwards. Probably the only reason his
shoes didn't strike sparks from the pavement was because they
were rubber-heeled.

He hadn't intended going in where he finally did. You could tell
that by the abrupt way he braked as he came opposite to it. There
was no other word for the way he halted; it was as though a brace
down his leg had locked jamming him still. He probably wouldn't
have even noticed the place if the intermittent neon over it hadn't
glowed on just then, as he was passing. It said "Anselmo's" in
geranium-red, and it dyed the whole sidewalk under it as though
someobdy had spilled a bottle of ketchup.

He swerved aside, on what was obviously an impulse, and went
barging in. He found himself in a long low-ceilinged room, three
or four steps below street-level. It wasn't a large place nor, at the
moment, a crowded one. It was restful on the eyes; the lighting
was subdued, amber-coloured, and directed upwards. There was a
line of little bracketed nooks with tables set in them running down
both walls. He ignored them and went straight back to the bar,
which was semicircular, facing toward the entrance from the rear
wall. He didn't look to see who was at it, or whether anyone was
at it at all. He just dumped his topcoat on top of one of the tall
chairs, dropped his hat on top of it, and then sat down on the next
one over. His attitude plainly implied he was there for the night.

A blurred white jacket approached just above the line of his
downcast vision, and a voice said, "Good-evening sir."

"Scotch," he said, "and a little water. I don't give a damn how
little."

The water stayed on untouched, after its companion-glass was
empty.

He must have, subconsciously at the moment of sitting down,
glimpsed a bowl of pretzels or some sort of accessory like that over
to his right. He reached out that way without looking. His hand
came down, not on a twisted baked shape, but on a straight, smooth
one that moved slightly.

He swung his head around, took his hand off the other one that had just preceded his into the bowl. "Sorry," he grunted. "After you."

He swung his head around to his own business once more. Then he turned again, gave her a second look. He kept on looking from then on, didn't quit after that. Still in a gloomy, calculating way, though.

The unusual thing about her was the hat. It resembled a pumpkin, not only in shape and size, but in colour. It was a flaming orange, so vivid it almost hurt the eyes. It seemed to light up the whole bar, like a low-hanging garden-party lantern. Stemming from the exact centre of it was a long, thin cockerel feather, sticking straight up like the antenna of an insect. Not one woman in a thousand would have braved that colour. She not only did, she got away with it. She looked startling, but good, not funny. The rest of her was toned down, reticent in black, almost invisible against that beacon of a hat. Perhaps the thing was a symbol of some sort of liberation, to her. Perhaps the mood that went with it was, "When I have this on, watch out for me! The sky's the limit!"

Meanwhile she was nibbling a pretzel and trying to seem unaware of his steady scrutiny. When she broke off nibbling, that was the only sign she gave of being aware that he had quitted his own chair, come over, and was standing beside her.

She inclined her head very slightly, in a listening attitude, as if to say: "I'm not going to stop you, if you try to speak. Whether I do after that or not depends on what you have to say."

What he had to say, with terse directness, was: "Are you doing anything?"

"I am, and I'm not." Her answer was well-mannered, but not encouraging. She didn't smile nor commit herself to receptiveness in any way. She carried herself well; whatever else she was, she wasn't cheap.

There was no trace of the masher in his own manner, either. He went on, briskly impersonal, "If you've got an engagement, just say so. I'm not trying to annoy you."

"You're not annoying me—so far." She got her meaning across perfectly: my decision is still held in the balance.

His eyes went to the clock up over the bar, facing both of them. "Look, it's ten after six, right now."

Her own eyes sought it in turn. "So it is," she agreed neutrally.

He had taken out a wallet, meanwhile, extracted a small oblong envelope from one of the compartments. This he opened in turn, and prodded forward two salmon-coloured pasteboard strips, forking them apart as he did so. "I have two perfectly good tickets here for the show at the Casino. Row Double-A, aisle-seats. Care to take it in with me?"

"You're abrupt about it." Her eyes went from the tickets to his face.

"I have to be abrupt about it." He was scowling as deeply as ever. He wasn't even looking at her at all; he was looking at the tickets, with an air of resentment. "If you have a previous engagement say so, and I'll try to find somebody else to share them with me."

A flicker of interest showed in her eyes. "These tickets must be used up at all costs?"

"It's a matter of principle." he said sullenly.

"This could be mistaken for a very crude attempt at, shall we say, striking up an acquaintanceship," she let him know. "The reason I don't think it is, is it's so blunt, so unvarnished, it couldn't be anything but just what you say it is."

"It isn't." His face was still set in flinty lines.

She had veered slightly toward him on her chair by now. Her way of accepting was to remark, "I've always wanted to do something of this sort. I'd better do it now. The chance mayn't recur— at least not in a genuine form—for a long time."

He armed her down. "Shall we make an agreement before we start? It may make it simpler afterward, when the show is over."

"That depends on what it is."

"We're just companions for an evening. Two people having dinner together, seeing a show together. No names, no addresses, no irrelevant personal references and details. Just—"

She supplied: "Two people seeing a show together, companions for an evening. I think that's a very sensible, in fact necessary, understanding, so let's abide by it. It does away with a great deal of self-consciousness, and perhaps even an occasional lie." She offered him her hand, and they shook briefly on it. She smiled for the first time. She had a rather likeable smile; reserved, not too sugary.

He motioned the barman over, tried to pay for both drinks.

"I'd already paid for mine before you came in," she told him. "I was just coasting along on it."

The barman took a small tablet out of the pocket of his jacket, pencilled. "1 Scotch—60" on the top leaf, tore it off and presented it to him.

They were numbered, he noticed, and he saw that he'd drawn a large, beetling, black "13" in the upper corner. He gave a wry grin, handed it back with the requisite amount, turned and went after her.

She had preceded him toward the entrance. A girl ensconced with a companion in one of the wall-booths leaned slightly outward to stare after the glowing hat as it went by. He, coming up in the rear, was just in time to catch that.

Outside she turned to him questioningly. "I'm in your hands."

He forefingered a taxi waiting a few car-lengths away. One cruising past at the moment, for whom the signal had not been intended, tried to chisel in on the hail. The first one frustrated it by rolling up into position ahead of it, but not without a slight scraping of fenders and snatches of belligerent repartee. By the time the competition had sidled off again and the first driver had cooled sufficiently to turn his attention to his fares-to-be, she was already ensconced inside.

Her host had waited a moment by the driver's seat to give him the destination. "Maison Blanche," he said, and then followed her in.

The light was on, and they let it stay that way. Perhaps because to have turned it out would have been a suggestion of intimacy, neither one felt a dim-out was appropriate to the occasion.

Presently he heard her give a little gratified chuckle, and, following the direction of her eyes, grinned sparingly in accompaniment. Cabmen's licence-photos are seldom examples of great portrait-beauty, but this one was a caricature, with its pitcher-ears, receding chin, and pop-eyes. The name identifying it was memorably curt and alliterative: "Al Alp."

His mind took note of it, then let it go again.

The Maison Blanche was an intimate-type dining-room, renowned for the excellent of its food. It was one of those places over which a hush of appreciation seems to hang, even at their busiest hours. No music nor distraction of any other sort was allowed to interfere with its devotees' singleness of purpose.

In the foyer she separated from him. "Will you excuse me a moment while I go in and repair the ravages of Time? Go in and sit down a while; don't wait. I'll find you."

As the powder-room door opened to admit her, he saw her hands start upward toward her hat, as if she intended to remove it. The door closed after her before she completed the gesture. It occurred to him that a temporary lapse of courage was probably the real reason behind this whole manœuvre; that she had separated from him and was about to remove the hat in order to be able to enter the dining-room singly after he did, and thereby attract a degree less attention.

A head-waiter greeted him at the dining-room entrance. "One, sir?"

"No, I have a reservation for two." And then he gave the name. "Scott Henderson."

He found it on his list. "Ah yes." He glanced over the guest's shoulder. "Are you alone, Mr. Henderson?"

"No," Henderson answered noncommittally.

It was the only vacant table in sight. It was in a secluded position, set back into an indentation in the wall, so that its occupants could only be seen frontally, were screened from the rest of the diners on three sides.

When she appeared at the dining-room entrance presently, she was hatless, and he was surprised at how much the hat had been able to do for her. There was something flat about her. The light had gone out; the impact of her personality was soggy, limp. She was just some woman in black, with dark-brown hair; something that blocked the background, that was all. Not homely, not pretty, not tall, not small, not chic, not dowdy; not anything at all, just plain, just colourless, just a common denominator of all feminine figures everywhere. A cipher. A composite. A Gallup poll.

Not a head that turned remained turned a second longer than necessary, or carried back any continuing memory of what it had seen.

The head-water, momentarily engaged in tossing a salad, was not on hand to guide her. Henderson stood up to show her where he was, and she did not strike directly through the room, he noticed, but made her way unobtrusively around two sides of it, which was the longer but the far less conspicuous way.

The hat, which she had been carrying at arm's length beside her, she placed on the third chair of their table, and partly covered it with the edge of the cloth, possibly to protect it from stains.

"Do you come here often?" she asked.

He pointedly failed to hear her.

"Sorry," she relented, "that comes under the heading of personal background."

Their table-waiter had a mole on his chin. He couldn't help noticing that.

He ordered for them without consulting her. She listened attentively, gave him an appreciative glance when he had finished.

It was uphill work getting started. There were heavy restrictions on her choice of topics, and she had his laden mood to combat as well. Man-like, he left most of the effort to her, made very little attempt to keep his own end up. Though he gave a sketchy appearance of listening, his thoughts were obviously elsewhere most of the time. He would bring them back again each time, and with an effort that was almost a physical wrench, only when his abstraction had become so noticeable it threatened to be flagrantly discourteous.

"Don't you want to take your gloves off?" he said at one point. They were black, like everything else about her but the hat. They hadn't appeared awkward with the cocktail or purée, but with the sole came a slice of lemon that she was trying to mash with her fork.

She stripped the right one off immediately. She took a little longer with the left, seemed about to leave it on after all. Then finally, with a touch of defiance, she followed suit with that.

He carefully refrained from seeing the wedding-band, looked out and across at something else. But he could tell she knew that he had.

She was a good conversationalist, without being spectacular about it. She was dexterous, too, managed to eschew the obvious, the banal, the dry; the weather, the newspaper headlines, the food they were engaged with.

"This crazy South American, this Mendoza, in the show we're seeing tonight: when I first saw her a year or so ago, she had hardly any accent at all. Now, with every engagement she has up here, she seems to unlearn more English, acquire a heavier one than the time before. One more season and she'll be back in pure Spanish."

He gave one-third of a smile. She was cultured, he could tell that about her. Only someone cultured could have gotten away with what she was doing tonight and not made a ghastly mess of it, either in one direction or the other. She had balance, to take the place of either propriety or recklessness. And there again, if she had leaned a little more one way or the other, she would have been more memorable, more positive. If she had been a little less well bred, she would have had the piquancy, the raffishness, of the parvenu. If she had been a little more, she would have been brilliant—and therefore memorable in that respect. As it was, polarized between the two, she was little better than two-dimensional.

Toward the end he caught her studying his necktie. He looked down at it questioningly. "Wrong colour?" he suggested. It was a solid, without any pattern.

"No, quite good, in itself," she hastened to assure him. "Only, it doesn't match—it's the one thing that doesn't go with everything else you—Sorry, I didn't mean to criticize," she concluded.

He glanced down at it a second time, with a sort of detached curiosity, as though he hadn't known until now, himself, just which one it was he had put on. Almost as though he were surprised to find it on him. He destroyed a little of the total clash she had indicated by thrusting the edge of his dress-handkerchief down out of sight into his pocket.

He lit their cigarettes, they stayed with their cognacs awhile, and then they left.

It was only in the foyer—at a full-length glass out in the foyer—that she finally put her hat on again. And at once she came alive, she was something, somebody again. It was wonderful, he reflected, what that hat could do to her. It was like turning on the current in a glass chandelier.

A gigantic theatre-doorman, fully six-four, opened the cab-door for them when it had driven up, and his eyes boggled comically as the hat swept past, almost directly under them. He had white walrus-rusk moustaches, almost looked like a line-drawing of a theatre-doorman in the *New Yorker*. His bulging eyes followed it from right to left as its wearer stepped down and brushed past him. Henderson noted this comic bit of optic by-play, to forget it again a moment later. If anything is ever really forgotten.

The completely deserted theatre-lobby was the best possible criterion of how late they actually were. Even the ticket-taker at the door had deserted his post by now. An anonymous silhouette against the stage-glow, presumably an usher, accosted them just inside the door, sighted their tickets by flashlight, then led them down the aisle, trailing an oval of light backhand along the floor to guide their advancing feet.

Their seats were in the first row. Almost too close. The stage was an orange blur for a moment or two, until their eyes had grown used to the foreshortened perspective.

They sat patiently watching the montage of the revue, scene blending into scene with the superimposed effect of motion-picture dissolves. She would beam occasionally, even laugh outright now and then. The most he would do was give a strained smile, as though under obligation to do it. The noise, colour, and brilliance of lighting reached a crescendo, and then the curtains rippled together, ending the first half.

"The house-lights came on, and there was a stir all around them as people got up and went outside.

"Care for a smoke?" he asked her.

"Let's stay where we are. We haven't been sitting as long as the rest of them." She drew the collar of her coat closer around the back of her neck. The theatre was stifling already, so the purpose of it, he conjectured, was to screen her profile from observation as far as possible.

"Come across some name you've recognized?" she murmured presently, with a smile.

He looked down and found his fingers had been busily turning down the upper right-hand corner of each leaf of his programme, one by one, from front to back. They were all blunted now, with neat little turned-back triangles superimposed one on the other. "I always do that, fidgety habit I've had for years. A variation of doodling, I guess you'd call it. I never know I'm doing it, either."

The trap under the stage opened and the orchestra started to file back into the pit for the second half. The trap-drummer was nearest to them, just across the partition-rail. He was a rodent-like individual, who looked as though he hadn't been out in the open air for ten years past. Skin stretched tight over his cheekbones, hair so flattened and glistening it almost looked like a wet bathing-cap with a white seam bisecting it. He had a little twig of a moustache that almost seemed like smudge from his nose.

He didn't look outward into the audience at first; busied himself adjusting his chair and tightening something or other on his instrument. Then, set, he turned idly, and almost at once became aware of her and of the hat.

It seemed to do something to him. His vapid unintelligent face froze into an almost hypnotic fascination. His mouth even opened slightly, like a fish's; stayed that way. He would try to stop staring at her every once in a while, but she was on his mind; he couldn't keep his eyes away very long; they would stray back to her each time.

Henderson took it in for a while, with a sort of detached, humorous curiosity. Then finally, seeing that it was beginning to make her acutely uncomfortable, he put a stop to it in short order, by sending such a sizzling glare at him that he turned back to his music rack forthwith and for good. You could tell, though, even with his head turned the other way, that he was still thinking about her, by the rather conscious, stiff way he held his neck.

"I seem to have made an impression," she chuckled under her breath.

"Perfectly good trap-drummer ruined for the evening," he assented.

The gaps behind them had filled up again now. The house-lights dimmed, the foots welled up, and the overture to the second act began. He went ahead moodily pleating the upper corners of his dog-eared programme.

Midway through the second half there was a crescendo build-up, then the American house-orchestra laid down its instruments. An exotic thumping of tom-toms and rattling of gourds on stage took its place, and the main attraction of the show, Estela Mendoza, the South American sensation, appeared.

A sharp nudge from his seat-mate reached him even before he had had time to make the discovery for himself. He looked at her without understanding, then back to the stage again.

The two women had already become mutually aware of the fatal fact that was still eluding his slower masculine perceptions. A cryptic whisper reached him: "Just look at her face. I'm glad there are footlights between us. She could kill me.

There was a distinct glitter of animosity visible in the expressive black eyes of the figure on stage, over and above her toothsome smile, as they rested on the identical replica of her own headgear, flaunted by his companion there in the very first row, where it couldn't be missed.

"Now I understand where they got the inspiration for this particular creation," she murmured ruefully.

"But why get sore about it? I should think she'd be flattered.

"It's no use expecting a man to understand. Steal my jewellery, steal the gold-fillings from my teeth, but don't steal my hat. And over and above that, in this particular case it's a distinctive part of her act, part of her trademark. It's probably been pirated; I doubt that she'd give permission to—"

"I suppose it is a form of plagiarism." He watched with slightly heightened interest, if not yet complete self-forgetfulness.

Her art was a simple thing. As real art always is. And as getting away with something at times is too. She sang in Spanish, but even in that language there was very little intellect to the lyric. Something like this:

> "Chica chica boom boom
> Chica chica boom boom."

Over and over. Meanwhile she kept rolling her eyes from side to side, throwing one hip out of joint at every step she took, and throwing little nosegays out to the women members of the audience from a flat basket she carried slung at her side.

By the time she had run through two choruses of the thing, every woman in the first two or three rows was in possession of one of her floral tokens. With the notable exception of Henderson's companion. "She purposely held out on me, to get even for the hat," she whispered knowingly. And as a matter of fact, every time the hitching, heel-stamping figure on the stage had slowly worked her way past their particular vantage-point, there had been an ominous flash, an almost electrical crackling, visible in her fuse-like eyes as they glided over that particular location.

"Watch me call her on it," she remarked under the breath for his benefit. She clasped her hands together, just below her face, in vise-formation.

The hint was patently ignored.

She extended them out before her, at half arm's length, held them that way in solicitation.

The eyes on the stage slitted for a minute, then resumed their natural contour, strayed elsewhere.

Suddenly there was a distinct snap of the fingers from Henderson's companion. A crackling snap, sharp enough to top the music. The eyes rolled back again, glowered maniacally at the offender. Another flower came out and winged over, but still not to her.

"I never know when I'm beaten," he heard her mutter doggedly. Before he knew what she meant, she had risen to her feet, stood there in her seat, smiling beatifically, passively claiming her due.

For a moment there was a deadlock between the two. But the odds were too unequal. The performer, after all was said and done, was at the mercy of this individualistic spectator, for she had an

illusion of sweetness and charm to maintain at all costs in the sight
of the rest of the audience.

The alteration in the stature of Henderson's seat-mate also had
an unforeseen result in another respect. As the hiphiker slowly
made the return trip, the spotlight, obediently following her and
slanted low, cut across the head and shoulders of this lone vertical
impediment, standing up on the orchestra floor. The result was that
the similarity of the two hats was brought explosively to everyone's
attention. A centripetal ripple of comment began to spread outward, as when a stone is dropped into heretofore still waters.

The performer capitulated and capitulated fast, to put an end to
this odious comparison. Up came a blackmail-extorted flower, out
it went over the footlights in a graceful little curve. She covered up
the omission by making a rueful little moue, as if to say, "Did I
overlook you? Forgive me, I didn't mean to." Behind it, however,
could be detected the subcutaneous pallor of a lethal tropical rage.

Henderson's companion had deftly caught the token and sub-
sided into her seat again with a gracious lip-movement. Only he
detected the wordage that actually emerged: "Thank you—you
Latin louse!" He choked on something in his throat.

The worsted performer slowly worked her way off into the wings
with little spasmodic hitches, while the music died down like the
clatter of train-wheels receding into the distance.

In the wings they glimpsed a momentary but highly revealing
vignette, while the house was still rocking with applause. A pair of
shirt-sleeved masculine arms, most likely the stage-manager's, were
bodily restraining the performer from rushing back on stage again.
Obviously for some purpose over and above merely taking bows.
Her hands, held down at her sides by his bear-hug embrace, were
visibly clenched into fists and twitching with punitive intent. Then
the stage blacked out and another number came on.

At the final curtain, as they rose to go, he tossed his programme
into the discard, on to the seat he had just quitted.

To his surprise she reached down for it, added it to her own,
which she was retaining. "Just as a memento," she remarked.

"I didn't think you were sentimental," he said, moving slowly
up the choked aisle at her heels.

"Not sentimental, strictly speaking. It's just that—I like to gloat
over my own impulsiveness at times, and these things will help."

Impulsiveness? Because she had joined forces with him for the
evening, without ever having seen him before, he supposed. He
shrugged—inwardly, if not visibly.

As they were fighting their way toward a taxi, in the mêlée
outside the entrance, an odd little mischance occurred. They had
already claimed their cab, but before they could get into it a blind
beggar approached, hovered beside her in mute appeal, alms-cup

all but nudging her. The lighted cigarette she was holding was jarred from her fingers in some way, either by the beggar himself or someone nearby, and fell into the cup. Henderson saw it happen, she didn't. Before he could interfere the trustful unfortunate had thrust probing fingers in after it, and then snatched them back again in pain.

Henderson quickly dug the ember out for him himself, and put a dollar bill in his hand to make amends. "Sorry, old timer, that wasn't intentional," he murmured. Then noting that the sufferer was still blowing ruefully on his smarting finger, he added a second bill to the first, simply because the incident could have been so easily misconstrued as the height of calloused mockery, and he could tell by looking at her it hadn't been intended as such.

He followed her into the cab and they drove off. "Wasn't that pathetic?" was all she said.

He had given the driver no direction as yet.

"What time is it?" she asked presently.

"Going on quarter of twelve."

"Suppose we go back to Anselmo's, where we first met. We'll have a night-cap and then we'll part there. You go your way and I'll go mine. I like completed circles."

They're usually empty in the middle, it occurred to him, but it seemed ungallant to mention this, so he didn't.

The bar was considerably more crowded now, when they got there, than it had been at six. However, he managed to secure a stool for her all the way around at the very end of the bar, up against the wall, and posted himself at her shoulder.

"Well," she said, holding her glass just an inch above bar-level and eyeing it speculatively, "hail and farewell. Nice having met you."

"Nice of you to say so."

They drank: he to completion, she only partially. "I'll remain here for a short while," she said by way of dismissal. She offered him her hand. "Good-night—and good luck." They shook briefly, as acquaintances of an evening should. Then just as he was about to turn away, she crinkled her eyes at him in remonstrative after-thought. "Now that you've got it out of your system, why don't you go back and make up with her?"

He gave her a slightly surprised look.

"I've understood all evening," she said quietly.

On that note they parted. He moved toward the door, she turned back to her drink. The episode was over.

He glanced back, when he had reached the street entrance, and he could still see her sitting there, all the way over against the wall, at the end of the curved bar, looking down pensively, probably fiddling idly with the stem of her glass. The bright orange of the hat showed through a V-shaped opening left between two pairs of shoulders around the turn of the bar from her.

That was the last thing of all, the bright orange of her hat peering blurredly through the cigarette-haze and shadows, all the way back there behind him, as in a dream, as in a scene that wasn't real and never had been.


# TWO

# The Hundred and Fiftieth Day Before the Execution

### MIDNIGHT

Ten minutes later and only eight blocks away in a straight line— two straight lines: seven blocks up one way and then one over to the left—he got out of the cab in front of an apartment house on the corner.

He put the change left over from the fare into his pocket, opened the vestibule-door with his own key, and went inside.

There was a man hanging around in the lobby waiting for somebody. He was on his feet, drifting aimlessly around, from here to there, from there to the next place, the way a man waiting in a lobby does. He didn't live in the building; Henderson had never seen him before. He wasn't waiting for the car to take him up, because the indicator was unlighted; it was motionless somewhere up above.

Henderson passed him without a second glance, and pushed the button for himself, to bring it down.

The other had found a picture on the wall now, and was staring at it far beyond its merits. He stood with his back to Henderson. In fact, he made it a point to seem unaware there was anyone else in the lobby with him at all, which was overdoing it a little.

He must have a guilty conscience, Henderson decided. That picture wasn't worth all that close attention. He must be waiting for someone to join him down there, someone whom he had no right to escort out.

Henderson thought: What the hell did he care, what was it to him, anyway?

The car arrived and he stepped in. The heavy bronze door swung closed by itself after him. He thumbed the six-button, the top of the rack. The lobby started to drop from sight, seen through the little diamond-shaped glass insert let into the shaft-door. Just before it did so he saw the picture-gazer, evidently impatient at being kept waiting this long by his prospective date, finally detach himself and take a preliminary step over toward the switchboard. Just a vignette, that was no possible concern of his.

He got out on the sixth floor and fumbled for his latch-key. The hall was quiet; there wasn't a sound around him but the slight tinkle of the loose change in his own pocket as he sought for the key.

He fitted it into his own door, the one to the right as you came off the car, and opened it. The lights were out, it was pitch-dark on the other side of it. At this, for some reason or other, he gave a sound of scornful disbelief, deep in his throat.

He snapped a light-switch, and a small, neat foyer came into existence. But the light only took care of just this one cubicle. Beyond the arched opening facing him across it, it was still as dark, as impenetrable, as ever.

He closed the door behind him, flung down his hat and coat on a chair out there. The silence, the continuing darkness, seemed to irritate him. The sullenness was starting to come back into his face again, the sullenness that had been so conspicuously there at six, out on the street.

He called out a name, called it through into the darkness lying beyond the inscrutable arched opening. "Marcella!" He called it imperatively, and not particularly friendlily.

The darkness didn't answer.

He strode into it, speaking in that same harsh, demanding tone as he went. "Come on, cut it out! You're awake. Who do you think you're kidding? I saw the light in your bedroom window, from the street just now. Grow up. This isn't going to get us anywhere!"

The silence didn't answer.

He cut diagonally through the dark, toward some particular point on the wall, known to him by heart. He was grumbling in a less strident voice now. "Until I come back you're wide awake! The minute you hear me you're sound asleep! That's just dodging the issue!"

His arm was reaching out before him. The click came before it had touched anything. The sudden bath of light made him jump slightly; it had come too soon, before he was expecting it.

He looked along his own arm, and the switch was still inches out past it; they hadn't come together yet. There was a hand just leaving it, sidling away from it along the wall. His eyes raced up the sleeve the hand protruded from and found a man's face.

He gave a startled half-turn, and there was another one looking at him from that direction. He gave an additional turn, still further rearward, having nearly reversed himself now, and there was a third, directly behind him. The three stood impassive, motionless as statues, in a half-circle around him.

He was so stunned for a minute by the triple, deathly silent apparition that he stared questioningly around the room in search of recognition, of orientation, to see if he was in the right place at all, if it was his own apartment he'd entered.

His eyes came to rest on a cobalt-blue lamp-base on a table over by the wall. That was his. On a low-slung chair cocked out from a corner. That was his. On a photograph folder standing on a cabinet. One panel held the face of a beautiful, pouting, doe-eyed girl with masses of curly hair. The other held his own face.

The two faces were looking in opposite directions, aloofly, away from one another.

So it was his own home he'd come back to.

He was the first one to speak. It seemed as if they were never going to. It seemed as as if they were going to stand staring at him all night. "What're you men doing in my apartment?" he rapped out.

They didn't answer.

"Who are you?"

They didn't answer.

"What do you want here? How'd you get in?" He called her name again. This time parenthetically, as though demanding of her an explanation of their presence here. The door toward which he'd turned his head as he did so, the only other door that broke the walls besides the arched opening through which he'd just come, remained obliviously closed. Secretively, inscrutably closed.

They'd spoken. His head snapped back to them. "Are you Scott Henderson?" They had narrowed the semi-circle about him a little now.

"Yes, that's my name." He kept looking around toward that door that didn't open. "What is it? What's up?"

They continued, with maddening deliberation, to ask their own questions instead of answering his. "And you live here, is that right?"

"Certainly I live here!"

"And you're the husband of Marcella Henderson, is that right?"

"Yes! Now listen, I want to know what this is about."

One of them did something with his palm, made some sort of gesture with it that he failed to get in time. It only struck him after it was already over.

He tried to get over to that door and found that one of them, somehow, was in his way. "Where is she? Is she out?"

"She's not out, Mr. Henderson," one of them said quietly.

"Well, if she's in there, why doesn't she come out?" His voice rose exasperatedly. "*Talk*, will you? Say something!"

"She can't come out, Mr. Henderson."

"Wait a minute. What was that you showed me just now, a police badge?"

"Now take it easy, Mr. Henderson." They were executing a clumsy sort of a group dance, the four of them. He'd shift a little one way, and they'd shift with him. Then he'd shift back again the other way, and again they'd shift with him.

"Take it easy? But I want to know what's happened! Have we been robbed? Has there been an accident? Was she run over? Take your hands off me. Let me go in there, will you?"

But they had three pairs of hands to his one. Each time he'd get rid of one pair, two more would hold him back somewhere else. He was rapidly working himself up into a state of unmanageable excitement. The next step would have been blows. The rapid breathing of the four of them filled the quiet room.

"I live here, this is my home! You can't do this to me! What right've you got to keep me out of my wife's bedroom—?"

Suddenly they'd quit. The one in the middle made a little sign to the one nearest the door, said with a sort of reluctant indulgence: "All right, let him go in. Joe."

The obstructive arm he had been pressing against dropped so suddenly he opened the door and went through almost off balance, careening the first step or two of the way.

Into a pretty place, a fragile place, a place of love. All blue and silver, and with a sachet clinging to the air that he knew well. A doll with wide-spread blue satin panniers, sitting plumped on a vanity table, seemed to look over at him with helpless wide-eyed horror. One of the two crystal sticks supporting blue silken shades had fallen athwart her lap. On the two beds, blue satin coverlets. One flat and smooth as ice, the other rounded over someone's hidden form. Someone sleeping, or someone ill. Covered up completely from head to foot, with just a stray wisp or two of curly hair escaping up at the top, like bronze foam.

He'd stopped short. A look of white consternation crossed his face. "She's—she's done something to herself! Oh, the little fool!" He glanced fearfully at the nightstand between the two beds, but there was nothing on it, no drinking-glass or small bottle or prescription-box.

He took sagging steps over to the bedside. He leaned down, touched her through the coverlet, found her rounded shoulder, shook it questioningly. "Marcella, are you all right—?"

They'd come in past the doorway after him. Vaguely he had an impression everything he did was being watched, being studied. But he had no time for anyone, anything but her.

Three pairs of eyes in a doorway, watching. Watching him fumble with a blue satin coverlet. His hand whipped down a narrow triangular corner of it.

There was a hideous, unbelievable moment, enough to scar his heart for life, while she grinned up at him. Grinned with a cadaverous humour that had become static. Her hair was ripping about her on the pillows in the shape of an open fan.

Hands interfered. He went backwards, draggingly, a step at a time. A flicker of blue satin and she was gone again. For good, for ever.

"I didn't want *this* to happen," he said brokenly. "*This* wasn't what I was looking for—"

Three pairs of eyes exchanged glances, jotted that down in the notebooks of their minds.

They took him out into the other room and led him over to a sofa. He sat down on it. Then one of them went back and closed the door.

He sat there quietly, shading his eyes with one hand as though the light in the room was too strong. They didn't seem to be watching him. One stood at the window, staring out at nothing. The other was standing beside a small table, leafing through a magazine. The third one was sitting down across the room from him, but not looking at him. He was prodding at one of his finger-nails with something, to clean it. The way he pored over it, it seemed the most important thing in the world to him at the moment.

Henderson took his shielding hand away presently. He found himself looking at her wing of the photograph port-folio. It slanted his way. He reached over and closed it.

Three pairs of eyes completed a circuit of telepathic communication.

The ceiling of leaden silence began to come down closer, to weigh oppressively. Finally, the one sitting across from him said, "We're going to have to talk to you."

"Will you give me just a minute more, please?" he said wanly. "I'm sort of shaken up—"

The one in the chair nodded with considerate understanding. The one by the window kept looking out. The one by the table kept turning the pages of a woman's magazine.

Finally, Henderson pinched the corners of his eyes together as if to clear them. He said, quite simply: "It's all right now. You can begin."

It began so conversationally, so offhandedly, it was hard to tell it had even begun at all. Or that it was anything but just a tactful chat, to help them fill in a few general facts. "Your age, Mr. Henderson?"

"Thirty-two."

"Her age?"

"Twenty-nine."

"How long were you married?"

"Five years."

"Your occupation?"

"I'm in the brokerage business."

"About what time did you leave here tonight, Mr. Henderson?"

"Between five-thirty and six."

"Can you come a little closer than that?"

"I can narrow it for you, yes. I can't give you the exact minute the door closed after me. Say, somewhere between quarter of and five of six. I remember I heard six o'clock striking when I'd got down as far as the corner; from the little chapel over in the next block."

"I see. You'd already had your dinner?"

"No." A split second went by. "No—I hadn't."

"You had your dinner out, in that case."

"I had my dinner out."

"Did you have your dinner alone?"

"I had my dinner out, without my wife."

The one by the table had come to the end of the magazine. The one by the window had come to the end of the interest the view held for him. The one in the chair said with tactful over-emphasis, as if afraid of giving offence: "Well, er, it wasn't your usual custom, though, to dine out without your wife, was it?"

"No, it wasn't."

"Well, as long as you say that, how is it you did tonight?" The detective didn't look at him, looked at the cone of ash he was knocking off his cigarette into a receptacle beside him.

"We'd arranged to take dinner out together tonight. Then at the last minute she complained of not feeling well, of having a headache, and—I went alone."

"Have words, anything like that?" This time the question was inaudible, it was so minor-keyed.

Henderson said, in an equally minor key. "We had a word or two, yes. You know how it is."

"Sure." The detective seemed to understand perfectly how little domestic misunderstandings like that went. "But nothing serious, that right?"

"Nothing that would make her do anything like this, if that's what you're driving at." He stopped, asked a question in turn, with a momentary stepping-up of alertness. "What was it, anyway? You men haven't even told me yet. What caused—?"

The outside door had opened and he broke off short. He watched with a sort of hypnotic fascination, until the bedroom door had closed. Then he made a half-start to his feet. "What do *they* want? Who are they? What are they going to do in there?"

The one in the chair had come over and put his hand to his shoulder so that he sat down again; without, however, any undue pressure being exerted. It was more like a gesture of condolence.

The one who had been by the window looked over, mentioned: "A little nervous, aren't you, Mr. Henderson?"

A sort of instinctive natural dignity, to be found in all human beings, came to Henderson's aid. "How should I be—at ease, self-possessed?" he answered with rebuking bitterness. "I've just come home and found my wife dead in the house." .

He'd made that point. The interlocutor by the window noticeably had nothing further to say on that score.

The bedroom door had opened again. There was awkward, commingled motion in it. Henderson's eyes dilated, they slowly coursed the short distance from door to arched opening, leading out into the foyer. This time he gained his feet fully, in a spasmodic jolt. "No, not like *that!* Look what they're doing! Like a sack of potatoes. And all her lovely hair along the floor. She was so careful of it—!"

Hands riveted to him, holding him there. The outer door closed muffledly. A little sachet came drifting out of the empty bedroom, seeming to whisper: "Remember? Remember when I was your love? Remember?"

This time he sank down suddenly, buried his face within his two gouging, kneading hands. You could hear his breath. The tempo was all shot to pieces. He said to them in helpless surprise, after his hands had dropped again. "I thought guys didn't cry—and now I just have."

The one who had been in the chair before passed him a cigarette, and even lit it for him. His eyes looked bright, Henderson's, in the shine of the match.

Whether it was that that had interrupted it, or it had died out of its own accord for lack of anything further to feed on, the questioning didn't resume. When they resumed talking again, it was pointless, inane, almost as though they were talking just to kill time, for the sake of having something to say.

"You're a very neat dresser, Mr. Henderson," the one in the chair observed at random.

Henderson gave him a half-disgusted look, didn't answer.

"It's great the way everything you've got on goes together."

"That's an art in itself,' the former magazine-reader chimed in.

"Socks and shirt, and pocket-handkerchief—"

"All but the tie," the one by the window objected.

"Why do you have to discuss anything like that at a time like this?" Henderson protested wearily.

"It should be blue, shouldn't it? Everything else is blue. It knocks your whole get-up silly. I'm not a fashion-plate, but y'know just looking at it does something to me—" And then he went on innocently. "How'd you happen to slip up on an item as important as the tie, when you went to all the trouble of matching everything else up? Haven't you got a blue tie?"

Henderson protested almost pleadingly, "What're you trying to do to me? Can't you see I can't talk about trifles like—?"

He'd asked the question again, as tonelessly as before. "Haven't you got a blue tie, Mr. Henderson?"

Henderson ran his hand up through his hair. "Are you trying to drive me out of my mind?" He said it very quietly, as though this small-talk was almost unendurable. "Yes, I have a blue tie. Inside, on my tie rack, I think."

"Then how'd you come to skip it when you were putting on an outfit like this? It cries out for it." The detective gestured disarmingly. "Unless, of course, you did have it on to begin with, changed your mind at the last minute, whipped it off and put on the one you're wearing instead."

Henderson said. "What's the difference? Why do you keep this up?" His voice went up a note. "My wife is dead. I'm all cracked up inside. What's the difference what colour tie I did or didn't put on?"

It went on, as relentlessly as drops of water falling one by one upon the head. "Are you sure you didn't have it on originally, then change your mind—?"

His voice was smothered. "Yes. I'm sure. It's hanging from my tie-rack in there."

The detective said guilelessly, "No, it isn't hanging from your tie-rack. That's why I'm asking. You know those little verticle notches running down your tie-rack, like a fish's backbone? We found the one it belongs on, the one you usually kept it strung through, because that was the only vacant one on the whole gadget. And that was the lowest one of all; in other words, all the ties on the upper ones overlapped it as they hung down straight. So, you see, it was removed from *under* all the other ties, which means you must have gone there and selected it originally, not just pulled it off at random from the top. Now, what bothers me is why, if you went to all the trouble of lifting up all your other ties and selecting that one from underneath, and withdrawing it from the rack, you then changed your mind and went back to the one you'd already been wearing all day at business, and which didn't go with your after-dark outfit."

Henderson hit himself smartly at the ridge of the forehead with the heel of one hand. He sprang up. "I can't stand this!" he muttered. "I can't stand any more of it, I tell you! Come out with what you're doing it for, or else stop it! If it's not on the tie-rack, then where is it? I haven't got it on! Where is it? You tell me, if you know! What's the difference where it is anyway?"

"A great deal of difference, Mr. Henderson."

There was a long wait after that; so long that he started to get pale even before it had come to an end.

"It was knotted tight around your wife's neck. So tight it killed her. So tight it will have to be cut loose with a knife to get it off."

# THREE

# The Hundred and Forty-ninth Day Before the Execution

### DAYBREAK

A thousand questions later, the early light of day peering in the windows made the room look different somehow, although everything in it was the same, including the people. It looked like a room in which an all-night party had taken place. Cigarette-ends spilling over in every possible container, and many that weren't intended as such. The cobalt-blue lamp was still there, looking strange in the dawn with its halo of faded electric light. The photographs were still there; hers a lie now, a picture of someone that no longer existed.

They all looked and acted like men suffering from a hangover. They had their coats and vests off, and their shirt-collars open. One of them was in the bathroom, freshening up at the cold-water tap. You could hear him snorting through the open door. The other two kept smoking and moving restlessly around. Only Henderson was sitting quiet. He was still sitting on the same sofa he'd been on all night. He felt as though he'd spent all his life on it, had never known what it was to be anywhere but in this one room.

The one in the bathroom—his name was Burgess—came to the door. He was pressing drops of excess water out of his hair, as though he'd ducked his whole head in the wash-basin. "Where're all your towels?" he asked Henderson, with odd-sounding commonplaceness.

"I was never able to find one on the rack myself," the latter admitted ruefully. "She—I'd always be given one when I asked for it, but I don't know to this day just where they're kept."

The detective looked around helplessly, dripping all over the doorsill. "D'you mind if I use the edge of the shower-curtain?" he asked.

"I don't mind," Henderson said with a sort of touching wistfulness.

It began again. It always began again just when it seemed to have finally stopped for good.

"It wasn't just about two theatre tickets. Why do you keep trying to make us believe it was that?"

He looked up at the wrong one first. He was still used to the parliamentary system of being looked at when spoken to. It had come from the one who wasn't looking at him.

"Because it was that. What should I say it was about, if that's all it was about? Didn't you ever hear of two people having words about a pair of theatre tickets? It can happen, you know."

The other one said, "Come on Henderson, quit stalling. Who is she?"

"Who is who?"

"Oh, don't start that again," his questioner said disgustedly. "That takes us back an hour and a half or two hours, to where we were about four this morning. Who is she?"

Henderson dug wearied fingers through his hair, let his head droop over in futility.

Burgess came out of the bathroom, tucking his shirt in. He took his wrist-watch out of his pocket, strapped it on. He scanned it idly, then he drifted aimlessly out into the foyer. He must have picked up the house-phone. His voice came back. "All right now, Tierney." Nobody paid any attention, least of all Henderson. He was half asleep there with his eyes open, staring down at the carpet.

Burgess sauntered in again, moved around after that as if he didn't know what to do with himself. Finally he ended up at the window. He adjusted the shade a little to get more light in. There was a bird on the sill outside. It quirked its head at him knowingly. He said, "C'mere a minute, Henderson. What kind of a bird is this, anyway?" And then when Henderson didn't move the first time. "C'mere. Hurry up, before he goes away." As though that were the most important thing in the world.

Henderson got up and went over and stood beside him, and thus his back was to the room. "Sparrow," he said briefly. He gave him a look as if to say: That wasn't what you wanted to know.

"That's what I figured it was," Burgess said. And then, to keep him looking forward, "pretty decent view you got from here."

"You can have it, bird and all," Henderson said bitterly.

There was a noticeable lull. All questioning had stopped.

Henderson turned away, then stopped where he was. There was a girl sitting there on the sofa, in the exact place where he'd just been himself until now. There hadn't been a sound to mark her arrival. Not the creak of a door-hinge, not the rustle of a garment.

The way the eyes of the three men dug into his face, all the skin should have peeled off it. He got a grip on it from the inside, held it steady. It felt a little stiff, like cardboard, but he saw to it that it didn't move.

She looked at him, and he at her. She was pretty. She was the Anglo-Saxon type, more so even than the Anglo-Saxon themselves are any more. Blue-eyed, and with her taffy-coloured hair uncurled and brushed straight across her forehead in a clean-looking sweep. The part was as distinct as a man's. She had a tan camel-hair coat drawn over her shoulders, with the sleeves left empty. She was hatless, but was clutching a handbag. She was young, at that stage when they still believe in love and men. Or maybe she always would, was of an idealistic temperament. You could read it in the way she looked at him. There was practically incense burning in her eyes.

He moistened his lips slightly, nodded barely perceptibly, as to a distant acquaintance, whose name he could not recall, nor where they had met, but whom he didn't want to slight.

He seemed to have no further interest in her after that.

Burgess must have made some esoteric sign in the background. All of a sudden they were alone together, there was no one else in the room with them any more.

He tried to motion with his hand, but it was too late. The camel-hair coat was already propped up empty in the corner of the sofa, without her inside it. Then it slowly wavered and collapsed into a huddle. She had flung herself against him like some sort of a projectile.

He tried to get out of the way, side-step. "Don't. Be careful. That's just what they want. They're probably listening to every word—"

"I have nothing to be afraid of." She took him by the arms and shook him slightly. "Have you? Have you? You've got to answer me!"

"For six hours I've been fencing to keep your name out of it. How did they come to drag you into it? How did they hear of you?" He smacked himself heavily on the shoulder. "Damn it. I would have given my right arm up here to keep you out!"

"But I want to be in things like this with you, when you're in them. You don't know very much about me, do you?"

The kiss kept him from answering. Then he said. "You've kissed me before you even know whether or not—"

"No, I haven't," she insisted, breathing close to his face. "Oh, I couldn't be *that* wrong. Nobody could be. If I could be that wrong, then my heart ought to be put in an institution for mental defectives. And I've got a smart heart."

"Well, tell your heart for me it's okay," he said sadly. "I didn't hate Marcella. I just didn't love her enough to go on with her, that's all. But I couldn't have killed her. I don't think I could kill anyone, not even a man—"

She buried her forehead against his chest, in a sort of ineffable gratitude. "Do you have to tell me that? Haven't I seen your face when a stray dog came up to the two of us on the street? When a dray-horse standing at the kerb—Oh, this is no time to tell you, but why do you suppose I love you? You don't think it's because you're so handsome, do you? Or so brilliant? Or so dashing?" He smiled and kept stroking her hair. And he'd interrupt the strokes, softly, with his lips. "It's all inside you, what I love, where no one but me can see it. There's so much goodness in you, you're such a swell fellow—but it's all inside, for me alone to know, to have to myself."

She raised her face at last, and her eyes were all wet.

"Don't do that," he said gently. "I'm not worth it."

"I'll set my own price-tags; don't try to jew me down," she rebuked him. She glanced over at the oblivious door, and the light on her face dimmed a little. "What about *them*? Do they think—?"

"I think it's about fifty-fifty, so far. They wouldn't have kept at me this long—How did they come to drag you into it?"

"Your message was there from six o'clock, when I got in last night. I hated to go to sleep without knowing one way or the other, so finally I called you back here, around eleven. They were already here in the place, and they sent someone right over to talk to me. I've had someone with me ever since."

"That's great, keeping you up all night long!" he said resentfully.

"I wouldn't have wanted to be asleep, knowing you were in trouble." Her fingers swept the curve of his face. "There's only one thing that matters. Everything else is beside the point. It'll be straightened out, it's got to be. They must have ways of finding out who actually did it. How much have you told them?"

"About us, you mean? Nothing. I was trying to keep you out of it."

"Well, maybe that's what the hitch has been. They could sense you were leaving out something. I'm in it now, so don't you think it's better to tell them everything there is to know about us? We have nothing to be ashamed or afraid of. The quicker you do, the quicker it'll be over with. And they've probably already guessed, from my own attitude, we're pretty off-base about each—"

She stopped short. Burgess was back in the room. He had the pleased look of a man who has gained his point. When the other two followed him in, Henderson even saw him give one of them the wink.

"There's a car downstairs that'll take you back to your own address, Miss Richman."

Henderson stepped over to him. "Look, will you keep Miss Richman out of this? It's unfair; she really has nothing—"

"That depends entirely on yourself," Burgess told him. "We only brought her over here in the first place because you made it necessary for us to remind you—"

"Anything I know, anything I can tell you, is yours," Henderson assured him earnestly, "if you see that she's not annoyed by newspapermen, that they don't get hold of her name and make a big thing of it."

"Always providing it's the truth," Burgess qualified.

"It will be." He turned to her, said in a softer voice than the one he'd been using. "You go now, Carol. Get some sleep, and don't worry; everything'll be all right in a little while."

She kissed him in front of all of them, as though proud to show the way she felt toward him. "Will you let me hear from you? Will you let me hear from you as soon as you can—some time right today if you can?"

Burgess went to the door with her, said to the cop posted outside it: "Tell Tierney nobody is to come near this young lady. No name, no questions answered, no information of any kind."

"Thanks," Henderson said fervently when he'd come back, "you're a regular guy."

The detective eyed him without acknowledgment. He sat down, took out a notebook, ran a wavy cancellation-line down two or three closely scribbled pages, turned over to a fresh one. "Shall we start in?" he said.

"Let's start," Henderson acquiesced.

"You said you had words. Does that stand?"

"That stands."

"About two theatre tickets? Does that stand?"

"About two theatre tickets and a divorce. That stands."

"Now that comes in it. Then there was bad feeling between you?"

"No feeling of any kind, good or bad. Call it a sort of numbness. I'd already asked her for a divorce some time ago. She knew about

Miss Richman. I told her. I wasn't trying to hide anything. I was trying to do it the decent way. She refused the divorce. Walking out was no good. I didn't want that. I wanted Miss Richman for my wife. We stayed away from each other all we could, but it was hell, I couldn't stand it. Is all this necessary?"

"Very."

"I had a talk with Miss Richman night before last. She saw it was getting me. She said, 'Let me try, let me talk to her.' I said no. She said, 'Then you try again yourself. Try in a different way this time. Talk to her reasonably, try to win her over.' It went against the grain, but I gave it a spin. I telephoned from work and reserved a table for two at our old place. I bought two tickets to a show, first row on the aisle. At the last minute I even turned down an invitation from my best friend to go out on a farewell party with him. Jack Lombard, he's going to be in South America for the next few years; it was my last chance of seeing him before he sailed. But I stuck to my original intention; I was going to be nice to her if it killed me.

"Then when I got back here, nothing doing. She wasn't having any reconciliation. She liked things the way they were, and she was going to keep them that way. I got sore, I admit. I blew up. She waited until the last minute. Let me go ahead and shower and change clothes. Then she just sat there and laughed. 'Why don't you take *her* instead?' she kept needling me. 'Why waste the ten dollars?' So I phoned Miss Richman from here, right in front of her.

"I didn't even have that satisfaction. She wasn't in. Marcella laughed her head off. She made me know it.

"You know how it is when they laugh at you. You feel like a fool. I was so sore I couldn't see straight any more. I yelled: 'I'm going out on the street and invite the first girl I run into to come with me in your place! The first thing in curves and high heels that comes along, no matter who it is!' And I slammed on my hat and slammed out the door."

His voice ran down like a clock that needs winding. "And that's all. I can't do any better than that for you, even if I tried. Because that's the truth, and the truth can't be improved on."

"And after you left here, does that time-table of your movements you already gave us still go?" Burgess asked.

"That still goes. Except that I wasn't alone; I *was* with someone. I did what I'd told her I'd do: stepped up to someone and invited her along. She accepted, and I was with her from then until just about ten minutes before I came back here."

"What time did you meet her, about?"

"Only a few minutes after leaving here. I stopped in at some bar or other, over on Fiftieth Street, and that was where I met her."

He did something with his finger. "Wait a minute. I just remembered. I can give you the exact time I met her. We both looked at the clock together, as I was showing her the theatre tickets. It was ten after after six, to the dot."

Burgess ran his nail along underneath his lower lip. "What bar was this?"

"I couldn't say, exactly. It had a red come-on over it, that's all I can remember at the moment."

"Can you prove you were in there at ten after six?"

"I've just told you I was. Why? Why is that so important?"

Burgess drawled: "Well, I could string you along, but I'm funny that way. I'll give it to you. Your wife died at exactly *eight after six*. The small wrist-watch she wore shattered against the edge of the vanity-table as she fell to her death. It stopped at exactly—" He read from something: "6–08–15." He put it away again. "Now, nothing with two legs, or even wings, could have been here at that time, and over on Fiftieth Street one minute and forty-five seconds later. You prove you were over there at ten past, and all this is over."

"But I've told you! I looked at the clock."

"That isn't proof, that's an unsupported statement."

"Then what would proof be?"

"Corroboration."

"But why does it have to be at that end? Why can't it be at this?"

"Because there's nothing at this end to show that anyone but you did it. Why do you suppose we've been sitting up with you all night?"

Henderson let his wrists dangle limp over his knees. "I see," he breathed at last. "I see." The silence coursed and swirled around the room after that for a while.

Burgess spoke again at last. "Can this woman you say you met in the bar corroborate you on what time it was?"

"Yes. She looked at the clock when I did. She must remember that. Yes, she can."

"All right, then that's all there is to it. Providing she satisfies us her corroboration is given in good faith, and you didn't put her up to it. Where does she live?"

"I don't know. I left her where I first met her, back at the bar."

"Well, what was her name?"

"I don't know. I didn't ask, and she didn't give it to me."

"Not even a first name, not even a nickname? You were with her for six hours, what did you call her?"

" 'You,' " he answered glumly.

Burgess had got out his notebook again. "All right, describe her for us. We'll have to send out after her ourselves and have her brought in."

There was a long wait.

"Well?" he said finally.

Henderson's face was getting paler by the minute. He swallowed hard, "My God, I can't!" he blurted out finally. "I've lost her completely, she's rubbed out." He circled his hand helplessly in front of his own face. "I could have told you when I first came back here last night, maybe, but now I can't any more. Too much has happened since. The shock of Marcella. And then you guys pegging away at me all night. She's like a film that's been exposed to too much light, she's completely faded out. Even while I was with her I didn't notice her very closely, my mind was too full of my own affairs." He looked from one to the other of them, as if in search of help. "She's a complete blank!"

Burgess tried to help him out. "Take your time. Think hard. Now, here. Eyes?"

Henderson flexed his clenched hands open, in futility.

"No? All right, hair then. What about hair? What colour hair?"

He plastered hands to his eye-sockets. "That's gone too. Every time I start to say one colour, it seems to me it was another; and then when I start to say the other, I think it was the first again. I don't know; it must have been sort of in between. Not brown, not black. Most of the time she had it under a hat." He looked up half hopefully. "I can remember the hat better than anything else. An orange hat, will that do any good? Yeah, orange, that's it."

"But suppose she's taken it off since last night, suppose she don't show up anywhere in it for the next six months? Then where are we? Can't you remember anything about *her* herself?"

Henderson kneaded his temples in brain-agony.

"Was she fat? Skinny? Tall? Short?" Burgess peppered at him.

Henderson writhed his waist, first to one side, then the other, as if to get away from the questions. "I can't, that's all, I can't!"

"I think you're taking us for a ride, aren't you?" one of the others suggested stonily. "It was only last night. Not last week or last year."

"I never did have a very good memory for faces, even when I'm—at peace, nothing to bother me. Oh, she had a face, I suppose—"

"No kidding?" the one who had assumed the rôle of end-man jeered.

He kept going from bad to worse, because he was making the mistake of thinking aloud, instead of rehearsing his words. "She was shaped like other women, that's about all I can tell you—"

That did it. Burgess' face had been slowly lengthening for some time, without his giving any other sign of truculence. He was evidently of a slow-moving temperament. Instead of reclipping his stymied pencil into his pocket, he flung it with a sort of angered deliberateness, almost as if taking aim, at the wall opposite him. Then he got up and went over and got it. His face had turned good and red. He shrugged into his long-discarded coat, pulled the knot of his tie around frontward.

"Come on, boys," he said surlily. "let's get out of here, it's getting late."

He stopped a moment at the arched opening leading out to the foyer, eyed Henderson flintily. "What do you take us for, anyway?" he growled. "Easy-marks? You're out with a woman, for six solid hours, only last night, and yet you can't tell us what she looked like! You're sitting shoulder-to-shoulder with her at a bar, you're sitting across a table from her for a whole table d'hôte meal from celery to coffee, you're in the seat right next to her for three full hours at a show, you're in the same taxi with her coming and going—but her face is just a blank space under an orange hat! You expect us to swallow that? You try to hand us a myth, a phantom, without any name or form or height or width or eyes or hair or anything else, and we're supposed to take your word for it you were with *that* and not home here when your wife was getting killed! You're not even plausible about it. A ten-year-old kid could see through what you're trying to put over. It's one of two things. Either you weren't with any such person, and just made her up out of your own mind. Or more likely still, you weren't with any such person but *did* see her in the crowd around you some time during the evening, and are trying to foist her on us as having been with you, when she wasn't at all. Which is why you're purposely making her blurred, so we can't get a very good line on her and find out the truth!"

"Come on, sir!" one of the others ordered Henderson, in a voice like a buzz-saw going through a pine-knot. "Burge don't burn very often," he added half humorously, "but when he does he burns good and strong."

"Am I under arrest?" Scott Henderson asked Burgess as he got up and moved toward the door in the grasp of the other man.

Burgess didn't answer him directly. The answer was to be found in the parting instruction he gave the third man, over his shoulder.

"Turn out that lamp, Joe. There won't be anybody using it around here for a long time to come."

# FOUR

## The Hundred and Forty-ninth Day Before the Execution

### SIX P.M.

The car was standing waiting there by the corner when the unseen belfry somewhere close at hand began tolling the hour. "Here it comes," Burgess said. They'd been waiting about ten minutes for this, motor running.

Henderson, neither free nor indicted yet, sat on the rear seat between him and one of the other two headquarters men who had taken part in the questioning up at his apartment the previous night and morning.

A third man whom they referred to as "Dutch" stood outside the car, on the sidewalk, in a sort of fatuous idleness. He had been kneeling crouched in mid-sidewalk tightening up his shoelaces just before the first stroke sounded. He straightened now.

It was the same kind of a night like the one before. The get-together hour, the sky with its make-up on in the west, everyone going some place all at one time. Henderson gave no sign, sitting there between two of his captors. It must have occurred to him, though, what a difference a few hours can make.

His own address was just a few doors behind them, at the next corner to the rear. Only he didn't live there any more; he lived in a detention-cell in the prison attached to police headquarters now.

He spoke dully. "No, a store-length further back," he said to Burgess. "I'd just come up to that lingerie-store window when the first stroke hit. I can remember that, now that I'm looking at it—and hearing the same sound—over again."

Burgess relayed it to the man on the sidewalk. "Back up one store-length and take it from there, Dutch. That's it. All right, start walking!" The second stroke of six had sounded. He did something to the stop-watch he was holding in his hand.

The tall, rangy, red-headed man on the sidewalk struck out. The car at the same time eased into gliding motion, keeping abreast of him out beyond the kerb.

"Dutch" looked self-conscious for a moment or two, his legs worked a little stiffly; then it wore off gradually.

"How is he for pace?" Burgess asked presently.

"I think I was a little faster than that," Henderson said. "When I'm sore I walk fast, I notice, and I was going at a pretty good clip last night."

"Quicken it up a little, Dutch!" Burgess coached.

The rangy one accelerated slightly.

The fifth stroke sounded, then the last.

"How is it now?" Burgess asked.

"That's about me," Henderson concurred.

An intersection sidled past under them. A light held the car up. Not the walker. Henderson had disregarded them the night before. The car caught up with him midway down the next block.

They were on Fiftieth now. One block of it ticked off. Two.

"See it yet?"

"No. Or if I have, it doesn't click. It was awfully red, redder than that one. The whole sidewalk was like red paint."

The third block. The fourth.

"See it?"

"It doesn't click."

Burgess warned: "Watch what you're doing now. If you string it out very much longer, even your theoretical alibi won't be any good. You should have been inside it already by now; it's eight and a half past."

"If you don't believe me anyway," Henderson said dryly, "what's the difference?"

"It don't hurt to figure out the exact walking-time between the two points," the man on the other side of him put in. "We might just happen to find out when you *actually* got there, and then all we do is subtract."

"Nine minutes past!" Burgess intoned.

Henderson was holding his head low, scanning the slowly moving belt of sidewalk fronts from under the car ceiling.

A name drifted by, colourless glass tubes unlighted. He turned quickly after it. "That's it! I think that's it, but it's out. Anselmo's, it was something like that, I'm almost sure of it. Something foreign—"

"In, Dutch!" Burgess hollered. He drove the plunger down, killed his stop-watch. "Nine minutes, ten and a half seconds," he announced. "We'll give you the ten and a half seconds to allow for variations, such as the density of the crowd you had to buck and the cross-traffic at intersections, which is never the same twice. Nine minutes flat, walking-time, from the corner below your apartment to this bar. And we'll give you another minute from the apartment itself down to that first corner, where the first chime-stroke caught you. We've already tested that lap out. In other words"—he turned and looked at him—"you find some way of proving that you got into this bar as late as *six-seventeen*—but no later—and you'll still clear yourself automatically, even now."

Henderson said: "I can prove I got in here as early as six-ten, if I can only find that woman."

Burgess swung open the car door. "Let's go inside," he said.

"Ever seen this man before?" Burgess asked.

The barman held his chin in a vice. "Looks kind of familiar," he admitted. "But then, my whole job is just faces, faces, faces."

They gave him a little more time. He took an angle-shot at Henderson. Then he went around the opposite side and took it from there. "I don't know," he still hesitated.

Burgess said, "Sometimes the frame counts as much as the picture. Let's try it differently. Go on back behind the bar, barman."

They all went over to it. "Which stool were you on, Henderson?"

"Somewhere along about here. The clock was straight over, and the pretzel-bowl was about two up from me."

"All right, get on it. Now try it, barman. Forget about us; take a good look at him."

Henderson inclined his head morosely, stared down at the surface of the bar, the way he had the other time.

It worked. The barman snapped his fingers. "That did it! Gloomy Gus. I remember him now. Only last night, wasn't it? Must have been just a one-drink customer, didn't stick around long enough to sink in."

"Now we want the time."

"Some time during my first hour on duty. They hadn't thickened up yet around me. We had a late start last night; sometimes happens."

"What is your first hour on duty?"

"Six to seven."

"Yeah, but how long after six, that's what we want to know."

He shook his head. "I'm sorry, gents. I only watch the clock toward the *end* of my shift, never around the beginning. It might have been six, it might have been six-thirty, it might have been six-forty-five. It just wouldn't be worth a damn for me to try to say."

Burgess looked at Henderson, raised his eyebrows slightly. Then he turned to the barman again. "Tell us about this woman that was in here at that time."

The barman said with catastrophic simplicity, "What woman?"

Henderson's complexion went slowly down the colour-scale, from natural to pale to dead white.

A flick of Burgess' hand held him mute.

"You didn't see him get up and go over and speak to a woman?"

The barman said, "No, sir. I didn't see him get up and go over and speak to anyone. I can't swear to it, but my impression was there was no one else at the bar at that time *for* him to speak to."

"Did you see a woman sitting here by herself, without seeing him get up and go over to her?"

Henderson pointed helplessly two bar-stools over. "An orange hat," he said, before Burgess could stop him.

"Don't do that," the detective warned him.

The barman was suddenly becoming irritable, for some reason or other. "Look," he said. "I've been in this business thirty-seven years. I'm sick of their damn faces, night after night, just opening and closing, opening and closing, throwing the booze in. Don't come in and ask me what colour hats they had on, or if they picked each other up or not. To me they're just orders. To me they're just drinks, see, to me they're just drinks! Tell me what she had and I'll tell you if she was in here or not! We keep all the tabs. I'll get 'em from the boss's office."

They were all looking at Henderson now. He said, "I had Scotch and water. I always have that, never anything else. Give me just a minute now, to see if I can get hers. It was all the way down near the bottom—"

The barman came back with a large tin box.

Henderson said, rubbing his forehead. "There was a cherry left in the bottom of the glass and—"

"That could be any one of six drinks. I'll get it for you. Was the bottom stemmed or flat? And what colour was the dregs? If it was a Manhattan the glass was stemmed and dregs, brown."

Henderson said, "It was a stem-glass, she was fiddling with it. But the dregs weren't brown, no, they were pinklike."

"Jack Rose," said the barman briskly. "I can get it for you easy, now." He started shuffling through the tabs. It took a few moments; he had to sift his way through them in reverse, the earlier ones were at the bottom. "See, they come off the pads in order, numbered at the top," he mentioned.

Henderson gave a start, leaned forward. "Wait a minute!" he said breathlessly. "That brought something back to me, just then. I can remember the number printed at the top of my particular pad. Thirteen. The jinx-number. I remember staring at it for a minute when he handed it to me, like you would with that number."

The barman put down two tabs in front of all of them. "Yeah, you're right," he said. "Here you are. But not both on the same tab. Thirteen—one Scotch and water. And here are the Jack Roses, three of them, on number seventy-four. That's one of Tommy's tabs, from the shift before, in the late afternoon; I know his writing. Not only that, but there was some other guy with her. Three Jack Roses and a rum, this one says, and no one in their right mind is going to mix those two drinks."

"So?" Burgess suggested softly.

"So I still don't remember seeing any such woman, even if she stayed over into my shift, because she was Tommy's order, not mine. But if she *did* stay over, my thirty-seven years' experience tending bar tells me he didn't get up and go over and speak to her, because there was already a guy with her. And my thirty-seven years' experience also tells me he was with her to the end, because nobody buys three Jack Roses at eighty cents a throw and then walks out and leaves his investment behind for somebody else to cash in on." And he took a definitive swipe to the counter with his bar-rag.

Henderson's voice was shaking. "But you remembered *me* being here! If you can remember me, why can't you remember her? She was even better to look at."

The barman said with vicious logic: "Sure I remembered you. Because I'm seeing you now over again, right before my eyes. Bring her back in front of me the same way, and I'll probably remember her too. I can't without that."

He was hanging on to the rim of the bar with both hands, like a drunk with unmanageable legs. Burgess detached one of his arms, grunted. "Come on, Henderson."

He still clung to it with the other, straining toward the barman. "Don't do this to me!" he protested in a choked voice. "Don't you know what the charges are? Murder!"

Burgess quickly sealed a hand to his mouth. "Shut up, Henderson," he ordered curtly.

They led him out backward. He kept straining away from them toward that bar.

"You sure did draw the thirteen tab," one of them grunted in a wry undertone, as they emerged to the street with him, pressed closely around him in a sort of perambulatory vice.

"Even if she shows up from now on, at any later point in the evening, it's already too late to do you any good," Burgess warned him as they sat waiting for the taxi-driver to be traced and brought in. "It had to be in that bar by six-seventeen. But I'm curious to see whether she will show up at some later point, and, if so, just how long after. That's why we're going to retrace your movements, step by step, throughout the entire evening, from beginning to end."

"She will, she's got to!" Henderson insisted. "*Somebody*'ll remember her, in one of the other places we went that night. And then, once you get hold of her in that way, she herself will be able to tell you just where and at what time she first met me."

The man Burgess had sent out on the assignment came in, reported: "The Sunrise Company has two drivers on the line outside

Anselmo's. I brought them both down. Their names are Budd Hickey and Al Alp."

"Alp," Henderson said. "That's the funny name I've been trying to think of. That's the name I told you we both laughed at."

"Send Alp in. Tell the other guy never mind."

He was as funny-looking in real life as on his licence picture; even funnier, for he was in full colour in real life.

Burgess said, "Did you have a haul last night from your stand to the Maison Blanche Restaurant?"

"Mason Blantch, Mason Blantch—" He was going to be a little doubtful at first. "I pick 'em up and put 'em down so many times a night—" Then a memory-quickening method of his own seemed to come to his aid. "Mason Blantch; about sixty-five cents on a dry night," he mumbled. He went back into full voice again. "Yeah, I did! I had a sixty-five cent haul last night, in between two thirty-cent pulls."

"Look around you. See anyone here you gave it to?"

His eyes slid past Henderson's face. Then they came back again. "It was him, wasn't it?"

"We're asking you, don't ask us.

He took the question-mark off. "It was him."

"Alone or with somebody else?"

He took a minute with that. Then he shook his head slowly. "I don't remember noticing nobody else with him. Alone, I guess."

Henderson gave a lurch forward, like somebody who suddenly turns an ankle. "You must have seen her! She got in ahead of me and she got out ahead of me, like a woman does—"

"Sh, quiet," Burgess tuned him out.

"Woman?" the driver said aggrievedly. "I remember you. I remember you perfect, because I got a dented fender picking you up—"

"Yes, yes," Henderson agreed eagerly, "and maybe that's why you didn't see her step in, because your head was turned the other way. But surely when we got there—"

"When we got there," the driver said sturdily, "my head *wasn't* turned the other way; no cabman's ever is when it comes time to collect a fare. *And I didn't see her get out either.* Now how about it?"

"We had the light on, all the way over," Henderson pleaded. "How could you help seeing her, sitting there in the back of you? She must have shown in your rear-sight mirror or even against your windshield—"

"Now I *am* sure," the driver said. "Now I'm positive—even if I wasn't before. I been hacking eight years. If you had the top-light on, you were by yourself. I never knew a guy riding with a woman to leave the top-light on yet. Any time the top-light's on you can bet the guy behind you is a single."

Henderson could hardly talk. He was feeling at his throat as though it bothered him. "How could you remember my face and not remember hers?"

Burgess stepped all over that before the man could even answer. "You didn't remember her face yourself. You were with her six solid hours—*you* say. He had his back to her for twenty minutes." He ended the interview. "All right, Alp. Then that's your statement?"

"That's my statement. *There was nobody with this man when I had him in my cab last night.*"

They hit the Maison Blanche at the dismantlement stage. The cloths were off the tables, the last long-lingering gourmets had departed. The help was eating in the kitchen, judging by the unbridled sounds of crockery and silverware in work that emanated from there.

They sat down at one of the denuded tables, drawing up chairs like a peculiar ghost-party of diners about to fall to without any visible utensils or comestibles.

The head-waiter was so used to bowing to people that he bowed now as he came out to them, even though he was off duty. The bow didn't look so good because he'd removed his collar and tie, and had a lump of food in one cheek.

Burgess said. "Have you seen this man before?"

His black-pitted eyes took in Henderson. The answer came like a finger-snap. "Yes, surely."

"When was the last time?"

"Last night."

"Where did he sit?"

He picked out the niche-table unerringly. "Over there."

"Well?" Burgess said. "Go on."

"Go on with what?"

"Who was with him?"

"Nobody was with him."

There was a line of little moist needle-pricks starting out along Henderson's forehead. "You saw her come in a moment or two after me, and join me. You saw her sitting there during the whole meal. You must have. Once you even passed close by and bowed and said, "Everything satisfactory, m'sieu?' "

"Yes. That is part of my duties. I do it to each table at least once. I distinctly recall doing it to you, because your face was, how shall I say, a little discontented. I also distinctly recall the two vacant chairs, one on each side of you. I believe I straightened one a little. You have quoted me yourself. And if I said 'monsieur,' as

I did, that is the surest indication there was no one with you. The correct inquiry for a lady and gentleman together is 'm'sieu-et-dame.' It is never altered."

The black centres of his eyes were as steady as buckshot fired deep into his face and lodged there. He turned to Burgess. "Well, if there is any doubt, I can show you my reservation list for last night. You can see for yourselves."

Burgess said with an exaggeratedly slow drawl that meant he liked the idea very much, "I don't think that would hurt."

The head-waiter went across the dining-room, opened a drawer in a buffet, brought back a ledger. He didn't go out of the room, he didn't go out of their sight. He handed it to them unopened, just as he had found it; let them open it for themselves. All he said was, "You can refer to the date at the top."

They all formed a cluster of heads over it but himself. He remained detached. It was kept in impromptu pencil, but it was sufficient for its purpose. The page was headed "5–20, Tues." Then there was a large corner-to-corner X drawn across the page, to show that it was over and done with. It cancelled without impairing legibility.

There was a list of some nine or ten names. They went like this, columnarly:

Table 18—Roger Ashley, for four. (Lined out.)
Table 5—Mrs. Rayburn, for six. (Lined out.)
Table 24—Scott Henderson, for two. (Not lined out.)

Beside the third name was this parenthetic symbol: (1).

The head-waiter explained. "That tells its own story. When a line is drawn through, that means the reservation has been completed, filled up. When there is no line drawn through, that means they never showed up. When there is no line drawn through, and a number is added, that means only part of them showed up, the rest are still expected. Those things in the little brackets are for my own guidance, so I will know where they go when they do show up, where to put them, without having to ask a lot of questions. No matter if they come only at the dessert, so long as they come at all, the line goes through. What you see here means, therefore; m'sieu had a reservation for two, m'sieu showed up by himself, and the other half of his party never reached here."

Burgess traced hypersensitive finger-pads over that particular section of the page, feeling for erasures. "Texture unmarred," he said.

Henderson pronged his hand, elbow to table-top; let it catch his head as it toppled forward.

The head-waiter shovelled with his hands. "My book is all I have to go by. My books says—to me—Mr. Henderson was alone in this dining-room last night."

"Then your book says that to us too. Take his name and address, usual stuff, case wanted further questioning. All right, next. Mitri Maloff, table-waiter."

A change of figures before Henderson's eyes, that was all. The dream, the practical joke, the whatever it was, went on and on.

This was going to be comedy stuff. To the rest of them, anyway, if not to him. He caught sight of one of them writing something down. He hooked his finger around to his thumb, like in that old hair-tonic ad. "No, no. Beg pardon, shentlemen. There is a D in it. It is silent, you don't speak it."

"Then what's the good of having it?" one of them wondered to the man next to him.

"I don't care what there is in it," Burgess said. "All I want to know is, do you have table twenty-four?"

"From ten, over there, all the way around to twenty eight, that is me."

"You waited on this man at twenty-four last night?"

He was going to make a social introduction of it. "Ah, sure, certainly!" he lighted up. "Good-evening! How are you? You coming back again soon, I hope!" He evidently didn't recognize them as detectives.

"No, he isn't," said Burgess brutally. He flattened his hand, to kill the flow of amenities. "How many were there at the table when you waited on him?"

The waiter looked puzzled, like a man who is willing to do his best but can't get the hang of what is expected of him. "Him," he said. "No more. Shust him."

"No lady?"

"No, no lady. What lady?" And then he added, in perfect innocence. "Why? He lose one?"

It brought on a howl. Henderson parted his lips and took a deep breath, like when something hurts you unbearably.

"Yeah, he lost one all right," one of them clowned.

The waiter saw he had made a hit, batted his eyes at them coyly, but still, apparently, without any very clear idea of how he had chalked up his success.

Henderson spoke, in a desolate, beaten-down sort of voice. "You drew out her chair for her. You opened the menu-card, offered it to her." He tapped his own skull a couple of times. "I *saw* you do those things. But no, you didn't see her."

The waiter began to expostulate with Eastern European warmth, and lavishness of gesture, but without any rancour: "I draw out a chair, yes, when there is a lady there for it. But when there is no lady there, how can I draw out a chair? For the air to sit down on it, you think I'm going to draw out a chair? When is no face there, you think I'm going to open bill-of-fare and push it in front of?"

Burgess said, "Talk to us, not him. He's in custody."

He did, as volubly as ever, simply switching the direction of his head. "He leave me tip for one and a half. How could there be lady with him? You think I'm going to be nice to him today if is two there last night and he leave me tip for only one and a half?" His eyes lit with Slavonic fire. Even the supposition seemed to inflame him. "You think I forget it in a horry? I remember it for next two weeks! Hah! You think I ask him to come back like I do? Hah!' he snorted belligerently.

"What's a tip for one and a half?" Burgess asked with jocular curiosity.

"For one is thirty cents. For two is sixty cents. He give me forty-five cents, is tip for one and a half."

"Couldn't you get forty-five cents for a party of two?"

"Never!" he panted resentfully. "If I do, I do like this." He removed an imaginary salver from the table, fingers disdainfully lifted as if it were contaminated. He fixed a baleful eye on the imaginary customer, in this case Henderson. Sustained it long enough to shrivel him. His thick underlip curled in what was meant for a lopsided leer of derision. "I say, "Thank you, sor. Thank you very motch, sor. Thank you *very, very* motch, sor. You sure you able to do this?' And if is lady with him, he feels like two cents, he stick in some more."

"I kind of would myself," Burgess admitted. He turned his head. "How much do you say you left, Henderson?"

Henderson's answer was forlornly soft-spoken. "What he says I did; forty-five cents."

"One thing more," Burgess said, "just to round the whole thing out, I'd like to see the cheque for that particular dinner. You keep them, don't you?"

"Manager got them. You have to ask him." The waiter's face took on an expression of conscious virtue, as though now he felt sure his veracity would be sustained.

Henderson was suddenly leaning alertly forward, his licked list-lessness was gone again.

The manager brought them out himself. They were kept in sheaves, in little oblong clasp-folders, one to a date, apparently to help him tally his accounts at the end of each month. They found it without difficulty. It said "Table 24. Waiter 3. 1 Table d'hote— 2.25." It was stamped in faint purple, "Paid—May 20th" in a sort of oval formation.

There were only two other cheques for table twenty four in that day's batch. One was "1 tea—0.75," from late afternoon, just before the dinner hour. The other was dinner for four, a party that had evidently come in late, just before closing.

They had to help him get back into the car. He walked in a kind of stupor. His legs were balky. Again there was the dream-like glide of unreal buildings and unreal streets moving backward past them, like shadows on glass.

He broke out suddenly. "They're lying—they're killing me, all of them! What did I ever do to any of them—?"

"Y'know what it reminds me of?" one of the said in an aside. "Them Topper pictures, where they fade off and on the screen right in front of your eyes. Did y'ever see one of them, Burge?"

Henderson shuddered involuntarily and let his head go over.

There was a show going on outside, and the music, and laughter, and sometimes handclapping, would trickle into the small, cluttered office, diluted.

The manager was sitting waiting by the phone. Business was good, and he tried to look pleasantly at all of them, savouring his cigar and leaning far back in his swivel-chair.

"There can be no question that the two seats were paid for," the manager said urbanely. "All I can tell you is that nobody was seen going in with him—" He broke off with sudden anxiety. "He's going to be ill. Please get him out of here as quickly as you can. I don't want any commotion while there's a performance going on."

They opened the door and half carried, half walked Henderson toward it, his back inclined far over toward the floor. A gust of singing from out front surged in.

"Chica chica boom boom
Chica chica boom boom—"

"Ah, don't, he pleaded chokingly."I can't stand any more of it!" He toppled on to the back seat of the police sedan, made a knot of his two hands, gnawed at them as if seeking assistance for his sanity.

"Why not break down and admit there *was* no dame with you?" Burgess tried to reason with him. "Don't you see how much simpler it would be all around?"

Henderson tried to answer him in a rational, even voice, but he was a little shaky at it. "Do you know what the next step would be after that, if I did, if I *could*, make such an admission as you're asking me to? My sanity would start to leave me. I'd never be sure of anything again in my life. You can't take a fact that you know to be true, as true as—as that your name is Scott Henderson"—he clapped himself on the thigh—"as true as that this is my own leg, and let yourself begin to doubt it, deny it, without your mental balance going overboard. She was beside me for six hours. I touched her arm. I felt it in the curve of my own." He reached out and briefly tweaked Burgess' muscular underarm. "The rustle of her dress. The words she spoke. The faint fragrance of her perfume. The clink of her spoon against her *consommé*-plate. The little stamp of her chair when she moved it back. The little quiver of the shaky taxi-chassis when she stepped down from it. Where did the liquor go to that my eyes saw in her glass when she raised it? When it came down again it was empty." He pounded his fist against his knee three, four, five times. "She was, she was, she was!" He was almost crying; at least his face was wreathed in those lines. "Now they're trying to tell me she *wasn't*!"

The car glided on through the never-never land it had been traversing all evening.

He said a thing that few, if any, suspects have ever said before. Said it and meant it with his whole heart and soul. "I'm frightened; take me back to the detention-pen will you? Please, fellows, take me back. I want walls around me that you can feel with your hands. Thick, solid, that you can't budge!"

"He's shivering," one of them pointed out with a sort of detached curiosity.

"He needs a drink," Burgess said. "Stop here a minute. One of you go in and bring him out a couple fingers of rye. I hate to see a guy suffer like that."

Henderson gulped it avidly, as though he couldn't get it down fast enough. Then he slopped back against the seat. "Let's go back, take me back,' he pleaded.

"He's haunted," one of them chuckled.

"That's what you get when you raise a ghost."

Nothing further was said until they were out of the car again and filing up the steps at Headquarters in phalanx. Then Burgess steadied him with a hand to his arm as he fumbled one of the steps. "You better get a good night's sleep. Henderson," he suggested. "And a good lawyer. You're going to need both."

# FIVE

# The Ninety-first Day Before the Execution

". . . You have heard the defence try to claim that the accused met a certain woman, in a place called Anselmo's Bar, at ten minutes after six on the night the murder was committed. In other words, two minutes and forty-five seconds after the time established by police investigation as that of the death of the victim. Very clever. You can see at once, ladies and gentlemen of the jury, that *if* he was at Anselmo's Bar, Fiftieth Street, at ten past six, he could not have been at *his own* apartment two and three-quarter minutes before then. Nothing on two legs could have covered the distance from one to the other in that length of time. No, nor on four wheels, nor with wings and a propeller either, for that matter. Again I say, very clever. *But*—not clever enough.

"Convenient, wasn't it, that he should just happen to meet her on that one night, and not any other night during the year? Almost as though he had a premonition he was going to need her on that particular night. Strange things, premonitions, aren't they? You have heard the defendant admit, in answer to my questions, that he did *not* go out and accost unknown women other nights of the year. That he had never done such a thing before during the entire course of his married life. Not once, mind you. Those are the accused's own words, not mine. You heard them yourselves, ladies and gentlemen. Such a thought had never entered his mind until then. It was not his habit to do that sort of thing. It was foreign to his nature. On this one night of all nights, however, they would have us believe that he did. Quite a handy coincidence, what? Only—"

Shrug, and a long pause.

"Where is the woman? We've all been waiting to see her. Why don't they show her to us? What's keeping them? Have they produced such a woman here in court?"

Singling out a juror at random with index-finger. "Have *you* seen her?" Another. "Or you?" A third, in the second tier. "Or you?" Gesture of empty-handed helplessness. "Has anyone of us seen her? Has she been up there on that witness-chair at any time from first to last? No, of course not, ladies and gentlemen. Because—"

Another long pause.

"Because there *is* no such woman. There never was. They can't produce a person who doesn't exist. They can't breathe life into a figment, a figure of speech, a nebula, a thing that *isn't*. Only the good Lord can create a full-grown woman in all her height and breath and thickness. And even He needs eighteen years to do it, not two weeks."

Laughter from all parts of the room. Brief smile of grateful appreciation on his part.

"This man is being tried for his life. If there was such a woman, do you think they would have neglected to bring her here? Wouldn't they have seen to it that she was on the job here, speaking her piece at the right time? You bet they would! *If*—"

Dramatic pause.

"—there was such a woman. Let's leave ourselves out of it. We're here in a court-room, miles from the places that he insists he visited with her that night, and months have passed. Let's take the word of those who were right there, *at* those same places, *at* the same time, as he supposedly was with her. Surely they should have seen her, if anyone did. *Did* they? You heard for yourself. They saw him, yes. Every one of them can recall, no matter how vaguely, no matter how hazily, glimpsing him, Scott Henderson, that night. It seems to end there, as though they all had a blindness in one eye. Doesn't that strike you as a little odd, ladies and gentlemen? It does me. When people travel around in pairs, one of two things happens: either neither one of them is remembered afterward, or, if one is, then the other is also. How can the human eye see one person without seeing the other—if the other is right there alongside the first at the time? That violates the law of physics. I can't account for it. It baffles me."

Coy bunching of the shoulders.

"I'm open to suggestions. In fact, I'll make a few myself. Possibly her skin was of a peculiar transparency that let the light through, and so they looked right through her to the other side without—"

General laughter.

"Or possibly she just didn't happen to be there with him. Nothing more natural than that they should fail to see her if she didn't happen to be there at the time."

Change of manner and of voice. General tightening up.

"Why go ahead? Let's keep this serious. A man's on trial here for his life. I'm not anxious to make a farce out of it. The defence is the one that seems to be. Let's leave hypotheses and theories and go back to facts. Let's stop talking about phantoms and will-o'-the-wisps and mirages; instead let's talk about a woman of whose existence there has never at any time been any doubt. Everybody saw Marcella Henderson in life, and everybody saw her just as plainly afterward in death. *She* was no phantom. She was murdered. The police have photographs showing that. That's the first fact. All of us see that man over there in the prisoner's dock, with his head bowed low through all of this—no, now he's raising it to stare defiantly over at me. He's on trial here for his life. That's the second fact."

In a confidential, theatrical aside: "I like facts much better than fancies, don't you, ladies and gentlemen? They're much easier to handle.

"And the third fact? Here's the third fact. He murdered her. Yes, that's as concrete, as undeniable, a fact as the first two. Every detail of it is a fact, already proven once here in this room. We're not asking you to believe in phantoms, in wraiths, in hallucinations,

like the defence!" Raising his voice. "We have documents, affi-
davits, evidence, for every statement we make every step of the
way!" Bringing his fist crashing down on the rail before the jury-
box.

Impressive pause. Then in a quieter voice. "You've already been
made acquainted with the circumstances, the domestic background,
immediately preceding the murder. The accused himself doesn't
deny their accuracy. You've heard him confirm them; under pressure, unwillingly perhaps, but confirm them nevertheless. There
hasn't been a false statement made about them; don't take my
word for that, take his. I asked him that yesterday on the stand,
and you all heard his answer. I'll run over them once more, briefly,
for you.

"Scott Henderson fell in love outside of his own home. He's not
up here for having done that. The girl he fell in love with is not on
trial here. You've noticed that her name hasn't been mentioned in
this court-room; she hasn't been dragged forward, compelled to
testify, involved in any way in this brutal, inexcusable murder.
Why? Because she doesn't deserve to be. She had nothing to do
with it. It's not our purpose to punish the innocent here in this
court-room, to subject her to the notoriety and humiliation that
would follow. The crime was his—that man whom you see there—
and his alone. Not hers. She's blameless. She's been investigated
both by the police and by the prosecution, and absolved of any
connection, or incitement, or even knowledge of what had happened, until it was all over. She's suffering enough right now
through no fault of her own. We're in general agreement on that
one point, all of us, defence as well as prosecution. Her name and
identity is known to us, but we've called her "The Girl" throughout,
and we'll continue to do so.

"Very well. He was already dangerously in love with The Girl
by the time he remembered to tell her he was married. Yes, I say
dangerously—from his wife's viewpoint. The Girl wouldn't have
him on those terms. She was, and is, a decent person, a fine human
being; every one of us who has spoken to her feels that way strongly
about her. I do myself, ladies and gentlemen; she's a lovely, unfortunate person who happened to meet the wrong man. So, as I
say, she wouldn't have him on those terms. She didn't want to hurt
anyone else. He found he couldn't have his cake and eat it too.

"Very well, he went to his wife and he asked her to divorce him.
Cold-bloodedly, just like that. She refused him a divorce. Why?
Because, to her, marriage, was a sacred institution. Not just a
passing affair, to be broken off short at a whim. Strange wife,
wasn't she?

"The Girl's suggestion, when he told her this, was that they
forget all about one another. He couldn't see it that way. He found

himself caught between the horns of a dilemma. His wife wouldn't give him up, and he wouldn't give The Girl up.

"He bided his time and then he tried once more. And if you'd speak of the first method as cold-blooded, what would you say of the way he went about it the second time? He put himself out to *entertain* her the way a customer's man entertains an out-of-town buyer with whom he is trying to transact a business deal. That should give you a good insight into his character, ladies and gentlemen; that should tell you what calibre man he is. That was all a scrapped marriage, a broken home, a discarded wife, were worth to him. An evening's paltry entertainment.

"He bought two tickets for the theatre, he reserved a table at a restaurant. He came home and told her he was taking her out. She couldn't understand this sudden attentiveness. She mistakenly thought, for a moment, that perhaps there was a reconciliation in the air. She sat down at her mirror and she began to get ready.

"A few moments later he returned to the room and he found her still sitting there at her dressing table, without going any further in her preparations. She understood a little better what his purpose was now

"She told him that she wouldn't give him up. She told him, in effect, that she valued her home higher than two orchestra seats and a course dinner. In other words, without giving him time to ask her, she had refused him a divorce a second time. That was one time too many.

"He was at the final stage of his own preparations. He had his necktie open in his hands, measured off, ready to insert it under his collar. Instead, in a blind, ungovernable rage at being out-guessed and outgeneralled, he dropped it over her head as she sat there at her mirror. He tightened it around her neck, he twined the ends together with unimaginable cruelty and strength and will to kill. The police officers have told you how it had to be cut off, practically *pared* off, it was so embedded in her soft throat. Did you ever try to tear one of these sevenfold rep silk ties between your hands, ladies and gentlemen? It can't be done; the edges will slice your fingers like a knife, but you can't sever them.

"She died. She flung her arms out once or twice, just in the beginning, and then she died there, between her husband's hands. The man that had sworn to cherish and protect her. Don't forget that.

"He held her like that, upright at her own mirror, letting her look at her own death-struggles, so to speak, for long minutes. Long, long minutes. So that she was dead long before he let her fall over from that upright position he'd held her in. Then when he was sure that she was dead, that she was good and dead, that she was dead beyond recall, that she was out of his way once and for all—what did he do then?

"Did he try to bring her back, did he feel any remorse, did he show any regret? No, I'll tell you what he did. *He calmly went ahead and finished his own dressing*, right there in the room with her. He picked up another necktie and put that on, to take the place of the one he'd garrotted her with. He put on his hat and his coat, and just before he left he called The Girl up. Luckily for her, and it was the luckiest thing that ever happened to her in her life, she wasn't there at the time to get that call. She never knew about it until hours afterward. And why did he call her up, with his hands still moist and reeking from taking his wife's life? Not in remorse, not to confess what he'd just done and ask her to help him or advise him. No, no. To use her for a cat's-paw. To make a living alibi out of her, without her knowledge. To ask her to go out with him instead, on those same tickets, on that same table reservation. He probably would have set his own watch back, just before meeting her, and commented on it, so that she would be sure to remember afterwards, and come forward in good faith and shield him with her honestly given testimony.

"Is that a murderer for you, ladies and gentlemen, or isn't it?

"But that didn't work; he couldn't get her. So he did the next best thing. He went out alone, cold-bloodedly went through the whole routine he had prepared for himself and his wife, without missing a single stop, from six to midnight. At the time it didn't occur to him to do what he now says he did: pick up some stray along the way and use her for his alibi. He was too excited, too confused, just then. Or perhaps it did enter his mind, but he lacked the nerve; was afraid to trust a stranger, afraid his manner would betray him. Or then again maybe it was because he reasoned that it was already too late for that to do him any good; too much time had passed by now since he'd left his own house. His living alibi could have been made just as easily to count against him as for him, once the crime was more than just a few minutes old. A little adroit questioning would have been able to extract the exact time he had *really* met her, and not the time he wished it to be believed he had met her. He thought of all that.

"So what was better than that, even? Why; an imaginary companion, of course. A phantom at his side, purposely left vague, left blurred, so that she could never be retrieved later on to damn his story of when they had met. In other words, which was preferable for his purposes: an unsupported alibi or a refuted one? I leave that up to you yourselves, ladies and gentlemen. An unsupported one could never be completely confirmed, but it would always seem to leave a reasonable doubt open. A refuted one would be automatically cast back in his face and leave him no further defence.

That was the best he could do, that was the best he could get, and he made his decision accordingly.

"In other words, he deliberately injected a myth into the proceedings, *knowing* she did not exist, *knowing* she could never be found, and perfectly content to have her *not* found, for only while she remains *not* found is his fractional alibi of any service to him.

"In conclusion, let me ask you ladies and gentlemen just one simple question. Is it natural, is it likely, when a man's very life depends on his ability to remember certain details in the appearance of another, for him to be unable to recall a single, solitary one of them? Not one, mind you! He is unable to recall the colour of her eyes, or the colour of her hair, or the contour of her face, or her height, or her girth, or anything else about her. Put yourselves in his place. Would you be likely to forget so completely, so devastatingly, if your lives depended on it? Self-preservation can be a wonderful spur to the memory, you know. Is it at all plausible that he would forget her so totally, if he really wished her to be found? If she exists, or ever did, *to be* found? I leave you with that thought.

"I don't think there's much more I have to say to you, ladies and gentlemen of the jury. It's a simple case. The issue is clear, without anything to confuse it."

Pointing with dramatic prolongation. "The State accuses that man whom you see there, Scott Henderson, of murdering his wife.

"The State demands his life in return.

"The State rests its case."

# SIX

## The Ninetieth Day Before the Execution

"Will the accused please rise and face the jury.

"Will the foreman of the jury please stand.

"Ladies and gentlemen of the jury, have you reached a verdict?"

"We have, your honour."

"Do you find this defendant guilty or not guilty of the charge made against him?"

"Guilty, your honour."

Strangled voice from the direction of the prisoner's dock: "Oh, my God—no—!"

# SEVEN

## The Eighty-seventh Day Before the Execution

"Prisoner at the bar, have you anything to say before this court passes sentence upon you?"

"What is there to say, when they tell you you have committed a crime, and you and you alone know you haven't? Who is there to hear you, and who is there to believe you?

"You're about to tell me that I must die, and if you tell me I must, I must. I'm not more afraid of dying than any other man. But I'm just as afraid of dying as any other man. It isn't easy to die at all, but it's even harder to die for a mistake. I'm not dying for something I've done, but for a mistake. And that's the hardest way to die of all. When the times comes, I'll meet it the best I can; that's all I can do, anyway.

"But I say to you now, all of you, who won't listen and don't believe: I didn't do that. I didn't do it. Not all the findings of all the juries, not all the trials in all the courts, not all the executions in all the electric chairs—in the whole world—can make what isn't so, so.

"I'm ready to hear it now, your honour. Quite ready."

Voice from the bench, in a sympathetic aside: "I'm sorry, Mr. Henderson, I don't think I've ever heard a more compelling, dignified, manly plea from anyone who has stood before me for sentence. But the verdict of the jury in this cases gives me no alternative."

Same voice, slightly louder: "Scott Henderson, having been tried and found guilty of murder in the first degree, I hereby sentence you to die in the electric chair, in the State Prison at—, during the week beginning October 20th, said sentence to be carried out by the warden of the prison, and may God have mercy on your soul."

# EIGHT

## The Twenty-first Day Before the Execution

Low voice, just outside the cell in the Death House corridor: "Here he is, in this one."

Louder, above a jangle of keys: "Somebody here to see you, Henderson."

Henderson doesn't speak or move. Gate is opened, then closed again. Long, awkward pause, while they look at one another.

"Guess you don't remember me."

"You remember the people that kill you."

"I don't kill people, Henderson. I turn people who commit crimes over to those whose job it is to try them."

"Then you come around afterward to make sure they haven't gotten away, to satisfy yourself they're still there where you put them, getting it rubbed into them, day by day and minute by minute. It must worry you. Well, take a look. I'm here. I'm safe on ice. Now you can go away happy."

"You're bitter, Henderson."

"It doesn't sweeten you any to die at thirty-two."

Burgess didn't answer that. No one could have, adequately. He shuttered his eyes rapidly a couple of times to show that it had hit. He went over to the skinny canal of opening and looked out.

"Small, isn't it?" Henderson said, without turning his head to look.

Burgess promptly turned and came away from it, at that, as though it had closed up on him. He took something out of his pocket, stopped before the bunk the other was sitting crouched on. "Cigarette?"

Henderson looked up derisively. "What's the matter with them?"

"Ah, don't be like that," the detective protested throatily. He continued to hold them out.

Henderson took one grudgingly at last, more as if by doing so to get him to move away from him than because he really wanted one. His eyes were still bitter. He wiped the small cylinder insultingly on his sleeve before putting it to his mouth.

Burgess gave him a light for it. Henderson looked his scorn at him even for that, holding his eyes steady, above the small flame, on the other's face. "What's this, the day of the execution already?"

"I know how you feel—" Burgess began in mild remonstrance.

Henderson reared up suddenly on the slab. "*You* know how I

feel!" he flared. He snapped ashes down toward the detective's feet, by way of indicating them. "They can go anywhere they feel like!" He jabbed his thumb toward his own. "But *they* can't!" His mouth looped downward at one corner. "Get out of here. Get out. Go back and kill somebody else. Get fresh material, I'm second hand, I've been worked over once already."

He lay back again, blew a tracer of smoke out along the wall. It mushroomed when it hit the top of the bunk, came down toward him again.

They had quit looking at one another. But Burgess was standing still, hadn't gone. He said finally, "I understand your appeal's been turned down."

"Yes, my appeal's been turned down. Now there are no more hitches, no more impediments, nothing further to interfere with the ceremonial bonfire. Now I can skid straight down the chute without anything more to stop me. Now the cannibals won't have to go hungry. Now they can make a nice, swift, clean-cut job of it. Streamlined." He turned and looked at his listener. "What're *you* looking so mournful about? Sorry because the agony can't be prolonged? Sorry because I can't die twice over?"

Burgess made a wry face as though his cigarette tasted rotten. He stepped on it. "Don't hit below the belt, Henderson. My dukes aren't even up."

Henderson looked at him intently for a while, as though noticing something in his manner for the first time through the red haze of anger that had hovered over his perceptions until now. "What's on your mind?" he asked. "What brings you around here like this, anyway, months afterward?"

Burgess felt the back of his neck. "I don't know how to put it myself. It's a funny thing for a dick to do," he admitted. "I know my job with you ended when you were indicted by the Grand Jury and bound over for trial. It's sort of hard to bring out," he ended lamely.

"Why? It shouldn't be. I'm just a condemned guy in a cell."

"That's just why it is. I came up to—well, what I'm here to say is—" He stopped a minute, then blurted out: "I believe you're innocent. Well, there it is, for what it's worth, and it's not worth anything—to you or me either. I don't think you did it, Henderson."

Long wait.

"Well, say something. Don't just sit there looking at me."

"I don't know what to say when a guy digs up the corpse he helped to bury and says, 'Sorry, old man, I guess I've made a mistake.' You better tell me what to say."

"I guess you're right. I guess there's nothing to say. But I still claim I did my part of the job right, on the evidence there was to go by. I'll go further than that. I'd do the same thing over again tomorrow, if it had to be done a second time. My personal feelings don't count; my job is to work with concrete things."

"And what brought on this profound change of conviction?" Henderson asked, with a dull sort of irony.

"That's as hard to explain, to make clear, as any of the rest of it. It's been a slow thing, it's taken weeks and months to soak through me. About as slow as water soaking through a stack of blotters. It started in at the trial, I guess. It worked by a sort of reverse process. All the things that they made to count against you so heavily, they seemed to point the other way around, to me, later on when I ran over them in my own mind.

"I don't know if you can quite get what I mean. Framed alibis are always so clever, so smooth, so chockful of plausible details. Yours was so lame, so blank. You couldn't remember a single thing about this woman. A ten-year-old child would have been able to do a better job of description. As I sat in the back of the courtroom listening, it slowly dawned on me: hey, that must be the truth he's telling! Any lie, any lie at all, would have more meat on its bones than that. Only a man who was *not* guilty could frustrate his own chances as thoroughly as you did. The guilty are smarter than that. Your life was at stake, and all you could muster to protect yourself was two nouns and an adjective. 'Woman,' 'hat,' and 'funny.' I thought to myself, 'How true to life that is.' A guy is all riled up inside from a row at home, he picks up someone he's not interested in in the first place. Then right on top of that comes the mental cloudburst of finding out there's been a murder in his house and hearing himself accused of it—" He gestured expressively. "Which is more likely: that he'd remember such a stranger in exhaustive detail, or that what little impression remained of her in the first place would be completely washed away, leaving the slate blank?

"It's been on my mind a long time now. It's kept coming back to me with more and more pressure each time. Once before I already started to come up here, but then I turned around and backed out again. Then I talked to Miss Richman once or twice—"

Henderson elongated his neck. "I begin to see light."

The detective said, sharply and at once: "No, you don't at all! You probably think she came to see me and finally influenced me. It was the other way around. I first looked her up, and went to have a talk with her—to tell her pretty much what I've told you today. Since then, I admit, she's been to see me several times—not at Headquarters, but at my own place—and we've had several more talks about it. But that's neither here nor there. Miss Richman nor nobody else can put anything in my mind if it wasn't in there already. If there's any changing with me, it's got to be done on the inside, and not from the outside in. If I'm up here to see you today, it's on my own hook. I'm not here at her suggestion. She didn't know I was coming up here. I didn't myself—until I did."

He started to walk back and forth. "Well, I've got it off my chest now. I still won't retract, I did my part of the job the only way it could have been done, the way the evidence called for it to be done. And you can't ask any more of a man than that."

Henderson didn't answer. He sat staring moodily at the floor. It was a sort of quiescent brooding. He seemed less actively bitter than in the beginning. The shadow made by Burgess' pacing kept passing and repassing him. He didn't bother to look up at its source.

Then the shadow stood still, and he could hear the sound of coins jangling thoughtfully inside a pocket lining.

Burgess' voice said: "You've got to get hold of someone that can help you. That can work at it full time for you."

He jingled some more. "I can't, I've got work of my own. Oh, I know in movies and such there are these glorified detectives that chuck everything just to go off on some sideline of their own. I've got a wife and kids. I need my job. And you and me are strangers, after all."

Henderson didn't move his head. "I didn't ask you to," he murmured quietly.

Burgess quit jingling finally, came part of the way back to him. "Get someone that's close to you, that's all for you"—he tightened his fist and hoisted it in promise—"and I'll back him up all I can."

Henderson looked up for the first time, then down again. He said one word, dispiritedly. "Who?"

"It needs someone that'll put a passion into it, a belief, a fervour. Someone who isn't doing it for money, nor for his own advancement. Someone who's doing it for you because you're Scott Henderson, and no other reason. Because he likes you—yes, even loves you, because he'd almost rather die himself than have you die. Someone that won't be licked, even when he is. Someone that won't know it's too late, even when it is. That's the kind of flame it needs, that's the kind of juice. That and only that'll swing it."

His hand had come to rest on Henderson's shoulder while he spoke, in an accolade of insistence.

"You've got a girl that feels that way about you, I know. But she's just a girl. She's got the flame, but not the experience. She's doing what she can, but it isn't enough."

For the first time Henderson's bleak expression softened a little. He shot a brief look of gratitude, meant for her, by proxy at the detective. "I might have known—" he murmured.

"It needs a man. Someone that knows his way around. And yet has that feeling for you she has. You must have someone like that. Everyone has someone like that in his life.

"Yes, when they first start out. I used to, I guess, like everyone else. They seem to drop off along the way, as you get older. Especially after you get married."

"They don't drop off, if they're what I'm talking about," Burgess insisted. "Whether you keep in touch with them or not has nothing to do with it. If it's once there, it's there."

"There was a guy once; he and I were as close as brothers," Henderson admitted. "But that was in the past—"

"There's no time-limit on friendship."

"He isn't here right now, anyway. The last time I met him he told me he was leaving the next day for South America. He had a five-year contract with some oil company."

He quirked his head at the detective. "For a fellow in your line of work you seem to have quite a few illusions left intact, haven't you? That would be asking something, wouldn't it? Expect someone to come back three thousand miles and can his whole immediate future to go to bat for a friend at the drop of a hat. And not a current friend either, mind you. Remember, you get thicker-skinned as you get older. Some of the idealism peels off. The man of thirty-two isn't the same pal to you the lad of twenty-five was, and you're not to him."

Burgess cut across his objections. "Just answer one thing. Would he have once done it?"

"He would have once done it."

"Then if he would have once done it, he'll still do it. I tell you again there's no age-limit on that kind of loyalty. If he had it, then he has it. If he hasn't it, then that only proves he never did have it.

"But that's an unfair test, that's putting the hurdle too high."

"If he's the sort of a guy that would weigh a five-year contract against your life," Burgess argued, "then he's no good to you anyway. If he isn't, then he's the guy you need. Why not give him a chance to come through first, before you start to talk as though he won't?"

He took a memorandum-book out of his pocket, tore off a blank leaf, poised his knee for a writing-rest, foot to the edge of the bunk.

NN29 22 CABLE VIA NBN = ——, SEPT 20.
NLT JOHN LOMBARD =
Compania Petrolera Sudamericana
Head Office, Caracas, Venezuela.

Have been sentenced for Marcellas death since you left a certain key witness can clear me if found my lawyer here has reached the end of his resources this is to ask you to come up and help me have no one else to turn to and no other chance of pulling through sentence set for third week October and appeal has been turned down give me a hand will you.

SCOTT HENDERSON

# NINE

## Eighteenth Day Before the Execution

He still had some of the tan on him from warmer latitudes. He'd come up so quick he'd brought it with him, like people do when they travel nowadays; a cold in the head flies with them from the West Coast to the East; a three-day boil on the neck lasts from Rio to La Guardia Field before it pops.

He looked about the age Scott Henderson had once been; the former Scott Henderson of five or six months ago, not the pinched death-mask lingering on in a cell, who counted years by hours.

He was still wearing the clothes he'd put on in South America. A snowy panama that was out of season up here right now, and a grey flannel suit that was too light, both in shade and weight, for an American autumn. It needed the blazing Venezuelan sunshine to make it seem less conspicuous.

He was moderately tall, and easy-moving with it; no effort at all to get around. You could think of him as always chasing after a street-car, even when it was already a block away, because it was so easy for him to catch up with it. He was anything but a natty dresser, in spite of his vernal clothes. His small moustache could have stood a touch of the scissors, and his necktie needed steaming; it kept curling around on itself all the way down, like a spiral of spun-sugar candy. The impression he gave, in short, was that he'd be a lot better at bossing a crew of men or poring over a draughting-board than dancing on a ballroom floor with the ladies. There was a certain gravity about him that indicated that, if outward indications are ever any good. What used to be called, in the days of simpler cataloguing, a man's man.

"How's he taking it?" he asked the guard in an undertone as he followed him along the tier.

"Just about." Meaning, what can you expect?

"Just about, eh?" He shook his head, muttered under his breath: "Poor cuss."

The guard had reached it, was opening it up.

He held back a moment, swallowed hard as if to get his throat working smoothly, then turned the corner of the cell-grate into view. He went into the cell with a wry grin on his face and an outstretched hand leading the way. As though he was running into him in the lounge of the Savoy-Plaza.

"Well lookit old Hendy," he drawled. "What're you doing, trying to be funny?"

There was none of the bitterness present in Henderson's reaction there had been the day the detective had visited him. You could tell this man was an old friend. His drawn face lighted up. He answered him in kind. "I live here now. How d'you like that?"

They pumped hands as if they'd never get through. They were still working away at it after the guard had locked up and gone off again.

That link of hands carried messages for them, unspoken but plainly understood. Henderson's was a warmly grateful: "You came. You showed up. So that stuff about a real friend isn't the bunk."

And Lombard's was a fervent, encouraging: "I'm with you. I'm damned if they're going to do it."

After that they steered clear of the subject the first few minutes. They said everything but what they really wanted to. A sort of skittishness, a diffidence, that a particular topic, when it is too vital, bleeding, and raw, will sometimes bring about.

Thus Lombard said: "Gee, that was a dusty ride on the train, getting up here."

And Henderson: "You look good, Jack. Must agree with you down there."

"Agree, hell! Don't talk about it, will you? Of all the lousy, God-forsaken holes! And the food! *And* the mosquitoes! I was a sucker ever to sign up for five years like I did."

"But there was good money in it, I suppose, wasn't there?"

"Sure. But what am I going to do with it down there, anyway? Nowhere to spend it. Even the beer has a kerosene flavour."

Henderson mumbled. "I feel low, spiking it for you, though."

"You did me a favour," Lombard protested gallantly. "The contract's still on, anyway. This is just time off I wangled."

He waited a moment or two more. Then finally he edged up to it; the *it* that was on both their minds. He quit looking at his friend, looked somewhere else instead. "What about this thing, anyway, Hendy?"

Henderson tried to smile. "Well, there's a member of the Class of '30 going to take part in an electrical experiment two and a half weeks from today. What was it they gave me in the year-book? 'Most likely to get his name in the papers.' Good prophecy. I'll probably make every edition that day."

Lombard's eyes turned to stare at him truculently. "No you won't. Let's quit horsing around. We've known each other half our lives; may as well kick off our shoes and drop the company manners."

"Sure," Henderson agreed forlornly. "What the hell, life's so short." He belatedly realized the unintentional appropriateness of that, grinned sheepishly.

Lombard slung one hip across the rim of the washbowl in the corner and relieved the leg that supported it of floor duty. He took it by the ankle with both hands and held it up. "I only met her once," he said thoughtfully.

"Twice," Henderson corrected. "There was that time we ran into you on the street, remember?"

"Yeah, I remember. She kept pulling you by the arm, from behind, to break it up."

"She was on her way to buy some clothes, and you know how they are when that's in the wind. Neither time nor tide—" Then he apologized still further, on behalf of someone who was dead and gone, apparently without realizing how perfectly unimportant it was now. "We were always going to have you up for dinner, but I dunno—somehow—you know how those things are."

"I know how it is," Lombard agreed, with diplomatic understanding. "No wife ever yet liked her husband's pre-marriage friends." He took out the pow-wow cigarettes, threw them across the narrow cell. "Don't mind if they make your tongue swell up and your lips blister. They're from down there; part gunpowder and insecticide. I haven't had time to change back to ours yet."

He took a thoughtful drag. "Well, I guess you better give me the dope."

Henderson pulled up a sigh from way in. "Yeah, I guess I better. I've been over it so many times already, I think I could reel it off backwards, or in my sleep."

"To me it's like a blackboard without anything written on it yet. So don't skip anything if you can help it."

"That marriage of mine and Marcella's was just a prelim, not the main event it should have been at all. A guy don't usually go around admitting that, even to his friends, but this is the death-house and it seems foolish to have reticences here. A little over a year ago the main bout suddenly came up. And too late for me to take part in. You never met her, don't know her, so there's no reason for me to mention her name. They were decent enough to do that for me at the trial too. All through it they just called her The Girl. I'll do that here, I'll call her My Girl to you."

"Your Girl." Lombard assented. He had his arms folded, cigarette sticking out from behind his elbow, and was staring down himself broodingly at the floor, listening hard.

"My Girl, poor girl. It was It, the real thing, the McCoy. If you're not married, and It comes along—you're safe. Of if your marriage itself happens to be It, that's better still, you're on pure velvet. Or if you're married, and It never comes along—you're still safe, even if you're only half alive and don't know it. It's when you're married, and It shows up only after it's too late—that you want to look out."

"That you want to look out," murmured Lombard, with a sort of musing compassion.

"It was a clean little thing. I told My Girl about Marcella the second time I saw her. That was supposed to be the last time we saw each other. The twelfth time we saw each other we were still trying to make it the last time. We tried to steer clear of each other—like steel filings try to steer clear of a magnet.

"Marcella knew about her within thirty days after it had started. I saw to it that she did, I went and told her. It wasn't a case of any sudden shock, get that. She just smiled about it a little, and she waited. Like someone watching two flies under a tumbler turned upside town.

"I went to her and asked for a divorce. That was at about mid-point. That slow, thoughtful smile came out on her again. She hadn't seemed to set any particular store by me until then that I could notice. Just that thing that dropped shoes in the next aisle over from her. The weeks went by, the months. She took her time thinking it over, she kept me dangling like that. I'd get that slow, mocking smile every now and then. She was the only one of the three of us having a good time out of it.

"It was pulling me inside out. I'm a grown man, and I wanted Mr Girl. I wasn't going to let myself be gypped. I didn't want any affair, I wanted my wife. And the woman in my house, she wasn't my wife."

The hands before his face that he stared down through, they shook a little even at this late day.

"My Girl said to me, "There must be some way out. We're in her hands and she knows it. This sullen silence on your part, that's the wrong attitude. That brings out an equally sulky opposition on her part. Go to her as a man goes to a friend. Take her out some night, have a heart-to-heart talk with her. When two people once loved one another, as you and she did, there must be something left of it, if it's only a memory in common. There must be some vestige of good-will, of kindly feeling for you, you can reach in her. Make her see it's the best thing for her own sake, as well as yours and mine.""

"So I bought tickets for a show, and I reserved a table for us at our old place, where we used to go in the days before our marriage. And I went home and said, 'Let's go out together again, shall we? Let's go out tonight like we used to.'

"Came that slow smile again, and she said. 'Why not?' As I stepped into the shower she was sitting there at the glass beginning to get ready. All the old ways I knew by heart, the first little touches here and there. I whistled in the shower. I liked her very much in the shower. I realized that the trouble was; I saw I'd always liked her, and I'd mistaken it for love."

He let the cigarette fall from his hand, flattened it. Then kept looking there. "Why didn't she refuse at once? Why did she let me whistle in the shower? Watch me in the glass take pains with the part in my hair? Get satisfaction out of the way my handkerchief looked in the breast-pocket in my coat? Be happy all over for the first time in six months? Why did she pretend she was going, when she knew from the first she didn't intend to? Because that was her way. That was her. Because she loved to keep me dangling in suspense. Even about that smaller matter, as well at the larger one.

"I caught on little by little. Her smile reflected in the glass. The way she wasn't really getting anywhere with those little touches of hers. I was holding my necktie out in my hands, ready to sling it on. And finally even the little touches had quit; she was sitting there not moving her hands any more, just sitting there doing nothing. Only the smile stayed on, the smile at a man in love. A man in love and at your mercy.

"There are two stories, theirs and mine. And both are identical up to that point; not a hair's-breadth variation between the two. They didn't bring out a single detail that wasn't true. Every slightest motion I made up to there, they had down pat. They did their research-work well, perfect. And then, as I stood behind her looking into the same glass with my necktie stretched out between my hands, the two stories split, as far apart as the hands of a clock at six. Mine goes all the way over this way, their goes all the way over that.

"I'm telling you mine now. I'm telling you the true one.

"She was just waiting for me to ask her. That's all she was sitting there for like that. The smile, the still hands, demurely folded on the table-edge. Finally I did, after I'd watched her for a moment. I said, 'Aren't you going?'

"She laughed. Gee, how she laughed. How hard, how long and hearty. I'd never known until then what a terrible weapon laughter can be. I could see my face, over there above hers in the glass, getting white.

"She said, 'But don't waste the tickets. Why throw out good money? Take *her* instead. She can have the show. She can have the dinner. She can have you altogether. *But she can't have you in the only way she wants you.'*

"That was her answer. That was always going to be her answer from then on. I knew it then. For ever, for the rest of our lives. And that's an awful long time.

"Then here's what happened next. I clenched my teeth and drew my arm back, in a line with the side of her jaw. I don't remember what happened to the necktie I'd been holding. It must have dropped to the floor. I only know it *didn't* go around her neck.

"I never let fly. I couldn't. I'm not that way. She even tried to get me to. I don't know why. Or maybe because she knew she was safe, I was incapable of doing it. She'd seen me in the glass, of course; she didn't have to turn her head. She jeered, 'Go ahead, hit me. Casey at the bat. That won't get it for you either. Nothing will get it for you; whether you're sweet or whether you're sour, whether you're gentle or whether you're rough.'"

"Then we both said things we shouldn't have, like people do. But it was just mouth-fireworks, that was all. I never laid a hand on her. I said, 'You don't want me; then what the hell are you hanging on to me for?'

"She said. 'You might come in handy, in case of burglars.'

"I said, 'You bet that's all there'll be to it from now on!'

"She said, 'I wonder if I'll be able to tell the difference?'

"I said. "That reminds me. You've got something coming to you.' I took two dollars out of my wallet and I threw them on the floor behind her. I said, 'That's for being married to you! And I'll pay the piano-player on my way downstairs.'

"Sure, it was low, it was rotten. I grabbed my hat and coat and I got out of there fast. She was still laughing there at the glass when I left. She was laughing, Jack. She wasn't dead. I didn't touch her. Her laughter followed me through the door, even after I'd closed it. It drove me down the stairs on foot, without waiting for the car to come up. It drove me nuts. I couldn't get away from it fast enough. It even followed me all the way down to the next landing, and then finally it faded away."

He stopped for a long time, while the scene he had rekindled slowly cooled and died again, before he could go ahead. There were traces of sweat in the creases running across his contracted forehead.

"Then when I came back," he said quietly, "she was dead and they said I did it. They said it happened at eight minutes and fifteen seconds after six. Her watch told them. It must have happened within ten minutes after I'd slammed the door behind me. That part of it still gives me the creeps, even now, when I think of it. He must have been lurking right there inside the building already, whoever he was—"

"But you say you went down the stairs yourself?"

"He might have been hidden up on the last stretch, between our floor and the roof. I don't know. Maybe he heard the whole thing. Maybe he even watched me go. Maybe I slammed the door so hard it rebounded instead of catching on, and he got in that way. He must have been in on her before she knew it. Maybe the very sound of her own laughter helped to cover him up, kept her from hearing anything until it was late."

"That makes it sound like some sort of a prowler, doesn't it?"

"Yes, but what *for*? The cops were never able to figure out what for, that's why they wouldn't give it any serious consideration. It wasn't robbery; nothing was taken. There was sixty dollars in cash right in the drawer in front of her, not even covered over. It wasn't attack, either. She was killed right where she'd been sitting, and left right where she'd been killed."

Lombard said, "One or the other could have been intended, and he got frightened off before he carried out the object of the intrusion. Either by some outside sound or by the very act he had just committed itself. That's happened a thousand and one times."

"Even that won't do," Henderson said dully. "Her diamond solitaire was lying there *loose* on the dressing table the whole time. It wasn't even on her finger. All he had to do was scoop it up as he ran out. Frightened or not, how long would that take? It stayed behind." He shook his head. "The necktie damned me. It came out from underneath all the others on the rack. And the rack was fairly deep within the closet. And that particular tie went with every stitch I had on. Sure, because I took it out myself. But I didn't twist it around her. I lost track of it in the heat of the quarrel. It must have fallen unnoticed to the floor. Then I grabbed up the one I'd come home with, and whipped that around my collar and stormed out. Then he came creeping in, and it caught his eye as he advanced unsuspectedly on her, and he picked it up. God knows who he was, and God only knows why he did it!"

Lombard said, "It may have been some impulse without rhyme or reason, just an urge to kill for the sake of killing, unleashed in some stray mental case hanging around outside. It may have been whipped up by the very scene of violence between you, especially after he had detected that the door wasn't securely closed. He realized he could commit it almost with impunity, and you'd be blamed for it. There have been things like that, you know."

"If it was anything along those lines, then they'll never get him. Those kind of killers are the hardest to track down. Only some freak or fluke will ever open it up. Some day they may get him for something else entirely, and then he'll confess this one along with it, and that's the first inkling they'll have. Long after it'll do me any good."

"What about this key-witness you mentioned in your message?"

"I'm coming to that now. It's the one slim ray of hope in the whole thing. Even if they never get on to who really did it, there's a way for me to be cleared of it. The two findings aren't necessarily one and the same, in this case; they can be separate and distinct, and yet equally valid each in its own right."

He began punching one hand into the flat of the other, over and over while he spoke. "There's a certain woman, somewhere or other, right at this moment, as we sit here in this cell talking it over, who can clear me—simply by telling them at what time I met her at a certain bar eight blocks from where I lived. That time was ten minutes after six. And she knows it just as I know it; wherever and whoever she is, she knows it. They proved, by re-enacting it, that I couldn't have reached that bar at that time and still have committed the murder back at my house. Jack, if you hope to do anything for me, if you want to pull me through this, you've got to find that woman. She and she alone is the answer."

Lombard took a long time. Finally he said, "What's been done about finding her, so far?"

"Everything," was the devastating answer, "everything under the sun."

Lombard came over and slumped down limply on the edge of the bunk beside him. "Whew!" he said, blowing through his clasped hands. "And if the police failed, your lawyer failed, everyone and everything failed, right at the time it happened and with all the time they needed—what a chance I have, months after it's cold and with eighteen days to do it in!"

The guard had showed up. Lombard stood up, let his hand trail off Henderson's slumped shoulder as he turned away to be let out.

Henderson raised his head. "Don't you want to shake hands?" he said falteringly.

"What for? I'll be back again tomorrow."

"You mean you're going to take a fling at it anyway?"

Lombard turned and gave him a look that was almost scathing, as if irked by the obtuseness of such a question. "What the hell gave you the idea I wasn't?" he growled surlily.

# TEN

# The Seventeenth, the Sixteenth Days
# Before the Execution

Lombard shuffled around the cell, hands in pockets, looking down at his own feet as though he'd never noticed how they worked before. Finally he stopped and said, "Hendy, you've got to do better than that. I'm not a magician, I can't just pull her out of a hat from nothing."

"Listen," Henderson said weariedly. "I've gone over the thing in my own mind until I'm sick of it, until I dream about it at nights. I can't squeeze a drop more detail out of it."

"Didn't you look at her face *at all*?"

"It must have gotten in the way plenty of times, but it didn't take."

"Let's start it again at the beginning and run through it once more. Don't look at me like that; it's the only thing we *can* do. She was already sitting on a stool at the bar when you walked in. Suppose you give me your first impression of her if you can. Try to recapture it. Sometimes there's a clearer visualization to be gained from a fleeting first impression than from all the more deliberate studies you can make later on. Well then, your first impression?"

"A hand reaching for pretzels."

Lombard eyed him scathingly. "How can you leave your own bar-stool, walk over to another, and accost somebody, without seeing them? Show me that trick some time. You knew it was a girl, didn't you? You didn't think it was a mirror you were addressing? Well, *how* did you know it was a girl?"

"She had on a skirt, so she was a girl, and she wasn't using crutches, so she was able-bodied. Those were the only two things I cared about. I was looking through her, seeing My Girl in my mind's eye the whole time I was with her; what do you expect me to be able to tell you?" Henderson flared in turn.

Lombard took a minute off to let the two of them calm down. Then: "What was her voice like? Did that tell you anything? Where she came from? What her background was?"

"That she'd been to high-school. That she was city bred. She talked like we all do here. Pure metropolitan. About as colourless as boiled water."

"Then this was her home-town, if you couldn't notice any variation in accent. Whatever good that does us. In the taxi, what?"

"Nothing; the wheels went around."

"In the restaurant, what?"

Henderson arched his neck rebelliously. "Nothing. It's no use, Jack. Nothing. It won't come. I can't. I can't. She ate and she talked, that was all."

"Yes, but about what?"

"I can't remember. I can't remember a word of it. It wasn't meant to be remembered. It was just meant to pass the time, keep silence at a distance. The first was excellent. Wasn't the war terrible? No, she didn't care for another cigarette, thank you."

"You're driving me crazy. You sure must have loved Your Girl."

"I did. I do. Shut up about it."

"In the theatre, what?"

"Only that she stood up in her seat; I've already told you that three times. And you said yourself that doesn't tell you what she was like, that only tells you what she did at one point."

Lombard came in closer. "Yes, but *why* did she stand up? That keeps eluding you. The curtain was still up, you say. People don't stand like that for no reason."

"I don't know why she stood up. I wasn't inside her mind."

"You weren't even inside your own, from what I can gather. Never mind, we can come back to that later.

Once you've got the effect, the cause is bound to follow eventually. "He moiled around for a while, letting a brief pause rest them up.

"When she stood up like that, you looked at her then at least?"

"Looking is a physical act, with the pupils of the eyes; seeing is a mental one, with the cells of the brain. I looked at her all night long; I didn't see her once."

"This is torture," Lombard grimaced, squeezing the bridge of his nose up close beneath the brows. "I can't seem to get it from you. There must be *somebody* I can get it from, *some*body who saw you with her that night. Two people can't go around town for six hours together without *some*body at least seeing them."

Henderson smiled wryly. "That's what I thought too. I found out I was wrong. There must have been a case of mass-astigmatism all over town that night. Sometimes they've got me wondering myself if there really was such a person, or if she wasn't just an hallucination on my part, a vagary of my own feverish imagination."

"You can cut that out right now," Lombard ordered curtly.

"Time's up," a voice said from outside.

Henderson got up, picked up a charred match-stick from the floor, and carried it over to the wall, where there were rows of little charred dabs in parallel rows. The top lines had all been intercrosed with x's; the last few on the end were still single down-ward strokes. He added a cross-line to one, and made that into an x.

"And cut that out, too!" Lombard added. He spat forcefully into his own hand, took a quick step over, gave the wall a violent sweep, and the whole bunch of them, crossed and uncrossed, were gone at once.

"All right, move over," he said, taking out pencil and paper.

"I'll stand for a change," Henderson said. "There's only room for one on the edge of that thing."

"Now you know what I want, don't you? Raw material that hasn't already been worked over. Second-string witnesses, people who weren't subpœnaed to appear at the trial, people who were overlooked both by the cops and Gregory, your lawyer."

"You don't want much. Ghosts, once-removed. Second-degree ghosts to help us get a line on a first-degree ghost. We better get a medium in on this with us."

"I don't care if they only brushed elbows with you, walked past on one side of the street, while you two walked past on the other. The point is, I want to be the first to get to them, if possible. I don't want anyone else's left-overs. There must be some place we can drive a wedge in, split this thing open. I don't care how dia-phanous it is, I want to rig up some kind of a list between us. All right, here we go again. The bar."

"The inevitable bar," Henderson sighed.

"The barman's been used up already. Anyone else at it but the two of you?"

"No."

"Take your time. Don't try to force it. It won't come that way, when you try to force it. It drives it back."

(Four or five minutes.)

"Wait. A girl in a booth turned her head to look around after her. I noticed that as we were leaving. Want that?"

Lombard's pencil moved. "Give me that sort of thing. That's exactly the sort of thing I want. Can you tell me anything else about this girl?"

"No. Even less than the woman I was with. Just the turn of a head."

"Come on, now."

"The taxi. That's been used up. He was the big comic relief at the trial."

"The restaurant comes next. Was there a hat-cheque girl at this Maison Blanche?"

"She's one of the few with a legitimate excuse for not remem-

bering her. I *was* alone when I went up to her alcove; the phantom
had separated from me to go into the powder-room."

Lombard's pencil moved again. "There may have been an attendant in there. Still, if she wasn't noticed with you, there's even
less chance she was noticed without you. Now, how about the
restaurant; any heads turn there?"

"She joined me separately."

"That brings us to the theatre."

"There was a doorman with funny fish-hook moustaches, I remember that much. He did a double take-'em on her hat."

"Good. He's in."

He jotted something. "How about the usher?"

"We got there late. Just a pocket-light in the dark."

"No good. How about the stage itself?"

"You mean the performers? I'm afraid the show ran off too
fast."

"When she stood up like that it might have been seen. Were any
of them questioned by the police?"

"No."

"It won't hurt for me to check. We're not passing up anything
in this, understand, anything? If a *blind man* was anywhere near
you that night. I'd want—What's matter?"

"Hey," Henderson had said sharply.

"What is it?"

"You just brought something back to me then. One was. A blind
pan-handler tagged us as we were leaving—" Then as he saw
Lombard's pencil briefly scrawl something. "You're kidding," he
protested incredulously.

"Think so?" Lombard said levelly. "Wait and see." He cocked
his pencil once more.

"That's all there is, there isn't any more."

Lombard put the last away in his pocket, stood up. "I'll make a
dent in that somewhere along the line!" he promised grimly. He
went over and whacked at the grate, to be let out. "And keep your
eyes off that wall!" he added, catching the direction of Henderson's
inadvertent glance, over to where the erased box-score had once
been kept. "They're not going to get you in there." He thumbed
the opposite direction along the corridor from the one he was about
to take.

"They say they are," was Henderson's ironically murmured
answers.

*Personal Columns, all newspapers:*

"Will the young lady who was seated in a wall-booth at Anselmo's Bar with a companion, at or around 6.15 in the evening,

May 20th last, and who may recall an orange hat that caused her to turn her head as its wearer was leaving, kindly get in touch with me. She was facing toward the back. If she remembers this it is vital that I hear from her without delay. A person's happiness is involved. All replies held in strictest confidence. Communicate J. L., Box 654, care of this newspaper."

No replies.

# ELEVEN

## The Fifteenth Day Before the Execution

### LOMBARD

A blowsy woman with her greying hair in her eyes and an aura of cabbage around her, opened the door.

"O'Bannon? Michael O'Bannon?"

That was as far as he got. "Now listen, I've already been over to your office once today, and the man there said he'd give us until Wednesday We're not trying to gyp the poor, penniless company that needs the money so bad. Sure, it must be down to its last fifty thousand bucks, it must!"

"Madam, I'm not a collector. I simply wish to speak to the Michael O'Bannon who worked as doorman at the Casino last spring."

"Yes, I can remember when he had that job," she agreed caustically. She turned her head slightly aside, raised her voice a little, as if she wished someone other than Lombard to overhear her. "They lose one job, and then they never move the seat of their pants off the chair from that day on to try and get another. They sit and wait for it to come to them!"

What sounded like the hoarse grunt of a trained seal came from somewhere in the interior.

"Someone to see you, Mike!" she bellowed. And then to Lombard. "You better go in to him yourself, he's got his shoes off."

Lombard advanced, down a "railroad" hall that threatened to go on indefinitely but didn't. It ended finally in a room whose centre was occupied by an oilcloth-covered table.

Sidewise to this lolled the object of his visit, stretched across two straight-backed wooden chairs in a suspension-bridge arrangement, the unsupported part of him curving downward. He had off a good deal more than just his shoes; in fact, his upper attire consisted solely of an oatmeal-coloured union-suit with elbow-length sleeves, and immediately over that a pair of braces. Two white-toed socks tilted acutely upward from the chair-seat opposite him. He laid aside a pink racing-form and a rancid pipe as Lombard entered. "And what can I do for you, sirr?" he rumbled accommodatingly.

Lombard put his hat on the table and sat down without being asked. "A friend of mine wishes to get in touch with someone," he began confidentially. It would be poor policy, he felt, to overawe these people ahead of time with mention of death-sentences, consultations with the police, and all that; they might become intimidated and chary of telling him anything, even if they were able to. "It means a lot to him. It means everything. Now. This is why I'm here. Can you recall a man and woman getting out of a taxi in front of the theatre, while you were working there, one night in May? You held the door for them, of course."

"Well, now, I held the door for everybody that drove up; that was my job."

"They were a little late, probably the last people you greeted that particular night. Now, this woman had on a bright orange hat. A very peculiar hat, with a thin, tickler sticking straight up from it. It swept right in front of your eyes as she got out, she passed so close to you. Your eyes followed it like this: slowly, from one side over to the other. You know, like when something passes too close to you, and you can't make out what it is."

"Leave it to him," his wife put in challengingly from the doorway. "If it was anything on a pretty woman he'd do that anyway, whether he could make out what it was or not!"

Neither of the men paid any attention. "He saw you do that," Lombard went on. "He happened to notice it at the time, and he told me about it." He pressed his hands to the oilcloth, leaned toward him. "Can you remember? Does it come back to you? Can you remember her at all?"

O'Bannon shook his head ponderously. Then he gnawed his upper lip. Then he shook his head some more. He gave him a reproachful look. "D'ye know what you're asking man? All those faces night after night! Nearly always two by two, lady and gent."

Lombard continued leaning across the table toward him for long minutes, as though the intensity of his gaze would be enough to bring it back to him of itself. "Try, O'Bannon. Think back. Try, will you, O'Bannon? It means everything in the world to this poor guy."

The wife began to draw slowly nearer, at that, but still held her peace.

O'Bannon shook his head once more, this time with finality. "No," he said. "Out of my whole season there, out of all them people I opened car-doors for, I can only recall today one single individjule. A fellow who showed up by himself one night, full of booze. And that was because he fell out of the cab face first when I opened the door, and I had to catch him in me arms—"

Lombard stemmed the flow of unwanted reminiscence that he suspected was about to follow. He got to his feet. "Then you don't, and you're sure you don't?"

"I don't, and I'm sure I don't." O'Bannon reached for the reeking pipe and the racing-chart again.

The wife was at their elbows by now. She had been eyeing Lombard speculatively for some moments past. The tip of her tongue peered forth in calculation for an instant at the corner of her mouth as she spoke. "Would there have been anything in it for us, now, if he had been able to?"

"Well, yes. I don't suppose I would have minded doing a little something for you if you'd been able to give me what I wanted."

"D'ye hear that, Mike?" She pounced on her husband as though she were going to attack him. She began to shake him strenuously by one shoulder, using both hands for the purpose, as though she were kneading dough or massaging a sprain. "Try, Mike, try!"

He tried to ward her off, backing an arm defensively before his head. "How can I, with you rocking me like an empty rowboat? Even if it was in me head somewhere, lying low, you'd shake it clean out of me mind!"

"Well—no go, I guess," Lombard sighed. He turned away and moved disappointedly down the long defile of hall passage.

He heard her voice rise to an exasperated wail, there in the room behind him, as she renewed her assault on her husband's obdurate shoulder. "Look, he's going. Oh, Mike, what's the matter with you? All the man wants you to do is remember something, and you can't even do that!"

She must have vented her disappointment on the inanimate objects about him. There was a roar of anguished protest. "Me pipe! Me handicap sheet!"

Their voices were loud in disputation as Lombard closed the outer door after him. Then, suspiciously, there was a sudden conspiratorial hush. Lombard's face took on a slightly knowing look as he started down the stairs.

Sure enough, in a moment more there was a swift onrush of footsteps in his wake along the inner hall, the door was flung open, and O'Bannon's wife called hectically down the stairwell after him:

"Wait, mister! Come back! He just remembered! It just now came
to him!"

"Oh, it did, did it?" Lombard said dryly. He stopped where he
was and turned to look up at her, but without making any move to
reascend. He took out his wallet, ran his thumb tentatively along
its edge. "Ask him was it a black or a white sling she was holding
her arm in?"

She relayed the question resoundingly back into the interior. She
got the answer, sent it on down to Lombard—slight hesitancy of
voice and all. "White—for the evening, you know."

Lombard put his wallet away again unopened. "Wrong number,"
he said firmly, and resumed his descent.

# TWELVE

## The Fourteenth, Thirteenth, Twelfth Days
## Before the Execution

### THE GIRL

She'd already been perched on the stool several minutes when he
first became aware of her. And that was all the more unusual, in
that there were only a scattering of others at the bar as yet; her
arrival should have been that much more conspicuous. It only
showed how unobtrusively she must have approached and settled
into place.

It was at the very beginning of his turn of duty, so her arrival
must have occurred only moments after his own taking up of position behind the bar, almost as though she had timed it that way:
to arrive when he did. She had not yet been there when he first
stepped out of the locker-room in freshly starched jacket and
glanced about his domain-to-be, that much he was sure of. At any
rate, turning away from waiting on a man down at the other end,
he became aware of her sitting there quiescently, and immediately
approached.

"Yes, miss?"

Her eyes held his in a peculiarly sustained look, he thought. And
then immediately thought, in postscript, that he must be mistaken,

he must be only imagining it. All customers looked at him when they gave an order, for he was the means of bringing it to them.

In this gaze of hers there was a difference, though; the impression returned a second time, after having been discarded once. It was a personalized look. A look in its own right, with the giving of the order the adjunct, and not just an adjunct to the giving of the order. It was a look at *him*, the *man* to whom she was addressing the order meant for him in his own right. It was a look that said: "Take note of me. Mark me well."

She asked for a little whisky with water. As he turned away to get it, her eyes remained on him to the last. He had a trivial and fleeting feeling of being at a loss, of being unable to account for her bizarre scrutiny, that evaporated again almost as soon as it had risen. That did not bother him much; that was just there and gone again, at first.

Thus, the beginnings of it.

He brought her drink, and turned away immediately to wait on someone else.

An interval elapsed. An interval during which he did not think of her again, had forgotten her. An interval during which there should have been some slight alteration in her posiion, if only a shift of her hand, a raising or edging of her glass, a look elsewhere about the room. There wasn't. She sat there not moving. As still as a pasteboard cut-out of a girl seated on a bar-stool. Her drink was not touched, remained where he had left it, as he had left it. Only one thing moved: her eyes. They went wherever he went. They followed him about.

A pause came in his activities, and he encountered them again, for the first time since his original discovery of their peculiar fixity. He found now that they had been on him all the while, without his guessing it. It disconcerted him. He could find no meaning for it. He stole a look into the glass to see if there was anything awry with his countenance or jacket. There wasn't; he was as other times; no one else was looking at him in that prolonged steadfast way but she. He could find no explanation for it.

It was intentional, of that there could be no doubt, for it moved about as he moved about. It was no glazed, dreamy, inward-mulling stare that just happened to be turned his way; there was intelligence behind it, directed at him.

Awareness of it having once entered his mind, it could not be dislodged again; it remained with him to stay, and trouble him. He began watching her covertly from time to time himself now, each time thinking himself unobserved. Always he found her already looking at him when he did, always he left her continuing to look at him after he had already desisted. His sense of being at a loss deepened, became discomfort, little by little.

He had never seen a human being sit so still. Nothing about her moved. The drink remained as neglected as though he had not brought it at all. She sat there like a young feminine Buddha, eyes gravely, uninterruptedly on him.

Discomfort was beginning to deepen into annoyance. He approached her at last, stopped before her.

"Don't you care for your drink, miss?"

This was meant to be a hint, a spur to get her to move on. It failed; she blunted it.

Her answer was toneless, told nothing. "Leave it there."

The circumstances were in her favour, for she was a girl, and girls are under no compulsion to be repetitious spenders at a bar, as a man customarily is if he expects to continue to be welcome. Moreover, she was not flirting, she was not seeking to have her cheque lifted, she was not behaving reprehensibly in any way, he was powerless against her.

He drew away from her again, worsted, looking back at her all the way down the curve of the bar, and her eyes followed him as persistently as ever.

Discomfort was settling into something chronic now. He tried to shrug it off with a squirming of the shoulders, an adjustment of his collar about the nape of his neck. He knew she was still looking, and he wouldn't look over himself any more to confirm it. Which only made it worse.

The demand of other customers, the thicker they came, instead of harassing him, were a relief now. The necessary manipulations they brought on gave him something to do, took his mind off that harrowing stare. But the lulls would keep coming back, when there was no one to attend to, nothing that needed polishing, no glass that needed filling, and it was then that her concentration on him would make itself felt the most. It was then that he didn't know what to do with his hands or with his bar-cloth.

He upset a small chaser of beer as he was knifing it a-top the sieve. He punched a wrong key in the cash register.

At last, driven almost beyond endurance, he tackled her again, trying to come to grips with what she was doing to him.

"Is there anything I can do for you miss?" he said, with husky, choked resentment.

She spoke always without putting any clue into her voice. "Have I said there is?"

He leaned heavily on the bar. "Well, is there something you want from me?"

"Have I said I do?"

"Well, pardon me, but do I remind you of someone you know?"

"No one."

He was beginning to flounder. "I thought maybe there was, the way you keep looking at me," he said unsteadily. It was meant to be a rebuke.

This time she didn't answer at all. Yet neither did her eyes leave him. He finally was the one had to leave them again, withdraw as discomfited as ever.

She didn't smile, she didn't speak, she showed neither contrition nor yet outright hostility. She just sat and looked after him with the inscrutable gravity of an owl.

It was a terrible weapon she had found and she was using. It does not ordinarily occur to people how utterly unbearable it can be to be looked at steadily over a protracted period of time, say an hour or two or three, simply because it is a thing that never happens to them, their fortitude is not put to the test.

It was happening to him now, and it was slowly unnerving him, fraying him. He was defenceless against it, both because he was confined within the semicircle of the bar, couldn't walk away from it, and also because of its very nature. Each time he tried to buffet it back he found that it was just a look, there was nothing there to seize hold of. The control of it rested with her. A beam, a ray, there was no way of warding it off, shunting it aside.

Symptons that he had never noted in himself before, and would not have recognized by their clinical name of agoraphobia, began to assail him with increasing urgency; a longing to take cover, to seek refuge back within the locker-room, even a desire to squat down below the level of the bar-top where she could no longer see him readily. He mopped his brow furtively once or twice and fought them off. His eyes began to seek the clock overhead with increasing frequency, the clock that they had once told him a man's life depended on.

He longed to see her go. He began to pray for it. And yet it was obvious by now, had been for a long time past, that she had no intention of going of her own accord, would only go with the closing of the place. For none of the usual reasons that cause people to seek a bar were operating in her case, and therefore there was no reprieve to be expected of any of them. She was not there to wait for anyone, or she would have been met long ago. She was not there to drink, for that same untouched glass still sat just where he had set it hours ago. She was there for one purpose and one alone: to look at him.

Failing to be rid of her in any other way, he began to long for closing-time to come, to find his escape through that. As the customers began to thin out, as the number of counter-attractions about him lessened, her power to bring herself to his notice rose accordingly. Presently there were large gaps around the semicircle fronting him, and that only emphasized the remorseless fixity of that Medusa-like countenance all the more.

He dropped a glass, and that was a thing he hadn't done in months. She was shooting him to pieces. He glowered at her and cursed her in soundless lip movements as he stooped to gather up the fragments.

And then finally, when he thought it was never coming any more, the minute hand notched twelve, and it was four o'clock and closing-time had arrived. Two men engaged in earnest conversation, the last of all the other customers, rose unbidden and sauntered toward the entrance, without interrupting their flow of amicable low-voiced talk. Not she. Not a muscle moved. The stagnant drink still sat before her, and she sat on with it. Looking, watching, eyeing, without even a blink.

"Good-night gentlemen," he called out loudly after the other two, so that she would understand.

She didn't move.

He opened the control-box and threw a switch. The outer perimeter of lights went out, leaving just an inner glow coming from behind the bar where he was, a hidden sunset creeping up the mirrors and the tiers of bottles ranged against the wall. He became a black silhouette against it, and she a disembodied faintly luminous face peering in from the surrounding dimness.

He went up to her, took the hours-old drink away, and threw it out, with a violent downward fling of the hand that sent drops leaping up.

"We're closing up now," he said in a grating voice.

She moved at last. Suddenly she was on her feet beside the stool, holding it for a moment to give the change of position time to work its way through her circulatory system.

His fingers worked deftly down the buttons of his jacket. He said cholerically. "What was it? What was the game? What was on your mind?"

She moved quietly off through the darkened tavern toward the street entrance without answering, as though she hadn't heard him. He had never dreamed that such a simple causative as the mere sight of a girl quitting a bar could bring such utter, contrite, prostrate relief welling up in him. His jacket open all down the front, he supported himself there on one hand planted firmly down upon the bar, and leaned limply, exhaustedly out in the direction in which she had gone.

There was a night-light standing at the outer entrance, and she came back into view again when she had reached there. She stopped just short of the doorway, and turned, and looked back at him across the intervening distance, long and solemnly and with purposeful implication. As if to show that the whole thing had been no illusion; more than that, to show that this was not its end, that this was just an interruption.

He turned from keying the door locked, and she was standing there quietly on the sidewalk, only a few yards off. She was turned expectantly facing toward the doorway, as if waiting for him to emerge.

He was forced to go toward her, because it was in that direction his path lay on leaving here on a night. They passed within a foot of one another, for the sidewalk was fairly narrow and she was posted out in the middle of it, not skulking back against the wall. Though her face turned slowly in time with his passing, he saw that she would have let him go by without speaking, and, goaded by this silent obstinacy, he spoke himself, although only a second before he had intended ignoring her.

"What is it ye want of me?" he rumbled truculently.

"Have I said I want anything of you?"

He made to go on, then swung around on his heel to face her accusingly. "You sat in there just now, never once took your eyes off me! Never once the livelong night, d'ye hear me?" He pounded one hand within the other for outraged emphasis. "And now I find you outside here waiting around—"

"Is it forbidden to stand here in the street?"

He shook a thick finger at her ponderously. "I'm warning you, young woman! I'm telling you for your own good!"

She didn't answer. She didn't open her mouth, and silence is always so victorious in argument. He turned and shambled off, breathing heavily with his own bafflement.

He didn't look back. Within twenty paces, even without looking back, he had become aware that she was advancing in turn behind him. It was not difficult to do so, for she was apparently making no effort to conceal the fact. The ticking-off of her small brittle shoes was clear-cut if subdued on the quiet night pavement.

An up-and-down intersection glided by beneath him like a slightly depressed asphalt stream-bed. Then presently another. Then still another. And through it all, as the town slowly veered over from west to east, came that unhurried *tick-chick, tick-chick* behind him in the middle distance.

He turned his head, the first time simply to warn her off. She came on with maddening casualness, as though it were three in the afternoon. Her walk was slow, almost stately, as the feminine gait so often is when the figure is held erect and the pace is leisurely.

He went on again briefly, then turned once more. This time his entire body, and flung himself back toward her in a sudden flurry of ungovernable exasperation.

She stopped advancing, but she held her ground, made no slightest retrograde move.

He closed in and bellowed full into her face: "Turn back now, will ye? That's enough of this now, d'ye hear? Turn back, or I'll—"

"*I* am going this way too," was all she said.

Again the circumstances were in her favour. Had their rôles been reversed— But what man has sufficiently stout armour against ridicule to risk calling a policeman to complain that a solitary young girl is following him along the streets? She was not reviling him, she was not soliciting him, she was simply walking in the same direction he was; he was as helpless against her as he had been in the bar earlier.

He maintained his stance before her for a moment or two, but his defiance was of that face-saving kind that only marks time while it is waiting to extricate itself with the least possible embarrassment from a false situation. He spun around finally with a snort through his nose, meant to convey belligerence, but that somehow sounded a bit like windy helplessness. He drew away from her, resumed his homeward journeying.

Ten paces, fifteen, twenty. Behind him, as at a given signal, it recommenced again, steady as slow rain in a puddle. *Tich-chick, tich-chick.* She was coming after him once more.

He rounded the appointed corner, started up the roofed-over sidewalk stairway he used every night to reach his train. He halted up above, at the rear of the plank-floored station gallery that led through the tracks, scanning the chute-like incline he had just emerged from for signs of her.

The oncoming tap of her footfalls took on a metallic ring as her feet clicked against the steel rims guarding the steps. In a moment her head came into view above the midway break in the stair-line.

A turnstile rumbled around after him, and he turned there on the other side of it, at bay, took up a defensive position.

She cleared the steps and came on, as matter-of-factly, as equably, as though he wasn't to be seen there at all in the gap fronting her. She already held the coin pinched between her fingers. She came on until there was just the width of the turnstile-arm between them.

He backed his arm at her, swinging it up all the way past its opposite shoulder, ready to fling it loose. It would have sent her spinning about the enclosure. His lip lifted in a canine snarl. "Get outa here now. Gawan down below where ye came from!" He reached down and quickly plugged the coin-slot with the ball of his thumb just ahead of her own move toward it.

She desisted, shifted over to the adjoining one. Instantly he was there before her again. She shifted back to the original one. He reversed himself once more, again blocked it. The superstructure began to vibrate with the approach of one of the infrequent night trains.

This time he finally flung his arm out in the backsweep he had
been threatening at each confrontation. The blow would have been
enough to fell her if it had caught her. She turned her head aside
with the fastidious little quirk of someone detecting an unpleasant
odour. It fanned her face.

Instantly there was a peremptory rapping on glass somewhere
close at hand. The station agent thrust head and shoulder out of
the sideward door of his dingy little booth. "Cut that out, you.
Whaddye trying to do, keep people from using this station? I'll run
you in!"

He turned to defend himself, the taboo partially lifted since this
intercession wasn't of his own seeking. "This girl's nuts or something; she ought to be sent to Bellevue. She's been follying me
along the street. I can't get rid of her."

She said in that same dispassionate voice, "Are you the only one
that can ride the Third Avenue El?"

He appealed to the agent once more, continuing to hang slantwise out of the doorway at a sort of self-appointed arbiter. "Ask
her where she's going. She don't know herself!"

Her answer was addressed to the agent, but with an emphasis
that could not have been meant for him, that must have had some
purpose of its own. "I'm going down to Twenty-seventh Street.
Twenty-seventh Street between Second and Third Avenues. I have
a right to use this station, haven't I?"

The face of the man blocking her way had suddenly grown white,
as though the locality she had mentioned conveyed a shock of
hidden meaning to him. It should have. It was his own.

She knew ahead of time where he was going. It was useless
therefore to attempt to shake her off, outdistance her in any way.

The agent rendered his decision with a majestic sweep of his
hand. "Come on through, miss."

Her coin suddenly swelled up in the reflector and she had come
though the next one over, without waiting for him to clear the way
for her. A thing which he seemed incapable of doing at the moment,
no longer through obstinacy so much as through a temporary par-
alysis of movement with which his discovery of her knowledge of
his eventual destination seemed to have afflicted him.

The train had arrived, meanwhile, but it was on the opposite
side, not theirs. It ebbed away again, and the station breastworks
dimmed once more behind it.

She sauntered to the outer lip of the platform and stood there
waiting, and presently he had come out in turn, but digressing so
that he emerged two pillar-lengths to the rearward of her. Since
both were looking the same way, in quest of a train, he had her in
view but she did not have him.

Presently, without noticing what she was doing, she began to amble further rearward along the platform, relieving the monotony of the wait by aimless movement, as most people are inclined to do at such a time. This had soon taken her beyond the agent's limited range of vision, and out to where the station roof ended and the platform itself narrowed to a single-file strip of runway. Here she came to a halt again, and would have eventually turned and retraced her steps back toward where she had come from. But while standing there, peering trainward and with her back still to him, an unaccountable tension, a sense of impending danger of some sort, began slowly to come over her.

It must have been something about the way his tread sounded to her on the planks. He, too, was straying now in turn, and toward her. He was moving sluggishly, just as she had. It wasn't that; it was that his tread, while distinct enough in the unnatural stillness that reigned over the station, had some sort of a furtive undertone to it. It was in the rhythm, rather than in any actual attempt to muffle it. It was somehow a leashed tread, a tread of calculated approach trying to disguise itself as a meaningless ramble. She could not know how she knew; she only knew, before she had even turned, that something had entered his mind in the few moments since her back had been turned. Something that had not been there before.

She turned, and rather sharply.

He was still little better than his original two stanchion-lengths away from her. It was not that that confirmed her impression. She caught him in the act of glancing down into the track-bed beside him, where the third rail lay, as he drifted along parallel to it. It was that.

She understood immediately. A jostle of the elbow, a deft, tripping side-swipe of the foot, as they made to pass one another. She took in at a glance the desperate position she had unwittingly strayed into. She was penned against the far end of the station. Without realizing it she had cut herself off from the agent's protective radius of vision altogether. His booth was set back inside to command the turnstiles, could not command the sweep of the platform.

The two of them were alone on the platform. She looked across the way, and the opposite side was altogether barren, had just been cleared by the northbound train. There was no down-town train in sight yet, either, offering that dubious deterrent.

To retreat still further would be suicidal; the platform ended completely only a few yards behind her back, she would only wedge herself into a cul-de-sac, be more at her mercy than ever. To get back to the mid-section where the agent offered safety, she would have to go toward him, *pass* him, which was the very act he was seeking to achieve.

If she screamed now, without waiting for the overt act, in hopes of bringing the agent out on to the platform in time, she ran a very real risk of bringing on all the faster the very thing she was trying to prevent. He was in a keyed-up state, she could tell by the look on his face, on which a scream, more likely than not, would produce the opposite effect from that intended. This temporary aberration was due to sheer fright on his part more than rage, and a scream might frighten him still further.

She had frightened him badly, she had done her work only too well.

She edged warily inward, back as far as possible from the tracks, until she had come up close against the row of advertisements lining the guard-rail. She pressed her hips flat against them, began to sidle along them, turned watchfully outward toward him. Her dress rustled as it swept their surfaces one by one, so close did she cling.

As she drew within his orbit he began to veer in toward her on a diagonal, obviously to cut off her further advance. There was a slowness about both their movements that was horrible; they were like lazy fish swimming in a tank, on that deserted platform three stories above the street, with its tawny widely spaced lights strung along overhead.

He still came on, and so did she, and they were bound to meet in another two or three paces.

The turnstile drummed unexpectedly, around out of sight from them, and a coloured girl of dubious pursuits came out on the platform just a few short yards away from the two of them, bent almost lopsided as she moved to scratch herself far down the side of her leg.

They slowly melted into relaxation, each in the pose in which she had surprised them. The girl, with her back to the billboards, stayed that way, slumped a little lower, buckled at the knees now. He leaned deflatedly against a chewing-gum slot machine at hand beside him. She could almost see the recent fell purpose oozing out of him at every pore. Finally he turned away from his nearness to her with a floundering movement. Nothing had been said, the whole thing had been in pantomime from beginning to end.

That would never come again. She had the upper hand once more.

The train came flickering in like sheet-lightning, and they both boarded the same car, at opposite ends. They sat the full car-length away from one another, still recuperating from their recent crisis; he huddled forward over his lap, she with her spine held convex, staring upward at the ceiling lights. In between there was no one but the coloured girl, who continued to scratch at intervals and scan the station numbers, as though waiting to pick one at random to alight at.

They both left the car at the Twenty-eighth Street station, again at opposite ends. He was aware of her coming down the stairs in his wake. She could tell that he was, although he didn't look back. The inclination of his head told her that. He seemed passively acquiescent now to letting her have her way, follow him, the short rest of the way, if that was her intent.

They both went down Twenty-seventh Street toward Second, he on one side of the street, she on the other. He maintained a lead of about four doorways, and she let him keep it. She knew which entrance he would go into, and he knew that she knew. The stalk had now become a purely mechanical thing, with its only remaining unknown quantity the why. But that was the dominant factor.

He went in, was inked from sight, within one of the black door-slits down near the corner. He must have heard that remorse-less, maniacally calm *tich-chick, tich-chick* behind him on the other side of the street to the very last, but he refrained from looking back, gave no sign. They had parted company at last, for the first time since early evening.

She came on until she had used up the distance there had been between them, stood even with the house. Then she took up her position there, and stood in full sight on the sidewalk opposite, watching a certain two of the dozen-odd darkened windows.

Presently they had lighted, as in greeting at someone's awaited entry. Then within a moment they blacked out once more, as if the act had been quickly countermanded. They remained dark after that, though at times the greyish film of the curtains would seem to stir and shift, with the elusiveness of a reflection on the glass. She knew she was being watched through them by one or more persons.

She maintained her vigil steadfastly.

An elevated train wriggled by like a glow-worm up at the far end of the street. A taxi passed, and the driver glanced at her curiously, but he already had a fare. A late wayfarer came by along the opposite side of the street, and looked over at her, trying to discern encouragement. She averted her face angularly, only righted it again after he was well on is way.

A policeman suddenly stood at her elbow, appearing from no-where. He must have stood watching, undetected, for some little time before.

"Just a minute, miss. I've had a complaint from a woman in one of the flats over there that you followed her husband home from work, and have been standing staring at their windows for the past half-hour.

"I have."

"Well, y'd better move on."

"I want you to take hold of my arm, please, and walk me with you until we get around the corner, as though you were running me in." He did, rather half-heartedly. They stopped again when they were out of sight of the windows. "Here." She produced a piece of paper, showed it to him. He peered at it in the uncertain light of a nearby lamp-post.

"Who's this?" he asked.

"Homicide Squad. You can call him and check on it, if you want to. I'm doing this with his full knowledge and permission."

"Oh, sort of undercover work, hunh?" he said, with increased respect.

"And please ignore all future complaints from those particular people about me. You're apt to get a great many of them during the next few days and nights."

She made a phone-call of her own after he had left her.

"How is it working out?" the voice on the other end asked.

"He's already showing signs of strain. He broke a glass behind the bar. He nearly gave in to an impulse to throw me off the elevated platform just now."

"That looks like it. Be careful; don't go too close to him when there's no one else around. Remember, the main thing is, don't give him an inkling of what the whole thing's about, of what's behind it. *Don't put the question to him*, that's the whole trick. The moment he finds out what you're after it goes into reverse, loses its effect. It's the not knowing that keeps him on edge, will finally wear him down to where we want him."

"What time does he start out for work, as a rule?"

"He leaves the flat around five each afternoon," her informant said, as though with documentary evidence at his fingers to refer to.

"He'll find me on hand tomorrow when he does."

The third night the manager suddenly approached the bar to one side of her, unasked, and called him over.

"What's the matter? Why don't you wanna wait on this young lady? I been watching. Twenty minutes she's been sitting here like this. Couldn't you see her?"

His face was grey, and the seams were shiny. It got that way whenever he had to come this close to her now.

"I can't," he said brokenly, keeping his voice muted so that others wouldn't hear it. "Mr. Anselmo, it's not human—she's torturing me—you don't understand—" He coughed on the verge of tears, and his cheeks swelled out, then flattened again.

The girl, less than a foot away, sat looking on at the two of them, with the tranquil, guiltless eyes of a child.

"Three nights she's been in here like this now. She keeps looking at me—"

"Sure she keeps looking at you; she's waiting to get waited on," the manager rebuked him. "What do you want her to do?" He peered closer at him, detected the strangeness in his face. "What's the matter? You sick? If you're sick and want to go home, I'll phone Pete to come down."

"No, no!" he pleaded hurriedly, almost with a frightened sob in his voice. "I don't want to go home—then she'll only follow me along the streets, stand outside my windows all night again! I'd rather stay here where there are people around me!"

"You quit talking crazy, and take her order," the manager said brusquely. He turned away, with a single verifying glance at her to confirm how well behaved, how docile, how harmless she was.

The hand that set down the drink before her shook uncontrollably, and some of it spilled.

They neither of them said anything to one another, though their breaths all but mingled.

"Hello," the station agent said friendlily through the wicket, as she came to rest just outside it. "Say, it's funny you and that guy that just passed through ahead of you always seem to get here at about the same time, and yet you're never together. Did y' notice?"

"Yes, I've noticed," she answered. "We both come out of the same place each night."

She maintained contact with this shrine of his by resting the point of her elbow on the slab outside the wicket, as though there were some sort of protective virtue to be derived from the touch of it, while she chatted desultorily with him, whiling her train-wait away. "Nice night, isn't it? . . . How's your little boy getting along? . . . I don't think the Dodgers stand a chance." Occasionally she would turn her head and cast a glance at the platform outside, where a lone figure paced, or stood, or was lost to view at times, but she never ventured out on it herself.

Only when the train was in, and at a full stop, and the platform gates stood open, did she break away and make a little dashing scamper that carried her aboard. On an insulated straight line, along which nothing could possibly happen to her, for the third rail was sheathed now by the undercarriages of the cars themselves.

An elevated train wriggled by like a glow-worm at the far end of the street. A taxi sloughed by and the driver glanced at her curiously, but he didn't want any more fares because he was taking his cab to bed for the night. Two late wayfarers passed, and one of them called over jocularly: "What's matter, Toots? Did you get a raincheque?" Quiet descended again after they had lost themselves in the distance.

Suddenly without any warning the doorway, the doorway that belonged to the two windows, disgorged a woman, hair awry and rushing as though she were a projectile discharged by the long black bore of the hall. She had donned a coat over her nightdress, and her bare feet were thrust into improperly secured shoes that made a clattering noise at each purposefully quick step she took. She was brandishing the long pole of a denuded floor-brush, and she made unerringly for the lone figure standing across the way, with unmistakable intent to flail at her.

The girl turned and sped, down to the nearby corner and around it and along the next street, but with a neat economy of movement that robbed her going of all fear, made it just a precautionary withdrawal from someone in whom she had no interest.

The woman's railing screams, fleeter than their owner, winged after the girl, overtook her midway down the block. "For three days now you been hounding my monn! Come back here and I'll give it to you! Let me get my hands on you and I'll fix you, I will!"

She stood there in view for a moment or two, just past the corner, gesturing threats of dire antagonism with pole and arm. The girl slowed, stopped, dissolved into the gloom.

Presently the woman went back around the corner, sought her own house again.

Presently the girl was back again too, standing where she had been before, and as she had been before, staring upward at two windows of the house across the way, like a cat watching a mouse-hole.

An elevated train wriggled by. . . . A taxi passed. . . . A late wayfarer came along, passed, receded. . . .

Those blank window-panes staring sightlessly down at her had a look of helpless frustration now, somehow.

"Soon," the voice on the telephone said. "One more day, to make sure he's completely pulverized. Maybe by tomorrow night—"

It was his day off, and he had been attempting to shake her off for well over an hour now.

He was going to halt again. She saw it coming before it had even occurred, she already knew the signs so well by now. He halted in full sunshine this time, stood back against a building-wall, with shoppers streaming to and fro before him. He had already halted two or three times before this, but each time it had ended inconclusively. As it always did. He had gone on again; she had too.

This time she detected a difference. This time the halt almost seemed to be involuntary. As though some mainspring of endurance had finally snapped, then and there, at just that point, as he was passing it and he had suddenly found himself all unwound. As he backed to the wall the small flat parcel he had held bedded under his arm slowly overbalanced, slapped to the ground, and he allowed it to lie there unrecovered.

She halted a short distance from him, making no pretence, as usual, that her halt had anything to do but with him. She stood looking at him in her usual grave way.

The sun was streaming whitely into his face, and he was blinking his eyes against it. More and more rapidly, however.

Tears appeared unexpectedly, and suddenly he was weeping abjectly, in full view of all the passers-by, his face an ugly, brick-red, puckered mask.

Two people stopped, incredulous. The two became four, the four eight. He and the girl were both contained in the hollow core of the crowd that in no time at all had ringed them around, kept thickening, outer layer by outer layer.

He was past all ordinary sense of self-consciousness, humiliation; he appealed to the onlookers, almost as if asking help, protection against her.

"Ask her what she *wants* of me!" he bawled suddenly. "Ask her what she's *after*!" She's been doing this to me for days now—day and night, night and day! I can't stand it any more, I tell ya. I can't stand it any more—!"

"What is he, drunk?" a woman asked another, in a derisive undertone.

She stood there unshrinking, making no attempt to escape from the attention he was forcing her to share with him. She was so dignified, so grave, so fetching to the eye, and he was so grotesquely comical, it could have had only one result: the sympathies of the crowd could have gone only one way. Crowds are more often sadistic than not, anyway.

Grins appeared here and there. The grins became snickers. The snickers guffaws and outright jeers. In another moment the whole crowd was laughing pitilessly at him. Only one face in all that group remained impassive, sober, clinically neutral.

Hers.

He had only worsened his situation instead of bettering it by making this spectacle. He had thirty tormentors now instead of one.

"I can't stand it any more! I tell ya I'll *do* something to her!" Suddenly he advanced on her, as if to strike her, beat her back.

Instantly men leaped forward, caught his arms, flung him this way and that with surly grunts. For a moment there was a confused floundering of bodies around her. His head suddenly forced its way through, lower than normal, straining to get at her.

It might easily have developed into a multiple onslaught—on *him*.

She appealed to them, self-possessedly but loudly enough to be heard, and the calm clarity of her voice stopped them all short. "Don't. Let him alone. Let him go about his business."

But there was no warmth nor compassion about it, just a terrible steely impartiality. As if to say: Leave him to me. He's mine.

Arms fell away from him, poised fists relaxed, coats were shrugged back into place, and the angry inner nucleus within the greater one disintegrated. Leaving him alone again within the hollow circle. Alone with her.

He made several false moves in his torment and frustration, seeking an outlet through the massed figures around him. Then he found one, and forced his way through it, and went plunging out. He went *running* away from the scene full tilt, padding ponderously down the street; running away from the slender girl who stood there looking after him, her coat belted around her waist to the thickness of little more than a man's hand-span. The ultimate in degradation.

She didn't linger long behind him. She wasn't interested in the plaudits of the crowd, nor savouring any juvenile public triumph. She thrust those in her way aside with deft little passes of her arm, until she had gained clearance for herself. Then she set out after the heavily labouring figure ahead, at a blend of light running and graceful, energetic walking that carried her rapidly forward in his wake.

Strange pursuit. Incredible pursuit. Slim young girl hurrying after a stocky barman, in and out, out and in, through the swarming midday streets of New York.

He became aware almost at once that she had taken up the chase once more. He looked back, the first time in dismal apprehension. She waited for him to look again. When he did she flung up her arm straight overhead, in imperious summons to him to stop.

Now would be the time, now would be the moment Burgess would approve of, she felt sure. Now he was like wax as he ran through this bright midday sun. That crowd back there had taken away his last prop. He had tested it, found it no protection, and accordingly he no longer had a sense of immunity even in broad daylight on these bustling city streets.

The curve of his resistance might start upward again from here on, if she didn't act now while she had the chance. The law of diminishing returns might set in from here on. Familiarity might very well breed contempt, for all she knew.

Now was the time; it was simply a matter of pinning him against the nearest wall, putting in a quick call to Burgess, and having him take charge in time to be in at the death. "Are you ready to admit now that you did see a certain woman at the bar that night in company with the man Henderson? Why did you deny having seen her? Who paid or coerced you to deny it?"

He had stopped for a moment, down there ahead at the next corner, looking all about him for a way of escape like a trapped, scurrying animal. Panic was on him at white heat. She could tell by the abortive, zig-zag, false starts he kept making, looking for sanctuary. To him she was no longer a girl, something he could have buffeted senseless with one arm if he chose. To him she was Nemesis.

She threw up her arm again, as the distance rapidly closed between them. It only stung him like the flick of a whip to an added spurt of frenzied disorientation. He was walled in there on the corner by a thin but continuous line of people waiting to cross over, standing elbow to elbow along the kerb. There was an adverse light on above.

He gave one last look at her, rapidly nearing him now, and then plunged through them like a circus performer tearing through a paper hoop.

She stopped short, as short as though both her flailing feet had caught simultaneously in a hidden crevice along the sidewalk. A brake keened out along the asphalt, scorching itself to death.

She flung up both hands, ground them into her eye sockets, but not before she had seen his hat go up in the air in a surprisingly high loop, clear over everyone else's head.

A woman screamed for prelude, and then a vast bay of horrified dismay went up from the crowd in general.

# THIRTEEN

## The Eleventh Day Before the Execution

### LOMBARD

Lombard had been following him for the past hour and a half, and there's nothing slower to be followed on the face of the earth than a blind mendicant. He moved like a tortoise that counts its life-span by centuries, instead of a man that counts his by years. It took him an average of forty minutes to traverse each block-length, from one corner to the next. Lombard timed it with his watch several times.

He didn't have a seeing eye dog. He had to rely on his fellow-pedestrians to get him safely over the crossings each time he came to one. They never failed him. Cops held up traffic well into the green if he hadn't quite made it by the time the change-over came. Hardly anyone that passed failed to drop something into his cup, so it paid him to walk slow.

It was painful to Lombard in the extreme; he was active, unhandicapped, and with an acutely heightened sense of time-value these days. Several times it was all he could do to hang back in the wake of this endless, creeping progress, that was like a variation of the Chinese water-drop torture. But he curbed himself, kept him grimly in sight, sucking impatiently at cigarettes for a safety-valve, standing immobile for long stretches at a time in doorways and shop-windows indentations to let him accomplish some distance, then closing in rapidly again in a few hectic strides, and falling motionless once more, to once more let his quarry eke out a little further microscopic progress. Breaking it up that way into fits and starts took a little of the curse out of it.

It couldn't keep on for ever, he kept reminding himself. It couldn't last through the whole night. That figure up ahead of him was a human being in a human being's body. He had to sleep some time. He'd have to turn in out of the open and go behind walls and lie down to rest *some time*. His kind didn't beg straight through the night hours until daybreak; the law of diminishing returns alone would be enough to discourage that.

And finally it came. Lombard had thought it never would, but it did at last. He turned aside, went within walls, and quitted the open. It was in a sector that had unnoticeably become so derelict as they both advanced through it that no bounty could be expected from it. It was in need of alms itself, instead of being able to bestow. It was blocked off at one end by overhead railway tracks carried on a viaduct of rough-faced granite blocks.

His burrow was a mouldering tenement just short of this. Lombard had to be careful, although he hadn't realized even yet that the end was this close at hand. He'd had to remain well back, for the streets were desolate hereabouts, with few other footsteps to blur his own, and he knew they had supersensitive ears as a rule.

When he saw him enter, therefore, he was further back than he would have wished to be. He hurriedly closed in for the last time, trying to reach it in time to ascertain which floor it was, if possible. He stopped at the doorway and cautiously entered in turn, just deep enough within to be able to listen.

The cane-taps were still going up, with infinite slowness. They sounded a little like drops of water from a faulty spigot striking into an empty wooden bucket. He held his breath, listening. He counted four breaks in them, changes of tempo, one for each turn of the stairs. They were duller on the level landings than on the incline of the stairs themselves. Then they dwindled off to the back, not the front, of the building.

He waited until he'd heard the faint closing of a door up there somewhere, then he started up in turn, treading stealthily but fast, with all the energy he'd had to hold suppressed until now unleashed at last. The acutely tilted flights of worn stairs would have prostrated anyone else; he was hardly aware of them.

There were two of them at the back, but he could tell which it was, because one of them, even at this distance, was obviously a water-closet.

He waited a moment at the top step until his rapidity of breath was completely quelled again, then advanced carefully toward it. Again he reminded himself how acute of hearing they were said to be. But he accomplished his purpose to perfection; not a floorboard wavered, due more to his superb muscular co-ordination than to any particular lightness of weight. He was and always had been a swell machine; something that belonged under the hood of a racing car instead of in a flimsy sack of skin.

He put his ear over against the door-seam and listened.

There was no light coming from it, of course, because for him in there there was never any light, so it would have done him no good to put it on. But he could hear an occasional sound of moving about. It put him in mind of an animal that withdraws into a hole and then keeps turning for some little time afterward, getting itself comfortable before it finally settles down for good.

There were no sounds of voice. He must be in there alone.

This was long enough. Now for it. He knocked.

The moving around died instantly, and there was nothing more. A cessation. A place trying to make itself seem empty. A frightened, bated stillness that he knew would go on for as long as he was out there—if he permitted it to.

He knocked again.

"Come on," he said sternly.

His third knocking was harshly imperative. The fourth would be blows.

"Come on," he said brutally in the silence.

The flooring creaked timidly in there, and then a voice, almost with breath accompanying it, it was emitted so close to the door-seam, asked: "Who's out there?"

"A friend."

The voice became more frightened at that, instead of less. "I haven't any. I don't know you."

"Let me in. I won't hurt you."

"I can't do it. I'm alone in here and helpless. I can't let anyone in." He was worried about his day's gleanings, Lombard knew. You couldn't blame him for that. It was a wonder he hadn't lost them, in the way that he took this to be, long before now.

"You can let me in. Come on, open up a minute. I only want to talk to you."

The voice on the other side quavered. "Get away from here. Go on away from my door, or I'll holler down for help from the window". But it was pleading rather than threatening.

There was a short stalemate. Neither of them moved. Neither of them made a sound. They were acutely aware of each other's nearness. Fright on one side of the door, determination on the other.

Lombard took out his wallet finally, scanned it thoughtfully. The largest denomination in it was a fifty-dollar bill. There were some smaller ones he could have taken out in place of it; he chose the larger one instead. He dropped to his heels, worked it through the crack under the door until there was nothing left of it to hold on to any more.

He straightened up again, said: "Reach down and feel along the bottom of the door. Doesn't that prove I don't want to rob you? Now let me in."

There was a postscript of hesitancy, then a chain-head slid off its groove. A bolt sidled back, and last of all a key turned in the keyhole. It had been well barricaded.

The door opened grudgingly, and the sightless black lenses that he'd first marked out on the streets hours ago stared at him. "Anyone else with you?"

"No, I'm alone. And I haven't come here to harm you, so don't be nervous.'

"You're not an agent, are you?"

"No, I'm not a police agent. There'd be a cop with me if I was, and there's nobody with me. I just want to talk to you, can't you get that through your head?" He pushed his way in.

The room was invisible in the darkness, non-existent, a pall of sightlessness, just as the other's whole world must be. For a moment a wedge of dull amber-tan lying along the floor from the hall light outside helped a little, then that went, too, as the door closed.

"Put on a light, can't you?"

"No," the blind man said, "this makes us more even. If you just want to talk, what do you need a light for?" Lombard heard a decrepit bedspring sing out somewhere nearby as he sank down on it. He was probably sitting on his day's take, nested under the mattress.

"Come on, cut out the foolishness; I can't talk like this—" He groped around him at knee-level, finally located the arm of a rickety wooden rocker, shifted it over and sank into it.

"You said you wanted to talk," the other voice said tautly in the dark. "Now you're in, now go ahead and talk. You don't have to see to be able to talk."

Lombard's voice said, "Well, at least I can smoke, can't I? You don't object to that, do you? You smoke yourself, don't you?"

"When I can get it," the other voice said warily.

"Here take one of these." There was a click, and a small lighter-flame peered out in his hand. A little of the room came back.

The blind man was on the edge of the bed, his cane crosswise on his lap in case it should be required as a weapon.

Lombard's hand came away from his pocket holding, instead of cigarettes, a revolver. He held it in close, but pointed directly at the other. "Here, help yourself," he repeated pleasantly.

The blind man became rigid. The cane rolled off his knees and hit the floor. He made a spasmodic warding motion of the hands, up toward his face. "I knew you were after my money!" he said hoarsely. "I shouldn't have let you in—"

Lombard put the gun away again, as calmly as he had taken it out. "You're not blind," he said quietly. "I didn't need that stunt to prove it to myself either. But I needed it to prove to you that I was already on to you. The mere fact that you opened the door for a fifty-dollar bill was proof enough. You must have struck a match for a minute and scanned it. How could you know it wasn't a one-dollar bill if you weren't a fake? A one is the same size and shape, feels the same, as a fifty. A one wouldn't have made it worth your while to open the door; you probably came in with more than that on you yourself just now. But a fifty was worth taking a chance for; that was more than you'd collected."

He saw a mis-shapen remnant of a candle, went over and touched the lighter to it while he was still speaking.

"You are an agent," the beggar faltered, wiping sweat from his forehead harassedly with the back of his hand. "I might have known—"

"Not the kind you mean, interested in whether you're out taking the public money under false pretences or not. If that's any consolation to you." He came back and sat down again.

"Then what are you? What do you want with me?"

"I want you to remember something you saw—Mr. *Blind Man*," he added ironically. "Now listen to this. You were hanging around outside the Casino Theatre, working the audience as it came out, one night last May—"

"But I've been around there lots of times."

"I'm talking about one night only, one particular night. That's the only one I care about; I don't give a damn about the rest. This night that I mean a man and a woman came out together. Now, here's the woman; she had on a bright orange hat with a tall black feeler sticking up from it. You put the bite on them as they were getting into a taxi a few yards down from the entrance. Listen carefully now. Without thinking what she was doing, she dropped a lighted cigarette into the cup you shoved at her, instead of the donation she intended. It burned your finger. The man quickly dug it out for you, and to make it up to you gave you a couple of dollars. I think he said something like this: 'Sorry, old man, that was a mistake.' Now surely you remember that. It isn't every night your finger gets burned by a live cigarette landing in your cup, and it isn't every night you get two dollars in a lick from just one passer-by."

"Suppose I say I don't remember?"

"Then I'm going to haul you out of here with me right now and turn you in at the nearest police station as an impostor. You'll get a stretch in the workhouse, you'll be down on the police blotter from then on, and you'll be picked up each time they see you trying to work the streets."

The man on the bed clawed at his own face distractedly, momentarily displacing the dark glasses upward past his eyes. "But isn't that like forcing me to say I remember, whether I do or not?"

"It's only forcing you to admit what I'm sure you do remember anyway."

"Then suppose I say I do remember, what happens then?"

"First you tell me what you remember, then you repeat it to a certain plain-clothes-man, a friend of mine. I'll either bring him down here or take you up there with me to see him—"

The mendicant jolted with renewed dismay. "But how can I do that without giving myself away? Especially to a plain-clothes-man! I'm supposed to be blind; how can I say I saw them? That's the same as what you were threatening to do to me if I *didn't* tell you!"

"No, you'll just be telling it to this one guy, not the whole force at large. I can strike a bargain with him, get him to promise you immunity from prosecution. Now how about it? Did you or didn't you?"

"Yes, I did," the professional blind man admitted in a low voice. "I saw the two of them together. I usually keep my eyes closed, even behind the glasses, when I'm near bright lights, like there were outside that theatre. But the cigarette burn made me open them good and wide. I can see through the glasses, and I saw them both all right."

Lombard took something out of his wallet. "Is this him?"

The blind man hitched his glasses up out of the way, scrutinized the snapshot critically. "I'd say it was," he said finally. "Considering how short a glimpse I had of him, and how long ago it was, it looks to me like the same guy."

"What about her? You'd know her again if you saw her?"

"I already have. I only saw him that one night, but I saw her at least once more after that—"

"What!" Lombard was suddenly on his feet, leaning over him. The rocker swayed emptily behind him. He grabbed him by the shoulder, squeezing as if trying to get the information out of his skinny frame in that way. "Let me hear about it! Come on, quick!"

"It was not very long after that same night, that's how I knew it was she. It was in front of one of the big swanky hotels, and you know how bright *they* are. I heard a pair of footsteps coming down the steps, a man's and a woman's. I heard the woman say, 'Wait a minute. Maybe this'll bring me luck.' And I knew she meant me. I heard her footsteps turn aside and come over to me. A coin went in. A quarter. I can tell the different coins by the sounds they make. And then the funny part of it happened that made me know it was she. It's such a little thing I don't know if you'll be able to catch on like I did. She stood still for just a tiny minute there in front of me, and they never do. The coin was already in, so I knew she must be looking at me. Or something about me. I was holding the cup in my right hand, the one with the burn on it, and the burn was one of those big water-blisters by that time. I think it must have been that she saw on the side of my finger. Anyway, here's what happened. I heard her say under her breath—not to me, but to herself—'Why, how very odd!' And then her footsteps turned and went back to where the man's were. That was all—"

"But—"

"Wait a minute, I'm not finished yet. I opened my eyes just a slit to look down at the cup. *And she'd added a dollar bill to the original quarter she'd put in the first time.* I knew it was she because it hadn't been in there until then. Now, why should she change her mind and add a dollar bill after she'd already put in a quarter? It must have been the same woman; she must have recognized the blister and remembered what had happened a few nights be—"

"Must have, must have," gritted Lombard impatiently. "I thought you said you saw her, could tell me what she looked like!"

"I can't tell you what she looks like from the front because I didn't dare open my eyes. The lights were too bright around there, it would have been a give-away. After she turned away and I saw the dollar bill, I peered up a little higher under my lashes and saw her from the back, as she was getting into the car."

"From the back! Well, tell me that at least, what was she like from the back?"

"I couldn't see all of her even from the back. I was afraid to look up that high. All I saw was just the seam of a silk stocking and one heel as she raised it to step in. That was all that was in focus with my downcast eyelids."

"An orange hat one night. A stocking seam and the heel of her shoe another night, a week later?" Lombard gave him a fling back on to the bed. "At this rate, after about twenty years we'll have a whole woman to stick in between the two!"

He went over to the door, flung it open. He looked back at him balefully. "You can do a lot better than that, and I'm sure of it! What you need is the professional touch to bring it out. You certainly did see her full eye-width the first night, outside the theatre. And the second time you must have heard the address given to the driver of the car as she stepped in—"

"No, I didn't."

"You stay here, get it? Don't move from here. I'm going to call up this fellow I told you about. I want him to come over here and listen to this with me."

"But he's a bull, isn't he?"

"I told you that's all right. We're not interested in you, either one of us. You've got nothing to be nervous about. But don't try to run out before I get back, or then we will make it hot for you."

He closed the door after him.

The voice at the other end sounded surprised. "You got something already?"

"I've got something already, and I want you to hear it for what it's worth. I think you can probably get a lot more out of it than I can. I'm way up here at 123 St. and Park Avenue, the last house short of the railroad tracks. I'd like you to get over here as fast as you can, and see what you think of it. I've got the beat-cop posted at the door watching it for me until I can get back. I'm talking from around the corner, nearest phone I could find. I'll be waiting down there by the street entrance for you."

Burgess dropped off a patrol car with a running slow-down a few minutes later. The car went on without stopping and he came over to where Lombard and the cop were standing waiting in the doorway.

"In here," Lombard said, turning to go in without any further explanation.

"Well, I guess I can get back on the line," the cop said, turning away.

"Thanks a lot, officer," Lombard called out to him. They were already in at the stairs by that time. "All the way up at the top," he explained, taking the lead. "He's seen her twice, *that* night and another time a week later. He's a blind man; don't laugh, phoney of course."

"Well, that was worth coming over for," Burgess admitted.

They made the first turning, one behind the other, hands coasting along the rail. "Wants immunity—about the blindness. Scared of cops."

"We can work something out, if it's worth it." Burgess grunted.

Second landing. "One more," Lombard checked off gratuitously. They saved their breath for climbing on the next.

Third landing. "What happened to the lights from here on up?" Burgess heaved.

A hitched snagged the rhythm of Lombard's ascent. "That's funny. There was one still on when I came down. Either the bulb died, or it was tampered with, turned off."

"You sure it was still on?"

"Absolutely. I remember he had his room dark, but light from the hall came in through the open door."

"Better let me go first, I've got a pocket light." Burgess detoured around him, took the lead.

He must have been still in the process of getting it out. At the middle turn, between floors, where the stairs changed direction, he suddenly went floundering down on all fours. "Look out," he warned Lombard. "Step back."

The moon of his torch sprang up, bleaching the little oblong between end wall and bottom step. Spanning it lay an inert figure, grotesquely contorted. Legs trailing downward off the last few steps, torso proper on the level landing-place, but head bent backward at an unnatural and acute angle by the impediment of the end wall at the turn. Dangling from one ear, but miraculously unbroken, was a pair of dark glasses.

"That him?" he muttered.

"It's him," agreed Lombard tersely.

Burgess bent over the figure, probed awhile. Then he straightened up again. "Broken neck," he said. "Killed instantly." He shot his light up the stair incline. Then he went up there, jittered it around on the floor. "Accident," he said. "Missed his footing up here on the top step, went all the way down head-first, and crashed head-on into that wall backing the turn. I can see the skidmarks up here, over the lip of the top step."

Lombard climbed slowly up to where he was, blew out his breath in a disgusted snort. "Fine time for an accident! I no sooner contact him—" He stopped short, looked at the detective searchingly in the battery light-rays. "You don't think it could have been anything else, do you?"

"Did anyone pass you or that other guy while you were waiting down there at the door?"

"No one, in or out."

"Did you hear anything like a fall?"

"No, we would have come in and looked if we had. But at least twice while we were waiting for you long trains went by on those overhead tracks, and you couldn't hear yourself think until they'd gone by. It might have been during one of those times."

Burgess nodded. "That's what probably kept others in the building from hearing it too. Don't you see, there's too much coincidence in it for it to be anything but an accident. He could have hit his head against that same wall down there ten times over and still lived; just been stunned without breaking his neck. He just *happened* to be killed instantly, but it couldn't have been counted on."

"Well, where does the bulb come in? I think that's too much coincidence, isn't it? I know that I'm saying that light was still in working order when I tore down those stairs to phone you. If it hadn't been, I would have had to pick my way down, and I didn't; I went pretty fast."

Burgess shot his light along the wall until he'd found it; it was on a bracket, sticking out from the side. "I don't get what you mean," he said, staring up at it. "If he was supposed to be blind, or at least went around most of the time with his eyes closed, which amounts to the same thing, how does the bulb enter into it one way or the other? How would darkness be any disadvantage to him? In fact, he'd be more sure-footed in the dark, probably, than with the light left on; because he wasn't used to using his eyes."

"Maybe that's just it," Lombard said. "Maybe he came out fast, trying to make his get-away before I got back, and in his hurry forgot to close his eyes, left them open. With them open, maybe he was no better off than you or me."

"Now you're getting yourself all tangled up. For his sight to be dazzled, the light would have had to be on. And your whole kick has been that it isn't. What would be the point, either way? How could anyone *count* on his missing a step, any more than they could count on his hitting in such a way that his neck snapped?"

"All right, it was a freak accident." Lombard flung his hand out disgustedly as he turned to go down. "All I say is, I don't like its timing. I no sooner catch up with him—"

"They will happen, you know, and they usually pick their own time for it, not yours."

Lombard went thumping frustratedly down the stairs, letting his whole weight down at each step. "Whatever you might have been able to drill out of him is gone for good now."

"Don't let it throw you down. You may be able to turn up somebody else."

"From him, it's gone for good. And it was practically there, waiting to be found out." He'd reached the landing where the body lay by now. He turned suddenly to look back. "What happened? What was that?"

Burgess pointed to the wall. "The bulb lit up again. Your vibration on the staircase jarred it on. Which explains what happened to it the first time: his fall broke the current. The wiring must be defective. That takes care of the light." He motioned him on. "You may as well clear out. I'll report it by myself. No sense of you getting all mixed up in it, if you want to keep working on the other thing."

Lombard's tread went dejectedly on down the rest of the way toward the street, all the lilt gone out of it. Burgess stayed behind up there, waiting beside the motionless form on the landing.

# FOURTEEN

## The Tenth Day Before the Execution

### THE GIRL

It was on a slip of paper that Burgess had given her.

Cliff Milburn
house-musician, Casino Theatre, last season.
current job, Regent Theatre.

And then two telephone numbers. One a police precinct up until a certain hour. The other his own home number, in case she needed him after he'd gone off duty.

He'd said to her: "I can't tell you how to go about it. You'll have to figure that out for yourself. Your own instinct will probably tell you what to do, better than I can. Just don't be frightened, and keep your wits about you. You'll be all right."

This was her own way of going about it, here in front of the glass. This was the only way she could figure out, sight-unseen. The clean, tomboyish look was gone from her. The breezy sweep of the hair from an immaculate part over to the other side of her face, that was missing in its place was a tortured surface of brassy rolls and undulations, drenched with some sort of fixative and then hardened into a metallic casque. Gone, too, was the youthful, free-swinging, graceful hang there had always been to her clothes. Instead she had managed to achieve a skin-tight effect that appalled her, even alone here in her own room. Excruciatingly short, so that when she sat down—well, she would be sure to catch his eye in a way that would do the most good. A big red poker-chip on each cheek, as obvious as a pair of stop-lights, but whose effect was intended to be the opposite: go ahead. A string of beads that clacked around her throat. A handkerchief with too much lace on it, saturated in a virulent concoction that made her own nose crinkle in distate as she hastily stuffed it into her bag. She had made herself heavy-lidded with some blue stuff she had never used before.

Scott Henderson had been watching her throughout the proceeding from a frame to one side of the glass, and she was ashamed: "You wouldn't know me, darling, would you?" she murmured contritely. "Don't look at me, darling, don't look at me."

And now one final ghastly item to complete the catalogue of sleazy accessibility. She put up her leg and slipped a garter of violently pink satin complete with a rosette up it, left it at a point just below visibility. At least, when seated.

She turned away fast. His Girl shouldn't look like that thing she had just seen in the glass, not His Girl. She went around putting lights out, outwardly calm, inwardly keyed up. Only someone that knew her well could have guessed it. *He* would have known it at a glance. He wasn't here to see it.

When she came to the last one of all, the one by the door, she said the little prayer she always said each time she started out. Looking over at him there, in the frame, across the room.

"Maybe tonight, darling," she breathed softly, "maybe tonight."

She put out the light and closed the door, and he stayed behind there in the dark, under glass.

The marquee lights were on when she got out of the cab, but the sidewalk under them was fairly empty yet. She wanted to get in good and early, so she'd have time to work on him before the house lights went down. She only half-knew what was playing, and when it was over and she came out again she knew she wouldn't know very much more than she had when she sent in. Something called "Keep on Dancing."

She stopped at the box-office. "I have a reservation for tonight. First row orchestra, on the aisle. Mimi Gordon."

She'd had to wait days for it. Because this wasn't a matter of seeing the show, this was a matter of being seen. She took out the money and paid for it. "Now you're sure of what you told me over the phone? That's the side of the house the trap-drummer is on, and not the other?"

"That's right, I checked on it for you before I put it aside." He gave her the leer she'd known he would. "You must think quite a lot of him. Lucky guy, I'd say."

"You don't understand; it's not him personally. I don't even know him from Adam. It's—how'll I explain? Everybody has some sort of a hobby. Well, mine happens to be the trap-drums. Every time I go to a show I try to sit as close to them as I can get; I love to watch them being played; it does something to me. I'm an addict of the trap-drums; they've fascinated me ever since I was a child.

I know it sounds crazy, but"—she spread her hands—"that's how it is."

"I didn't mean to be inquisitive," he apologized, crest-fallen.

She went inside. The ticket-taker at the door had just come on duty, the usher had just come up from the locker-room downstairs, she was so early. Whatever the status of the balcony, where the unwritten rule of being fashionable late did not hold sway, she was definitely the first patron on the orchestra floor.

She sat there alone, a small gilt-headed figure lost in that vast sea of empty seats. Most of her gaudiness was carefully concealed, from three directions, by the coat she kept huddled about her. It was only from the front that she wanted it to have its full lethal effect.

Seats began to slap down behind her more and more frequently; there was that rustle and slight hum that always marks a theatre slowly filling up. She had eyes for one thing and one thing only: that little half-submerged door down there under the rim of the stage. It was over on the opposite side from her. Light was peering through the seams of it now, and she could hear voices behind it. They were gathering there ready to come out to work.

Suddenly it opened and they began filing up into the pit, each one's head and shoulders bent acutely to permit his passage. She didn't know which one was he; she wouldn't know until she saw him seat himself, because she'd never seen him. One by one they dropped into the various chairs, disposing themselves in a thin crescent around the stage-apron, heads below the footlights.

She was seemingly absorbed in the programme on her lap, head lowered, but she kept peering watchfully up from under her sooty lashes. This one, coming now? No, he'd stopped one chair too short. The one behind him? What a villainous face! She was almost relieved when he'd dropped off at the second chair down from her. Clarinet, or something. Well, then, this one, it must be he—no, he'd turned and gone the other way, bass viol.

They'd stopped emerging now. Suddenly she was uneasy. The last one out had even closed the door behind him. There weren't any more of them coming through. They were all seated, they were all tuning up, settling themselves for work. Even the conductor was on hand. And the chair at the trap-drum, the one directly before her, remained ominously vacant.

Maybe he'd been discharged. No, because then they'd get a substitute to take his place. Maybe he'd been taken ill, couldn't play tonight. Oh, just tonight this had to happen! Probably every night this week, until now, he'd been here. She mightn't be able to get this same particular seat again for weeks to come; the show was selling well and there was great demand. And she couldn't afford to wait that long. Time was so precious, was running so short; there was too little of it left.

She could overhear them discussing it among themselves in disparaging undertones. She was close enough to catch nearly everything they said, to get in under the tuning-up discords that covered them from the rest of the house.

"D'jever see a guy like that? I think he's been on time once since the season started. Fining don't do any good."

The alto saxophone said. "He probably chased some blonde up an alley and forgot to come out again."

The man behind him chimed in facetiously: "A good drummer is hard to get."

"Not that hard."

She was staring at the credits on her programme, without their focusing into type. She was rigid with suppressed anxiety. Ironical that every man in the orchestra should be on hand but the single one, the only one, that could do her any good.

She thought: "This is the same sort of luck poor Scott was in the night *he*—"

The lull before the overture had fallen. They were all set now, light-rods turned on over their scores. Suddenly, when she was no longer even watching it any more, it seemed so hopeless, the door giving into the pit had flickered open, closed again, so quickly it was like the winking of an intermittent light, and a figure scuttled deftly alongside the outside of the chairs to the vacant one before her, bent over both to increase its speed and to attract the conductor's attention as little as possible. Thus there was something rodent-like about him even at his first appearance within her ken, and he was to stay in character throughout.

The conductor gave him a sizzling look.

He wasn't abashed. She heard him pant in a breathless undertone to his neighbour, "Boy, have I got a honey for the second tomorrow! A sure thing."

"Sure, and the only sure thing about it is it won't come in," was the dry answer.

He hadn't seen her yet. He was too busy fiddling with his rack, adjusting his instrument. Her hand dropped to her side and her skirt crept up her thigh an unnoticeable fraction of an inch more.

He got through arranging his set-up. "How's the house to-night?" she heard him ask. He turned and looked out through the pit-railing for the first time since he'd come in.

She was ready for him. She was looking at him. She'd hit him. There must have been an elbow-nudge beyond her radius of downcast vision. She heard the other man's slurred answer. "Yeah, I know; I seen it."

She'd hit him hard. She could feel his eyes on her. She could have made a graph of the wavy line they travelled. She took her time. Not too fast now, not right away. She thought: "Funny how we know these things, all of us, even when we've never tried them before." She concentrated on a line on her programme as though she could never get enough of its mystic import. It was mostly dots, running from one side of the page over to the other. It helped to keep her eyes steady.

"*Victorine* ...................................................Dixie Lee."

She counted the dots. Twenty-seven of them, from character-name over to performer-name. There, that was about long enough. That had given it time to work. She let her lashes come up slowly and unveil her eyes.

They met his. They stayed with his. He had expected them to turn away, frost over. Instead, they accepted his glance, sustained it for as long as he cared to give it. They seemed to say: "Are you interested in me? All right, go ahead; I don't mind."

He was a shade surprised for a moment at this ready acceptance. He kept on looking for all he was worth. He even tried a tentative smile, that was ready to be rubbed out at a moment's notice too.

She accepted that in turn. She even sent him one back, of about the same degree as his. His deepened. hers did too.

The preliminaries were over, they were getting into— And then, damn it, the buzzer signalled from back-curtain. The conductor tapped out attention, spread his arms, holding them poised. Flounced them, and the overture was under way, he and she had to break it off.

That was all right, she consoled herself. So far so good. The show couldn't be straight music all the way through, no show was. There would be rest-spells.

The curtain went up. She was aware of voices, lights, figures. She didn't bother with what was going on on stage. She wasn't here to see a show. She minded her own business strictly, and her business was making a musician.

He turned and spoke to her at the start of the intermission, when they were filing out for a rest and a smoke. He was the furthest over, so he was the last to go; that gave him the chance to do it undetected behind the others' backs. The people next to her had gotten up and gone out, so he could tell she was alone, even if her conduct had left him any doubts on that point until now, which is certainly should not have.

"How do you like it so far?"

"It's real good," she purred.

"Doing anything afterwards?"

She pouted. "No, I only wish I was."

He turned to go out after his fellow-bandsmen. "You are," he assured her smugly, "now."

She gave her skirt a corrective downward hitch with considerable asperity as soon as he was gone. She felt as though she could have used a scalding shower and plenty of Lifebuoy.

Her face-lines slipped back to where they belonged. Even the make-up couldn't hide the alteration. She sat there, pensive, alone, at the end of the empty row of seats. Maybe tonight, darling, maybe tonight.

When the house lights went on again at the final curtain, she lingered behind, pretending to have dropped this, pretending to be adjusting that, while the rest of the audience siphoned slowly up through the aisles.

The band finished playing them out. He gave the cymbal atop his drum a final stroke, steadied it with his fingers, put down his drumsticks, snapped off the light over his rack. He was through for the night, he was on his own time now. He turned around to her slowly, as if already feeling himself the dominant factor in the situation. "Wait for me around at the stage-alley, lovely," he said. "Be with you in five minutes."

There was ignominy attached even to the simple act of waiting for him outside, for some reason she couldn't quite ascertain. Perhaps it was something about his personality that tinged everything that way. She felt crawly, walking up and down out there. And a little afraid. And the way all the other bandsmen, coming out ahead of him (he couldn't even spare her that embarrassment, he had to be the last one out), looked at her as they passed added to her discomfort.

Then suddenly he'd swept her off with him by surprise. That is to say, before she'd even seen him coming, he had her arm possessively under his and was towing her along with him, without even breaking stride. That was probably characteristic of him, too, she thought.

"How's my new little friend?" he began breezily.

"Fine, how's mine?" she gave him back.

"We'll go where the rest of the gang goes," he said. I'd catch cold without 'em." She got the idea. She was like a new *boutonnière* to him; he wanted to show her off.

This was at twelve.

By two o'clock she decided he'd been softened up enough by beer for her to begin to go to work on him. They were in the second of two identical places by then, the gang still in the offing. A peculiar sort of etiquette seemed to govern things of this sort. He and she had moved on when the rest of them moved, and yet once they were in the new place they continued their separateness at a table by themselves. He would get up and join the others every once in a while, and then come back to her again, but the others never came over and joined him, she noticed. Probably because she was his, and they were supposed to stay away from her.

She'd been watching carefully for her opening for some time. She knew she'd better get going at it; after all, the night wouldn't last for ever, and she couldn't face the thought of having to go through another one like it.

One offered itself finally, just what she wanted, in one of the rancid compliments he'd been shovelling at her all evening—whenever he thought of it. Somewhat like an absent-minded stoker keeping a fire going.

"You say I'm the prettiest thing ever sat in that seat. But there must have been other times you turned around and saw someone you liked sitting there right behind you. Tell me about some of them."

"Not in it with you; wouldn't waste my breath."

"Well, just for fun; I'm not jealous. Tell me: if you had your choice, out of all the attractive women you ever saw sitting behind you in that same seat where I was tonight, since you've been playing in theatres, which was the one you would have rather taken out?"

"You, of course."

"I knew you'd say that. But after me; which would your second choice be? I want to see just how far back you can remember. I bet you can't remember their faces from one night to the next."

"Can't I? Well, just to show you. I turn around one night and there's a dame sitting there right on the other side of the rail from me—"

Under the table she was holding the soft inside curve of her arm with her own hand, squeezing it tightly as though it ached unendurably.

"This was at the other house, the Casino. I don't know, something about her got me—"

A succession of attenuated shadows slipped across their table one by one; the last one of all stood still for a minute. "We're going to pitch a jam-session downwards in the basement. Coming?"

Her gripping hand relaxed its hold on her arm, fell away frustratedly down by the side of her chair. They'd all gotten up, were piling in through a basement entrance at the back.

"No, stay up here with me," she urged, reaching out to hold him. "Finish what you—"

He'd already risen. "Come on, you don't want to miss this, snooks."

"Don't you do enough playing all evening at the theatre?"

"Yeah, but that's for pay. This is for myself. You're going to hear something now."

He was going to leave her anyway, she saw; this had a stronger

pull than she had, so she rose reluctantly to her feet and trailed
after him down narrow brick-walled stairs to the restaurant basement. They were all in a large room down there, with instruments
in it already that they must have used at previous times. Even an
upright piano. There was a single large but smoky bulb hanging on
a loose wire from the centre of the ceiling, and to supplement this
they had candles stuck in bottles. There was a battered wooden
table in the middle, and they put bottles of gin on it, nearly one to
a man. One of them spread a piece of brown wrapping-paper out
and dumped quantities of cigarettes on to it, for anyone to help
themselves at will. Not the kind the world upstairs smoked;
black-filled things; reefers, she heard them call them.

They closed and bolted the door as soon as she and Milburn had
come in, to keep themselves free from interruption. She was the
only girl among them.

There were packing-cases and empty cartons and even a keg or
two to sit on. A clarinet tootled mournfully, and mania had begun.

The next two hours were a sort of Dante-esque Inferno. She
knew as soon as it was over she wouldn't believe it had actually
been real at all. It wasn't the music; the music was good. It was the
phantasmagoria of their shadows, looming black, wavering
ceiling-high on the walls. It was the actuality of their faces, pos-
sessed, demonic, peering out here and there on sudden notes, then
seeming to recede again. It was the gin and the marihuana cigarettes, filling the air with haze and flux. It was the wildness that got
into them that at times made her cower into a far corner or climb
up on a packing case with both feet. Certain ones of them would
come at her at times individually, crowding her back, driving her
before them shrinking against the wall singling her out because she
was a girl, blowing their wind-instruments full into her face, deaf-
ening her, stirring her hair with them, bringing terror into her soul.

"Come on, get up on the barrel and dance!"

"I can't! I don't know how!"

"It don't have to be your feet. Do it with what else you've got,
that's what it's for. Never mind your dress, we're all friends."

"Darling," she thought, sidling away from a rabid saxophone
player until he gave up following her any more with a final ceiling-
ward blat of unutterable woe, "Oh, darling, you're costing me
dear."

Futuristic rhythm, never on the beat,
Any near drum, in my eardrum, throws me off my feet."

She managed to work her way around two sides of the room
until she got to the boiler factory that was the trap-drum. She
caught his pistoning arms, held them down, restrained them long

enough to make herself heard. "Cliff take me out of here. I can't stand it! I can't stand any more of it, I tell you! I'm going to keel over in another minute."

He was already doped with marihuana. She could tell by his eyes. "Where'll we go, my place?"

She had to say yes; she could see that was the only thing that would get him out of there.

He got up, guided her before him toward the door, stumbling a little. He got it open for her, and she fled through it like something released from a slingshot. Then he came out after. He seemed free to leave at will, without an explanation or farewell. The rest didn't even seem to notice his defection. The closing of the door cut the frenzied turmoil in half, as with the clean sweep of a knife, and there was sudden silence, so strange at first.

"You're the unexpected, disconnected time,
    Let me think in, sleep and drink in—"

The restaurant upstairs was dark and empty, save for a night-light left burning far at the back, and when she had gained the sidewalk in front the open air made her almost light-headed, it was so cool and rare and crystal-clear after that fever-chamber. She thought she'd never breathed anything so sweet and pure before. She leaned there against the side of the building, drinking it in, her cheek pressed to the wall like someone prostrated. He took a moment longer to come out after her, adjusting the door or something.

It must have been four by now, but it was still dark and the town was asleep all around them. For a moment there was a temptation to flee for dear life down the street away from him, and have done with the whole thing. She could have outrun him, she knew; he was in no condition to go after her.

She stayed there, passive. She had seen a photograph in her room. She knew that was the first thing that would meet her eyes when she opened the door. Then he was beside her, and the chance was gone.

They went over in a cab. It was in one of a row of old houses done over into apartments, a single one to a floor. He took her up to the second floor and unlocked it and turned on the lights for her. It was a depressing sort of place; age-blackened flooring underneath a thin application of varnish, remote ceilings, high, coffin-like window embrasures. It wasn't a place to come to at four in the morning. Not with anyone, much less him.

She shivered a little and stood still, close by the door, trying not to be too aware of the over-elaborate way he was securing it on the inside. She wanted to keep her thinking as clear and as relaxed as she possibly could, and that thought would only muddy it.

He'd finished locking her in. "We don't need these," he said.

"No, leave it on," she said matter-of-factly. "I'm cold."

There wasn't very much time.

"What're you going to do, just stand there?"

"No," she said, with absent-minded docility; "no, I'm not going to just stand here." She moved one foot inattentively forward, almost like a skater trying out the ice.

She kept looking around. Desperately looking around. What would start it? The colour. Orange. Something orange.

"Well, what're you looking for?" he said querulously. "It's just a room. Didn't you ever see a room before?"

She'd found it at last. A cheap rayon shade on a lamp far over at the other end of the room. She went over to it, turned it on. It cast a small glow in the shape of a halo above itself against the wall. She put her hand on it, turned to him. "I love this colour."

He didn't pay any attention.

She kept her hand on it. "You're not listening. I said this is my favourite colour."

This time he looked blearily over. "All right, what about it?"

"I wish I had a hat this colour."

"I'll buy you one. T'morrow or the next day."

"Look, like this; this is how I mean." She picked up the small base bodily, held it riding on her shoulder with the light still on inside the shade. Then she turned toward him so that the shade seemed to be topping her head. "Look at me. Look at me good. Didn't you ever see anyone wearing a hat this colour? Doesn't this remind you of someone you once saw?"

He blinked twice, with owl-like solemnity.

"Keep looking," she pleaded. "Just keep looking like that. You can remember if you want to. Didn't you ever see anyone sitting right behind you in the theatre, in the same seat I was in tonight, wearing a hat this colour?"

He said, quite momentously, quite incomprehensibly. "Oh—that was that five hundred smackeroos I got!" And then suddenly shading his eyes with one hand as if in perplexity. "Hey, I wasn't supposed to tell anyone about that." Then he looked up and asked with a sort of trustful blankness. "Have I already told you?"

"Yes, sure." That was the only answer to give. He might balk at telling her the first time, but not at repeating it, if the damage was already done. Those cigarettes probably did something to their powers of memory.

She had to grab it on the fly, she daren't let it go by, even though she didn't know if this was it yet, or what this was. She put the lamp down fast, moved toward him equally fast, yet somehow managing to give an impression of leisureliness. "But tell me about it over again. I like to listen to it. Go on, you can tell me, Cliff, because you know I'm your new friend; you said so yourself. What harm is there?"

He blinked again. "What are we talking about?" he said helplessly. "I forgot for a minute."

She had to get his drug-disconnected chain of thought in motion again. It was like a feeder-line that slips its cogs every once in a while and dangles helplessly. "Orange hat. Look up, here. Five hundred—five hundred smackeroos, remember? She sat in the same seat I did."

"Oh yeah," he said docilely. "Right behind me. I just looked at her." He gave a maniacal laugh, stilled it again as suddenly. "I got five hundred smackeroos just for looking at her. Just for looking at her and not saying I did."

She saw that her arms were creeping slowly up his collar, twining around his neck. She didn't try to stop them; they seemed to be acting independently of her. Her face was close to his, turned upward looking into it. How close you can be to a thought, it occurred to her, without guessing what it is! "Tell me more about it, Cliff. Tell me more about it. I love to listen to you when you're talking!"

His eyes died away in the fumes. "I forgot again what I was saying."

It was off again. "You got five hundred dollars for not saying you looked at her. Remember, the lady in the orange hat? Did *she* give you the five hundred dollars, Cliff? Who gave you the five hundred dollars? Ah, come on, tell me."

"A *hand* gave 'em to me, in the dark. A hand and a voice, and a handkerchief. Oh yea, and there was one other thing: a gun."

Her fingers kept making a slow sweep to the back of his head, and then returning each time. "Yes, but whose hand?"

"I don't know. I didn't know then, and I never found out since. Sometimes I ain't even sure it really happened; I think it must 'a' been the weed made it *seem* like it happened. Then again, sometimes I know it did."

"Tell it to me, anyway."

"Here's what happened. I came home late one night, after the show, and when I came in the hall downstairs, where there's usually a light, it was dark. Like the bulb went out. Just as I feel my way over to the stairs, a hand reaches out and stops me. Kind of heavy and cold, laying on me hard.

"I backed against the wall and says, 'Who's there? Who are you?' It was a man, I could tell by the voice. After a while, when my eyes got a little more used to it, I could make out something white, like a handkerchief, up where his face should be. It made his voice sound all burry. But I could hear him all right.

"He gave me my own name first, and what my job was; he seemed to know everything about me. Then he asked me if I remember seeing a certain lady at the theatre a night ago, in an orange hat.

"I told him I wouldn't have if he hadn't reminded me, but now that he'd reminded me of it, I did.

"Then he said, still in that same quiet voice, without even getting excited at all: 'How would you like to be shot dead?'

"I couldn't answer at all, my voice wouldn't work. He took my hand and put it on something cold he was holding. It was a gun. I jumped, but he made me hold my hand there a minute until he was sure I got what it was. He said, 'That's for you, if you tell anyone that.'

"He waited a minute and then went on speaking. He said, 'Or would you rather have five hundred dollars?'

"I hear paper rustling and he puts something in my hand. 'Here's five hundred dollars,' he says. 'Have you got a match? Go ahead, I'll let you light a match, so you can see it for yourself.' I did, and it was five hundred dollars all right. Then when my eyes started to go up to where his face was, about, they just got as far as the handkerchief, and he blew the match out.

" 'Now you didn't see that lady,' he said. 'There wasn't any lady. No matter who asks you, say no, keep saying no—and you'll keep on living.' He waited a minute and then he asked me. 'Now if they ask you, what is it you say?'

"I said, 'I didn't see that lady. There wasn't any lady.' And I was shaking all over.

" 'Now go on upstairs,' he said. "Good-night.' The way it sounded through that handkerchief it was like something coming from a grave.

"I couldn't get inside my door fast enough. I beat it upstairs and locked myself in and kept away from the windows. I'd been blazing a reefer already before it happened, and you know what that does to you."

He gave another of those chilling jangles of laughter that always stopped dead again as suddenly. "I lost the whole five hundred on a horse the next day," he added abjectly.

He shifted harassedly, dislodging her from the chair-arm she'd been perched on. "You've brought it back again by making me talk about it. You've made me scared again and all shaky, like I was so many times afterwards. Gimme another weed, I want to blaze again. I'm going down and I need another lift."

"I don't carry marihuana on me."

"There must be some in your bag, from over there. You were

just over there with me, you must have brought some away with you." He evidently thought she'd been using them as well as he.

It was lying there on the table, and before she could get over and stop him he'd opened it and strewn everything out.

"No," she cried out in sudden alarm, "that isn't anything; don't look at it!"

He'd already read it before she could pull it away from him. It was the forgotten slip of paper from Burgess. His surprise was guileless for a moment, he didn't take in its full meaning at first. "Why, that's me! My name and where I work and ev—"

"No! No!"

He warded her off. "And to call the precinct house number first; if not there call—"

She could see the mistrust starting to film his face, cloud it over. It was coming up fast, almost like a storm, behind his eyes. Behind it in turn was something more dangerous: stark, unreasoning fright, the fright of drug-hallucination, the fright that destroys those it fears. His eyes started to dilate. The black centres of them seemed to swallow up the colour of the pupils. "They sent you on purpose, you didn't just happen to meet me. Somebody's after me, and I don't know who; if I could only remember who—Somebody's going to shoot me with a gun, somebody said they'd shoot me with a gun! If I could only think what I wasn't supposed to do—You made me do it!"

She'd had no experience with marihuana addicts before; she'd heard the word, but to her it had no meaning. She had no way of knowing the inflaming effect it has on emotions such as suspicion, mistrust and fear, expanding them well beyond the explosion-point, providing they are latent already in the subject. She could tell by looking at him that she had somebody irrational to deal with, that much was apparent. The unpredictable current of his thoughts had veered dangerously, and there was no way for her to dam it, turn it aside. She couldn't reach into his mind because she was sane, and he—temporarily—wasn't.

He stood misleadingly still for a moment, head inclined, looking up at her from under his brows. "I been telling you something I shouldn't. Oh, if I could only remember now what it was!" He palmed his forehead distractedly.

"No, you haven't; you haven't been telling me anything," she tried to soothe him. She had realized she'd better get out of the place without delay, and also, instinctively, that to make her purpose apparent was to invite interception. She began moving slowly backward, a surreptitious step at a time. She had placed her hands behind her back, so they would be in a position to find the door, try to unlock it, before he could realize her purpose. At the same time she tried to keep her gradual withdrawal from attracting his attention by staring fixedly into his face, holding his gaze with her own. She realized she was becoming increasingly taut at the horrible slowness of the manœuvre. It was like backing away from a coiled snake, fearful that if you move too fast it will lash out all the quicker, fearful that if you move too slow—

"Yes, I did; I told you something I shouldn't. And now you're going to get out of here and tell someone. Somebody that's after me. And they'll come and get me like they said they would—"

"No, honest you haven't; you only think you have." He was getting worse instead of better. Her face must be growing smaller in his eyes; she couldn't keep him from realizing she was drawing away from him much longer. She was up against the wall now; and her desperately circling hands, groping secretly behind her, found only smooth, unbroken plaster-surface instead of the doorlock. She'd aimed wrong, she'd have to change directions. Out of the corner of her eye she placed its dark shape a few yards to her left. If he'd only stand there like that, where she'd left him, a second or two longer—

It was harder to move sidewise without seeming to than it had been rearwards. She would sidle one heel out of true, then work the ball of the foot over after it, then do the same with the second foot, bringing them together again, all without letting any motion show in her upper body.

"Don't you remember, I was sitting on the arm of your chair, smoothing your hair, that's all I was doing. Ah, don't!" she whimpered in a desperate last-minute effort to forestall him.

It was only a few seconds since this minuet of terror had began. It seemed like all night. If she'd only had another of those devilish cigarettes to throw at him, maybe—

She grazed some small lightweight table or stance in her crabwise creep, and some little object fell off. That slight sound, that tick, that thud, that inadvertent betrayal of motion going on, did it; shattered the glaze, seemed to act as the signal his crazed nerves had been waiting for; unleashed what she'd instinctively known all along was coming from one moment to the next. He broke stance, like a figure in a waxworks toppling from its pedestal, came at her arms out, in a sort of off-balance lurch.

She floundered to the door with a muted, thin little cry that was no cry at all, only had time to ascertain one thing with her wildly flailing hands—the key still projected, had been left in. Then she had to go on past it; he gave her no time to do anything with it.

She broke away from the wall, cut the corner of the room and made for the window, which was set into that next side. There was a blind down over it, effacing the exact outline of its sash-frame, hampering the single, sketchy attempt to fling up the sash and scream out for help that was all his onrush allowed her. There was a stringy, dust-laden drape hanging on each side of the embrasure. She flung one behind her at him, and it slowed him for a moment until he could get its hampering folds off his neck and shoulder.

There was a derelict sofa standing out diagonally across the next wall angle. She got in behind that, and, before she could get out at the opposite end, he had sealed her in. They backed and filed along its length twice, she on her side, he on his, in a cat-and-mouse play, a Victorian beauty-and-the-beast pantominme, that she would have laughed at until five minutes ago as being something that just didn't occur, that belonged in "East Lynn," but that she would never laugh at again for the rest of her life—although that apparently would only be for another two or three minutes.

"Don't!" she kept panting. "No! Don't! You know what they'll do to you—if you do this to me up here—you know what they'll do to you!"

She wasn't talking to a man, she was talking to the after-effects of a narcotic.

He suddenly took a short-cut by planting one knee on the seat of the sofa and grasping for her across the top of it. There wasn't any room in the little triangle for her to withdraw far enough. His fingers caught under the neckline of her dress, at one shoulder. Before they could tighten, close on it, she had freed herself by flinging her body around in two or three complete revolutions. It pulled the whole thing down off her shoulder on that side, but the contact broke.

She flashed out past the gap at the lower end of the sofa while his body was still prone across the top of it, and skimmed along the wall on the fourth and final side of the room. She had now made a complete circuit of it, was coming back to the door again on the next side. To cut out into the middle was to go *toward* him again, at any particular point, for he had the inside position.

There was an unlighted opening on this last side, the doorway to either a closet or bath, but after her experience with the sofa just now she flashed past it without stopping, fearful of being trapped even more quickly in whatever narrower space was offered on the other side of it. Besides, the outer door, the only way to final safety, lay just ahead.

She caught at a spindling wooden chair in passage, swung it around, flung it down behind her, in hopes of overthrowing him. He saw it in time, went out around it. It only gained her five extra seconds.

She was wearing down now. As she reached the final wall angle, turned to go along the side where this interminable game of puss-in-corner had first started, he cut out ahead of her, turned, and blocked her. She couldn't reverse in time, went almost into him. He had her in a pocket now, between him and the wall. His arms scissored for her. She could go neither forward nor back, so she went down, the only direction there was left. She had dropped down through them before they could close, and darted out from below them, so close she grazed his side as she went.

She screamed a name. The one name of all that was most powerless to help her right now. "Scott! Scott darling!" The door was ahead, but she'd never get to it in time. And she was too spent to go on past it any further—

The little lamp was still there, the one she'd tried to light his memory with before. It was too light to be able to harm him much, but she picked it up and flung it back at him. It failed even to hit him, dropped futilely wide of the mark, and the bulb in it didn't even shatter against the dingy carpeting. He came on undeterred in the final surge that they both knew—

And then something happened. His toe must have caught in something. She didn't see these things at the time, but remembered about them later. The unbroken lamp bucked violently on the floor behind him, there was a flash of bright blue from the foot of the wall, and he went sprawling down full length between the two, arms at full reach.

There was a channel of clearance left between him and the blessed door. She was afraid to trust herself into it, but she was more afraid not to. Those hands of his, flat for a moment, lay partly in the way. She jumped around him, just past his clawing fingers, got to it.

An instant can be so long. An instant can be so short. For an instant he lay helpless like that, flat on his face, an instant only. She could feel her hands wrangling the key. Like something in a dream; they didn't seem to belong to her at all. She turned it the wrong way first, it wouldn't work; had to reverse it, bring it all the way around to the other side. He was rippling his belly along the floor, trying to close the couple of inches gap between them from where he lay, without getting up; trying to grab her by the ankles and bring her down to him.

The key clicked, she pulled, and the door swung in. Something pecked futilely across the rounded back of her shoe—it was like the tapping of finger-nails—as she plunged out through the new-made opening.

Then the rest was a blurred welter of mingled horror and relief; horror at anticipated pursuit that didn't come. She was careening down dimly lighted stairs, more by impetus than any clear sight of them. She found a door, opened it, and it was cool, and it was night, and she was safe, but she kept staggering on, away from that place of evil, that would haunt her a little bit for ever. She was zigzagging along an empty sidewalk, like a drunk, and she *was* drunk—with an overpowering terror.

She remembered turning a corner, and she wasn't sure where she was any more. Then she saw a light ahead and went toward it, running now, in order to get to it quick, before he had a chance to overtake her. She went in and found herself looking at glass cases holding salami and platters of potato salad, so it must have been an all night delicatessen.

There was no one in it but a man dozing behind the counter. He opened his eyes and found her standing there dazedly, her dress still diagonally down off one shoulder where he'd torn it. He jumped, came forward, peered, palms to counter.

"What's the matter, miss? You been in an accident? Something I can do for you?"

"Give me a nickel," she sobbed brokenly. "Please give me a nickel—to use your phone."

She went over and dropped it in, still sobbing by reflex diaphragm action.

The kindly old man called inside to the back: "Momma, come out front, yess? Is here a child in zome kind of trouble."

She got Burgess at his home; it was nearly five in the morning by now. She didn't even remember to tell him who she was, but he must have known. "Burgess, will you please come here for me? I've just had a terrible time, and I don't think I can manage it the rest of the way by myself—"

The delicatessen-keeper and his wife, the latter in curl-papers and bathrobe, were holding a diagnostic consultation over her in the background meanwhile. "Black coffee, you think?"

"Sure, iss the only thing. Aspirin we ain't got."

The woman went over and sat down across the table from her, patted her head sympathetically. "What they do to you, dolling? You got a mudder?"

She couldn't help smiling wanly at the thought, even while she continued to sniff. The only mother she had was a supposedly hard-boiled detective.

Burgess came in alone, collar up around his ears, to find her; huddled over a thick mug of steaming black coffee. Shivers that had nothing to do with the temperature that had set in, but were now waning again. He'd come by himself because this was not official; it was personal off-the-record stuff as far as he was concerned.

She greeted him with a little whimper of relief.

He sized her up. "Ah, poor kid," he said throatily, shoving out the chair next to her and sitting down on it sidewise. "Bad as all that, huh?"

"This is nothing; you should have seen me five or ten minutes ago." Then she brushed that aside, leaned over toward him absorbedly. "Burgess, it was worth it! He saw her! Not only that. Somebody came around afterward and bribed him. Some man, acting on her behalf I suppose. You can get all that out of him, can't you?"

"Come on," he said briskly. "If I don't it won't be for lack of trying. I'm going up there right now. I'll put you in a taxi first and—"

"No, no. I want to go back with you. It's all right now, I'm over it.

The delicatessen couple came out to the doorway after them, watched them go down the street together in the paling dawn. There was a dark disapproval of Burgess plainly to be read on both their faces.

"Yah, fine brudder, she's got!" the man snorted contemptuously. "First leaffs her out alone at fife in the morning! Now he comes when it's too late to make trouble with the fellow what done it! A loafer he iss if he can't look after her any better than that!"

Burgess moved stealthily up the stairs, well ahead of her, motioning her backhand to go easy. By the time she'd caught up to him he'd already been listening intently at the door for several moments, head bent over motionless against it.

"Sounds as if he's lammed out," he whispered. "Can't hear him. Get back a little; don't stand too close, in case he starts up with something."

She retreated a few steps lower down on the staircase until only her head and shoulders were above floor-level. She saw him take something to the door and work it carefully, with little sound if any. Suddenly a gap showed, he thrust his hand back to his hip, held it there and trod guardedly forward.

She came up on his wake, holding her breath for the flare-up of violence, even the ambushed onslaught, that she expected from one moment to the next. She was even with the threshold herself when the sudden flare of electric light through the opening made her jump spasmodically, though it was soundless. He'd lit the place up.

She peered through, in time to see him disappear into that doorway in the adjoining wall that she had bypassed herself in her mad circuit of the room a while ago. She ventured in past the door-sill, emboldened, for his uninterrupted transit showed this first room to be vacant.

There was a second soundless flare of electricity, and the dark place he'd gone into became a gleaming white-surfaced bathroom. She was in a straight line with it and him; for a moment she could see into it. She could see an old-fashioned four-legged tub. She could see the rump of a figure folded like a clothespin over the rim of it. The soles of its shoes were turned back and up; she could see them too. The tub could not have been marble, in such a place, and yet it gave a curious optical illusion of being marbled even on the outside. That might have been due to the thin red vein or two discernible down its outside surface. Red-veined marble—

For a moment she thought he'd gotten sick and passed out. Then, as she moved to go in after him, Burgess' sharp, "Don't come in here, Carol; stay where you are!" stopped her like the crack of a whip. He came back a step or two, gave the door a corrective push-to, narrowing it, enough to keep her from looking in any more, without closing it entirely.

He stayed in there a long time. She remained where she was, waiting. She noticed her own wrist was shaking a little, but it wasn't due to fear any more, it was with a sort of emotional tension. She knew what that was in there now. She knew what must have brought it about. A paroxysm of drug-magnified fear, insupportable once she'd made good her escape and the unseen tentacles of retribution seemed to be closing in on him. All the more dreadful because they were unidentifiable.

A scrap of torn paper lying there on the table that caught her eye confirmed it. Three almost illegible words, trailing off into a meaningless wavy line that overran the paper and ended in a pencil-stub lying on the floor. "Ther after me—"

The door widened grudgingly and Burgess came out to her again at last. His face looked whiter than before he'd gone in there, she thought. She noticed that he crowded her before him, without overtly seeming to so that she found herself moving backward toward the outer door without any volition of her own. "Did you see that?" she asked, about the note.

"Yeah, on the way in."

"Is he—?"

For answer he poked a finger up under one ear, then swept it all the way around his neck to the other.

She drew in her breath sharply.

"Come on, get out of here," he said with kindly meant gruffness. "This is no place for you." He was closing the outside door after the two of them, the way he'd found it just now. "That tub," she heard him murmur under his breath, as he guided her down the stairs to the fore of him with both hands to her shrinking shoulders. "I'll never be able to think of the Red Sea again without—" He realized that she was listening to him, and shut up.

He put her in a taxi around the corner. "This'll get you home. I've got to get right back and break out with the notification."

"It's no good now, is it?" she said almost tearfully, leaning toward him through the cab window.

"No, it's no good now, Carol."

"Couldn't *I* repeat what he told me—?"

"That would be just hearsay. You *heard* somebody say he'd seen her, been bribed to deny it. Second-hand evidence. It's no good that way; they won't accept it."

He'd taken a thickly folded handkerchief out of his pocket, opened it in the palm of his hand. She saw him looking at something resting within it.

"What's that?" she said.

"You tell me what it is."

"A razor-blade."

"Not enough."

"A—a safety-razor blade?"

"That's it. And when a man takes a swing at his throat with one of the old-fashioned open kind—such as I found lying under him at the bottom of the tub—what's one of these doing overlooked under the shelf-paper in the cabinet? A guy uses either one type or the other, not both." He put it away again. "Suicide, they'll say. And I think I'll let them—for the present. You go home, Carol. Whichever it is, you weren't here tonight; you're staying out of it. I'll see to that."

In the taxi, riding homeward through streets tinplated in the quickening dawn, she let her head hang futilely downward.

Not tonight, darling, not tonight, after all. But maybe tomorrow night, maybe the night after.

# FIFTEEN

## The Ninth Day Before the Execution

### LOMBARD

It was one of those incredible luxury hotels, its single slender tower rising to disdainful heights above the mass of more commonplace buildings like a tilted aristocratic nose. It was a plush-and-jewelled perch on which birds of paradise flying east from the movie colony were wont to alight. Bedraggled birds of equally rich plumage, flying west before the storm broke, had also sought refuge here in droves while they were still able to make it.

This, he knew, was going to require a finesse all its own. It needed just the right touch, just the right approach. He didn't make the tactical mistake of trying to gain admission on demand, sight unseen. It wasn't the kind of place in which anyone was ever received by anyone just at request or at first try. You had to campaign, pull wires.

He sought out the flower-shop first, therefore, entering it from the lobby itself through a curved door of blue glass. He said, "What would you say are Miss Mendoza's favourite flowers? I understand you deliver a great many to her."

"I couldn't say," the florist demurred.

Lombard peeled off a bill, repeated what he'd just said, as though he hadn't spoken loudly enough the first time.

Apparently he hadn't. "Callers are always sending up the usual sort of thing—orchids, gardenias. I happen to know, though, that in South America, where she comes from, those flowers aren't highly regarded, they grow wild. If you want a tip of real value"— he dropped his voice, as though this were of incalculable import— "the few times she has ordered flowers for herself, to brighten up her apartment, they have *always* been deep salmon-pink sweet peas."

"I want your whole stock," Lombard said immediately. "I don't want a single one left over. And let me have two cards."

On one he roughed out a brief message in English. Then, taking out a small pocket dictionary, he transcribed it into Spanish, word for word, on the second card. Then he threw the first away. "Put this in with them, and see that they go right up. About how long should that take?"

"They should be in her hands within five minutes. She's in the tower and the page will take an express up."

Lombard returned to the lobby and poised himself before the reception alcove, head bent to his watch like someone taking a pulse-count.

"Yes, sir?" the clerk inquired.

"Not yet," Lombard motioned. He wanted to strike her at white heat.

"*Now!*" he said after a moment's wait, so suddenly the clerk gave a startled jump backward. "Phone Miss Mendoza's suite and ask if the gentleman who sent the flowers may come up for a moment. Lombard's the name, but don't leave out about the flowers."

When the clerk came back again he seemed almost stunned with surprise. "She said yes," he reported limply. Apparently one of the unwritten laws of the hotel had just been broken. Somebody had been received at first try.

Lombard, meanwhile, was shooting upward like a rocket into the tower. He got out slightly shaky at the knees, and found a young woman standing waiting at an open door to receive him. Evidently a personal maid, judging by her black taffeta uniform.

"Mr. Lombard?" she inquired.

"That's me."

There was evidently a final customs inspection to be passed before he was cleared for admission. "It is not a press interview, no?"

"No."

"It is not an autograph, no?"

"No."

"It is not to obtain a testimonial, no?"

"No."

"It is not about some bill that has, er"—she hesitated delicately—"escaped the señorita's mind, no?"

"No."

This last point seemed to be the crucial one; she didn't go any further. "Just a moment." The door closed, then in due course reopened again. This time all the way. "You may come in, Mr. Lombard. The señorita will try to squeeze you in between her mail and her hairdresser. Will you sit down?"

He was by now in a room that was altogether remarkable. Not because of its size, nor the stratospheric view from its windows, nor the breath-taking expensiveness of its *décor*, though all those things were unusual; it was remarkable because of the welter of sounds, the clamour that managed to fill it while yet it remained unoccupied. It was, in fact, the noisiest empty room he had ever yet found himself in. From one doorway came a hissing and spitting sound, that was either water cascading from a tap or something frying in fat. Probably the latter, since a spicy aroma accompanied it. Mingled in with this were snatches of song in a vigorous but not very good baritone. From another doorway, this one of double width and which opened and closed intermittently, came an even more vibrant blend. This consisted, to the best of his ability to disentangle its various skeins, of a programme of samba music coming in over short waves, admixed with shattering shots of static; of a feminine voice chattering in machine-gun Spanish apparently without shopping to breathe between stanzas; of a telephone that seemed not to let more than two and a half minutes at a time go by without fluting. And finally, in with the rest of the *mélange*, every once in a while there was a nerve-plucking squeak, acute and unbearable as a nail scratching glass or a piece of chalk skidding on a slate. These last abominations, fortunately, only came at widely spaced intervals.

He sat patiently waiting. He was in now, and half the battle was won. He didn't care how long the second half took.

The maid came darting out at one point, and he thought it was to summon him, and half rose to his feet. Her errand, however, was apparently a much more important one than that, judging by her haste. She flitted into the region of the sputtering and baritone accompaniment to shriek warningly: "Not too much oil, Enrico! She says not too much oil!" Then raced back again whence she had come, pursued by malevolent bass tones that seemed to shake the very walls.

"Do I cook for her tongue or do I cook for the shaky clock on the bathroom floor she step on?"

Both coming and going she was accompanied by an intimate garment of feathery pink marabou, held extended in her hands as though someone were about to ensconce themselves in it, but which seemed to have nothing whatever to do with her mission. All the way over and back it shed generously, filling the air with small particles of feather which drifted lazily to the floor long after she was gone.

Presently the hissing stopped short with one final spit, there was a deep-drawn "Aaah!" of satisfaction, and a rotund coffee-coloured little man in a white jacket, towering chef's cap on his head and weaving his head with satisfaction, marched out, around, and in again at the next door up, carrying something on a domed salver.

There was a momentary lull after that. Momentary only. Then an upheaval that made the previous clamour seem to have been golden silence detonated. It had everything previous in it and some new additions of its own; soprano shrieks, baritone bellows, nail-head squeaks, and the deep, gong-like clash of a violently thrown chafing-dish cover striking the wall and rolling halfway around the room, after that giving out fractured chimes.

The small, rotund man came out, fast and outraged; no longer coffee-complected, but streaked with what looked like egg-yolks and red peppers. His arms were going around like windmills. "This time I go back! On the next ship I go back! This time she can get down on her broken knees to me and I do not stay!"

Lombard bent slightly forward in his chair and tried stopping up his ears with the points of his pinkeys to give them a rest. After all, the human ear-drum is a delicate membrane; it can stand just so much abuse and no more.

When he uncovered them again he found to his relief that the establishment had toned down once more to the state of only partial frenzy that was seemingly its norm. At least you could hear what you were thinking again. Presently the door-bell had rung by way of variation, instead of the telephone, and the maid admitted a dark-haired, daintily moustached individual who sat down and joined him in waiting. But with much less fortitude than Lombard himself was displaying. He got up again almost at once and began walking briskly back and forth, but with paces that were just a trifle too short to fit comfortably into the lap he was giving himself. Then he discovered one of the aggregations of Lombard's sweet peas, stopped, extracted one, and put it to his nose. Lombard at this point promptly broke of all further thought of entering into diplomatic relations, even if any had been contemplated.

"Will she be ready for me soon?" the newcomer demanded of the maid on one of her flying visits. "I have a new idea. I would like to get the feel of it between my hands before it escapes me."

"So would I," thought Lombard, eyeing his neck truculently.

The sweet-pea smeller sat down again. Then he stood up again, with every appearance of vibrating impatiently down around the knees. "It's leaving me," he warned. "I am losing it. Once it goes I will have to go back to the old way again!" The maid fled inside with these dire tidings.

Lombard murmured half audibly. "You should have gone back to the old way long ago."

It worked, at any rate. The maid came out again, beckoned with suppressed urgency, and he was in. Lombard swung at the sweet pea he had dropped, caught it neatly with the toe of his shoe, and kited it upward with grim zest, as though doing that made him feel a lot better.

The maid came out and bent over him confidentially, to salve his impatience. "She will positively squeeze you in between him and her costume-fitter. He's hard to handle, you know."

"Oh, I don't know," Lombard demurred, twitching his extended foot slightly and eying it longingly.

There was a good long lull after that. At least, comparatively. The maid only came out once or twice and the telephone only rang once or twice. Even the machine-gun Spanish only came in disconnected salvos now. The private chef who had been going back on the next ship appeared, more rotund than ever in beret, muffler, and fuzzy overcoat, but only to inquire with injured mien: "Ask if she is dining in tonight. I cannot do it myself, I am not speaking with her."

Lombard's predecessor emerged finally, small kit in hand, and departed. Not without detouring first and hijacking another one of the sweet peas. Lombard's foot crept toward the receptacle that held the rest of them, as though he was aching to let him have all of them at once, but he conscientiously curbed the impulse.

The maid reappeared outside the holy of holies, announced, "The señorita will see you now." He found, when he tried to stand up, that his legs had gone to sleep. He slapped at them fore and aft a couple of times, straightened his tie, shot his cuffs, and stepped through.

He had no more than glimpsed a figure stretched out Cleopatra-like on a chaise-longue, when a soft, furry projectile of some sort shot through the air at him and landed on his shoulder with a squeaking sound. One of those same nail-on-glass squeaks that had reached him outside every now and then. He shied nervously at the impact. Something that felt like a long velvet snake coiled itself affectionately around his throat.

The figure on the chaise beamed at him like a fond parent watching its offspring cut up. "Don't be alarmed, señor. Is unly little Bibi."

Giving it a pet name was only partial reassurance as far as Lombard was concerned. He kept trying to turn his head to get a look at it, but it was too close in. He managed a grin of strained geniality, for the sake of furthering his own cause.

"I go by Bibi," his hostess confided. "Bibi is, how you say it, my welcoam committee. If Bibi don't like, he duck under sofa; I get rid of them queek. If Bibi like, he jump to their neck; then is all right they stay." She shrugged disarmingly. "You he must like. Bibi, come down off the man's neck," she coaxed insincerely.

"No, let him stay; I don't mind him in the least," he drawled tolerantly. It would have been a *faux pas* of the first water, he realized, to have taken her reproach at face value. His nose had identified the encumbrance as a small monkey by now, in spite of the cologne it had been saturated with. The tail reversed, to rewind itself the other way around. He had evidently made a hit. He could feel strands of his hair being painstakingly separated and examined, as if in search of something.

The actress crowed delightedly. If anything could put her in a receptive mood, this simian seemed able to, so Lombard felt he couldn't afford to resent the way it was getting personal with him. "Sit down," she urged cordially. He walked rather stiffly to a chair and sank into it, careful not to disturb his head-balance. He got his first good look at her. She had on a shoulder-cape of pink marabou over black velvet pyjamas, each trouser-leg of which was the width of a full skirt. A somewhat horrifying arrangement that looked like molten lava had been deposited on top of her head by the sweet-pea fiend who had been in here before him. The maid was standing behind her, fanning at it with a palm-leaf as if to cool it off. "I have a minute while this sets," the wearer explained graciously. He saw her surreptitiously consult the card he had sent up with the flowers a while ago, to remind herself of his name.

"How nice it was to get my flowers in Spanish for a change, Señor Lombard. You say you have just come up from *mi tierra*. We met down there?"

She had, fortunately, glided past this point before it was necessary for him to commit himself outright. Her large dark eyes took on a soulful expression, went searchingly upward toward the ceiling; she made a cushion of her hands and pressed one cheek against them. "Ah, my Buenos Aires," she breathed, "my Buenos Aires.

How I miss it! The lights of the Calle Florida shining in the evening—"

Not for nothing had he spent several hours poring over travel folders before coming up here. "The beach at La Plata, down by the shore," he supplied softly, "the races at Palermo Park—"

"Don't," she winced. "Don't, you make me cry." She wasn't just acting. Or at least she wasn't entirely acting, he could tell. She was simply dramatizing emotions that were already there, that were basically sincere, as is the way with the theatrical temperament. "Why did I leave it, why am I opp here so far away?"

Seven thousand dollars a week and ten per cent of the show might have had something to do with it, it occurred to him, but he wisely kept that to himself.

Bibi, meanwhile, having failed to find anything that required exterminating on his scalp, lost interest, ran down his arm, and took a flying leap off on to the floor. It made conversation a lot easier, even though his thatch was left looking like a haystack that had been hit by a high wind. He refrained from smoothing it down, lest this give offence to the pest's mercurial mistress. She was now in as soft a mood as he could ever hope to get her into, on such short acquaintance, so he took the plunge.

"I have come to you because you are known to be as intelligent as you are talented and beautiful," he said, laying it on with a shovel.

"It is true, nobody has ever said I am a doll," the celebrity admitted with refreshing un-self-consciousness, studying her finger-nails.

He hitched his chair slightly forward. "You recall a number you did in last season's show, in which you threw nosegays, little flowers, to the ladies in your audiences?"

She poised a warning finger toward the ceiling. Her eyes sparkled. "Ah, *Chica Chica Boom!* Si, si! You like? Wasn't it good?" she agreed warmly.

"Perfect," he assented, with a concealed fluctuation of his Adam's apple. "Now one night a friend of mine—"

That was as far as he got on that try. The maid, who had just quit fanning a moment before, stepped in again. "William would like his orders for the day, señorita."

"Excuse me a minute." She turned her head toward the doorway. A stalwart individual in chauffeur's uniform stepped forward, stood at attention. "I won't nidd you until twelve. I go to the Coq Bleu for launch, so you be downstairs, at ten to." Then she added without any change of inflection, "And you better take that with you while you here, you left it behind."

He stepped over to the vanity-table she had indicated, removed a hammered-silver cigarette-case, spaded it into his pocket and stepped outside again, all with perfect nonchalance.

"It didn't come from the five-and-ten, you know," she called after him, with, it seemed to Lombard, a slight touch of asperity. Judging by the snap in her eyes, he didn't give William much longer.

She turned back to him again, let her filaments slowly darken.

"I was saying a friend of mine attended a performance one night with a certain woman. That is why I have come to you."

"Ah?"

"I am trying to find her for him."

She misunderstood. Her eyes corruscated with renewed zest. "Ah, a romance! I loave a romance!"

"I'm afraid not. It's a matter of life or death." As with all the rest, he was afraid to give her too many details, lest she shy away from it.

She seemed to like this even better. "Ah, a mees-tirry! I loave a mees-tirry"—she shrugged—"as long as it don't happen to me."

Something suddenly stopped her dead. Apparently some calamity, judging by the effect it had. She eyed a tiny diamond-studded particle on her wrist. Suddenly she had reared upright, begun snapping her fingers all over the place, like a string of firecrackers going off. The maid came running in on the fly. Lombard thought he was about to be unceremoniously dismissed in favour of the next comer.

"You know what time it is?" the dancer said accusingly. "I don't have told you to watch it closely? You are very careless. You nearly let it go past too far. The doctor said one itch hour, on the hour. Get the calomel—"

Before Lombard knew it, another of those seasonal typhoons that seemed to occur regularly in here was swirling around him full blast. Machine-gun Spanish, nail-head squeaks, and the maid going around and around the room after Bibi, until Lombard felt as though he were the centre-pole of a *carrousel*.

He finally raised his own voice and added it to the din. "Why don't you stop short and turn back the other way?" he shouted above the racket.

That did it. Bibi ran into the maid—and the calomel ran into Bibi.

When that was over with, and the patient was clinging forlornly to his mistress, both arms about her neck, giving her a momentary resemblance to a bearded lady, he resumed his own job.

"I realize how hopeless it is to expect you to remember any particular individual out of that sea of faces before you each night. I realize you played six nights a week and two matinees, all season long, to packed houses—"

"I have never play to an empty house in my hull career," she contributed, with more of her characteristic modesty. "Even a fire cannot compete with me. Once in Buenos Aires the theatre start to burn. You think they left—?"

He waited until that was out of the way. "My friend and this woman were sitting in the first row, on the aisle." He consulted something on a scrap of paper taken from his pocket. "That would be on your left, as you faced the audience. Now, the only help I can give you at all is this. She stood up in her seat—oh, along about the second or third chorus of the song."

A speculative glint flickering across her eyes. "She stood opp? While Mendoza was on stage? This interests me very much. I have never known it to happen before." Her shapely fingers, he noticed, were beginning to claw tentatively at the velvet of her trouser-leg, as if whetting themselves for reprisal. "She did not care for my singing, perhaps? She had a train to catch, perhaps?"

"No, no, no, you don't understand," he reassured her hastily. "Who could do that to you? No, here's what it was. It was during the *Chica Chica Boom* number. You forgot to throw one of the little souvenirs to her, and she stood up to attract your attention. For just a moment or two she stood there right in front of you, and we were hoping—"

She shuttered her eyes rapidly two or three times, trying to recapture the incident. She even poked one long finger just behind her ear, careful not to disturb the hair-do. "I see if I can remember it for you." She obviously was doing her best. She did all the things likely to be conducive to memory quickening. She even lit a cigarette, although she was not, judging by the stiff way she handled it, an habitual smoker. She simply held it, letting it burn down in her fingers.

"No, I cannot," she said finally. "I'm sorry. I try hard. For me last season is like twenty years ago." She shook her head morosely, clicked her tongue compassionately a couple of times.

He started to return the futile scrap of paper to his pocket, glanced at it as he did so. "Oh, and here's another thing—although I suppose it's no more help than the first. She had on the same hat that you did, my friend tells me. I mean a duplication of it, an exact copy."

She straightened suddenly, as though she were on the point of getting something from that. He obviously had her whole undivided attention at last, if he hadn't before. Her eyes narrowed speculatively. Then they glittered behind their thread-like constriction. He was almost afraid to move or breathe. Even Bibi looked at her curiously from a fur-huddle on the carpet at her feet.

Suddenly it came. She stabbed her cigarette out with a single vicious lunge. She emitted a strident, macaw-like cry that wouldn't

have been out of place in a jungle. "A-a-ai! *Now* I remember!
Now!" A flash-flood of Spanish swept her off his conversational
track. Finally, after a lot of eddying around, she got back on to it
in English again. "That *thing* that stood up there! That *criatura*
that stand in front of the hull house, in *my* hat, to show she is
wearing it! She even stop the spotlight, clip some of it off from me!
Hanh! Do I recall? You bet I recall! You think I'm going to forget
a thing like that in a horry? Hanh! You don't know Mendoza!"
She snorted with such violence that Bibi gave the appearance of
being swept across the floor for a distance of several feet like a
dried leaf, although it was probably a scuttle for shelter under his
own power.

The maid chose this most unpropitious moment to intrude. "The
costumer has been waiting for some time now, señorita."

She semaphored violently, crossing and recrossing her arms over
her head. "She should keep on wetting some more! I am listening
to something I don't like to hear!"

She climbed down the chaise-longe toward Lombard, balancing
on one bent knee over the lower end of it. She even seemed to
regard her own overheated state of mind as a prideful accomplish-
ment. She flung out her arms to show him, then tapped herself like
a woodpecker on the chest. "Look how I get! Look how angry it
still make me, even sotch a long time after! Look what it do!"

After which she rose to her feet, squeezed herself tightly around
the waist with both arms in a belligerent embrace, as if holding
herself in, and began to stalk back and forth, turning at the end of
each short heat with a great fanning-out of her wide trouser-bot-
toms. Bibi crouched in a far corner, head bowed in desolation and
his skinny arms flung up over it.

"And what you want her for, you and this friend of yours?" she
demanded suddenly. "You haven't told me yet!"

He could tell by her challenging inflection that if it was anything
that had to do with making the style-pirate happy he wasn't going
to get any help from Mendoza, even if she had been in a position
to give it. He wisely marshalled the facts in such a way that her
purpose would swing over to coincide with his, even though both
had not quite the same end in view. "He is in serious trouble,
believe me, señorita. I won't bore you with the details, but she is
the only one who can get him out of it. He has to prove that he
was with her that night, and not where they say he was. He only
met her that night; we don't know her name, we don't know where
she lives, we don't know anything about her. That's why we're
looking high and low—"

He could see her mulling it over. After a moment she informed
him: "I like to help you. I give anything to tell you who she is."
Then her face dropped, she spread her hands helplessly. "But I

never see her before. I never see her after. I just see her hand opp like that. That's all. I can't tell you no more about her than that." At least facially she seemed to be even more disappointed than he was about it.

"Did you notice him at all, the man with her?"

"No, I never give him a look. I couldn't say who was with her. He stay in the shadow down below."

"You see, there's as big a link as ever missing, only it's the other way around now. Most of the others remembered him, but not her. You remember her, but not him. It's still no good, wouldn't prove anything. Just that a woman stood up in a theatre one night. Any woman. She might have been alone. She might have been with someone else entirely. It doesn't mean a thing. I've got to get the two linked up together by *one* witness." He clapped his hands to his knees frustratedly, rose to leave. "Looks like it ends there, where it began. Well, thank you for your time."

"I keep trying for you, anyway," she promised, giving him her hand. "I don't know what I can do, but I keep at it."

He didn't either. He shook hands briefly, passed through the outer room in a mist of depression. He felt the let-down, the sudden reversal, all the more keenly because he had come closer to getting on to something tangible just now than he had at any other time so far; it had been almost within his grasp, only to be snatched away at the last moment. Now he was right back where he'd been before.

The operator had turned and was looking at him expectantly, so he knew he'd come all the way down without feeling it, and was supposed to get out of the car. Somebody propelled a door for him and he was outside in the street. He stood there for a moment without moving away from the entrance, simply because he couldn't decide which direction to take next. One offered as little as the other, so they checkmated each other. And his ability to make even such a minor decision as that was wallowing helplessly in a trough just then.

A taxi came along and he hailed it. It had someone in it; he had to wait for another. That kept him there a minute longer. And sometimes a minute can make an awful lot of difference. He hadn't left any tracer with Mendoza; she wouldn't have known where to contact him.

He was already seated in the second taxi and it was just about to take off when the revolving door of the hotel blurred like a propeller in motion and a bell-boy came darting out to him. "Are you the gentleman that just left Miss Mendoza's suite?" She called down a minute ago after you'd gone by. She'd like you to come back again, if you don't mind."

He went inside again and up fast. The same fur snowball

launched itself at him in fond recollection. He didn't even mind that this time. The pyjamas were gone and she was in the middle of trying something or other on. She looked like a half-finished lampshade standing in the middle of the floor, but he had no eye for any of that.

She was only mildly disconcerted, if at all. "I hope you're a married man? Pouf, if you're not, you will be some day, so it's all the same." He couldn't quite grasp the fine point of propriety involved, but let it go at that. She picked up a length of material and draped it negligently across one shoulder, where it would do the least good, as a protection. Then she dismissed some shadowy third person kneeling at her feet with a mouthful of pins.

"A minute after you left I got something," she told him as soon as they were alone. "I was still kind of"—she twisted her hand this way and that, as though she were trying a door-knob—"you know—sore."

"William," occurred to him unspoken at this point.

"So I let it out, like I always do when I'm sore, by breaking a couple of little things." She motioned with perfect unconcern to numerous crystal fragments littering the floor, with a disembodied atomizer bulb lying in their midst. "Then the funniest thing happen. It bring back another time I am sore, about that woman we were talking about. Because I throw things now, I remember how I throw things that other time." She hitched her shoulders. "Is peculiar, no? It remember to me what I do with the hat. I think maybe it help you to know."

He waited, shifting one foot out toward her in leashed intensity.

She shook an explanatory finger at him. "So that night, when that woman do like that to me, I go back to my dressing-room and, immh—" She inhaled deeply. "I nidd to be tied opp. I take everything on the table and I go like this!" She made a clean horizontal sweep with one arm. "You understand how I feel, no? You don't blem me?"

"I don't blame you at all."

She trip-hammered the flat of her hand between the circumflex accents formed by the brassière she had on. "You think anyone is going to do that to me in front of a houseful of people? You think I, Mendoza, let them get away with that?"

He didn't, now that he'd had a sample or two of her combustive temperament.

"They have to huld me back by both arms, the stage manager and my maid, to keep me from rushing out the stage door in my wrapper just like I am, to see if I can find her in front of the theatre, for to pull her to pieces betwinn my two hands!"

He'd half hoped, for a minute, that that was what it was going to develop had happened, that she'd tangled with the cipher at the theatre entrance. But he knew it hadn't, or Henderson would have mentioned it to him, and she herself would have recalled it sooner than this.

"I would have showed her a thing or two, you bet!" She still looked capable of doing it even at this late day. Lombard even drew back a precautionary step or two, the way she was crouched facing him, fingers working convulsively in lobster-claw formation. Bibi was clasping and unclasping his own tiny digits in apprehensive supplication.

She straightened, threw her arms outward in breast-stroke position. "The next day I'm still sore. With me it lasts. So I go to the modiste, the designer, that make opp the hat for me, and I blow off stimm there instead. I throw it in her face in front of hull room full of customers. I say, "So you make *me* an original for my production number, ha? The only one of its kind, ha? Nobody else is going to have one like it, ha?' And I wipe it all over her face, and when I leave she is still spitting out pieces of the material, she can't talk."

She shovelled her hands at him inquiringly. "So that's good for you, is no? That helps you, no? This cheat of a designer, she must know who is the person she sell the copy to. You go to her and you find out who this woman is you look for."

"Swell! Great! At last!" he yelled, so enthusiastically that Bibi dived head-first under the chaise and pulled his tail in after him. "What's her name? Give me her name!"

"Wait, I dig it opp for you." She tapped the side of her head apologetically. "I work in so many different shows, I have so many different costumers, I can't keep track." She called the maid in, instructed her: "Look among my bills for a hat from last year's show; see you can find one."

"But we don't keep them that long, do we, señorita?"

"You don't have to go all the way back to when it start from, stupid," said the star, as un-self-consciously as ever. "Look it opp among last month's; it probably still keep coming in.))

The maid came back after a moderately lengthy—and to Lombard excruciating—wait. "Yes, I found it; it did come in this month again. It says, 'One hat, a hundred dollars,' and the letter-head reads 'Kettisha.' "

"Good! That's it!" She passed it to Lombard. "You got it?" He copied the address, returned it to her. Her hands went into hysterics, and a blizzard of tiny pieces of paper snowed all over the floor. Then she ground her foot down into the middle of them. "I like the nerve! Still sending me bills a year later! She's got no shem, that woman!"

She looked up to find him already crossing the adjoining room on his way out. He was an opportunist; after all, her contribution had been made, she was of no further value to him. On to the next link.

She hastened to the boudoir doorway to deliver a parting benediction on his enterprise. One motivated by spite, however, and not altruism. She would have followed him all the way to the outside door, only the uncompleted hoopskirt she wore got stuck in the opening, wouldn't let her pass through. "I hope you catch opp with her!" she shrilled after him vengefully. "I hope she find herself in plenty of trouble!"

A woman will forgive you anything—but wearing the same hat as she does, at the same time.

He felt like a fish out of water when he walked into the place, but he didn't let it deter him. He would have stalked into far more unlikely places than this to attain his goal. It was one of those establishments on a side street, housed in a former private residence converted to commerical purpose, whose expensiveness and exclusiveness always seems to be in inverse ratio to their lack of conspicuousness. The entire ground floor was given over to the display-room, or whatever the trade name for it was. Having stated his business, he took shelter in a secluded corner of this the most secluded corner he was able to find.

He'd walked in right in the middle of a showing. Or maybe they had one every day at this hour, for all he knew. It didn't help to put him at his ease. He was the only man there, or at least the only one of service age. There was what appeared to be a desiccated septuagenarian present among the sprinkling of clients seated here and there. The charming young thing with him—his granddaughter, no doubt—must have brought him in with her to help her select a wardrobe. "The mind," thought Lombard, regarding him with a billious eye, "can certainly work wonders." But with that one exception it was all distaff. Even a girl doorman and girl pages.

The mannequins would come forward slowly, one by one, from the rear, and make a complete circuit of the forepart of the room, turning this way and that with little graceful swirls. For some reason—it may simply have been the corner he had chosen—he kept getting swirls and even full halts from every single one of them. He felt like saying, "I'm not here to buy anything," but didn't have the nerve. It made him actuely uncomfortable, the more so since he had to keep staring into their faces, and there were lots of other places he would have preferred staring.

The young woman he'd spoken to came back and rescued him at last. "Madame Kettisha will see you in her private office upstairs on the second floor," she whispered. A girl page showed him the way, knocked for him, then departed below again.

There was a buxom, middle-aged, red-headed Irish-woman sitting facing him from behind a large desk when he went in. She not only had nothing of the chic *couturier* about her; she even leaned slightly to the horsy dowdy side. She probably had once been Kitty Shaw in some back-street tenement, and she deserved plenty of credit, he told himself, sizing her up. She probably was a wizard at making money; only an unqualified success could have afford to flaunt such personal slovenliness as she was exhibiting. His first impression was altogether favourable and his relief was almost abject.

She was shuffling through a sheaf of crayon-coloured fashion sketches at lightning speed, discarding some to her right, okaying others to her left. Or *vice versa*. "Well, Mike, what can I do for you?" she grunted brusquely, without looking up.

He was all out of tact by now. It was still the same day as the Mendoza interviews, and he hadn't had time to recuperate from them yet. It was getting late, anyway; nearly five in the afternoon.

"I came straight down here from one of your former customers. The South American actress Mendoza."

She did look up at that. "Better use a whiskbroom," she suggested dourly.

"You did a hat for her for last year's show, remember? One hundred bucks, and I want to know who got the chaser on it."

She put the sketches out of harm's way first, before she cut loose. The accepts into a drawer, the discards into a waste-basket. She had a temper, evidently, that could be turned off and on at will, and with a time-limit set to it. At that he liked it better than Mendoza's brand. It was more forthright. Her hand came down on the desk-top with a bang like a hand-grenade. "Don't you gimme any of that!" she roared. "I've had enough trouble out of that hat! I said then there was no copy made, and I still say now there was no copy made. When I produce an original, it stays original! If there was a copy made, it wasn't run up in this establishment or with my knowledge, and I'm not responsible! I may soak 'em, but I don't double-cross them!"

"There was a copy made," he insisted. "It showed up in a theatre, face to face with hers across the footlights!"

She leaned down heavily over the desk, both elbows in air. "What does she want me to do, sue her for slander?" she shouted. "I will if she keeps this up! She's a liar, and you can go back and tell her I said so!"

Instead he took his hat and pitched it on to a chair over in the corner, to show her he intended staying until he had what he'd come here to get. He even unbuttoned his coat, to give himself plenty of free arm-action. "She has nothing to do with it, so let's just forget her. I'm here for purposes of my own. There was a copy, because a friend of mine was with the very woman that had it on in the theatre. So don't tell me there wasn't. I want to know who she is. I want her name from your list of customers."

"It isn't on it. It couldn't be, because there was no such transaction entered into by us. What're you going to do, keep this up all day?"

He hitched his chin out into second, brought his own hand down in an answering blow to hers that made the whole desk-structure jar. "For the love of God, there's a man counting his life by hours! What the hell do I care about your business ethics at such a time. You're not going to sit there and head me off, not if I've got to lock this door and stay in here with you all night! Don't you understand me? There's a man going to be executed in nine days' time! The wearer of that hat is the only one can save him. You've got to give me her name. It's not the hat, it's the woman I want!"

Her voice suddenly dropped to a reasonable level. She'd evidently turned her temper off. He'd caught her interest. "Who is he?" she asked curiously.

"Scott Henderson, for killing his wife."

She wagged her head in recognition. "I remember reading about that at the time."

He struck the desk again, less shatteringly than before. "The man's innocent. It's simply got to be stopped. Mendoza bought a certain specially designed hat here that couldn't have been reproduced elsewhere. Somebody popped up in the theatre with an exact copy of that same hat. He was with this somebody, he was with her all that evening, but he never found out her name or anything about her. Now I've got to find that person at all costs. She can prove that he wasn't home when it happened. Is that clear enough for you? If it isn't I can't make it any clearer!"

She gave him the impression of being a person with few, if any, moments of indecision. She was having one of them now, but it was of brief duration. She asked one more question, to safeguard herself. "You're sure this isn't some legal trick on that spick hellcat's part? The only reason I haven't filed suit against her for non-payment and also for assault that day she came down here was so that she wouldn't file cross-suit against me. The publicity would be harmful to my establishment's good name."

"I'm not a lawyer," he assured her. "I'm an engineer from South America. I can show you who I am, if you're in any doubt." He took things out of his pocket for identification purposes, presented them to her.

"Then I can talk confidentially to you," she decided.

"Absolutely. My only interest in the matter is Henderson. I'm sweating myself skinny to get him out of it. Your wrangle with her doesn't mean anything to me, from either party's side. It's just that it happens to lie across my own path of investigation."

She nodded. She glanced at the door to make sure it was discreetly closed. "Very well, then. Here's something that I wouldn't admit to Mendoza for the world, that I can't afford to, understand? There must have been a leak around here some place. The copying did originate here. But not officially; on the sly, by some member of the organization. Now I'm telling you this, but I don't want it to go any further. I'd have to deny it, of course, if it was ever brought out publicly. My designer, the girl that does the sketches, is in the clear; I know it wasn't she who sold us out. She's been with me ever since I first opened my own place; she's bought into it. It wouldn't pay her, for a measly fifty, seventy-five, or whatever it was, to peddle around her own ideas like that. She'd be competing against herself. The two of us, she and I investigated on the q.t. after Mendoza was down here raising an uproar that day, and we found that particular sketch gone from her album, missing, when we went to look. Somebody had deliberately swiped it to use over again. We figured it for the seamstress, the girl who did the actual needlework on that number in the shop. She denied it, naturally, and we had no evidence to prove it. She must have run the thing up at home on her own time. I suppose we caught her before she'd had time to slip the borrowed sketch back into the album again. Well, to be on the safe side, to make sure we didn't get into hot water like that again, we shipped her." She thumbed over her shoulder.

"So you see, Lombard—that your name, again?—as far as the sales records here in the office go, there never was any second buyer for that particular hat. That's dead on the level. I couldn't help you there if I wanted to. All I can suggest is, if you want that woman, your best bet is to tackle that former sewing apprentice of ours. As I say, I can't guarantee that she actually does know anything about it. All I know is we ourselves felt strongly enough convinced that she did, at the time, to dismiss her. If you want to take the chance, it's up to you."

Again it had jumped a lap ahead of him, just when he thought he was safely up to it at last. "I have to. I haven't any choice," he said dismally.

"Maybe I can give you a hand with it," she said helpfully. She snapped on her desk speaker. "Miss Lewis, look up the name of that girl we discharged right after we had all that trouble with Mendoza. Address too."

He leaned his head sideward, elbow to desk, while they were waiting. She must have seen something in his attitude. "You think quite a lot of him, I guess," she said, almost gently. It was a seldom-used inflection with her; she had to clear her throat to get it to transmit in the right key.

He didn't answer. That was one of those things that didn't need answering.

She shot a drawer, pulled out a squat bottle of Irish whisky. "The hell with that sissy champagne they serve downstairs. A nip of this is what's in order when you're up against something that needs tall bucking. It's an example I learned from my old man, rest his bones—"

The speaker signalled back. A girl's voice said: "That was Madge Peyton. The address on record for her when she worked here is four-nine-eight Fourteenth Street."

"Yeah, but which Fourteenth Street?"

"That's all it says here: Fourteenth Street."

"Never mind," he said, "there's only two to choose from, east and west." He took it down, went over and reclaimed his hat, buttoned up with renewed purpose, the brief rest-period over.

She was sitting there shading her eyes lengthwise. "Let me see if I can give you an angle on her. She won't come through willingly, you know." She dropped her hand, looked up. "Yeah, I've got her now. She was one of these quiet mousy little things. Shirtwaist-and-skirt type, know what I mean? They're the kind that are always apt to pull a stunt like that for money, quicker than the good-lookers are, because money don't come as easy to them. You'll find they're usually scared of guys, and don't give themselves a chance to get to know them; then when they do get in with one it's always the wrong kind, because they haven't had any previous sampling experience."

She was a shrewd woman, he had to admit. That was why she probably wasn't Kitty Shaw in some back-street tenement at this very moment.

"We soaked Mendoza a hundred for it originally. She probably didn't get more than fifty for repeating on it. There's an angle for you, right there. Try her with another fifty; that ought to get it out of her—if you can find her."

"If I can find her," he agreed, plodding dispiritedly down the stairs.

A rooming-house keeper opened a door painted black to resemble ebony, with a square of glass set into the upper half and a tawny roller-shade backing that. "Un?" she said.

"I'm looking for a Madge Peyton."

She just shook her head to conserve energy.

"A girl that—well, a sort of plain-looking mousy girl."

"Yeah, I know who you mean. No, she's not here any more. Used to be, but she's gone quite some time now." She kept scanning the street while she was talking to him. As if, now that she'd taken the trouble of coming to the door, she might as well get something out of it before she went back inside again. That was probably why she continued to stand there as long as she did, and not because of any interest in his problem.

"Any idea where she moved to?"

"Just left, that's all I can tell you. I don't keep strings on 'em."

"But there must be some sort of a trace. People don't just go up in smoke. What took her things away?"

"One arm and both her feet." She jerked a thumb. "Down that way, if it's any good to you."

It wasn't very much. There were three more intersecting avenues "down that way." And then a marginal thoroughfare. And then a river. And then fifteen to twenty States. And then an ocean.

She'd had enough air and sightseeing now. "I can make something up if you want me to," she offered. "But if it's facts you're after—" She bunched fingers to her lips, blew them apart to denote emptiness.

She started to close the door, added: "What's the matter, mister? You look kind of white."

"I feel kind of white," he assented. "Mind if I sit on your doorstep here a minute?"

"Help yourself, as long as you don't get in the way of anyone coming in or going out."

*Slam.*

# SIXTEEN

## The Eighth Day Before the Execution

# SEVENTEEN

## The Seventh Day Before the Execution

# EIGHTEEN

## The Sixth Day Before the Execution

He got off the train at the end of a three-hour ride from the city, looked around him doubtfully as soon as it had taken itself out of the way. This was one of those small outlying hamlets close to a large centre that, for some reason or other, often give an impression of far greater sleepiness and rusticity than places that are actually much further out. Possibly because the contrast is too sudden, the eye hasn't become conditioned to the change yet. It was still close enough in to have certain typical features of the metropolitan scene: a well-known five- and ten-cent store, an A and P, a familiar chain orange-juice concession. But they only seemed to emphasize its remoteness from the originals instead of tempering it.

He consulted the back of an envelope with a list of names jotted down it perpendicularly, each with an accompanying address. They were all approximations of one another, although in two different languages. All but the last two had been lined out. They ran something like this:

Marge, Payton, millinery (and address).
Marge Payton, millinery (and address).
Margaret Peyton, hats (and address)).
Madame Magdax, chapeaux (and address).
Madame Margot, chapeaux (and address).

He crossed the tracks to a filling-station, asked the grease monkey: "Know of anyone around here makes hats and calls herself Marguerite?"

"There's a boarder down at old Mrs. Hascom's got some sort of sign in the window. I don't know if it's hats or dresses, I never noticed it very closely. It's the end house on this side of the road. Just keep going straight down."

It was an unlovely-looking frame building with a pitiful hand-printed placard in a corner of one of the lower windows. "Marguerite, hats." A trade name, for a whistle-stop like this. Even in an out-of-the-way place like this, he reflected curiously, they still had to be French. Peculiar convention.

He went up under the gloomy porch-shed and knocked. The girl who came out was she herself, if Kettisha's description was to be trusted. Plain and timid-looking. Lawn shirtwaist and dark-blue skirt. He caught sight of a little metal cap topping one of her fingers; a thimble.

She thought he wanted the person who owned the house, told him unasked: "Mrs. Hascom's gone down to the store. She ought to be back in—"

He said, "Miss Peyton, I had quite a time finding you."

Instantly she was frightened, tried to withdraw and close the door. He blocked it with his foot. "I don't think you have the right person."

"I do think I have." Her fright alone was proof enough of that, although he couldn't understand the reason for it. She kept shaking her head. "All right, then I'll tell you. You used to work for Kettisha, in their sewing-room."

She got white as a sheet, so she had. He reached down and caught her by the wrist to keep her from running in even without being able to close the door, as he saw she was about to do.

"A woman approached you and induced you to copy a hat that had been made for Mendoza, the actress."

She kept swinging her head faster and faster; that was all she seemed capable of doing. She was straining terrifiedly away from him at an acute backward slant. His grip on her wrist was all that was holding her there in the door opening. Panic can be as stubborn as courage, its opposite.

"I just want that woman's name, that's all."

She was beyond reasoning with. He'd never seen anyone plunged headlong into such depths of terror. Her face was grey. Her cheeks were visibly pulsing, as though her heart were in truth in her mouth, as the expression went. It couldn't be the design-theft that was doing this to her. Cause and effect were too unrelated. A major apprehension for a minor infraction. He could sense vaguely that he'd stumbled on some other story, some other story entirely, lying across the path of this quest of his. That was the most he was able to make out of it.

"Just the name of the woman—" He could tell by her fear-blurred eyes that she didn't even hear the words. "You're in no danger of being prosecuted. You must know who it was."

She found her voice at last. A strangled distortion of one, anyhow. "I'll get it for you. It's inside. Let me go a minute—"

He held the door so that she couldn't close it. He opened the hand that had been choking her wrist, and instantly he was alone. She'd gone like something windswept, blown from sight.

He stood there waiting for just a moment, and then something that he was unable to account for, some tension that she'd left behind her in the air, made him spurt forward, rush down the gloomy central hallway, fling open the door to one side she had just closed behind her.

She hadn't locked it, fortunately. He swept it back just in time to see the shears flash in the air, a little over her head. He never knew how he got over in time, but he did. He managed to deflect the blow with an outward fling of his arm, slashing his sleeve and drawing a fleshy cut for his pains. He pulled them away from her and threw them over in the corner with a tinkle. They probably would have gone in deep enough to get her heart, at that, if she'd hit the right place.

"What was that for?" he winced, stuffing a handkerchief down his sleeve.

She caved in like a stepped-on ice-cream cone. She dissolved into a welter of tears and incoherence. "I haven't seen him since. I don't know what to do with it. I was afraid of him, afraid to refuse him. He told me just a few days and now it's been months. I've been afraid to come forward and tell anyone; he said he'd kill me—"

He clamped his hand across her mouth, held it there a minute. This was that other story, the one he didn't want. Not his. "Shut up, you frightened little fool. I only want the name, the *name* of the woman for whom you made a plagiarized hat at Kettisha's. Can't you get that through your head?"

The reversal was too sudden, the prospect of renewed security too tantalizing for her to be able to believe in it fully at once. "You're just saying that, you're just trying to trick me—"

A muted wailing, almost unnoticeable it was so thin, had started in somewhere nearby. Everything seemed to have power to frighten her. He saw her cheeks get white all over again at that, although it was scarcely loud enough to penetrate the ear-drum.

"What faith are you?" he asked.

"I was a Catholic." The tense she gave it held some kernel of tragedy, he could not tell.

"Have you a rosary? Bring it out." He saw he'd have to convince her emotionally, since he couldn't through reasoning.

She offered it to him resting in her hand. He placed his own two over and under it, without removing it. "Now, I swear that all I want of you is what I've told you. Nothing else. That I won't harm you in any other matter. That I'm not here on any other matter. Is that enough?"

She'd grown a little calmer, as though the contact of the object was a steadying influence in itself. "Pierrette Douglas, Six Riverside Drive," she said unhesitatingly.

The wailing was beginning to grow louder little by little. She gave him one last look of dubious apprehension. Then she stepped into a small curtained alcove to one side of the room. The wailing stopped short. She came back as far as the entrance, holding a long white garment or garments trailing from her enfolded arms. There

was a small pink face topping it, looking trustfully up at her. She
was still frightened, vastly so, when she looked at Lombard. But
when she looked downward at that face under her own, there was
unmistakable love in the look. Guilty, furtive, but stubborn; the
love of the lonely that grows steadily stronger, more unbreakable,
day by day and week by week.

"Pierrette Douglas, Six Riverside Drive." He was shuffling out
money. "How much did she give you?"

"Fifty dollars," she said absently, as if speaking of a long-forgotten thing.

He dropped it contemptuously into a reversed hat-shape she'd
been working on. "And next time," he said from the doorway,
"try to use a little more self-control. You're only laying yourself
wide open this way."

She didn't hear him. She wasn't listening. She was smiling, looking downward at an answering little toothless smile that met her
own.

It didn't bear the slightest resemblance to hers, that other little
face directly under her own. But it was hers, hers from now on;
hers to have and hers to keep and hers to banish loneliness with.

"Good luck to you," he couldn't resist calling back to her from
the outer door of the house.

It had taken him three hours to ride out. It only took thirty
minutes to ride back. Or so it felt. The wheels racketed around
under him, talking out loud the way train-wheels do. "Now I've
got her! Now I've got her! Now I've got her!"

A conductor stopped beside him one time. "Tickets, please."

He looked up, grinning blankly. "It's okay," he said. "Now I've
got her."

Now I've got her. Now I've got her. Now I've got her. . . .

# NINETEEN

## The Fifth Day Before the Execution

There was no sound of arrival. There was a sound of departure,
the faint hum of a car drawing away outside past the glass doors.
He looked up and there was someone already standing there in the
inner entrance, like a wraith against the glass doors. She'd partly

opened them to step through, was standing there half in, half out, head turned to look behind her at the receding vehicle that had brought her.

He had a feeling that it was she, with nothing further than that to substantiate it for a moment. The fact that she was coming in alone, like the lady free-lance he'd gathered she was. She was stunningly beautiful, so beautiful that all delight was taken from her beauty by its excess amount, as anything overdone is apt to. Just as the profile of a cameo or the head of a statue fails to move the emotions, except as an artistic abstraction, so did she. One had the feeling that, the law of compensation being what it is, she had few inner merits, must be full of flaws, to be that peerless on the outside. She was a brunette, and tall; her figure was perfection. Almost it must have made life barren to be without so many of the problems, the strivings, that plagued other women. She looked that way, as though life was barren, a burst soap-bubble leaving the unpleasant taste of soap upon her lips.

Her gown was like a ripple of fluid silver running down the slender gap between the wings of the door as she stood there between them. Then, the car having gone, she turned her head forward again and finished entering.

She had no look for Lombard, a wan "Good-evening" without spirit for the hallman.

"This gentlemen has been—" the latter began.

Lombard had reached her before he could finish it.

"Pierrette Douglas." He stated it as a fact.

"I am."

"I've been waiting to speak to you. I must talk to you immediately. It's urgent—"

She had stopped before the waiting elevator, with no intention, he could see, of allowing him to accompany her any further than that. "It's a little late, don't you think?"

"Not for this. This can't wait. I'm John Lombard, and I'm here on behalf of Scott Henderson—"

"I don't know him, and I'm afraid I don't know you either—do I? The "do I?" was simply a sop of urbanity thrown in.

"He's in the death-house of the State Penitentiary, awaiting execution." He looked across her shoulder at the waiting attendant. "Don't make me discuss it down here. Out of common ordinary decency—"

"I'm sorry. I live here; it's one-fifteen in the morning, and there are certain proprieties— Well, over here, then." She started diagonally across the lobby toward a small inset furnished with a settee and smoking-stands. She turned to him there, remained standing; they conferred erect.

"You bought a hat from a certain employee of the Kettisha

establishment, a girl named Madge Peyton. You paid her fifty dollars for it."

"I may have." She noticed that the hallman, his interest whetted, was doing his best to overhear from the outside of the alcove. "George!" she reprimanded curtly. He withdrew reluctantly across the lobby.

"In this hat you accompanied a man to the theatre one night."

Again she conceded warily. "I may have. I have been to theatres. I have been escorted by gentlemen to them. Will you come to the point, please?"

"I am. This was a man you'd only met that same evening. You went with him without knowing his name, nor he yours."

"Ah no." She was not indignant, only coldly positive. "Now you can be sure you are mistaken. My standards of conduct are as liberal as anyone else's, you will find. But they do not include accompanying anyone anywhere, at any time, without the formality of an introduction first. You have been misdirected, you want some other person." She thrust her foot out from underneath the silver hem, to move away.

"Please don't let's split hairs about social conduct. This man is under sentence of death, he's to be executed this week! You've got to do something for him!"

"Let's understand one another a little better. Would it help him if I falsely testify I was with him on one certain night?"

"No, no, no," he breathed, exhausted, "only if you rightly testify you were with him, as you were."

"Then I can't do it, because I wasn't."

She continued to gaze at him steadily. "Let's go back to the hat," he said finally. "You did buy a hat, a special model that had been made for somebody else—"

"But we're still at cross-purposes, aren't we? My admitting that has no bearing on my admitting that I accompanied this man to a theatre. The two facts are entirely unrelated, have nothing to do with one another."

That, he had to admit to himself, could very well be. A dismal chasm seemed to be on the point of opening at his feet, where he had seemed to be on solid ground until now.

"Give me some more details of this theatre excursion," she had gone on. "What evidence have you that the person accompanying him was myself?"

"Mainly the hat," he admitted. "The twin to it was being worn on the stage that very night by the actress Mendoza. It was an original made for her. You admit that you secured a duplication of it. The woman with Scott Henderson was wearing that duplication."

"It still does not follow that I was that woman; your logic is not

as flawless as you seem to believe." But that was simply by way of
an aside; her thoughts, he could see, were busy elsewhere.

Something had happened to her. Something was having a surprisingly favourable effect on her. Either something that he had
said, or something that had occurred to her in her own mind. She
had suddenly become strangely alert, interested, almost one might
say feverishly absorbed. Her eyes were sparkling watchfully.

"Tell me. One or two more things. It was the Mendoza show, is
that right? Can you give me the approximate date?"

"I can give you the exact date. They were in the theatre together
on the night of May twentieth last, from nine until shortly after
eleven."

"May," she said to herself, aloud. "You interest me strangely,"
she let him know. She motioned, even touched him briefly on the
sleeve. "You were right. You'd better come upstairs with me a
minute, after all.'

During the ride up in the car she only said one thing. "I'm very
glad you came to me with this."

They got out at the twelfth floor or so, he wasn't sure just which
one it was. She keyed a door and put on lights, and he followed
her in. The red fox scarf that had been dangling over her arm she
dropped carelessly over a chair. Then she moved away from him
over a polished floor that reflected her upside down like a funnel
of fuming silver being spilled out across it.

"May the twentieth, is that right?" she said over her shoulder.
"I'll be right back. Sit down."

Light came from an open doorway, and she remained in there
awhile while he sat and waited. When she returned she was holding
a handful of papers, bills they looked like, sorting them from hand
to hand. Before she had even reached him she had apparently
found one that suited her purpose more than any of the rest. She
tossed all but one aside, retained that, came over to him with it.

"I think the first thing to establish, before we go any further,"
she said, "is that I was not the person with this man at the theatre
that night. Suppose you look at this."

It was a bill for hospitalization for a period of four weeks com-
mencing on the thirtieth of April.

"I was in the hospital for an appendectomy from the thirtieth of
April to the twenty-seventh of May. If that isn't satisfactory you
can check with the doctors and nurses there—"

"That's satisfactory," he said, on a long breath of defeat.

Instead of moving to terminate the interview, she joined him in
sitting down.

"But it was you who bought the hat?" he said finally.

"It was I who bought the hat."

"What became of it?"

She didn't answer immediately. She seemed to become lost in thought. An odd sort of silence descended on the two of them alike. Under cover of it he studied her and her surroundings. She, also under cover of it, studied some inward problem of her own.

The room told him things. Luxury keeping its head above water only by the sheerest nerve. No compromise permitted. Outside, a good, if not the smartest of possible addresses. In here, not quite enough carpeting to cover the polished lake of the floor. Not quite enough period pieces to go around. Gaps where perhaps some had been sold off one by one. But no shoddier stuff allowed to fill out the spaces. And even on the woman herself, as he looked at her, there were the same tell-tale signs. Her shoes were forty-dollar custom-mades, but they had been worn too long. Something about the heels and lustre, you could tell that. The dress had lines that nothing in the lower brackets could have hoped for, but again it had been used too much. He could read it plainest of all in her eyes. They had an unhealthy alertness, as of one reduced to living by her wits; never knowing from which direction the next chance might come, and desperately afraid of not being quick enough to seize it when it did. These were the little things about her that stated the case, if one could read. All of them could be denied, singly, but taken together they told the tale irrefutably.

He sat there almost listening to her thoughts. Yes, listening to them. He saw her look at her hand. He translated it: She is thinking of a diamond ring that once adorned it. Where is it now? Pawned. He saw her raise one instep slightly and glance at it. What thought had occurred to her just then? Silk stockings, probably. Some daydream of being deluged with silk stockings, scores of pairs, hundreds of pairs, more than she could ever hope to use. He translated it: She is thinking of money. Money for all these things and more.

She has decided, he said to himself, watching her expression closely.

She answered his question. The silence ended. Only a moment had gone by.

"The story of the hat is simply this," she resumed. "I'd glimpsed it, it took my fancy, and I wangled a copy of it out of a girl down there. I'm a creature of impulse that way, when I can afford to be. I wore it once. I think, not more than that, and"—her shoulders glittered in a corruscating silver shrug—"it wasn't meant for me. It just wasn't, that was all. Something wrong about it. I wasn't the type. It wasn't very tragic. I didn't let it bother me too much. Then a friend of mine was up here one day, just before I went to the hospital. She came across it, happened to try it on. If you were a woman you'd understand how that sort of thing goes. While one is waiting for the other to finish her dressing we try on one another's latest buys. She fell in love with it at sight, and I let her have it."

Ending it, she shrugged again as she had near the beginning. As though that was all there was to it, there was to be no more.

"Who is she?" he asked quietly. Even as he spoke the simple casual words he knew they were both fencing with one another, that the answer wouldn't be given readily, that this was bargaining.

She answered him equally simply, equally causally. "Do you think that would be fair of me?"

"There's a man's life involved. He's dying Friday," he said in such a low, expressionless voice that it was almost wholly lip-motion.

"Is it because of her, is it through her in any way? Is she to blame, has she caused it? Answer me."

"No," he sighed.

"Then what right have you to involve her? There can be a form of death for women too, you know. Social death. Call it notoriety, loss of reputation, whatever you will. It isn't over with as quickly. I'm not sure it isn't worse."

His face was getting continually whiter with strain. "There must be something in you I can appeal to. Don't you *care* if this man dies? Do you realize that if you withold this information—"

"After all, I *do* know the woman and I don't know the man. She is my friend, he isn't. You're asking me to jeopardize her to save him."

"Where does the jeopardy come in?" She didn't answer. "Then you refuse to tell me?"

"I have neither refused, nor agreed to, *yet*?"

He was suffocating with a sense of his own helplessness. "You're not going to do this to me. This is homebase. It ends here. You know, and you're going to tell me!" They had both risen to their feet. "You think because I can't hit you, like I would a man, I can't get it out of you. I'm going to get it out of you. You're not going to stand here like this and—"

She glanced meaningfully down at her own shoulder. "See here," she said with cold indignation.

He relaxed his grip on it. She readjusted the silver peninsula that clothed it. She looked him straight in the eye, in withering dispar-agement. A blundering, easily dealt with male. "Shall I call down and have you removed?"

"If you want to see a good brawl up here, try it."

"You can't *compel* me to tell you. The choice rests with me."

That was true up to a point, and he knew it.

"I'm a free agent in the matter. What're you going to do about it?"

"This."

Her face changed for a minute at sight of the gun, but it was just the flicker of a shock that would have crossed anyone's. It changed right back again to normal. She even sat down slowly, but not in the crumpled way of the vanquished; in a way that expressed patient assurance; as though this would take some time and she intended sitting it out.

He'd never seen anyone like her before. After that first momentary contraction of the facial muscles she was still the one remaining in control of the situation, not he, gun or no gun.

He stood over her with it, trying to bear down on her mentally if nothing else. "Aren't you afraid to die?"

She looked up into his face. "Very much," she said with perfect composure. "As much as anyone at any time. But I'm not in any danger right now. You can't afford to kill me. People are killed to *keep* them from telling something they know. They are never killed to *force* them to tell something they know. For then how can they tell it afterward? That gun still leaves the decision with me, not with you. I could do many things. I could call the police. But I won't. I'll sit and wait until you put it away again."

She had him.

He put it away, scrubbed a hand across his eyebrows. "All right," he said thickly.

She uttered a note of laughter. "Which one of us got most of the effects of that? My face is dry, yours is shining. My colour is unchanged, yours is pale."

About all he could find to say, once more, was: "All right, you win."

She continued to hammer the point home. Or, rather, tap it delicately, hammering being a heavy-handed procedure at best; and she was deft, she was chic. "You see, you can't threaten me." She paused, to permit him to hear between the lines. "You can interest me."

He nodded. Not to her, in inward confirmation to himself. He said, "Can I sit here a minute?" and motioned to a small table-desk. He took something out of his pocket and snapped it open. He carefully tore out something along a punctured line. Then he snapped the folder closed again and returned it to his pocket. A blank oblong remained before him. He uncapped a fountainpen and began to write across it.

He looked up once to ask: "Am I boring you?"

She gave him the wholly natural, unforced smile that comes when two people understand one another perfectly. "You're being very good company. Quiet but entertaining."

This time he was the one who smiled, to himself. "How do you spell your name?"

"B-e-a-r-e-r."

He gave her a look, then bent to his task once more. "Not quite phonetic, is it?" he murmured deprecatingly.

He had written the numeral "100". She had come closer, was looking down on the bias. "I'm rather sleepy," she remarked, and yawned artifically and tapped her hand over her mouth once or twice.

"Why don't you open the window? It may be a little close in here."

"I'm sure it isn't that." She crossed over to them, however, and did so. Then came back to him again.

He had added another cipher. "How do you feel now, better?" he questioned with ironic solicitude.

She glanced briefly downward. "Considerably refreshed. You might almost say revivified."

"It takes so little, doesn't it?" he agreed acidly.

"Surprisingly little. Next to nothing at all." She was enjoying her own pun.

He didn't go ahead writing. He allowed the pen to flatten against the desk without taking his hand from it. "This is preposterous, you know."

"I haven't gone to you for anything. You've come to me for something." She nodded. "Good-night."

The pen up-ended again in his hand.

He was standing in the open doorway, facing inward in the act of taking leave of her when the car arrived and the elevator door opened in answer to his ring. He was holding a small tab of paper, a leaf torn from a memo-pad, folded once and held within the pronged fingers of one hand.

"I hope I haven't been rude," he was saying to her. A rueful smile etched into his profile for a minute. "At least I know I haven't bored you. And please overlook the exceptional hour of the night. After all, it was rather an exceptional matter." Then in answer to something that she said, "You don't have to worry about that, I wouldn't bother writing a cheque if I were going to stop payment on it afterward. That's a pretty small dodge, any way you look at—"

"Down, sir?" the attendant reminded him, to attract his attention.

He glanced over. "Here's the car." Then back to her again. "Well, good-night." He tipped his hat to her decorously and came away, leaving the door ajar behind him. She closed it lingeringly in his wake, without looking out after him.

In the car he raised the tab of paper and glanced at it.

"Hey, wait a minute," he blurted out, with a stab of the hand toward the carman. "She only gave me one name here—"

The operator slowed the car, prepared to reverse it. "Did you want to go back again, sir?"

For a moment he seemed about to assent. Then he scanned his watch. "No, never mind. I guess it'll be all right. Go ahead down."

The car picked up speed again and resumed its descent.

In the lobby below he stopped long enough to consult the hall-man, flashing the paper at him for a moment. "Which way is this from here, up or down; any idea?"

On it were two names and a number. "Flora," the number, and "Amsterdam."

"It's finally over," he was telling Burgess breathlessly on the phone a minute or two later from an all-night drug-store on Broadway. "I thought I had it, and there was one last link, but this time it's the last. No time to tell you now. Here's where it is. I'm on my way there now. How soon can you be there?"

Burgess, overreaching himself in the headlong sweep of the patrol car that had brought him over, recognized Lombard's car standing out by itself in front of one of the buildings, at first sight empty; jumped hazardously off in full flight and came back. It was only when he'd gained the sidewalk and approached from that direction that he made him out sitting there on the running-board, screened from the roadway by the car-body at his back.

He thought he was ill at first, the way he was sitting there in a huddle on the car-step; bowed over his own lap, head lowered toward the sidewalk underfoot. His posture suggested someone in the penultimate stages of being sick to his stomach; everything but the final climax.

A man in suspenders and undershirt was standing a few steps off, regarding him sympathetically, arrested pipe in hand, a dog peering out from around his legs.

Lombard looked up wanly as Burgess' hastening footfalls drew up beside him. Then he turned his head away again, as though it were too much effort even to speak.

"Is this it? What's the matter? You been in there yet?"

"No, it's that one back there." He indicated a cavernous opening occupying almost the full width of the building it was set into. Within, to one side, could be made out a glistening brass upright set into the bare concrete flooring. Across the façade, in gilt letters backed with black sandpaper, was inscribed the legend: "Fire Department, City of New York."

"That's Number—," Lombard said, flourishing the tab of paper he still held in his hand.

The dog, a spotted Dalmatian, edged forward at this point to muzzle at it inquiringly.

"And that's Flora, these men tell me."

Burgess opened the car door and pulled it out behind him, forcing him to his feet to avoid being unseated.

"Let's get back," he commented tersely. "And fast."

He was flinging himself bodily against the door, with futile wrenches of breath, when Burgess came up with the pass-key and joined him outside it.

"Not a sound from in there. Has she answered them below on the announcer yet?"

"They're still ringing."

"She must have lammed."

"She can't have. They would have seen her leave, unless she went out some roundabout way—Here, let me use this. You'll never get it that way."

The door opened and they floundered inside. Then they stopped short, taking the scene in. The long living-room, which was a continuation of the entrance gallery with simply a one-step drop in height, was empty, but it was mutely eloquent. They both got it right away.

The lights were all on. An unfinished cigarette was still alive and working, sending up lazy spirals of bluish-silver from the rim of an ash-stand with a hollow stem. The floor-length windows were open to the night, showing an expanse of black, with a large star piercing it in one corner, a smaller one in another, like a black-out cloth held in place by a couple of shiny thumb-tacks.

Directly before the windows lay a silver shoe, turned on its side like a small capsized boat. The long, narrow runner of rug that bisected the polished flooring, from just past the drop-step to just short of the windows, showed corrugated ridges, frozen "ripples" that marred its evenness, at one end. As though a mis-step had sent a disturbance coursing along it.

Burgess went to the window, detouring around the side of the room to get there. He leaned out over the low, inadequate, decorative guard-rail on the outside of it, stayed that way, bent motionless, for long minutes.

Then he straightened, turned back into the room again, sent a quiet nod across it to where Lombard had remained, as if incapable of further movement. "She's all the way down below there. I can see her from here in the service alley between two deep walls. Like a rag off a clothes-line. Nobody seems to have heard it; all the windows on this side are still dark."

He didn't do anything about it, strangely enough; didn't even report it at once.

There was only one thing moving in the room, outside himself. And it wasn't Lombard. It was the skein from the cigarette. It was that fact, perhaps, that attracted his eye to it. He went over to it, picked it up. There was still enough to hold, a fraction of an inch. He murmured something under his breath that sounded like: "Must have happened as we got here."

The next thing, he had taken out a cigarette of his own, was holding the two upright side by side, their bases even, with the fingers of the same hand. He took a pencil, notched off the length of the remnant against the intact one.

Then he put the latter into his own mouth, lit it, and took a single, slightly ritualistic puff to get it going. After which he carefully set it down in the same curved trough the former one had occupied, left it there, and glanced at his watch.

"What're you doing that for?" Lombard asked in the listless voice of someone for whom nothing holds any interest any more.

"Just a home-made way of figuring out how long ago it happened. I don't know if it's reliable or not, if any two of these things burn down at the same rate of speed. Must ask some of the guys about that."

He went over, glanced closely at it once, moved away again. The second time he came back he picked it up, looked at it in air like a thermometer, looked at his watch, then tapped it out and discarded it, its purpose served.

"She fell out exactly three minutes before we got in here. That's taking off a full minute while I was looking out the window, before I got over to it and measured it. And that's giving her just one puff, as I took. If she took more, then that brings it down even closer."

"It may have been a King size," Lombard said from a great distance away.

"It's a Lucky; there's enough of the trade-mark left down at the mouth end to be visible. Think I would have wasted my time doing it if I hadn't seen that before I started?"

Lombard didn't answer, was back in the distance again.

"This makes it look as though it was our very ring on the downstairs announcer that killed her," Burgess went on. "Startled her and caused her to make that false move in front of the window that sent her over. The whole story's here in front of our eyes, without words. She'd gone over to them and was standing there looking out, possibly in an expansive mood, drinking in the night air, making plans, when the ring came from downstairs. She did something wrong. Turned in too much of a hurry, or with her weight thrown badly. Or maybe it was her shoes did it. This one looks a little warped, unsteady from overlong wear. Anyway the rug skidded over the waxed flooring. One or both of her feet shot out from under her, riding the rug. The shoe came off completely, went up in the air. She over balanced backwards. It wouldn't have been anything if she hadn't been that close to the open windows. What

would have been otherwise just a comical little sit-down became a
back somersault into space and a death-fall."

Then he said, "But what I don't get is about the address part of
it. Was it a practical joke or what? How'd she act; you were with
her."

"Nah, she wasn't kidding," Lombard said. "She was serious
about wanting that money; it was written all over her."

"I could understand her giving you a spiked address that would
take you a long time to investigate, so she'd have time to cash the
cheque and beat it. But a thing like this, only a few blocks from
here—she might've known you'd be back in five or ten minutes.
What was the angle?"

"Unless she figured she could get more from the lady in question
herself, more than I was offering, by warning her, tipping her off,
and just wanted to get me out of the place long enough to dicker
with her."

Burgess shook his head as though he found this unsatisfactory,
but he contented himself with repeating what he'd said to begin
with. "I don't get it."

Lombard hadn't waited to listen. He'd turned away and was
moving listlessly off to the side with the dragging shamble of a
drunk. The other man watched him curiously. He seemed to have
lost all interest in what was going on around him, to have gone
completely flat. He arrived at the wall and stood there for a moment
before it, sagging, like someone who has been disappointed too
often, is finally licked, finally ready to quit.

Then before Burgess could guess his purpose he had tightened
one arm, drawn it back, and sent it crashing home into the inanimate surface before him, as though it were some kind of an enemy.

"Hey, you fool!" Burgess yelped in stupefaction. "What're you
trying to do, bust your hand? What'd the walls do to you?"

Lombard, writhing in the crouched position of a man applying
a corkscrew to a bottle, his face contorted more by helpless rage
than pain even yet, answered in a choked voice while he nursed his
flaming hand against his stomach: "*They* know! They're all that's
left that knows now—and I can't get it out of them!"

# TWENTY

## The Third Day Before the Execution

The last-minute drink he'd gulped just now right after getting off
the train at the prison-stop wasn't any help. What could a drink
do? What could any number of drinks do? It couldn't alter facts.
It couldn't turn bad news into good. It couldn't change doom into
salvation.

He kept wondering as he trudged up the steep road toward the
gloomy pile of buildings ahead: How do you tell a man he's got to
die? How do you tell him there's no more hope, the last ray has
just faded out? He didn't know, and he was on his way right now
to find out—by first-hand experience. He even wondered whether
it wouldn't have been kinder not to come near him again at all, to
let him go without seeing him this useless one last time.

This was going to be ghastly, and he knew it. He was in the place
now, and he already had the creeps. But he'd had to come; he
couldn't be that yellow about it. Couldn't leave him dangling in
suspense for three agonizing days more; couldn't let him be led out
on Friday night still looking back over his shoulder the whole way,
metaphorically speaking, for the last-minute cancellation that
would never come now.

He passed the back of his hand slowly across his mouth as he
trudged after the guard up to the second-floor tier. "Am I going to
get drunk tonight after I leave here!" he swore bitterly to himself.
"I'm going to get so full I'll be an alcoholic case at one of the
hospitals until it's over and done with!"

And now the guard was standing by, and he went in to face the
music. Funeral music.

This was the execution right now. A bloodless, white one preceding the other by three days. The execution of all hope.

The guard's footsteps receded hollowly. After that the silence
was horrible. Neither of them could have stood it for very long.

"So that's it," Henderson said quietly at last. He'd understood.

The rigor mortis was broken, at least. Lombard turned away
from the window, came over and clapped him on the shoulder.
"Look, fellow—" he started to say.

"It's all right," Henderson told him. "I understand. I can tell by
your face. We don't have to talk about it."

"I lost her again. She slipped away—this time for good."

"I said you don't need to talk about it," Henderson urged

patiently. "I can see what it's done to you. For the love of Pete, let's drop it." He seemed to be the one trying to buck Lombard up, instead of *vice versa*.

Lombard slumped down on the edge of the bunk. Henderson, being the "host," let him have it, got up and stood leaning the curve of his back against the wall opposite.

The only sound in the cell for a while after that was the rustle of cellophane as Henderson kept continuously folding over the edge of an emptied cigarette package back on itself until he'd wound it up tight, then undoing it again pleat by pleat until he had it open once more. Over and over, endlessly, apparently just to give his fingers something to do.

No one could have stood it for long in that atmosphere. Lombard said finally. "Don't, will you? It's making me go nuts."

Henderson looked down at his own hands in surprise as though unaware until then what they'd been up to. "That's my old habit," he said sheepishly. "I never was able to break myself of it, even in good times. You remember, don't you? Any time I ever rode a train the time-table would end up like that. Any time I had to sit and wait in a doctor's or a dentist's office the magazines would end up like that. Any time I ever sat in a theatre the programme—" He stopped short, looked dreamily across at the wall, just over Lombard's head. "That night at the show with *her*, I can remember doing it that night too. It's funny how a little thing like that should come back to me now, this late, when all the more important things it might have helped me to remember all along— What's the matter; what are you looking at me like that for? I've quit doing it." He threw the tormented wrapper aside to show him.

"But you threw it away, of course? That night with *her*. You left it behind you, on the seat or on the floor, as people usually do?"

"No, she kept both programmes. I can remember that. It's funny, but I can. She asked me to let her have them. She made some remark to the effect of wanting to glory in her impulsiveness. I can't recall just what it was. But I know she kept them; I distinctly saw her put them in her bag."

Lombard had risen to his feet. "There's a little something there if we only knew how to get at it."

"What do you mean?"

"It's the only thing we know for sure she has in her possession."

"We don't know for sure she still has it in her possession, do we?" Henderson corrected.

"If she kept it to begin with, then it's likely she still has it. People either do or don't keep such things as theatre programmes. Either they throw them away at once or they keep them indefinitely, for years after. If there was only some way we could make this thing the bait. What I mean is, it's the only common denominator linking her to you—because it will have its upper right hand corners neatly winged back from cover to cover, without missing a page. If we could only get her to come forward with it, without guessing—she will stand revealed to us automatically."

"By advertising, you mean?"

"Something along those lines. People collect all sorts of things: stamps, sea-shells, pieces of furniture full of wormholes. Often they'll pay any price for things that to them are treasures, but to others are trash. They lose all sense of proportion once the collector's lust gets hold of them."

"Well?"

"I'm a collector of theatre programmes, say. A freak, an eccentric, a millionaire throwing my money away right and left. It is more than a hobby; it is an obsession with me. I must have complete sets of programmes for every play produced at every theatre in town, all the way back, season by season. I suddenly appear from nowhere, I open a little clearing depot, I advertise. Word spreads around. I'm a nut. I'm giving away something for nothing. There's a free-for-all to get in on it while it lasts. The papers'll probably puff it up, with pictures; one of those screwball incidents that pop up every now and then."

"Your whole premise is full of flaws. No matter how phenomenal the prices you offer, why should that attract her? Suppose she's well off?"

"Suppose she no longer is well off?"

"I still don't see how she can fail to smell a rat."

"To us the programme is 'hot.' To her it isn't. Why should it be? She may never even notice those tell-tale little folds up at the corner, or, if she does, never dream that they'll tell us what we want to know. You didn't remember about it yourself until just a few minutes ago. Why should she? She's not a mind-reader; how is she going to know that you and I are here together in this cell talking about it right now?"

"The whole thing is too flimsy."

"Of course it's flimsy," Lombard agreed. "It's a thousand-to-one shot. But we have to take it. Beggars can't be choosers. I'm going to try it, Hendy. I have a strange feeling that—that this'll work, where everything else has failed.

He turned away, went over to the bars to be let out.

"Well, so long—" Henderson suggested tentatively.

"I'll be seeing you," Lombard called back.

As he heard his tread recede outside behind the guard's, Henderson thought: "He doesn't believe that. And neither do I."

*Boxed Advertisement, All Morning and Evening Papers:*

# TWENTY-ONE

## The Day of the Execution

At nine-thirty, for almost the first time all day, the line had dwindled to vanishing-point, a straggler or two had been disposed of, and there was a breathing-spell, with nobody in the shop but Lombard and his young assistant.

Lombard slumped limply in his chair, thrust out his lower lip, and blew breath exhaustedly up across his face, so that it stirred the disarranged hair overhanging his forehead. He was in his vest, shirt-collar open. He dragged a handkerchief out from the pocket he was sitting on and popped it at his face here and there. It came away grey. They didn't bother dusting them off before they dumped them in front of him. They seemed to think the thicker the dust, the more highly they would be valued. He wiped his hands on the handkerchief, threw it away.

He turned his head, said to somebody hidden from view behind him by towering, slantwise stacks of programmes: "You can go now, Jerry. Time's about up; I'm closing in another half-hour. The rush seems to be over."

A skinny youth of nineteen or so straightened up in a sort of trench left between two parapets of the accumulation, came out, put on his coat.

Lombard took out some money. "Here's the fifteen dollars for the three days, Jerry."

The boy looked disappointed. "Won't you be needing me any more tomorrow, mister?"

"No. I won't be here tomorrow," Lombard said broodingly. "Tell you what you can do, though. You can have these to sell for waste-paper; some rag-picker might give you a few jits for them."

The boy looked at him pop-eyed. "Gee, mister, you mean you been buyin 'em up for three days straight just to get rid of them?"

"I'm funny that way," Lombard assented. "Keep it under your hat until then, though."

The boy went out, giving him awed backward glances all the way to the sidewalk. He thought he was crazy, Lombard knew. He didn't blame him. He thought he was crazy himself. For ever thinking that this would work, that she'd fall for it, show up. The whole idea had been hare-brained to start with.

A girl was passing along the sidewalk as the boy emerged. That was the only reason Lombard happened to notice her, because his eyes were on his departing assistant and she cut between them. Nobody. Nothing. Just a girl. A stray pedestrian. She gave a look in as she passed the doorway. Then, with just a momentary hesitation, probably caused by curiosity, went on again, passed from view beyond the vacant shop-window. For a moment, though, he had almost thought she was about to enter.

The lull ended and an antediluvian in beaver-collared coat, black-stringed eyeglasses, and an incredibly high collar came in, walking-stick to side. Behind him, to Lombard's dismay, appeared a cab-driver dragging in a small ancient trunk. The visitor halted before the bare wooden table. Lombard was using for a desk, and struck a pose so hammy that for a minute Lombard couldn't believe it was intended seriously, wasn't just a burlesque.

Lombard rolled his eyes upward. He'd been getting this type all day long. But never with a whole trunkful of them at a time, until now.

"Ah, sir," began the relic of the gas-lit footlights, in a richly resonant voice that would have been something if only he'd kept his hands down, "you are indeed lucky that I read your advertisement. I am in a position to enrich your collection immeasurably. I can add to it as no one else in this city can. I have some rarities here that will warm your heart. From the old Jefferson Playhouse, as far back as—"

Lombard motioned a hasty refusal. "I'm not interested in the Jefferson Playhouse. I've got a full set."

"The Olympia, then. The—"

"Not interested, not interested. I don't care what else you've got; I'm all bought up. I only need one item more before I put out the lights and lock up. Casino, 1941–42. Have you one?"

"Casino, hah!" the old man sputtered in his face, with a little more than just expelled breath. "You say Casino to me? What have I to do with trashy modern reviews? I was once one of the greatest tragedians on the American stage!"

"I can see that," Lombard said dryly. "I'm afraid we can't do business with one another."

The trunk and the cab-driver went out again. The trunk's owner stopped in the doorway long enough to express his contempt by way of the floor. "Casino—*thut!*" Then he went out too.

Another short hiatus, then an old woman who had the appearance of being a charwoman came in. She had bedecked herself for the occasion with a large floppy hat topped by a cabbagy rose, that looked as though it had either been picked up from the ash-can or taken out of a storage closet where it had lain forgotten for decades. She had applied a circular fever-spot of rouge to the leathery skin of each cheek with the uncertain hand of one trying to indulge in a long-forgotten practice.

As he raised his eyes to her, half compassionately, half unwillingly, he caught a sight over her rounded shoulder of the same girl as before, once again passing outside the shop, this time in the opposite direction. Again she turned and glanced in. This time, however, she did more than that. She came to a full halt, if only for a second or two; even went back a single step to bring herself more fully in line with the open entrance. Then, having scanned the interior, she went on. She was obviously interested in what was going on. Still, he had to admit there had been enough publicity attending the enterprise to make a chance passer-by conscious of it, cause her to give a second look. There had even been photographers sent around early in the event. And she may have simply been coming back from wherever she had been bound the first time she passed; if you went some place, you usually followed the same route on the way back; there was nothing unusual in that.

The old drudge before him was faltering timidly, "Is it on the level, sir? You really pay money for old programmes?"

He brought his attention back to her. "Certain ones, yes."

She fumbled in a knitted market-bag hanging over her arm. "I have only a few here, sir. From when I used to be in the chorus myself. I kept them all; they mean a lot to me. The Midnight Rambles, and the Frolics of 1911." She was trembling with apprehension as she put them down. She turned one of the yellowed leaves as though to add to the veracity of her story. "See, this is me here, sir. Dolly Golden, that used to be my name. I played the Spirit of Youth in the final tableau—"

Time, he thought, is a greater murderer than any man or woman. Time is the murderer that never gets punished.

He looked at her raw, toil-worn hands, not the programmes at all. "A dollar apiece," he said gruffly, feeling for his bill-fold.

She was nearly overcome with joy. "Oh, bless you, mister! It will come in so handy!" She had swept up his hand before he could stop her and put her lips to it. The rouge started to elongate into pink tears. "I didn't dream they were worth that much!"

They weren't. They weren't worth a plugged nickel "Here you are, mother," he said compassionately.

"Oh, now I'm going to eat—I'm going to eat a big dinner!" She staggered out almost drunk with the unexpected windfall. A younger woman was standing there quietly waiting as she gave place before him. She must have come in unnoticed behind her just now; he hadn't seen her enter. It was the same one who had passed the doorway twice already, once in each direction. He was almost sure of it, although the previous optical snapshots he had had of her had been too brief to focus properly.

She had looked younger out there in the middle distance than she did now, directly before him at close range. That was because she had retained a slimness of figure after almost everything else was gone. She was ravaged, almost as ravaged as the charwoman who had just preceded her, if in a different way.

A prickling sensation lightly stirred the fuzz below the hairline on his neck. He tried not to stare at her too blatantly, looked down again after one all-comprehensive sweep of the eyes, so she wouldn't detect anything on his face.

His composite impression was this: she must have been pretty until just recently. It was rapidly leaving her now. There was an air of sub-surface refinement, perhaps even culture, still emanating from her, but there was a hard crust, a shell of courseness and cheapening, forming on the outside that would soon smother it, extinguish it for good. Probably it was already too late to save her from the process. It was being accelerated, as far as he could tell at sight, either by alcohol in destructive daylong floods, or by acute and unaccustomed destitution; or perhaps by an attempt to dull the one with the other. There were traces of a third factor still discernible, and this perhaps had been the predecessor, the causative, of the other two, but it seemed to be no longer the determining one, had been superseded by the other two; unbearable distress of mind, mental misery, fear admixed with some sort of guilt, and prolonged endlessly over a period of months. It had left its mark, but it was dying out now; the strictly physical dissipations were the current ones. She was jaunty now, she was rubbery and unbreakable with the resiliency of the gutters and the bars, and of those who can go no lower, and that would suffice to see her through to the end. Probably a gas-tube in some rooming-house.

She looked as though she hadn't been eating regularly. There was a shadowed hollow in each cheek, and the whole bone-structure of the face showed through the thin covering. She was entirely in black, but not the black of widowhood nor yet the black of fashion; the rusty black of slovenliness, adhered to because it doesn't show soil. Even her stockings were black, with a white crescent of hole showing above the back of each shoe.

She spoke. Her voice was ruined, raucous with cheap whisky gulped inordinately all day and night. Yet even here there was a ghost of cultivation left. If she used slang now it was from choice, from contact with those she associated with, and not because she didn't know any better. "You got any jack left to pay on programmes or am I too late?"

"Let's see what you've got," he said guardedly.

There was a snap of her shoddy, oversized handbag, and a pair of them were planked down. Companion pieces from the same night. A musical show at the Regina, season before last. I wonder who she was with that night, he thought. She probably was secure yet and comely, she didn't dream—

He pretended to consult a reference list giving his needs, the gaps that remained to be filled in his "sets."

He saw her eyes glitter. He'd hoped that would get her.

"Got any more?" he suggested craftily. "This is your last chance, you know. I'm closing up this place tonight."

She hesitated. He saw her eyes go to her bag. "Well, do you bother buying just one at a time?"

"Any number."

"As long as I'm in here—" She opened the bag once more, tilted the flap over against her so that he couldn't look down into it, pulled an additional programme out. She snapped the bag shut again, first of all, before she did anything else. He noted that. Then she spaded the folder at him. He took it, reversed it his way.

## CASINO THEATRE

It was the first one that had showed up in the full three days. He leafed through it with pretended casualness past the preliminary filler columns to where the play-matter itself began. It was dated by the week, as all theatrical programmes are. "Week beginning May 17th." His breath log-jammed. That was the week. The right week. It had been on the night of the twentieth. He kept his eyes down so they wouldn't give him away. Only—the upper right-hand corners of the pages were untouched. It wasn't that they'd been smoothed out; that would have left a tell-tale diagonal seam. They'd never been folded over in the first place.

It was hard to keep his voice casual. "Got the mate to it? Most of them come in twos, you know, and I could make you a better offer."

She gave him a searching look. He even caught the little uncom-

pleted start her hand made toward the snap of her pocket-book.
Then she forced it down again. "What d'you think I do, print
them?"

"I prefer to buy duplicates, doubles, whenever possible. Didn't
anyone go with you to this particular show? What became of the
other pro—?"

There was something about it she didn't like. Her eyes darted
suspiciously around the store as if in search of a trap. She edged
warily backwards a step or two from the table. "Come on, one is
all I got. Do you wanna buy or don't you?"

"I can't give you as much as I could have given you for a pair—"

She was obviously in a hurry to get outside into the open again.
"All right, anything you say—" She even arched over to reach for
the money from where she was standing; he couldn't get her to
close in toward the purchasing table again.

He let her get as far as the door with it. Then he called after
her, but in a quietly modulated voice, unwarranted to cause alarm:
"Just a moment. Could I ask you to come back here a moment,
there's something I forgot."

She stopped short for a single instant, cast a look of sharp distrust
back over her shoulder at him. It was more than just the look of
automatic response one gives to a summons; it was a look of
wariness. Then as he rose, crooking his finger at her, she gave a
stifled cry, broke into a scampering run, rounded the store entrance, and fled from sight.

He flung the impediment of the table bodily over to one side to
get quick clearance, dashed out after her. Behind him several of
the top-heavy stacks of programmes reared by the boy wavered
from the vibration of his violent exit, crumbled, and spilled all over
the floor in snowdrifts.

She was chopsticking it down toward the next corner when he
got out on the sidewalk, but her high heels were against her. When
she glanced back and saw him coming full tilt behind her, she gave
another cry, louder this time, and was stung into an added spurt of
velocity that carried her around into the next street before he had
quite halved the distance.

But he got her there, only a few yards past where his own car
had been standing waiting all day, in hopes of just such an event-
uality as this. He overlapped her, blocked her off, gripped her by
the shoulders, and then swung her in with him against the building
front, pinning her there in a sort of enclave of his arms.

"All right now, stand still—it's no use," he breathed heavily.

She was less able to speak than he was; alcohol had killed her
wind. He almost thought she was going to choke for a minute.
"Lemme—'lone. What—uf I done?"

"Then what did you run for?"

"I didn't like"—her head hung over his arms, trying to get air—
"the way you looked."

"Lemme see that bag. Open that pocket-book! Come on, open
up that pocket-book, or I'll do it for you!"

"Take your hands off me! Leave me alone!"

He didn't waste any more time arguing. He yanked it so violently
from under her arm that the frayed loop-strap she had it suspended
by tore off bodily. He opened it, plunged his hand in, crowding
her back with his body so that she couldn't escape from the position
he had her backed into. It came up again with a programme identical to the one she had just sold him in the store. He let the
pocket-book drop to free his hands. He tried to flutter the leaves
to open it, and they adhered. He had to pry them away from one
another. All the inner ones, from cover to cover, were notched,
were neatly folded over at their upper right-hand tips. He peered
in the uncertain street light, and the date-line was the same as the
other.

Scott Henderson's programme. Poor Scott Henderson's programme, returning at the eleventh hour, like bread cast upon the
waters.


# TWENTY-TWO

## The Hour of the Execution

10.55 p.m. The last of anything—ah, the last of anything—is always
so bitter. He was cold all over, though the weather was warm, and
he was shivering, though he was sweating, and he kept saying to
himself over and over, "I'm not afraid," more than he was listening
to the chaplain. But he was, and he knew he was, and who could
blame him? Nature had put the instinct to live in his heart.

He was stretched out face downward on his bunk, and his head,
with a square patch shaved on the top, was hanging down over the
edge of it toward the floor. The chaplain was sitting by him, one
hand pressed consolingly against his shoulder as if to keep the fear
in, and every time the shoulder shook the hand would shake in
sympathy with it, although the chaplain was going to live many
more years yet. The shoulder shook at regular spaced intervals. It's
an awful thing to know the time of your own death.

The chaplain was intoning the Twenty-Third Psalm in a low voice. "Green pastures, refresh my soul—" Instead of consoling him, it made him feel worse. He didn't want the next world, he wanted this one.

The fried chicken and the waffles and the peach shortcake that he'd had hours ago felt like they were all gummed up somewhere behind his chest, wouldn't go down any further. But that didn't matter; it wouldn't give him indigestion; there wouldn't be time enough for it to.

He wondered if he'd have time to smoke another cigarette. They'd brought in two packs with his dinner; that had been only a few hours ago, and one was already crumpled and empty, the second half gone. It was a foolish thing to worry about, he knew, because what was the difference if he smoked one all the way down or had to throw it away after a single puff? But he'd always been thrifty about things like that, and the habits of a lifetime die hard.

He asked the chaplain, interrupting his low-voiced chant, and instead of answering directly the chaplain simply said, "Smoke another, my boy," and struck the match and held it for him. Which meant there really wasn't time.

His head flopped down again and smoke came out of the hidden grey gash of his lips. The chaplain's hand pressed down on his shoulder once more, steadying the fear, damming it. Footsteps could be heard coming quietly and with horrible slowness along the stone-floored passage outside, and a sudden hush fell over Death Row. Instead of coming up, Scott Henderson's head went down even further. The cigarette fell and rolled away. The chaplain's hand pressed down harder, almost riveting him there to the bunk.

The footsteps had stopped. He could sense they were standing out there looking in at him, and, though he tried not to look, he couldn't hold out; his head came up against his will and turned slowly. He said, "Is this it now?"

The cell door started to ease back along its grooves, and the warden said: "This is it now, Scott."

Scott Henderson's programme. Poor Scott Henderson's programme, returning like bread cast upon the waters. He stared at it. The handbag he had wrenched from her lay unnoticed at his feet.

The girl, meanwhile, was writhing there beside him, trying to break the soldered grip of his hand on her shoulder.

He put it carefully away in his inside pocket first of all. Then he took two hands to her, trundled her roughly along the sidewalk and over to where his car stood waiting. "Get in there, you heartless apology for a human being! You're coming with me! You know what you've nearly done, don't you?"

She threshed around for a moment on the running board before he got the door open and pushed her in. She went sprawling knees first, turned and scrambled upwards against the seat. "Let me go, I tell you!" Her voice went keening up and down the street. "You can't do this to me! Somebody come here! Aren't there any cops in this town to stop a guy like him—!"

"Cops? You're getting cops! All the cops you want! You'll be sick of the sight of them before I get through with you!" Before she could squirm out at the oppsoite side he had come in after her, yanked her violently back so that she floundered against him and crashed the door shut after him.

He took the back of his hand to her twice to silence her: once in threat, the second time in fulfilment. Then he bent to the dashboard. "I never did that to a woman before," he gritted. "But you're no woman. You're just a bum in feminine form. A no-good bum." They swerved out from the kerb, straightened and shot off. "Now you're going to ride, whether you want to or not, and you better see that you ride quiet. Every time you howl or try anything while I'm bucking this traffic I'll give you another one of those if I have to. It's up to you."

She quit wild-catting, deflated suddenly against the seat leather, glowered there while they cut around corners, by-passed car after car going the same way they were. Once, when a light held them up for a minute, she said defeatedly, without renewing her previous attempts to escape, "Where're you heading with me?"

"You don't know, do you?" he said cuttingly. "It's all news to you, isn't it?"

"*Him*, hunh?" she said with quiet resignation.

"Yeah, *him*, hunh! Some specimen of humanity you are!" He crushed the accelerator flat once more, and both their heads went back in unison. "You ought to be beaten raw for being willing to let an innocent man go to his death when you could have stopped it at any time from first to last, just by coming forward and telling them what you know!"

"I figured it was that," she said dully. She looked down at her hands. After a while she said, "When is it—tonight?"

"Yes, tonight!"

He saw her eyes widen slightly in the reflected dashboard light as though she hadn't realized until now it was that imminent. "I didn't know it was—going to be that soon," she gulped.

"Well, it isn't now!" he promised harshly. "Not as long as I've got you with me at last!"

Another light stopped them. He cursed it, sat there wiping his face with a large handkerchief. Then both their heads flung back together again.

She sat there staring steadily before her. Not at anything before or beyond the car. Yet not at anything below the windshield either, although it was there her eyes were fixed. He could see her in the mirror on her side. She was staring inwardly at something. The past, perhaps. Summing up her life. There was no bar whisky at hand now to provide her with an escape. She had to sit and face it while the car raced on.

"You must be something made of sawdust, without any insides at all!" he told her once.

She answered, unexpectedly and at length. "Look what it did to me. You haven't thought of that, have you? Haven't I suffered enough for it already? Why should I care what happens to him or to anyone else! What is he to me, anyway? They're killing him tonight. But *I've* been killed for it already! I'm dead, I tell you, dead! You've got someone dead sitting in the car next to you."

Her voice was the low growl of tragedy striking in the vitals; no shrill woman's whine or plaint; a sexless groan of suffering. "Sometimes in dreams I see someone who had a beautiful home, a husband who loved her, money, beautiful things, the esteem of her friends, security; above all, security, safety. That was supposed to go on until she died. That was supposed to *last*. I can't believe it was me. I know it wasn't me. And yet the whisky-dreams sometimes tell me that it was. You know how dreams are—"

He sat eyeing the darkness that came streaming toward them, to part in the middle over the silver prow of the headlights and come together again behind them like a mystic undulating tide. His eyes were grey pebbles that didn't move, didn't hear, didn't give a rap about her trouble.

"Do you know what it means to be thrown out into the street? Yes, literally thrown out, at two in the morning, with just the clothes you have on your back, and to have the doors locked behind you and your own servants warned not to admit you again on pain of dismissal! I sat on a park bench all night the first night. I had to borrow five dollars from my own former maid the next day so that I could get a room, find shelter at least."

"Why didn't you come forward then, at least? If you'd already lost everything, what more did you have to lose?"

"His power over me didn't end there. He warned me that if I opened my mouth, did anything to bring notoriety or disgrace on his good name, he'd sign me over into an institution for alocholics. He could easily do it too; he has the influence, the money. I'd never get out again. Strait-jackets and cold-water treatments."

"All that's no excuse. You must have known we were looking for you; you couldn't have avoided knowing it. You must have known this man was going to die. You were yellow, that's what you were. But if you never did a decent thing in your life before, and if you never do a decent thing in your life again, you're going to do one now. You're going to speak your piece and save Scott Henderson!"

She was silent for a long moment. Then her head went over slowly. "Yes," she said at last, "I am. I want to—now. I must have been blind all these months not to see it as it really is. Somehow I didn't think of him all along until now; I only thought of myself, what I had to lose by it." She looked up at him again. "And I *would* like to do one decent thing at last—just for a change."

"You're going to," he promised grimly. "What time did you meet him at the bar that night?"

"Six-ten, by the clock in front of us."

"Are you going to tell them that? Are you willing to swear to that?"

"Yes," she said in an exhausted voice, "I'm going to tell them that. I'm willing to swear to that."

All he answered was, "God forgive you for what you've done to that man!"

Then it came. It was as though something frozen within her had melted, crumbled. Or maybe it was that hard crust that he had noticed forming on the outside of her, smothering her slowly to death. Her hands flew up to her already lowered face, stayed that way, covering it. She made very little sound. He'd never seen anyone shake so. As though she was being torn apart internally. He thought she was never going to stop shaking like that.

He didn't speak to her. He didn't look at her, except by indirection in the mirror.

After a while he could tell it was over. Her hands had dropped again. He heard her say, more to herself than him, "It makes you feel so clean when you're going to do a thing you've been afraid to do."

They raced on in silence, just the two of them in the faint dashlight. Traffic was thinner now and all coming one way—toward them, instead of along with them, as heretofore. They were out past the city limits, flying along the sleek, straight artery that led up-country. The cars passing them left streaks of light on their side windows, they were going so fast.

"Why are we going this far out?" she asked presently, with only dulled awareness. "Isn't the Criminal Courts Building the place where—?"

"I'm taking you straight up there to the penitentiary," he answered tautly. "It's the quickest in the end. Cut through all the red tape—"

"It's right tonight—you said?"

"Some time within the next hour and a half. We'll make it.

They'd hit full wooded country now; trees with white-washed waistbands to give the road a boundary in the dark. No more terrain lights, only an occasional inbound car blurring into incandescence as it approached, then dousing its lights in that wayside salute so reminiscent of an ambulant tipping his hat.

"But suppose something happens to delay us? A tyre goes out or something? Wouldn't it be better to telephone?"

"I know what I'm doing. You sound quite anxious all at once."

"Yes, oh yes, I am," she breathed. "I've been blind. Blind. I see which was the dream now and which the reality."

"Quite a reformation," he said grudgingly. "For five months you didn't lift a finger to help him. And now all at once, within fifteen minutes, you're all hot and bothered."

"Yes," she said submissively. "It doesn't seem to matter all at once. About my husband, or the threat of being put into an institution, or any of the rest of it. You've made me see the whole thing in a different light." She drew the back of one hand weariedly across her brow, said with infinite disgust: "I want to do at least one brave thing; I'm so sick of being a coward all my life!"

They rode in silence after that. Until presently she asked, almost with anxiety. "Will just my sworn testimony be enough to save him?"

"It'll be enough to postpone—what they have scheduled for tonight. Once that's been accomplished we can turn it over to the lawyers; they'll see it through the rest of the way."

Suddenly she noticed they had swung off left at a fork on to a desolate, poorly surfaced cross-country "feeder." It had already occurred several moments before by the time she became aware of it. The motion of the car had become less even. The occasional passing road-mate had diminished to none. There was no sign of life on it.

"But why this? I thought the north-and-south highway we were on was the one that takes you up to the State Prison. Isn't he at—?"

"This is a short-cut," he answered briefly. "A sort of shuttle that'll save time."

The humming of the wind seemed to rise a little, take on an apprehensive moaning quality, as they rushed through, displacing it.

He spoke again, chin almost to wheel, eyes motionless and emotionless over it. "I'll get you where we're going in plenty of time."

There were no longer just two of them in the car. At some indeterminate point in the previous silence a third presence had entered it, was in it now, sitting between them. The icy, shrouded shape of fear, its unseen arms enfolding the woman in cold embrace, its frigid fingertips seeking out her windpipe.

There hadn't been any lights but their own for ten minutes past now. There hadn't been any word between them. The trees were a smoky, billowing mass on each side of them. The wind was a warning message, unheeded until too late. Their two faces were ghosts reflected side by side on the windshield before them.

He slowed, backed, turned aside once more, this time on to an unpaved dirt lane, little better than a defile through the trees. They jounced along over its unevenness of surface, dried leaves hissing in their wake, stirred by the exhaust tube; the wheels climbing over half-submerged roots, the fenders grazing trunks impinging on the right-of-way. The headlights played over a grotto-like profundity of trees, bleaching the nearer ones into dazzling stalagmites, leaving the inner ones black and enshrouded. It was like some evil, bewitched glade in a fairy-tale for children, woods of supernatural import where bad things were about to happen.

She said in a smothered voice, "Now what're you doing—?" Fear locked its embrace about her tighter, breathed glacially down her neck. "I don't like the way you're acting. What're you doing this for?"

Suddenly they'd stopped and it was over. The sound of the brakes only reached her senses after the fact had been accomplished. He killed the engine, and there was stillness all around. Inside the car and out. They were motionless, all of them—the car, and he and she, and her fear.

Not quite; there was one thing moving. The three fingers of his hand that had remained upon the wheel-rim kept fluttering restlessly, rising and falling in rotation, like somebody striking successive keys on the piano over and over.

She turned and began to pummel at him in impotent fright. "What is it? Say something! Say something to me! Don't just sit there like that! What did we stop here for? What are you thinking? Why are you looking like that?"

"Get out." He gave the order with a hitch of his chin.

"No. What are you going to do? No." She sat there staring at him in ever-widening fright.

He reached across her and unlatched the door on that side. "I said get out."

"No! You're going to do something. I can see it on your face—"

He flung her before him with one stiffly locked arm. A moment later they were both standing there beside the car, toe-deep in sandpapery tan and yellow leaves. He cracked the car door shut again after him. It was damp and penetrating under the trees, pitch-black around them in all directions but one: the ghostly tunnel ahead made by the projecting headlight beams.

"Come this way," he said quietly. He started walking down it. He held her by the elbow to make sure that she accompanied him. The leaves sloshed and spit under them in the unnatural quiet. The car fender fell behind them; they were clear of it now, walking ahead. She turned unnaturally sidewise, staring into his unanswerable face. She could hear her own breath echoing under the canopy of the trees. His was quieter.

They walked like that in silent, unexplained pantomime until they'd reached a point where the projected headlight shine thinned out, was about to disappear. On this boundary-line between light and shadows he stopped, took his hand off her. She went down convulsively a few inches; he caught her, straightened her, took his hand off her a second time.

He took out a cigarette and offered it to her. She tried to refuse. "Here," he insisted roughly, thrusting it at her mouth. "Better take one! He lit it for her, holding his hands cupped over the matchflame. There was something ritualistic about the little attention that only struck redoubled fear into her, instead of reassuring her. She took one puff, then the cigarette dropped from her unmanageable lips: she wasn't able to retain it. He made a precautionary pass at it with his foot, ground it out because of the leaves.

"All right," he said. "Now go back to the car. Walk up that pathway of light from here, and get back in the car, and wait for me in it. And *don't look around*; just keep walking straight ahead."

She didn't seem to understand, or else was too undone by terror to be able to move of her own volition. He had to give her a slight push away from him to start her off. She tottered a few uncertain steps through the shuffling leaves.

"Go ahead, keep walking straight back along those lights like I told you," his voice came after her." *"And don't look back!"*

She was a woman and a frightened one. The admonition had an opposite effect to that intended; it brought her head around uncontrollably.

He already had the gun out in his hand, although he hadn't quite brought it all the way up yet; it was still at half-position. It must have come out silently behind her back as she was moving away.

Her scream was like a bird, clawed and dying, that manages to spiral up through the trees for one last flutter before it drops down dead. She tried to close it toward him again, as though nearness was a guarantee of immunity and the danger lay in being detached from him.

"Stay there!" he warned flintily. "I tried to make it as easy for you as I could; I told you not to look back."

"Don't! What for?" she wailed. "I told you I'd tell them everything you want me to! I *told* you I would! I will. I will—!"

"No," he contradicted with horrifying calm, "you won't, and I'll make sure you don't. Tell it to him instead when he catches up to you in the next world, about half an hour from now." His arm stretched out at firing position with the gun.

She made a perfect silhouette against the fuzzy headlight glare. Trapped, unable even to flee aside into the protective darkness beyond the beams in time, for they were so wide, she floundered around where she stood in a complete befuddled circle that brought her around facing him once more as she had been before.

That was all there was time for.

Then the shot echoed thunderously under the ceiling of trees overhead. Her scream was its counterpoint.

He must have missed, as fairly close to one another as they were. There was no smoke at his end, as there should have been, though her mind had no time to reason about that. She felt nothing; she still stayed up, too dazed to run or do anything but waver there, like a ribbon streamer before an electric fan. He was the one stumbled sideways against a nearby tree-trunk, leaned there inertly for a minute, face pressed against the bark, as though in remorse for what he had just attempted. Then she saw that he was holding his shoulder with the other hand. The gun winked harmlessly from the bed of leaves where he had dropped it, like a lump of coal in the light-flare.

A man's figure glided swiftly past her from the rear, went down the path of light toward him. He was holding a gun of his own, she saw, centred on the crumbling figure against the tree. He dipped for a minute, and the wink was gone from the leaves underfoot. Then he stepped in close, there was a flash of reflected light down by their wrists, and something made the sound of a twig snapping. Lombard's sagging figure came away from the tree, leaned suddenly against him, then straightened itself.

In the leaden quiet the second man's voice reached her clearly.

"I arrest you for the murder of Marcella Henderson!"

He put something to his lips, and a whistle sounded with doleful, long-drawn out finality. Then the silence came down on the three of them again.

Burgess leaned down solicitously and raised her from the kneeling position she had collapsed into on the bed of leaves, hands pressed tightly over her sobbing face.

"I know," he said soothingly. "I know it was pretty bad. It's over now. It's over. You did the job. You've saved him. Lean on me, that's it. Have a good cry. Go to it. You've got it coming to you."

Woman-like, she stopped then and there. "I don't want to now. I'm all right now. It's just that—I didn't think anyone would get here in time to—"

"They wouldn't have just by tailing the two of you. Not the way he drove." A second car had braked somewhere further up the lane only moments before; its occupants hadn't even reached the spot yet. "I couldn't take any chances on that. I was riding right with you the whole way out, didn't you know that? I was right in the trunk compartment. I heard the whole thing. I've been in it ever since you first walked inside the store."

He raised his voice, shouted back to where flashlights were winking fitfully under the trees as the second party descended. "Is that Gregory and the rest of you fellows? Go back—don't waste time getting out and coming over here. Get over the highway fast and get on the nearest telephone. Get the District Attorney's office. We only have a few minutes. I'll follow you in the other car. Tell them I'm holding a guy named John Lombard, self-confessed killer of Mrs. Henderson, to get word to the warden—"

"You haven't got a bit of evidence against me," Lombard growled, wincing with pain.

"No? What more do I need than what you've just given me? I caught you in the very act of murdering in cold blood a girl whom you never even set eyes on until just an hour ago! What could you have possibly had against her, except that her evidence was the one thing that could have still saved Henderson, absolved him of the crime? And why were you determined not to let that happen? Because that would have meant reopening the whole case, and your own immunity would have been endangered. That's my evidence against you!"

A State trooper came thudding up to them. "Need a hand here?"

"Carry the girl over to the car. She's just been through a pretty rocky experience and needs looking after. I'll take care of the guy."

The husky trooper picked her up bodily, cradled her in his arms. "Who is she?" he asked over his shoulder, as he led the way back along the glowing headlight carpet.

"A pretty valuable little person," Burgess answered from the rear, jarring his prisoner along beside him, "so walk gently with her, officer, walk slow. That's Henderson's girl, Carol Richman, you're holding in your arms. The best man of us all."

# TWENTY-THREE

## One Day, After the Execution

They were together in the living-room of Burgess' small flat in Jackson Heights. That was the scene of their first meeting, following

the release. He'd arranged it that way for them. He'd had her there
waiting for Henderson when the latter came down on the train. As
he expressed it to her, "Who wants to meet outside a prison gate?
You two have had enough of that stuff already. Wait for him over
at my place. It may be only instalment-plan furniture, but at least
it's non-penal."

They were sitting close together on the sofa, in soft lamplight,
in a state of profound—if still somewhat dazed—peace. Henderson
had his arm around her, and her head was resting in the notch of
his shoulder.

Something about the two of them gave Burgess a choking feeling
in the throat when he came in and saw them. "How's it coming,
you two?" he asked gruffly, in order not to show it.

"Gee, everything's so *good-looking*, isn't it?" Henderson mar-
velled. "I'd almost forgotten how *good-looking* everything is. Car-
pets on the floor. Soft light coming from a lampshade. A sofa-
cushion behind me. And look, the best-looking thing of all." He
nudged the top of her head with his chin. "It's all mine; I've got
it all back again, and it's good for another forty years yet!"

Burgess and the girl exchanged a side glance of unspoken
compassion.

"I just came here from the District Attorney's office," Burgess
said. "They finally got the full confession out of him down there.
Sealed, signed, and delivered."

"I still can't get over it," Henderson said, shaking his head. "I
still can hardly believe it. What was in back of it? Was he in love
with Marcella? She'd never met him more than twice in her whole
life, as far as I know."

"As far as you know," Burgess said dryly.

"You mean it was one of those things on the side?"

"Didn't you notice she was out a lot?"

"Yes, but I didn't think anything of it. She and I weren't living
on cordial terms any more."

"Well, that was it, right there." He took a turn or two about the
room. "There's one thing I think ought to be made clear to you,
though, Henderson. For what it's worth at this late date. It was
strictly a one-sided affair. Your wife was not in love with Lombard.
If she had been, most likely she would still be alive today. She was
not in love with anyone but herself. She liked admiration and
flattery; she was the type that likes to flirt and string people along,
without meaning it seriously. That's a harmless game with nine
men. And with the tenth it's dangerous. To her he was just someone
to go out with, and a handy way of getting back at you in her own
mind: to show herself that she didn't need you. Unfortunately, he
was the tenth man. He was the wrong type for it altogether. He'd
spent most of his life around oilfields in God-forsaken parts of the

world; and he hadn't had much experience with women. He didn't have any sense of humour about things like that. He took her seriously. And of course she liked that part of it all the better, that made the game more real.

"There's no question about it, she gave him a raw deal. She led him on until the very last, long after she must have seen where it was leading. She let him arrange his whole future around her, knowing darn well she wasn't going to be there to share it with him. She let him sign on for five years with this oil company in South America. Why, he even had the bungalow they were going to live in down there picked out and furnished up for them. The understanding was she was to divorce you as soon as they got there, and marry him. After all, when a guy's that age, and not a kid any more, he takes it hard when you kick his heart around like that.

"Instead of tapering off, breaking it to him by degrees, giving him a sporting chance to get over it, she went about it the worst possible way. She hated to give up her cake any sooner than she had to: his rings on the phone, their luncheon meetings, their dinner-dates, his kisses in a taxi. Her ego needed all that. She got used to it, and she would have missed it. So she put off and put off. *She waited until the very night they were due to sail together to South America*; waited until he called for her at the flat—as soon as you'd gone—to take her to the pier with him.

"I'm not surprised it cost her her life. I would have been surprised if it hadn't. He says he got there even before you left, side-stepped you by waiting on the upper flight of stairs, past your floor until after you'd come storming out. It just so happened there was no hallman on duty that night; the former one had just been drafted, and they hadn't gotten a replacement yet. So no one saw him come in. And as we all very well know, no one saw him leave again either.

"Well, anyway, she let him in, went back to her mirror again, and, when he asked her if she was all packed and ready, laughed at him. That seems to have been her day for laughing at people. She asked him if he'd really seriously believed she was going to bury herself in South America, place herself at his mercy, to marry or not as he saw fit, once her bridges were burned behind her. Above all, free you to go to someone else. She liked the situation the way it was. She wasn't giving up a sure thing for a gamble.

"But more than anything else it was the laughter that did it. If she'd cried when she told him all this, or even if she'd just kept a straight face, he says he thinks he would have let it go at that. Just gone out and drunk himself stone-blind, maybe, but she would still have been alive behind him. And I think so too."

"So he killed her," Henderson said quietly.

"So he killed her. Your discarded necktie was still lying there on the floor behind her, where you'd dropped it. He must have absently picked it up at one point or another just before this, been holding it in his hands without noticing it, when the snap came." He gave an expressive snap of his own fingers.

"I don't blame him altogether," Carol breathed, looking down at the floor.

"I don't either," Burgess admitted. "But that was no excuse for doing what he did next. For deliberately turning on the man who had been his lifelong friend, going out of his way to see that he was framed for it."

"What did I do to him?" Henderson asked, without any trace of rancour.

"What it amounts to is this. He didn't understand then, and he still doesn't today yet, even this long after, what it really was that made her act the way she did. Jilt him so heartlessly. He failed to see that it was in perfect keeping with her own character to do so, that that was the way she was built. He mistakenly thought it must be because of a renewal of her love for you. Therefore he blamed you for it. You were responsible for his losing her. That made him hate you. He wanted to take it out on you. A distorted form of jealousy that was only made more insane by the coveted one's death is about the closest you can get to it."

"Whew!" said Henderson softly.

"He came out of there unseen, and he deliberately set out after you to try and overtake you. That quarrel which he'd overheard from the stairs was too good an opportunity to be passed up. Too good an opportunity of saddling you with what he'd just done. His original idea, he says, was to join you as if by accident, as if he'd just happened to run into you, and stick around with you long enough to give you a chance to convict yourself out of your own mouth. At least implicate yourself seriously. He would have said, 'Hullo, I thought your wife was going to be with you.' And then, quite naturally, you would have answered, 'I had a fierce row with her before I left.' It was necessary for that row to come out. He wanted it to. He couldn't bring it out otherwise without implicating himself as having been within eavesdropping distance out on the stairs. It had to come through *your* telling *him*, in the first person, do you understand?

"He would have seen to it that you got quite tanked—if you still needed any additional encouragement—while he was with you. Then he would have accompanied you back to your own door. So that when you made the grim discovery he'd be there: be on hand to reluctantly repeat to the police what he'd heard you say about having a terrific blow-up with her just before leaving. You would have been acting as a shock-absorber for him. That's a neat little touch there, that idea of accompanying the husband back to where he's just finished murdering the wife. Automatically relegating himself to the position of innocent bystander at someone else's crime. It would have been practically foolproof as a suspicion disinfectant.

"All this he tells quite freely—and I've got to admit quite unremorsefully even yet—in his confession."

"Nice," said Carol sombrely.

"He thought you'd be alone. He already knew two of the places you'd said you'd be. You'd mentioned that afternoon, when you ran into him, that you were taking the missis to the Maison Blanche for dinner, and then afterward to the Casino. The bar he didn't know about, because you didn't yourself until you turned and went in there on the spur of the moment.

"He went straight to the Maison, and he cased it cautiously from the foyer, without showing himself. He saw you in there. You must have just arrived. He saw you were with someone. That changed things around. He not only could not join you now with any hope of profiting from any possible revelation on your part, but this unknown third person might even provide you with a degree of immunity altogether, depending on just how soon you'd met her after leaving your own door. In other words, that early, almost at sight, he sensed her paramount importance in the matter, both from his point of view and your own. And acted accordingly.

"He withdrew, and hovered around outside on the street, far enough away to command the entrance without any danger of being caught sight of himself. He knew your next stop was slated to be the Casino Theatre, but he couldn't be sure, of course. Couldn't afford to take it for granted.

"The two of you came out, taxied over, and he taxied over in your wake. He followed you *into* the theatre. Listen to this, it's an exciting thing. He bought a standing-room ticket, as people often do who have only time to catch one act. He stood up back there at the rear of the orchestra, sheltered by a post, and kept the back of your heads in sight throughout the performance.

"He saw you leave when you did leave. He almost lost you in the crowd when you left, but luck was with him. The little incident of the blind man he missed altogether, for he dared not tread that closely behind you. Your taxi had such a hard time pulling clear of the jam that he was able to keep you in sight from another.

"You led him back to Anselmo's finally, although he still didn't know that that was the pivot of the whole thing. Again he loitered outside, for in the closer quarters of the bar he couldn't have hoped to avoid your spotting him. He saw you leave her there, presently, and could guess by that fact alone, if he hadn't already, that you'd carried out the threat he'd heard you yell back at the apartment: that you'd invite the first stranger you met along in your wife's place.

"He had to decide quickly now whether to keep on after you, and run the risk of losing her in the shuffle, or to switch his attention to her, find out just how much good she could do you, how much harm she could do him.

"He didn't hesitate long. Again his good luck held, and he did the right thing almost by instinct. It was too late to attach himself to you any more with any degree of plausibility. Instead of helping to incriminate you, he'd only be incriminating himself. His ship was being warped out of the pier at that very minute, and he should have been on it by this time.

"So he let you go and he chose her, never dreaming how unterringly right he was, and he bided his time outside, watching her covertly, knowing she could not stay in the bar all night, knowing she would have to have some final destination.

"Presently she emerged, and he drew back out of sight to give her leeway enough. He was shrewd enough not to accost her then and there; he would only be identifying himself to her. In case it turned out she could absolve you, he would only be incriminating himself indelibly for later on by the mere fact of having questioned her on the subject at all, shown any interest in it. So he wisely decided that this was the thing to do: learn her identity and destination first of all, so that he would know where to find her again when he wanted her. That much done, leave her undisturbed for a short while. Then discover, if possible, just how much protection she was able to give you. This by retracing your steps of the evening, seeking to ferret out if possible your original meeting-place, and above all how soon after your leaving the apartment the meeting had taken place. Then thirdly, if the weight she could throw in the matter was enough to count, take care of it by a little judicious erasing. Seek her out wherever it was he had traced her to the first time, and ascertain whether or not he could persuade her to remain silent. And if she proved not amenable, he admits there was already a darker method of erasure lurking in the back of his mind. Immunizing one crime by committing a second.

"So he set out after her. She went on foot, for some inscrutable reason, late as the hour was; but this only made it easier for him to keep her in sight. At first he thought it might be because she lived in the immediate vicinity, a stone's throw away from the bar, but as the distance she covered slowly lengthened he saw that couldn't be it. Presently he wondered if it mightn't be that she had become aware there was someone following her, and was deliberately trying to mislead them, throw them off the track. But even this, he finally decided, couldn't be the case. She showed absolutely no awareness nor alarm about anything; she was sauntering along too aimlessly, almost dawdling, stopping to scan the contents of unlighted showcases whenever she happened upon them, stopping to stroke a stray cat, obviously improvising her route as she went along, but under no outward compulsion whatever. After all, had she been seeking to rid herself of him, it would have been simple enough for her to have hopped into a cab or stepped up to a policeman' and said a word or two. Several of them drifted into sight along the way and she didn't. There was nothing left for him to ascribe her erratic movements to, finally, than that she had no fixed destination, she was wandering at random. She was too well dressed to be homeless, and he was completely at a loss what to make of it.

"She went up Lexington to Fifty-seventh, then she turned west there as far as Fifth. She went north two blocks and sat for some time on one of the benches on the outside of the quadrangle around the statue of General Sherman, just as though it were three in the afternoon. She was finally driven off from there again by the questioning slowing-up of about every third car that passed her on its way in or out of the park. She ambled east again through Fifty-ninth, absorbedly memorizing the contents of the art-shop windows along there, with Lombard slowly going mad behind her.

"Then at last, when he almost began to think she intended going over the Queensborough Bridge on foot into Long Island, she suddenly turned aside into a very grubby little hotel at the far end of Fifty-ninth, and he detected her in the act of signing the register when he peered in after her. Showing that this was as much of an improvisation as all the rest of her meandering had been.

"As soon as she was safely out of sight, he went in there in turn and, as the quickest way of finding out what name she'd given and what room she'd been assigned to, took one for himself. The name immediately above his own, when he'd signed for it, was 'Frances Miller' and she'd gone into 214. He managed to secure the one adjoining, 216, by a deft process of elimination, finding fault with the two or three that were shown him at first until he'd secured the one he had his eye on. The place was in the last stages of deterioration, little better than a lodging-house, so that was excusable enough.

He went up for a short while, chiefly to watch her door from the hallways outside his own and convince himself that she was finally settled for the rest of the night and would be here when he came back. He couldn't have hoped for more proof than he obtained. He could see the light in her room peering out through the opaque transom over the door. He could without any difficulty in that weather-beaten place, hear every move she made, almost guess what she was doing. He could hear the clicking of the wire hangers in the barren closet as she hung her outer clothing up. She had come in without any baggage, of course. He could hear her humming softly to herself as she moved about. He could even detect now and then what it was she was humming. *Chica Chica Boom*, from the show you had taken her to earlier that night. He could hear the trickle of the water as she busied herslef preparing to retire. Finally the light went out behind the transom, and he could even hear the creak of the springs in the decrepit bed as she disposed herself on it. He goes into all this at great and grim length in the final draft of his confession.

"He crossed his own unlighted room, leaned out the window, which overlooked a miserable blind shaft, and scrutinized what he could see of her room from that direction. The shade was down to within a foot of the sill, but her bed was in such a position that by straddling the sill of his own and leaning far out he could see the glint of the cigarette she held suspended over the side of the bed in the darkness in there. There was a drain-pipe running down between their two windows, and the collar-like fastening which held it to the wall offered a foot-rest at one point. He made a note of that. Made note it was possible to get in there in that way, if he should find it necessary, when he came back.

"Sure of her now, he came out of the place again. This was a little before two o'clock in the morning.

"He hurried straight back to Anselmo's in a cab. The place was going into the death-watch now, and there was plenty of opportunity to become confidential with the bar-tender and find out what, if anything, he knew. In due course he let drop some casual remark about her; you know the sort of thing. "Who was that lonely looking number I saw sitting up at the end there all by herself a little whole ago?" or something on that order. Just as an opening wedge.

"They're a talkative race anyway, and that was all the barman needed to go the rest of the way under his own speed. That she'd been in there once before, around six, gone out with someone, he'd brought her back, and then he'd left her.

"An adroit further question or two brought out the point he was mainly interested in. That you had accosted her without any time-lag, immediately upon coming in, and that it had been only a very few minutes past six. In other words, his worst fears were exceeded. She was not only a potential protection to you; she was your absolute, unqualified salvation. It would have to be taken care of. And without delay." He broke off to ask, "Am I boring you by rehashing it at this length?"

"It was my life," Henderson observed dryly.

"He didn't let any grass grow under his feet. He made the first deal then and there, under the very eyes of the few remaining customers still lingering in the place. The barman was the type that bribes easy, anyway, as the saying goes; he was ripe and ready to fall into his hand. A few guarded words, a palming of hands across the bar, and it was done. 'How much would you take to forget you saw that woman meet that fellow in here? You don't need to forget *he* was in here, just forget she was.' The barman allowed he'd take a modest enough sum. 'Even if it turned out to be a police matter?' The barman wasn't quite so sure after he'd heard that. Lombard made up his mind for him with a sum of fifty times larger than he'd expected to get out of it. He gave him a *thousand dollars in cold cash*. He had a considerable wad of it on him, ready at hand, the stake he'd been intending to use to set the two of them up in South America. That cinched it as far as the barman was concerned, of course. Not only that, Lombard cemented it with a few quiet-spoken but blood-chilling threats. And he was evidently a good threatener. Maybe because his threats weren't idle; they were the McCoy, and his listener could sense that.

"That barman stayed fixed from then on, long after he knew all the facts in the case, and nothing we nor anyone else could do could get a word out of him. And it wasn't entirely due to the thousand dollars by any means. He was good and frightened, and so were all the rest of them. You saw the effect it finally had on Cliff Milburn. There was something grim about this Lombard. He was a man with absolutely no sense of humour. He'd stayed too close to nature all his life.

"The barman taken care of, he went on from there, back-tracking over the route you had taken not very many hours before. There's no need of giving you all the details at this late date. The restaurant and the theatre were closed, of course, by that time of night, but he managed to learn the whereabouts of the individuals he was after and seek them out. In one case he even made a quick trip all the way out to Forest Hills and back, to get one of them out of bed. By four o'clock that morning the job was complete; he'd contacted three more of the key figures whose collusion it was necessary for him to have: the taxi-driver Alp, the head-waiter from the Maison Blanche, and the box-office man from the Casino. He gave them varying amounts. The taxi-driver simply to deny having seen her. The head-waiter to give a split to the table-waiter, whose job depended on him after all, and make sure that he stayed in line. The box-office man he fixed so liberally he practically made him an ally. It was through him that Lombard learned one of the house-musicians had been heard shooting his mouth off, bragging what a hit he'd made with this particular woman—as he saw it—and added a suggestion that perhaps he'd better be taken care of too. Lombard wasn't able to get around to that until the second night after the murder, but luckily for him we had overlooked the man entirely, so there was no harm done by the delay.

"Well, now it's an hour before daybreak and his job's done—he's caused her to disappear from view, as far as it's humanly possible.

The only one who remained to be taken care of was she herself. He went back there where he'd left her, to attend to that part of it. And he admits his mind was already made up. He wasn't going to buy her silence; he was going to make sure of it in a more lasting way—by death. Then the rest of his structure wouldn't be in any danger. Any of the others could welsh, but there wouldn't be any proof left.

"He let himself back into the room he'd taken next to hers, and sat there in the dark for a moment or two, thinking it out. He realized that he ran a far greater risk of being detected as the murderer in this case than in the case of your wife, but only as an unknown man who had signed the register downstairs under an assumed name, not as John Lombard. He intended overtaking his ship; he would never be seen around here again, so what chance was there of identifying him later? It would be suspected that 'he' had killed her, but it wouldn't be known who 'he' was. See what I mean?

"He went outside and listened at her door. The room was quiet, she was asleep by now. He tried it very carefully, but, as he'd half-expected, the door was locked, he couldn't get in that way. There remained that drainpipe stepping-stone outside their two windows, which had been in the back of his mind all along, anyhow.

"The shade was still down to within a foot of the sill, as it had been before, when he looked out. He climbed quietly and agilely out the window, rested his foot on the necessary drainpipe support, and was able without very much difficulty to swing himself on to her sill and lower himself into the room under the shade. He didn't take anything with him; he intended using just his bare hands and the bedclothes.

"In the dark he edged his way to the bed, and he poised his arms, and he gripped the tortured mass of of the bedclothes tight to prevent any outcry. They collapsed under him; they were empty. She wasn't there. She'd gone. As erratically as she'd come into this place she'd gone again, in the hour before dawn, after lying in the bed awhile. Two cigarette butts, a few grains of powder on the dressing-stand, and the rumpled bedclothes were all that was left of her.

"When the worst part of the shock had worn off and he went downstairs again and asked about it more or less openly, they told him she'd come down not long before his return, handed in her key, and calmly walked out to the street once more. They didn't know which way she'd gone, nor where she'd gone, nor why she'd gone; only that she'd gone—as strangely as she'd come.

"His own game had boomeranged on him. The woman whom he had spent all night and hundreds of dollars in trying to turn into a ghost as far as you, Henderson, were concerned *had* turned into a ghost—but as far as he himself was concerned now. Which wasn't what he'd wanted at all. It left things too dangerously indefinite. She might pop back into the picture at any moment.

"He went through hell in those few short hours that were all he could spare before he had to plane out, if he was still to overtake his ship. He knew how hopeless it was. He knew, as you and I know, what a place New York is to find someone in on short order.

"He hunted for her high and low, with the remorselessness of a maniac, and he couldn't find her again. The day went, and the second night went, and his time was up, he couldn't stay behind any longer. So he had to let it go under the heading of unfinished business. An axe hanging over him from then on, threatening to fall at any moment.

"He planed out of New York the second day after the murder, made the short over-water hop from Miami to Havana that same day, and was just in time to board his own ship when it touched there on the third day out. His excuse to the shipboard officials was that he'd got drunk the night of sailing and missed it.

"That was why he was so ripe for that come-on message I sent in your name; that was all he needed to drop everything and come back. He'd been panicky all along, and that gave him the finishing touch. They talk about murderers being drawn back to the scene of their crime. This pulled him back like a magnet. Your asking for help gave him just the excuse he needed. He could come back openly now and help you 'look' for her. Finish the death-hunt he hadn't had time to complete the first time. Make sure that if she was ever found, she'd be found dead.''

"Then you already suspected him when you came to my cell that day and drafted that cable in my name. When did you first begin to suspect him?"

"I can't put my finger on it and give you the exact day or hour. It was a very gradual thing, that came on in the wake of my change of mind about your own guilt. There was no conclusive evidence against him from first to last; that's why I had to go at it in the roundabout way I did. He left no finger-prints at the apartment; must have wiped the few surfaces he touched off clean. I remember we found several door-knobs without any marks on them at all.

"To start off with he was just a name you'd dropped in the course of being questioned yourself. An old-time friend, whose invitation to join him in a farewell tour of the town you'd conscientiously passed up, much to your regret, on *her* account. I had a routine inquiry made for him, more to have him help us fill in a little of your background for our record than anything else. I learned he'd sailed, as you'd mentioned he intended to. But I also found out, quite unintentionally, from the steamship line that he'd missed the sailing here and caught up with his ship at Havana three days later. And one other thing. That he'd originally booked passage for two, himself and a wife, but that when he'd overtaken the ship he was alone, and had finished out the rest of the trip unaccompanied. Incidentally, there was no record of his ever having been married or having had a wife up here, when I checked a little further.

"Now, there was not necessarily anything glaringly suspicious in all that, you understand. People do miss ships, especially when they celebrate too copiously just before sailing-time. And people's brides-to-be do change their minds at the last minute, back out, or the contemplated marriage is postponed by mutual consent.

"So I didn't think any more about it. And yet on the other hand I did. That little detail of his missing the ship and then overtaking it alone lodged in the back of my mind and stayed with me from then on. He had, a little bit unluckily for himself, managed to attract my attention. Which seldom turns out to be beneficial, with cops. Then later, when my belief in your own guilt began to evaporate, there was a vacuum left behind. And a vacuum is something that has to be filled, or it will fill by itself. These facts about him began to trickle out, and before I knew it the empty space had begun to fill up again."

"You sure kept me in the dark," Henderson admitted.

"I had to. There wasn't anything definite enough until just recently. In fact, until that night he drove Miss Richman into the woods with him. Confiding in you would have been a bad risk. Most likely you wouldn't have shared my feelings about him, and for all I knew might have warned him off in some burst of misguided loyalty. Or even if you had strung along with me, had shared my belief, knowledge of what was up might have made you a poor actor. He might have detected something in your manner toward him, and our hands would have been tipped. You were under a terrific strain, you know. I felt the safest thing to do was to work *through* you, using you as a sort of unconscious medium, without letting you realize the purpose of what you were doing yourself. And it wasn't easy. Take that stunt with the theatre programmes, for instance—"

"I thought you were crazy—or I would have if I was normal myself—the way you rehearsed me and rehearsed me and rehearsed me, every little act, every little word, that was to lead up to it. You know what I thought you were doing it for? As a pain-killer, to keep my mind off the approaching dead-line. So I fell in with it, and did as you told me, but with my tongue in my cheek."

"Your tongue in your cheek, and my heart in my mouth," Burgess chuckled grimly.

"Did he have anything to do with those peculiar accidents that kept dogging you all along the way, as far as you were able to find out?''

"Everything. The strange part of that is, the one that seemed most like a murder, the Cliff Milburn affair, proved to be a *bona-fide* suicide when we got through investigating it; and, of course, the barman was killed accidentally. But the two that seemed most like accidents turned out to be murders. Murders that he committed. I'm speaking of the deaths of the blind man and Pierrette Douglas. Both were murders without weapons, in the usual sense. The death of the blind man was a particularly horrible piece of business.

"He left him there in the room for a moment or two, ostensibly to chase down to the street and call me. He knew the man had an aversion to the police, typical of his kind of fraudulent panhandling. He knew the first thing he'd do would be to try to escape from there. He counted on his doing that. As soon as he was on the other side of the door he attached a strong black thread, the kind tailors use, across the top step, at about ankle height. Knotted it around the banister leg on one side, a projecting nail-head on the other. Then he turned out the light, knowing now the blind man had the use of his eyes, made a receding drum-beat of his foot-steps—you know that old stunt—and crouched there waiting on the lower flight, just out of sight below the landing.

"The blind man came out fast and incautiously, in a hurry to put himself out of reach before Lombard returned with his police friend, and the thing worked just as he'd intended it to. The thread caught him short and sent him toppling down the whole flight and into the foreshortened landing-wall head first. The thread had snapped, of course, but that didn't save him. The fall didn't kill him; he simply got a nasty crack on the skull and lay there stunned. And so Lombard hurriedly came back up to the landing again, stepped over him, went on to the head of the stairs, removed the tell-tale ends of loose thread from both sides.

"Then he went back to the senseless man, explored with his hands, found he was still breathing. His head was forced back at an unnatural angle by the wall against which it rested, and there was a strain on his neck. It was like a suspension-bridge, you understand, between his shoulders flat on the floor and his head semi-upright against the wall. He located the position of the neck, and then he straightened up, raised one leg so that his heavy shoe was poised just over it, and—"

Carol turned her head sharply aside.

"I'm sorry," Burgess murmured.

She turned back again. "It's part of the story. We should know it."

"Then and only then he went out and called me. And when he

came back he stayed down at the street door, and was careful to engage the cop on the beat in conversation the whole time he was waiting for me, to establish that he'd remained down there in full sight, if it became necessary."

"Did you get what it was right away?" Henderson asked.

"I examined the body down at the Morgue later that night, after I'd sent him home, and I saw the little red nick across each shin the thread had made. I saw the traces of dust on the back of his neck too. I figured what it was then. It was just a matter of building it up from those two points. It would have been hard to get him on it, though. It might have been done. I preferred to wait and get him for the main thing. I couldn't have got him for the main thing on the strength of that blind man incident, that was a cinch. And I didn't want to grab him prematurely only to see him get away again. Once I had him I wanted to hang on to him. So I kept my mouth closed and went on paying out rope."

"And the thing about that reefer-smoker you say he had nothing to do with?"

"In spite of the discrepancy of razors, that was only what it seemed. Cliff Milburn slashed his own throat in a fit of drug-induced depression and fear. The safety blade must have been a discard berthed under the shelf-paper either by a former tenant or by some friend of his who came in and used his bathroom to shave in. A behaviourist would be interested. Even when it came to suicide, he instinctively avoided using his own implement for anything other than what it was intended for. That's a trait common to all of us; that's why we get so sore when our wives sharpen pencils with them."

Carol murmured softly, "I'll never be able to go near one again, after that night.

"But the death of Mrs. Douglas was his doing?" Henderson questioned interestedly.

"That was even more adroit than the other one. A long strip of runner of carpeting ran across the highly polished floor-surface in her place, from the foyer stepdown at one end to directly under the French windows at the other. What first put the idea into his head was that he skidded, slightly himself on the quite dangerous flooring a little earlier in the proceedings, and she had laughed at him. Eye measurement did the rest, while he was talking to her. The straight line-sweep of the rug, of course, was almost an invitation. He marked an invisible X on it to show where she must stand in order to have the greater part of her length go outside the window when she was overbalanced, and carefully retained its exact location in his mind from then on. Which is not the easy feat it sounds when you are engaged in moving about yourself and talking with someone, and can only give it part of your attention.

"This isn't hypothetical reconstruction on my part. I have all this from him at first hand, in black and white. From that point on there was a sort of minuet of death danced by the two of them, during which he delicately manœuvred her into just the right position. When he had completed writing out the cheque, he stood up with it and returned toward the window, as if to have the fresh air hasten its drying. Then he shifted until he was precisely to one side of the position he wanted her to take, but off the rug. Then he drew her on from where she had remained by seeming to offer her the cheque. Passively extending it toward her, but without moving his own feet, so that she had to come forward for it. It's the same principle they use in bull-fighting. The bull follows the cape away from the fighter's body. She followed the cheque up to one side of his body. When she had fallen into the exact spot he wanted her to, he relaxed his fingers and let the cheque pass to her.

"Her attention was taken up in scanning it for a moment or two; she stood motionless. He quickly moved away from her, strode the whole length of the room, as if taking an abrupt departure then and there. Then when he'd reached the far end of it and was on the step clear of it, he turned to look back at her and called 'Good-bye!' That brought her head up from the cheque, that caused her to turn toward him—and at the same time present her full back to the window. She was now in the exact position it was necessary for her to be. For if she'd gone out frontwards or sidewards she might have been able to cling to the window-frame and arrest herself. Backwards it was an impossibility; the human armsocket doesn't work that way.

"He dipped down, flung up the rug at full arm's length overhead, let it drop again; that was all he had to do. She went out like a puff of wind. She didn't even have time to scream, he says. He must have caught her on the out-breath. She was already gone by the time her flown-off shoe ticked back again to the floor."

Carol crinkled up the corners of her eyes. "Those things are worse than the ones with knife and gun; there's so much more treachery involved in them!"

"Yes, but much harder to prove to a jury. He didn't lay a hand on her, he killed her from twenty or twenty-two feet away. The clue was still in the rug itself, of course. I saw it the minute I got in there. The ripples were at his end. Where she had stood it was smooth, only just shifted further back along the floor. If it had been an honest skid or mis-step, it would have been the other way around. The pleats would have been at her end, where her feet kicked the rug back on itself. His end would have been flat and undisturbed; the agitation couldn't possibly have transferred itself that far over.

"There was a cigarette left burning there, as if by her. That was to make it seem that the fall had occurred just previous to our arrival, whereas he had telephoned me some fifteen minutes before. Or if I wanted to disregard that, he had been continuously in my company for fully eight to ten minutes before, counting from the time I met him in front of the fire-station.

"It didn't fool me for a moment, but the mechanics of how he'd done it gave me three full days' work before I could figure it out satisfactorily. The ash-stand had an orifice in its centre through which ashes were meant to drop, all the way down through the long stem into the hollow base which was meant for that purpose. There was supposed to be a trap, but he jammed that so it would stay open. He simply took three ordinary-size cigarettes, removed a little tobacco from the mouth end of the two foremost ones, and telescoped them together to form one triple the usual length, but retaining the trade-mark of a small-size cigarette at the far end, in case there should be enough left to investigate. Then he lit it, left it spearing the top of the stand in a long inclined plane, one end down into the open stem and resting against it. A cigarette left burning like that in a slanted position, and over an opening, will seldom go out, even when it's not fanned by the breath as in smoking. The slow ember simply worked its way back from cigarette to cigarette without a break. As the first two were consumed they dropped off down the stem without leaving a trace. The third, which was resting wholly on the tilted perimeter of the smoke-stand, remained in place to the end, forming just what he wanted it to, a perfect one-cigarette butt by the time we got there.

"This alibi, however, handicapped him in another way. It would have been better if he'd skipped it. It limited how far away he could go on the fool's errand she was supposed to have sent him; he had to be sure of getting back soon enough for it to be of any use to him. He had to pick some place in the immediate vicinity, and he had to pick some place that would at sight be identifiable as a complex hoax, so there would be no excuse for the two of us to linger around investigating or asking questions. Hence the fire-house gag. One look was enough, and we beat it back again to her place.

"In other words, by tying himself down with that cigarette alibi, he weakened the plausibility of his story in another respect. Why would she do a thing like that, send him just a stone's throw away and to a glaringly fake address? She would have either given him the real address, refused to give him any address at all, or—if she intended fleecing him out of the cheque—given him a fake address and name that would have taken him all the rest of the night and the better part of the next day to run down, thus giving herself a comfortable head start. Well, he preferred to cauterize the murder angle a little even at the expense of shooting the credibility of her behaviour to hell. After all, there was the precedent of the blind man by this time, and I guess he was afraid to have the pitcher go to the well once too often.

"Apart from that one bad flaw, he did a fairly competent job. Let the elevator boy overhear him talking to an empty room, even gave the door a delayed-action swing behind him, so that she seemed to be closing it after he'd already left it.

"I suppose I could have pinned him down with it." Then he concluded: "But that still wouldn't have meant getting him for the killing of your wife, necessarily. So I played dumb again. It was just a matter of getting him to repeat himself—but on someone that we sicked on to him, and held the strings to, instead of on someone that he'd picked for himself without our full knowledge."

"Was that your idea, to use Carol like that?" Henderson queried. "It's a good thing I didn't know about it ahead of time. If I had you wouldn't have gotten me to—"

"That was her idea, not mine. I'd arranged to hire some outside girl to play the part of decoy. She muscled in on it. She came storming in to where we were posted, watching him in the magazine shop that last night just before the deadline, and told me flatly she was going to be the one to go in there and tackle him, or else! She said she was going ahead whether she had my okay or whether she didn't. Hell, I couldn't stop her, and I couldn't afford to have two of them walking in there one behind the other, so I had to let her have her way. We called in a make-up expert from one of the theatres and had him give her a good going over, and we sent her on in."

"Imagine," she said rebelliously to the room at large. "I should sit back on my hands and take a chance on some two-dollar extra gumming the whole thing up with her hamminess! There was no more time left by then to go wrong any more; we'd used it all up."

"Never did show up, did she?" Henderson mused. "I mean the real one. Strangest thing. Whoever she is, wherever she is, she sure played out her little game of hide-and-seek to the end."

"She wasn't trying to, she wasn't even playing one," Burgess said. "That's what's stranger about it still."

Henderson and the girl both jolted slightly, leaned forward alertly. "How do you know? You mean you finally got wind of her? You've found out who she is?"

"Yes, I got wind of her," Burgess said simply. "Quite some time ago. I've know it for weeks, months now—who she was."

"Was?" breathed Henderson. "Is she dead?"

"Not in the way you mean. But she's as good as, for all practical purposes. Her body's still alive. She's in an asylum for the hopelessly insane."

He reached slowly into his pocket, began to sift through envelopes and papers, while the two of them stared, transfixed.

"I've been up there myself, not once but several times. I've talked to her. You can hardly tell it in her manner. Just a little vague, dreamy. But she can't remember yesterday; the past is blurred, all fogged out. She would have been no good to us, no good at all; she couldn't have testified. That's why I had to keep it to myself, play the thing out the way we did. It was our only chance, to get him to convict himself out of his own mouth, by substituting someone for her."

"How long—?"

"She was committed within three weeks after that night with you. It had been intermittent up to then, then the curtain dropped for good."

"How did you—?"

"In a roundabout way that doesn't really matter now any more. The hat showed up by itself in one of these bundle shops. You know, thrift shops where they sell things for a few cents. One of my men spotted it. We traced it back link by link, just as he did later, working in the opposite direction. Some old hag had picked it up out of an ash-can, peddled it to the thrift shop. We canvassed all the houses in the vicinity, after she'd pointed out the general site of the ash-can to us. It took weeks. Finally we found a maid who had thrown it out. Her employer had been committed to an asylum not long before. I questioned her husband, the members of her family. Nobody knew of the exact incident with you but herself, but they told me enough to show it was she all right. She'd been behaving erratically like that for some time past, staying out alone all night, going to hotels by herself. Once they found her sitting on a park bench at daybreak.

"I got this from them."

He handed Henderson a snapshot. A snapshot of a woman.

Henderson looked at it long and hard. He nodded finally, but more to himself than to them. "Yes," he said softly, "yes—I guess so."

Carol took it away from him suddenly. "Don't look at her any more. She's done enough to you for one lifetime. Stay as you are, keep her unremembered. Here, here's your snapshot back."

"It helped, of course," Burgess said, putting it away again, "when we were getting Carol ready that night, to go in and pinch-hit for her. The make-up man was able to give her a superficial resemblance to this person. Enough to fool him, anyway. He'd only seen her at a distance and in uncertain light that night."

"What was her name?" Henderson asked.

Carol made a quick pass with her hand. "No, don't tell him. I don't want her with us. We're starting out new—no ghosts."

"She's right," Burgess said. "It's over. Bury it."

Even so, they fell silent for a few moments, the three of them, thinking about her, as they would probably continue to think about her, every so often, for the rest of their lives. It was one of those things that stays with you.

At the door when they were leaving, Carol's arm linked to his, Henderson turned back to Burgess for a minute, his forehead querulously creased. "But there should be some lesson in the whole thing, some *reason*. You mean she and I went through all we did— for nothing? There must be some moral in it somewhere?"

Burgess gave him an encouraging slap on the back to speed him on his way. "If you've got to have a moral, I give you this: don't ever take strangers to the theatre unless you've got a good memory for faces."

# STUDENTS OF DISASTER

## Michael Z. Lewin

## I

The separation of a man from his wife takes a long time. Slowly too comes the ability to find the words that truly sum up the grounds for the gap growing between them.

Tim Bluffton was married for twelve years before he faced the body of mood which meant that he and Barbara had drifted apart. The crystallizing seed had to do with the summer vacation which each year the Blufftons spent at home. Tim would build and mend things around the house, while Barbara read about crimes and disasters.

But as their thirteenth summer approached, Tim found that he felt like a change. He wanted to get out and do something, like go camping. Before they were too old. Pack the bags and see the country.

Barbara took a deep breath and drew the line. Cart her books around in a suitcase? Read by flashlight? No way.

So Tim spent the vacation replacing the gutters while Barbara read volumes one and two of *One Thousand True Crimes*.

At the top of his ladder, outside the guest room he'd built on top of the garage, Tim was first struck by the burst of cold, bright perception. "I am a participator," he thought, "and Barbara is a spectator."

Simple words, but they covered the countless situations in which Tim and Barbara crossed swords, and recently with less and less ceremony.

When he finished the gutter brackets, Tim went inside and took the book from Barbara's hands. "There's no point in moaning and fighting for the rest of our lives," he said. "We only live once and we're still young enough to do something about us."

"Good idea," Barbara said acidly, as she grabbed at her tome. "If you hate living with me so much, then leave. Larry Hartford left Mary last spring and Mary says that it's like having two hundred pounds off her chest."

But there was the rub.

Tim didn't want to leave. It wasn't Barbara he would miss, but the house he'd worked so hard in for twelve years. He had created an intricate, personal castle hardly recognizable as the assembly line shell they'd started with. The idea of leaving his house to Barbara, letting it rust and rot and rupture while she sat reading thrillers.... Tim could contemplate almost anything but that.

"Look," he said, "our fights can't be fun for you either. Why don't we admit we have problems, and look for help. How about a marriage counsellor? At least we would be trying to make things better instead of just sitting around and watching life get worse."

"You go, if you've got so many problems," Barbara said. And to be fair, she was studying the details of the Atlanta child murder, a far more compelling situation of grief and tragedy than anything she should relate to Tim Bluffton.

# II

"Marriage," said Mr. Mauzy, "is a two-way street. Give and take. Share and share alike. To get from marriage, you have to give. Now tell me about your wife. Tell me about yourself. What does she like? What do you like? What did you like about each other when first you plighted your troth?"

The fact the counsellor was a man comforted Tim at first. But then he felt naked, alone before this peer. He had made the appointment, invited Barbara to come with him. Then begged her.

But she stayed at home, curled up with a new book on the Kennedy assassinations.

"It seems so long ago," Tim said dimly.

"Try!" said Mr. Mauzy, and as he strained to comply Tim brought the young Barbara back to mind and mouth, gave an architect's drawing of the marriage as he saw it.

"So she reads a lot," Mr. Mauzy said carefully. "What kind of books does she read?"

"About crimes mostly."

"Thrillers. I see."

"Not just fiction. She studies real crimes too. And disasters. She'll spend hours reading about disasters and listening to news reports. You can't tear her away when there's something big, like Three Mile Island."

"A compelling interest," Mr Mauzy said. "Rather like yours in repairing, maintaining and expanding your house."

"Well," Tim said, "if you put it like that...."

"You see, you share an approach to things. It's just the subject of your respective interests that has diverged. Do you ever read thrillers, Mr Bluffton?"

"No. Never."

"A lot of people, your wife included, get pleasure and satisfation from them."

"I suppose so."

Mr Mauzy sat back in his chair. "You've come to me because you want to find some way to cope, to help you feel better about

continuing in marriage with your wife. Why not make a real effort
to participate in your wife's interest? It may be hard going at first,
but I think that if you stick at it you will find that you will come to
enjoy life more yourself and that gradually your wife will respond
more to your interests. Do you see what I mean?''

"I do," Tim said, a look of resolution on his face as the full
significance of the suggestion first burst upon him.


# III


When Tim got home Barbara looked up from her book and
asked, "How was your marriage doctor? Did he tell you you were
sick?"

Tim hung his coat up in silence and then came into the living
room. He gently pulled Barbara's feet off the couch and onto the
floor. He sat next to her and took one of her hands in his. "The
counsellor made me realize that I must try to be more interested in
your life and interests." Tim said.

"He what?"

"After all, we're still young. We have a lot of time ahead of us
to spend together."

From the evening of Tim's return from the marriage counsellor
the pattern of life at the Blufftons changed.It was not that Barbara,
when not gossiping with her friends, had stopped reading her books
on Dr. Crippin and the Air Florida crash in Washington D.C. Nor
that Tim was any different with his friends at work.

But at home Tim too now read. Working slowly into the books
Barbara finished, forcing himself to read and, gradually, to find an
interest.

"That terrible Jones man in Guyana," Tim would say now and
Barbara couldn't fault him. She harbored suspicions, but the first

few times she dismissed Tim as not being genuinely interested, he exposed her by offering a tidbit of information or interpretation which had slipped through her own fine net. He made obvious mistakes at first too, and she couldn't resist correcting them, thereby involving herself in his participation in her interest.

"He's a different man," Barbara said to Mary Hartford when she ran into her at the drugstore one day. "All of a sudden he's showing a real interest in life instead of spending all his waking hours fiddling with wood and mixing cement."

"I've got a lot of things that need fixing since Larry left," Mary said wistfully. "If he's run out around your house...."

"I don't imagine for a moment that it will last," Barbara said. "But it is nice to have someone around the house to talk to for a change."


# IV


The crunch came two months later when a chemical plant exploded in the northern part of the state. The news came through late in the afternoon and Barbara, feeling girlish again, could hardly wait until Tim got home.

"Have you heard --" she began. But she could tell by his eyes that he had.

"Isn't it awful!" he exulted. "Do you know yet how many injuries there have been?"

"No, but they're afraid of another explosion. "Then she looked at him. "Tim, what's wrong?"

"I was just wondering..." he said shyly.

"What?" He acted just as he used to when, in the old days, he was going to make some damn fool suggestion like horseback riding or learning how to play badminton. Oh God! she thought. And things had been going so nicely. I knew it wouldn't last for ever.

"Never mind," he said. It had been a long time since he suggested they do anything, and you'd think she would have given him a little credit. But perhaps too early to harvest anything from what he had sown.

Maybe I'm wrong, she thought. "Go on Tim. What were you going to say?"

"Just that I wondered whether you might want to drive up to the site, look at what is happening. If we left now we could be there by ten. See it while it was still burning or at least glowing. We could stay in a motel...."

"But --" she began, torn. And stopped.

There it was. Crunch. Make or break.

It made.

Actually to see a big disaster herself, while it was happening!

"What about work?" she asked.

"I can fix that," he said.

And he did. They went upstate and spent two whole days watching the disaster recovery operation.

"Oh Tim," Barbara said, as they left for home. "That was wonderful. You get so much more than ever you can on television. It's so much bigger being there yourself. It really makes you feel your humanity, your mortality."

For Barbara it seemed like the dawn of a new era.

## V

"So I said to him," Barbara told her neighbor, Flora Tipton, over coffee one morning, "If I'd known you were interested I would have just adored to go to Detroit and see where the riots were.' And he said, 'Let's go now, see where it happened, 'and I said, `Why not?' so we're going up this weekend. We've decided not to take any vacation as such in the summer but to save up the days in case we need them. You know, depending on what comes up."

"You're so lucky," said Flora Tipton feelingly. "Tim is such a wonderful husband to you. I can't get my Norris to do anything, not anything at all. He just sits around and looks at the tube. It drives me crazy."

"Well," Barbara began, and hesitated because she'd never put the thought into words before. "In a good marriage, you have to share interests. Have you tried going to a marriage counsellor?"

"Good heavens, no!" Flora Tipton said.

"You should try it. It did wonders for us."

"Did...was the counsellor...I mean did he ask embarrassing questions?"

"Well," Barbara said, "I didn't actually go myself, but Tim went. Just the once. And it's been wonderful ever since."

"That puts it out of the question for us," said Flora sadly. "Norris wouldn't go anywhere. He'd be too afraid of missing 'The A Team' or a 'Mash' rerun."

Barbara smiled contentedly.

## VI

The contentment continued unabated. Indeed, grew, through visits to a train derailment, two Interstate pile-ups, three local fires, a large pig farm devastated by swine vesicular disease, a flood, a pop festival, and two murder homes.

It was a full and busy life, rich with giggles and tears and frissons.

After a few months the Blufftons decided to join a common interest society, The League of Students of Human and Natural Disaster. Through the League they received newsletters and material prepared on special subjects, particularly foreign catastrophes. They went to League lectures. The first was on the bombing patterns in Northern Ireland. And they also spent a congenial weekend with a party of League members following the Strangler Trail in Boston.

In all the period of contentment covered thirteen calendar months. But one morning, while Barbara was studying her Poisoner's Map of The Middle West, she heard the car screech to a halt in the driveway. She stood up quickly, felt the urgency. And she was right. Tim rushed in the door. "Get your bag," he said. "Emergency. Plane crash in West Virginia."

She could tell by the way he spoke that it was a big one. "God!" Barbara said, "How awful!" and she ran to pick up the ready-packed overnight case she kept at the bottom of her closet.

Tim explained what he knew as they drove. "A 747, only a little way out of Cleveland when it just blew up. There were 187 people on board, including lots of women and children. It was in the mountains just north of Wheeling. I picked up a map on the way home, but you know about these things. The bodies could be scattered for miles."

"Ooo, how terrible," Barbara said. She turned on the radio and settled herself in for the drive.

# VII

They got to the base camp of the Emergency Operations Center about two hours before sunset and sensed immediately the familiar chaos common to major disaster scenes. Ambulances and official vehicles prowled restlessly as if unable to choose which positive thing to do.

"What are the chances of there being survivors?" Barbara asked an official as he walked from one tent to another.

An experienced man, he thought she was a reporter. It was an aura Barbara cultivated carefully. She had considered writing about her techniques for the League newsletter. But there never seemed to be time.

"From what we know so far, I wouldn't want to raise anybody's hopes," the official told her.

"Have you found any bodies yet?" Tim asked.

"No. But we're only just getting ourselves organized," the official said. Then he turned to them. "Off the record, they are going to be scattered all over the damn place. It's going to take us weeks to gather them up."

"Where do you expect to find the bulk of the wreckage?" Tim asked and he produced his map and a pen.

The official paused. The last thing he wanted was the critical area to be located in the press. It would mean the mountain roads would be clogged by gawkers. But he felt obliged to cooperate, so he marked the spot on Tim's map where he knew the wreck to be. "Please don't publish it," he said. A compromise.

"We won't," Barbara promised eagerly.

It was Tim's idea that they spend the remaining daylight looking for bodies themselves. "It seems the least we can do," he said. "To try to help.''

"Since we're here,'' Barbara said nodding.

# VIII

They got near the area designated by the official within half an hour and at a convenient place they pulled off the road to think out what they wanted to do.

As they looked at the map, an emergency vehicle passed them and Barbara said, "Let's go see what he's found.''

But Tim spotted a service road cut through the trees ahead of them to the right. "The light won't last forever,'' he said. "If we go up that track and have a look round ourselves now, we can go on up to the wreckage site later on. They are bound to have it well lit.''

It seemed reasonable and they turned off the main road.

A few hundred yards along, Tim stopped the car and they got out.

"We'll spend twenty or thirty minutes. If we don't come up with anything, we'll go back.''

"All right,'' Barbara said. But she was rather uneasy. Woods were full of things and she hated the idea of them. It was one reason she would never give a moment's thought to camping. Yet...if there were people out there, who had landed in something soft, who were still alive...

Together the Blufftons walked into the woods.

After a few minutes Tim said, "I think I see something.''

"Where?'' Barbara asked, her heart racing.

"Over in that hollow. Come on.''

Tim went ahead, and as Barbara arrived he faced her, looking disappointed. "It was only this branch," he said. It was a short thick piece of wood, dead but not rotten.

"Oh," she said, clearly disappointed.

"Look," Tim said, "shall we go back? Would you rather we did that?"

"Yes please," Barbara said.

"All right."

Barbara turned to lead the way back to the comfort and security of their car.

# IX

As she did so, Tim felled her from behind with the branch.
Tim spent an hour stripping identifying articles from the body and making it look as if it had fallen from the sky.

As he gathered wedding ring, watch and purse, he felt satisfied. The way he always felt after finishing a job well done.

He returned to the car and drove home. It was a long drive and in the dark, but he didn't feel tired. He was happy and fully awake and on a long deserted stretch of Interstate he pulled onto the shoulder and threw the ring and watch into the long grass, and dumped his crash map. It was the first of many exultant disposings.

Or rather, the second.

He slept when he got home and shortly after waking he went to the police station and reported his wife's absence.

"We went on a trip yesterday and got back in the early hours. But when I woke up this morning, she was gone!"

When Barbara didn't return after several days, there was some local interest. It was an unexpected happening with upsetting overtones, the kind of thing people are interested in.

"They were so happy," Flora Tipton said to Mary Hartford. "At least for this past year or so."

"Yes," Mary said thoughtfully. "Barbara did get happy all of a sudden. But now, now that this has happened, I begin to wonder if she could have... you know...found someone."

"You mean a man!" Flora asked, astonished at the thought. "I never thought of that. You don't really think... Oh, but it makes sense. The little minx. And to think she suggested that I send my Norris off to a marriage counsellor. And all that time...!"

"Oh, the poor man," Mary said. "And now he's all alone. And him so good with his hands. I wonder whether he's eating enough. You know, I have some left-over goulash I could take round to him."

"Oh, you are kind," said Flora, whose mind wasn't really up to certain kinds of deviousness.

For his part, Tim's mind was freed from complications. Eyes forward. Life to come. There were more than a year's neglected repairs to get on with, for a start. Quite apart from the complete and precise expunging of everything around the house that had anything to do with his Barbara. The late and unlamented.

# Murder In Blue

Coleman said: "Eight ball in the corner."

There was soft click of ball against ball and then sharper click as the black ball dropped into the pocket Coleman had called.

Coleman put his cue in the rack. He rolled down the sleeves of his vividly striped silk shirt and put on his coat and a pearl gray velour hat. He went to the pale fat man who slouched against a neighboring table and took two crisp hundred dollar notes from the fat man's outstretched hand, glanced at the slim, pimpled youth who had been his opponent, smiled thinly, said: "So long," went to the door, out into the street.

There was sudden roar from a black, curtained roadster on the other side of the street; the sudden ragged roar of four or five shots close together, a white pulsing finger of flame in the dusk, and Coleman sank to his knees. He swayed backwards once, fell forward onto his face hard; his gray hat rolled slowly across the sidewalk. The roadster was moving, had disappeared before Coleman was entirely still. It became very quiet in the street.

Mazie Decker curved her orange mouth to its best "Customer" smile. She took the little green ticket that the dark-haired boy held out to her and tore off one corner and dropped the rest into the slot. He took her tightly in his arms and as the violins melted to sound and the lights dimmed they swung out across the crowded floor.

Her head was tilted back, her bright mouth near the blue smoothness of his jaw.

She whispered: "Gee—I didn't think you was coming."

He twisted his head down a little, smiled at her.

She spoke again without looking at him: "I waited till one o'clock for you last night." She hesitated a moment then

411

went on rapidly: "Gee—I act like I'd known you for years, an' it's only two days. What a sap I turned out to be!" She giggled mirthlessly.

He didn't answer.

The music swelled to brassy crescendo, stopped. They stood with a hundred other couples and applauded mechanically.

She said: "Gee—I love a waltz! Don't you?"

He nodded briefly and as the orchestra bellowed to a moaning foxtrot he took her again in his arms and they circled towards the far end of the floor.

"Let's get out of here, kid." He smiled do a thin line against the whiteness of his skin, his large eyes half closed.

She said: "All right—only let's try to get out without the manager seeing me. I'm supposed to work till eleven."

They parted at one of the little turnstiles; he got his hat and coat from the check-room, went downstairs and got his car from a parking station across the street.

When she came down he had double-parked near the entrance. He honked his horn and held the door open for her as she trotted breathlessly out and climbed in beside him. Her eyes were very bright and she laughed a little hysterically.

"The manager saw me," she said. "But I said I was sick—an' it worked." She snuggled up close to him as he swung the car into Sixth Street. "Gee—what a swell car!"

He grunted affirmatively and they went out Sixth a block or so in silence.

As they turned north on Figueroa she said: "What've you got the side curtains on for? It's such a beautiful night."

He offered her a cigarette and lighted one for himself and leaned back comfortably in the seat.

He said: "I think it's going to rain."

It was Very dark at the side of the road. A great pepper tree screened the roadster from whatever light there was in the sky.

Mazie Decker spoke softly: "Angelo. Angelo—that's a beautiful name. It sounds like angel."

The dark youth's face was hard in the narrow glow of the dashlight. He had taken off his hat and his shiny black hair looked like a metal skullcap. He stroked the heel of his

412

hand back over one ear, over the oily blackness and then he took his hand down and wriggled it under his coat. His other arm was around the girl.

He took his hand out of the darkness of his coat and there was brief flash of bright metal; the girl said: "My God!" slowly and put her hands up to her breast. . . .

He leaned in front of her and pressed the door open and as her body sank into itself he pushed her gently and her body slanted, toppled through the door, fell softly on the leaves beside the road. Her sharp breath and a far quavering "Ah!" were blotted out as he pressed the starter and the motor roared; he swung the door closed and put on his hat carefully, shifted gears and let the dutch in slowly.

As he came out of the darkness of the dirt road on to tie highway he thrust one hand through a slit in the side-curtain, took it in and leaned forward over the wheel.

It was raining, a little.

R F Winfield stretched one long leg out and planted his foot on a nearby leather chair. The blonde woman got up and walked unsteadily to the phonograph. This latter looked like a grandfather clock, had cost well into four figures, would probably have collapsed at the appellation "phonograph"—but it was.

The blonde woman snapped the little tin brake; she lifted the record, stared empty-eyed at the other side.

She said: " 's Minnie th' Moocher. Wanna hear it?"

Mr Winfield said: "Uh-huh." He tilted an ice and amber filled glass to his mouth, drained it. He stood up and gathered his very blue dressing-gown about his lean shanks. He lifted his head and walked through a short corridor to the bathroom, opened the door, entered.

Water splashed noisily in the big blue porcelain tub. He braced himself with one hand on the shower-tap, turned off the water, slipped out of the dressing-gown and into the tub.

The blonde woman's voice clanged like cold metal through the partially open door.

"Took 'er down to Chinatown; showed 'er how to kick the gong aroun'."

Mr Winfield reached up into the pocket of the

413

dressing-gown, fished out a cigarette, matches. He lighted the cigarette, leaned back in the water, sighed. His face was a long tan oblong of contentment. He flexed his jaw, then mechanically put up one hand and removed an upper plate, put the little semi-circle of shining teeth on the basin beside the tub, ran his tongue over thick, sharply etched lips, sighed again. The warm water was soft, caressing; he was very comfortable.

He heard the buzzer and he heard the blonde woman stagger along the corridor past the bathroom to the outer door of the apartment. He listened but could hear no word of anything said there; only the sound of the door opening and closing, and silence broken faintly by the phonograph's "Hi-de-ho-oh, Minnie."

Then the bathroom door swung slowly open and a man stood outlined against the darkness of the corridor. He was bareheaded and the electric light was reflected in a thin line across his hair, shone dully on the moist pallor of his skin. He wore a tightly belted raincoat and his hands were thrust deep into his pockets.

Winfield sat up straight in the tub, spoke tentatively "Hello!" He said "hello" with an incredulous rising inflection, blinked incredulously upward. The cigarette dangled loosely from one corner of his mouth.

The man leaned against the frame of the door and took a short thick automatic out of his coat pocket and held it steadily, waist high.

Winfield put his hands on the sides of the tub and started to get up.

The automatic barked twice.

Winfield half stood, with one hand and one leg braced against the side of the tub for perhaps five seconds. His eyes were wide, blank. Then he sank down slowly, his head fell back against the smooth blue porcelain, slid slowly under the water. The cigarette still hung in the corner of his clenched mouth and as his head went under the water it hissed briefly, was gone.

The man in the doorway turned, disappeared.

The water reddened. Faintly, the phonograph lisped: "Hi de ho. . . ."

414

Doolin grinned up at the waiter. "An' see the eggs are four minutes, an' don't put any cream in my coffee."

The waiter bobbed his head sullenly and disappeared through swinging doors.

Doolin unfolded his paper and turned to the comic page. He read it carefully, chuckling audibly, from top to bottom. Then he spread pages two and three across the counter and began at the top of page two. Halfway across he read the headline: Winfield, Motion Picture Executive, Slain by Sweetheart: Story continued from page one.

He turned to the front page and stared at a two-column cut of Winfield, read the accompanying account, turned back to page two and finished it. There was another cut of Winfield, and a woman. The caption under the woman's picture read: "Elma O'Shea Darmond, well-known screen actress and friend of Winfield, who was found unconscious in his apartment with the automatic in her hand."

Doolin yawned and shoved the paper aside to make room for the eggs and toast and coffee that the sour-faced waiter carried. He devoured the eggs and had half-finished his coffee before he saw something that interested him on page three. He put his cup down, leaned over the paper, read: "Man shot in Glendale Mystery. H J (Jake) Coleman, alleged gambler, was shot and killed as he came out of the Lyric Billiard Parlors in Glendale yesterday evening. The shots were fired from a mysterious black roadster which the police are attempting to trace."

Doolin read the rest of the story, finished his coffee. He sat several minutes staring expressionlessly at his reflection in the mirror behind the counter, got up, paid his check and went out into the bright morning.

He walked briskly down Hill Street to First, over First, to the Los Angeles Bulletin Building. He was whistling as the elevator carried him up.

In the back files of the *Bulletin* he found what he was looking for, a front-page spread in the Home Edition of December 10th:

## MASSACRE IN NIGHTCLUB
### Screen-stars Duck for Cover as Machine-guns Belch Death

Early this morning The Hotspot, famous cabaret near Culver City, was the scene of the bloodiest battle the local gang war has afforded to date. Two men who police believe to be Frank Riccio and Edward (Whitey) Conroy of the Purple Gang in Detroit were instantly killed when a private room in the club was invaded by four men with sub-machine guns. A third man, a companion of Riccio and Conroy, was seriously wounded and is not expected to live.

Doolin skimmed down the column, read:

R. F. Winfield, prominent motion-picture executive, who was one of the party in the private room, said that he could not identify any of the killers. He said it all happened too quickly to be sure of any of them, and explained his presence in the company of the notorious gangsters as the result of his desire for first-hand information about the underworld in connection with a picture of that type which he is supervising. The names of others in the party are being withheld. . . .

Under a sub-head Doolin read:

H. J. Coleman and his companion, Miss Mazie Decker, were in the corridor leading to the private room when the killers entered. Miss Decker said she could positively identify two of them. Coleman who is near-sighted, was equally positive that he could not. . . .

An hour and a half later, Doolin left the Bulletin Building. He had gone carefully through the December file, and up to the middle of January. He had called into service the City Directory, Telephone Book, Dun & Bradstreet, and the telephone, and he had wheedled all the inside dope he could out of a police-reporter whom he knew casually.

He stood on the wide stone steps and looked at the sheet of paper on which he had scrawled notes. It read:

*People in private room and corridor who might be able to identify killers of Riccio and Conroy:*

*Winfield. Dead.*

416

*Coleman. Dead.*

*Martha Grainger. Actress. In show, in N. Y.*

*Betty Crane. Hustler. Died of pneumonia January 4th.*

*Isabel Dolly. Hustler and extra-girl. Was paralyzed drunk during shooting; probably not important. Can't locate.*

*Mazie Decker. Taxi-dancer. Works at Dreamland on Sixth and Hill. Failed to identify killers from rogues-gallery photographs.*

*Nelson Halloran. Man-about-town. Money. Friend of Winfield's. Lives at Fontenoy, same apartment-house as Winfield.*

Doolin folded and creased the sheet of paper. He wound it abstractedly around his forefinger and walked down the steps, across the sidewalk to a cab. He got into the cab and sat down and leaned back.

The driver slid the glass, asked: "Where to?"

Doolin stared at him blankly, then laughed. He said: "Wait a minute," spread the sheet of paper across his knee. He took a stub of pencil out of his pocket and slowly, thoughtfully, drew a line through the first five names; that left Mazie Decker and Nelson Halloran.

Doolin leaned forward and spoke to the driver: "Is that Dreamland joint at Sixth an' Hill open in the afternoon?"

The driver thought a moment, shook his head.

Doolin said: "All right, then—Fontenoy Apartment—on Whitley in Hollywood."

Nelson Halloran looked like Death. His white face was extremely long, narrow; his sharp chin tapered upward in unbroken lines to high sharp cheek-bones, great deep-sunken eyes; continued to a high, almost degenerately narrow, forehead. His mouth was wide, thin, dark against the whiteness of his skin. His hair was the color of water. He was six-feet-three inches tall, weighed a hundred and eighty.

He half lay in a deeply upholstered chair in the living room of his apartment and watched a round spot of sunlight move across the wall. The shades were drawn and the apartment was in semi-darkness. It was a chaos of modern furniture, books, magazines, papers, bottles; there were several good but badly hung reproductions on the pale walls.

Halloran occasionally lifted one long white hand languidly to his mouth, inhaled smoke deeply and blew it upward into the ray of sunlight.

417

When the phone buzzed he shuddered involuntarily, leaned sidewise and took it up from a low table.

He listened a moment, said: "Send him up." His voice was very low. There was softness in it; and there was coldness and something very far-away.

He moved slightly in the chair so that one hand was near his side, in the folds of his dressing gown. There was a Luger there in the darkness of the chair. He was facing the door.

With the whirl of the buzzer he called: "Come in."

The door opened and Doolin came a little way into the room, closed the door behind him.

Halloran did not speak.

Doolin stood blinking in the half-light, and Halloran watched him and was silent.

Doolin was around thirty; of medium height, inclined to thickness through all the upper part of his body. His face was round and on the florid side and his eyes were wide-set, blue. His clothes didn't fit him very well.

He stood with his hat in his hand, his face expressionless, until Halloran said coldly: "I didn't get the name."

"Doolin. D—double o-l-i-n." Doolin spoke without moving his mouth very much. His Voice was pleasant; his vowels colored slightly by brogue.

Halloran waited.

Doolin said: "I read a couple of things in the paper this morning that gave me an idea. I went over to the *Bulletin* an' worked on the idea, an' it pans out you're in a very bad spot."

Halloran took a drag of his cigarette, stared blankly at Doolin, waited. Doolin waited, too. They were both silent, looking at one another for more than a minute. Doolin's eyes were bright, pleased.

Halloran finally said: "This is a little embarrassing." He hesitated a moment. "Sit down."

Doolin sat on the edge of a wide steel and canvas chair against the wall. He dropped his hat on the floor and leaned forward, put his elbows on his knees. The little circle of sunlight moved slowly across the wall above him.

Halloran mashed his cigarette out, changed his position a little, said: "Go on."

"Have you read the papers?" Doolin took a cellophane-wrapped cigar out of his pocket and ripped off the wrapper, clamped the cigar between his teeth.

Halloran nodded, if moving his head the merest fraction of an inch could be called a nod.

Doolin spoke around the cigar: "Who rubbed Riccio and Conroy?"

Halloran laughed.

Doolin took the cigar out of his mouth. He said very earnestly: "Listen. Last night Winfield was murdered—an' Coleman. You're next. I don't know why the people who did it waited so long—maybe because the trial of a couple of the boys they've been holding comes up next week. . . ."

Halloran's face was a blank white mask.

Doolin leaned back and crossed his legs. "Anyway—they got Winfield an' Coleman. That leaves the Decker broad—the one who was with Coleman—an' you. The rest of them don't count—one's in New York an' one died of pneumonia an, one was cockeyed. . . ."

He paused to chew his cigar, Halloran rubbed his left hand down over one side of his face, slowly.

Doolin went on: "I used to be a stunt-man in pictures. For the last year all the breaks have been bad. I haven't worked for five months." He leaned forward, emphasized his words with the cigar held like a pencil: "I want to work for you."

There was thin amusement in Halloran's voice: "What are your qualifications?"

"I can shoot straight, an' fast, an' I ain't afraid to take a chance—any kind of a chance! I'd make a hell of a swell bodyguard."

Doolin stood up in the excitement of his sales-talk, took two steps towards Halloran.

Halloran said: "Sit down." His voice was icy. The Luger glistened in his hand.

Doolin looked at the gun and smiled a little, stuck the cigar in his mouth and backed up and sat down.

Halloran said: "How am I supposed to know you're on the level?"

Doolin slid his lower lip up over the upper. He scratched his nose with the nail of his thumb and shook his head slowly, grinning.

"Anyway—it sounds like a pipe dream to me," Halloran went on. "The paper says Miss Darmond killed Winfield." He smiled. "And Coleman was a gambler—any one of a half dozen suckers is liable to have shot him."

Doolin shrugged elaborately. He leaned forward and picked up his hat and put it on, stood up.

Halloran laughed again. His laugh was not a particularly pleasing one.

"Don't be in a hurry," he said.

They were silent a while and then Halloran lighted a cigarette and stood up. He was so tall and spare that Doolin stared involuntarily as he crossed, holding the Luger loosely at his side, patted Doolin's pockets, felt under his arms with his free hand. Then Halloran went to a table across a corner of the room and dropped the Luger into a drawer.

He turned and smiled warmly at Doolin, said: "What will you drink?"

"Gin."

"No gin."

Doolin grinned.

Halloran went on: "Scotch, rye, bourbon, brandy, rum, Kirsch, champagne. No gin."

Doolin said: "Rye."

Halloran took two bottles from a tall cabinet, poured two drinks. "Why don't you go to the Decker girl? She's the one who said she could identify the men who killed Riccio and Conroy. She's the one who needs a bodyguard."

Doolin went over to the table and picked up his drink. "I ain't had a chance," he said. "She works at Dreamland downtown, an' it ain't open in the afternoon." They drank.

Halloran's mouth was curved to a small smile. He picked up a folded newspaper, pointed to a headline, handed it to Doolin.

Doolin took the paper, a late edition of the *Morning Bulletin*, read:

## MURDERED GIRL
## IDENTIFIED AS
## TAXI-DANCER

The body of the girl who was found stabbed to death

on the road near Lankershim early this morning, has been identified as Mazie Decker of 305 S. Lake Street, an employee of the Dreamland Dancing Studio.

The identification was made by Peggy Galbraith, the murdered girl's room-mate. Miss Decker did not return home last night, and upon reading an account of the tragedy in the early editions, Miss Galbraith went to the morgue and positively identified Miss Decker. The police are . . .

Doolin put the paper down, said: "Well, well. . . . Like I said. . . ." There was a knock at the door, rather a curious rhythmic tapping of fingernails.

Halloran called: "Come in."

The door opened and a woman came in slowly, closed the door. She went to Halloran and put her arms around him and tilted her head back.

Halloran kissed her lightly. He smiled at Doolin, said: "This is Mrs Sare." He turned his smile to the woman. "Lola—meet Mr Doolin—my bodyguard."

Lola Sare had no single feature, except her hair, that was beautiful; yet she was very beautiful.

Her hair was red, so dark that it was black in certain lights. Her eyes slanted; were so dark a green they were usually black. Her nose was straight but the nostrils flared the least bit too much; her mouth red and full; too wide and curved. Her skin was smooth, very dark. Her figure was good, on the slender side. She was ageless; perhaps twenty-six, perhaps thirty-six.

She wore a dark green robe of heavy silk, black mules; her hair was gathered in a large roll at the nape of her neck.

She inclined her head sharply towards Doolin, without expression.

Doolin said: "Very happy to know you, Mrs Sare."

She went to one of the wide windows and jerked the drape aside a little; a broad flat beam of sunshine yellowed the darkness.

She said: "Sorry to desecrate the tomb." Her voice was deep, husky.

Halloran poured three drinks and went back to his chair

and sat down. Mrs Sare leaned against the table, and Doolin, after a hesitant glance at her, sat down on the chair against the wall.

Halloran sipped his drink. "The strange part of it all," he said, "is that I couldn't identify any of the four men who came in that night if my life depended upon it—and I'm almost sure Winfield couldn't. We'd been on a bender together for three days—and my memory for faces is bad, at best. . . ."

He put his glass on the floor beside the chair, lighted a cigarette. "Who else did you mention, besides the Decker girl and Coleman and Winfield and myself, who might . . . ?"

Doolin took the folded sheet of paper out of his pocket, got up and handed it to Halloran.

Halloran studied it a while, said: "You missed one."

Mrs Sare picked up the two bottles and went to Doolin, refilled his glass.

Doolin stared questioningly at Halloran, his eyebrows raised to a wide inverted V.

"The man who was with Riccio and Conroy," Halloran went on. "The third man, who was shot. . . ."

Doolin said: "I didn't see any more about him in the files—the paper said he wasn't expected to live. . . ."

Halloran clicked the nail of his forefinger against his teeth, said: "I wonder."

Mrs Sare had paused to listen. She went to Halloran and refilled his glass and put the bottles on the floor, sat down on the arm of Halloran's chair.

"Winfield and I went to The Hotspot alone," Halloran went on. "We had some business to talk over with a couple girls in the show." He grinned faintly, crookedly at Mrs Sare. "Riccio and Conroy and this third man—I think his name was Martini or something dry like that—and the three girls on your list, passed our table on their way to the private-room. . . ."

Doolin was leaning forward, chewing his cigar, his eyes bright with interest.

Halloran blew smoke up into the wedge of sun. "Winfield knew Conroy casually—had met him in the East. They fell on one another's necks, and Conroy invited us to join their party. Winfield went for that—he was doing a gangster picture and Conroy was a big shot in the East—Winfield figured he could get a lot of angles. . . ."

Doolin said: "That was on the level, then?"

"Yes," Halloran nodded emphatically. "Winfield even talked of making Conroy technical expert on the picture—before the fireworks started."

"What did this third man—this Martini, look like?"

Halloran looked a little annoyed. He said: "I'll get to that. There were eight of us in the private room—the three men and the three girls and Winfield and I. Riccio was pretty drunk, and one of the girls was practically under the table. We were all pretty high."

Halloran picked up his glass, leaned forward. "Riccio and Martini were all tangled up in some kind of drunken argument and I got the idea it had something to do with drugs—morphine. Riccio was pretty loud. Winfield and I were talking to Conroy, and the girls were amusing themselves gargling champagne, when the four men—I guess there were four—crashed in and opened up on Riccio and Conroy. . . ."

"What about Martini?" Doolin's unlighted cigar was growing rapidly shorter.

Halloran looked annoyed again. "That's the point," he said. "They didn't pay any attention to Martini—they wanted Riccio and Conroy. And it wasn't machine-guns—that was newspaper color. It was automatics. . . ."

Doolin said: "What about Martini?"

"For Christ's sake—shut up!" Halloran grinned cheerlessly, finished his drink. "Riccio shot Martini."

Doolin stood up slowly, said: "Can I use the phone?"

Halloran smiled at Mrs Sare, nodded.

Doolin called several numbers, asked questions, said "Yes" and "No" monotonously.

Halloran and Mrs Sare talked quietly. Between two calls, Halloran spoke to Doolin; "You've connections—haven't you." It was an observation, not a question.

Doolin said: "If I had as much money as I have connections, I'd retire."

He finished after a while, hung up and put the phone back on the low round table.

"Martinelli," he said, "not Martini. Supposed to have been Riccio and Conroy's partner in the East. They had the drug business pretty well cornered. He showed up out here around the last of November, and Riccio and Conroy came in December tenth, were killed the night they got in. . . ."

Halloran said: "I remember that—they were talking about the trip."

Doolin took the cigar out of his mouth long enough to take a drink. "Martinelli was discharged from St. Vincent's Hospital January sixteenth—day before yesterday. He's plenty bad—beat four or five murder raps in the East and was figured for a half dozen others. They called him The Executioner. Angelo Martinelli—The Executioner."

Mrs Sare said: "Come and get it."

Doolin and Halloran got up and went into the little dining room. They sat down at the table and Mrs Sare brought in a steaming platter of bacon and scrambled eggs, a huge double-globe of bubbling coffee.

Doolin said: "Here's the way it looks to me: If Martinelli figured you an' Winfield an' whoever else was in the private room had seen Riccio shoot him, he'd want to shut you up; it was a cinch he'd double-crossed Riccio and if it came out at the trial, the Detroit boys would be on his tail."

Halloran nodded, poured a large rosette of chili-sauce on the plate beside his scrambled eggs.

"But what did he want to rub Coleman an' Decker for?"

Halloran started to speak with his mouth full, but Doolin interrupted him: "The answer to that is that Martinelli had hooked up with the outfit out here, the outfit that Riccio and Conroy figured on moving in on. . . ."

Halloran said: "Martinelli probably came out to organize things for a narcotic combination between here and Detroit, in opposition to our local talent. He liked the combination here the way it was and threw in with them—and when Riccio and Conroy arrived Martinelli put the finger on them, for the local boys. . . ."

Doolin swallowed a huge mouthful of bacon and eggs, said: "Swell," out of the corner of his mouth to Mrs Sare.

He picked up his cigar and pointed it at Halloran. "That's the reason he wanted all of you—you an' Winfield because you'd get the Detroit outfit on his neck if you testified; Decker an' Coleman because they could spot the L A boys.

He didn't try to proposition any of you—he's the kind of guy who would figure killing was simpler."

Halloran said: "He's got to protect himself against the two men who are in jail too. They're liable to spill their guts. If everybody who was in on it was bumped there wouldn't be a chance of those two guys being identified—everything would be rosy."

They finished their bacon and eggs in silence.

With the coffee, Doolin said: "Funny he didn't make a pass at you last night—before or after he got Winfield. The same building an' all. . . ."

"Maybe he did." Halloran put his arm around Mrs Sare who was standing beside his chair. "I didn't get home till around three—he was probably here, missed me."

Doolin said: "We better go downtown an' talk to the D A. That poor gal of Winfield's is probably on the grill. We can clear that up an' have Martinelli picked up. . . ."

Halloran said: "No." He said it very emphatically.

Doolin opened his eyes wide, slowly. He finished his coffee, waited.

Halloran smiled faintly, said: "In the first place, I hate coppers." He tightened his arm around Mrs Sare. "In the second place I don't particularly care for Miss Darmond—she can God damned well fry on the griddle from now on, so far as I'm concerned. In the third place—I like it. . . ."

Doolin glanced at Mrs Sare, turned his head slowly back towards Halloran.

"I've got three months to live," Halloran went on—"at the outside." His voice was cold, entirely unemotional. "I was shell-shocked and gassed and kicked around pretty generally in France in 'eighteen. They stuck me together and sent me back and I've lasted rather well. But my heart is shot, and my lungs are bad, and so on—the doctors are getting pretty sore because I'm still on my feet. . . ."

He grinned widely. "I'm going to have all the fun I can in whatever time is left. We're not going to call copper, and we're going to play this for everything we can get out of it. You're my bodyguard and your salary is five hundred a week, but your job isn't to guard me—it's to see that there's plenty of excitement. And instead of waiting for Martinelli to come to us, we're going to Martinelli."

Doolin looked blankly at Mrs Sare. She was smiling in a very curious way.

Halloran said: "Are you working?"

Doolin smiled slowly with all his face. He said: "Sure."

Doolin dried his hands and smoothed his hair, whistling tunelessly, went through the small cheaply furnished living room of his apartment to the door of the kitchenette. He picked up a newspaper from a table near the door, unfolded it and glanced at the headlines, said: "They're calling the Winfield kill 'Murder in Blue' because it happened in a blue bathtub. Is that a laugh!"

A rather pretty fresh-faced girl was stirring something in a white sauce-pan on the little gas stove. She looked up and smiled and said: "Dinner'll be ready in a minute," wiped her hands on her apron and began setting the table.

Doolin leaned against the wall and skimmed through the rest of the paper. The Coleman case was limited to a quarter column—the police had been unable to trace the car. There was even less about Mazie Decker. The police were "working on a theory. . . ."

The police were working on a theory, too, on the Winfield killing. Miss Darmond had been found near the door of Winfield's apartment with a great bruise on her head, the night of the murder; she said the last she remembered was opening the door and struggling with someone. The "Best Minds" of the Force believed her story up to that point; they were working on the angle that she had an accomplice.

Doolin rolled up the paper and threw it on a chair. He said: "Five hundred a week—an' expenses! Gee!—is that swell!" He was grinning broadly.

The girl said: "I'm awfully glad about the money, darling—if you're SURE you'll be safe. God knows its about time we had a break." She hesitated a moment. "I hope it's all right. . . ."

She was twenty-three or four, a honey-blonde pink-cheeked girl with wide gray eyes, a slender well-curved figure.

Doolin went to her and kissed the back of her neck.

"Sure, it's all right, Mollie," he said. "Anything is all right when you get paid enough for it. The point is to make it

426

last—five hundred is a lot of money, but a thousand will buy twice as many lamb chops."

She became very interested in a tiny speck on one of the cheap white plates, rubbed it industriously with a towel. She spoke without looking up: "I keep thinking about that Darmond girl—in jail. What do you suppose Halloran has against her?"

"I don't know." Doolin sat down at the table. "Anyway—she's okay. We can spring her any time, only we can't do it now because we'd have to let the Law in on the Martinelli angle an' they'd pick him up—an' Halloran couldn't have his fun."

"It's a funny kind of fun." The girl smiled with her mouth.

Doolin said: "He's a funny guy. Used to be a police reporter in Chi—maybe that has something to do with it. Anyway, the poor bastard's only got a little while to go—let him have any kind of fun he wants. He can afford it. . . ."

They were silent while the girl cut bread and got the butter out of the Frigidaire and finished setting the table.

Doolin was leaning forward with his elbows on the table, his chin in his hands. "As far as the Darmond gal is concerned, a little of that beef stew they dish up at the County will be good for her. These broads need a little of that—to give them perspective."

The girl was heaping mashed potatoes into a big bowl. She did not speak.

"The way I figure it," Doolin went on—"Halloran hasn't got the guts to bump himself off. He's all washed up, an' he knows it—an' the idea has made him a little batty. Then along comes Martinelli—a chance for him to go out dramatically—the way he's lived—an' he goes for it. Jesus! so would I if I was as near the edge as he is. He doesn't give a god-damn about anything—he doesn't have to. . . ."

The girl finished putting food on the table, sat down. Doolin heaped their plates with chops and potatoes and cauliflower while she served salad. They began to eat.

Doolin got up and filled two glasses with water and put them on the table.

The girl said: "I'm sorry I forgot the water. . . ."

Doolin bent over and kissed her, sat down.

"As far as Halloran is concerned," he went on—"I'm just another actor in his show. Instead of sitting and waiting for Martinelli to come to get him—we go after Martinelli. That's Halloran's idea of fun—that's the kind of sense of humor he's got. What the hell!—he's got nothing to lose. . . ."

The girl said: "Eat your dinner before it gets cold."

They were silent a while.

Finally she said: "What if Martinelli shoots first?"

Doolin laughed. "Martinelli isn't going to shoot at all. Neither am I—an' neither is Mr Halloran."

The girl lighted a cigarette, sipped her coffee. She stared expressionlessly at Doolin, waited.

"Halloran is having dinner with Mrs Sare," Doolin went on. "Then they're going to a show an' I'm picking them up afterwards—at the theatre. Then Halloran an' I are going to have a look around for Martinelli."

He finished his coffee, refilled both their cups. "In the meantime I'm supposed to be finding out where we're most likely to find him—Halloran is a great believer in my 'connections.' "

Doolin grinned, went on with a softly satisfied expression, as if he were taking a rabbit out of a hat: "I've already found Martinelli—not only where he hangs out, but where he lives. it was a cinch. He hasn't any reason to think he's pegged for anything—he's not hiding out."

The girl said: "So what?"

He stood up, stretched luxuriously. "So I'm going to Martinelli right now." He paused dramatically. "An' I'm going to tell him what kind of a spot he's in—with half a dozen murder raps hanging over his head, and all. I'm going to tell him that plenty people besides myself know about it an' that the stuff's on the way to the D A's office an' that he'd better scram toot sweet. . . ."

The girl said: "You're crazy."

Doolin laughed extravagantly. "Like a fox," he said. "Like a fox. I'm doing Martinelli a big favor—so I'm set with him. I'm keeping Halloran from running a chance of being killed—an' he'll think he's still running the chance, an' get his throb out of it. I'm keeping five hundred smackers coming into the cash register every week as long as Halloran lives, or as long as I can give him a good show. An' everybody's happy. What more do you want?"

"Sense." The girl mashed her cigarette out, stood up. "I never heard such a crazy idea in all my life! . . ."

Doolin looked disgusted. He walked into the living room, came back to the doorway. "Sure, it's crazy," he said. "Sure, it's crazy. So is Halloran—an' you—an' me. So is Martinelli—probably. It's the crazy ideas that work—an' this one is going to work like a charm."

The girl said: "What about Darmond? If Martinelli gets away she'll be holding the bag for Winfield's murder."

"Oh, no, she won't! As soon as the Halloran angle washes up I'll turn my evidence over to the D A an' tell him it took a few weeks to get it together—an' be sure about it. It's as plain as the nose on your face that Martinelli killed all three of them. Those chumps downtown are too sappy to see it now but they won't be when I point it out to them. It's a set-up case against Martinelli!"

The girl smiled coldly. She said: "You're the most conceited, bull-headed Mick that ever lived. You've been in one jam after another ever since we were married. This is one time I'm not going to let you make a fool of yourself—an' probably get killed. . . ."

Doolin's expression was stubborn, annoyed. He turned and strode across the living room, squirmed into his coat, put on his hat and jerked it down over his eyes.

She stood in the doorway. Her face was very white and her eyes were wide, round.

She said: "Please. Johnny. . . ."

He didn't look at her. He went to the desk against one wall and opened a drawer, took a nickel-plated revolver out of the drawer and dropped it into his coat pocket.

She said: "If you do this insane thing—I'm leaving." Her voice was cold, brittle.

Doolin went to the outer-door, went out, slammed the door.

She stood there a little while looking at the door.

Angelo Martinelli stuck two fingers of his left hand into the little jar, took them out pale, green, sticky with Smoothcomb Hair Dressing. He dabbed it on his head, held his hands stiff with the fingers bent backwards and rubbed it vigorously into his hair. Then he wiped his hands and picked up a comb, bent towards the mirror.

Martinelli was very young—perhaps twenty-four or -five. His face was pale, unlined; pallor shading to blue towards his long angular jaw; his eyes red-brown, his nose straight and delicately cut. He was of medium height but the high padded shoulders of his coat made him appear taller.

The room was small, garishly furnished. A low bed and two or three chairs in the worst modern manner were made a little more objectionable by orange and pink batik throws; there was an elaborately wrought iron floor lamp, its shade made of whiskey labels pasted on imitation parchment.

Martinelli finished combing his hair, spoke over his shoulder to a woman who lounged across the foot of the bed:

"Tonight does it. . . ."

Lola Sare said: "Tonight does it—if you're careful. . . ."

Martinelli glanced at his wrist-watch. "I better get going—it's nearly eight. He said he'd be there at eight."

Lola Sare leaned forward and dropped her cigarette into a half-full glass on the floor.

"I'll be home from about eight-thirty on," she said. "Call as soon as you can."

Martinelli nodded. He put on a lightweight black felt hat, tilted it to the required angle in front of the mirror. He helped her into her coat, and then he put his arms around her, kissed her mouth lingeringly.

She clung to him, whispered: "Make it as fast as you can, darling."

They went to the door and Martinelli snapped off the light and they went out.

Martinelli said: "Turn right at the next corner."

The cab driver nodded; they turned off North Broadway into a dimly lighted street, went several blocks over bad pavement.

Martinelli pounded on the glass, said: "Oke."

The cab slid to an abrupt stop and Martinelli got out and paid the driver, stood at the curb until the cab had turned around in the narrow street, disappeared.

He went to a door above which one pale electric globe

glittered, felt in the darkness for the button, pressed it. The door clicked open; Martinelli went in and slammed it shut behind him.

There were a half dozen or so men strung out along the bar in the long dim room. A few more sat at tables against the wall.

Martinelli walked to the far end of the bar, leaned across it to speak quietly to a chunky bald-headed man who sat on a high stool near the cash register:

"Chief here?"

The bald man bobbed his head, jerked it towards a door behind Martinelli.

Martinelli looked surprised, said mildly: "He's on time for once in his life!"

The man bobbed his head. His face was blank.

Martinelli went through the door, up two short flights of stairs to a narrow hallway. At the end of the hallway he knocked at a heavy steel-sheathed fire-door.

After a little while the door opened and a voice said: "Come in."

Doolin stood on his toes and tried to make out the number above the door but the figures were too faded by weather, time; the electric light was too dim.

He walked down the dark street a half block and then walked back and pressed the button beside the door; the door clicked open and he went through the short passageway into the long barroom.

A bartender wiped off the stained wood in front of him, questioned with his eyes.

Doolin said: "Rye."

He glanced idly at the men at the bar, at the tables, at the heavily built bald man who sat on a stool at the far end of the bar. The little bald man was stooped over a wide-spread newspaper.

The bartender put a glass on the bar in front of Doolin, put a flat brightly labeled flask beside it.

Doolin said: "Seen Martinelli tonight?"

The bartender watched Doolin pour his drink, picked up the bottle and put it under the bar, said: "Yeah. He came in a little while ago. He's upstairs."

Doolin nodded, tasted the rye. It wasn't too bad. He finished it and put a quarter on the bar, sauntered towards the door at the back of the room.

The little bald man looked up from his paper.

Doolin said: "Martinelli's expecting me. He's upstairs—ain't he?"

The little man looked at Doolin. He began at his face and went down to his feet and then back up, slowly. "He didn't say anything about you." He spat with the admirable precision of age and confidence into a cuspidor in the corner.

Doolin said: "He forgot." He put his hand on the doorknob.

The little man looked at him, through him, blankly.

Doolin turned the knob and opened the door, went through, closed the door behind him.

The stairs were dimly lighted by a sputtering gas-jet. He went up slowly. There was one door at the top of the first flight; it was dark; there was no light under it, no sound beyond it. Doolin went up another flight very quietly. He put his ear against the steel-sheathed door; he could hear no sound, but a little light filtered through under the door. He doubled up his fist, knocked with the heel of his hand.

Martinelli opened the door. He stood a moment staring questioningly at Doolin and then he glanced over his shoulder, smiled, said: "Come in."

Doolin put his hands in his overcoat pockets, his right hand holding the revolver tightly, went forward into the room.

Martinelli closed the door behind him, slid the heavy bolt.

The room was large, bare; somewhere around thirty-five by forty. It was lighted by a single green-shaded droplight over a very large round table in the center; there were other tables and chairs stacked in the dusk of the corner. There were no windows, no other doors.

Halloran sat in one of the four chairs at the table. He was leaning slightly forward with his elbows on the table, his long waxen hands framing his face. His face was entirely cold, white, expressionless.

Martinelli stood with his back against the door, his hands behind him.

432

Doolin glanced over his shoulder at Martinelli, looked back at Halloran. His eyebrows were lifted to the wide V, his mouth hung a little open.

Halloran said: "Well, well—this is a surprise."

He moved his eyes to Martinelli, said: "Angelo. Meet Mr Doolin—my bodyguard. . . ." For an instant his wide thin mouth flickered a fraction of an inch upward; then his face became a blank, white mask again. "Mr Doolin—Mr Martinelli. . . ."

Martinelli had silently come up behind Doolin, suddenly thrust his hands into Doolin's pockets, hard, grabbed Doolin's hands. Doolin bent sharply forward. They struggled for possibly half a minute, silently except for the tearing sound of their breath; then Martinelli brought his knee up suddenly, savagely; Doolin groaned, sank to his knees, the nickel-plated revolver clattered to the floor, slid halfway across the room.

Martinelli darted after it.

Halloran had not appeared to move. He said: "Wait a minute, baby. . . ." The blunt Luger that Doolin had experienced in the afternoon glittered on the table between his two hands.

Martinelli made an impatient gesture, stooped to pick up Doolin's gun.

"Wait a minute, baby." Halloran's voice was like a cold swift scythe.

Martinelli stood up very straight.

Doolin got to his feet slowly. He bent over and held the middle of his body, rolled his head toward Martinelli, his eyes narrow, malevolent. He said very quietly, as if to himself: "Dirty son of a bitch—dirty, *dirty* son of a bitch!"

Martinelli grinned, stood very straight. His hands, cupped close to his thighs, trembled rigidly.

Halloran said slowly: "Don't do it, baby. I'll shoot both your eyes out before you get that shiv of yours into the air—and never touch your nose."

Martinelli looked like a clothing store dummy. He was balanced on the balls of his feet, his hands trembling at his sides; his grin artificial, empty.

Doolin laughed suddenly. He stood up straight and looked at Martinelli and laughed.

Halloran moved his eyes to Doolin, smiled faintly.

He said: "Gentlemen—sit down."

Martinelli tottered forward, sank into one of the chairs.

Halloran said: "Put your hands on the table, please."

Martinelli obediently put his hands on the table. The empty grin seemed to have congealed on his face.

Halloran turned his eyes towards Doolin. Doolin smiled, walked gingerly to the other chair and sat down.

Halloran said: "Now. . . ." He put one hand up to his face; the other held the Luger loosely on the table.

Doolin cleared his throat, said: "What's it all about, Mr Halloran?"

Martinelli laughed suddenly. The empty grin exploded into loud high-pitched mirth. "What's it all about! Dear God—what's it all about! . . ."

Halloran was watching Doolin, his shadowed sunken eyes half closed.

Martinelli leaned forward, lifted his hands and pointed two fingers at Doolin. "Listen—wise guy. . . . You've got minutes to live—if you're lucky. That's what it's all about!"

Doolin regarded Martinelli with faint amusement.

Martinelli laughed again. He moved his hand slowly until the two fingers pointed at Halloran. "He killed Coleman," he said. "He shot Coleman an' I drove the car. An' he killed Winfield himself. An' his outfit killed Riccio an' Conroy. . . ."

Doolin glanced at Halloran, turned back to smile dimly, dumbly at Martinelli.

"He propositioned me into killing the dance-hall dame," Martinelli went on—"an' now he's going to kill you an' me. . . ."

Doolin grinned broadly but it was all done with his mouth. He didn't look like he felt it very much. He looked at Halloran. Halloran's face was white and immovable as plaster.

"Listen—wise-guy!" Martinelli leaned forward, moved his hand back to point at Doolin. He was suddenly very intense; his dark eyes burned into Doolin's. "I came out here for Riccio to make connections to peddle M——a lot of it—an' I met Mr Halloran." Martinelli moved his head an eighth of an inch towards Halloran. "Mr Halloran runs the drug racket out here—did you know that?"

Doolin glanced swiftly at Halloran, looked back at Martinelli's tense face.

"Mr Halloran aced me into double-crossing Frankie Riccio an' Conroy," Martinelli went on. "Mr Halloran's men rubbed Riccio an' Conroy, an' would've taken care of me if Riccio hadn't almost beat 'em to it. . . ."

Halloran said coldly, amusedly: "Oh—come, come, Angelo. . . ."

Martinelli did not look at Halloran. He said: "I met Riccio an' Conroy at the train that night an' took them to that joint in Culver City to talk business to Mr Halloran—only I didn't know the kind of business Mr Halloran was going to talk. . . ."

"Is it quite necessary to go into all this?" Halloran spoke sidewise to Martinelli, smiled at Doolin. It was his first definite change of expression since Doolin had come into the room.

Martinelli said: "Yes," emphatically. He scowled at Halloran, his eyes thin black slits. "Bright-boy here" he indicated Doolin with his hand—"wants to know what it's all about. I'd like to have somebody know—besides me. One of us might leave here alive—if I get this all out of my system it's a cinch it won't be Bright-boy."

Halloran's smile was very cheerful. He said: "Go on."

"One of the men the Law picked up for the Hotspot shooting was a good guess—he's on Mr Halloran's payroll," Martinelli went on. He was accenting the "Mr" a little unnecessarily, a little too much. "When I got out of the hospital Mr Halloran suggested we clean things up—move Coleman an' Decker an' Winfield—anybody who might identify his man or testify that Riccio shot me—out of the way. He hated Winfield anyway, for beating his time with the Darmond gal—an' he hated her. . . ."

Halloran was beaming at Doolin, his hand tight and steady on the Luger. Doolin thought about the distance across the big table to Halloran, the distance to the light.

Martinelli was leaning forward, talking swiftly, eagerly: "I brought eighty-five grand worth of morphine out with me, an' I turned it over to his nibs here when we threw in together. I ain't had a nickel out of it. That's the reason I went for all this finagling—I wanted my dough. I was

435

supposed to get it tonight, but I found out about ten minutes ago I ain't going to get it at all. . . ."

Martinelli smiled at Halloran, finished: "Mr Halloran says it was hi-jacked." He stood up slowly.

Halloran asked: "All through, baby?"

Martinelli was standing very stiff and straight, his hands cupped at his sides.

Doolin ducked suddenly, exerted all his strength to upset the table. For a moment he was protected by the edge, could see neither Martinelli nor Halloran; then the big round table-top slid off its metal base, crashed to the floor.

Halloran was holding Martinelli very much in the way a great ape would hold a smaller animal. One long arm was out stiff, the long white hand at Martinelli's throat, almost encircling it. Halloran's other hand held Martinelli's wrist, waved it back and forth slowly. The blade of a short curved knife glistened in Martinelli's hand. Except for the slow waving of their two hands they were as if frozen, entirely still. There was nothing human in their position, nothing human in their faces.

Doolin felt in that instant that Halloran was not human. He was mad, insane; but it was not the madness of a man, it was the cold murderous lust of an animal.

The Luger and Doolin's revolver were on the floor near their feet. Doolin circled until he was behind Halloran, moved slowly towards them.

As he dived for one of the guns Halloran swung Martinelli around swiftly, kicked viciously at Doolin's head. He missed once, but the second caught Doolin's hand as it closed over the Luger, sent the Luger spinning to a corner.

As Doolin half rose, Halloran's long leg lashed out again, his heavy shoe struck the side of Doolin's head. Doolin grunted, fell sidewise to the floor.

Doolin lay on his back and the room went around him. Later, in remembering what followed, it was like short strips of motion-picture film, separated by strips of darkness.

Halloran backed Martinelli slowly to the wall. It was as if they were performing some strange ritualistic dance; their steps were measured; Halloran's face was composed, his expression almost tender. Martinelli's face was darkening from the pressure on his throat. Halloran waved the hand holding the knife slowly back and forth.

The next time the darkness in Doolin's head cleared, they were against the wall, his head high, at a curious twisted angle above Halloran's white relentless hand, his face purpling. Halloran's other hand had slipped down over Martinelli's chest.

Martinelli's eyes bulged. His face was the face of a man who saw death coming, and was afraid. Doolin could no longer see Halloran's face. He watched the knife near Martinelli's chest, slowly.

Martinelli, some way, made a high piercing sound in his throat as the knife went into him. And again as Halloran withdrew the knife, pressed it in again slowly. Halloran did not stab mercifully on the left side, but on the right puncturing the lung again and again, slowly.

Doolin rolled over on his side. The revolver lay on the floor midway between him and Halloran. He shook his head sharply, crawled towards it.

Halloran suddenly released Martinelli, stepped back a pace. Martinelli's knees buckled, he sank slowly down, sat on the floor with his back against the wall, his legs out straight. He sucked in air in great rattling gasps, held both hands tightly against his chest, tightly against the shaft of the knife.

He lifted his head and there was blood on his mouth. He laughed; and Doolin forgot the gun, stopped, stared fascinated at Martinelli. Martinelli laughed and the sound was as if everything inside him was breaking. His head rolled back and he grinned upward with glazing eyes at Halloran, held his hands tightly against his chest, spoke:

"Tell Lola we can't go away now. . . ." He paused, sucked in air. "She's waiting for me. . . . Tell her Angelo sends his regrets. . . ." His voice was thick, high-pitched, but his words were telling, deadly, took deadly effect.

Halloran seemed to grow taller, his great shoulders seemed to widen as Doolin watched.

Martinelli laughed again. He said: "So long—sucker. . . ."

Halloran kicked him savagely in the chest. He drew his

long leg back and as Martinelli slumped sidewise he kicked his face, hard, repeatedly.

Doolin scrambled swiftly forward, picked up the revolver, raised it.

Halloran turned slowly.

Doolin held the revolver unsteadily in his right hand, aimed at Halloran's chest while the muzzle described little circles, pulled the trigger twice.

Halloran came towards him. Doolin made a harsh sound in his throat, scuttled backwards a few feet, held the revolver out limply and fired again.

Halloran's face was cold, impassive; his eyes were great black holes in his skull. He came towards Doolin slowly.

Doolin tried to say something but the words stuck in his throat, and then Halloran was above him and there was a terribly crushing weight against Doolin's forehead and it was suddenly dark.

Slowly, Doolin came to, lay a little while with his eyes closed. There were sharp twisting wires of pain in his head; he put his hand up, took it away wet, sticky.

He opened his eyes. It was entirely dark, a cold penetrating darkness; entirely still.

Suddenly he laughed, a curious hysterical sound in the quiet room; and as suddenly, panic seized him. He struggled to his knees, almost fell down again as the pain in his head throbbed to the swift movement. He got to his feet slowly, fumbled in his pockets and found a match, lighted it.

Martinelli's body was slumped in the angle of floor and wall at one side of the room. There was no one else. Doolin's revolver shone dimly on the floor in the flare of the match. The door was ajar.

Doolin lighted another match and picked up his revolver, his hat. He took out a handkerchief and wiped his face and the handkerchief was wet, dark. He walked, unsteadily to the door, down the dark stairs.

One faint globe burned above the deserted bar. Doolin felt his way along the wall, lifted the heavy bar across the outside door and went out, closed the door behind him. It was raining lightly a thin cold drizzle.

He took air into his lungs in great gulps, soaked the handkerchief in a little puddle of rainwater and tried to

438

clean his face. Then he went down the dark street swiftly towards Broadway.

The druggist looked at him through thick spectacles, gestured towards the back of the store.

Doolin said: "Fix me up some peroxide an' bandages an' stuff—I had an accident." He went back to the telephone booth, found the number of the Fontenoy, called it, asked for Mrs Sare.

The operator said Mrs Sare didn't answer.

Doolin hung up and went out and cleaned the blood from his face in front of a mirror. A little girl stared at him wide-eyed from the soda fountain; the druggist said: "Automobile . . . ?"

Doolin nodded.

The druggist asked: "How much bandage do you want?"

Doolin said: "Let it go—it's not as bad as I thought it was."

He put his hat on the back of his head and went out and got into a cab, said: "Fontenoy Apartments—Hollywood. An' make it snappy."

Lola Sare's voice said: "Yes," with rising inflection.

Doolin opened the door, went in.

She was sitting in a long low chair beneath a crimson-shaded bridge lamp. It was the only light in the room. Her arms were bare, straight on the arms of the chair, her hands hanging limply downward. Her dark head was against the back of the chair and her face was taut, her eyes wide, vacant.

Doolin took off his hat, said: "Why the hell don't you answer your phone?"

She did not speak, nor move.

"You'd better get out of here—quick." Doolin went towards her. "Halloran killed Martinelli—an' Martinelli opened up about you before he died. Halloran will be coming to see you. . . ."

Her blank eyes moved slowly from his face to some place in the dusk behind him. He followed her gaze, turned slowly.

Halloran was standing against the wall near the door. The door had covered him when Doolin entered; he put out one hand and pushed it gently, it swung closed with a sharp click.

As Doolin's eyes became used to the dimness of the room he saw Halloran clearly. He was leaning against the wall and the right shoulder and breast of his light gray suit was dark, sodden. He held the short blunt Luger in his left hand.

He said: "You're a little late. . . ."

The Luger roared.

Lola Sare put her hands up to the middle of her breast, low; her head came forward slowly. She started to get up and the Luger leaped in Halloran's hand, roared again.

At the same instant Doolin shot, holding the revolver low. The two explosions were simultaneous, thundered in the dark and narrow room.

Halloran fell as a tree falls; slowly, stiffly, his arm stiff at his sides; crashed to the floor.

Doolin dropped the revolver, walked unsteadily towards Lola Sare. His knees buckled suddenly and he sank forward, down.

There was someone pounding at the door

Doolin finished dabbing iodine on his head, washed his hands and went into the little living room of his apartment. A first dull streak of morning grayed the windows. He pulled down the shades and went into the kitchenette, lighted the gas under the percolator.

When the coffee was hot he poured a cup, dropped four lumps of sugar into it absently, carried it into the living room. He sat down on the davenport and put the coffee on an endtable, picked up the phone and dialed a number.

He said: "Hello, Grace? Is Mollie there? . . ." He listened a moment, went on: "Oh—I thought she might be there. Sorry I woke you up. . . ." He hung up, sipped his steaming coffee.

After a few minutes he picked up the phone, dialed again, said. "Listen, Grace—please put Mollie on. . . . Aw nuts! I know she's there—please make her talk to me. . . ."

Then he smiled, waited a moment, said: Hello darling . . . Listen—please come on home—will you? . . . Aw listen, Honey—I did what you said—everything's all right. . . . Uh-huh. . . . Halloran's dead—an' Martinelli . . . . Uh-huh. . . . The Sare dame is shot up pretty bad,

but not too much to give evidence an' clean it all up. . . .
Uh-huh. . . ."

He reached over and picked up the cup and took a long drink of coffee, smiled into the phone, said: "Sure—I'm all right—I got a little scratch on my head but I'm all right. . . . Sure. . . . Sure—we were right. . . . All right, Honey—I'll be waiting for you. Hurry up. . . . G'bye. . . ."

He hung up, curved his mouth to a wide grin, finished his coffee, lit a cigarette and waited.

# The NO EXIT PRESS Prize Crossword

Here's your chance to win a complete set of NO EXIT PRESS books. The first correct entry out of the bag on January 31st 1990 will win every NO EXIT title in print at that date! But don't despair every correct entry received by June 30th 1990 will receive a free mystery book. Incidentally a Reilly or suitable crime reference book wouldn't go amiss for some of the more obscure clues.

Completed entries (we will accept photocopies if you don't want to rip your book apart) to: *Prize Crossword, No Exit Press, 18 Coleswood Road, Harpenden, Herts, AL5 1EQ.*


Name:


Address:


Postcode:

## ACROSS:

1. A mixed up red room from the man who gave you 'Time to Kill' (7)
5. Cain's (the other one) novel of speed (4,3)
9. Unpleasant relation (4,5)
10. The Japanese superintendent (5)
11. Cornell's Country pseudonym (5)
12. Erle Stanley's moody female (5,4)
14. Annoyed Ronay or aggrieved Spengler (10,4)
17. Namesake of author of 10 across is a whale of a writer (6,8)
21. A strange situation from one holding another to ransom (2,7)
23. To follow. Found in raft error (5)
24. Asch's creator (5)
25. Kenneth Royce's strange fellow owing secret allegiance (6,3)
26. Repentance (7)
27. & 1 Down
    Carroll John Daly's royal bad guy (7,2,4)

## DOWN:

2. Drop the black in threat while sending a letter (7)
3. A criminal haven, no place to be alone in (5,4)
4. Upset sieved mince to give you these forceful people (8,3)
5. A P.I.'s bill (3)
6. Mix up tory's and get a narrative (5)
7. Go train rearranged for public speaking (7)
8. Reginald Hill's novel in the singular. A criminal's last word (4,4)
13. These people have virtually no idea of fashion (6,5)
15. Get rid of at summit. Then move around paint to do (2,2,2,3)
16. I see the maker of candles in a high window (8)
18. Le Queux's 1909 coloured living space (3,4)
19. Bill Cranes creator (7)
20. One who trims roses (6)
22. He gave life to Scott Jordan (5)
25. Stark a man of many names - this is his shortest (3)

# INTRODUCTION

The people and events in "The Specialty of the House" are, in the words of the fine old disclaimer, entirely imaginary. The restaurant, however, is real. Its name is Gage and Tollner's, and it may be found not far from Brooklyn's Borough Hall where it has stood for the past seventy-three years. The management solemnly affirms that the installation of electric lighting is the only real change in the room during those years. I can solemnly affirm that the food is superb, and that what God hath wrought in an oyster, clam, or lobster, Gage and Tollner's will never undo.

"The Specialty of the House" was born in that restaurant one evening in October, 1946, when my wife and I were eating dinner there, and talking about stories and storytelling. It was her contention that not only were there sermons in stones, and books in running brooks, but an anthology of stories in the old room around us. That stout gentleman, for example, remarking that as an amateur chef he'd enjoy visiting the kitchen, and the waiter explaining that it would be difficult to arrange during dinner hour, but perhaps some other time . . .

I started the story the next day and finished it three weeks later. The New Yorker rejected it promptly, and again my incomparable wife played a key role by suggesting Ellery Queen's Mystery Magazine as the best possible market. One week later Fred Dannay, the editor, phoned me and announced his decision to buy the story, and his desire to have me enter it in the magazine's annual contest. It won the prize as Best First Story in the contest that year, 1947, and brought me three hundred dollars, plus the peculiar distinction of always being introduced in company as "the one who wrote 'The Specialty of the House,'" although I have had a number of stories published since then, and a couple of novels as well.

I have not yet decided whether it is an asset or not to travel always with Mr. Sbirro saddled, like an Old Man of the Mountain, to my back. I leave that decision to you.

STANLEY ELLIN

# THE SPECIALITY OF THE HOUSE

*by Stanley Ellin*

"AND THIS," said Laffler, "is Sbirro's." Costain saw a square brownstone façade identical with the others that extended from either side into the clammy darkness of the deserted street. From the barred windows of the basement at his feet, a glimmer of light showed behind heavy curtains.

"Lord," he observed, "it's a dismal hole, isn't it?"

"I beg you to understand," said Laffler stiffly, "that Sbirro's is the restaurant without pretensions. Besieged by these ghastly, neurotic times, it has refused to compromise. It is perhaps the last important establishment in this city lit by gas jets. Here you will find the same honest furnishings, the same magnificent Sheffield service, and possibly, in a far corner, the very same spider webs that were remarked by the patrons of a half century ago!"

"A doubtful recommendation," said Costain, "and hardly sanitary."

"When you enter," Laffler continued, "you leave the insanity of this year, this day, and this hour, and you find yourself for a brief span restored in spirit, not by opulence, but by dignity, which is the lost quality of our time."

Costain laughed uncomfortably. "You make it sound more like a cathedral than a restaurant," he said.

In the pale reflection of the street lamp overhead, Laffler peered at his companion's face. "I wonder," he said abruptly, "whether I have not made a mistake in extending this invitation to you."

Costain was hurt. Despite an impressive title and

large salary, he was no more than clerk to this pompous little man, but he was impelled to make some display of his feelings. "If you wish," he said coldly, "I can make other plans for my evening with no trouble."

With his large, cowlike eyes turned up to Costain, the mist drifting into the ruddy, full moon of his face, Laffler seemed strangely ill at ease. Then "No, no," he said at last, "absolutely not. It's important that you dine at Sbirro's with me." He grasped Costain's arm firmly and led the way to the wrought-iron gate of the basement. "You see, you're the sole person in my office who seems to know anything at all about good food. And on my part, knowing about Sbirro's but not having some appreciative friend to share it is like having a unique piece of art locked in a room where no one else can enjoy it."

Costain was considerably mollified by this. "I understand there are a great many people who relish that situation."

"I'm not one of that kind!" Laffler said sharply. "And having the secret of Sbirro's locked in myself for years has finally become unendurable." He fumbled at the side of the gate and from within could be heard the small, discordant jangle of an ancient pull-bell. An interior door opened with a groan, and Costain found himself peering into a dark face whose only discernible feature was a row of gleaming teeth.

"Sair?" said the face.

"Mr Laffler and a guest."

"Sair," the face said again, this time in what was clearly an invitation. It moved aside and Costain stumbled down a single step behind his host. The door and gate creaked behind him, and he stood blinking in a small foyer. It took him a moment to realize that the figure he now stared at was his own reflection in a gigantic pier glass that extended from floor to ceiling. "Atmosphere," he said under his breath and chuckled as he followed his guide to a seat.

447

He faced Laffler across a small table for two and peered curiously around the dining room. It was no size at all, but the half-dozen guttering gas jets which provided the only illumination threw such a deceptive light that the walls flickered and faded into uncertain distance.

There were no more than eight or ten tables about, arranged to insure the maximum privacy. All were occupied, and the few waiters serving them moved with quiet efficiency. In the air were a soft clash and scrape of cutlery and a soothing murmur of talk. Costain nodded appreciatively.

Laffler breathed an audible sigh of gratification. "I knew you would share my enthusiasm," he said. "Have you noticed, by the way, that there are no women present?"

Costain raised inquiring eyebrows.

"Sbirro," said Laffler, "does not encourage members of the fair sex to enter the premises. And, I can tell you, his method is decidedly effective. I had the experience of seeing a woman get a taste of it not long ago. She sat at a table for not less than an hour waiting for service which was never forthcoming."

"Didn't she make a scene?"

"She did." Laffler smiled at the recollection. "She succeeded in annoying the customers, embarrassing her partner, and nothing more."

"And what about Mr Sbirro?"

"He did not make an appearance. Whether he directed affairs from behind the scenes, or was not even present during the episode, I don't know. Whichever it was, he won a complete victory. The woman never reappeared nor, for that matter, did the witless gentleman who by bringing her was really the cause of the entire contretemps."

"A fair warning to all present," laughed Costain.

A waiter now appeared at the table. The chocolate-dark skin, the thin, beautifully moulded nose and lips,

448

the large liquid eyes, heavily lashed, and the silver white hair so heavy and silken that it lay on the skull like a cap, all marked him definitely as an East Indian of some sort, Costain decided. The man arranged the stiff table linen, filled two tumblers from a huge, cut-glass pitcher, and set them in their proper places.

"Tell me," Laffler said eagerly, "is the special being served this evening?"

The waiter smiled regretfully and showed teeth as spectacular as those of the majordomo. "I am so sorry, sair. There is no special this evening."

Laffler's face fell into lines of heavy disappointment. "After waiting so long. It's been a month already, and I hoped to show my friend here . . ."

"You understand the difficulties, sair."

"Of course, of course." Laffler looked at Costain sadly and shrugged. "You see, I had in mind to introduce you to the greatest treat that Sbirro's offers, but unfortunately it isn't on the menu this evening."

The waiter said, "Do you wish to be served now, sair?" and Laffler nodded. To Costain's surprise the waiter made his way off without waiting for any instructions.

"Have you ordered in advance?" he asked.

"Ah," said Laffler, "I really should have explained. Sbirro's offers no choice whatsoever. You will eat the same meal as everyone else in this room. Tomorrow evening you would eat an entirely different meal, but again without designating a single preference."

"Very unusual," said Costain, "and certainly unsatisfactory at times. What if one doesn't have a taste for the particular dish set before him?"

"On that score," said Laffler solemnly, "you need have no fears. I give you my word that no matter how exacting your tastes, you will relish every mouthful you eat in Sbirro's."

Costain looked doubtful, and Laffler smiled. "And consider the subtle advantages of the system," he said.

449

"When you pick up the menu of a popular restaurant, you find yourself confronted with innumerable choices. You are forced to weigh, to evaluate, to make uneasy decisions which you may instantly regret. The effect of all this is a tension which, however slight, must make for discomfort.

"And consider the mechanics of the process. Instead of a hurly-burly of sweating cooks rushing about a kitchen in a frenzy to prepare a hundred varying items, we have a chef who stands serenely alone, bringing all his talents to bear on one task, with all assurance of a complete triumph!"

"Then you have seen the kitchen?"

"Unfortunately, no," said Laffler sadly. "The picture I offer is hypothetical, made of conversational fragments I have pieced together over the years. I must admit, though, that my desire to see the functioning of the kitchen here comes very close to being my sole obsession nowadays."

"But have you mentioned this to Sbirro?"

"A dozen times. He shrugs the suggestion away."

"Isn't that a rather curious foible on his part?"

"No, no," Laffler said hastily, "a master artist is never under the compulsion of petty courtesies. Still," he sighed, "I have never given up hope."

The waiter now reappeared bearing two soup bowls which he set in place with mathematical exactitude, and a small tureen from which he slowly ladled a measure of clear, thin broth. Costain dipped his spoon into the broth and tasted it with some curiosity. It was delicately flavoured, bland to the verge of tastelessness. Costain frowned, tentatively reached for the salt and pepper cellars, and discovered there were none on the table. He looked up, saw Laffler's eyes on him, and although unwilling to compromise with his own tastes, he hesitated to act as a damper on Laffler's enthusiasm. Therefore he smiled and indicated the broth.

"Excellent," he said.

Laffler returned his smile. "You do not find it excellent at all," he said coolly. "You find it flat and badly in need of condiments. I know this," he continued as Costain's eyebrows shot upwards, "because it was my own reaction many years ago, and because like yourself I found myself reaching for salt and pepper after the first mouthful. I also learned with surprise that condiments are not available in Sbirro's."

Costain was shocked. "Not even salt!" he exclaimed.

"Not even salt. The very fact that you require it for your soup stands as evidence that your taste is unduly jaded. I am confident that you will now make the same discovery that I did: by the time you have nearly finished your soup, your desire for salt will be nonexistent."

Laffler was right; before Costain had reached the bottom of his plate, he was relishing the nuances of the broth with steadily increasing delight. Laffler thrust aside his own empty bowl and rested his elbows on the table. "Do you agree with me now?"

"To my surprise," said Costain, "I do."

As the waiter busied himself clearing the table, Laffler lowered his voice significantly. "You will find," he said, "that the absence of condiments is but one of several noteworthy characteristics which mark Sbirro's. I may as well prepare you for these. For example, no alcoholic beverages of any sort are served here, nor for that matter any beverage except clear, cold water, the first and only drink necessary for a human being."

"Outside of mother's milk," suggested Costain dryly.

"I can answer that in like vein by pointing out that the average patron of Sbirro's has passed that primal stage of his development."

Costain laughed. "Granted," he said.

"Very well. There is also a ban on the use of tobacco in any form."

"But good heavens," said Costain, "doesn't that make

Sbirro's more a teetotaller's retreat than a gourmet's sanctuary?"

"I fear," said Laffler solemnly, "that you confuse the words, *gourmet* and *gourmand*. The gourmand, through glutting himself, requires a wider and wider latitude of experience to stir his surfeited senses, but the very nature of the gourmet is simplicity. The ancient Greek in his coarse chiton savoring the ripe olive; the Japanese in his bare room contemplating the curve of a single flower stem—these are the true gourmets."

"But an occasional drop of brandy or pipeful of tobacco," said Costain dubiously, "are hardly over-indulgences."

"By alternating stimulant and narcotic," said Laffler, "you seesaw the delicate balance of your taste so violently that it loses its most precious quality: the appreciation of fine food. During my years as a patron of Sbirro's, I have proved this to my satisfaction."

"May I ask," said Costain, "why you regard the ban on these things as having such deep aesthetic motives? What about such mundane reasons as the high cost of a liquor licence, or the possibility that patrons would object to the smell of tobacco in such confined quarters?"

Laffler shook his head violently. "If and when you meet Sbirro," he said, "you will understand at once that he is not the man to make decisions on a mundane basis. As a matter of fact, it was Sbirro himself who first made me cognizant of what you call 'aesthetic' motives."

"An amazing man," said Costain as the waiter prepared to serve the entrée.

Laffler's next words were not spoken until he had savoured and swallowed a large portion of meat. "I hesitate to use superlatives," he said, "but to my way of thinking, Sbirro represents man at the apex of his civilization!"

Costain cocked an eyebrow and applied himself to

452

his roast which rested in a pool of stiff gravy ungarnished by green or vegetable. The thin steam rising from it carried to his nostrils a subtle, tantalizing odour which made his mouth water. He chewed a piece as slowly and thoughtfully as if he were analyzing the intricacies of a Mozart symphony. The range of taste he discovered was really extraordinary, from the pungent nip of the crisp outer edge of the peculiarly flat yet soul-satisfying ooze of blood which the pressure of his jaws forced from the half-raw interior.

Upon swallowing he found himself ferociously hungry for another piece, and then another, and it was only with an effort that he prevented himself from wolfing down all his share of the meat and gravy without waiting to get the full voluptuous satisfaction from each mouthful. When he had scraped his platter clean, he realized that both he and Laffler had completed the entire course without exchanging a single word. He commented on this, and Laffler said: "Can you see any need for words in the presence of such food?"

Costain looked around at the shabby, dimly lit room, the quiet diners, with a new perception. "No," he said humbly, "I cannot. For any doubts I had I apologize unreservedly. In all your praise of Sbirro's there was not a single word of exaggeration."

"Ah," said Laffler delightedly. "And that is only part of the story. You heard me mention the special which unfortunately was not on the menu tonight. What you have just eaten is as nothing when compared to the absolute delights of that special!"

"Good Lord!" cried Costain. "What is it? Nightingale's tongues? Fillet of unicorn?"

"Neither," said Laffler. "It is lamb."

"Lamb?"

Laffler remained lost in thought for a minute. "If," he said at last, "I were to give you in my own unstinted words my opinion of this dish, you would judge me completely insane. That is how deeply the mere thought of it affects me. It is neither the fatty chop, nor the too solid leg; it is, instead, a select portion of the rarest sheep in existence and is named after the species—lamb Amirstan."

Costain knit his brows. "Amirstan?"

"A fragment of desolation almost lost on the border which separates Afghanistan and Russia. From chance remarks dropped by Sbirro, I gather it is no more than a plateau which grazes the pitiful remnants of a flock of superb sheep. Sbirro, through some means or other, obtained rights to the traffic in this flock and is, therefore, the sole restauranteur ever to have lamb Amirstan on his bill of fare. I can tell you that the appearance of this dish is a rare occurrence indeed, and luck is the only guide in determining for the clientele the exact date when it will be served."

"But surely," said Costain, "Sbirro could provide some advance knowledge of this event."

"The objection to that is simply stated," said Laffler. "There exists in this city a huge number of professional gluttons. Should advance information slip out, it is quite likely that they will, out of curiosity, become familiar with the dish and thenceforth supplant the regular patrons at these tables.

"But you don't mean to say," objected Costain, "that these few people present are the only ones in the entire city, or for that matter, in the whole wide world, who know of the existence of Sbirro's!"

"Very nearly. There may be one or two regular patrons who, for some reason, are not present at the moment."

"That's incredible."

"It is done," said Laffler, the slightest shade of menace in his voice, "by every patron making it his solemn obligation to keep the secret. By accepting my invitation this evening you automatically assume that obligation. I hope you can be trusted with it."

Costain flushed. "My position in your employ should

454

vouch for me. I only question the wisdom of a policy which keeps such magnificent food away from so many who would enjoy it."

"Do you know the inevitable result of the policy *you* favour?" asked Laffler bitterly. "An influx of idiots who would nightly complain that they are never served roast duck with chocolate sauce. Is that picture tolerable to you?"

"No," admitted Costain, "I am forced to agree with you."

Laffler leaned back in his chair wearily and passed his hand over his eyes in an uncertain gesture. "I am a solitary man," he said quietly, "and not by choice alone. It may sound strange to you, it may border on eccentricity, but I feel to my depths that this restaurant, this warm haven in a coldly insane world, is both family and friend to me."

And Costain, who to this moment had never viewed his companion as other than tyrannical employer or officious host, now felt an overwhelming pity twist inside his comfortably expanded stomach.

\*     \*     \*

By the end of two weeks the invitations to join Laffler at Sbirro's had become something of a ritual. Every day, at a few minutes after five, Costain would step out into the office corridor and lock his cubicle behind him; he would drape his overcoat neatly over his left arm, and peer into the glass of the door to make sure his Homburg was set at the proper angle. At one time he would have followed this by lighting a cigarette, but under Laffler's prodding he had decided to give abstinence a fair trial. Then he would start down the corridor, and Laffler would fall in step at his elbow, clearing his throat. "Ah, Costain. No plans for this evening, I hope."

"No," Costain would say, "I'm footloose and fancy-free," or "At your service," or something equally inane.

He wondered at times whether it would not be more tactful to vary the ritual with an occasional refusal, but the glow with which Laffler received his answer, and the rough friendliness of Laffler's grip on his arm, forestalled him.

Among the treacherous crags of the business world, reflected Costain, what better way to secure your footing than friendship with one's employer. Already, a secretary close to the workings of the inner office had commented publicly on Laffler's highly favourable opinion of Costain. That was all to the good.

And the food! The incomparable food at Sbirro's! For the first time in his life, Costain, ordinarily a lean and bony man, noted with gratification that he was certainly gaining weight; within two weeks his bones had disappeared under a layer of sleek, firm flesh, and here and there were even signs of incipient plumpness. It struck Costain one night, while surveying himself in his bath, that the rotund Laffler, himself, might have been a spare and bony man before discovering Sbirro's.

So there was obviously everything to be gained and nothing to be lost by accepting Laffler's invitations. Perhaps after testing the heralded wonders of lamb Amirstan and meeting Sbirro, who thus far had not made an appearance, a refusal or two might be in order. But certainly not until then.

That evening, two weeks to a day after his first visit to Sbirro's, Costain had both desires fulfilled: he dined on lamb Amirstan, and he met Sbirro. Both exceeded all his expectations.

When the waiter leaned over their table immediately after seating them and gravely announced: "Tonight is special, sair," Costain was shocked to find his heart pounding with expectation. On the table before him he saw Laffler's hands trembling violently. But it isn't natural, he thought suddenly. Two full grown men, presumably intelligent and in the full possession of their senses, as jumpy as a pair of cats waiting to have their meat flung to them!

"This is it!" Laffler's voice startled him so that he almost leaped from his seat. "The culinary triumph of all times! And faced by it you are embarrassed by the very emotions it distills."

"How did you know that?" Costain asked faintly.

"How? Because a decade ago I underwent your embarrassment. Add to that your air of revulsion and it's easy to see how affronted you are by the knowledge that man has not yet forgotten how to slaver over his meat."

"And these others," whispered Costain, "do they all feel the same thing?"

"Judge for yourself."

Costain looked furtively around at the nearby tables. "You are right," he finally said. "At any rate, there's comfort in numbers."

Laffler inclined his head slightly to the side. "One of the numbers," he remarked, "appears to be in for a disappointment."

Costain followed the gesture. At the table indicated a grey-haired man sat conspicuously alone, and Costain frowned at the empty chair opposite him.

"Why, yes," he recalled, "that very stout, bald man, isn't it? I believe it's the first dinner he's missed here in two weeks."

"The entire decade more likely," said Laffler sympathetically. "Rain or shine, crisis or calamity, I don't think he's missed an evening at Sbirro's since the first time I dined here. Imagine his expression when he's told that, on his very first defection, lamb Amirstan was the *plat du jour*."

Costain looked at the empty chair again with a dim discomfort. "His very first?" he murmured.

"Mr Laffler! And friend! I am so pleased. So very, very pleased. No, do not stand; I will have a place made." Miraculously a seat appeared under the figure standing there at the table. "The lamb Amirstan

457

will be an unqualified success, hurr? I myself have been stewing in the miserable kitchen all the day, prodding the foolish chef to do everything just so. The just so is the important part, hurr? But I see your friend does not know me. An introduction, perhaps?"

The words ran in a smooth, fluid eddy. They rippled, they purred, they hypnotized Costain so that he could do no more than stare. The mouth that uncoiled this sinuous monologue was alarmingly wide, with thin mobile lips that curled and twisted with every syllable. There was a flat nose with a straggling line of hair under it; wide-set eyes, almost oriental in appearance, that glittered in the unsteady flare of gaslight; and long, sleek hair that swept back from high on the unwrinkled forehead—hair so pale that it might have been bleached of all colour. An amazing face surely, and the sight of it tortured Costain with the conviction that it was somehow familiar. His brain twitched and prodded but could not stir up any solid recollection.

Laffler's voice jerked Costain out of his study. "Mr Sbirro. Mr Costain, a good friend and associate." Costain rose and shook the proffered hand. It was warm and dry, flint-hard against his palm.

"I am so very pleased, Mr Costain. So very, very pleased," purred the voice. "You like my little establishment, hurr? You have a great treat in store, I assure you."

Laffler chuckled. "Oh, Costain's been dining here regularly for two weeks," he said. "He's by way of becoming a great admirer of yours, Sbirro."

The eyes were turned on Costain. "A very great compliment. You compliment me with your presence and I return same with my food, hurr? But the lamb Amirstan is far superior to anything of your past experience, I assure you. All the trouble of obtaining it, all the difficulty of preparation, is truly merited."

Costain strove to put aside the exasperating problem of that face. "I have wondered," he said, "why with

458

all these difficulties you mention, you even bother to present lamb Amirstan to the public. Surely your other dishes are excellent enough to uphold your reputation."

Sbirro smiled so broadly that his face became perfectly round. "Perhaps it is a matter of the psychology, hurr? Someone discovers a wonder and must share it with others. He must fill his cup to the brim, perhaps, by observing the so evident pleasure of those who explore it with him. Or," he shrugged, "perhaps it is just a matter of good business."

"Then in the light of all this," Costain persisted, "and considering all the conventions you have imposed on your customers, why do you open the restaurant to the public instead of operating it as a private club?"

The eyes abruptly glinted into Costain's, then turned away. "So perspicacious, hurr? Then I will tell you. Because there is more privacy in a public eating place than in the most exclusive club in existence! Here no one inquires of your affairs; no one desires to know the intimacies of your life. Here the business is eating. We are not curious about names and addresses or the reasons for the coming and going of our guests. We welcome you when you are here; we have no regrets when you are here no longer. That is the answer, hurr?"

Costain was startled by his vehemence. "I had no intention of prying," he stammered.

Sbirro ran the tip of his tongue over his thin lips. "No, no," he reassured, "you are not prying. Do not let me give you that impression. On the contrary, I invite your questions."

"Oh, come, Costain," said Laffler. "Don't let Sbirro intimidate you. I've known him for years and I guarantee that his bark is worse than his bite. Before you know it, he'll be showing you all the privileges of the house—outside of inviting you to visit his precious kitchen, of course."

"Ah," smiled Sbirro, "for that, Mr Costain may have to wait a little while. For everything else I am at his beck and call."

Laffler slapped his hand jovially on the table. "What did I tell you!" he said. "Now let's have the truth, Sbirro. Has anyone, outside of your staff, ever stepped into the sanctum sanctorum?"

Sbirro looked up. "You see on the wall above you," he said earnestly, "the portrait of one to whom I did the honour. A very dear friend and a patron of most long standing, he is evidence that my kitchen is not inviolate."

Costain studied the picture and started with recognition. "Why," he said excitedly, "that's the famous writer—you know the one, Laffler—he used to do such wonderful short stories and cynical bits and then suddenly took himself off and disappeared in Mexico!"

"Of course!" cried Laffler, "and to think I've been sitting under his portrait for years without even realizing it!" He turned to Sbirro. "A dear friend, you say? His disappearance must have been a blow to you."

Sbirro's face lengthened. "It was, it was, I assure you. But think of it this way, gentlemen: he was probably greater in his death than in his life, hurr? A most tragic man, he often told me that his only happy hours were spent here at this very table. Pathetic, is it not? And to think the only favour I could ever show him was to let him witness the mysteries of my kitchen, which is, when all is said and done, no more than a plain, ordinary kitchen."

"You seem very certain of his death," commented Costain. "After all, no evidence has ever turned up to substantiate it."

Sbirro contemplated the picture. "None at all," he said softly. "Remarkable, hurr?"

With the arrival of the entrée Sbirro leaped to his feet and set about serving them himself. With his eyes alight he lifted the casserole from the tray and sniffed at the fragrance from within with sensual relish. Then, taking great care not to lose a single drop of gravy, he filled two platters with chunks of dripping meat. As if exhausted by this task, he sat back in his chair, breathing heavily. "Gentlemen," he said "to your good appetite."

Costain chewed his first mouthful with great deliberation and swallowed it. Then he looked at the empty tines of his fork with glazed eyes.

"Good God!" he breathed.

"It is good, hurr? Better than you imagined?"

Costain shook his head dazedly. "It is impossible," he said slowly, "for the uninitiated to conceive the delights of lamb Amirstan as for mortal man to look into his own soul."

"Perhaps"—Sbirro thrust his head so close that Costain could feel the warm, fetid breath tickle his nostrils—"perhaps you have just had a glimpse into your soul, hurr?"

Costain tried to draw back slightly without giving offence. "Perhaps." He laughed. "And a gratifying picture it made: all fang and claw. But without intending any disrespect, I should hardly like to build my church on *lamb en casserole*."

Sbirro rose and laid a hand gently on his shoulder. "So perspicacious," he said. "Sometimes when you have nothing to do, nothing, perhaps, but sit for a very little while in a dark room and think of this world— what it is and what it is going to be—then you must turn your thoughts a little to the significance of the Lamb in religion. It will be so interesting. And now"—he bowed deeply to both men—"I have held you long enough from your dinner. I was most happy," he said, nodding to Costain, "and I am sure we will meet again." The teeth gleamed, the eyes glittered, and Sbirro was gone down the aisle of tables.

Costain twisted around to stare after the retreating figure. "Have I offended him in some way?" he asked.

461

Laffler looked up from his plate. "Offended him? He loves that kind of talk. Lamb Amirstan is a ritual with him; get him started and he'll be back at you a dozen times worse than a priest making a conversion."

Costain turned to his meal with the face still hovering before him. "Interesting man," he reflected. "Very."

It took him a month to discover the tantalizing familiarity of that face, and when he did, he laughed aloud in his bed. Why, of course! Sbirro might have sat as the model for the Cheshire cat in *Alice*!

\*     \*     \*

He passed this thought on to Laffler the very next evening as they pushed their way down the street to the restaurant against a chill, blustering wind. Laffler only looked blank.

"You may be right," he said, "but I'm not a fit judge. It's a far cry back to the days when I read the book. A far cry, indeed."

As if taking up his words, a piercing howl came ringing down the street and stopped both men short in their tracks. "Someone's in trouble there," said Laffler. "Look!"

Not far from the entrance to Sbirro's two figures could be seen struggling in the near darkness. They swayed back and forth and suddenly tumbled into a writhing heap on the sidewalk. The piteous howl went up again, and Laffler, despite his girth, ran towards it at a fair speed with Costain tagging cautiously behind.

Stretched out full length on the pavement was a slender figure with the dusky complexion and white hair of one of Sbirro's servitors. His fingers were futilely plucking at the huge hands which encircled his throat, and his knees pushed weakly up at the gigantic bulk of a man who brutally bore down with his full weight.

Laffler came up panting. "Stop this!" he shouted. "What's going on here?"

The pleading eyes almost bulging from their sockets

462

turned towards Laffler. "Help, sair. This man—
drunk——"

"Drunk am I, ya dirty——" Costain saw now that
the man was a sailor in a badly soiled uniform. The air
around him reeked with the stench of liquor. "Pick
me pocket and then call me drunk, will ya!" He dug
his fingers in harder, and his victim groaned.

Laffler seized the sailor's shoulder. "Let go of him,
do you hear! Let go of him at once!" he cried, and the
next instant was sent careening into Costain, who staggered back under the force of the blow.

The attack on his own person sent Laffler into immediate and berserk action. Without a sound he leaped
at the sailor, striking and kicking furiously at the un-
protected face and flanks. Stunned at first, the man
came to his feet with a rush and turned on Laffler. For
a moment they stood locked together, and then as
Costain joined the attack, all three went sprawling to
the ground. Slowly Laffler and Costain got to their
feet and looked down at the body before them.

"He's either out cold from liquor," said Costain, "or
he struck his head going down. In any case, it's a job
for the police."

"No, no, sair!" The waiter crawled weakly to his
feet, and stood swaying. "No police, sair. Mr Sbirro
do not want such. You understand, sair." He caught
hold of Costain with a pleading hand, and Costain
looked at Laffler.

"Of course not," said Laffler. "We won't have to
bother with the police. They'll pick him up soon
enough, the murderous sot. But what in the world
started all this?"

"That man, sair. He make most erratic way while
walking, and with no meaning I push against him.
Then he attack me, accusing me to rob him."

"As I thought." Laffler pushed the waiter gently
along. "Now go on in and get yourself attended
to."

The man seemed ready to burst into tears. "To you, sair, I owe my life. If there is anything I can do——"

Laffler turned into the areaway that led to Sbirro's door. "No, no, it was nothing. You go along, and if Sbirro has any questions send him to me. I'll straighten it out."

"My life, sair," were the last words they heard as the inner door closed behind them.

"There you are, Costain," said Laffler, as a few minutes later he drew his chair under the table, "civilized man in all his glory. Reeking with alcohol, strangling to death some miserable innocent who came too close."

Costain made an effort to gloss over the nerve-shattering memory of the episode. "It's the neurotic cat that takes to alcohol," he said. "Surely there's a reason for that sailor's condition."

"Reason? Of course there is. Plain atavistic savagery!" Laffler swept his arm in an all-embracing gesture. "Why do we all sit here at our meat? Not only to appease physical demands, but because our atavistic selves cry for release. Think back, Costain. Do you remember that I once described Sbirro as the epitome of civilization? Can you now see why? A brilliant man, he fully understands the nature of human beings. But unlike lesser men he bends all his efforts to the satisfaction of our innate natures without resultant harm to some innocent bystander."

"When I think back on the wonders of lamb Amirstan," said Costain, "I quite understand what you're driving at. And, by the way, isn't it nearly due to appear on the bill of fare? It must have been over a month ago that it was last served."

The waiter, filling the tumblers, hesitated. "I am so sorry, sair. No special this evening."

"There's your answer," Laffler grunted, "and probably just my luck to miss out on it altogether the next time."

Costain stared at him. "Oh, come, that's impossible."

"No, blast it." Laffler drank off half his water at a gulp and the waiter immediately refilled the glass. "I'm off to South America for a surprise tour of inspection. One month, two months, Lord knows how long."

"Are things that bad down there?"

"They could be better." Laffler suddenly grinned. "Mustn't forget it takes very mundane dollars and cents to pay the tariff at Sbirro's."

"I haven't heard a word of this around the office."

"Wouldn't be a surprise tour if you had. Nobody knows about this except myself—and now you. I want to walk in on them completely unsuspected. Find out what flimflammery they're up to down there. As far as the office is concerned, I'm off on a jaunt somewhere. Maybe recuperating in some sanatorium from my hard work. Anyhow, the business will be in good hands. Yours, among them."

"Mine?" said Costain, surprised.

"When you go in tomorrow you'll find yourself in receipt of a promotion, even if I'm not there to hand it to you personally. Mind you, it has nothing to do with our friendship either; you've done fine work, and I'm immensely grateful for it."

Costain reddened under the praise. "You don't expect to be in tomorrow. Then you're leaving tonight?"

Laffler nodded. "I've been trying to wangle some reservations. If they come through, well, this will be in the nature of a farewell celebration."

"You know," said Costain slowly, "I devoutly hope that your reservations don't come through. I believe our dinners here have come to mean more to me than I ever dared imagine."

The waiter's voice broke in. "Do you wish to be served now, sair?" and they both started.

"Of course, of course," said Laffler sharply, "I didn't realize you were waiting."

465

"What bothers me," he told Costain as the waiter turned away, "is the thought of the lamb Amirstan I'm bound to miss. To tell you the truth, I've already put off my departure a week, hoping to hit a lucky night, and now I simply can't delay any more. I do hope that when you're sitting over your share of lamb Amirstan, you'll think of me with suitable regrets."

Costain laughed. "I will indeed," he said as he turned to his dinner.

Hardly had he cleared the plate when a waiter silently reached for it. It was not their usual waiter, he observed; it was none other than the victim of the assault.

"Well," Costain said, "how do you feel now? Still under the weather?"

The waiter paid no attention to him. Instead, with the air of a man under great strain, he turned to Laffler. "Sair," he whispered. "My life. I owe it to you. I can repay you!"

Laffler looked up in amazement, then shook his head firmly. "No," he said, "I want nothing from you, understand? You have repaid me sufficiently with your thanks. Now get on with your work and let's hear no more about it."

The waiter did not stir an inch, but his voice rose slightly. "By the body and blood of your God, sair, I will help you even if you do not want! *Do not go into the kitchen, sair.* I trade you my life for yours, sair, when I speak this. Tonight or any night of your life, do not go into the kitchen at Sbirro's!"

Laffler sat back, completely dumbfounded. "Not go into the kitchen? Why shouldn't I go into the kitchen if Mr Sbirro ever took it into his head to invite me there? What's all this about?"

A hard hand was laid on Costain's back, and another gripped the waiter's arm. The waiter remained frozen to the spot, his lips compressed, his eyes downcast.

"What is all *what* about, gentlemen?" purred the

voice. "So opportune an arrival. In time as ever, I see, to answer all the questions, hurr?"

Laffler breathed a sigh of relief. "Ah, Sbirro, thank heaven you're here. This man is saying something about my not going into your kitchen. Do you know what he means?"

The teeth showed in a broad grin. "But of course. This good man was giving you advice in all amiability. It so happens that my too emotional chef heard some rumour that I might have a guest into his precious kitchen, and he flew into a fearful rage. Such a rage, gentlemen! He even threatened to give notice on the spot, and you can understand what that would mean to Sbirro's, hurr? Fortunately, I succeeded in showing him what a signal honour it is to have an esteemed patron and true connoisseur observe him at his work firsthand, and now he is quite amenable. Quite, hurr?"

He released the waiter's arm. "You are at the wrong table," he said softly. "See that it does not happen again."

The waiter slipped off without daring to raise his eyes and Sbirro drew a chair to the table. He seated himself and brushed his hand lightly over his hair. "Now I am afraid that the cat is out of the bag, hurr? This invitation to you, Mr Laffler, was to be a surprise; but the surprise is gone, and all that is left is the invitation."

Laffler mopped beads of perspiration from his forehead. "Are you serious?" he said huskily. "Do you mean that we are really to witness the preparation of your food tonight?"

Sbirro drew a sharp fingernail along the tablecloth, leaving a thin, straight line printed in the linen. "Ah," he said, "I am faced with a dilemma of great proportions." He studied the line soberly. "You, Mr Laffler, have been my guest for ten long years. But our friend here——"

Costain raised his hand in protest. "I understand

467

perfectly. This invitation is solely to Mr Laffler, and naturally my presence is embarrassing. As it happen., I have an early engagement for this evening and must be on my way anyhow. So you see there's no dilemma at all, really."

"No," said Laffler, "absolutely not. That wouldn't be fair at all. We've been sharing this until now, Costain, and I won't enjoy this experience half as much if you're not along. Surely Sbirro can make his conditions flexible, this one occasion."

They both looked at Sbirro who shrugged his shoulders regretfully.

Costain rose abruptly. "I'm not going to sit here, Laffler, and spoil your great adventure. And then too," he bantered, "think of that ferocious chef waiting to get his cleaver on you. I prefer not to be at the scene. I'll just say goodbye," he went on, to cover Laffler's guilty silence, "and leave you to Sbirro. I'm sure he'll take pains to give you a good show." He held out his hand and Laffler squeezed it painfully hard.

"You're being very decent, Costain," he said. "I hope you'll continue to dine here until we meet again. It shouldn't be too long."

Sbirro made way for Costain to pass. "I will expect you," he said. "*Au 'voir.*"

Costain stopped briefly in the dim foyer to adjust his scarf and fix his Homburg at the proper angle. When he turned away from the mirror, satisfied at last, he saw with a final glance that Laffler and Sbirro were already at the kitchen door, Sbirro holding the door invitingly wide with one hand, while the other rested, almost tenderly, on Laffler's meaty shoulders.

# THE NO EXIT PRESS DIARY FOR 1990

## compiled by Graham Lovatt

The compiler and publisher would like to apologise in advance for any offence caused to readers whose favourite authors or films are not included in this diary.

Do not get upset or do anything as drastic as taking a contract out on us but write, instead, with any snippets of information which you think ought to be included in next year's diary.

Have a criminally good 1990.

GJL

N.B.   All film titles are shown thus: 'The Maltese Falcon'.
        r. indicates U.S. release date.

# JANUARY

**1  MONDAY**

**2  TUESDAY**  *Isaac Asimov b. 1920*

**3  WEDNESDAY**

**4  THURSDAY**  *Vincent Starrett d. 1974 'High Sierra' r. 1941*

**5  FRIDAY**  *James Melville b. 1931 Arthur Lyons b. 1946*

**6  SATURDAY**  *Sherlock Holmes birthday (according to the Baker Street Irregulars) Francis M. Nevins Jr. b. 1943*

**7  SUNDAY**  *David Goodis d. 1967*

# JANUARY

**8 MONDAY**      *Wilkie Collins b. 1824*

**9 TUESDAY**     *Phoebe Atwood Taylor d. 1976*
*Gil Brewer d. 1983*

**10 WEDNESDAY** *Dashiell Hammett d. 1961*

**11 THURSDAY**  *Manfred B. Lee (one half of Ellery Queen)*
*b. 1905 Los Angeles, 1936: Chandler &*
*Hammett are introduced to each other at a*
*dinner for Black Mask' contributors.*

**12 FRIDAY**    *Trevanian (Rodney Whitacker) b. 1925 Agatha*
*Christie d. 1976 'Shadow of a Doubt' r. 1943*

**13 SATURDAY**  *Ted Willis b. 1918 Amanda Cross b.1926*
*Ron Goulart b.1933*

**14 SUNDAY**

## JANUARY

**15 MONDAY** *Michael Collins b. 1924*

**16 TUESDAY** *Carroll John Daly d. 1958 'I Wake Up Screaming' r. 1942*

**17 WEDNESDAY** *Roy Lewis b. 1933   Colin Watson d. 1982*

**18 THURSDAY** *File On Thelma Jordan' r. 1950*

**19 FRIDAY** *Edgar Allen Poe b. 1809  Patricia Highsmith b. 1921  Patricia Moyes b. 1923*

**20 SATURDAY**

**21 SUNDAY** *Niagara' r. 1953*

# JANUARY

**22 MONDAY**
*Joseph Wambaugh b. 1973 'Dead Reckoning'*
*r. 1947 'T Men' r. 1948*

**23 TUESDAY**
*Humphrey Bogart b. 1899 Dick Donovan d. 1934*
*'Lady in the Lake' r. 1947 'Nightfall' r. 1957*

**24 WEDNESDAY**

**25 THURSDAY**
*The Woman in the Window' r. 1945*

**26 FRIDAY**
*Brian Garfield b. 1939*

**27 SATURDAY**

**28 SUNDAY**
*Richard Hoyt b. 1941 Tim Heald b. 1944*
*Patricia Wentworth d. 1961*

## JANUARY / FEBRUARY

**29 MONDAY**     *'You Only Live Once' r. 1937*

**30 TUESDAY**     *Margaret Yorke b. 1924   J.S. Fletcher d. 1935*

**31 WEDNESDAY**

**1 THURSDAY**     *Colin Watson b. 1920*

**2 FRIDAY**

**3 SATURDAY**     *E. Phillips Oppenheim d. 1946*

**4 SUNDAY**     *Brett Halliday d. 1977*

# FEBRUARY

**5  MONDAY**  *Margaret Millar b. 1915*

**6  TUESDAY**  *'Fallen Angel' r. 1946 'He Walked By Night' r. 1949*

**7  WEDNESDAY**  *Charles Dickens b. 1812  J.S. Fletcher b. 1863 'Ministry Of Fear' r. 1945*

**8  THURSDAY**

**9  FRIDAY**

**10 SATURDAY**  *Julian Rathbone b. 1935  Edgar Wallace d. 1932*

**11 SUNDAY**  *John Buchan d. 1940*

# FEBRUARY

**12 MONDAY** *Andrew Garve b. 1908 Janwillem van de Wetering b. 1931*

**13 TUESDAY** *Josephine Tey d. 1952 Arthur Upfield d. 1964*

**14 WEDNESDAY**

**15 THURSDAY** *Anthony Gilbert b. 1899 B.M. Gill b. 1921*

**16 FRIDAY**

**17 SATURDAY** *Ronald Knox b. 1888 Elleston Trevor b. 1920 Ruth Rendell b. 1930 'Phantom Lady' r. 1944*

**18 SUNDAY** *Len Deighton b. 1929 Ngaio Marsh d. 1982 'Call Northside 777' r. 1948*

# FEBRUARY

**19 MONDAY**    *Ross Thomas b. 1926 'Johnny Eager' r. 1942*

**20 TUESDAY**    *Bill Knox b. 1928*

**21 WEDNESDAY**    *'The Thirteenth Letter' r. 1951*

**22 THURSDAY**    *Edward D. Hoch b. 1930 'Knock On Any Door' r. 1949*

**23 FRIDAY**

**24 SATURDAY**    *August Derleth b. 1909 'The Enforcer' r.1951*

**25 SUNDAY**    *John Wainwright b. 1921*

## FEBRUARY / MARCH

**26 MONDAY**

**27 TUESDAY**    *John Dickson Carr d. 1977*

**28 WEDNESDAY**

**1 THURSDAY**

**2 FRIDAY**    *Jonathan Ross b. 1916   David Goodis b. 1917*

**3 SATURDAY**    *Max Allan Collins b. 1948*

**4 SUNDAY**    *'Naked City' r. 1948*

# MARCH

**5 MONDAY**

---

**6 TUESDAY** *William F. Nolan b. 1928*

---

**7 WEDNESDAY** *Sara Woods b. 1922 'The Long Godbye' r. 1973*

---

**8 THURSDAY**

---

**9 FRIDAY** *William Campbell Gault b. 1910 Edward Grierson b. 1914 MIckey Spillane b. 1918 Anthony Berekely d. 1971*

---

**10 SATURDAY**

---

**11 SUNDAY** *Erle Stanley Gardner d. 1970 Fredric Brown d. 1972*

## MARCH

**12 MONDAY**

**13 TUESDAY**

**14 WEDNESDAY**

**15 THURSDAY**     *Lillian de la Torre b. 1902  'The Fall Guy'*
*r. 1947*

**16 FRIDAY**

**17 SATURDAY**     *Patrick Hamilton b. 1904*

**18 SUNDAY**     *Richard Condon b. 1915*

# MARCH

**19 MONDAY**

**20 TUESDAY** *Ernest Bramah b. 1868*

**21 WEDNESDAY**

**22 THURSDAY** *E.W. Hornung d. 1921*

**23 FRIDAY**

**24 SATURDAY** *Leigh Brackett d. 1978*

**25 SUNDAY**

## MARCH / APRIL

**26 MONDAY**      *Raymond Chandler d. 1959*

**27 TUESDAY**      *'Johnny O'Clock' r. 1947*

**28 WEDNESDAY** *Joyce Porter b. 1924*

**29 THURSDAY**      *Raymond Postgate d. 1971 'Madigan' r. 1968*

**30 FRIDAY**      *E.C. Bentley d. 1956*

**31 SATURDAY**      *Lionel Davidson b. 1922*

**1 SUNDAY**      *Edgar Wallace b. 1875*

# APRIL

**2  MONDAY**     *C.H.B. Kitchin d. 1967*

**3  TUESDAY**     *Reginald Hill b. 1936*

**4  WEDNESDAY**

**5  THURSDAY**     *Robert Bloch b. 1917  Earl Derr Biggers d. 1933*

**6  FRIDAY**

**7  SATURDAY**

**8  SUNDAY**

## APRIL

**9  MONDAY**     *Jacques Futrelle b. 1875  'The Dark Corner'*
*r. 1946  'The Big Clock' r. 1948*

**10 TUESDAY**

**11 WEDNESDAY** *R. Austin Freeman b. 1862  Peter O'Donnell b.*
*1920  S.S. Van Dine d. 1939  Freeman Wills*
*Crofts d. 1957*

**12 THURSDAY**

**13 FRIDAY**     *Bill Prnzini b. 1943*

**14 SATURDAY**   *Horace McCoy b. 1897  William R. Cox b. 1901*

**15  SUNDAY**    *Howard Browne b. 1908  Jacques Futrelle*
*d. 1912*

# APRIL

**16 MONDAY**

**17 TUESDAY**

**18 WEDNESDAY**

**19 THURSDAY**   *Gladys Mitchell b. 1901  'The Blue Dahlia'*
*r. 1946*

**20 FRIDAY**

**21 SATURDAY**   *John Mortimer b. 1923*

**22 SUNDAY**   *'The Crooked Way' r. 1949*

# APRIL

**23 MONDAY**  *Ngaio Marsh b. 1899*

**24 TUESDAY**

**25 WEDNESDAY**  *Richard Deming b. 1915  W.R. Burnett d. 1982*

**26 THURSDAY**

**27 FRIDAY**  *Nicholas Blake (Cecil Day Lewis) b. 1904*

**28 SATURDAY**

**29 SUNDAY**  *Anthony Boucher d. 1968*

## APRIL / MAY

**30 MONDAY**   *'D.O.A.' r. 1950*

**1 TUESDAY**   *Andrew Coburn b. 1932*

**2 WEDNESDAY**   *'The Postman Always Rings Twice' r. 1946*

**3 THURSDAY**   *Edgar Lustgarten b. 1907   Frederick Nebel d. 1967*

**4 FRIDAY**

**5 SATURDAY**   *Miles Tripp b. 1923.*

**6 SUNDAY**

# MAY

**7  MONDAY**    *A. E.W. Mason b. 1865*

**8  TUESDAY**

**9  WEDNESDAY**

**10 THURSDAY**

**11 FRIDAY**

**12 SATURDAY**    *Leslie Charteris b. 1907*

**13 SUNDAY**    *Daphne Du Maurier b. 1907 'This Gun For Hire' r. 1942*

# MAY

**14 MONDAY**

---

**15 TUESDAY**

---

**16 WEDNESDAY** *While The City Sleeps' r. 1956*

---

**17 THURSDAY** *'In A Lonely Place' r. 1950*

---

**18 FRIDAY** *Phoebe Atwood Taylor b. 1909 'Kiss Me Deadly' r. 1955*

---

**19 SATURDAY**

---

**20 SUNDAY** *Margery Allingham b. 1904 'The Killing' r. 1956*

# MAY

**21 MONDAY**   *'Touch of Evil' r. 1958  'French Connection II' r. 1975*

**22 TUESDAY**   *Sir Arthur Conan Doyle b. 1859   Nicholas Blake (Cecil Day Lewis) d. 1972*

**23 WEDNESDAY**

**24 THURSDAY**   *Edward Grierson d. 1975*

**25 FRIDAY**   *Robert Ludlum b. 1927*

**26 SATURDAY**

**27 SUNDAY**   *Dashiell Hammett b. 1894  Tony Hillerman b. 1925*

## MAY / JUNE

**28 MONDAY**  *Dick Donovan b. 1842  G.K. Chesterton b. 1874
Ian Fleming b. 1908*

**29 TUESDAY**

**30 WEDNESDAY**  *Paul Cain b. 1902  Julian Symons b. 1912*

**31 THURSDAY**

**1  FRIDAY**

**2  SATURDAY**  *Michael Underwood b. 1916*

**3  SUNDAY**

# JUNE

**4 MONDAY**

---

**5 TUESDAY** *Craig Rice b. 1908 Ken Follett b: 1949 ' Fury' r. 1936*

---

**6 WEDNESDAY**

---

**7 THURSDAY** *E.W. Hornung b. 1866*

---

**8 FRIDAY** *David Williams b. 1926 The Asphalt Jungle' r. 1950*

---

**9 SATURDAY** *Charles Dickens d. 1870 John Creasey d. 1973*

---

**10 SUNDAY** *Brian Freemantle b. 1936 Leo Bruce d. 1979*

# JUNE

**11 MONDAY** *George Baxt b. 1923*

**12 TUESDAY** *Henry Slesar b. 1927*

**13 WEDNESDAY** *Rex Burns b. 1935*

**14 THURSDAY** *G.K. Chesterton d. 1936*

**15 FRIDAY** *'Conflict' r. 1945*

**16 SATURDAY** *Victor Canning b. 1911*

**17 SUNDAY**

## JUNE

**18 MONDAY**

**19 TUESDAY**

**20 WEDNESDAY** *Leo Bruce b. 1903  Celia Fremlin b. 1914*
*Catherine Aird b. 1930  Dorothy Simpson b. 1933*

**21 THURSDAY** *'Chinatown' r. 1974*

**22 FRIDAY** *Hilary Waugh b. 1920*

**23 SATURDAY** *Paul Cain d. 1966  Jonathan Latimer d. 1983*
*'Mask of Dimitrios' r. 1944*

**24 SUNDAY** *Nigel Morland b. 1905  June Thomson b. 1930*
*Lawrence Block b. 1938*

## JUNE / JULY

**25 MONDAY**   *Erskine Childers b. 1870  Barry Perowne b. 1908*

**26 TUESDAY**   *Colin Wilson b. 1931  Peter Cheyney d. 1951 'Sweet Smell Of Success' ("Match Me Sidney") r. 1957*

**27 WEDNESDAY** *Ernest Bramah d. 1942 'Friends Of Eddie Coyle' r. 1973*

**28 THURSDAY**  *Eric Ambler b. 1909 'They Live By Night' r. (as 'The Twisted Road') 1948*

**29 FRIDAY**

**30 SATURDAY**  *Margery Allingham d. 1966 'Strangers On A Train' r. 1951*

**1 SUNDAY**   *James M. Cain b. 1892  Wiliam L. DeAndrea b. 1952  Alan Pinkerton (founder of Pinkerton's National Detective Agency) d. 1884*

# JULY

**2  MONDAY**     *William Le Queux b. 1864 'The Prowler' r. 1951*
*'Night Moves' r. 1975*

**3  TUESDAY**     *Gwen Moffat b. 1924  Evelyn Anthony b. 1928*

**4  WEDNESDAY**  *August Derleth d. 1971*

**5  THURSDAY**    *Anthony Berkeley b. 1893   Georgette Heyer*
*d. 1974*

**6  FRIDAY**

**7  SATURDAY**    *Sir Arthur Conan Doyle d. 1930*

**8  SUNDAY**      *Fergus Hume b. 1859*

# JULY

**9 MONDAY**  *John Franklin Bardin d. 1981*

**10 TUESDAY**  *E.C. Bentley b. 1875*

**11 WEDNESDAY** *Ross MacDonald d. 1983*

**12 THURSDAY**  *Donald Westlake b. 1933*

**13 FRIDAY**  *Dorothy L. Sayers b. 1893  Fergus Hume d. 1932*

**14 SATURDAY**

**15 SUNDAY**

# JULY

**16 MONDAY**  *John P. Marquand d. 1960 'Key Largo' r. 1948*

**17 TUESDAY**  *Erle Stanley Gardner b. 1889  James Cagney b. 1899  Michael Gilbert b. 1912*

**18 WEDNESDAY**  *Sydney Horler b. 1888*

**19 THURSDAY**  *Chester Himes b. 1909  Joseph Hansen b. 1923*

**20 FRIDAY**

**21 SATURDAY**  *Michael Lewin b. 1942 'The Stranger' r. 1946*

**22 SUNDAY**  *Bartholomew Gill b. 1943*

# JULY

**23 MONDAY** — *Raymond Chandler b. 1888  Elspeth Huxley b. 1907*

**24 TUESDAY** — *Francois Eugene Vidocq (world's first private detective) b. 1775  John D. Mac Donald b. 1916 Barry N. Malzberg b. 1939  Roger Busby b. 1941*

**25 WEDNESDAY**

**26 THURSDAY**

**27 FRIDAY** — *Jack Higgins b. 1929  Gladys Mitchell d. 1983*

**28 SATURDAY**

**29 SUNDAY**

## JULY / AUGUST

**30 MONDAY**

---

**31 TUESDAY**    *Brett Halliday b. 1904*

---

**1 WEDNESDAY**    *W. J. Burley b. 1914  Carter Brown b. 1923*

---

**2 THURSDAY**    *Joseph Hayes b. 1918*

---

**3 FRIDAY**    *P.D. James b. 1920*

---

**4 SATURDAY**    *' Kiss Tomorrow Goodbye' r. 1950 'Panic In The Streets' r. 1950*

---

**5 SUNDAY**

# AUGUST

**6 MONDAY**     *F. Tennyson Jesse d. 1958*

**7 TUESDAY**     *Anthony Lejeune b. 1928 William R. Cox d. 1988*

**8 WEDNESDAY**     *'City That Never Sleeps' r. 1953*

**9 THURSDAY**     *Laurence Meynell b. 1899*

**10 FRIDAY**     *Hugh Pentecost b. 1903 Dorothy B. Hughes b. 1904*

**11 SATURDAY**

**12 SUNDAY**     *Ian Fleming d. 1964*

# AUGUST

**13 MONDAY**    *Alfred Hitchcock b. 1899*

**14 TUESDAY**    *Sapper (Herman Cyril McNeile) d. 1937 J.B. Priestly d. 1984 'I, The Jury' r. 1953*

**15 WEDNESDAY**

**16 THURSDAY**    *Georgette Heyer b. 1902 Anthony Price b. 1928*

**17 FRIDAY**

**18 SATURDAY**

**19 SUNDAY**

# AUGUST

**20 MONDAY**   *'Farewell My Lovely' r. 1975*

**21 TUESDAY**   *Anthony Boucher b. 1911   Robert L. Fish b. 1912*

**22 WEDNESDAY**   *'Notorious' r. 1946*

**23 THURSDAY**

**24 FRIDAY**   *Ronald Knox d. 1957*

**25 SATURDAY**   *Cyril Hare d. 1958*

**26 SUNDAY**   *John Buchan b. 1875   Earl Derr Biggers b. 1884 1987: Major crime-fiction publishing event ! First No Exit Press titles ("Fast One" & "Dead Don't Care") are issued.*

# AUGUST / SEPTEMBER

**27 MONDAY**     *Ira Levin b. 1929  Lady Antonia Fraser b. 1932*

**28 TUESDAY**     *Craig Rice d. 1957 'The Killers' r. 1946*

**29 WEDNESDAY**

**30 THURSDAY**

**31 FRIDAY**     *'The Big Sleep' r. 1946*

**1  SATURDAY**     *Arthur Upfield b. 1888 'Sorry, Wrong Number'*
*r. 1948*

**2  SUNDAY**     *'White Heat' r. 1949*

# SEPTEMBER

**3  MONDAY**  *Frederick Dannay (one half of Ellery Queen) d. 1982*

**4  TUESDAY**  *Cyril Hare b. 1900*

**5  WEDNESDAY**  *Richard Deming d. 1983 'Beyond A Reasonable Doubt' r. 1956*

**6  THURSDAY**  *Richard Hull b. 1896  Elizabeth Ferrars b. 1907*

**7  FRIDAY**  *'Double Indemnity' r. 1944*

**8  SATURDAY**

**9  SUNDAY**

## SEPTEMBER

**10 MONDAY** *Peter Lovesey b. 1936*

**11 TUESDAY** *John Lutz b. 1939*

**12 WEDNESDAY**

**13 THURSDAY** *J.B. Priestley b. 1894*

**14 FRIDAY** *Carroll John Daly b. 1889*

**15 SATURDAY** *Agatha Christie b. 1890 Loren D. Estleman b. 1952 Edmund Crispin d. 1978*

**16 SUNDAY**

# SEPTEMBER

**17 MONDAY** *John Creasey b. 1908 Robert B. Parker b. 1932 'Rogue Cop' r. 1954*

**18 TUESDAY** *'Point Blank' r. 1967*

**19 WEDNESDAY**

**20 THURSDAY**

**21 FRIDAY**

**22 SATURDAY** *Mary Roberts Rinehart d. 1958*

**23 SUNDAY** *Baroness Orczy b. 1865 Patrick Hamilton d. 1962*

# SEPTEMBER

**24 MONDAY**

**25 TUESDAY**

**26 WEDNESDAY**

**27 THURSDAY**    *'Dark Passage' r. 1947*

**28 FRIDAY**    *Sapper (Herman Cyril McNeile) b. 1888 Ellis Peters b. 1913 R. Austin Freeman d. 1943 'Mildred Pierce' r. 1945*

**29 SATURDAY**    *Elizabeth Peters b. 1927 Colin Dexter b. 1930 Stuart Kaminsky b. 1934 'Cry Of The City' r. 1948*

**30 SUNDAY**    *Michael Innes b. 1906 Jonathan Gash b. 1933*

# OCTOBER

**1  MONDAY**

**2  TUESDAY**  *Graham Greene b. 1904  Edmund Crispin b. 1921*

**3  WEDNESDAY**  *'The Maltese Falcon' r. 1941*

**4  THURSDAY**  *Talmage Powell b. 1920 'Union Station' r. 1950*

**5  FRIDAY**

**6  SATURDAY**  *Stanley Ellin b. 1916*

**7  SUNDAY**  *Edgar Allen Poe d. 1849 'French Connection' r. 1971*

## OCTOBER

**8  MONDAY**    *Lord Peter Wimsey marries Harriet Vane (in D.
L. Sayers' "Busman's Honeymoon") 1937*

**9  TUESDAY**    *James McClure b. 1939 ' Nightmare Alley'
r. 1947*

**10 WEDNESDAY**

**11 THURSDAY**    *Elmore Leonard b. 1925 'Laura' r. 1944*

**12 FRIDAY**    *James Crumley b. 1939  Paula Gosling b. 1939*

**13 SATURDAY**    *William Le Queux d. 1927 'Night Has A
Thousand Eyes' r. 1948*

**14 SUNDAY**    *'The Big Heat' r. 1953*

# OCTOBER

**15 MONDAY** *Ed McBain b. 1926 'The Glass Key' r. 1942*

**16 TUESDAY**

**17 WEDNESDAY** *C.H.B. Kitchin b. 1895*

**18 THURSDAY** *Mark Hebden b. 1916 'Dark Mirror' r. 1946*

**19 FRIDAY** *John Le Carre b. 1931*

**20 SATURDAY** *Frederic Dannay (one half of Ellery Queen)
b. 1905*

**21 SUNDAY**

# OCTOBER

**22 MONDAY**    *E. Phillips Oppenheim b. 1866 ' Marlowe'*
*r. 1969*

**23 TUESDAY**    *Jonathan Latimer b. 1906*

**24 WEDNESDAY**    *Ted Allbeury b. 1917 1958: Chandler begins*
*work on "The Poodle Springs Story", his*
*last - unfinished - book.*

**25 THURSDAY**

**26 FRIDAY**    *Vincent Starrett b. 1886*

**27 SATURDAY**    *Elizabeth Lemarchand b. 1906 Michael*
*Avallone b. 1924 Sydney Horler d. 1954 Rex*
*Stout d. 1975 James M. Cain d. 1977*

**28 SUNDAY**    *Simon Brett b. 1945*

## OCTOBER / NOVEMBER

**29 MONDAY**    *Fredric Brown b. 1906 'Kiss The Blood Off My Hands' r. 1948*

**30 TUESDAY**

**31 WEDNESDAY** *Dick Francis b. 1920  H.R.F. Keating b. 1926*

**1 THURSDAY**    *'Nobody Lives For Ever' r. 1946*

**2 FRIDAY**

**3 SATURDAY**    *Frederick Nebel b. 1903  John Bingham b. 1908 Martin Cruz Smith b. 1942*

**4 SUNDAY**

# NOVEMBER

**5 MONDAY**

**6 TUESDAY**    *Raymond Postgate b. 1896 'Detective Story'*
*r. 1951 1889: The play "Sherlock Holmes",*
*starring William Gillette, opens at the Garrick*
*Theatre in New York*

**7 WEDNESDAY**

**8 THURSDAY**    *Jon L. Breen b. 1943*

**9 FRIDAY**

**10 SATURDAY**    *John P. Marquand b. 1893 'I Am A Fugitive*
*From A Chain Gang' r. 1932*

**11 SUNDAY**

# NOVEMBER

**12 MONDAY**     *Charlotte Macleod b. 1922 Baroness Orczy d. 1947 Chester Himes d. 1984*

**13 TUESDAY**     *Vera Caspary b. 1904 George V. Higgins b. 1939*

**14 WEDNESDAY**

**15 THURSDAY**

**16 FRIDAY**

**17 SATURDAY**

**18 SUNDAY**     *William P. McGivern d. 1982*

# NOVEMBER

**19 MONDAY**

**20 TUESDAY**  *John Gardner b. 1926*

**21 WEDNESDAY**

**22 THURSDAY**  *Joel Townsley Rogers b. 1896  Raoul Whitfield b. 1898  Jon Cleary b. 1917  A.E.W. Mason d. 1948 'The Letter' r. 1940*

**23 FRIDAY**  *Robert Barnard b. 1936  Jonathan Valin b. 1948*

**24 SATURDAY**  *Harry Kemelman b. 1908  William F. Buckley b. 1925  Erskine Childers d. 1922*

**25 SUNDAY**  *W.R. Burnett b. 1899  Francis Durbridge b. 1912 Clive Egleton b. 1927  Gerald Seymour b. 1941 'Out Of The Past' r. 1947*

## NOVEMBER / DECEMBER

**26 MONDAY**

**27 TUESDAY**

**28 WEDNESDAY**

**29 THURSDAY**

**30 FRIDAY**       *John Dickson Carr b. 1906  John Franklin*
*Bardin b. 1916*

**1 SATURDAY**     *Rex Stout b. 1886*

**2 SUNDAY**

## DECEMBER

**3  MONDAY**

**4  TUESDAY**

**5  WEDNESDAY**

**6  THURSDAY**  *William P. McGivern b. 1922*

**7  FRIDAY**  *Leigh Brackett b. 1915*

**8  SATURDAY**  *Josephine Bell b. 1897*

**9  SUNDAY**  *Anthony Gilbert d. 1973*

# DECEMBER

**10 MONDAY**

**11 TUESDAY**

**12 WEDNESDAY**

**13 THURSDAY**     *Ross MacDonald b. 1915*

**14 FRIDAY**

**15 SATURDAY**     *Horace McCoy d. 1955  Edgar Lustgarten d. 1978*

**16 SUNDAY**     *Peter Dickinson b. 1927*

# DECEMBER

**17 MONDAY**      *Christianna Brand b. 1907   Richard Sale b. 1911*
*Dorothy L. Sayers d. 1957*

**18 TUESDAY**      *' Murder My Sweet' r. (as ' Farewell My Lovely')*
*1944*

**19 WEDNESDAY**

**20 THURSDAY**

**21 FRIDAY**      *Lawrence Treat b. 1903*

**22 SATURDAY**

**23 SUNDAY**      *'The Wrong Man' r. 1956   'Dirty Harry' r. 1971*

# DECEMBER

**24 MONDAY**     *James Hadley Chase b. 1906 Mary Higgins Clark b. 1929 Nicholas Meyer b. 1945*

**25 TUESDAY**     *'Cornered' r. 1945 'A Double Life' r. 1947 'High Wall' r. 1947*

**26 WEDNESDAY**

**27 THURSDAY**     *'Johnny Angel' r. 1945*

**28 FRIDAY**

**29 SATURDAY**

**30 SUNDAY**

## DECEMBER

**31 MONDAY**     *Helen Eustis b. 1916*

# THE MORGUE'S OUR HOME

*Blackmailers had forced Nixey Duncan to sign a murder-confession that
spelled certain doom for her in the electric chair—so she hollered for
help, and Race Williams. But guns, not frame-documents, were that big
dick's specialty. And for once he had no gun—plus being shackled by
chains to the very man who had sworn to kill him!*

## CHAPTER ONE

### Hell on the Roof

**B**LACKMAIL'S a dirty, slimy business. I hate it. Yet, there are times
when I have to be the pay-off man
for poor fools who pay, over and over, and
never get the damaging evidence they pay

for. With me—I pay once and get the
goods. This time it was letters—three of
them—and a frantic wife and mother
about ready to kill herself and her child.
Fear of exposure has caused more suicides,
and even madness, than the police suspect.

But here I was sitting straight across
the desk from Joseph T. Lyman, attorney

# A Race Williams Novel

## by
# Carroll John Daly

*Author of "City of Blood," etc.*

**—frantically tried to twist that
chain into the flesh of his neck.**

at law, who used to have the handling of
some pretty good estates until he began
buying up witnesses, and fixing crooked
officials.

"Joe, I don't know why you sent the

woman word to use me," I said. "Since I knocked you down a flight of stairs, and threatened to put lead in your stomach, we haven't been overfriendly."

"Not we, just you—Race Williams, the city's private investigator de luxe. I forgave that little display of temper of yours long ago. A party, whom I do not know, has three letters to sell to a party that you do know. We simply give one person money, and the other peace of mind."

"Well, she does want those three letters," I had to agree. "I've got the five thousand dollars right here. If I didn't think she'd do something desperate, I'd advise her to stick it out. She's almost a wreck. Yet, the letters seem harmless enough."

"To you and me, yes. But to her husband and those high-nosed relatives of his—well, they'd bust up her home. You know, Race, if I wasn't perfectly sincere about helping this woman and—"

"Let that ride," I told him. "I'm here for the pay-off."

"So"—he blinked small eyes—"in my client's interest, and because of your heart-rending description of the woman's desperate plight, don't you think I should jump the price—say, from five thousand to ten?"

I just looked at him—his pleasant smile, his little blue eyes, the twinkle in them. Then I spoke very seriously. "Joe, I never kid about blackmail. You and I have an agreement. Men in the blackmail business don't break agreements with me—and live."

He threw back his head and laughed. 'You're straight and honest, and that's why I rang up the woman and had her hire you. Blackmailers have no conscience. If this client, whom I really do not know, felt that the pay-off could be ten grand, he'd never have made it five. She's had hard work getting that, I understand."

"That's right." I took out the money

and laid it on his desk. I watched him count the bills and put them right back in the same position. Was I afraid that he'd cop the money? No. I trusted to his good sense. I'd have shot his fingers off if he had tried to. The money stayed on the desk.

Joe reached down and came up with three letters. He tossed them over to me. I took my time as I compared the handwriting on each letter with the samples of the woman's I had brought with me.

Finally, I put the magnifying glass back in my pocket, shoved the letters in after it and came to my feet.

"O. K., Joe," I said.

JOE LYMAN followed me as I walked to the door. "You and I helped an unfortunate woman today, Race," he said. "Of course, we placed some money in dishonest hands. But blackmailers we will always have. Someone must help their victims."

"Yeah," I looked at him. "You act like a man who has done this stuff before. Look out, Joe, that some blackmailer—perhaps the big shot they've been talking about—doesn't rope you in as his steady lawyer. You'd be digging your own grave, then."

Joe Lyman nodded very seriously. "True, and, under such circumstances, it would be nice to have you as my friend —as a protector." His hands came far apart. "You're known for your honesty, Race—square dealings even with crooks. There might be big money in it, Race. Could I recommend your name to this client if I ever hear from him again?"

"Sure," I told Joe at the door, "providing he's not particular whether he gets a belly full of lead or not."

"Good boy." He patted me on the shoulder. "How about having supper with me tonight? Could I count on you joining me at midnight at the Budapest Casino?"

I told him the truth. "Sorry, Joe, but I've got an engagement. Yes, one I'm paid for." But I didn't tell him any more than that of the truth. As a matter of fact, I knew little more of the truth myself.

Someone had sent me one thousand dollars in cash, and a key, with the request that I spend that night in a certain walk-up apartment. Would I do it? Would I take a chance like that for a thousand dollars? Sure, I would. For fifty bucks more, I'd let Public Enemy No. 1 share half the bed with me.

THAT evening, when the woman's husband was out at a meeting, I brought her the letters, watched her read, then burn them. The ice-cold hands gripped mine, and tears streamed down her face.

"You'll wait for your fee, as you said?" she finally spoke. "Just how much will it be?"

I looked her straight in the eyes. There was no use to warn or caution her now. I said: "The fee is ten percent—five hundred dollars. You will send it to me when you can save the money without arousing your husband's suspicions." Spotting the thanks in her eyes, and then the question most women ask, I finished: "No, never tell him. Under no circumstances, tell him the truth."

From here, I went searching through the top floor of the badly furnished walk-up apartment. No one was hiding there— not even a circus midget. I put the chain across the front door, and this left the fire-escape the only remaining entrance. I hesitated about closing that window, then left it open. Someone might wish to enter that way—an enemy or a friend. Both were welcome. I went into the bedroom, got undressed, climbed into bed. The message had distinctly said to sleep there. I like to sleep.

Many people have their little peculiarities. Mine was holding a loaded gun in my hand while I slept.

Sure, I woke up.

It seemed as if they raised hell all over the roof before light feet started down the fire-escape. I was out of bed, across to the living-room, and had snapped on the lights, when the curtains at the window parted and she burst into the room.

She was nice to look at in her riding-habit, but it didn't seem just the time for it—two A.M. Short, straight, black hair banged down over her forehead—just as severe covering her ears. I don't go in for bangs much, but it fitted her face. She said, red lips trembling: "Don't let them find me—get me." A quick, frightened look from me to the window and then, "I'll give you anything."

I looked her over, said quickly: "Do you mean give or pay? Cash?"

"Pay. Cash," she gulped, looked around like a frightened animal—and by that I don't mean jack rabbit but more a cornered wildcat. Feet beat upon steel outside. I nodded toward my bedroom door, said, "Close it and keep quiet," and added, "It's five stories, so don't jump out the window. You're quite safe."

She went into the room. The door closed, and I stepped behind the curtains by the fire-escape window that pounding feet must soon enter. My hands were sunk deep in my bathrobe pockets. They were big pockets. They had to be—they held big guns. I earn my living by holding big guns.

The feet on the fire-escape were not overly quiet. The curtains waved slightly, then I heard a hoarse whisper say: "You'll stick, of course. We haven't any rights."

A gruff laugh answered this. "I'll make the right. Come on."

THEY came into the room swiftly. One was a tall, dignified man of perhaps thirty-five, the other a hard-visaged, mean-faced, determined police inspector. I knew him, and didn't like him. He didn't like me, either. That was one thing we both agreed on.

"Stay here, Mr. Hopper," Inspector Iron Man Nelson said. "I'll try the front door." He took quick strides out. They were quicker coming back, and he wore a grin that grew broader as he looked into the kitchen and bathroom.

Then Nelson voiced the astounding solution. "The kitchen's empty, and so's the bathroom. She couldn't have gone out by the hall door—there's a chain across the inside of it. She must have come in here and gone in that room there."

He walked straight toward the bedroom door, motioning to the dignified Mr. Hopper who was straightening his tie and jerking at the lapels of his coat without losing the nice balance of his cane.

Inspector Nelson stretched his hand toward the knob of that door, gripped it and stopped dead. I just stepped from behind the curtains and said: "Don't do it, Nelson."

Nelson swung, half reached for his inside jacket pocket, then dropped his hand. He was looking straight down the nose of my .44. His eyes blazed; his mouth hung open.

"Come on," I told him. "Snap your hand off that doorknob."

Nelson didn't like it, but he obeyed. "You're obstructing justice, Race Williams. That girl stole this man's wallet, and we followed her into your apartment."

"What girl?" I tossed big innocent eyes on him. "I was asleep, heard the commotion on the roof, got up, and you two pounded in the window. I stand for law and order. Where's your warrant?"

"Do you think every officer chasing a thief needs a warrant to catch him?"

"He needs one here." I moved closer to Nelson and let him have it straight. "I know my rights. No loud-mouthed cop

can toss himself through my window and give orders. If you think you can—well, go try a crack at that bedroom door."

"Perhaps we've made a mistake, Inspector," said the dressy guy. "Maybe she went in the apartment below."

"By God, Race I'll use force. I'll have the police up." Nelson was ill-tempered.

"O. K." I nodded. "There's the phone—use it. Get Detective Sergeant O'Rourke on the phone for me. He might like to help you." O'Rourke was my friend. "So they've got you chasing purse-snatchers, eh, Nelson? The commissioner knows his business."

FOR a minute I felt I had overstepped the mark. Not that I minded, particularly. Everybody on the force knew how Nelson and I felt about each other—the private investigator and the officer of the law. If he drew a gun, it was his life or mine. Iron Man Nelson was no rat like the underworld produces. If he went for a gun, he'd use it. If he used it, I'd be dead.

He hesitated, his right hand close to his left lapel, for he was not in uniform. It's just these few seconds of indecision that stand between life and death. A lad would be a fool to wound a man like Nelson, and I mean a dead fool.

But he didn't go for the gun. Hopper stepped between us, pulled Nelson to the far corner of the room. Hopper's words were too low to hear, but Nelson was hot under the collar, and buzzed his answers like a giant horsefly.

Hopper stiffened, then smiled. He said to me: "You and I, Mr. Williams, are business men. We work for the same thing —money. You could use a hundred dollars, couldn't you?"

"I could use five hundred."

"Ah." The smile became real now. We were on his specialty—money. "Very well, Mr. Williams"—he had the "stolen" wallet in his hand—"let us not quibble. We can't have notoriety. So we'll say five hundred dollars for inspecting your bedroom—every part of it."

Harvey Hopper, smooth or not, was a man who didn't waste time. He lifted five one-hundred-dollar bills out of his wallet, tossed them on a table and walked toward the door. I sort of liked Harvey, then. The feel of the bills was pleasant.

THEY found the girl, of course. In fact, she jumped out on them when Nelson got feeling around in the clothes' closet. She shoved the stunned inspector back and slapped his face when he was about to speak some words of wisdom. Yep, she left the prints of her fingers on his thick cheek and her words in his thicker brain. "How dare you maul me around like that!" and, to Harvey, "Who is this man, and what does he mean by putting his hands all over me?"

"He's a police officer, Nixey." Harvey Hopper smiled. "He and I have come to take you home." He looked over her riding-habit. "All day in that—running around the city! How did you ever happen to reach this apartment?"

She looked at me. "You weren't much good. But why should you help a dame you didn't even know? They knocked you around, I suppose?"

"No, they didn't knock me around and wouldn't be apt to. It was a matter of cash." As her little face, with the turned-up nose, grew furious, I explained: "Saving ladies in distress is a business with me, not a pleasure."

She turned to Harvey. "What does he mean?"

Harvey put an arm around her shoulder which she didn't shake off. "You were fortunate, my dear, in entering the apartment of a well-known detective. Mr. Race Williams."

"Race Williams." Her eyes brightened.

"That's what he meant then—about money!" She suddenly dashed across the room and placed both hands on my shoulders. "You're mine, then. I hired you when I came in. Why, you've the reputation of never letting a client down!"

"Are you my client?" I started to smile, then stopped, remembering how I happened to be here in this apartment for a thousand-dollar fee. I finally said: "You don't have to leave, if you don't wish. You can talk to me alone."

"You're mad." Harvey came across the room and took her arm. "Come on, Inspector. We've got to get her out of here. I paid Williams five hundred dollars to deliver the girl."

I said: "Just a minute." Nelson came toward me so fast that the end of my gun nearly broke one of his ribs. I told Harvey: "You paid for a look in the bedroom. You've even had conversation with the girl. There was nothing in our bargain about your taking her away with you. Now—both of you—get out quick."

Nelson made a face with his hard pan, but moved out into the living-room. Whatever he said stuck in his throat. It was something about her father, and, if he had his way, he'd lock her up out of harm.

Harvey Hopper held his temper. "You knew we wanted the girl, Williams. We thought we paid for that. Certainly, you didn't have any idea that—" He came close to the girl now, touched her shoulder lightly. "You must let me handle this thing, Nixey. Tell Mr. Williams you're going along with me. Your father suggested the inspector come with me. Come, Nixey. I want you to come."

She swung from me suddenly. I waited to see her hand go up and leave the mark of those fingers across his face. But the hand didn't go up. She just threw herself into his arms and rested her head against his shoulder.

"No, Harvey," she cried. "I'm alone. I've got to do it alone. You're all against me now." She stepped back, turned sidewise, slipped through the bedroom door. It closed; the lock clicked. This time she had discovered the inside latch.

I turned to Harvey. "Here." I handed him back the five hundred. "You heard what the lady said. There's no deal. I have a client. Miss Nixey"—and after a wait wherein no one supplied the name— "I'm working for her now."

"But she hasn't any—"

We all raised our heads, listened, then dashed toward that door together. There was a crash, a sharp report, and another, as if small guns had exploded in that bedroom.

## CHAPTER TWO

### The Big Blow

THREE bodies pounded against that door together. The lock snapped like a toy one, and, regaining our balance, we all stared at the open window. Nelson and Hopper jumped to that window and looked out into the darkness, far down into the court below. I didn't. I was looking at the huge, heavy floor-lamp leaning against the window—almost over the sill. "She shot herself and fell out the window," Nelson was saying.

"Nonsense." Harvey's voice was high-pitched. "She wouldn't do that—she's too good a sport." He was frantically searching about the room, in the closet and under the bed. But the girl wasn't in sight.

Nelson was examining the lamp. He leaned out the window and pulled in the fifteen or twenty feet of heavy-wire cord that was attached to the base of the lamp.

"I shot the flash into the court below. No body there," he said stiffly. "By God, she could have tossed the heavy cord down almost to the window below, and, by giving herself a little push, could have dropped smack on the lower fire-escape, easily. The little fool had a break. It's a wonder she made it," and, to Harvey Hopper who joined him, "Bulbs broken clean out of the lamp, glass on the windowsill."

They were as ready to leave now as they had been determined to stay before. The hall door just slammed behind them. They were gone when I slipped the chain back across it and returned to the bedroom.

I took another look at that lamp-cord and admitted the escape might be made— just made, understand—by one who was indifferent to death. Anyway, the girl was gone.

I threw up my head and listened. Yep, I heard it plainly. Noise beyond the living-room—in the kitchen, of course. What now! I jerked out a gun, stepped softly across the living-room floor, down the little hall. There was a light in the kitchen. The hall was in darkness. I swung before that door, chucked up my gun and let it drop again.

Nixey was there—with the refrigerator door open!

SHE pointed to the kitchen table, said: "Sit down, Race." She tossed off a glass of milk and took a chew at a slab of cheese on rye. "Surprised to see me? Why, it was just a kid trick. I simply lifted the lamp to the window, tossed the wire out, busted the bulbs and pressed myself flat against the wall—behind that door—when you crashed it open. Since you all ran to the window, why I stepped into the living-room, then hid in the kitchen. Anyway, what are you doing here?"

"Me?" I said. "Didn't you know I was going to be here?"

"How would I know you were here? A boy friend of mine hired this apartment furnished, but gave it up only yesterday." She looked down at her riding-habit

"Tough outfit to hide out in, but I wear it driving the car. I intend to get something different in the morning. Anyway, I look good in it. I thought I might park here tonight, but Harvey and that big, pawing flatfoot grabbed me almost before I entered the front door downstairs. They weren't so good on the steps up. My idea was to beat it down the fire-escape. I did, saw the window open and dashed in to hide."

Sharp, intelligent, yet vengeful eyes watched me. Evidently, she wasn't the client who sent me the thousand bucks to stay in that apartment.

"What a big washout you nearly turned out to be, Race Williams. Now that I know you, I mean business. There's ten thousand dollars in it for you to start. What do you say to that."

"It's too much," I told her.

"It's not too much. I don't want someone buying you out from right under my nose. If someone should jack up the price, let me know. I'll ride with the raise." She added, with a smile that made her almost beautiful—almost, understand: "Ten thousand isn't too much to pay you to kill a man."

"You talk like a gunman's moll," I kidded her.

"Do you need one?" She eyed me sharply. "Why shouldn't I? Father's money came out of the bodies of overworked men. Take a guess, Race."

"You're Nixey Duncan." I nodded. "Your father's James R. Duncan. Copper."

"Tin," she said. "Just tin. Everything about us is tin. If you banged a finger against my chest now, you'd hear the false ring of it. By the way, were you ever blackmailed?"

"No. I'd hardly permit a live man to blackmail me. A dead one couldn't."

"You mean you wouldn't permit a man, who was blackmailing you, to live. But blackmailing me is different. God!" She jerked out the word as if it tore her apart inside. "It grips you night and day. They get you and they hold you until you put a bullet in your own head. Would you call it murder to kill blackmailers? There must be hundreds of people paying these vultures."

"There are hundreds of thousands"— I gave her the truth—"and little can be done unless someone will testify against them."

"I've heard that. Testify to the very thing you'd die to hide! Yes, I know about police protection, too. I had to get money from my father. I couldn't take it from Harvey any more or the man I'm going to marry. I got him mixed up in it. He didn't care what I had written or done. He loves me. He was the one who delivered the money to them—sometimes."

"What do you mean 'sometimes'?"

"Oh, sometimes I paid it—when they

just took the money from him and laughed in his face."

"Who were your letters to—these letters which you consider so valuable?"

She bit her lip. "To Harvey."

"And what was so terrible about them?"

"I was a kid. I thought I loved him, and —well, his wife was alive, then."

"He wrote letters to you, also?"

"Yes. They were the sort of letters Harvey would write—full of kindness, understanding and advice." She changed her soft mood, suddenly, and a hardness, almost a viciousness, crept in. "But they'd sound like hell to anyone else, and ruin him. Harvey gave mine back to me, when I asked for them. After that, they were stolen. Then it was money, the police— privacy and protection. Why, the commissioner even went into Harvey's business! I heard him talking once with my father. Harvey doesn't have as much money as he used to have. How would he? Yes, they even discussed Harvey as the blackmailer and watched him day and night."

"I see." She gave me something to think about. "And the man you are going to marry, Harvey and your father approve of him?"

"Not Harvey. But Father approves— anything to get me off his hands. But he doesn't want me to marry Miles Lewis until Miles' grandmother dies. She'll leave him millions, if he lives a life that meets with her approval. If she knew the truth now, she'd cut his allowance to a lead nickel a year." She breathed deeply, shook her shoulders as if the weight of the world rested on them. "Miles isn't much, but he's the best a girl like I am can get. Besides, he worships me. You and I must go to him tonight. He's gone into danger to help me. I'm afraid something has happened to him and he needs us."

"O. K.," I told her as we left the apartment. "We'll take a look at Miles."

IN her car before the door, she took out a checkbook, wrote carefully and handed the check to me. After I got a look at it, I waved it for the ink to dry. Yes, the check was for ten thousand dollars. A lot of jack? Sure, it was. But she insisted upon giving it to me, and, since everybody else seemed to be sticking their fingers in the Duncan money, why not me? For that ten grand I gave her good advice.

"Here's the lay," I told her. "From now on neither you nor your father pay these blackmailers any more money unless it comes through my hands. When I go after letters with heavy dough, I either bring back the letters or the money. Maybe I leave a corpse behind—never anything else."

She shoved the key into the lock, turned the ignition, and the car rocked—the pavement rocked. For a moment, I thought we were blown to pieces. Then I knew different. I could look up through the alley to the top floor and see the burst of flames, the falling brick. People were screaming on the floor below. Somewhere, a police whistle blew, and a couple of harness-bulls passed us on the run and went straight into that building. After that, came the screech of a siren, the arrival of engines. Yep, they work it out in seconds, not minutes, in the old home town.

"Step on it," I said to the girl. "I hope the cheese on rye makes good."

Nixey Duncan seemed stunned, but started the car.

I rubbed at my chin. The single grand, and the instructions to stay in that apartment, meant one thing. Someone had prepared to give me the big blow. Was it Miles Lewis, the girl's boy friend, who sent me the money, or was it Harvey? I tried to remember if Harvey seemed in a hurry to leave.

"Kid," I said, as we drove along, "ten thousand bucks is a lot of money. The letters don't seem important enough. Why not hop a ship for Europe and let the scandal ride? It isn't much of a one. I doubt if the papers would give it much of a play." I gave it to her straight. "The name of Nixey Duncan has furnished some pretty rough copy. You've raised hell up and down Broadway. A few love letters of yours wouldn't make much news. It would need murder."

"Yes, I know." She spoke very quickly, as we turned a corner. "That's the real trouble. I got back the letters, but I signed a confession of murder."

That was a jolt.

"I had to do it." She gripped my arm. "It was a terrible night. I was promised the letters. I went with the money, myself. There were three men. One gave me the letters, let me examine them, then held them while I crawled back into the bushes where I had hidden the money. We exchanged letters for money. Then they laughed. One of them grabbed me. I was desperate—half crazy. I struggled and kicked and fought, and one of them stuck a gun in my side. I grabbed at it, twisted his wrist, and—well, I don't know. There was a single shot—then the man was there, dead, and the gun was in my hand. The other two men threatened to hit me on the head and leave me lying near the dead man, the gun beside me. They were so scared they let me keep the letters."

"Yet, they made you write a confession —under the threat of leaving you there?"

"That's right. I don't know just what I wrote."

"Where did this take place?"

"Someplace up near those empty lots by the Jerome Avenue Subway—far uptown. I'm so confused—have been ever since—that I don't remember."

"Then there's just one letter now—a confession of murder?" I asked. "What did your father and Harvey Hopper say to that?"

"They didn't know. I didn't tell them.

I still let them think they were just those other letters. I—" She paused, jerked the car to the curb. "Here's the house Miles was to meet them in tonight. He's trying to make arrangement for the price of that confession—and the assurance that the confession will be returned. I was to come if he was delayed. It's long after the time now."

When we climbed from the car, I asked her: "Did he know I would come with you?"

"No," she snapped, "nor did I suspect you'd come. Oh, I wanted to go to you in the beginning, but they were against it."

"Who was against it?"

"Harvey and father. Father called in the police. He knew the commissioner."

"Your fiancé didn't kick about your wanting me?"

"No. He hinted there was a good reason for Harvey not wanting you. But, then, why wouldn't he?" She smiled contentedly as if she enjoyed the situation. "He was jealous of those letters. I read them to him. Besides, he knew I always do what I want to." She gave a short laugh. "The inspector was to bring me back home, and see that I stayed there."

## CHAPTER THREE

### Williams, Meet Murder

THE girl led me through a vacant lot along a row of other houses, keeping close in the shadows, and then to a cellar window. "We go in this way." To my question that she knew a lot about sneaking in on blackmailers, she added: "They made no secret about it. We can go upstairs easily enough, then pass through thick curtains into a room. They used to sit under a light and paint the picture of the scandal. Now, perhaps it will be the electric chair."

"You'd have a self-defense plea that

would acquit you," I told her. "But it would be a dirty mess."

She nodded at that, pointed out the open cellar window, and we slid quickly to the floor inside. She insisted upon leading the way, too. She said over shoulder, as we reached the floor above: "You got your check. The man I'm going to marry is short, slim, with a trick blond mustache and a squeaky voice."

"What's that got to do with it?"

"If they see us and kill me, I expect you're paid enough to kill everyone else in the house. There should only be two of them."

Fair enough, you think? Well, maybe it was. But my business is saving clients' lives—not avenging their deaths. I'd hate to have a girl shot from right under my nose.

But she knew her way in the dark, and I held her belt until we reached the lighted hallway. After that, she moved up to thick curtains. I got a look through them from the corner almost at the same minute she peeked through the middle.

She had described her fiancé well—all but the whine. He was in a chair, looking silly or dizzy. Then, one of the two big men, who stood flat-footed before him, leaned over, fastened huge fingers on his shirt collar and jerked him to his seat.

"Listen"—this mugg had to hold him erect, his knees trembled so—"we want that hundred thousand dollars. The big boss won't wait." He paused, knocked him straight again. Neither one held him now. They just knocked him around, gave him a boost up every time he would have fallen to the floor, or jerked him erect as he started back toward the chair. Then came the smack from the hand of the broadest man. "How do you like that one?"

I stepped into the room and said to that broad back: "How do you like *that* one?"

Sure, I cracked him a backhanded wallop with the nose of my gun that damn near tore the head off his shoulders. The only thing that kept him erect was his friend, whose teeth he nearly knocked out. Then his friend swung and saw me—just in time to take a backhand right across his own face. It wasn't a particularly nice blow and he had nothing to block his passage to the floor, but the wall. He hit that and slid to a sitting position.

"I'm out for business, boys," I started in to give them their warning, when the girl yelled.

I half swung to the curtains, but no one was there. Then I saw the girl struggling with the other man—the first man I hit.

"Help—help! Look out, Race!"

Then came the shot. I pivoted slightly, and the second shot parted my hair before I even saw the gun in the hand of the lad I had knocked to a sitting position by the wall.

No time to waste, then. Somehow, the girl had either been grabbed by Broad Back, who I thought was too dizzy to even stand on his feet, or had grabbed him.

I COULDN'T let the man in the corner fire again, so I squeezed lead and blew his brains out. Then I swung, started to call to the other man to toss up his fists. But he wasn't standing there. He was flat on the floor—a gun close to his arm. I leaned down, turned him over. Someone had blasted a hole in his middle.

"What happened?" I said to the girl, who was wiping Miles' head with a handkerchief.

She turned her head away, said, as if trying to think: "I don't know. I saw him pull out the gun. I was afraid for your life or Miles'. I dashed forward, grasped his arm. We struggled, and he dropped the gun after it exploded. It was terrible."

"*Wasn't* it?" I stared at her for a long time. She sure had a habit of struggling with guys—tough guys—who shot themselves.

"Both these dead men were with the man—who died before," she said. "They won't ever talk."

"That's a comforting thought," I agreed from my kneeling position beside the man. I saw the single holster beneath his left shoulder. It held a fully loaded gun. I picked up the one on the floor, said to the girl: "I'm not even hinting, but can this gun here—the one that killed him—get you into trouble? Ownership traced, fingerprints—anything?"

Her eyes grew wide. For a moment I believed her myself when she said: "But how could they have anything to do with me?"

WE left after that. I'm not one to give law and order a jingle too soon. There was one pleasant thing about the whole affair. I recognized the broadshouldered bird with the unpleasant face—unpleasant stomach now, too. I knew he was wanted for murder. If I could only get Sergeant O'Rourke to take the credit for those shootings!

I stood looking down at the gun by the dead man's side. I saw the pellet of lead. Yep, the damned bullet must have plowed right through the body of Eddie Koft, alias Broad Shoulders, wanted for murder. I picked it up, looked around for the shell and picked that up, too, for the gun was an automatic. Why? I don't know. I'd see what O'Rourke had to say. Also, I had ideas about that gun I left there.

I've got an eye like an eagle when I leave the scene of a bit of shooting. I even asked Miles if anything of his was around. Yet, we had hardly started down the hall, when the girl gasped: "My handkerchief—back in the room."

She was gone like a shot—back, through those curtains then out again, a handkerchief dangling in her hand, before I could even stir. After that, we moved out of the place and all climbed into the car.

It was taking a chance, but there wasn't much traffic, and, tremble or not, I made this Miles drive. We started off and I said to the girl. "Give me the rod, and don't turn those Aladdin lamps on me. There isn't going to be any struggle this time. I've got a weak stomach."

Was she mad? Not a bit. She smiled, dug a hand someplace into that riding-habit and handed me a heavy .45. "Don't misunderstand me, Race." She moved close to me. "I guess I must have touched it. But I think it was the way I jerked free that made him—kill himself." I didn't speak. "Where are you going to take me?" she asked.

"I'm taking you home," I told her.

"No." She gripped at my arm. "If you don't stick with me, Race, the morgue's our home. I'll never be let out again, if you take me to my house. I won't be able to see you, and there is so much to be done."

"Much to be done—sure!" My laugh was not a good one. "I've got to cover that little bit of killing. Who's got your confession now? The three muggs with knowledge in their heads are dead, but your problem remains the same."

"I know. You've got to help me. My father must never know the truth—the real truth. But he must put up the money to pay them."

"I think you had better tell your father," I told her. "I'll handle the dead. If your father's dough is big enough, we'll get your confession back. But I've got to do the work myself, because the knowledge in the man's head may be as bad as the confession you wrote. I've got to find the head man and tell him things will happen to him as soon as he even threatens to talk."

But she didn't want to go home, and I

gave her the horselaugh about that. "You're over twenty-one, and the law is with me. When you want out, you'll get out."

"But you don't know my father—the Tin King," through her teeth.

"And your father doesn't know me—the Lead King."

I let Miles Lewis beat it and told him to be at my office in the morning.

I WENT into the house with Nixey and met her old man, Duncan. He was fat, smooth and even the tin had not thickened the smoothness of his oil. That he was perturbed about his daughter showed on his sudden rising and falling chins. Besides, he was downstairs the minute we entered. He gave me a nod which was supposed to freeze me up, then we went into his library. Old Duncan was ready to shoot his face off, so I got my words in first.

"Your daughter did not wish to come home, Mr. Duncan. She had some idea that you might attempt to detain her here by force. I dismissed all such stupidity from her mind." I laughed easily, and, before he could let out his blast, said: "She's over twenty-one. Even your knowing the commissioner wouldn't help."

"It wouldn't?" Duncan exploded. "And just what would you do if the police were here—come in, anyway?"

"Certainly," I grinned pleasantly. "She's my client. Oh, I won't say you couldn't make a nasty mess out of it for the newspapers. I prefer a different method. I just want your word that she comes and goes as she pleases, and that I see her in the morning. If you don't give me that word, she leaves with me now."

That was that. He puffed a bit, but finally gave me his word. I nodded at the girl. "You need sleep, Miss Duncan. I will see you in the morning." After she left the room, I pounded a finger against Tin King Duncan's chest—probably the first finger that had been there in years. "Now, for the tough part, Mr. Duncan. Your daughter's in trouble. I won't go into details. The letters, er—the letters she's been trying to buy—are far more important than you think. They will cost you plenty. Maybe a hundred thousand dollars—maybe more. My advice is to pay the price."

He stiffened and led the way to the hall. His voice was loud, booming. "I am not aware, Mr. Williams, that I engaged your services. Oh, I was told by Inspector Nelson that Nixey visited your apartment early this morning, and I was told other things about you by the inspector. I must warn you to stay away from this house. My daughter is not of independent means. Perhaps that will save you the trouble of visiting her in the morning. Good-night, Mr. Williams." He pulled his dressing-gown tightly about him.

Nixey called to me from the stairs. She was leaning over the bannister. Her hair brushed my cheek as she bent far over and whispered: "Think well of me, Race. Just a girl who was foolish, a woman who was desperate, and one who is held together by that terrible binding fear of letting down even for a moment. I've shocked you tonight—the great Race Williams. Take a grip on yourself—there's a far greater shock coming to you in the morning."

There was. The next morning, her check bounced—bounced right back through the bank teller's window and exploded in my face.

## CHAPTER FOUR

### Just Plain Killing

THE boy friend, Miles, was at my office the next A.M. I didn't tell him about the check—I just talked. What Nixey Duncan saw in this lightweight, I didn't know. Every once in a while, he'd give himself a shake as if he were mixing drinks. I don't like to waste time, so I came down to facts with him. A shake finished, I asked him: "Dope?"

"No—no," he said. "Fear—fear for Nixey."

"About this blackmail stuff. You've delivered the money for her. Why?"

"Why? I've known Nixey since we were kids. Then this Harvey Hopper came along and—and—Nixey and I were sort of engaged even then."

"Did you send me a thousand dollars to stop at your apartment?" I shot my question.

"Me? No." His eye widened. "So that's the reason the place was blown up."

"That was the reason," I told him. "Now, listen—"

I leaned forward, put a hand on his chest, when Jerry stuck his head in the door and said: "A Mr. Harvey Hopper to see you—very important. My guess is he's a tailor."

"Wrong," I told Jerry. "You're no better detective than I am. I'll see him." Then I whispered: "Follow this Harvey when he leaves. Keep on his tail." I started toward the door.

Miles grabbed my arm. "Mr. Williams! I don't know anything, understand—not a thing. But, once—well, I paid over money to— God Mr. Williams, it couldn't be him—not Mr. Hopper! He's such a rich man."

I just looked at the kid and thought of the line I had gotten on Harvey less than half an hour ago. He was not a rich man —not by a damned sight—at present, anyway. He had just come through a bad financial crisis and was still sitting on the top of a volcano. I said: "Wait here. I'll be back in a minute."

I saw Harvey in the office down the hall. A sort of storeroom, maybe, but I

called it an office. He was dressed ready for the parade, even to the posy in his lapel, if you want to be poetic. I couldn't find much wrong with his face. That was it. He looked too decent—yes, far too decent to be real.

He chirped first: "I would like to engage your services on this blackmail case. It has come to me that I need you—and, at present, Miss Duncan is no longer your client. I'll engage your services and buy that check from you for the full ten thousand dollars."

I looked steadily at him, took the check from my pocket, tore it into tiny pieces and set fire to it in the ashtray.

"Now, what?" I asked him.

"Now"—his smile was rather tired— "Miss Duncan has realized the mistake she made in drawing that check and asked me to correct her error!"

"I will see Miss Duncan today and let her correct her own error."

"I'm afraid that you will not see her." He shook his head. "I have just been to the house. Although a friend of the family for years, I was refused admittance."

I let my eyebrows go up. "You put money into getting back these letters yourself, didn't you?"

He hesitated, then said: "Yes."

"And personally you didn't think they were very damning. You are a widower. Mr. Duncan is a very wealthy man, and the girl was in love with you."

"Nixey was infatuated with me," he said.

"And, now that is passed, she's to marry the squirt. You know Miles?"

"I know Miles. And, since you're getting around to it"—he stiffened—"I'm against the marriage. It would not bring Nixey happiness."

"But *you* would, eh?"

"No, I'm afraid not. God knows I would have tried." He smiled. "She's far too young. You see, Mr. Williams, I

am—well, I am very much in love with the girl."

"Yeah." I swung a foot easily over my desk. "That's why you dished out the dough for the letters. Now"—I turned my head toward the window, swung back suddenly and pounded the question at him —"did her father return this money to you?"

"Why, no, he didn't," he answered, surprised.

"Because he thought you were paying it to yourself—was that why he didn't?"

"That idea came from the police. When I could no longer afford the useless payments, Nixey had to go to her father. I didn't even want him to know I had given her money. She told him. He gave some money, then went to the police. They advised him to meet the demands. I carried the money, the blackmailer took it, and that was all. Miles Lewis carried much more. I'd watch him, Mr. Williams." He shrugged. "But since Nixey has no money to pay for your services, and you don't accept mine, I guess that leaves you out."

The squirt came running out of my office, grabbed me by the arm. His eyes were wide, staring.

"Don't go with him, Mr. Williams! Don't go with him!"

Harvey paused in the doorway, stepped toward the youth, and I thrust the trembling lad back into my office. When I turned, Harvey Hopper was gone.

I TOLD Miles Lewis: "From now on, you're out of this. No more money on your part. No more trying to fix things." He was little more than a boy. Yet there were things written on his face—not nice things. Harvey hadn't exactly hinted things about him. But, then, Harvey was an experienced man of the world.

"Mr. Williams, men have died—three of them," Miles Lewis pleaded like an hysterical woman. So he knew about the girl's first shot. "I won't say now. I won't tell now. But if any more money is to be delivered, have me take it. Follow me, or I'll tell you where I'm to go. The blackmailer has lost his contact-men. He will have to deal directly himself now. Help me, and I'll help you catch him red-handed. It means everything to Nixey. Please, Mr. Williams. I'm certain he'll use me. They're not afraid of me, but if you—"

"All right. All right." I shoved him out.

THEN I did some thinking. Did Miles, or the polished man of the world, Harvey, have a hand in this? Yep, I did some thinking and I'd have done some more but Sergeant O'Rourke walked in—tall, broad, with a thick neck, his chin protruding and defiant. The squarest cop on the force.

"You get worse and worse, Race." He shook his head. "One of those guys was wanted for murder; the other was on parole. They've been suspected of being in the blackmail racket. The other lad you wanted to know about—the lad you said was killed up by Jerome Avenue—we've been looking for, for over a year. He was close to the head of this blackmail bunch—a small crowd, we think."

"Ah," I nodded. "Then there was a guy shot up by Jerome Avenue—through the stomach just like this last one?"

O'Rourke shook his head. "It didn't happen near Jerome Avenue. It happened miles away in Prospect Park, Brooklyn, and he wasn't shot through the stomach at close range. He was smacked through the back of the skull while he was running away. But I can't take the blame nor the credit for that stiff, for the body was found and a report made on it over a month ago. Three men were running, when one was shot dead. There was a witness to the shooting, and the medical-examiner's report that he was smacked

three times in the body before he took the final dose."

"Interesting, but not up my alley." I shook my head at O'Rourke. "My man was shot up on Jerome Avenue."

"It's up your alley all right, Race." He took the gun I had given him the night before—the one I had taken from the girl—and handed it to me.

"If that's the gun that blasted the insides out of Eddie Kopt in the house uptown, then it's the same gun that popped over the running figure in Prospect Park. Don't shake your head. Fredericks, the best man in the ballistic department, put his O. K. on it. We had both hunks of lead, you know."

And I was stunned. It didn't make sense. I didn't open my trap for a few minutes. Then I said to O'Rourke: "There was a witness to this shooting?" I took a breath, waiting. And, for a second, I thought it was all right—for a second.

"That's right—a lad in a car. He was parked with a dame," he said. "Four people were talking huddled close to a cluster of bushes. Two men walked away. He saw their figures plainly in the moonlight. He thought there was a struggle between the two that were left. Anyway, he heard a laugh, saw a small figure lying on the grass, then the bigger figure turn and start to walk away.

"Then came the fireworks. Two men disappeared to the left, the other staggered, gripped something tight he held in his hand, jerked out a gun, moved his hand quickly from side to side, then turned and ran. After that, the shots were fast. The guy in the car saw the running man twist, jump, and finally drop like a log.

"The figure with the gun moved then, ran across the grass, knelt by the side of the dead man and lifted something long and white from his hand."

I gulped, said: "Did he recognize the figure? Did he do anything?"

"Sure, he did something. He got out of the car, started across the grass, saw the kneeling figure rise and the gun blaze in its hand. He heard the bullet, too— heard it smack against the hood of his car. Then—"

"Then, what?" I was interested.

O'Rourke shrugged his shoulders. "He took the hint. He jumped back in the car and drove away. His description was fair —at least, how the killer was dressed. We covered every riding academy in Brooklyn—the race tracks, too."

"Why such places?" There wasn't much of a question in my voice.

"The killer wore 'riding-pants,' as the witness called them. Looked more like a boy than a man. This dead guy had a record, and we suspected him of being in this blackmail ring. Hardly a ring—just a vicious little circle—a few known criminals for the heavy work, a collector or two, and a man who keeps himeslf in the background. There's the gun, Race. It's the same gun that killed the man in Prospect Park and killed the man who was shot through the stomach, early this morning. Here's the gun, as I promised."

I put the gun in my pocket, said: "Just cover me, O'Rourke. This blackmailer will be wanted dead or alive?"

"That's right." O'Rourke nodded. "But I want him alive."

"I know." I wasn't especially thinking of anything, but I finally said: "If I find him, it's easy enough to destroy written evidence. But this lad carries knowledge in his head. I wouldn't dare turn him over to you with this same knowledge still in his head. I have a client to think of." And I was thinking of Nixey Duncan. She'd lied to me about having to sign a confession at the scene of the shooting. The witness had said the two men ran away. So how did she happen to write it?

O'Rourke sighed. "That means you'll blow the knowledge out of his head. Just plain killing—gun him out."

I shook my head sadly, too. I knew O'Rourke. I said: "Of course, I could let him live—let him free while he kept that knowledge secret. He'd talk if he were locked up."

"That's right. You're always right, Race. The slimy rats."

"Then it's a bargain. You'll take the credit if there's killing. Or, if things don't work out that way, you'll tell the commissioner it was your orders."

O'Rourke pulled himself erect. "Go shoot him to death, Race," he said almost viciously. "I hate blackmailers more than murderers."

## CHAPTER FIVE

### The Price to Slay

AT eleven o'clock exactly, I walked up the steps of the James R. Duncan residence. The butler opened the door a crack, started to close it, and I did the rest. No putting a foot in to keep the door from closing—that's for salesmen. I just lifted my foot and let the door have it. Then I walked into the hall. The butler was sailing ungracefully across the highly polished wood until he struck a small rug and continued his passage on that.

Rough? Of course it was rough. But if you're going to force your way into a place, let it be determined. Let them be damned thankful that you didn't shoot your way in.

Mr. Duncan burst out the door of the library, started in on the butler, and, seeing me, suddenly changed his tune. He hit the high spots, stepped right up to me threatening bodily harm, even pulled up his sleeves when he must have known that one poke in his stomach would have silenced him for hours.

I laid the finger hard on him, took his

wind, and talked myself. "Locking me out, eh? I'm here to tell you, Mr. Duncan, that your daughter is in deadly peril." When he tried that annoyed laugh I added: "All right, laugh this off. They'll be arresting her for murder unless—"

Then he got his breath and was in on me. "Where is my daughter? It was your idea that she come and go as she pleased. Well, she got a call on her private phone, and left sometime before dawn. Don't try to glare me down, my man. I want to know where she went. Where—" He stopped, looked at my staring eyes and said to the butler: "You may take Mr. Williams to Miss Nixey's room. Let him search the house if he wishes. You to protect my daughter!" As he turned back toward the library, and I started up the stairs, he flung over his shoulder: "I'll see you in the library for a moment, Mr. Williams, before you leave."

"It will cost you money to talk to me, if your daughter's gone," I said.

The girl was gone, all right. There were no two ways about that. The dumb faces of the servants were even more convincing than the bed she had not slept in. I found the note addressed to me. It was under the pillow. It was a surprise. I read—

Darling Race:

If you are a real detective, you will find this. Somehow, through you I am to get my single "letter" back. I am to see it and identify the handwriting and put my mark of approval on the transaction. Better tell Dad the truth. It will cost plenty. But Dad must pay—must, understand, Race.

Yours, for a good struggle,
Nixey.

It was pretty bad. There was no flippancy in that letter. The kid was breaking fast. The next struggle for a gun might be her last. She might even want it that way.

I walked into the library, copped a couple of expensive cigars, slipped them into my pocket, and, lighting a cigarette, sat down. Duncan's front was still hostile, so I broke the ice.

"You don't have to play the heavy parent with me, Mr. Duncan," I said. "Your girl's in a jam. The cops can't help her. It's gone far beyond that stage."

"Harvey Hopper said that this morning when I ordered him from the house," the old man replied. "He demanded I give him the money he had already paid out for this blackmail. He shook his finger in my face and said it would cost me plenty now. I have known Harvey and his family for years. He told me I was sacrificing Nixey's career, her future—perhaps her life—for money."

I didn't give him much sympathy. "That was certainly telling you."

He did a bit of squirming, but he took it. "You hinted at something dreadful in the hall."

"Hinted!" I started, and stopped. The butler was at the door, almost apologetic. A gentleman wished to see Mr. Duncan. He was quite insistent, talked vaguely of Miss Duncan's interest, and presented his card.

I looked over Duncan's shoulder, and saw the card—*Joseph T. Lyman, Attorney at Law.*

"See him," I said at once. Things were moving fast. The blackmailer was ready to strike or collect. When they hired Lyman, they meant business—quick business.

TWO minutes later Joe Lyman, stout, round-faced, smiling, all honest appearing except for those little watery-blue eyes, breezed in. "Well, well, well." He drew off suede gloves and shook the limp hand Mr. Duncan gave him. "You're in good company, sir—very good company. Mr. Williams—Race Williams, a connoisseur of rare and precious documents."

"I am afraid"—Mr. Duncan stood up just as Joe Lyman, attorney at law, dropped uninvited into a chair—"that I have not had the pleasure of meeting you before, nor do I know if—"

"If you wish to meet me now." Blue eyes popped, fat cheeks reddened, and Lyman, opening his mouth, laughed good-naturedly. "I know you, Mr. Duncan, and I know the unpleasantness of lawyers popping in. One doesn't know what to expect." He laughed again, and Duncan sat down and tapped on the desk.

"A man of business, eh?" Lyman nodded pleasantly. "I like that. I have a client who has a rare piece of writing which he believes you would very much wish to purchase." He extended a long, sealed envelope to Duncan, who just held it in his hand and stared.

"We have our stamp collectors, our patrons of the arts," Lyman went on affably. "Now, though worth nothing to posterity, the original of that typewritten document you have there is worth a great deal to you. At least I am told that. I have not seen the contents of that envelope"—this as Duncan was reading it— "but I understand the price is two hundred thousand dollars."

Duncan came to his feet, dropped back against the wall. His face grew white, then a pasty yellow. "Murder," he whispered. "Murder."

Joe Lyman was smoking a cigar, leaning against the bookcase mumbling over some rare volume. I picked up the paper and read it. A quick glance was enough. It was Nixey's confession, just as O'Rourke had told it. The end of it stuck with me.

I fired five times—then he fell. I took the envelope from his hand. In it were my letters. A man jumped from a car. I turned and fired a shot to frighten him. Then I ran away. . . . I am making this confession of my own free will, so that someone else

will not suffer for a crime I committed. I shot him through the back of the head.

Nixey Duncan.

It was all typewritten.

I shut Duncan up when he started to shout about the police, and having Lyman disbarred.

"Why, my dear chap, I had no idea there was anything offensive," Lyman's voice grew cold. "Give me that paper." When I merely handed it back to Duncan, Lyman said: "Well, the owner has the original. Good-day. I will tell him you can't use it. I am sure that he can."

I took Lyman over in the corner and talked to him like a Dutch uncle. He grinned his appreciation.

"Certainly, you can handle it, Race. Delighted to have you associated with me. So understanding. Remember, I am simply delivering a scroll—a very expensive piece of handwriting."

"That's right," I told Lyman. "You know my business, and how I do it. I'll want to meet this blackmailer"—and seeing his horrified look—"this client of yours, personally, before delivering the money."

"But I don't know him. I serve in this capacity, occasionally, solely to help the unfortunate."

"Sure." I believed Lyman had never seen the blackmailer. If I were in that kind of a business, Lyman would never see me, either. But I went on: "It's this way, Joe. This lad has knowledge as well as written evidence. I got to see him and tell him he's dead five minutes after he tries to sell that knowledge or threatens to use it again."

"You can take my word for it, Race—can't you?"

I hesitated a moment, then said: "Yes, if you can take my lead."

It was his turn to hesitate, but finally he said: "All right, Williams. It will have to be like that for a bit."

Joe Lyman waited out in the hall while I talked to Duncan.

"Nixey couldn't do these things." He must have read that note over and over. "It's a fake. My daughter did—"

"Did a good job." I stood up for the kid. "It shocked me, too, Mr. Duncan, when I first thought of a young girl—and a gun and a dead body. It took guts just the same. Still, there's her confession, which God only knows why she wrote, or how she came to write. But I'm telling you, Duncan, she wrote the original. It's a dirty mess all around. You can't deal the police in now. There's the law. The papers would tie your tin factory to her tail and drag it through the streets of New York."

Duncan nodded and finally agreed that I do the job.

MONEY after that—just talk of money. Duncan blew up, and I'm not sure to this day if it were the girl or the tin business he was thinking about. Anyway, I went into the hall and talked to Lyman. One hundred grand was all Duncan could put up. Joe Lyman raised hell all over that hall. Tin-plate, millions and everything else was brought into it. He wanted to go back and talk to Duncan. Then I admitted that Duncan could raise one hundred twenty-five thousand, but my fee came out of that, for Duncan wouldn't be so easy to work on once his daughter was safe.

We finally did reach an agreement. If Lyman could swing the deal at a hundred grand, he could work ten percent from us as well as taking his cut from the blackmailer. Yes, he squawked all over his face, but finally agreed he might fix it up if Duncan would draw the money out of the bank that afternoon. More trouble there. Duncan, like all big men, didn't have cash to that amount. But he could raise it easily in the morning with-

out causing any unpleasant talk that might reach the police.

"Sure," I said. "Mr. Duncan can get it through his partner—the police are watching him."

The "police" did the trick. Lyman laid a hunk of fish in my mitt—at least his wet, cold hand felt like that—and the talk was over. The blackmailer would know they were dealing with me—dealing with death.

## CHAPTER SIX

### A Fool for Trouble

I WENT back to my office and into my private room. Jerry took his feet off the desk and shot a cigarette butt through the window. "I got a report on this Harvey Hopper," he said. "He's harmless enough."

"I guess so. About Miss Nixey Duncan—did she telephone?" I was beginning to worry about that girl. With good reasons, you'll admit. She might do anything from shooting a gun, getting shot herself or taking a high dive off the George Washington Bridge.

Jerry was giving his report. I pretended to listen. After all, he was supposed to be a detective. I caught some of his story, and jerked erect. Jerry was saying: "Harvey walked straight into the Latham Building, took the elevator to the seventeenth floor, and must have delivered the large envelope he carried to Joseph T. Lyman, for Harvey wasn't carrying it when he came out."

Surprised? Sure, I was surprised. Maybe I had suspected him. Nelson and Duncan already had done so. Now, it flashed over me. There was big money in it for Harvey. He gave the girl money in the beginning—money that had been handed right back to him through others. The money he had given Miles had also come back to him. Then he demanded back from Duncan what he had spent to help Nixey. Now, finally, he was after one hundred thousand dollars cash. Yep, Harvey was smooth and slick.

I WENT straight to Harvey Hopper's office. It appeared prosperous. A studious-looking lad sat behind the little gate that protected *Harvey Hopper, Private* from the general public. He stood up when I pressed the catch and tore the gate from its hinges. He sat down again when I parted his hair with my elbow and busted into that private office. I like the melodramatic. It's real stuff in the rackets, but to Harvey's type it might be new.

Harvey swung the chair, sort of smiled, then screwed up his face. My gun pounded against his chest. I spoke my piece. "Your number's up, Harvey. I'll blow a hole straight—" Then I stopped.

The expression of his face never changed. He said very quietly: "You're making yourself ridiculous, Williams. Half the office force are already in the doorway behind you." Then he spoke in a louder voice: "Now, Mr. Williams, just what is it you wish?"

Maybe I was stumped, but at that his smiled seemed a little painted. If I hadn't had a client, I'd have at least poked him. But I had no proof—only a gun which I couldn't use. I held back the curses and asked: "Did you bring a long envelope to a lawyer this afternoon?"

"So that's it! Well—yes. My instructions were not to open it. Anything else?"

"I'd like to see you alone." I had hard work getting those words out.

"I am afraid that's impossible. I'm very busy."

"I can make you a lot busier," I snarled.

"Don't play the fool, Williams," he said, then louder: "I had your letter—sold your bonds. That is all they were

worth. Your request was to sell at the market. They were not active bonds. You were fortunate to get the amount you did. Are you here to sell or buy?"

If there were a hint in his voice that he meant selling out the girl, or buying the confession, I didn't get it. But I had been a fool to tip my hand. I said simply: "I'll be buying, tomorrow."

"Good." He came to his feet, took my arm and walked me through the office workers, who stared at us. The doorman followed closely behind us, a belligerent look on his hard face. Harvey led me to the elevator that gave entrance right into his offices, and, before the door opened, spoke to the broad-shouldered guard who had taken my other arm.

"No, Edward." Harvey shook his head. "There are many people who, knowing nothing of finance, blame their misfortune on those they deal with at the time. It affects some people differently. We must understand that."

The door closed. I was in the elevator, going down, Edward with me. Once I tossed off the huge, knuckled hand that gripped my arm—then I didn't bother with it. I was thinking I had been a fool. The car reached the ground floor. We were the only passengers.

"Just keep the door closed a minute, Frank," Edward, my companion, told the elevator operator. "This is a smart guy who tried to beat my boss out of money. Pushed the secretary around and—"

Damn it, Edward did it. He started smacking me around just as those bruisers smacked the trembling squirt Miles around.

The pent-up anger at making an idiot of myself hit top—and Edward got it. I jumped a left into his stomach, then tore up a right and damn near stove his head through the side of that car. Then, as the birdies started to sing to Edward, I told the operator: "Open that door, before I knock your head through it."

Thirty seconds later I walked out of the building.

WHEN I came back to my office I had a caller. He was moving his long legs up and down the office, face red, blue eyes blazing with anger. It was the lawyer, Joe Lyman. He shot his life's history at me.

"Maybe you know it, Williams—maybe you don't," he began. "Once I was a well thought of lawyer. But things went bad with me, just as it did with our big mortgage companies. Nothing criminal, you understand. Let us say a little unethical. On top of that, a client of mine was blackmailed. There was nothing to do but fix it. Otherwise, it would have broken a dear old lady's heart. I had attended to her business for years. I knew this blackmail was the truth, and charged her nothing for my services."

"Charged her nothing?"

"No. This is a hard confession to make, Race, but it's little different than your business, right now. You are the go-between for the criminal and the honest citizen. I took my fee from the blackmailer."

"Added it onto what the client would pay, eh?"

"Oh, no. I insisted on my fee—a small amount—or I would advise my client not to pay a cent and face the scandal. The blackmailer believed me, of course, for there was nothing in the scandal for me."

"So what? Why this history of your wrong?" I asked.

"Well, this blackmailer used me again and again. I swear, Race, that I did it for the best interest of those he threatened. And I played square with all of them—just as I did with you last week. Just as I would have done with you tonight."

"What do you mean 'would have done' with me?"

"We've been double-crossed, Williams. James R. Duncan is not giving you the money to carry. This thief must have gotten in touch with him direct—through his daughter or someone else. Now, I never take a double-cross lying down. There must have been some purpose for it."

"This blackmailer doesn't trust you maybe," I suggested.

"Or he knows of that extra twenty-five grand that you and I are splitting. I had him on the phone. He agreed to the one hundred thousand dollars. A few hours later, he rang me back. He told me to keep my nose out of it and hung up. He didn't like your being in this, Race. I guess he's expecting to continue this blackmail of Miss Duncan, for sometime. There's knowledge in his head, as you said. I am no longer willing to take your lead."

"Now, what?" I watched the greed in those small eyes.

"I've come to you to make a deal," he said. "I've fully protected myself. I'll lead you to this man—lead you to his meeting with Miss Nixey and the man they've picked to carry the money."

"Can't you guess who this blackmailer is? Just guess."

"I have talked with him in the dark and might guess, but I won't," he answered. "If he thought that I knew him, it would mean my death. Suppose you and I be at this meeting-place before him. He has arranged to get the money tonight. Let us wait in the room until he comes with the confession and the other arrives with the money. Then you get the confession and shoot the knowledge out of his head. You'll have to kill him, for he's a dangerous man. Besides, I must think of myself, Williams."

"I don't doubt that statement," I told

him, lifted the phone, and, when he grabbed at my wrist, said: "I'm going to call James R. Duncan."

"No, no. If you do that you'll—this blackmailer will know."

I shook my head and dialed my number. I got Mr. Duncan. I said: "This is Race Williams. Everything's O. K. as arranged for tomorrow night, Mr. Duncan?"

"Why do you ask that?" he said sharply. "Of course, it is—only one change."

"And the change?"

"It's Inspector Nelson and the police. I'm leaving town for a day or two. They were rather curious today. Nelson was at my office twice. The money will be ready for you. My secretary—Mr. Slatery, at the office—will give you the envelope any time after twelve tomorrow. Of course, he knows nothing."

"All right," I said easily. "Don't worry. There is nothing to alarm you. Have a good rest."

I DROPPED the phone back in its cradle, frowning. Mr. Duncan had not been so polite to anyone in years—nor had his voice ever contained such a tremor. I was sure of that, and something else—he was lying to me.

"You're correct, Lyman," I told him. "He's been frightened. You must remember his daughter is not home. This blackmailer may have her. You're positive you know where this meeting is to take place?"

"To the least detail," he nodded. "I am more familiar with his routine than you might imagine. I have kept my eyes open. There is the matter of the police later, which you will arrange with O'Rourke I presume." Yes, Lyman was well informed. "And there is the matter of the hundred thousand dollars—which I will arrange."

So Lyman had it all planned out. The blackmailer, who would kill him in a second if he knew of his conversation with me, would not be in a position to kill him if I turned on the heat. Also, Lyman would have one hundred thousand dollars in cash. Yes, he was a bad man to doublecross. But I took the heart out of him. I said: "There will be fifteen thousand dollars in it for you, and ten in it for me."

When he started to holler for more money, I went on: "Oh, I'll tell Duncan the part you played and try to double your fee. Anyway, you can share the headlines with O'Rourke if this blackmailer gets knocked over." I gave him the sound of it: "Sergeant O'Rourke, with the assistance of the noted lawyer, Joseph T. Lyman, kills—"

"I think I'll work on the money—not the publicity," said Lyman. "Tonight, then, at eleven o'clock exactly, I will be at your apartment for you."

"Eleven exactly," I agreed. "But I'm not promising to kill him. That's up to him." As Lyman looked at me, I added: "Oh, I'll get his word that he won't harm you."

"And you?" Lyman said.

I shrugged my shoulders. "He won't have to promise me anything. He's entitled to kill somebody—or at least have a try at it."

Joe Lyman, attorney at law, looked at me for a long moment. Then he said: "You are an extraordinary man, Mr. Williams. I am almost afraid to go with you."

"You'd be more afraid to go without me," I grinned.

He opened his mouth once or twice to speak, but didn't. Finally, he put on his hat, gripped his stick and left me.

YEP, Lyman was a bright man, but what would prevent him taking that one hundred grand himself and leaving the country? Duncan couldn't squawk to the police, without bringing the whole thing into the public eye now. Mr. Blackmailer would have trouble in finding a guy who had plenty of leisure, and at least a hundred thousand dollars, to spend moving about. I grabbed a taxi, trotted straight up to Mr. Tin Can Duncan, and, after giving the butler another ride on the floor, walked into the library and watched the brandy roll suddenly down Duncan's chin when he saw me.

I started to give it to him and then stopped. I didn't need to.

He spoke right out, said: "If you feel there is any charge, Mr. Williams, why I'll pay it. I faced this thing as long as I could outside, but inside it was getting me. I love my daughter, strange as it may seem to you. I'd love her if everything written on that paper is true. I lied about raising that money, hoping I'd see her and that she would tell me it wasn't true. That I won't be using you is a fact."

"Never mind that. Do you intend to give that money to Lyman without my knowledge?"

"Good God, no! Neither with, nor without your knowledge. I don't even know this Lyman. He came and you suggested — and I — I was helpless. Since then, a message has come directly from the blackmailer for the money to go to him by someone else."

"How do you know the message came directly from the blackmailer?"

"Because of the person who brought the message—and because of the telephone message from my daughter to give the money to that person."

"Was she held someplace by force?"

"No." He thought a long moment. "She said she would be over to see me shortly after the money was delivered. The person went away while I raised the money, but she didn't come here afterward."

"You gave it to this man your daughter sent—the money—one hundred thousand dollars!" I gasped.

"Why, yes. It was someone my daughter trusted, and I—knew. No, Mr. Williams—from now on, I remain silent. I am going the whole way for Nixey."

## CHAPTER SEVEN

### Behind the Locked Door

JOE LYMAN picked me up at eleven o'clock, drove me several blocks, parked his car, took a taxi, hopped a subway and got into another taxi again. "There," he said. "We couldn't have been followed. I'll have this taxi leave us a couple of blocks from the house we must visit. We'll find our way home—if we ever do get home. You're armed, of course?"

"Do you know any more jokes?" I asked him. Was I armed? Joe was nervous all right.

"Come, Joe," I told him, "get down to cases. Just what is the line-up for tonight's game? You seem to think this lad's pretty bad."

"Pretty bad!" he cried. "He has let people die even when they had no more money to pay him. He has spread scandal after he had sucked his victim dry of every penny. He either wanted to send the clipping to some client who wouldn't pay or wanted his victims to betray his friends to him. I tell you, Race Williams, I want this man dead. He's a fiend."

"So that's why you dragged me along tonight? He's got something on you."

Joe Lyman faced me for a long time in the dimness of flashing street lights. He looked like a very determined man. He lifted a gun from his pocket, and I was so surprised that I damn near shot the side of his face off.

But Joe didn't notice me. He said: "All knowledge that he has about me is in his head, too. I know little about guns. But perhaps, after all, you won't have to tax your conscience tonight."

We left the taxi and walked two blocks east, turned left, did another block and started down the side street of brownstone fronts, finally stopping before one house—the house.

It wasn't quite ten minutes to twelve and Lyman told me we had nothing to fear. No one guarded its doors. The blackmailer, perhaps using the psychology of the hour, always entered the house at twelve and came directly up the stairs. We would hear him from the room above.

Despite Lyman's assurance of safety, we entered by the back door to which he had a key, showed no light as we went along the hall and started up the worn carpeted stairs to the floor above. Once I felt Lyman's hand on my arm. His fingers trembled there, then were gone.

He flashed a small pocket-light on the second floor, found the room he wanted. We stepped inside. A light popped on over the door, the moment we entered. I stepped quickly out of its glare, cursed once, waited. Lyman was plainly visible on the edge of the circle of light. It was a cinch that light went on automatically when the door was opened.

"More light," I told him abruptly. "Pull down the shades, or something. What the hell! A little light can be seen outside as well as a big one. I want to look the room over." I'm a man who generally gets what he wants.

Lyman said, and, despite that former exhibition of trembling fingers, his voice was steady: "We'll have plenty of light. It won't show from outside." A button clicked. Another light showed. This was a sixty-watt with a huge green shade shooting the glare directly down upon a desk and chair, and forming a brilliant circle of light—perhaps three feet out around that chair—and along the floor.

I DID'NT get enough time to complain or explain that when I hid out in a room, waiting for a desperate man, or men to come, I wanted a look all over that room first. There was another pop, and a central light on the ceiling went on —a light that didn't even leave the dust hidden.

There was one other chair in the corner of the room, and two windows with steel curtains from top to bottom. Like the desk and chair, these steel curtains were new. The room seemed soundproof, and also there seemed no possibility of a light showing outside the house.

Apart from the door we had come in, there was another door across the big room, to the far side of the windows. I walked to this door, turned the knob, jerked, felt old wood give, but the door was locked.

"Closet?" I asked. "Or what?"

"Closet," Lyman explained. "Locked."

"Locked." I looked at him. "Don't I know that? But there's no key."

Lyman shrugged his shoulders. "Nothing of importance there, I imagine. I have seen it open at times. Old newspapers—perhaps reference to this fiend's victims."

"We've got a few minutes," I said. "I'll tear that door off its hinges easy enough."

"You'll break it in."

"Not me," I told him, took one careful look around that room, jerked a gun from a shoulder holster into my left hand and said: "Watch the hall door, Lyman. I'm a guy who never lets the unexpected happen."

I gripped the knob of that door with my right hand, pulled once, felt old boards give, then, raising my left foot against the wall, I gave one more jerk.

I'm a strong man, and that was a rotten door. I tore the lock loose as if it were papier-mâché—had the door open. I stepped back so as to watch both the closet, the main door and—yes, even Lyman, as I raised my gun.

It was a small closet. My breath whistled far back in my throat. Small as that closet was, something was in it—something was coming out of it.

It was the girl, Nixey. She was smothering to death before my eyes. My left hand caught her slender body and held it. My right hand tore the handkerchief from across her mouth. Then my fingers almost dove down into her throat, and, as I jerked out the dirty piece of wet rag, I heard a breath.

"All right, kid," I told her. "You're safe now—"

She tried to speak and couldn't. Did she look back over my shoulder? Did she look toward the door? But in her eyes was a message for me—fear, terror, horror.

But it was too late. The lights went out. Darkness came—complete darkness. Then a million lights were steadying and becoming the same single glare of the big ceiling light. The girl slipped from my arms to the floor, my sagging knees straightened, and then sagged again. This time I knew the terrible truth. Something had pounded down on my head with terrific force.

What would become of the girl now? What had happened to Joe Lyman? Another blow smashed, and I folded up like an army cot and hit the floor.

## CHAPTER EIGHT

### Master of Massacre

WHAT a sap! Those were the three words that rang through my head. The unexpected had happened. I had been ready for any sort of an attack when I tore open that closed door and raised my gun in my left hand. But the falling girl had taken one off guard.

But what about Joe Lyman? He had been right beside, and almost directly behind, me. He had only to holler once to have me turn and shoot the lad to death who came in and knocked me cold. Imagine a guy walking across that floor and pounding me on the head. But why blame anyone but myself? No doubt, Joe, too, was surprised by the sudden appearance of the girl and had been watching her as closely as I was. But what had happened to Joe Lyman who had brought me along to protect him?

Things cleared as I lay there. Not for the better, understand. My hands were cuffed at the wrists with a thick, rather long length of chain, and, as I moved my feet, I could feel more chains—cuffs about my ankles.

I shook my head again to keep what wits I had left in it. My blurred eyes saw the bulb pop over the door, and a tall figure who stood in that doorway under the light. I didn't see his face, for the man peered back into the darkness of the hall. Then he turned his head. It was Harvey Hopper.

For a full ten seconds, he stood motionless. I saw the gun in his right hand, strained as if he were listening. Then he swung. There was the sudden report of a gun, as if he shot down the hall. But, with the report of that gun, the light went out. I listened for an answering shot, or a falling body. There was none.

I moved back against the wall, drew myself to a sitting position. I heard a groan, felt hair close to my face, whispered hoarsely: "Nixey. You got guts, kid. You're not afraid. Can you make it? Crawl toward that door. I think a lad was shot outside. Now you—"

Her voice was kind of weak, but there

was no hysteria in it, and it didn't break. This girl had plenty of what it takes. "I'm chained, too," she said. "I should never have trusted him."

I was feeling all right in the head now, but mad. I sat there like a fool, and kept sticking my manacled hands up under my armpits, though I had known from the moment I first came to that my guns were gone.

"What will he do with us?" she asked. "He wouldn't dare kill me."

I didn't answer that one. Why lie to the kid?

We both straightened. There was a funny scraping sound across the room. The dame didn't recognize it, but I did. It was the heels of someone being dragged over that floor. Then there was a thump of a body not far from me—about ten feet.

I cursed.

A man laughed: "Keep your mouth shut, Williams. Die like a gentleman. Your entrance into this case meant death for all."

I knew the voice all right. There was no doubt of that. It was Harvey Hopper.

A man cried out, a body upon the floor struggled. Faint cries came, and feet moved across the room.

"Why did you come?" the girl whispered. "I had things safe—I thought. You see, I discovered the identity of the blackmailer. I made a deal with him. I'd pay the one hundred thousand dollars for the return of my confession. I lied to you a little about that shooting, Race. Then I made another agreement with him. I would keep his identity secret, while he kept his knowledge about me secret."

I bit my lips, tried to see her in the darkness, but couldn't. And she didn't know why she was there? This blackmailer—Harvey—was going to kill her. But I wanted to make certain it was Harvey. I started: "The blackmailer was—"

I stopped dead. The light went on above the desk. It shone directly down on the man who sat in the chair—a pasty-faced young man. He was sitting very straight and stiff. His eyes blinked, but the hands he laid upon the desk were steady enough—as if he were hopped up. Yes, it was the squirt, Miles Lewis.

HAD I been wrong about Harvey, then? But Miles was talking, sitting there in the blaze of light—with complete blackness behind him. He spoke, his head bent forward now as if he read from a paper. "My grandmother is very wealthy. She is eighty-four—should have died years ago. Her money would have been mine. I had money and spent it. It was not hard for anyone to dig into my past to find things that would cause my grandmother to disinherit me. Someone did that. But that person was surprised to know that most of my own money was spent, and that my grandmother put me on a strict allowance."

Miles paused. His laugh was hollow. He went on: "The joke, then, was on this blackmailer—but not for long. I had to face the scandal and the loss of over a million dollars, or work for this slimy —" He bowed his head. "I have caused many people suffering, and, most of all, the girl I was to marry—Nixey Duncan. It was to me she came when she found the letters were stolen—stolen by me, of course. She came to me, for I had once told her of being blackmailed, and she had given me money, and advised me to go to you, Race Williams. But I don't think she paid because of those letters. I think she paid for the adventure—to discover this blackmailer and so protect other victims."

Now, that was a damn fine speech for a hopped-up guy. He was sure dumping the wagon over, spilling his guts, which meant, of course, that he expected to kill us.

"My reward for working for this blackmailer was Nixey and my dead grandmother's money—which this blackmailer could then take away from me," he went on. "But now Nixey knows who he is. I felt that Nixey had suspected me for sometime. She forced the real name of the blackmailer from me today by the point of a gun. Worse, he knew it—read it in my eyes. He had me trap her here." The boy began to laugh. "He couldn't kill me because of my grandmother's wealth and his greed. He knew I was simply a coward. He started me on the use of drugs. He loaded me up so that I could read this paper to you tonight. Yes, my grandmother would die, and he would get the money from me. I know that, but he'll never get that money. I have courage tonight—courage that he gave me in a little white powder—courage to die, but first to kill."

Miles Lewis jumped to his feet, swung toward the darkness behind him and pressed the trigger. There was no sound. He pressed it again and again, cursing into the darkness.

"Courage, boy," a voice spoke. "Courage to die."

Miles Lewis raised both his hands in the air and rushed back toward the darkness. I saw the splash of orange-blue flame—once, twice, three times—four times, even—as the shadow of Miles came out of the darkness and sank slowly to its knees. There was another shot, and Miles rolled over in the light, his head turning, his eyes facing us. It took a sixth and final shot to kill him.

A LONG silence after that, broken by sharp clicks and a single thud upon the floor. I didn't have to be a mind reader to know that an inexperienced man was reloading a gun, that he had dropped a bullet to the floor—and I also recalled that it had taken him six shots to kill

Miles. God, for a chance to have a gun on a lad like that!

Now, what? From the way Miles had spoken, Harvey was not the blackmailer.

Then the truth came—the truth which should have pushed me in the face long before. Yes, I knew before the figure moved into the light and sat down in that chair. I knew before the ring of light widened, and two others, beside myself, were disclosed there on the floor.

I had my back against the wall. Beside me, her head very close to my shoulder, was Nixey Duncan. Her face was white in the sudden light. On the other side of me, stretched out flat upon the wood, was the man who had been dragged across that floor. There was a little pool of blood beside his body, and his hands and feet were bound tightly. He turned his head and looked at me. It was Harvey Hopper. He had been shot down in that doorway when I thought he had shot someone.

"What of the envelope you delivered to Lyman?" I said without thinking.

"It came through the mail to me with a letter of instructions to bring it to Joseph Lyman—that he would be handling things for Nixey through her father," he was gasping.

Not bad stuff, eh? Harvey, delivering the envelope, was just to make me suspect Harvey and so fall an easy victim to the blackmailer's trap--which I sure had done, all right.

Harvey was groaning.

"I'm helpless to save Nixey," he said. "I let her associate with that rat, Miles. Williams, I don't care what happens to me! But get Nixey out of this, and I'll pay you—yes, I can raise twenty-five thousand dollars."

"Really." The man beneath the light juggled a great roll of bills when he spoke. "I have one hundred thousand dollars here so kindly given to poor Miles by

Mr. Duncan—which Mr. Williams can simply pick up from the desk if he can get you out of here, Mr. Harvey Hopper."

I looked at this man. The smack on my head was explained now. No one else could have done it. But how cleverly he had gotten me there! How cleverly he had us both apparently shoved out of the job by Mr. Tin Can Duncan. Sap—sure I was. Perhaps, I should have guessed it. I don't know. But as I looked at Joseph T. Lyman, attorney at law, sitting there, I knew that, any way you looked at it, I was dumber than hell.

## CHAPTER NINE

### One Way to Die

JOE Lyman laughed easily, said: "Outsmarted you, eh, Race? But why not? The dead boy here held a college degree. The girl was well educated, considered exceptionally bright. Mr. Harvey Hopper is unquestionably one of the ablest bondmen on the Street. He suspected the boy, Miles, I think. Because of that, he fell for my invitation to come here tonight. Miss Nixey not only suspected Miles—she had become *certain* of him. I believe she did after she signed that confession of murder.

"Good work, that confession. There was a witness to the little affair in Prospect Park. I discovered that through the police. Nixey had seen him, but she was surprised when Miles told her that the witness had seen and recognized her from her pictures so often in the papers. Miles also told her that the witness was hardworking and honest, heard the story of her being blackmailed, and, if he could protect himself, wouldn't talk. This witness—there was my only mistake, for I met her and represented myself as the witness—wanted no money, just the assurance that, in case he was arrested and

tried for murder, he would have proof that he had nothing to do with it. Miss Duncan wrote the confession gladly. It was that, or this witness going directly to the police. If she didn't write it, the murder would come out at once. If she did, it might never come out at all—at least so she thought. Smart, eh?"

"And she fell for it all," I cut in. "Your posing as the witness in the car and pretending that you had recognized her?"

"Wrong, Williams." Lyman shook his head. "She might have fallen for it at first. But early this morning she left her home, stuck a gun in Miles' stomach and made him tell her my name. It may be that she only pleaded with him. But that was his story, and, knowing the young lady, and knowing that she came straight to my office and threatened to kill me, I can very easily believe her. We had to be rather rough with her.

"That's about the whole thing. I even had Miles arrange for her to come and see him knocked around so she would trust him. Miles had told me that the girl was going to bring you into the case against everyone's advice. So, to appear innocent, I told Miles to encourage her to hire you.

"It was I who fixed up that small blackmail deal with you—to see if I could trap you later, if other plans failed. It was I who sent you the thousand dollars to stay at Miles' apartment, and invited you out that night for supper to be sure from your answer that you were going to stay there. The bomb was planted and timed. I had no idea that the girl would be driven, by the police and Harvey, to hide there. Nor that she would bring you to the house where they were abusing Miles."

"And it was you, of course, who arranged for Miles to carry the money instead of me. Why?"

"I was the blackmailer whom you

would kill. This way I was a friend whom you would protect. It made it easier for me to dispose of you." He took a long envelope from his pocket and laid it on the desk. "The girl's confession left here will confuse things. I am going to kill you, of course."

"You can't get away with that," Harvey Hopper said.

"I am going to try to, Mr. Hopper." Joe Lyman nodded gravely, lifted the gun from his desk. "Which one of you is to die first?"

"Harvey should take it first," I said, as I pushed my feet under me and staggered erect, leaning against the wall.

"Really?" Joe Lyman's eyebrows went up. "I thought you would be the first to die, Williams. Noble, self-sacrificing, and all that. But we'll have Harvey first, if you suggest it. You will all stand up against the wall, please. Tut, tut, Williams—you are not very gallant."

THE girl and I pitched to the floor as I tried to lift her. She looked at me rather peculiarly—perhaps disdainfully—and, as I struggled to help her to her feet, I whispered: "You want to live. There's a chance if Harvey dies first."

"It is certain death, anyway," she said. "Let me go first."

"Come on." Lyman seemed slightly annoyed. "The rôle of a killer is not exactly new to me, Race." He waved a hand toward Harvey. "I shot him, as he stood in the doorway. I didn't know he was hurt badly. I'll kill him later if he insists on lying there." This last as Harvey, trying to climb to his knees, pitched to the floor again.

"It's you or the young lady—which first? You'll have to come to the desk, you know. I'm not much with a gun."

"I know that. I'll come first." I took a step forward and fell, and, much to Lyman's amusement, started crawling

along. I didn't need to crawl. That's why I wanted Harvey to go first. I had a plan —if you could call it a plan—but, without Harvey's death, I didn't know if I would get the opportunity to try it.

"Look at your hero—and a most expensive hero." Lyman chuckled at the girl, as I snaked slowly toward the desk. "I've waited for a long time, Race—a very long time. I've never forgotten that beating you gave me, nor your threat to kill me. I'm not a very good shot, so get on your feet. There, that's far enough."

I came to my feet. He leaned his elbow on the desk and leveled the gun straight at my middle. I saw the way he held it and the peculiar position of his finger, as it began to tighten upon the trigger. Then I dropped to my knees, half staggered—and was five feet nearer the desk when I came to my feet again.

"Any last words from the condemned?" Lyman's teeth gleamed.

The desk was four or five feet away. The man who would deal death was on the other side of it, leaning forward now, half over it. His gun was stretched out, moving undecidedly up and down my body, but never toward my head. He wasn't that sure of his shooting. But there was nothing of fear in his eyes.

What could I do? Hands and feet, manacled. I wondered if it would take six shots for him to kill me, and if he'd purposely make a slow job of it. I raised my hands far above my head, and his finger loosened on the trigger.

"That isn't necessary," he said. "I'm not expecting you to draw a gun. Now—"

I held my hands high, said: "You wanted my last words. I've got some for you. There's been a note left behind that—"

"Nonsense." He laughed. "That's an old story. Imagine you suspecting me before you came here!"

"Look at my eyes, Lyman. Look at the

eyes of a man who is going to die. Look at eyes that will—" I got the suggestion over as my voice broke. His eyes raised for a fraction of a second and rested on mine.

I expected death. But I did the thing, anyhow.

I let out one horrible, ear-piercing shriek—a shriek that startled him rigid for a split second. Then I took a hop forward with both feet and flung my, body out and over that desk, as his finger closed upon the trigger. And it worked, at least so far. The sudden shriek had paralyzed him for that single moment. Oh, I don't know where the lead hit me. I only know that, if it tore me apart inside, I did not feel it.

Nor was I a fool when I made that leap over the desk. I didn't try to crash the cuffs into his face and knock him from the chair. Not me. I spread my arms and wrists out and drove the chain over his head tightly down against the back of his neck. Then I jerked my body backward. I brought his body and his exploding gun back over the desk with me. We hit the floor in the very center of that light—and I mean hit it.

Then we were struggling on the hard wood.

"Harvey—Harvey!" I cried out. "The chains—your chains! Bang them against his head."

But Harvey never moved, and I twisted and turned my body and did everything possible to break his damned neck. But the gun—where was that deadly gun? Twice I drove up my knees. Chains or no chains, they struck like twin pistons. He twisted his feet around my legs and pounded his hands against my face. Both his hands, understand—not one hand, but two flaying fists. That meant just one thing. The gun had bounced from his hand when we hit the floor. He was no longer armed.

HE was a stronger man than I thought. The chains and irons interfered or perhaps the knock on my head had actually affected me. Then I thought of my wound—thought of it only because there was blood on the floor.

Joe Lyman made a mistake. My fingers now were tightly fastened against the back of his neck and the side of his throat. He must have forgotten about the chain that held them there, for, with both his hands, he tried to break my arms away. Constantly, I kept jerking back my body and bringing those chains hard against the back of his neck. Then, as I went forward, I'd pound my head into his face.

Joe was breathing hard now. I thought I had him. Then he twisted his body suddenly. As we turned on our sides like the Siamese twins, I saw what he was after—the thing that my manacled hands prevented me from grasping. The gun had been jarred from his hand. It was lying there in a tiny smudge of red. His gun—my blood.

His hand was close to it. His arm was snaking along the floor directing that hand. I saw the girl standing, swaying, her eyes staring straight at the gun.

"Good girl, Nixey," I cried out. But, even as my words formed, she had hopped from the wall and was throwing her body toward that gun, chained hands outstretched.

Then I saw Lyman's fingers twist about that gun and grip it.

I lost my head, then, forgot that the girl's body would pound down on his hand just the same, break his fingers, his wrist—at least knock the gun away. Yes, I forgot all that. I acted through instinct. I made a desperate effort, jerked my body over and pulled Joe's hand away just as the girl's manacled hands struck the red spot.

I jerked his hand away, but the gun was held tightly in that hand. The girl had given me the break, and I didn't take it. Now, we were all to die.

Joe Lyman had a gun in his hand. He had only to press against any part of my body and finish our struggle. I could not bring a hand down to prevent it nor move a finger from around his neck. After that, I'm not sure what happened. Anyway, I cut loose, hands chained about his neck or not. I wasn't going to take that dose of lead without a struggle—even a useless one. I just started rolling over, pulling him with me.

No shot came, as our bodies whirled across that room. No shot came as we crashed against the wall. No shot came as I twisted that length of chain and we were on our knees, my body tight against his.

Then it did come—a single shot, and somehow we got up to our feet.

I went mad. I jerked and jumped, staggered, straightened—somehow went into a spin. I tried to shake the man from me, as a terrier does a rat. Joe Lyman's feet left the floor. He was swinging around in a wide circle, his neck held as if in a vice by the chains about my wrists.

I saw his face before me, felt my own body spinning as I frantically tried to twist that chain into his neck. My body was bent far back, my manacled legs seemed to have settled hard upon the floor. Nixey was crying: "Stop—stop!"

I heard the desk crack, break, then crash, and knew that Lyman's feet had struck it. The chain broke with a metallic clink, held a minute—finally twisted with a crunching sound around Lyman's neck.

After that, the weight was no longer at the end of my arms. A heavy body left me, struck something solid. I shot backward, hit the floor, turned a complete somersault and wound up flat against the wall.

Queer thoughts, then.

Somehow, I had failed. Lyman was free. I tried to climb to my feet, but only reached my knees. I saw Lyman, his heels there by the wrecked desk. Then I saw the back of his feet, the back of his body as if he lay upon his face. But I could see his face, too. Though his body was prone upon that floor, his neck was twisted clean around, sightless eyes staring up into the light—a light they did not see, would never see. I had not only broken the blackmailer's neck, but, God, in Heaven, I had twisted it clear around on his body!

I lay down on my stomach, but, unlike Joe Lyman, who also lay on his stomach, my eyes did not glare up at the light. They did not glare at anything. I was out cold.

## CHAPTER TEN

### Bill for a Broken Neck

THE cuffs were off me, and also off Harvey, who lay in that single chair near the desk. Nixey was buttoning up my shirt, saying: "I took the keys from Lyman's pocket. Why, the bullet hardly scraped you. There, Race, take it easy. Harvey was hit in the leg. We'll need you to carry him. Wait, I'll get more water."

She left the room, and I got up off the floor and wobbled over toward Harvey. "What—happened? I had an illusion, I guess. Lyman lying—"

Harvey pointed down at a pair of feet. There was a coat thrown over the upper part of the body. I lifted it, then tossed it back and turned to Harvey. I felt pretty good.

"Boy," I said, "I don't remember just what happened, but I certainly handed Joe Lyman a dose he won't forget."

Harvey's face paled. He ducked his head into his hands, straightened again.

"It was the most brutal and most horrible—and yet the most courageous thing I ever saw. You must have gone mad. The two of you hit that wall hard enough to kill both of you—yet you staggered to your feet. Then you stumbled and whirled, and Lyman tried to get his gun up. Here comes Nixey. I hope she kept her eyes closed when that terrible—"

Nixey had a pitcher of water for me and a bottle of brandy.

I drank a half gallon of water, but left some of the brandy for Harvey. I didn't listen to her explanation of how Miles had the bottle there in the afternoon. I was interested in the present.

First, I took a match and struck it to the confession. Harvey just watched me. Then I picked the phone off the floor, put it together, and, after a bit, got Sergeant O'Rourke. I told him where to come, clamped down the phone and said to Nixey: "You got those letters about you and Harvey—that mush stuff?"

"Home. I can get them," she said.

"Good. I'm counting on you to finish this job, Nixey." She was beginning to look white under the gills, but she pepped up almost at once. "We'll forget about this burned murder confession, and tell O'Rourke of the letters only. The D. A. should give you a break and keep your name out of it. But he'll talk to you. Just tell him the truth—everything but the killing. Go home and go to bed and remain unconscious until I prop up your story." I turned to Harvey. "You go with her. You just tell the truth. You don't know much—you're too dumb." I had to get that in. He had to take it, too.

Brave little Nixey. I saw her to Harvey's car, got Harvey into it, and asked if she could make the drive.

Her chin went up. "I'll be a rag doll when I get to bed, Race, but I'll hold out until then. Some of the servants can carry Harvey into my house. You don't think much of me, but I can take it."

"You're all right, kid." I hesitated, then pushed the hundred grand into her hand. "It's your old man's. Yes, I know—a big slice of it is coming my way, but the cops might search me. On your way."

I didn't tell her, as she drove off that Harvey had slid gently to the floor in the rear of the car. After all, there wasn't much wrong with him. I sat down on the front steps and lit a butt.

O'Rourke drove up almost the same moment the medical examiner arrived. Doc Ritter wasn't a lad who complained of getting out of bed at night or missing a meal, or the things medical-examiners generally are supposed to complain about. At times, I think he rather liked it. Now, he spotted me and grinned.

"Williams, eh? Race Williams. That

always means a neat, clean job. Through the forehead, I suppose—right between his eyes. I like your work, Race."

O'Rourke and I followed the hustling doctor up the stairs. Two cops came behind us. I buzzed O'Rourke, gave him the office that he had been wanting to break this case, get this Lyman for a long time, and that I had helped him.

"He's dead?" O'Rourke asked the coroner as he stood up from the body of Joe Lyman.

"Yes, I think we can safely call him dead." The doctor added quickly: "If you want an unofficial report on the cause of his death, I'd say he turned his head too quickly."

NIXEY was downstairs when I arrived at the house the next afternoon. Harvey was still occupying the guestroom. As for me, I felt fair. The doctor who dug the lead out of my side and patched up the flesh wound a little above my knee, must have helped dig the Panama Canal.

James R. Duncan drew me aside. "Thank you for what you've done, Mr. Williams. I am very grateful. And your keeping the twenty-five thousand as your fee is a little unusual—but quite all right."

"Unusual for me, too," I told him. "But quite all right."

"Why did you get out of bed?" I grabbed Nixey's arm. "The D. A. has been here and questioned you. Now, for trouble."

She looked at me almost sweetly.

"He was such a nice man—and so understanding when I couldn't remember anything. Shock, you know." And before we reached Harvey's bedroom she gripped both my hands, held them tightly. I never heard such earnestness in her voice—any woman's voice for that matter when she said: "I remember everything. I will always remember everything. There isn't anything I want to forget. You—you—" She jumped up suddenly and kissed me full upon the lips. "I'll never forget you."

And, as we entered Harvey's room, she said: "There's your twenty-five grand on the dresser. I told father you had already taken it. He's tight at times, but he's going to pay Harvey back. Here's Harvey." She jumped onto the bed and put an arm about him. "Marriage bells." She looked almost defiantly at me.

"So you're going to get married?"

"I'm going to marry him, if that's what you mean." Nixey stuck her face close to his. "I've still got those letters, and that's the price he'll pay."

After I taught them their routine with the D. A., and started to leave, Harvey said: "Can't you give some advice to a man about to be married?"

"Sure," I told him. "Search her every night before retiring."

# NO EXIT PRESS

There is an extensive list of NO EXIT PRESS crime titles to choose from. All the books can be obtained from Oldcastle Books Ltd, 18 Coleswood Road, Harpenden, Herts AL5 1EQ by sending a cheque/P.O. (or quoting your credit card number and expiry date) for the appropriate amount + 10% as a contribution to Postage & Packing.

Alternatively, you can send for FREE details of the NO EXIT PRESS CRIME BOOK CLUB, which includes many special offers on NO EXIT PRESS titles and full information on forthcoming books. Please write clearly stating your full name and address.

## NO EXIT PRESS Vintage Crime

Classic crime novels by the contemporaries of Chandler & Hammett that typify the hard-boiled heyday of American crime fiction.

**FAST ONE — Paul Cain £3.95pb, £9.95hb**
Possibly the toughest, tough-guy story ever written. Set in depression Los Angeles, it has a surreal quality that is positively hypnotic. It is the saga of gunman-gambler Gerry Kells and his dipsomaniacal lover, S Granquist (she has no first name), who rearrange the L.A. underworld and disappear in an explosive climax that matches their first appearance. The pace is incredible and the complex plot, with its twists and turns, defies summary.

**SEVEN SLAYERS — Paul Cain £3.99pb, £9.95hb**
A superb collection of seven stories about seven star crossed killers and the sole follow up to the very successful Fast One. Peopled by racketeers, con men, dope pushers, private detectives, cops, newspapermen and women of some virtue or none at all. Seven Slayers is as intense a 'noir' portrait of depression era America as those painted by Horace McCoy and James M Cain.

**THE DEAD DON'T CARE — Jonathan Latimer £3.95pb, £9.95hb**
Meet Bill Crane, the hard-boiled P.I., and his two sidekicks, O'Malley and Doc Williams. The locale of the cyclonic action is a large Florida estate near Miami. A varied cast includes a former tragic actress turned dipso, a gigolo, a 'Babe' from Minsky's, a broken down welterweight and an exotic Mayan dancer. Kidnapping and murder give the final shake to the cocktail and provide an explosive and shocking climax.

**HARD TRADE — Arthur Lyons £2.99pb**
LA's most renowned detective, Jacob Asch is on the street once
more in a startling tale of Californian political corruption. A
troubled woman hires Asch to uncover the truth about the man
she is to marry. When Asch discovers the man is gay and the
woman is run down on her way to a hastily called meeting with
Asch, it becomes clear something big is at stake. Serious money
real estate schemes, the seamy side of LA gay life and a murder
frame involve Asch in a major political scandal that costs him his
licence and nearly his life.

**THE KILLING FLOOR — Arthur Lyons £2.99pb**
David Fein, owner of Supreme Packing, a slaughterhouse in a
grimy little Californian town had a problem . . . he was a com-
pulsive gambler. First he couldn't cover his losses from the takings
so he got a loan and went into debt. By the time he took in
Tortorello, a clean cut Harvard type but with 'Family' connections
he was in big trouble. Now he had been missing for 4 days and
his wife was frantic. Jake Bloom, old family friend puts her in
touch with Jacob Asch, who figures Fein is on a bender or in the
sack with another woman — he's heard and seen it all before.
But that's before he finds a body on the killing floor.

**DEAD RINGER — Arthur Lyons £2.99 (available 5/89)**
Jacob Asch is called in by boxing promoter Jack Schwartz to
help out Carlos Realango, a South American heavyweight whose
career is on the skids. He has been receiving threatening phone
calls and Susan Mezzano his manager and mistress thinks her
husband is responsible. Asch shows them how to tap their own
phone and leaves it at that. Two weeks later Asch is called to
Reno to prevent Realango tearing the husband apart only to find
it is too late as Realango has been shot at Moonfire ranch, a
fancy brothel, owned by the husband. The police say justifiable
homicide, but Asch smells murder and something more than a
lovers' quarrel.
"Lyons belongs up there with . . . Ross Macdonald" New York
Times.

**THE LADY IN THE MORGUE — Jonathan Latimer £3.99pb, £9.95hb**

Crime was on the up. People sang of Ding-Dong Daddy, skirts were long and lives were short, violin cases mostly sported machine guns. Bill Crane thought it was a pretty wonderful time. He was in the Chicago morgue at the height of summer, trying to cool off and learn the identity of its most beautiful inmate. So-called Alice Ross had been found hanging, absolutely naked, in the room of a honky tonk hotel. His orders were to find out who she really was. Alice was stolen from her slab that night! Thus began the crazy hunt for a body and a name, through lousy hotels, dancehalls and penthouses, with occasional side trips to bed to bar to blonde and back again.

**MURDER IN THE MADHOUSE — Jonathan Latimer £3.99pb, £9.95hb**

Hard drinking, hard living Bill Crane in his first case has himself committed incognito to a private sanitarium for the mentally insane to protect rich, little Ms Van Camp. Terror, violence and sudden death follow when a patient is found strangled with a bathrobe cord. The murderer strikes again but makes a fatal error in killing pleasant little mute, Mr Penny. The local police doubt Crane is a bonafide detective and believe he is suffering from delusions, the non-alcoholic kind. Despite all this, Crane breaks the case in a final scene of real dramatic fury.

**HEADED FOR A HEARSE — Jonathan Latimer £3.99pb, £9.95hb**

Death row, Chicago county jail. Robert Westland, convicted of his wife's murder, is six days from the 'chair'. What seems an iron clad case against Westland begins to fall apart as Bill Crane races against time to investigate the background of the major players and prove Westland's innocence. Westland's two brokerage partners; his hard drinking, hard riding cousin; enigmatic and exotic Ms Brentino; the amiable Ms Hogan; a secretive clerk; a tight-lipped valet and a dipso widow all have plenty to explain. Aided by a lime squeezer, a quart of whisky, a monkey wrench, a taxi cab, a stop watch and a deep sea diver, Crane cracks the case in this locked room classic.

### RED GARDENIAS — Jonathan Latimer £2.99pb.

Bill Crane's fifth and final mystery finds him teamed up again
with Doc Williams and Ann Fortune, his boss's niece, who poses
as his wife, to investigate a murder and a death threat to the
family of an industrial magnate. On the way to cracking the case
in his own, inimitable way he learns the secret of the gardenia
perfume, the lipstick marks on the dead man's face, the crimson
cat, the three shelves and the hairpin! Latimer's deft blending of
humour and suspense has been described as "masterful — the
proper proportion of dry vermouth to produce a fine martini, all
without bruising the gin!"

### BLUES FOR A PRINCE — Bart Spicer £2.99pb

The Prince was dead. Harold Morton Prince, great jazz and blues
composer had been killed in the studio of his sprawling, palatial
home. From coast to coast, the papers carried his life story and
every band was playing his blues pieces. But already ugly rumours
threatened his name. Carney Wilde, P.I., had reasons to doubt
the official story of how The Prince died and they centred on the
people closest to him: His daughter Martha, his musician
colleagues, The Prince's patient and dying father and the deadly
Hollie Gray. Threads from each of these led Wilde along the
dark road to the killer.

### NO EXIT PRESS Contemporary Crime

A companion to Vintage Crime in the popular pocket book format
that highlights both the classic and exciting new books from the
past twenty years of American Crime Fiction. Contemporary Crime
will feature in 1989 such titles as Day of the Ram by William
Campbell Gault, Ask the Right Question by Michael Z Lewin,
Act of Fear by Michael Collins, Dead Ringer and Castles Burning
by Arthur Lyons all costing just £2.99.

**OUT OF TIME — Michael Z. Lewin £2.99**
Albert Samson feels life is looking up when he gets two clients in
one afternoon. The first is an eccentric old man obsessed with his
home computer who lives in an expensive apartment and asks
Samson to investigate a young man suspected of running with the
wrong crowd. The second is wealthy banker, Douglas A. Belter,
whose wife has discovered that her birth certificate is a fake. For
48 years she has believed she is the daughter of Ella and the late
Earl Wilmott Murchison. Now she wonders if she has any identity
at all. Samson is intrigued by this latter case and his investigations
lead him, via dusty archives, a sentimental might club owner, the
police and the press, to the 1930s and '40s and to an old murder.
In turn it leads Samson to suspect that a recent 'natural' death is
in fact a cold blooded killing.
"Consistently readable entertainment" H. R. F. Keating, The
Times.
"Very assured and satisfying" Sunday Times.

**ASK THE RIGHT QUESTION — Michael Z. Lewin £2.99**

When 16-year-old Eloise Crystal asks Albert Samson, an
Indianapolis P.I. whose career has languished to the point of
extinction to find her biological father, he's not sure whether it's
a childish whim or a serious proposal. Some quick checking reveals
the Crystal background to be far from crystal clear. There is the
puzzling stipulation in her grandfather's will, the sudden trips her
parents made to France where Eloise was conceived and to New
York where she was born. Samson's digging turns up much more
than a mix up in genes and he finds himself in the family closet
rattling too many skeletons for his own good. ASK THE RIGHT
QUESTION was an Edgar nominee for Best First Novel and
introduces a detective who for sheer determination ranks with
Lew Archer and Philip Marlowe.

**DAY OF THE RAM — William Campbell Gault £2.50**

Brock Callahan, ex guard for the L.A. Rams, is now a tough
private eye, weighing in at 220 pounds with a passion for Einlicher
beer. In DAY OF THE RAM, Callahan becomes involved with
Johnny Quirk, ace quarterback of his old team, the Rams. Quirk
fears he is being blackmailed by 'The Syndicate' into fixing the
games and when Quirk turns up in the morgue, Callahan moves
in to find his client's killer.
"A sharp, smooth blend of violence and murder, fashioned by
one of America's most skilful mystery experts"
"Brock Callahan is a memorable believable character notable for
his directness and integrity" — Art Scott.

**ACT OF FEAR — Michael Collins £2.99 (available 6/89)**
Act of Fear won an Edgar for the best first novel and introduces
the one-armed New York City detective, Dan Fortune.
Two seemingly simple events — the mugging of a policeman and
the disappearance of a neighbourhood youth, a possible witness
— inexorably lead Fortune to a more serious matter as one of
the witness's friends, a kid, hires Dan to find the missing boy.
Two girls, an innocent old man are murdered and Fortune's client
lands up in hospital. Then the killers go after Dan and he finds
himself in the middle of a bitter dispute between rival Mafia
factions.
"A notable writing talent" Ross Macdonald.

**THREE WITH A BULLET — Arthur Lyons £2.99**

A top LA music promoter hires Jacob Asch to find out who is
methodically trying to destroy him by cancelling appointments and
bookings. Then a faded superstar is found dead — apparently
from a drug overdose — and the promoter is the prime suspect.
Then two more bodies surface. Asch enters the glitzy, frenzied,
music world where the sex, drugs and rock 'n' roll combine with
ruthlessly competitive professional ambitions to create a murderous
mixture.
"Lyons writes with grace and energy" John D. MacDonald.
"Lyons belongs up there with . . . Ross Macdonald" New York
Times.
"Some of the best side of the mouth similes this side of Chandler"
Newsweek.

**CASTLES BURNING — Arthur Lyons £2.99 (available 5/89)**
A young L.A. artist hires Jacob Asch to track down the wife and
infant son he deserted years ago to make amends, now he has
made good. Asch finds her in the plush sybaritic world of Palm
Springs, remarried to a wealthy businessman. He finds the son
was killed in a car crash, driven by his mother. The case seems
closed until the teenage son of her second marriage is kidnapped
and Asch's client mysteriously disappears.
"Lyons writes with grace and energy" John D. MacDonald.
"Lyons belongs up there with . . . Ross Macdonald" New York
Times.
"Some of the best side of the mouth similes this side of Chandler"
Newsweek.

**GREEN ICE — Raoul Whitfield £3.99pb, £9.95hb**
Watch out for Mal Ourney: where Mal goes, murder follows. It
is on his heels as he walks out of Sing Sing after taking a man-
slaughter rap for a dubious dame and follows him all the way on
the trail of some sizzling hot emeralds — 'Green Ice'. "naked
action pounded into tough compactness by staccato, hammer-like
writing" Dashiell Hammett.

**DEATH IN A BOWL — Raoul Whitfield £3.99pb, £9.95hb**
Maestro Hans Reiner is on the podium, taking the fiddle players
through a big crescendo. Then something goes off with a bang
and it isn't the tympani! Reiner finds himself with a load of lead
in the back — and a new tune: The Funeral March.

**THE VIRGIN KILLS — Raoul Whitfield £3.99pb, £9.95hb**
Millionaire gambler Eric Vennel's yacht sets sail for the regatta
at Poughkeepsie with an oddball assortment of uneasy companions:
Hardheaded sportswriter Al Conners; beautiful Hollywood ham,
Carla Sard; Sard's nemesis tart-tongued scribbler Rita Veld; big
ugly out of place bruiser Mick O'Rourke, and a glittering cross-
section of east and west coast society. Rumours of Vennel's heavy
betting on the regatta and a midnight attack by a masked intruder
raise the tension . . . to the point of murder!

**HALO IN BLOOD — Howard Browne £3.99pb, £9.95hb**
Meet Paul Pine, Chicago P.I. Three seemingly unrelated events
-— the funeral of a pauper at which 12 clergymen from different
faiths are the only mourners; Pine being hired by John Sandmark
to dig up some dirt on the man intending to marry his daughter,
Leona; and a run-in with the gangster, D'Allemand, where Pine
is nearly killed delivering a $25,000 ransom in counterfeit bills —
are woven into a complex and web of events that produces some
explosive twists to the finale.

**HALO FOR SATAN — Howard Browne £3.99pb, £9.95hb.**

Raymond Wirtz has something everyone wants! His grace, the
Bishop of Chicago; Lola North, "a girl who could turn out to be
as pure as an easter lily or steeped in sin and fail to surprise you
either way"; Louis Antuni, Chicago Godfather; Constance
Benbrook, who "wasn't the type to curl up with anything as
inanimate as a novel" and mysterious super criminal, Jafar Baijan
— all want what Wirtz has . . . the ultimate religious artefact.
Private Eye, Paul Pine is right in the middle. In the middle of a
deadly obstacle race strewn with corpses, cops and beautiful
women.

## THE LADY IN THE CAR WITH GLASSES AND A GUN —
### Sebastian Japrisot £2.99

Dany Longo is 26, blonde, beautiful and short-sighted. After borrowing her employer's car to drive to the south of France, she is confronted with one terrifying incident after another. She is handed the coat she forgot yesterday, the garage man checks the car he repaired the day before and a policeman asks her if she got back to Paris on time the previous night . . . when she had been there all day!

When she is attacked, her glasses smashed, her hand crushed and then she is confronted by a man in the boot of her car, Dany belives she is going mad. Japrisot brilliantly developes this into a tangled mystery story that won 'Le Prix d'Honneur' when first published.

NO EXIT CRIME CUTS brings the very best in crime writing, old and new at unbeatably low prices!

### FAST ONE — Paul Cain (New Edition) £1.99

### WAX APPLE — Tucker Coe (aka Donald Westlake) £1.99

Mitch Tobin, ex NYPD policeman was sacked for neglect that resulted in the death of his partner and friend. Racked by guilt, Tobin retires into a grim artificial world of his own until he is drawn out to investigate a series of suspicious fatal accidents at the Midway sanatorium. Five minutes after arriving Tobin is a victim himself, left with a broken arm, a headache and no idea where to begin. Then the fire escape collapses and the dirty game becomes murder!

### LITTLE CAESAR — W. R. Burnett £1.99

CHICAGO. Girls and pimps, bootleggers and booze, killers and 'typewriters'. Go down the mean dark streets and see the cats sniffing the corpes. Go down the alleys and meet Rico, and Otero, Bat Carillo and Baa Baa Otavio, Killer Pepi and Kidney Bean. There are the squirrels, flapping to stay alive – Blondy Belle and Seal-Skin, Blue Jay and Olga. All playing for power. All certain to die! Little Caesar is the prototype underworld novel that inspired a whole generation of gangster films.

### BURGLARS CAN'T BE CHOOSERS — Lawrence Block £1.99

Introducing Bernie Rhodenbarr, New York City's prince of thieves – who really should have known better!

When the mysterious pear-shaped man with a lot of uncomfortably accurate information about Bernie and his career offered him 5 big ones to liberate a blue leather box – unopened – it would have been a good time to plead a previous engagement, but times were tough. Everything was straightforward until two men in blue coats arrived before the liberation. Still all was not lost, there was always a way to work things out – but then they discover the body in the bedroom!

# NO EXIT PRESS

## MATCH ME SIDNEY –
### The 1990 No Exit Press Crime Compendium

A Marvellous mix of all things NO EXIT! Features a full length novel by Cornell Woolrich (Phantom Lady – filmed with Franchot Tone), short stories by Stanley Ellin, Max Allan Collins, Loren Estelman, Sue Grafton, John Lutz, Arthur Lyons, Michael Z Lewin, Paul Cain, Bill Pronzini and many others. In addition there is the Murder One Top 30 books of the year, the 1990 No Exit Press Crime Diary, the No Exit Prize Crime Crossword plus much more.

592pp/Crime Fiction/£8.95pb/216x135mm/0 948353 59 7/November 1989

Barry Came

## RICE WINE

Paul Stenmark is sent by a Washington agency to a village in Luzon in the Philippines during the last years of the Marcos era to determine whether to fund a new dam project.

Fr Frank Enright and village elder Alfredo Dantog aided by the communist insurgents led by Ka Larry, oppose the project while Marcos stooge, Lt Col Rosales is eager to push the project through. All these elements combine against the backdrop of a terrifying monsoon to make for a tremendous adventure thriller with elements of Robert Stone, Wilber Smith and Philip Caputo.

'... a riveting story, told with sure skill and charged with insight. It is a novel of passion and Politics, of American innocence abroad and of the victims of that innocence. Full blooded and fully realised, it is at once highly readable entertainment and an important work, one which takes the reader beyond the international headlines for a behind the scenes look at the morality play being staged in developing countries throughout the world' – **Nicholas Proffitt** (author of *Gardens of Stone*)

304pp / Fiction / £3.99pb / 178x111mm ('A' format) / 0 948353 58 9/ January 1990

Lawrence Block

## THE BURGLAR IN THE CLOSET

Bernie Rhodenbarr, introduced in *Burglars can't be Choosers* (available from No Exit) is back. The so-called professional has got himself locked in the clothes cupboard of a smart New York apartment, while thieving it. And there was his swag all neatly packed, not in hand and not at hand but on the opposite side of the bedroom! By the time Bernie has picked the lock he was not best pleased to find the loot gone and more alarmingly the beautiful owner, Crystal Sheldrake lying very dead in their former resting place!

192pp/Crime Fiction/£3.50pb/'A' format/0 948353 70 8/June 1990

Sebastien Japrisot

## 10.30 FROM MARSEILLES
## TRAP FOR CINDERELLA

Two more classic sixties thrillers from Japrisot, whose new novel *Women in Evidence* is to be published by Secker. *10.30 from Marseilles* was Japrisot's first novel and is an excellent example of the police procedural. It was filmed starring Yves Montand and Simone Signoret. *Trap for Cinderella* is an exceedingly complex psychological thriller that won the Grand Prix de la Litterature de Policiere, similar in style to *The Lady in the Car with Glasses and a Gun*, also published by No Exit.
256pp/Crime Fiction/£3.99 each/'A' format/0 948353 73 2 *(10.30 Marseilles)*, 79 1 *(Trap for Cinderella)*/ March 1990.

Arthur Lyons

## THE DEAD ARE DISCREET

Asch is back on the trail, investigating the gruesome murders of socialite Shiela Warren and her boyfriend, film producer, Randy Folsom. All clues point to Shiela's distraught husband as the killer. Then Asch discovers Shiela has been dabbling in witchcraft prior to her death and then of a porno film starring Shiela now in the hands of an arcane set of Satanists, whose uncanny rites suggest a completely different motive for the crime.
'The best L.A. detective novel of the year' – **Los Angeles Times**
224pp/Crime Fiction/£3.50pb/'A' format/0 948353 72 4/June 1990

Stuart Kaminsky

## BURIED CAESARS

Hollywood P.I., Toby Peters in his 13th case receives a call from General Douglas MacArthur who wants Peters to investigate the theft, by one of his own aides, of some papers and campaign funds, that will destroy the General's budding political career. Peters is helped by one Dashiell Hammett, an ex Pinkerton man looking to kill some time in sunny California. The aide turns up dead and they trace it back to the mysterious Mr Pintacki, a desert tycoon who has his own very special plans for the future of America. Then Hammett is kidnapped by Pintacki's torpedoes and Peters must act alone – and fast.
192pp / Crime Fiction / £3.50pb / 'A' format / 0 948353 75 9 / May 1990(Early export edition), July 1990(home)

### Arthur Lyons
## ALL GOD'S CHILDREN

Jacob Asch's first ever case leads him on a search for attractive 18 year old runaway to the L.A. fringe life of Jesus freaks and vicious motor bike gangs.
'A thoroughly professional job ... Lyons writes lean prose' – **N.Y. Times Book Review**
224pp/Crime Fiction/£3.50pb/'A' format/0 948353 66 X/January 1990

### Pele, with Herb Resnicow
## THE WORLD CUP MURDER

A marvellously entertaining thriller set around the World Cup Final with a mix of football lore, big business and murder as the deeply unpopular manager of the World Cup Finalists, America(!!), Yugoslav entrepreneur, Gregor Ragusic is murdered on the eve of the final. Pele brings his years of knowledge and skill to a story line deftly crafted by Herb Resnicow that adds up to a Dick Francis of football thrillers.
320pp/Crime Fiction/£3.99pb/'A' format/0 948353 74 0/May 1990

### Dorothy B Hughes
## IN A LONELY PLACE

*Accepted as one of the best portraits ever of a psychopathic serial killer.*
Dix Steele, recently demobbed lives in someone else's apartment in L.A. and uses their possessions and periodically follows women round the city. Dix looks up his old war buddy, now L.A. detective, Brub Nicolai. Dix feels an unreasonable resentment to Nicolai's lovely wife, Sylvia, but continues to see him often in the company of would be actress, Laurel, who he is fiercely possessive of.
When Laurel betrays Dix, the serial killings that Nicolai has been investigating and keeping his friend Dix informed of, step up in pace!
*In a Lonely Place* was filmed by Nicholas Ray in 1950, starring Humphrey Bogart.
192pp/Crime Fiction/£3.99pb/'A' format/0 948353 67 8

## STILL TO COME:

Mirror, Mirror on the Wall – Stanley Ellin
Child Proof – Michael Lewin
Murder among Children – Tucker Coe
At the Hands of Another – Arthur Lyons

NO EXIT PRESS

BOOK TOKEN

NO EXIT PRESS

NO EXIT PRESS Tokens allow the regular reader of NO EXIT PRESS titles to benefit. Each token at the end of the book is worth 50p. Just tear out the page, complete the order form, listing the titles you require and send it DIRECT to Oldcastle Books, 18 Coleswood Road, Harpenden, Herts AL5 1EQ. Please note this offer is ONLY available DIRECT from the publishers.

There is no limit to the number of tokens you can use against each book. For example if you have 6 tokens (value £3) you can send for a £2.99 book – and it won't cost you a penny – not even the postage! Alternatively you can use just one token and the price would be £2.99 less £0.50 = £2.49+£0.25 (10% p&p) = Total cost of £2.74.

Please note only the original page from the book is acceptable – no photocopies allowed.

## ORDER FORM

1) ........................................................ £

2) ........................................................ £

3) ........................................................ £

4) ........................................................ £

Book Total ............................................... £

Add 10% p&p contribution ....................... £

Total ....................................................... £

Less ... Tokens @ £0.50 each .................... £

NET TOTAL ENCLOSED ....................... £

Please make cheques, P.O.s payable to Oldcastle Books Ltd or quote your credit card no. and expiry date.

VISA/ACCESS Expiry Date ☐☐☐☐

Card No. ☐☐☐☐☐☐☐☐☐☐☐☐☐

Signature ................................................................

Name ......................................................................

Address ..................................................................

............................................................. Postcode ..........

Title of Book from which token comes from:

Name of Bookshop where Book bought:

# The NO EXIT PRESS Prize Crossword

Here's your chance to win a complete set of NO EXIT PRESS books. The first correct entry out of the bag on January 31st 1990 will win every NO EXIT title in print at that date! But don't despair every correct entry received by June 30th 1990 will receive a free mystery book. Incidentally a Reilly or suitable crime reference book wouldn't go amiss for some of the more obscure clues.

Completed entries (we will accept photocopies if you don't want to rip your book apart) to: *Prize Crossword, No Exit Press, 18 Coleswood Road, Harpenden, Herts, AL5 1EQ.*

Name:

Address:

Postcode:

## ACROSS:

1   A mixed up red room from the man who gave you 'Time to Kill' (7)

5   Cain's (the other one) novel of speed (4,3)

9   Unpleasant relation (4,5)

10   The Japanese superintendent (5)

11   Cornell's Country pseudonym (5)

12   Erle Stanley's moody female (5,4)

14   Annoyed Ronay or aggrieved Spengler (10,4)

17   Namesake of author of 10 across is a whale of a writer (6,8)

21   A strange situation from one holding another to ransom (2,7)

23   To follow. Found in raft error (5)

24   Asch's creator (5)

25   Kenneth Royce's strange fellow owing secret allegiance (6,3)

26   Repentance (7)

**27 & 1 Down**
    Carroll John Daly's royal bad guy (7,2,4)

## DOWN:

2   Drop the black in threat while sending a letter (7)

3   A criminal haven, no place to be alone in (5,4)

4   Upset sieved mince to give you these forceful people (8,3)

5   A P.I.'s bill (3)

6   Mix up tory's and get a narrative (5)

7   Go train rearranged for public speaking (7)

8   Reginald Hill's novel in the singular. A criminal's last word (4,4)

13   These people have virtually no idea of fashion (6,5)

15   Get rid of at summit. Then move around paint to do (2,2,2,3)

16   I see the maker of candles in a high window (8)

18   Le Queux's 1909 coloured living space (3,4)

19   Bill Cranes creator (7)

20   One who trims roses (6)

22   He gave life to Scott Jordan (5)

25   Stark a man of many names - this is his shortest (3)